一山不容二 ONE MOUNTAIN CANNOT ABIDE TWO TIGERS

MY NAME IS LIM CHIN SIONG.

I WAS ONCE A FIERY ORATOR IN THE CHINESE DIALECT OF HOKKIEN.

I HELD SWAY OVER THOUSANDS THROUGH THE POWER OF MY WORDS AND THE DEDICATION OF MY ACTIONS.

THERE WAS A MOMENT IN HISTORY WHEN I MIGHT HAVE BECOME THE *PRIME MINISTER* OF SINGAPORE.

WHO ARE YOU?

BUT THEY CALLED ME A *COMMUNIST* AND LOCKED ME AWAY.

IN PRISON, I WAS OVERCOME BY DEPRESSION AND ATTEMPTED SUICIDE.

AFTER THAT, I LEFT FOR ENGLAND, WHERE I BECAME A FRUIT SELLER.

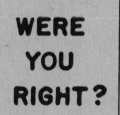

I AM *NOT A* COMMUNIST.

WERE YOU RIGHT?

I AM A *PATRIOT.*

I FOUGHT FOR MY COUNTRY AND MY FELLOW COUNTRYMEN.

YES, SINGAPORE HAS HAD GREAT ECONOMIC SUCCESS UNDER LEE KUAN YEW...

MANY MATERIAL THINGS HAVE IMPROVED...

BUT WHEN YOU LOOK IN THE MIRROR, WHAT DO YOU SEE?

NO WE MUST NOT

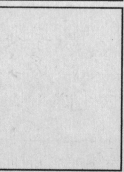

IN 1996, I DIED OF A HEART ATTACK.

Previous pages

ONE MOUNTAIN CANNOT ABIDE TWO TIGERS

1998

Chan Hock Chye

Unpublished

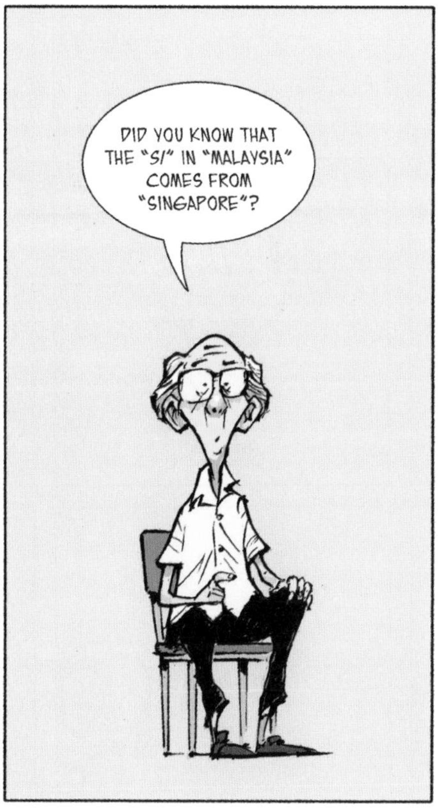
DID YOU KNOW THAT THE "SI" IN "MALAYSIA" COMES FROM "SINGAPORE"?

Charlie Chan Hock Chye, aged 72, 2010

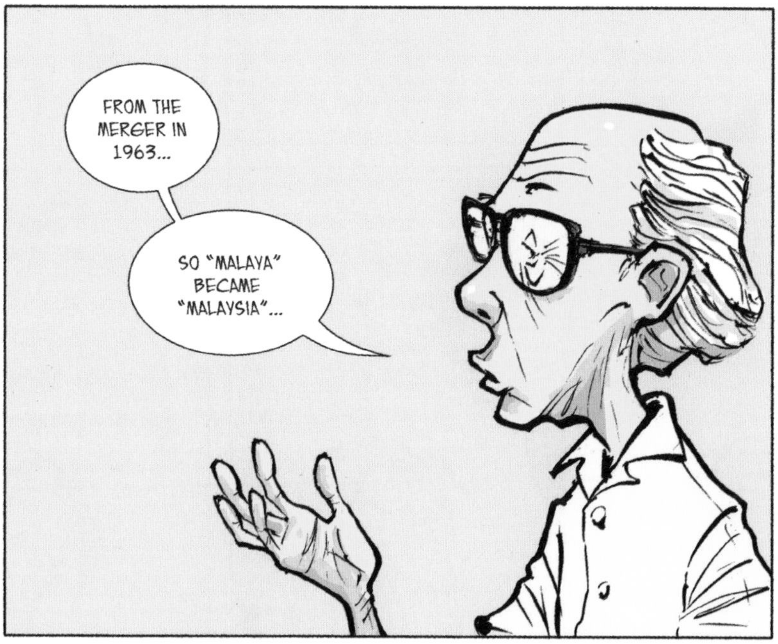
FROM THE MERGER IN 1963...
SO "MALAYA" BECAME "MALAYSIA"...

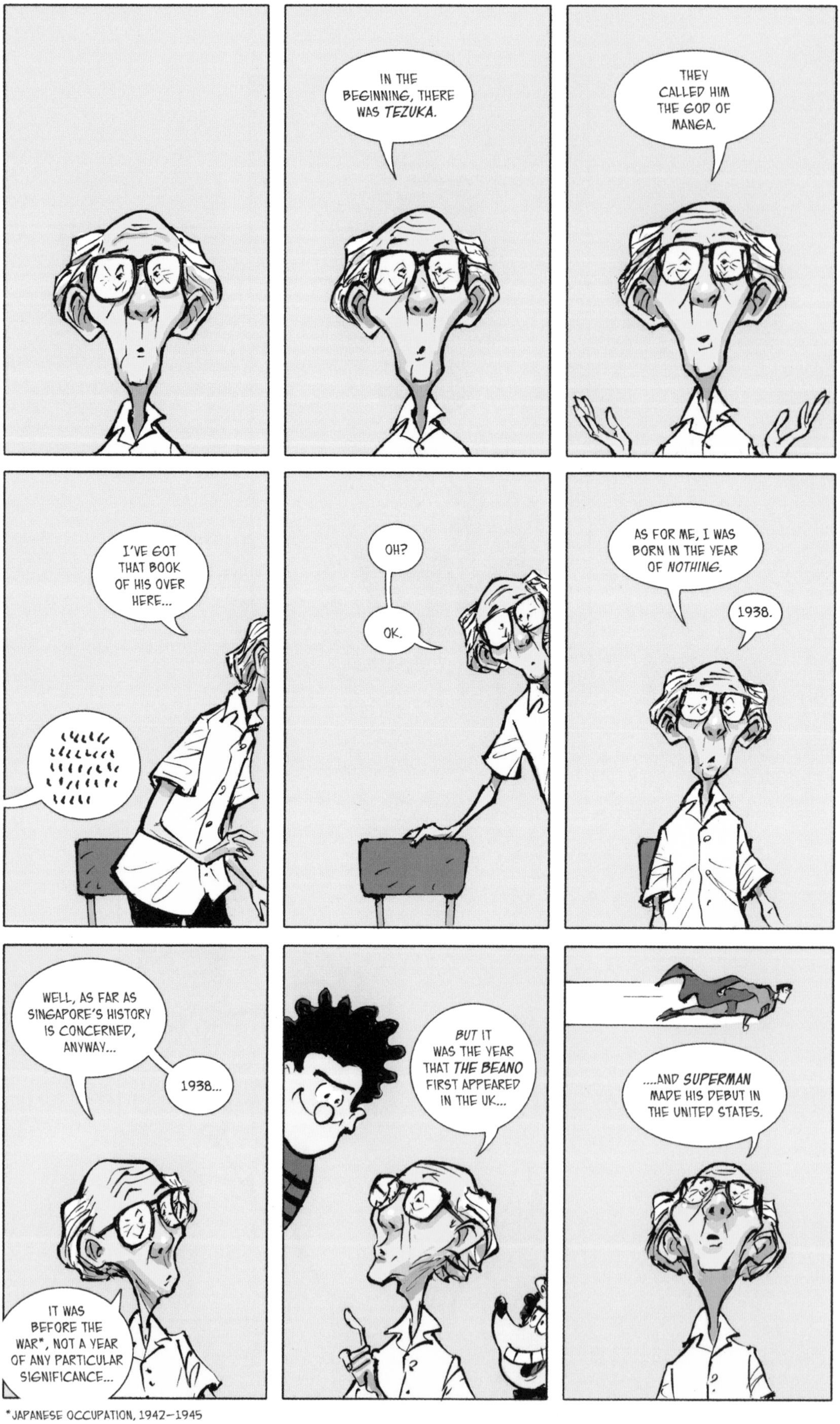
IN THE BEGINNING, THERE WAS TEZUKA.
THEY CALLED HIM THE GOD OF MANGA.
I'VE GOT THAT BOOK OF HIS OVER HERE...
OH?
OK.
AS FOR ME, I WAS BORN IN THE YEAR OF NOTHING.
1938.
WELL, AS FAR AS SINGAPORE'S HISTORY IS CONCERNED, ANYWAY...
1938...
IT WAS BEFORE THE WAR*, NOT A YEAR OF ANY PARTICULAR SIGNIFICANCE...
BUT IT WAS THE YEAR THAT THE BEANO FIRST APPEARED IN THE UK...
....AND SUPERMAN MADE HIS DEBUT IN THE UNITED STATES.

*JAPANESE OCCUPATION, 1942–1945

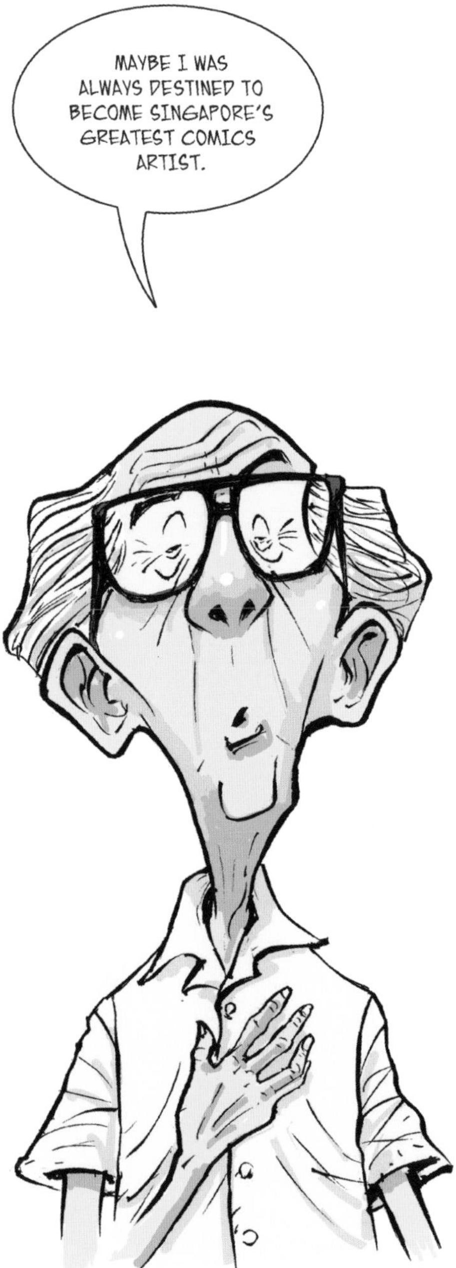
MAYBE I WAS ALWAYS DESTINED TO BECOME SINGAPORE'S GREATEST COMICS ARTIST.

THE ART OF
CHARLIE CHAN
HOCK CHYE

presented by
SONNY LIEW

PANTHEON BOOKS
NEW YORK

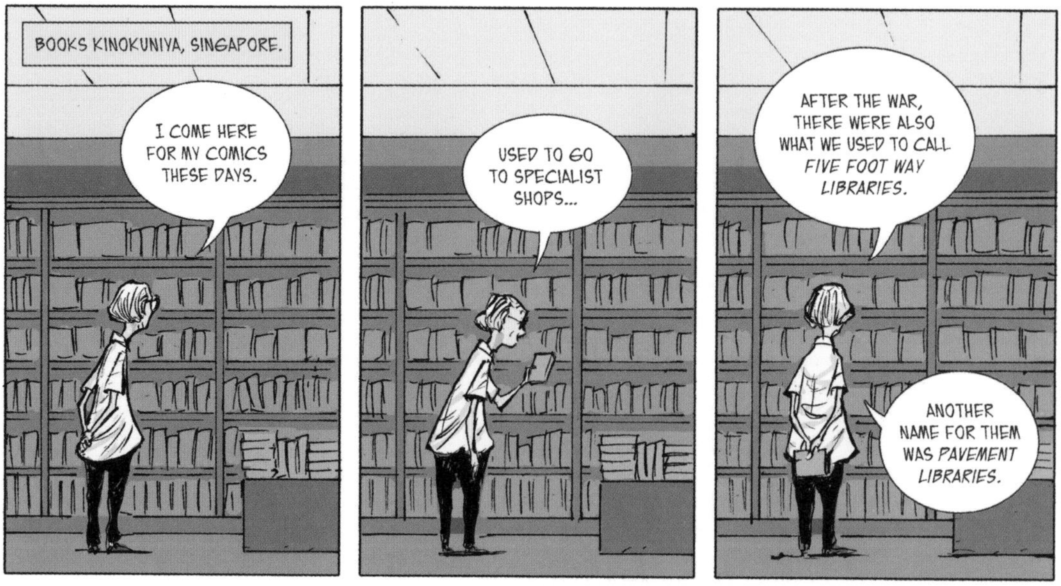
BOOKS KINOKUNIYA, SINGAPORE.
I COME HERE FOR MY COMICS THESE DAYS.
USED TO GO TO SPECIALIST SHOPS...
AFTER THE WAR, THERE WERE ALSO WHAT WE USED TO CALL *FIVE FOOT WAY LIBRARIES.*
ANOTHER NAME FOR THEM WAS *PAVEMENT LIBRARIES.*

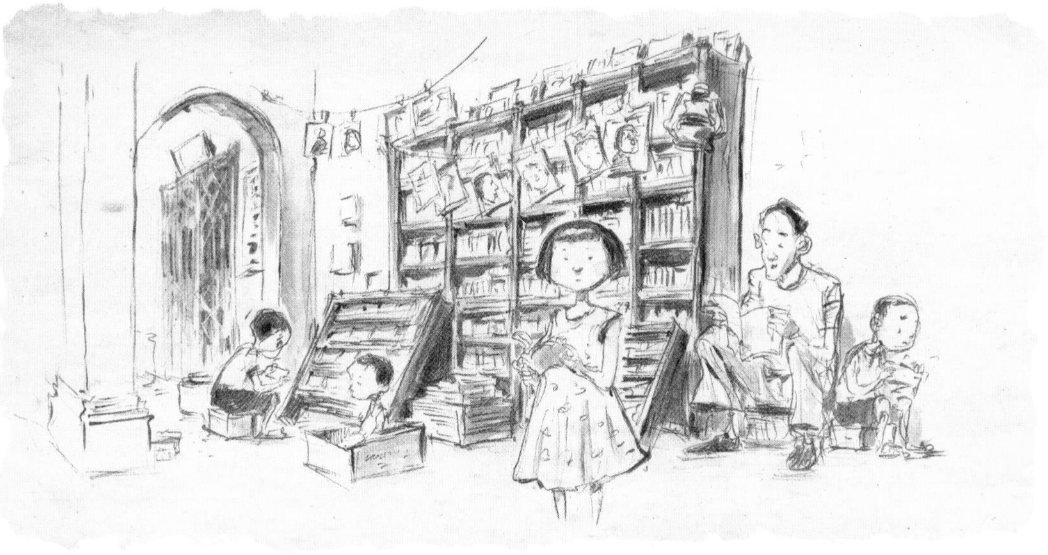

FIVE FOOT WAY LIBRARY (1966) | Chan Hock Chye | Ink and wash on paper

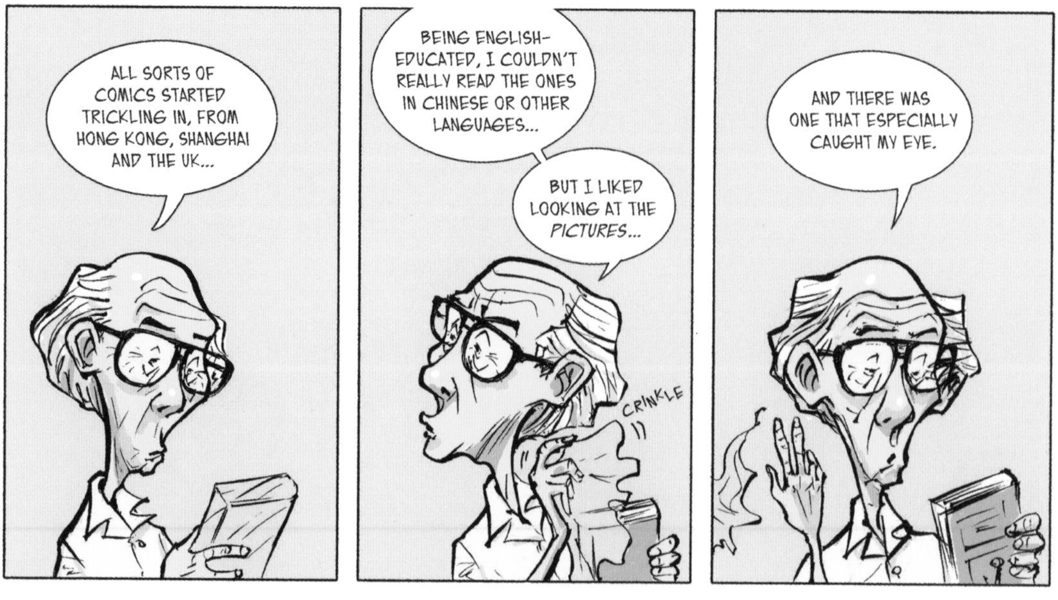
ALL SORTS OF COMICS STARTED TRICKLING IN, FROM HONG KONG, SHANGHAI AND THE UK...
BEING ENGLISH-EDUCATED, I COULDN'T REALLY READ THE ONES IN CHINESE OR OTHER LANGUAGES...
BUT I LIKED LOOKING AT THE *PICTURES*...
CRINKLE
AND THERE WAS ONE THAT ESPECIALLY CAUGHT MY EYE.

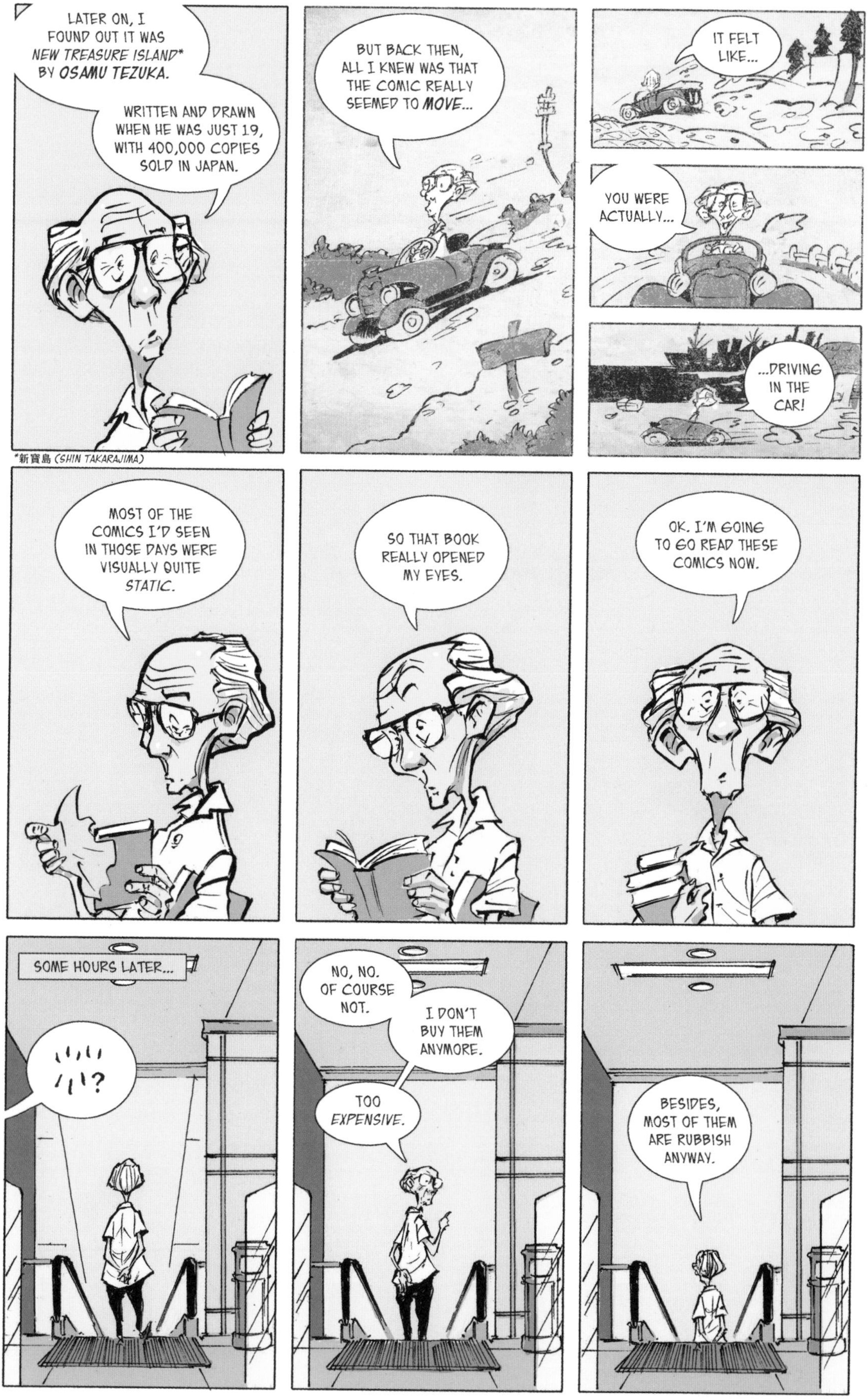
LATER ON, I FOUND OUT IT WAS NEW TREASURE ISLAND* BY OSAMU TEZUKA.
WRITTEN AND DRAWN WHEN HE WAS JUST 19, WITH 400,000 COPIES SOLD IN JAPAN.
*新寶島 (SHIN TAKARAJIMA)
BUT BACK THEN, ALL I KNEW WAS THAT THE COMIC REALLY SEEMED TO MOVE...
IT FELT LIKE...
YOU WERE ACTUALLY...
...DRIVING IN THE CAR!
MOST OF THE COMICS I'D SEEN IN THOSE DAYS WERE VISUALLY QUITE STATIC.
SO THAT BOOK REALLY OPENED MY EYES.
OK. I'M GOING TO GO READ THESE COMICS NOW.
SOME HOURS LATER...
!!!!
!!?
NO, NO. OF COURSE NOT.
I DON'T BUY THEM ANYMORE.
TOO EXPENSIVE.
BESIDES, MOST OF THEM ARE RUBBISH ANYWAY.

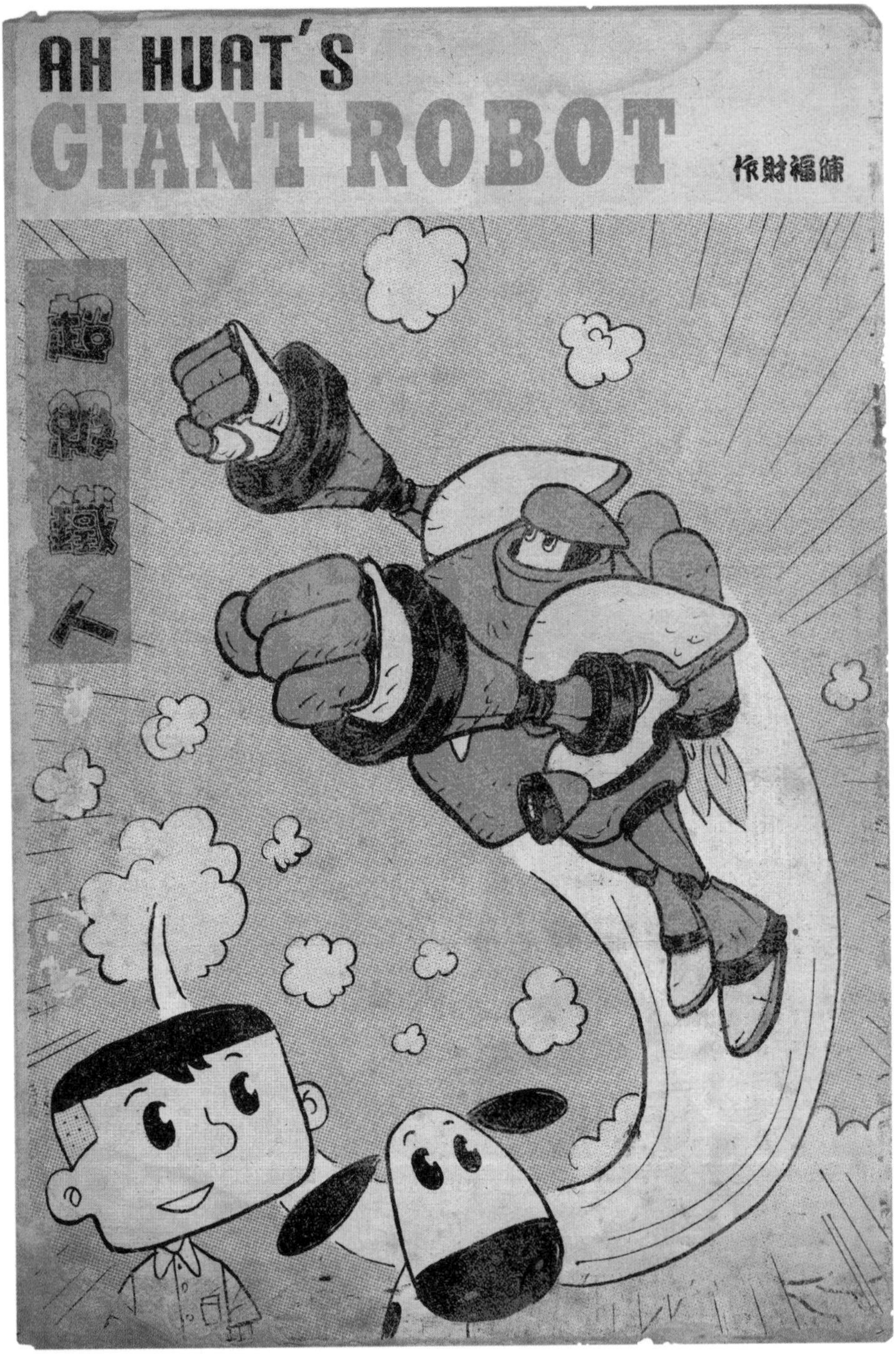
AH HUAT'S
GIANT ROBOT
陳福財作

Above
AH HUAT'S GIANT ROBOT Vol. 1
1956
Chan Hock Chye
Stones Throw Press

Opposite
AH HUAT'S GIANT ROBOT: AWAKENINGS
1954
Chan Hock Chye
Tiger Press

Ah Huat's Giant Robot: Awakenings was Chan's first published work. Written and drawn when he was 16, the 34-page comic first appeared as an extract in *Qian Jin* (*"Forward!"*) magazine, before being printed in its entirety as *Ah Huat's Giant Robot Vol. 1* by Stones Throw Press.

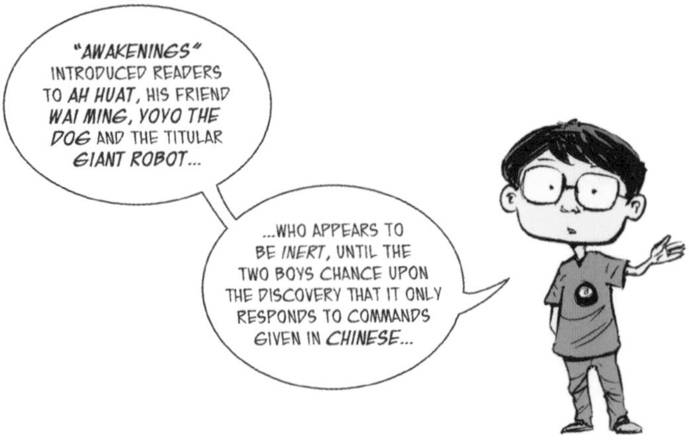
"AWAKENINGS" INTRODUCED READERS TO AH HUAT, HIS FRIEND WAI MING, YOYO THE DOG AND THE TITULAR GIANT ROBOT...
...WHO APPEARS TO BE INERT, UNTIL THE TWO BOYS CHANCE UPON THE DISCOVERY THAT IT ONLY RESPONDS TO COMMANDS GIVEN IN CHINESE...

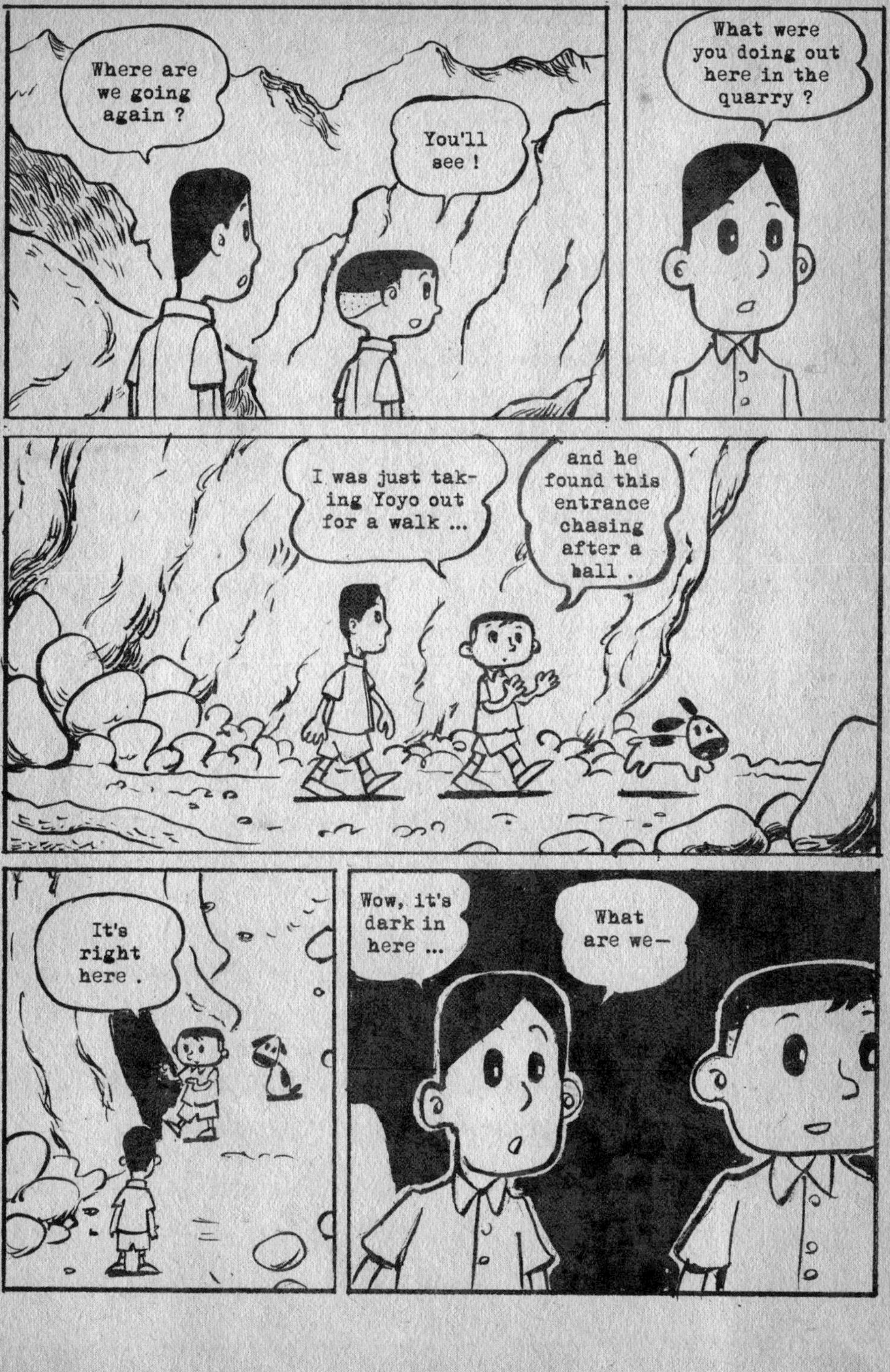
Where are we going again ?
You'll see !
What were you doing out here in the quarry ?
I was just tak-ing Yoyo out for a walk ...
and he found this entrance chasing after a ball .
It's right here .
Wow, it's dark in here ...
What are we—

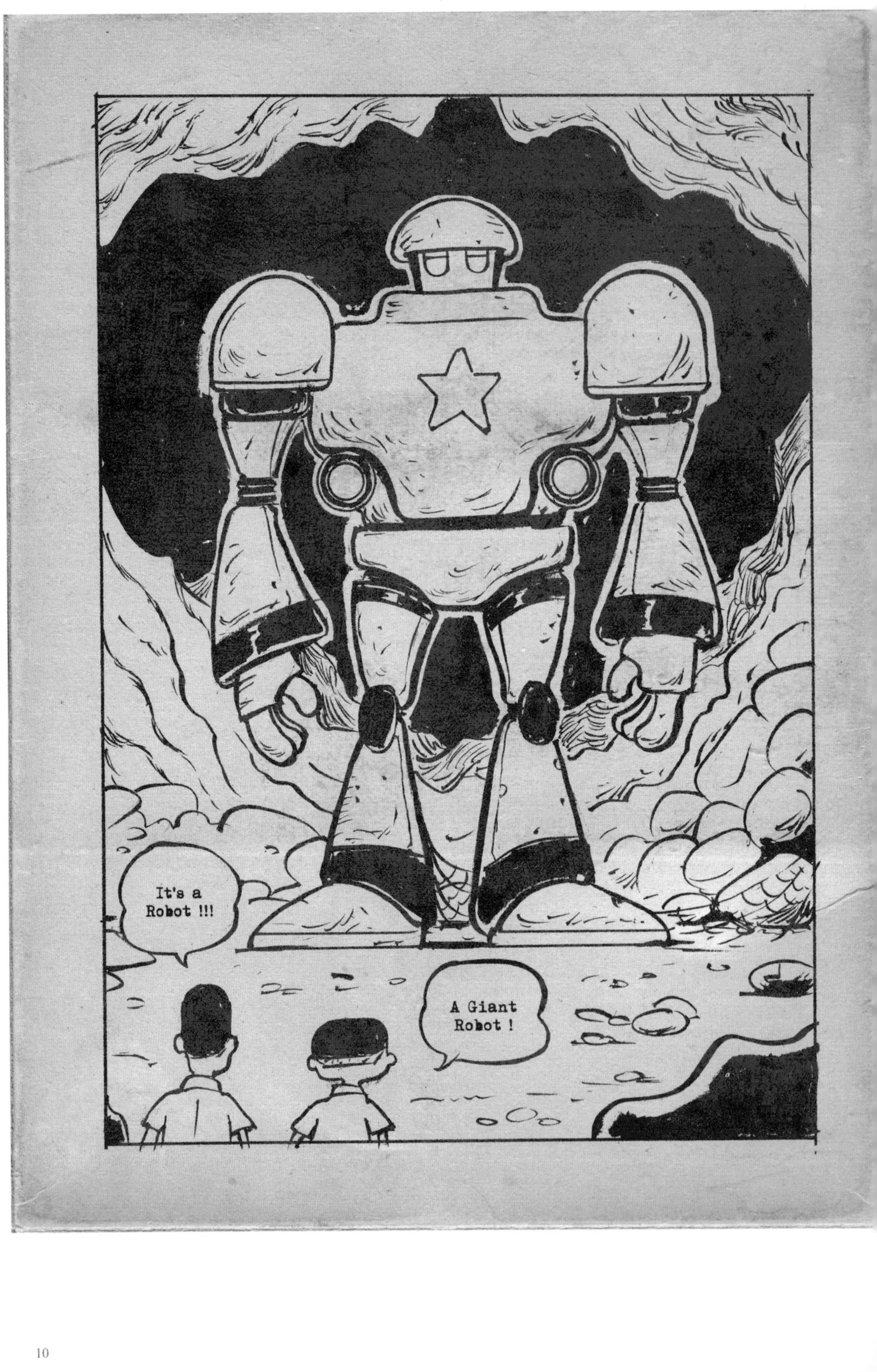
It's a Robot !!!
A Giant Robot !

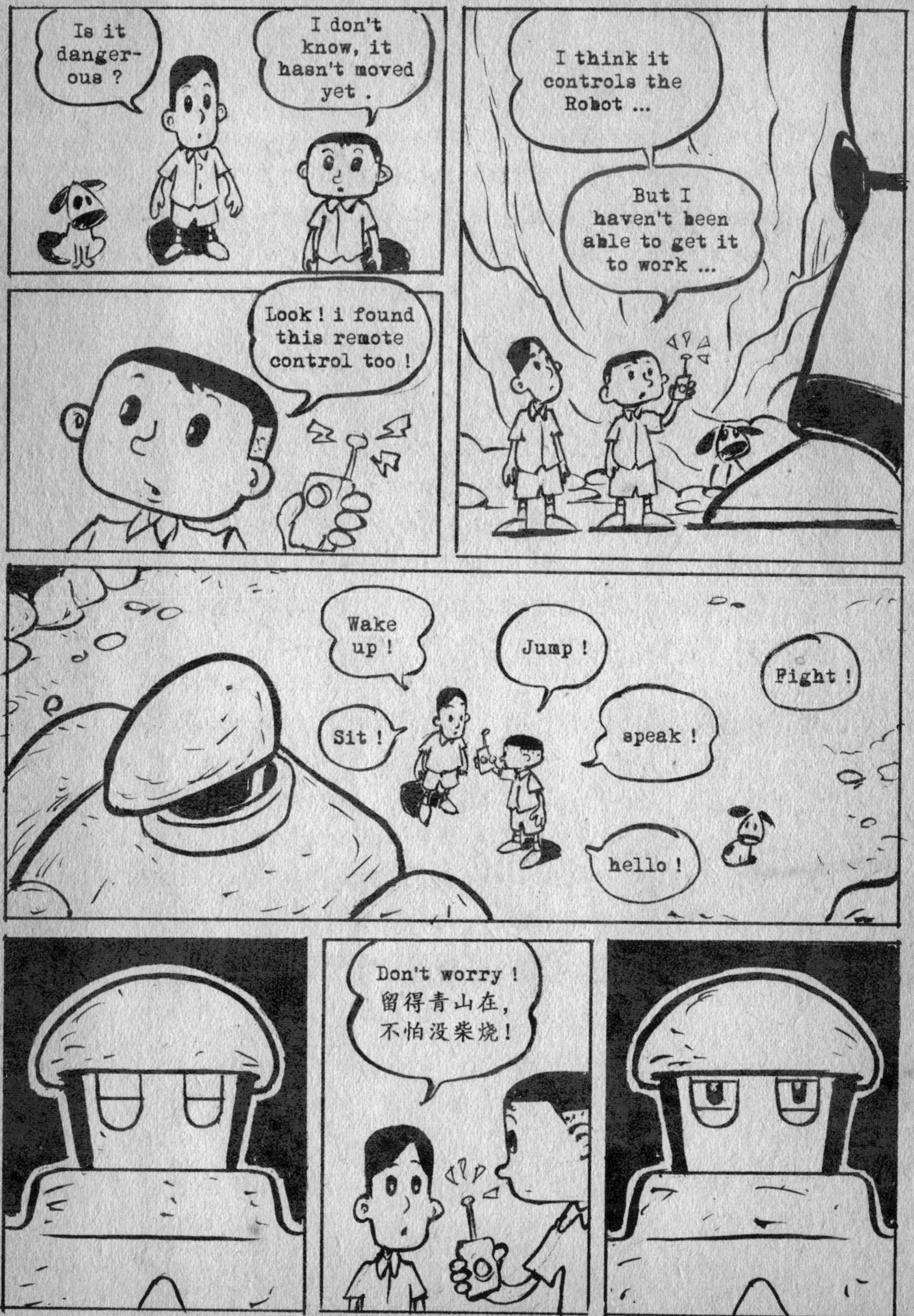
Is it danger-ous ?
I don't know, it hasn't moved yet .
Look ! i found this remote control too !
I think it controls the Robot ...
But I haven't been able to get it to work ...
Wake up !
Jump !
Fight !
Sit !
speak !
hello !
Don't worry ! 留得青山在, 不怕没柴烧！

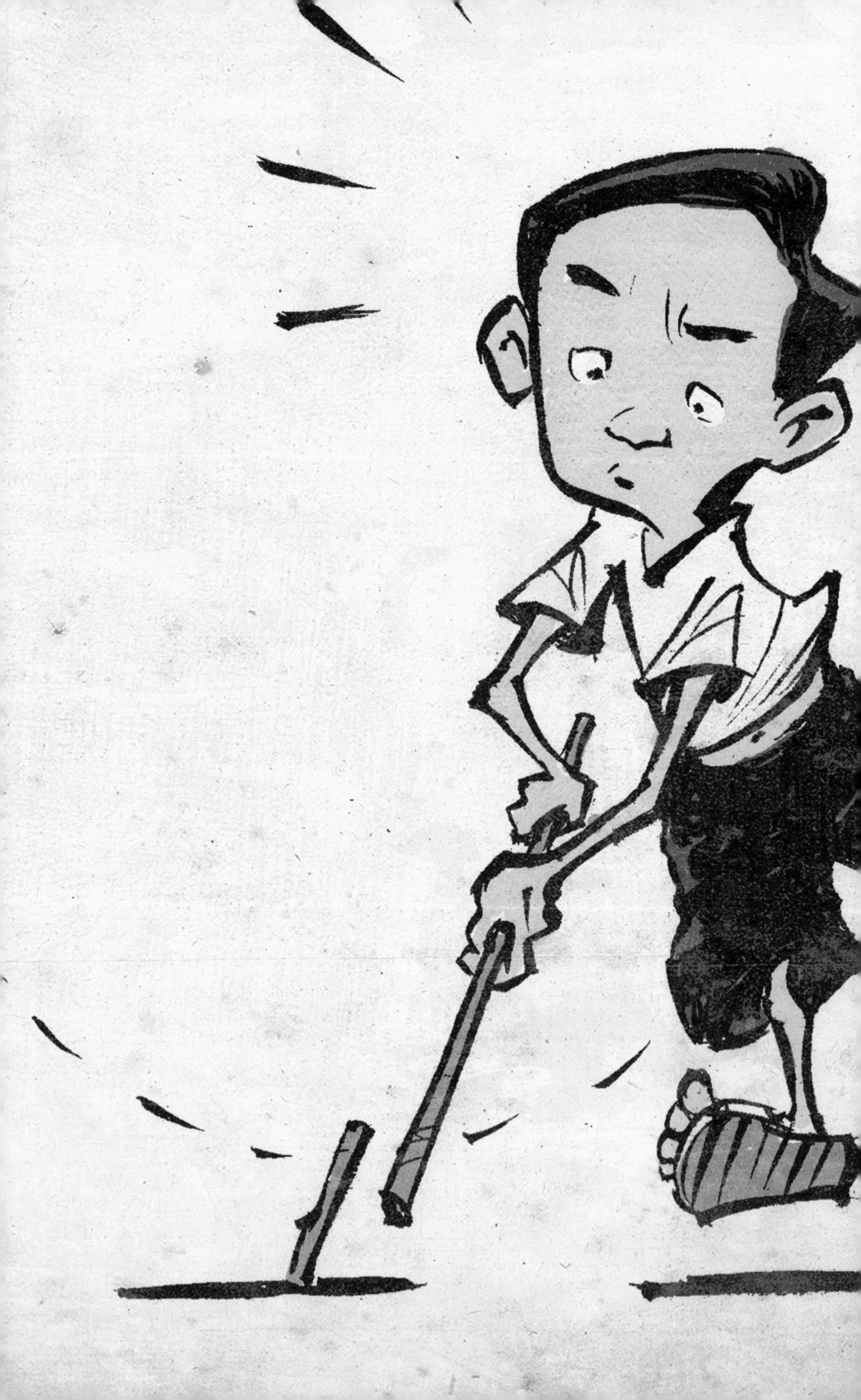

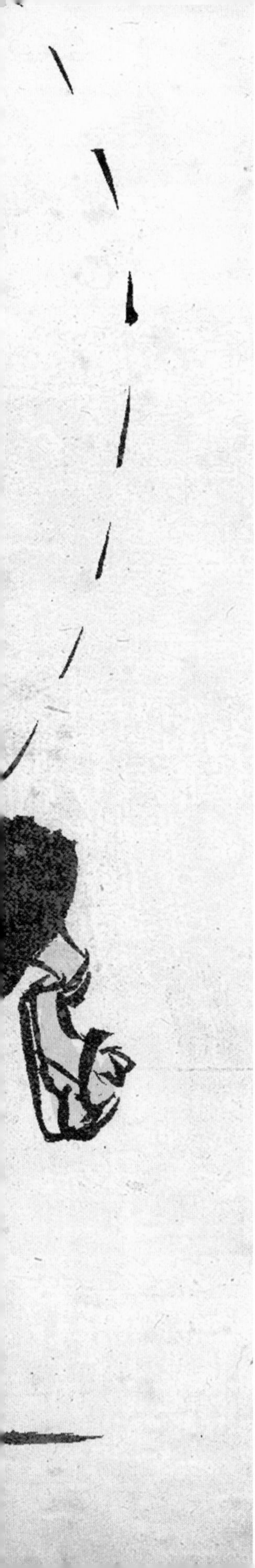

Chapter One

FIGHTING SPIDERS, LONGKANG FISH

童真年代

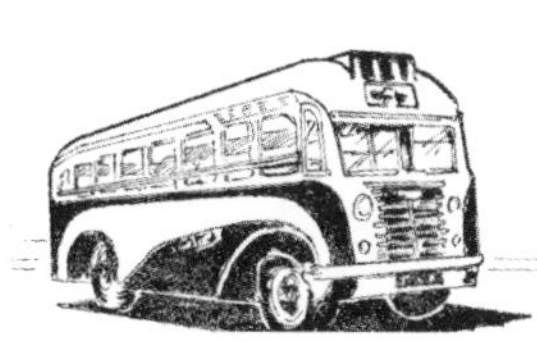

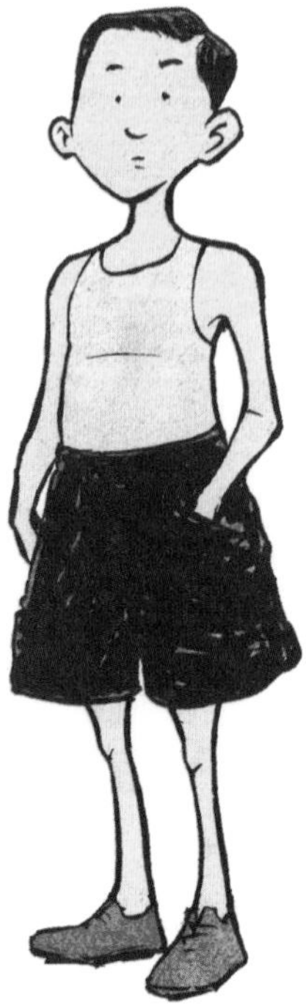

Charlie Chan Hock Chye, aged 10, 1948

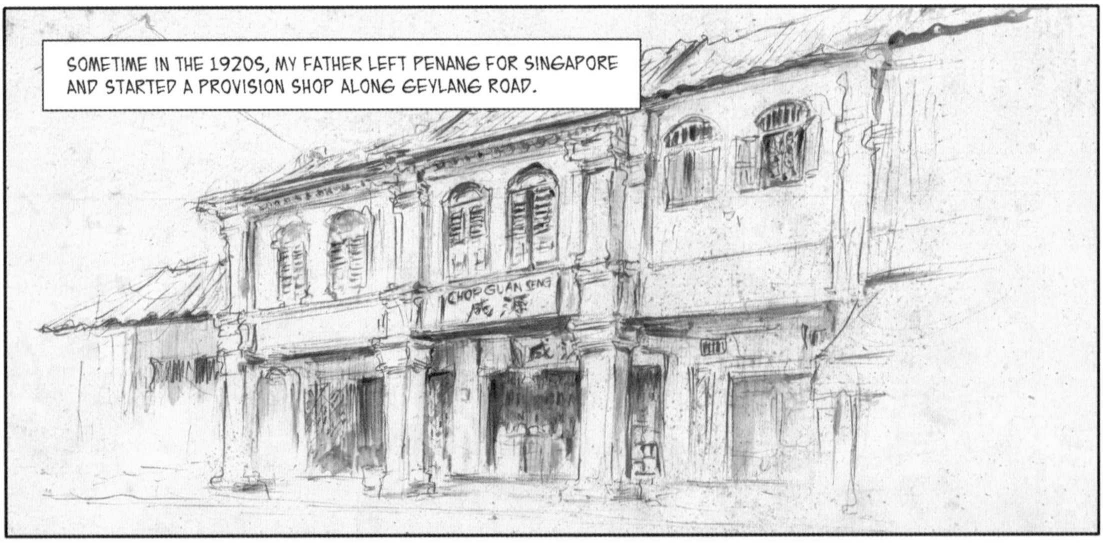
SOMETIME IN THE 1920S, MY FATHER LEFT PENANG FOR SINGAPORE AND STARTED A PROVISION SHOP ALONG GEYLANG ROAD.
CHOP GUAN SENG

GEYLANG PROVISION SHOP (1987) | Chan Hock Chye | Ink and wash on paper | Drawn from memory and photographs

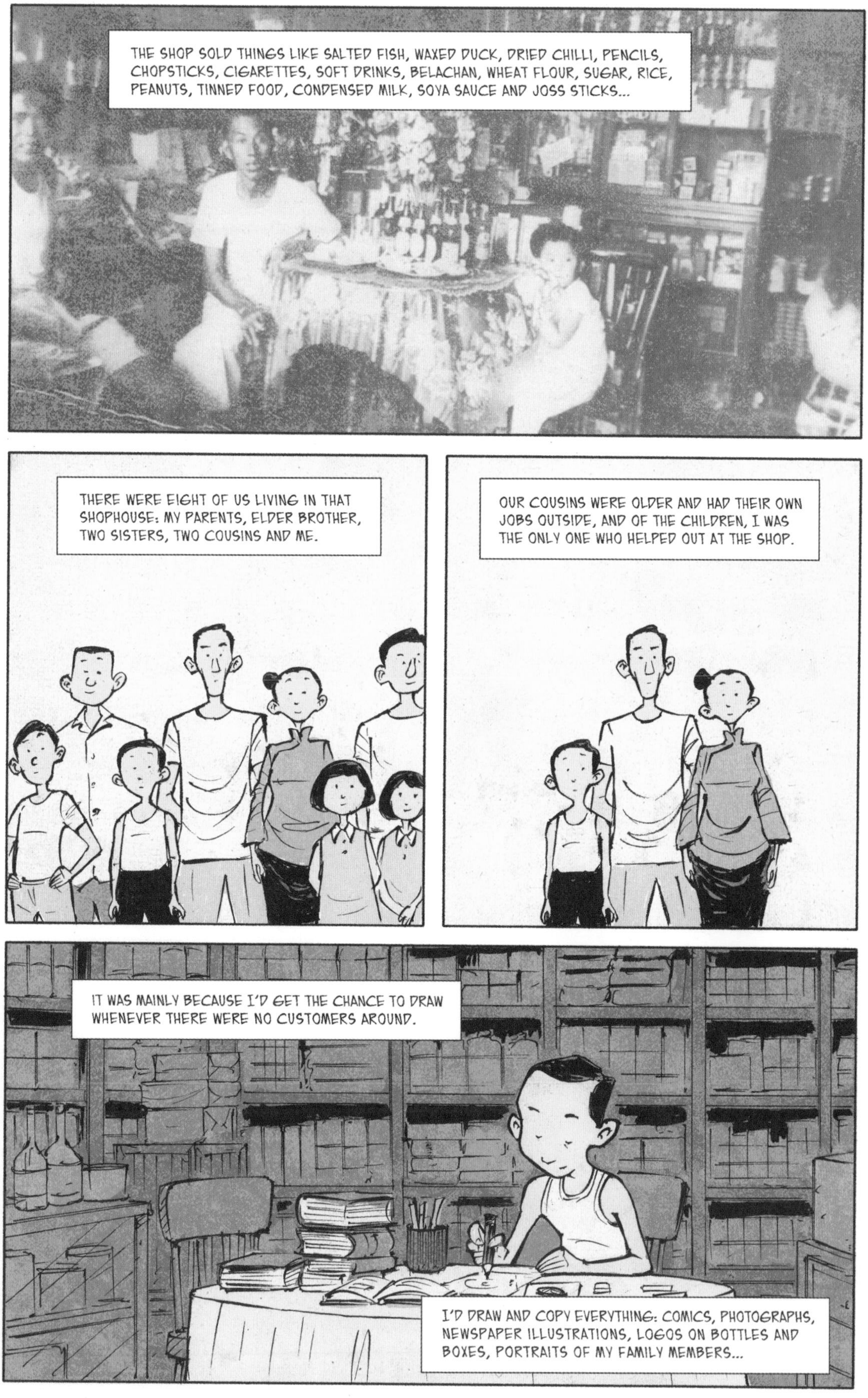
THE SHOP SOLD THINGS LIKE SALTED FISH, WAXED DUCK, DRIED CHILLI, PENCILS, CHOPSTICKS, CIGARETTES, SOFT DRINKS, BELACHAN, WHEAT FLOUR, SUGAR, RICE, PEANUTS, TINNED FOOD, CONDENSED MILK, SOYA SAUCE AND JOSS STICKS...
THERE WERE EIGHT OF US LIVING IN THAT SHOPHOUSE: MY PARENTS, ELDER BROTHER, TWO SISTERS, TWO COUSINS AND ME.
OUR COUSINS WERE OLDER AND HAD THEIR OWN JOBS OUTSIDE, AND OF THE CHILDREN, I WAS THE ONLY ONE WHO HELPED OUT AT THE SHOP.
IT WAS MAINLY BECAUSE I'D GET THE CHANCE TO DRAW WHENEVER THERE WERE NO CUSTOMERS AROUND.
I'D DRAW AND COPY EVERYTHING: COMICS, PHOTOGRAPHS, NEWSPAPER ILLUSTRATIONS, LOGOS ON BOTTLES AND BOXES, PORTRAITS OF MY FAMILY MEMBERS...

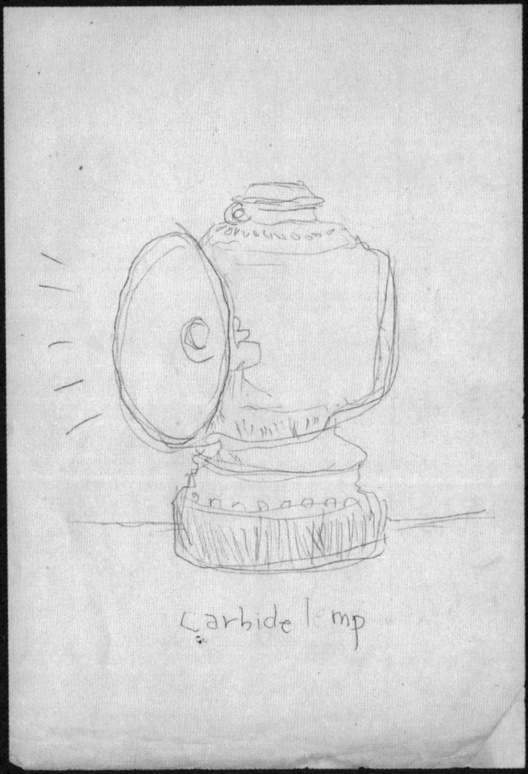
Carbide lamp

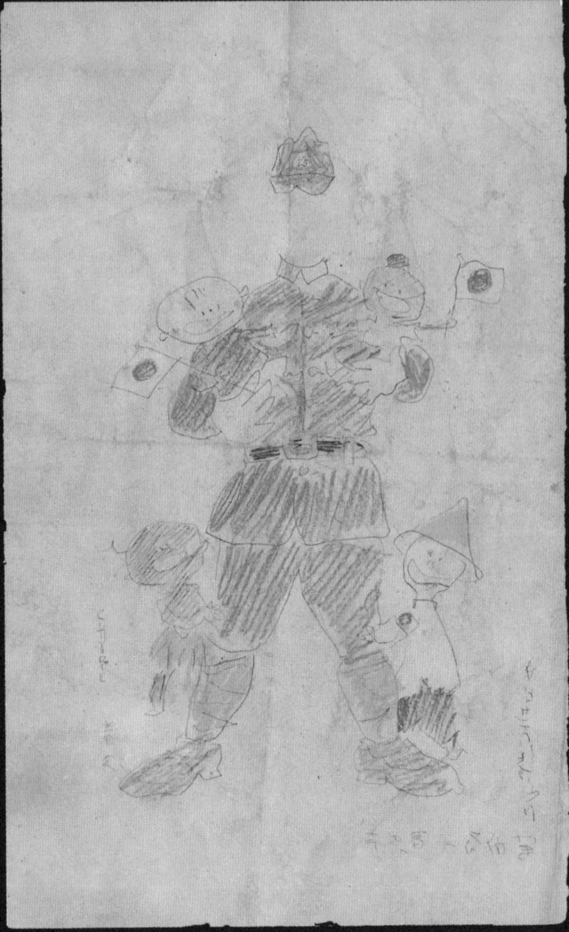

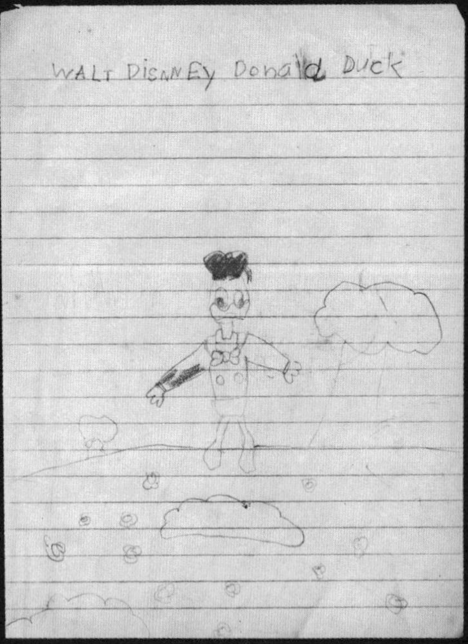
WALT DISNEY Donald Duck

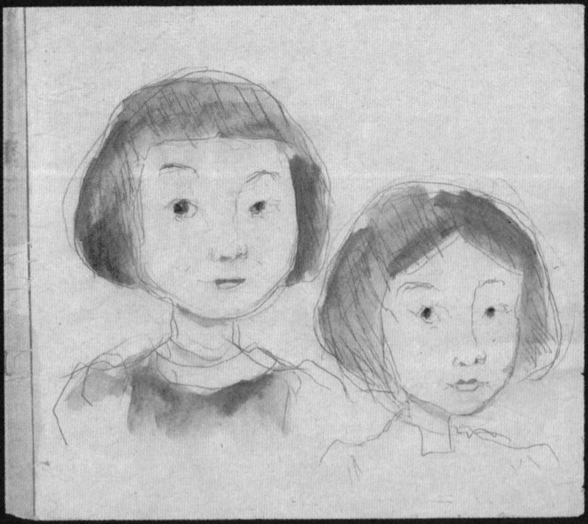

Top left
CARBIDE LAMP
1947

Bottom left
WALT "DISNNEY" DONALD DUCK
1944

Top right
GREATER FAR EASTERN CO-PROSPERITY SPHERE
1945
Copied from a Japanese propaganda magazine

Bottom right
MY SISTERS
1949

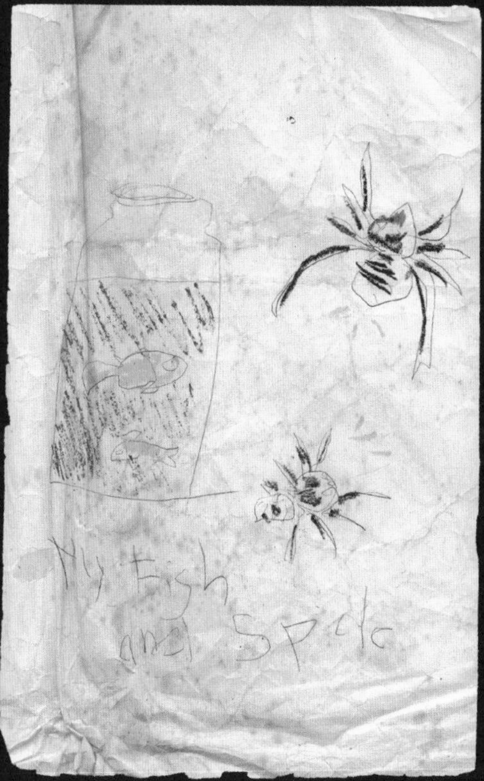

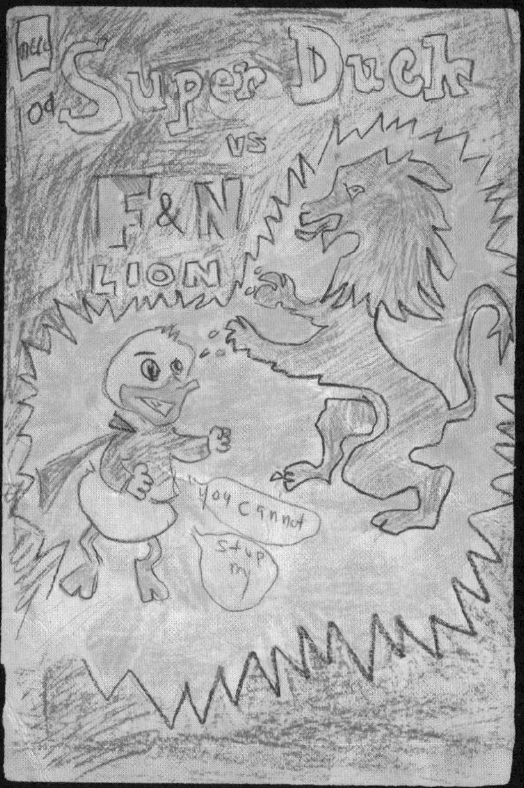
10d
Super Duck
vs
F&N
LION
you cannot
stup my

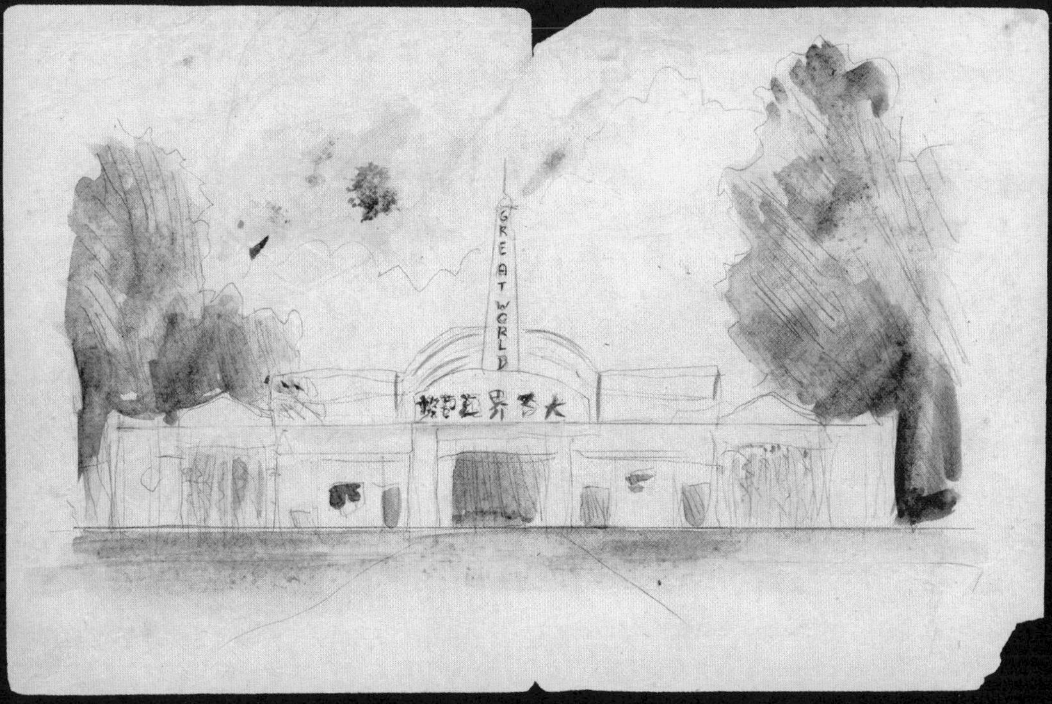
GREAT WORLD

Top left
FIGHTING SPIDERS, LONGKANG FISH
1944

Top right
SUPER DUCK VS. F&N LION
1948

Bottom right
GREAT WORLD AMUSEMENT PARK
1949
Copied from postcard

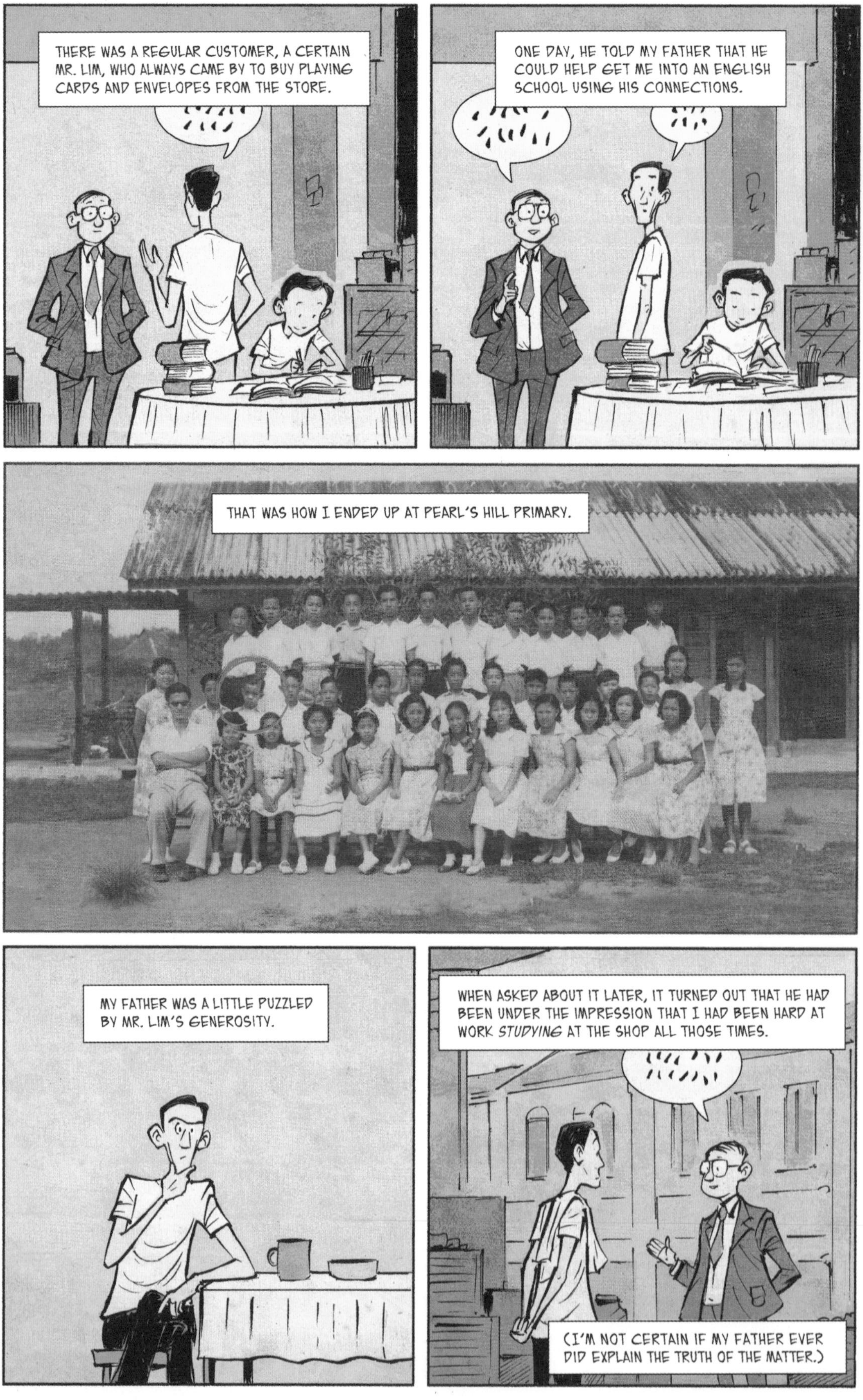
THERE WAS A REGULAR CUSTOMER, A CERTAIN MR. LIM, WHO ALWAYS CAME BY TO BUY PLAYING CARDS AND ENVELOPES FROM THE STORE.
ONE DAY, HE TOLD MY FATHER THAT HE COULD HELP GET ME INTO AN ENGLISH SCHOOL USING HIS CONNECTIONS.
THAT WAS HOW I ENDED UP AT PEARL'S HILL PRIMARY.
MY FATHER WAS A LITTLE PUZZLED BY MR. LIM'S GENEROSITY.
WHEN ASKED ABOUT IT LATER, IT TURNED OUT THAT HE HAD BEEN UNDER THE IMPRESSION THAT I HAD BEEN HARD AT WORK *STUDYING* AT THE SHOP ALL THOSE TIMES.
(I'M NOT CERTAIN IF MY FATHER EVER DID EXPLAIN THE TRUTH OF THE MATTER.)

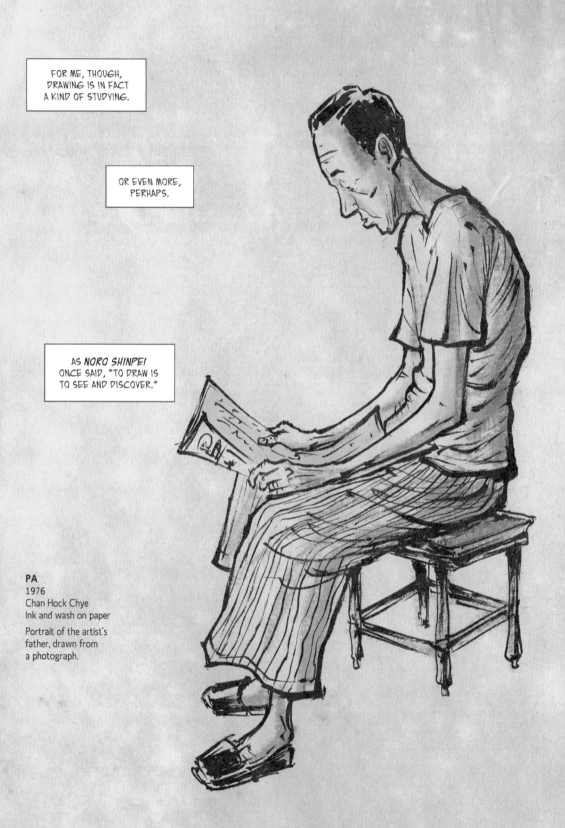

FOR ME, THOUGH, DRAWING IS IN FACT A KIND OF STUDYING.

OR EVEN MORE, PERHAPS.

AS *NORO SHINPEI* ONCE SAID, "TO DRAW IS TO SEE AND DISCOVER."

PA
1976
Chan Hock Chye
Ink and wash on paper

Portrait of the artist's father, drawn from a photograph.

"To draw is to see and discover. Every time you draw, you discover something new."
— Noro Shinpei, Japanese manga artist (1915–2002)

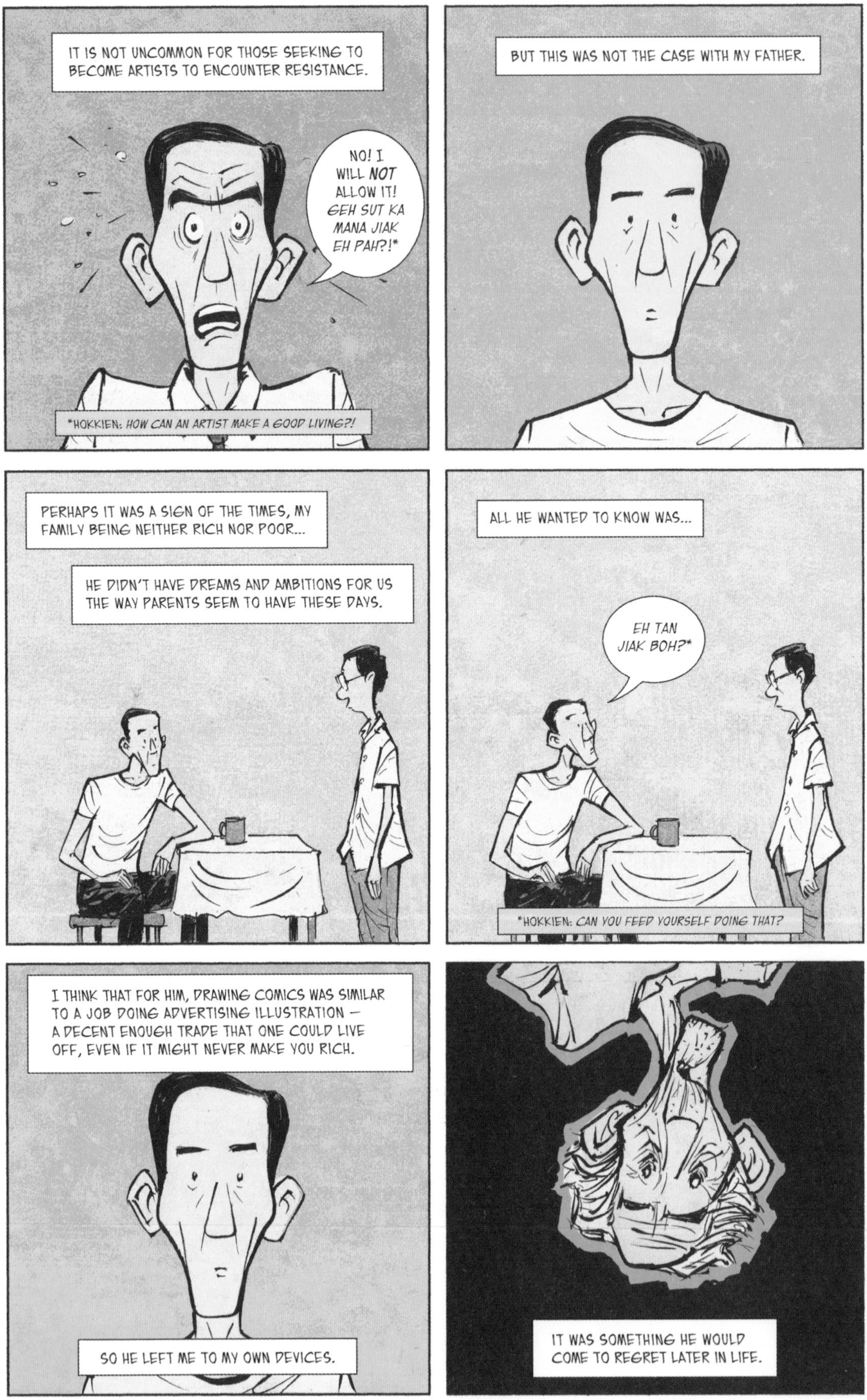
IT IS NOT UNCOMMON FOR THOSE SEEKING TO BECOME ARTISTS TO ENCOUNTER RESISTANCE.
NO! I WILL NOT ALLOW IT! GEH SUT KA MANA JIAK EH PAH?!*
*HOKKIEN: HOW CAN AN ARTIST MAKE A GOOD LIVING?!
BUT THIS WAS NOT THE CASE WITH MY FATHER.
PERHAPS IT WAS A SIGN OF THE TIMES, MY FAMILY BEING NEITHER RICH NOR POOR...
HE DIDN'T HAVE DREAMS AND AMBITIONS FOR US THE WAY PARENTS SEEM TO HAVE THESE DAYS.
ALL HE WANTED TO KNOW WAS...
EH TAN JIAK BOH?*
*HOKKIEN: CAN YOU FEED YOURSELF DOING THAT?
I THINK THAT FOR HIM, DRAWING COMICS WAS SIMILAR TO A JOB DOING ADVERTISING ILLUSTRATION — A DECENT ENOUGH TRADE THAT ONE COULD LIVE OFF, EVEN IF IT MIGHT NEVER MAKE YOU RICH.
SO HE LEFT ME TO MY OWN DEVICES.
IT WAS SOMETHING HE WOULD COME TO REGRET LATER IN LIFE.

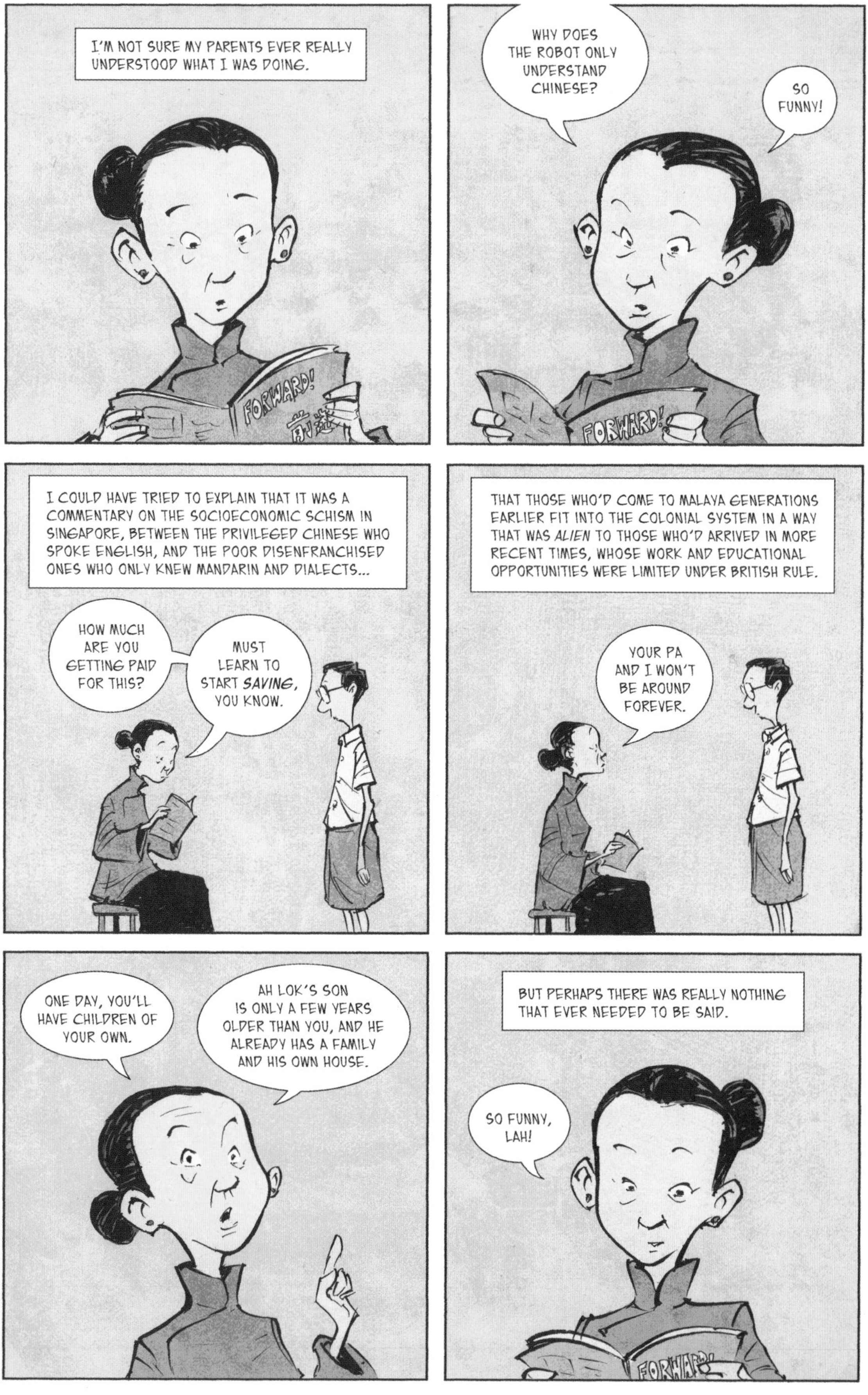
I'M NOT SURE MY PARENTS EVER REALLY UNDERSTOOD WHAT I WAS DOING.
FORWARD!
WHY DOES THE ROBOT ONLY UNDERSTAND CHINESE?
SO FUNNY!
FORWARD!
I COULD HAVE TRIED TO EXPLAIN THAT IT WAS A COMMENTARY ON THE SOCIOECONOMIC SCHISM IN SINGAPORE, BETWEEN THE PRIVILEGED CHINESE WHO SPOKE ENGLISH, AND THE POOR DISENFRANCHISED ONES WHO ONLY KNEW MANDARIN AND DIALECTS...
HOW MUCH ARE YOU GETTING PAID FOR THIS?
MUST LEARN TO START *SAVING*, YOU KNOW.
THAT THOSE WHO'D COME TO MALAYA GENERATIONS EARLIER FIT INTO THE COLONIAL SYSTEM IN A WAY THAT WAS *ALIEN* TO THOSE WHO'D ARRIVED IN MORE RECENT TIMES, WHOSE WORK AND EDUCATIONAL OPPORTUNITIES WERE LIMITED UNDER BRITISH RULE.
YOUR PA AND I WON'T BE AROUND FOREVER.
ONE DAY, YOU'LL HAVE CHILDREN OF YOUR OWN.
AH LOK'S SON IS ONLY A FEW YEARS OLDER THAN YOU, AND HE ALREADY HAS A FAMILY AND HIS OWN HOUSE.
BUT PERHAPS THERE WAS REALLY NOTHING THAT EVER NEEDED TO BE SAID.
SO FUNNY, LAH!

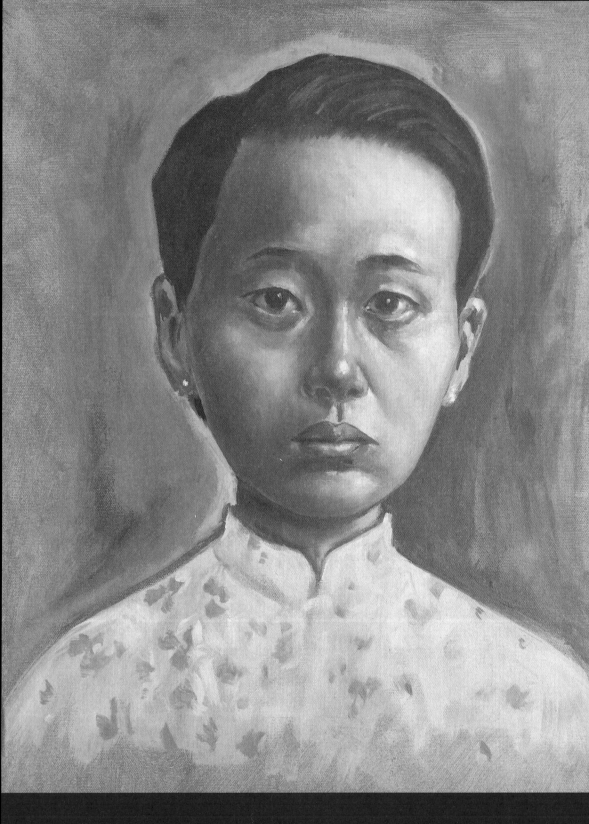

Above
MA
1983
Chan Hock Chye
Oil on canvas

Portrait of the artist's mother
as a young woman, painted
from a photograph.

Opposite & following
GEYLANG HILL
1986
Chan Hock Chye
Self-published

From a chapbook collection
of Chan's short stories.

GEYLANG HILL 芽籠山

BY CHAN HOCK CHYE

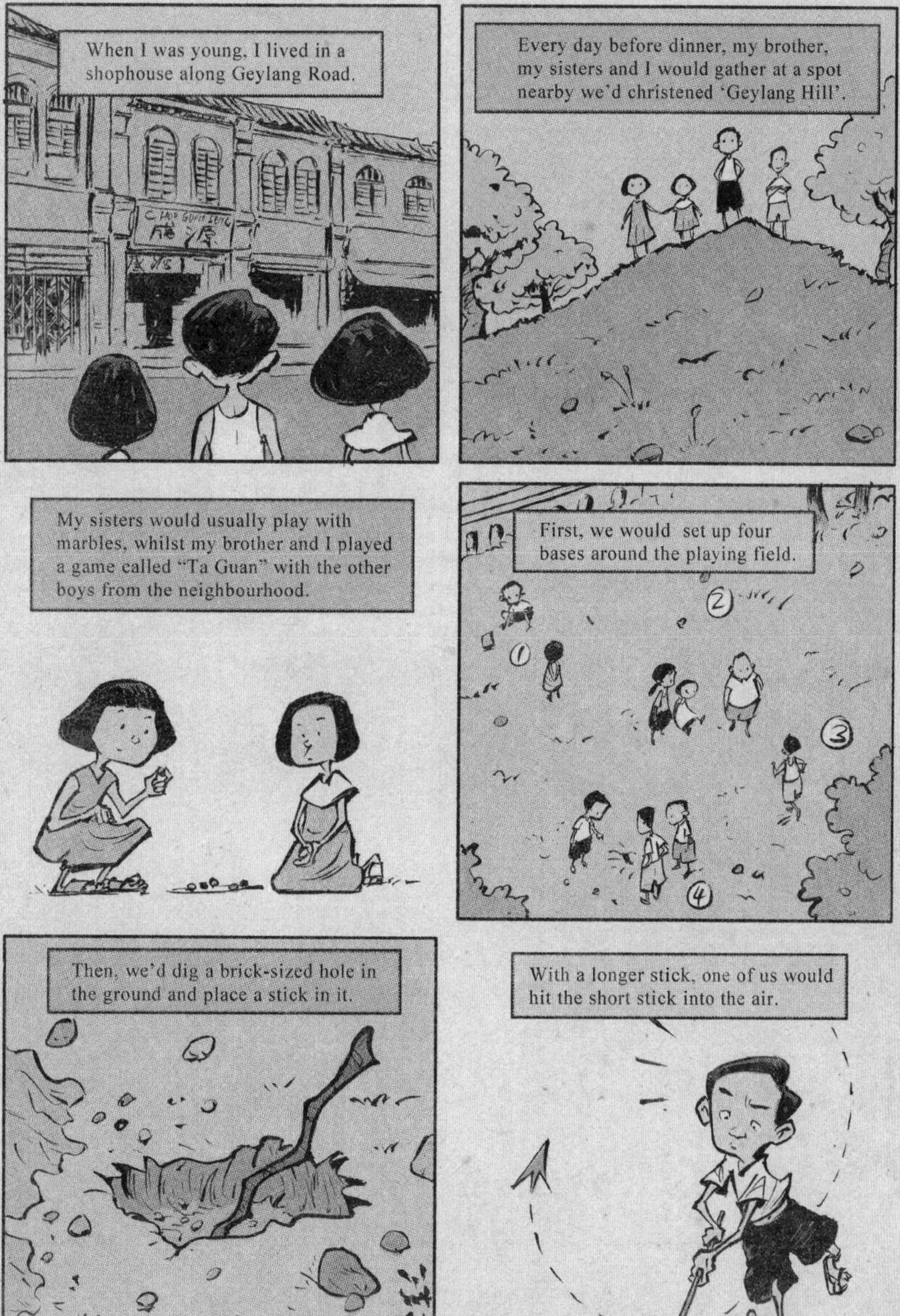
When I was young, I lived in a shophouse along Geylang Road.
Every day before dinner, my brother, my sisters and I would gather at a spot nearby we'd christened 'Geylang Hill'.
My sisters would usually play with marbles, whilst my brother and I played a game called "Ta Guan" with the other boys from the neighbourhood.
First, we would set up four bases around the playing field.
Then, we'd dig a brick-sized hole in the ground and place a stick in it.
With a longer stick, one of us would hit the short stick into the air.

Note: "Ta Guan" – Cantonese, literally meaning "Hitting Sticks"

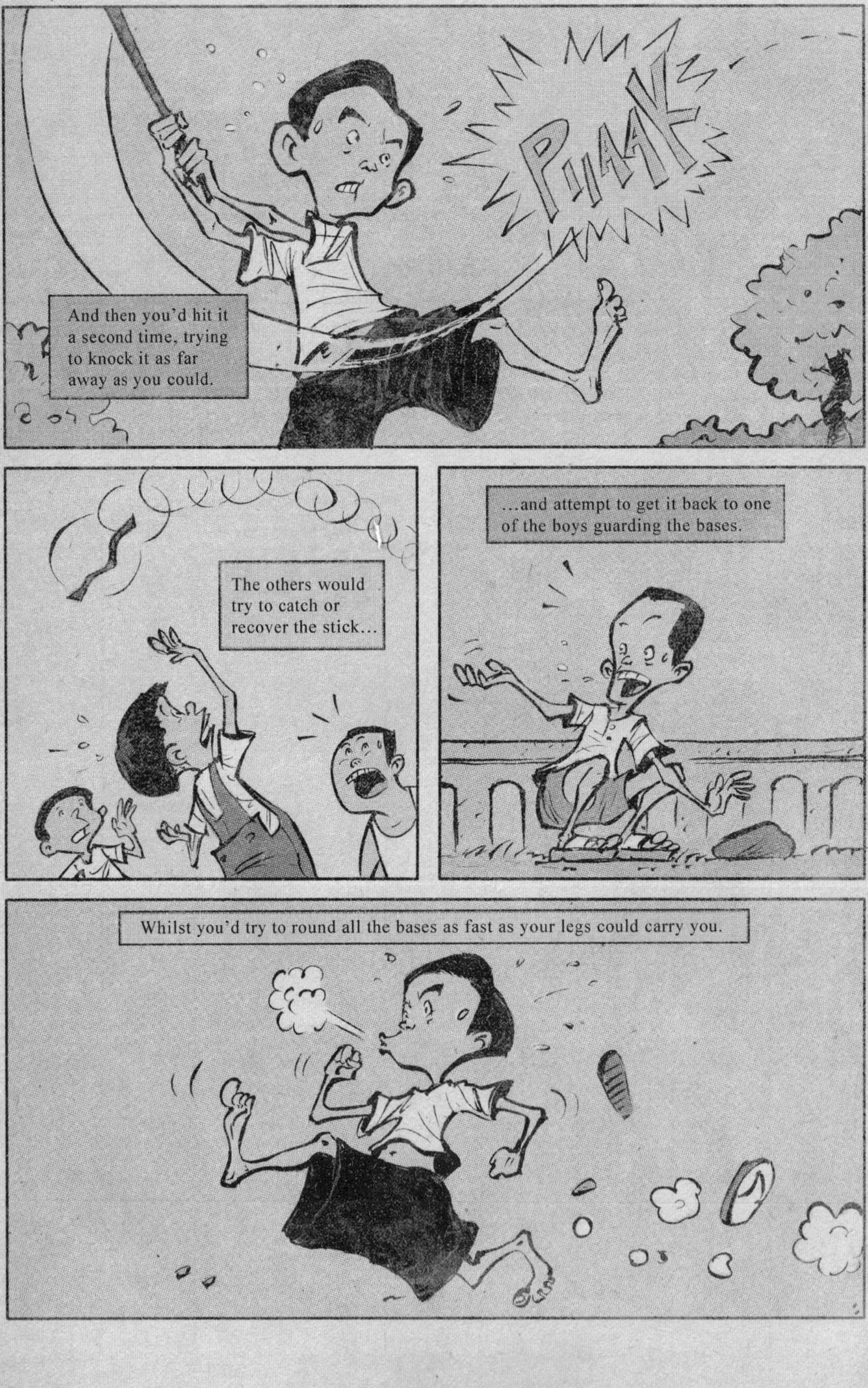
PUAAK
And then you'd hit it a second time, trying to knock it as far away as you could.
The others would try to catch or recover the stick...
...and attempt to get it back to one of the boys guarding the bases.
Whilst you'd try to round all the bases as fast as your legs could carry you.

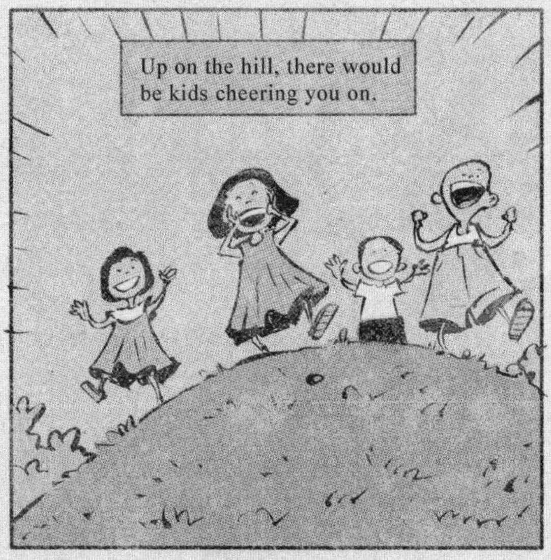
Up on the hill, there would be kids cheering you on.

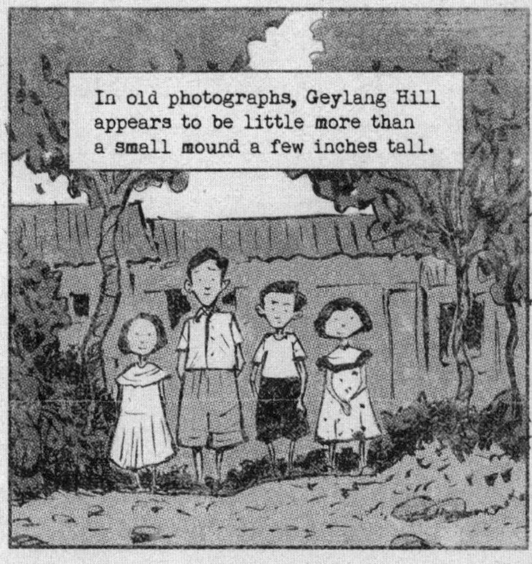
In old photographs, Geylang Hill appears to be little more than a small mound a few inches tall.

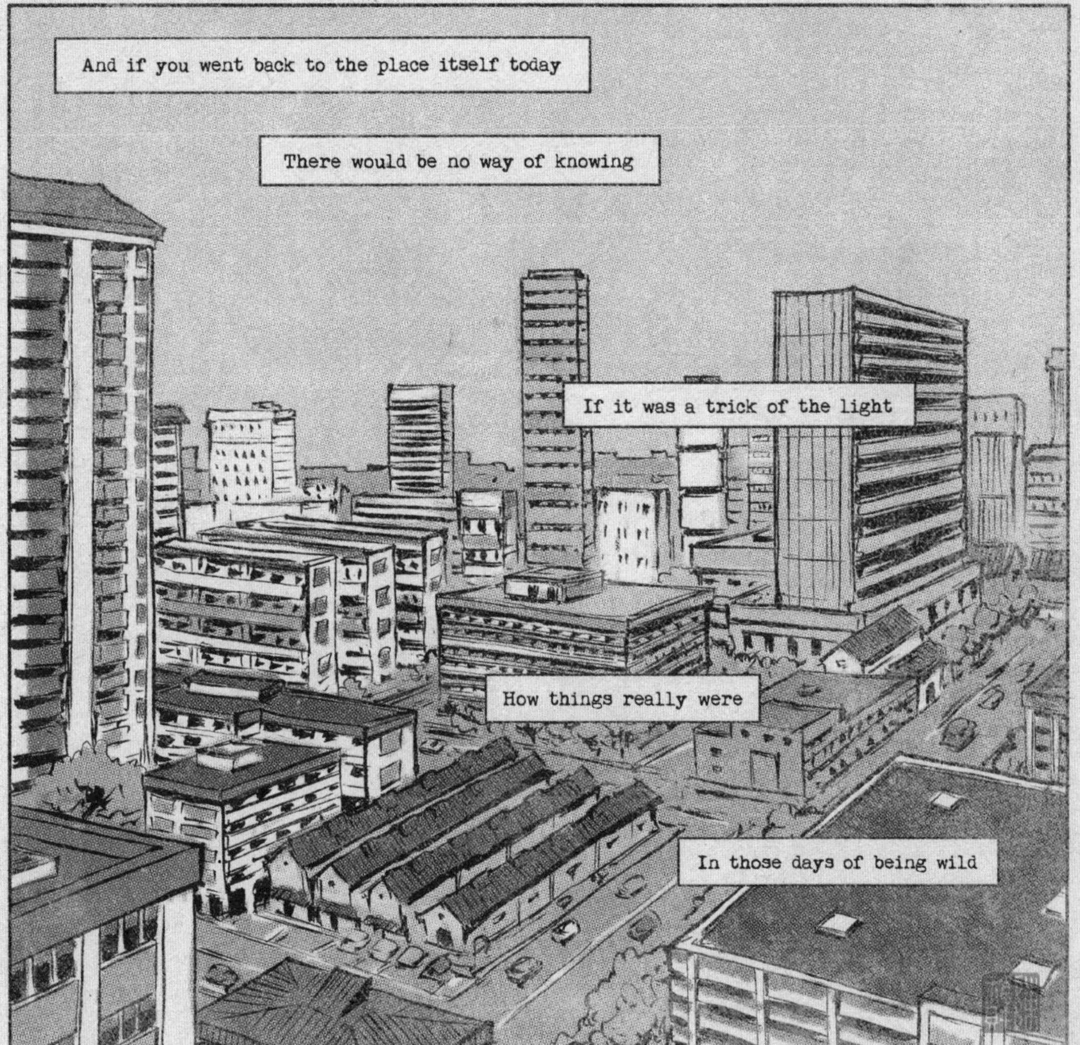
And if you went back to the place itself today
There would be no way of knowing
If it was a trick of the light
How things really were
In those days of being wild

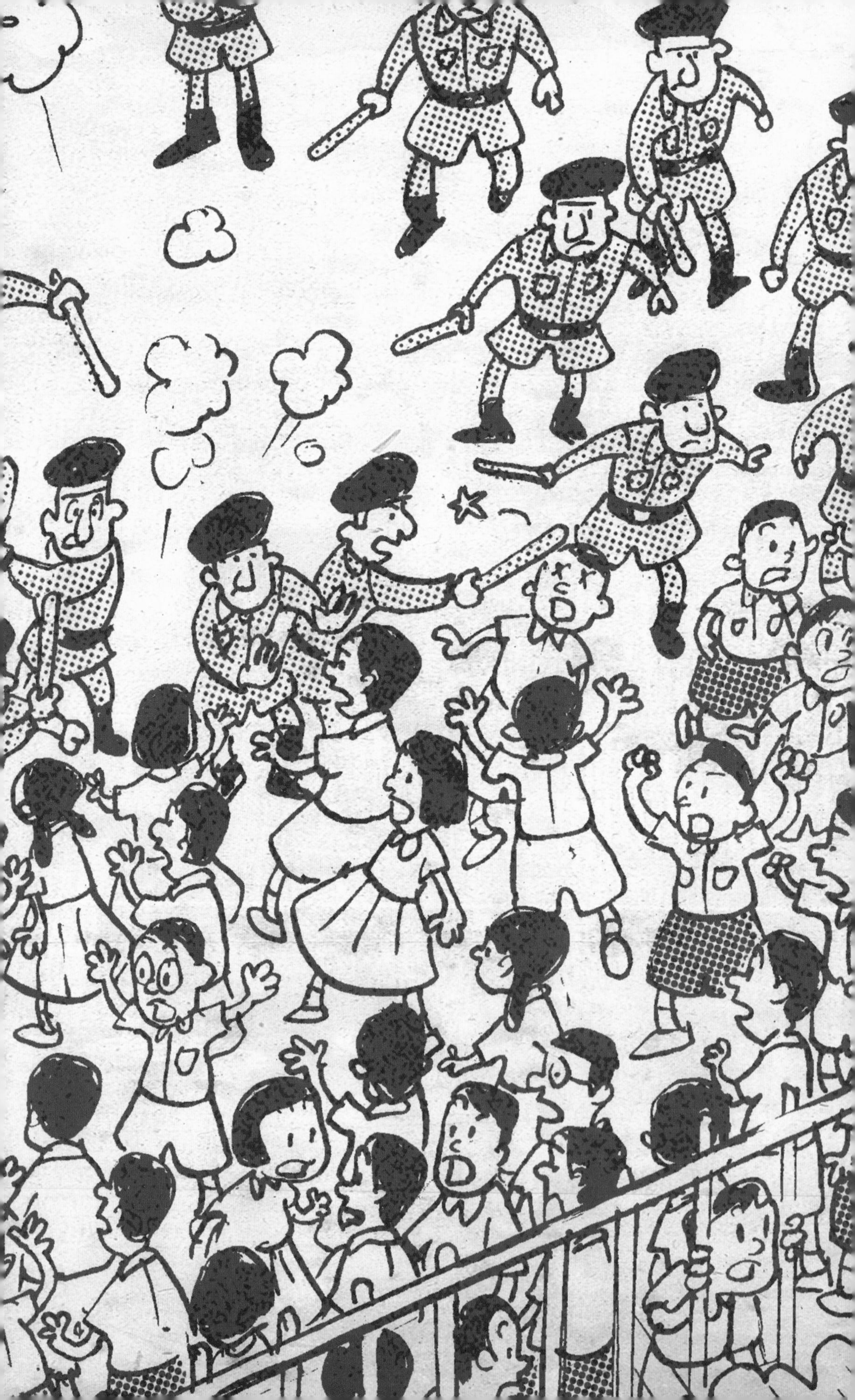

Chapter Two

CHARLIE JOINS THE REVOLUTION

置身革命

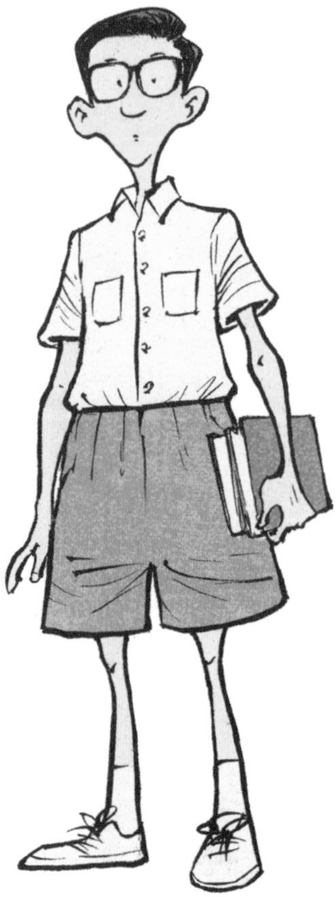

Charlie Chan Hock Chye, aged 16, 1954

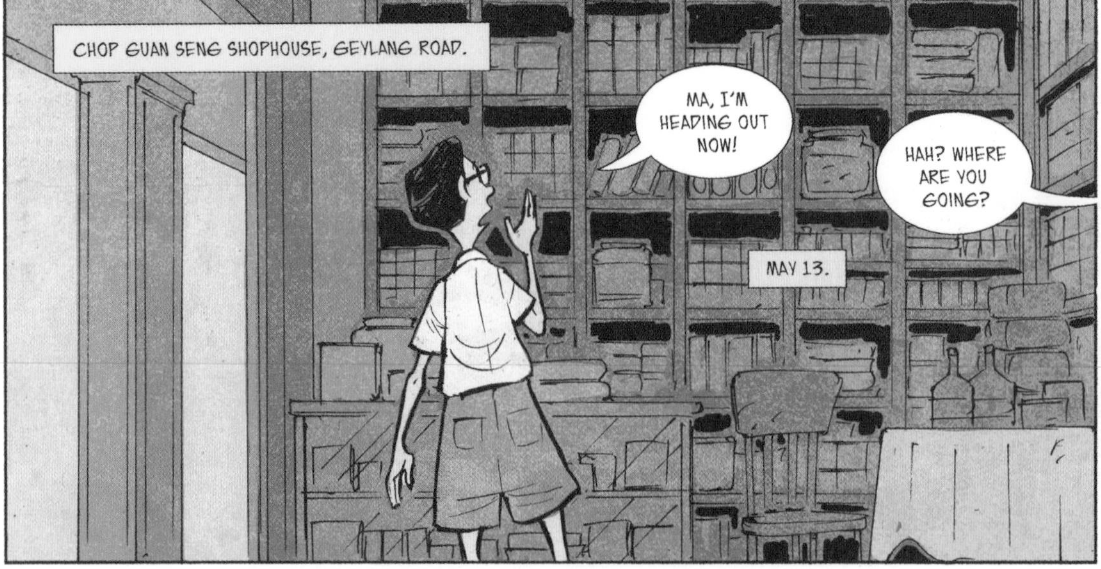
CHOP GUAN SENG SHOPHOUSE, GEYLANG ROAD.
MA, I'M HEADING OUT NOW!
HAH? WHERE ARE YOU GOING?
MAY 13.

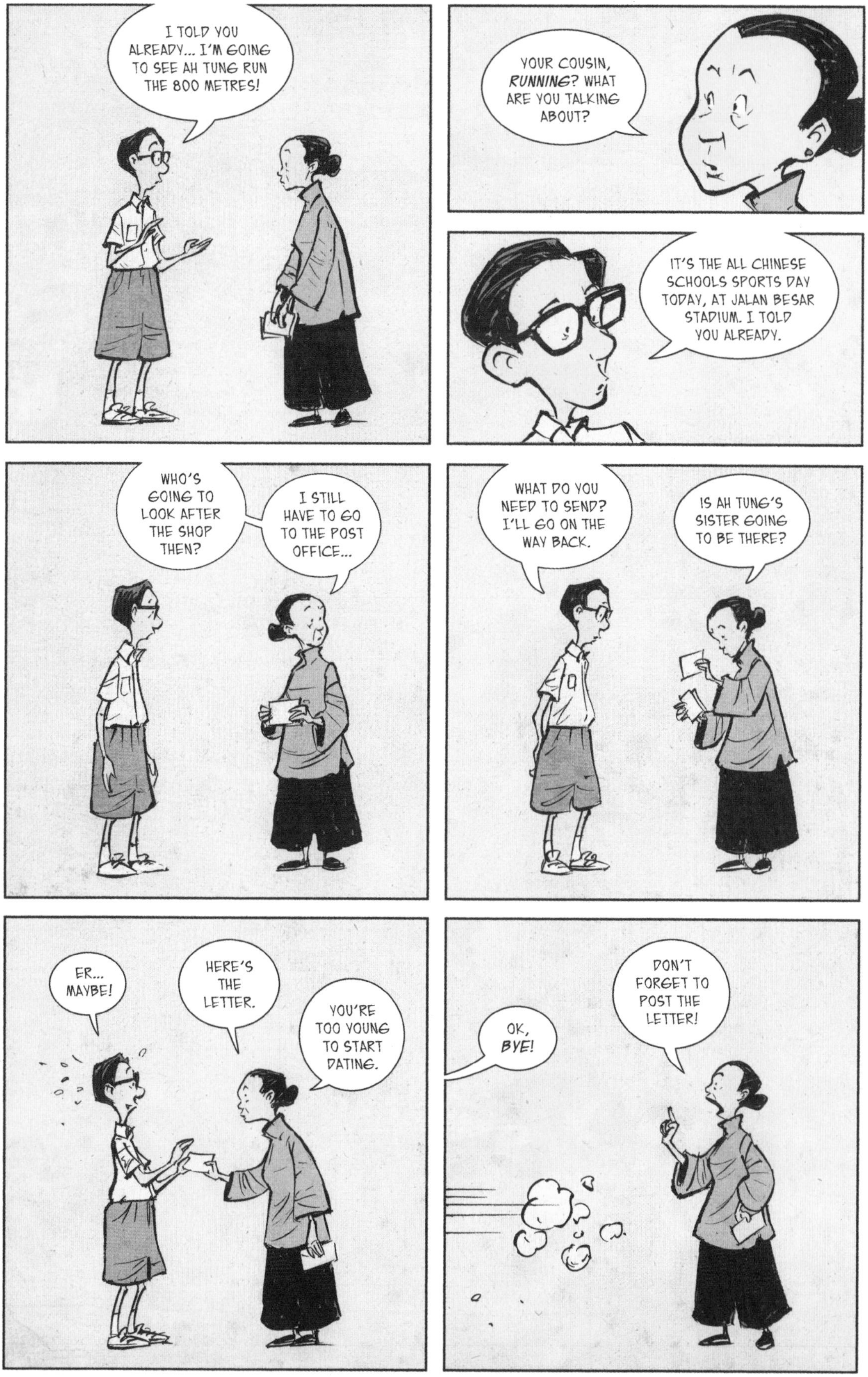
I TOLD YOU ALREADY... I'M GOING TO SEE AH TUNG RUN THE 800 METRES!
YOUR COUSIN, *RUNNING*? WHAT ARE YOU TALKING ABOUT?
IT'S THE ALL CHINESE SCHOOLS SPORTS DAY TODAY, AT JALAN BESAR STADIUM. I TOLD YOU ALREADY.
WHO'S GOING TO LOOK AFTER THE SHOP THEN?
I STILL HAVE TO GO TO THE POST OFFICE...
WHAT DO YOU NEED TO SEND? I'LL GO ON THE WAY BACK.
IS AH TUNG'S SISTER GOING TO BE THERE?
ER... MAYBE!
HERE'S THE LETTER.
YOU'RE TOO YOUNG TO START DATING.
OK, *BYE*!
DON'T FORGET TO POST THE LETTER!

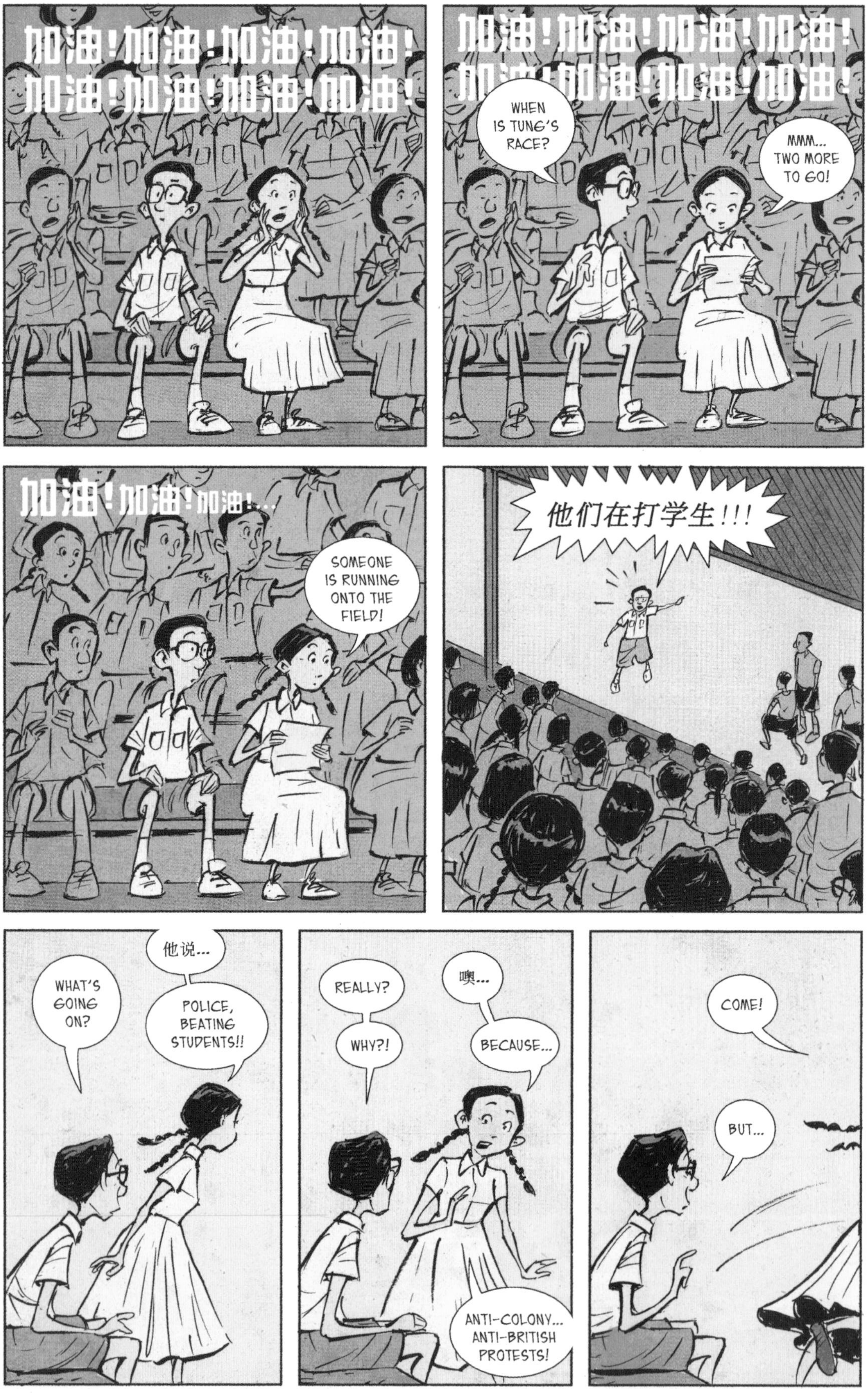
加油！加油！加油！加油！加油！加油！加油！加油！
加油！加油！加油！加油！加油！加油！加油！加油！
WHEN IS TUNG'S RACE?
MMM... TWO MORE TO GO!
加油！加油！加油！...
SOMEONE IS RUNNING ONTO THE FIELD!
他们在打学生!!!
WHAT'S GOING ON?
他说...
POLICE, BEATING STUDENTS!!
REALLY?
WHY?!
噢...
BECAUSE...
ANTI-COLONY... ANTI-BRITISH PROTESTS!
COME!
BUT...

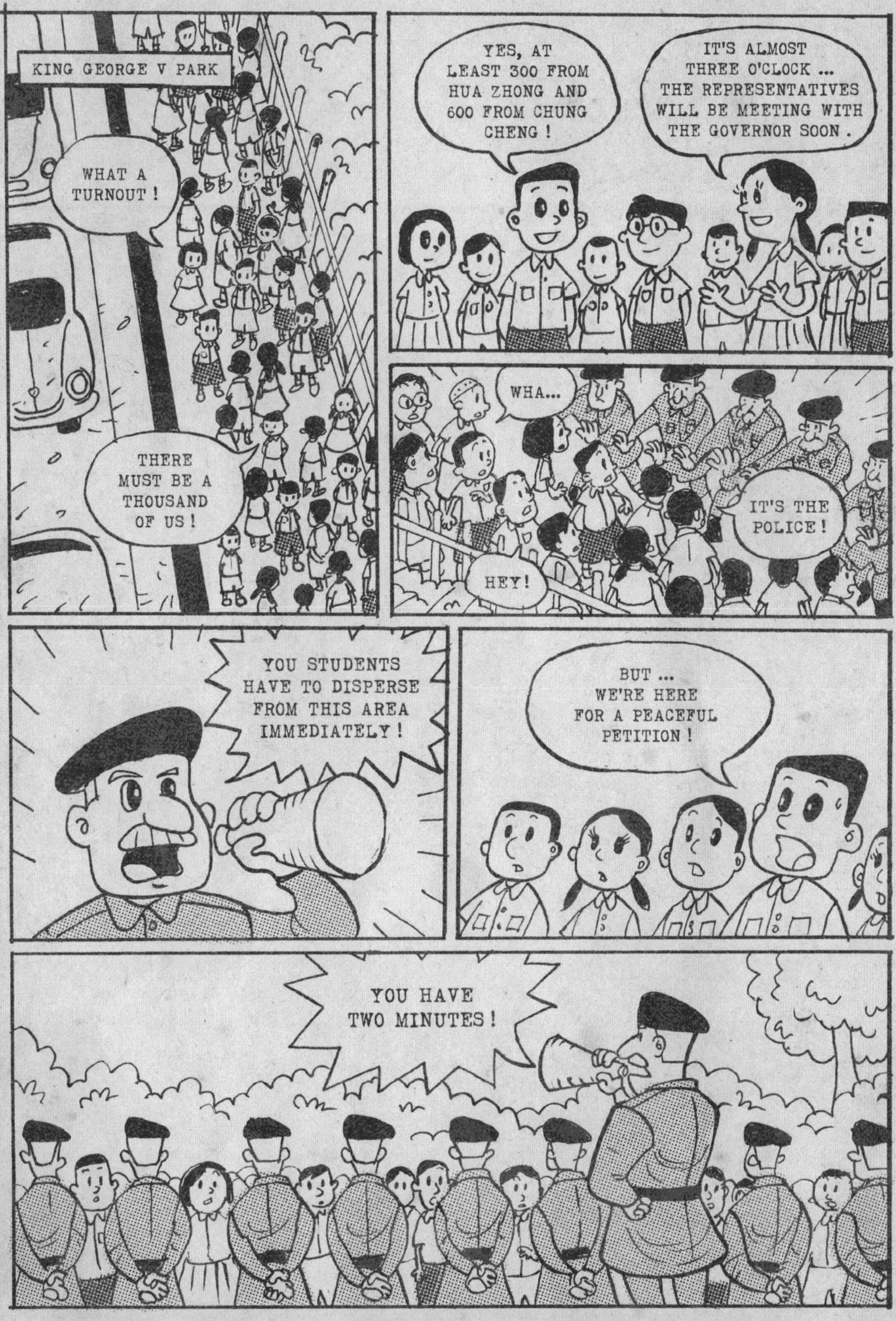
KING GEORGE V PARK
WHAT A TURNOUT !
THERE MUST BE A THOUSAND OF US !
YES, AT LEAST 300 FROM HUA ZHONG AND 600 FROM CHUNG CHENG !
IT'S ALMOST THREE O'CLOCK ... THE REPRESENTATIVES WILL BE MEETING WITH THE GOVERNOR SOON .
WHA...
IT'S THE POLICE !
HEY!
YOU STUDENTS HAVE TO DISPERSE FROM THIS AREA IMMEDIATELY !
BUT ... WE'RE HERE FOR A PEACEFUL PETITION !
YOU HAVE TWO MINUTES !

Above & following **AH HUAT'S GIANT ROBOT Vol. 1** (1956) | Chan Hock Chye | Stones Throw Press

Partly based on Chan's own experience of the May 13 incident of 1954, the comic depicts the actions taken by the police against students who had gathered at King George V Park (renamed Fort Canning Park in 1981) as an unprovoked attack.

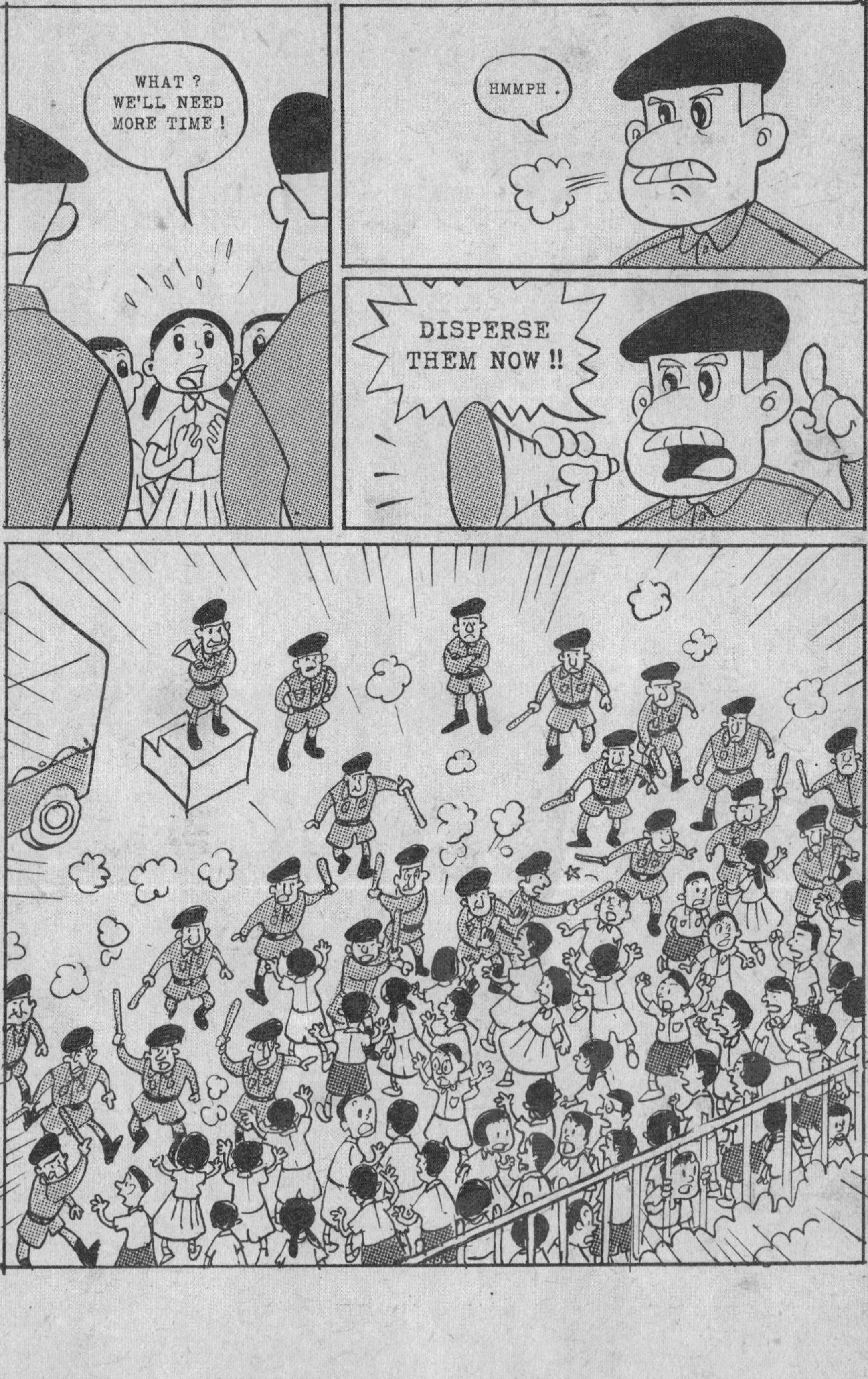
WHAT ? WE'LL NEED MORE TIME !
HMMPH .
DISPERSE THEM NOW !!

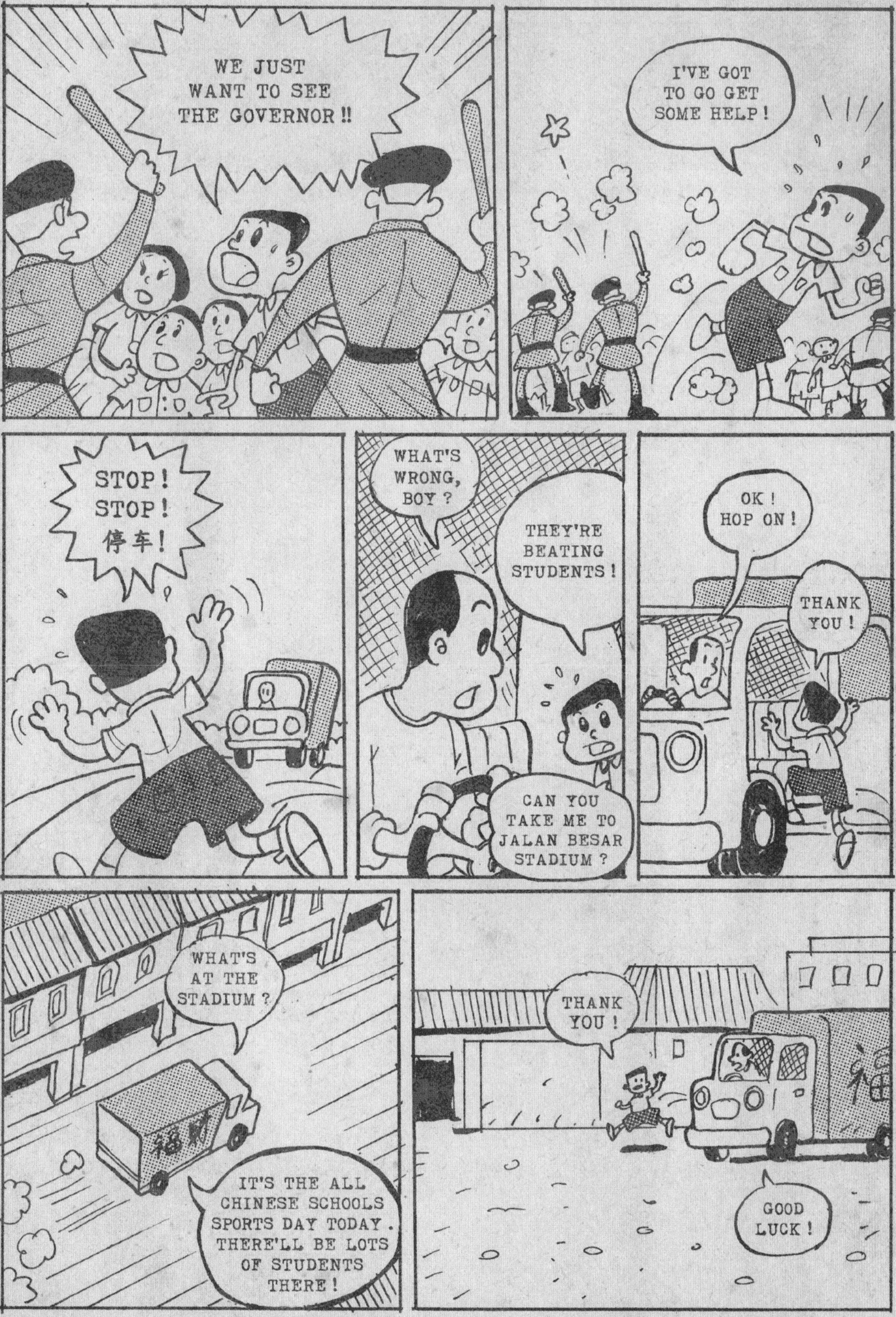
WE JUST WANT TO SEE THE GOVERNOR !!
I'VE GOT TO GO GET SOME HELP !
STOP ! STOP ! 停车 !
WHAT'S WRONG, BOY ?
THEY'RE BEATING STUDENTS !
CAN YOU TAKE ME TO JALAN BESAR STADIUM ?
OK ! HOP ON !
THANK YOU !
WHAT'S AT THE STADIUM ?
福财
IT'S THE ALL CHINESE SCHOOLS SPORTS DAY TODAY. THERE'LL BE LOTS OF STUDENTS THERE !
THANK YOU !
GOOD LUCK !

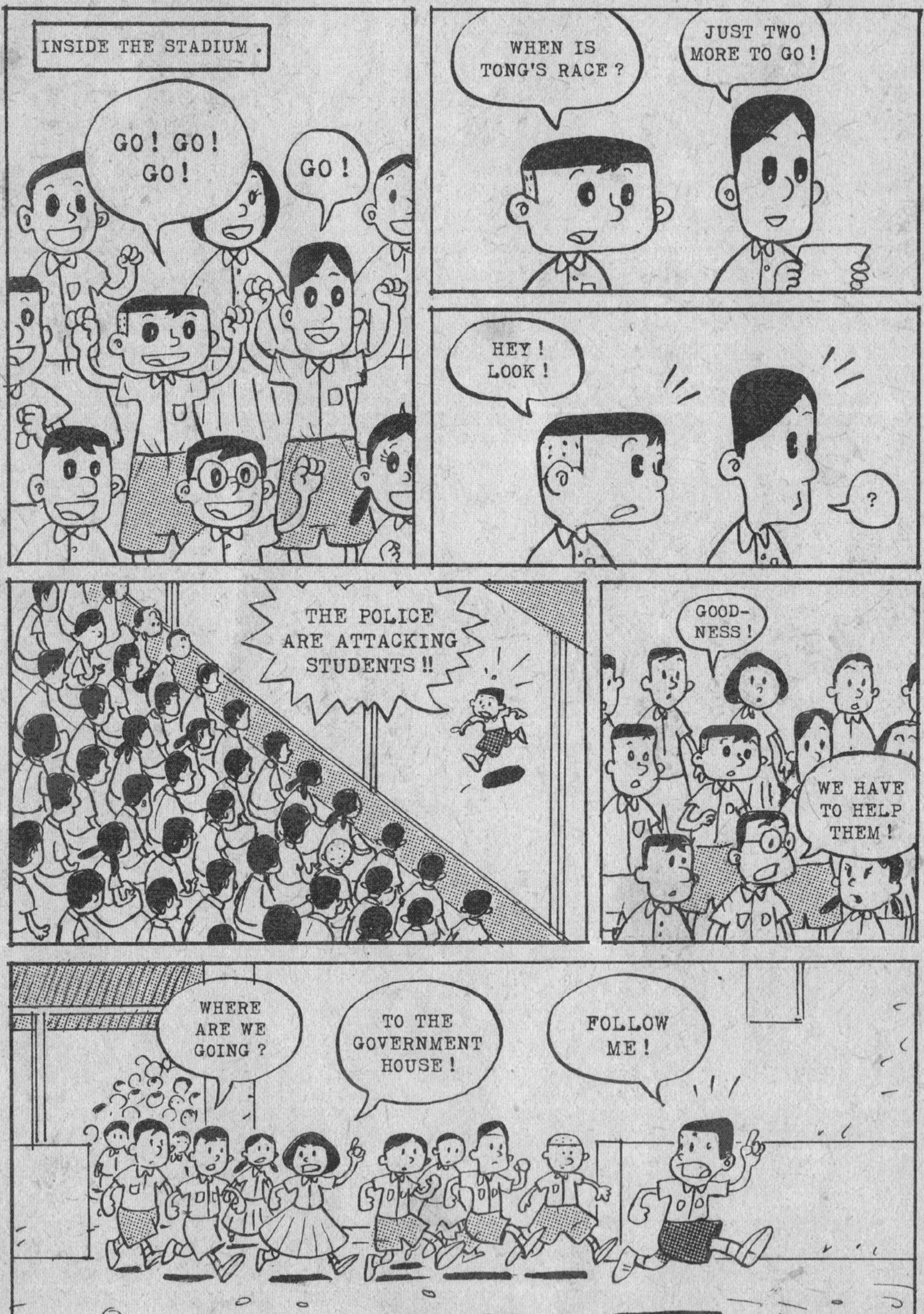
INSIDE THE STADIUM .
GO! GO! GO!
GO !
WHEN IS TONG'S RACE ?
JUST TWO MORE TO GO !
HEY ! LOOK !
?
THE POLICE ARE ATTACKING STUDENTS !!
GOOD-NESS !
WE HAVE TO HELP THEM !
WHERE ARE WE GOING ?
TO THE GOVERNMENT HOUSE !
FOLLOW ME !

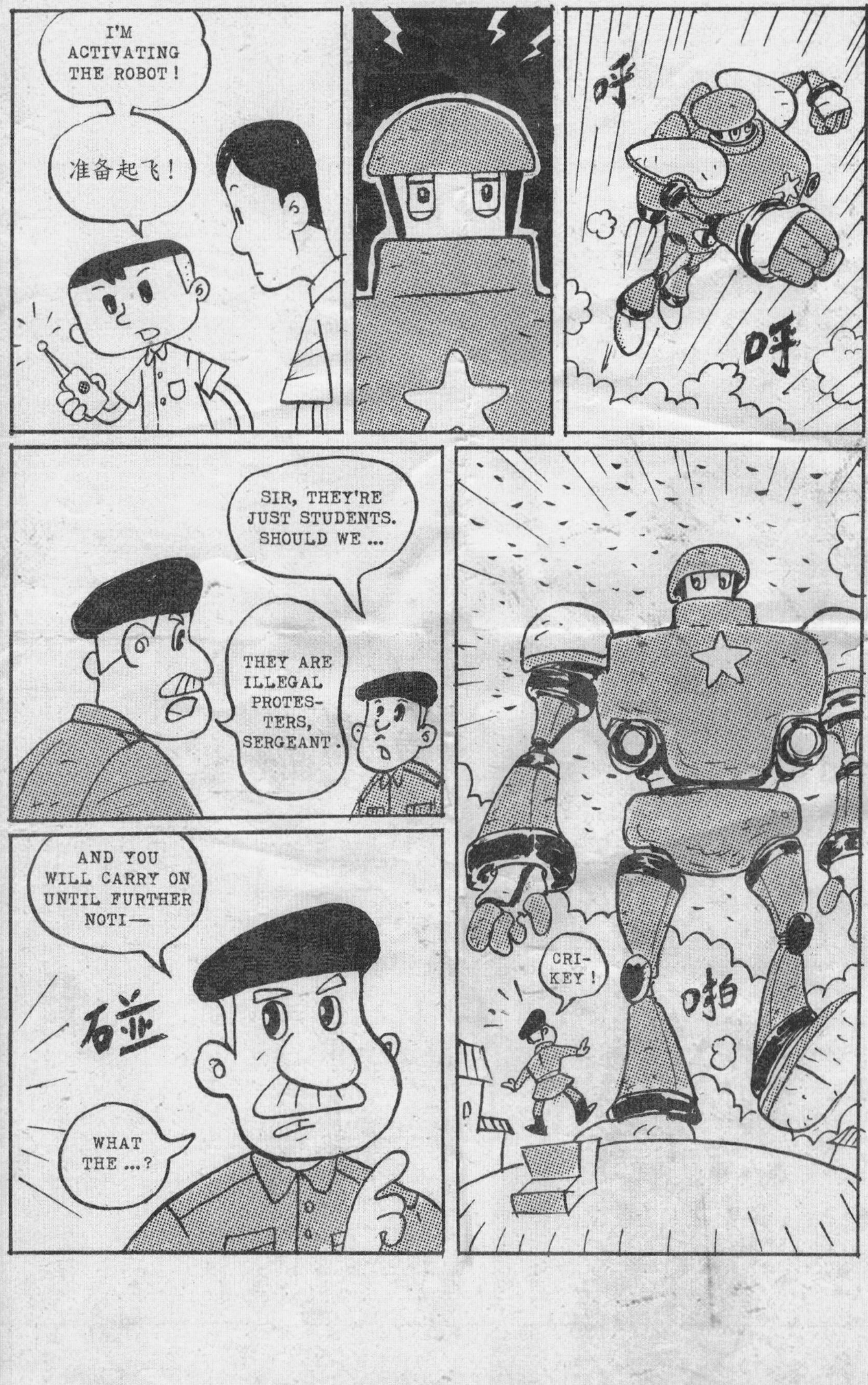
I'M ACTIVATING THE ROBOT!
准备起飞!
呼
呼
SIR, THEY'RE JUST STUDENTS. SHOULD WE ...
THEY ARE ILLEGAL PROTES-TERS, SERGEANT.
AND YOU WILL CARRY ON UNTIL FURTHER NOTI—
碰
WHAT THE ...?
CRI-KEY!
啪

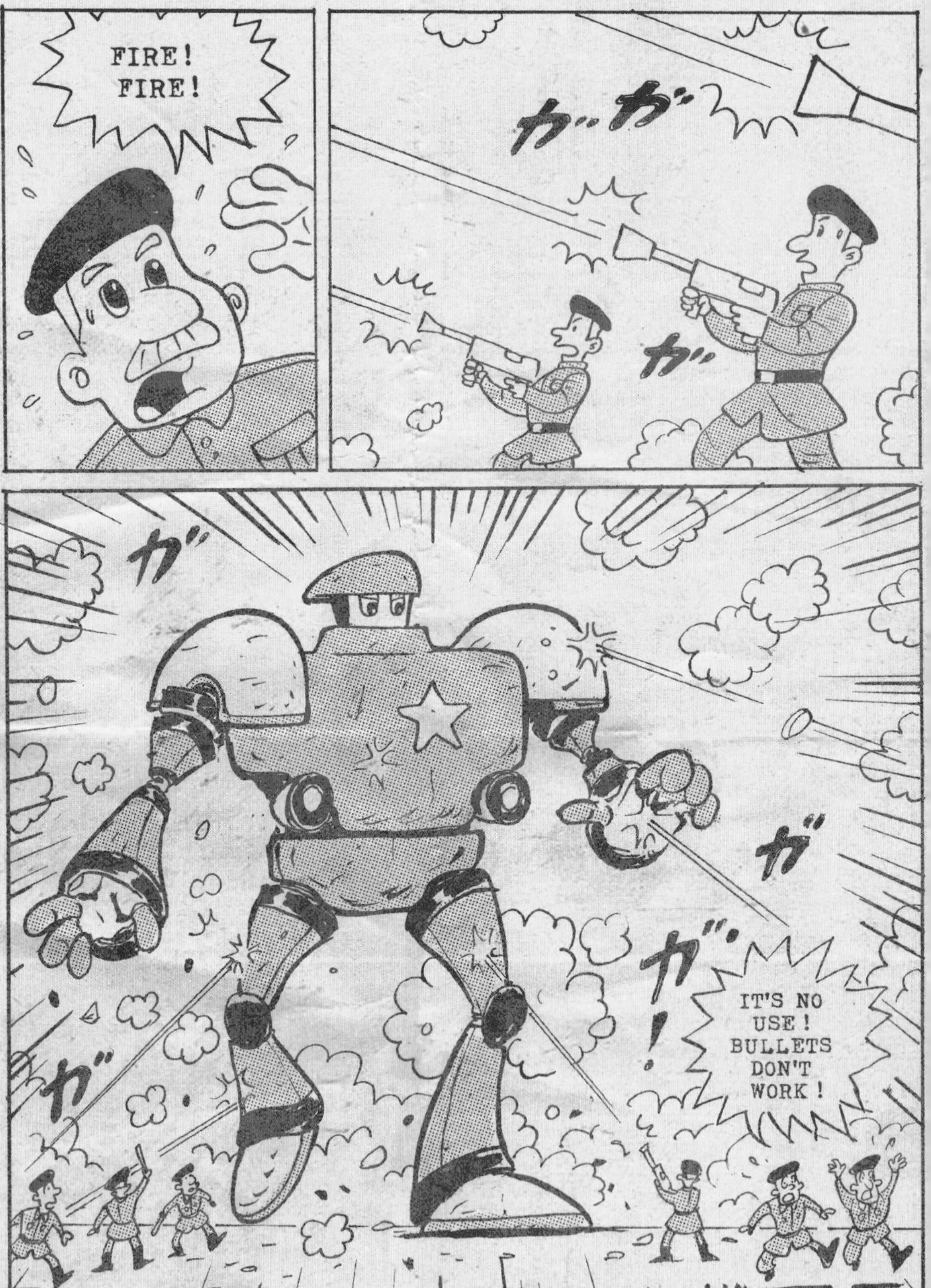
FIRE!
FIRE!
ガが
ガ
ガ
ガ
IT'S NO USE! BULLETS DON'T WORK!
ガ!
が
ザ
ザ

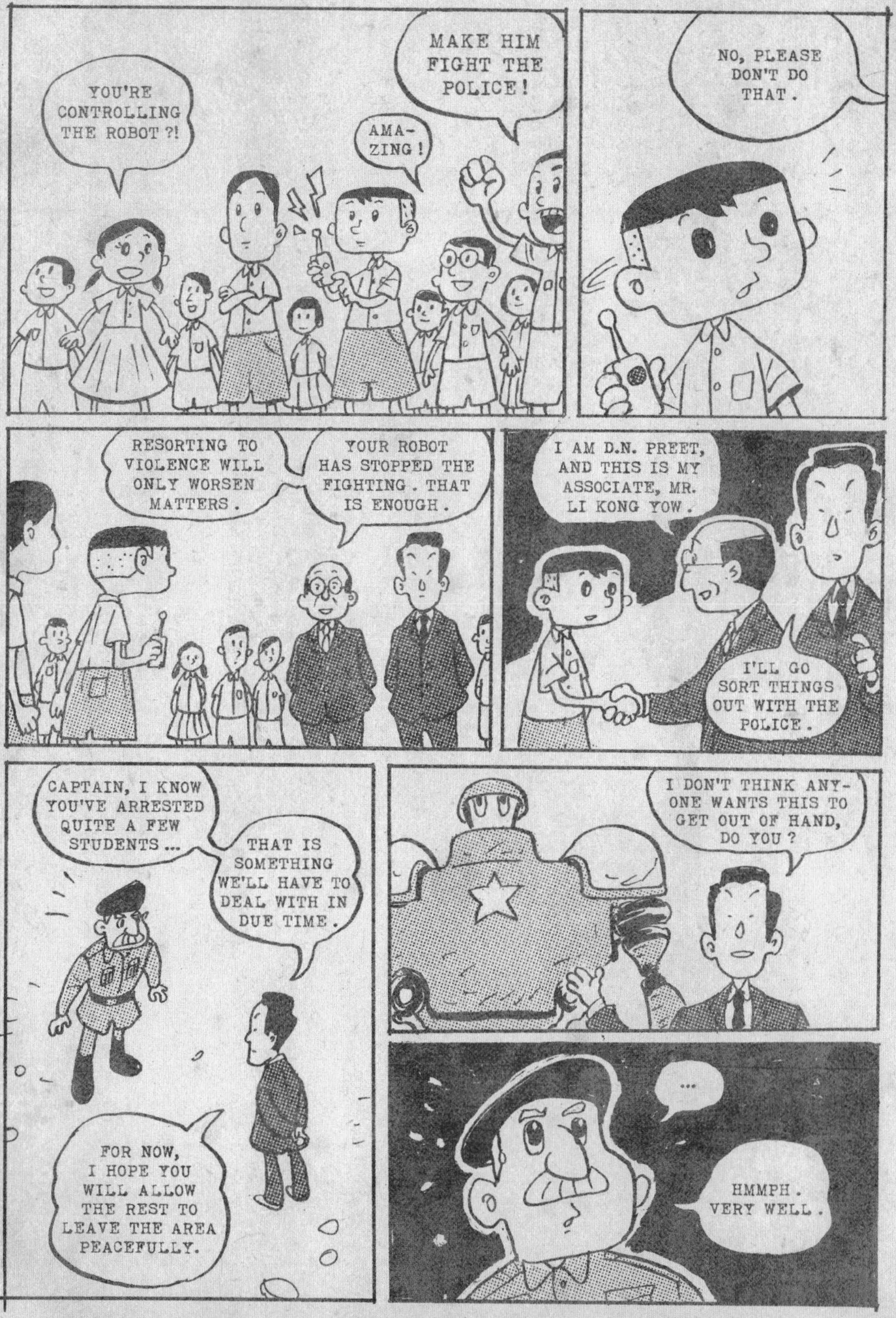
YOU'RE CONTROLLING THE ROBOT ?!
AMA-ZING !
MAKE HIM FIGHT THE POLICE !
NO, PLEASE DON'T DO THAT.
RESORTING TO VIOLENCE WILL ONLY WORSEN MATTERS.
YOUR ROBOT HAS STOPPED THE FIGHTING. THAT IS ENOUGH.
I AM D.N. PREET, AND THIS IS MY ASSOCIATE, MR. LI KONG YOW.
I'LL GO SORT THINGS OUT WITH THE POLICE.
CAPTAIN, I KNOW YOU'VE ARRESTED QUITE A FEW STUDENTS...
THAT IS SOMETHING WE'LL HAVE TO DEAL WITH IN DUE TIME.
FOR NOW, I HOPE YOU WILL ALLOW THE REST TO LEAVE THE AREA PEACEFULLY.
I DON'T THINK ANY-ONE WANTS THIS TO GET OUT OF HAND, DO YOU ?
...
HMMPH. VERY WELL.

Thinly disguised versions of British Queen's Counsel **D.N. Pritt** and legal assistant **Lee Kuan Yew** are shown offering advice at the May 13 scene itself in this fictionalised version of events. In reality, the two lawyers only got involved at a later date, when they agreed to act as legal counsels for the 48 students arrested during the incident.

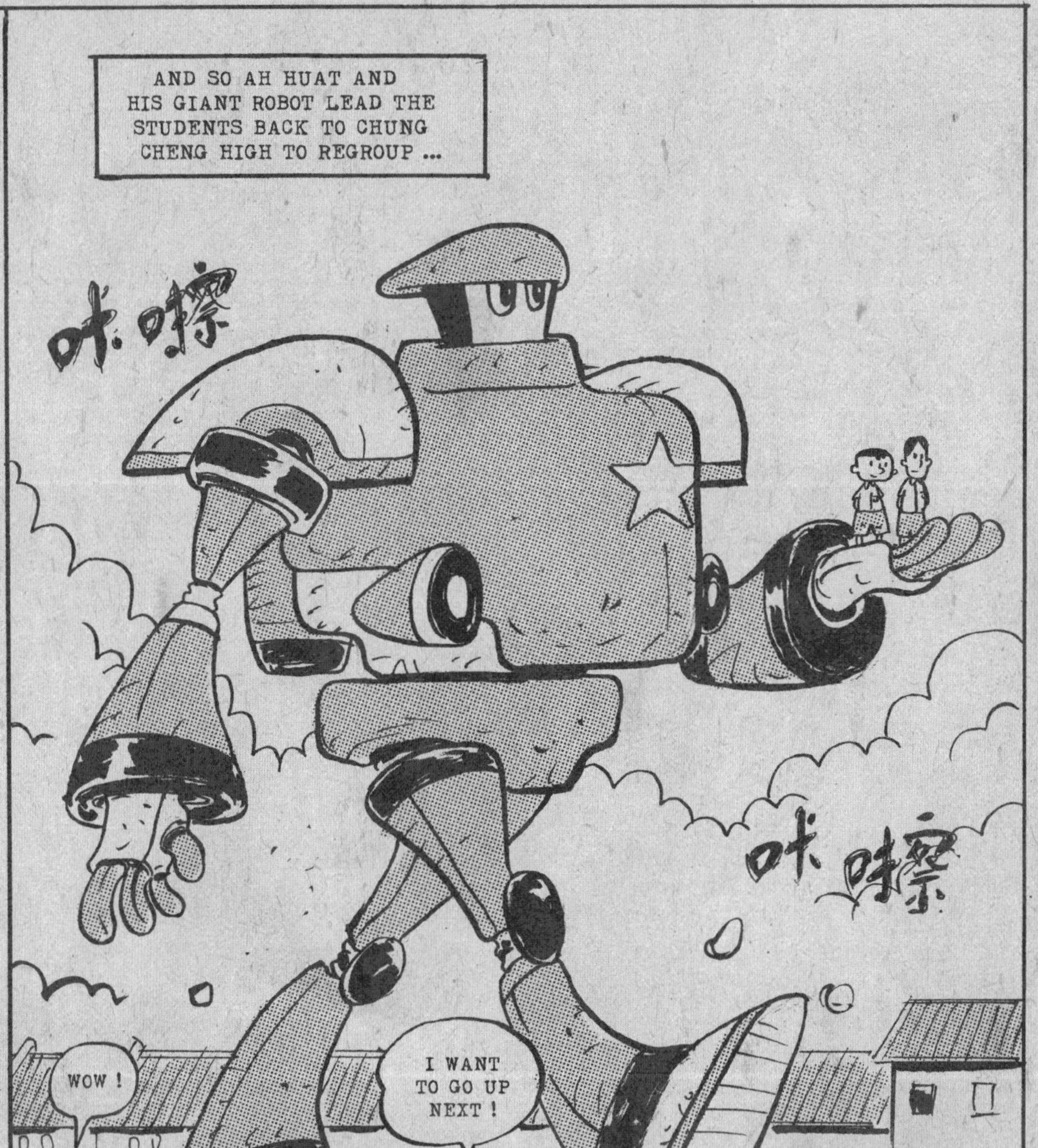
AND SO AH HUAT AND HIS GIANT ROBOT LEAD THE STUDENTS BACK TO CHUNG CHENG HIGH TO REGROUP ...
咔嚓
咔嚓
WOW !
I WANT TO GO UP NEXT !
HE'S GIGANTIC !

CHUNG CHENG HIGH SCHOOL, GOODMAN ROAD, 2011.

YES, YES...

THIS WAS THE PLACE, ALL THOSE YEARS AGO...

IN REALITY, WE NEVER MADE IT TO FORT CANNING, BECAUSE THE POLICE HAD SET UP *ROADBLOCKS*.

SO WE GATHERED HERE INSTEAD, ARRIVING ON FOOT, IN LORRIES AND ON BUSES.

MUST HAVE BEEN A *THOUSAND* OF US, AT LEAST.

I KEPT TRYING TO FIND OUT WHAT WAS GOING ON.

||||/|| ||/|||| |||| ?

NO, NO. IT'S ALL CHANGED NOW. NOTHING MORE TO SEE INSIDE.

ABOUT TIME FOR LUNCH, ANYWAY.

EVENTUALLY, I LEARNT THAT THE STUDENTS HAD BEEN TRYING TO SUBMIT A *PETITION* TO THE GOVERNOR.

IT WAS A PROTEST AGAINST AN ORDER FOR YOUTHS TO BE REGISTERED FOR *NATIONAL SERVICE*...

...TO SERVE IN THE *BRITISH* ARMY, BASICALLY.

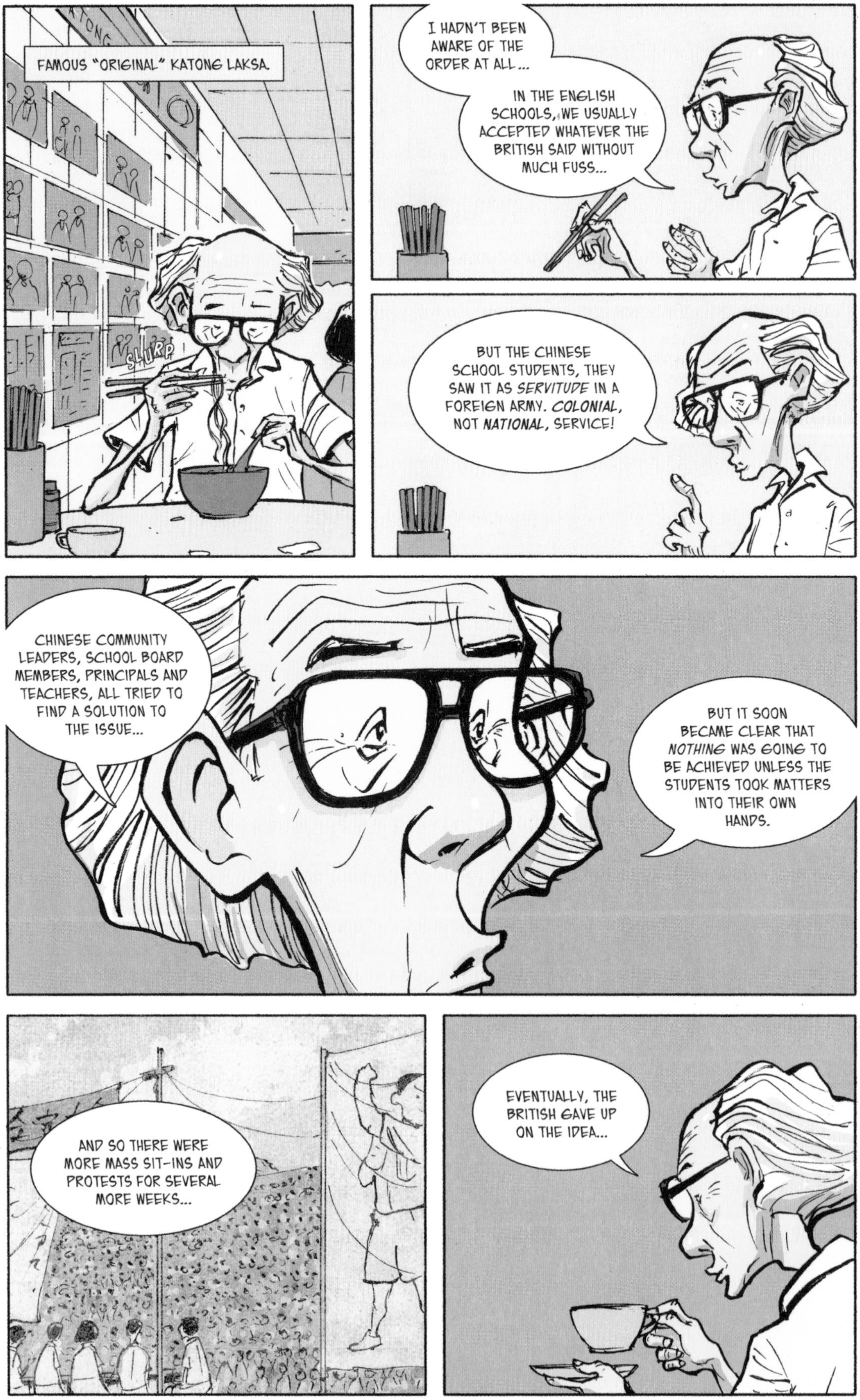
KATONG
FAMOUS "ORIGINAL" KATONG LAKSA.
SLURP
I HADN'T BEEN AWARE OF THE ORDER AT ALL...
IN THE ENGLISH SCHOOLS, WE USUALLY ACCEPTED WHATEVER THE BRITISH SAID WITHOUT MUCH FUSS...
BUT THE CHINESE SCHOOL STUDENTS, THEY SAW IT AS *SERVITUDE* IN A FOREIGN ARMY. *COLONIAL*, NOT ***NATIONAL***, SERVICE!
CHINESE COMMUNITY LEADERS, SCHOOL BOARD MEMBERS, PRINCIPALS AND TEACHERS, ALL TRIED TO FIND A SOLUTION TO THE ISSUE...
BUT IT SOON BECAME CLEAR THAT *NOTHING* WAS GOING TO BE ACHIEVED UNLESS THE STUDENTS TOOK MATTERS INTO THEIR OWN HANDS.
AND SO THERE WERE MORE MASS SIT-INS AND PROTESTS FOR SEVERAL MORE WEEKS...
EVENTUALLY, THE BRITISH GAVE UP ON THE IDEA...

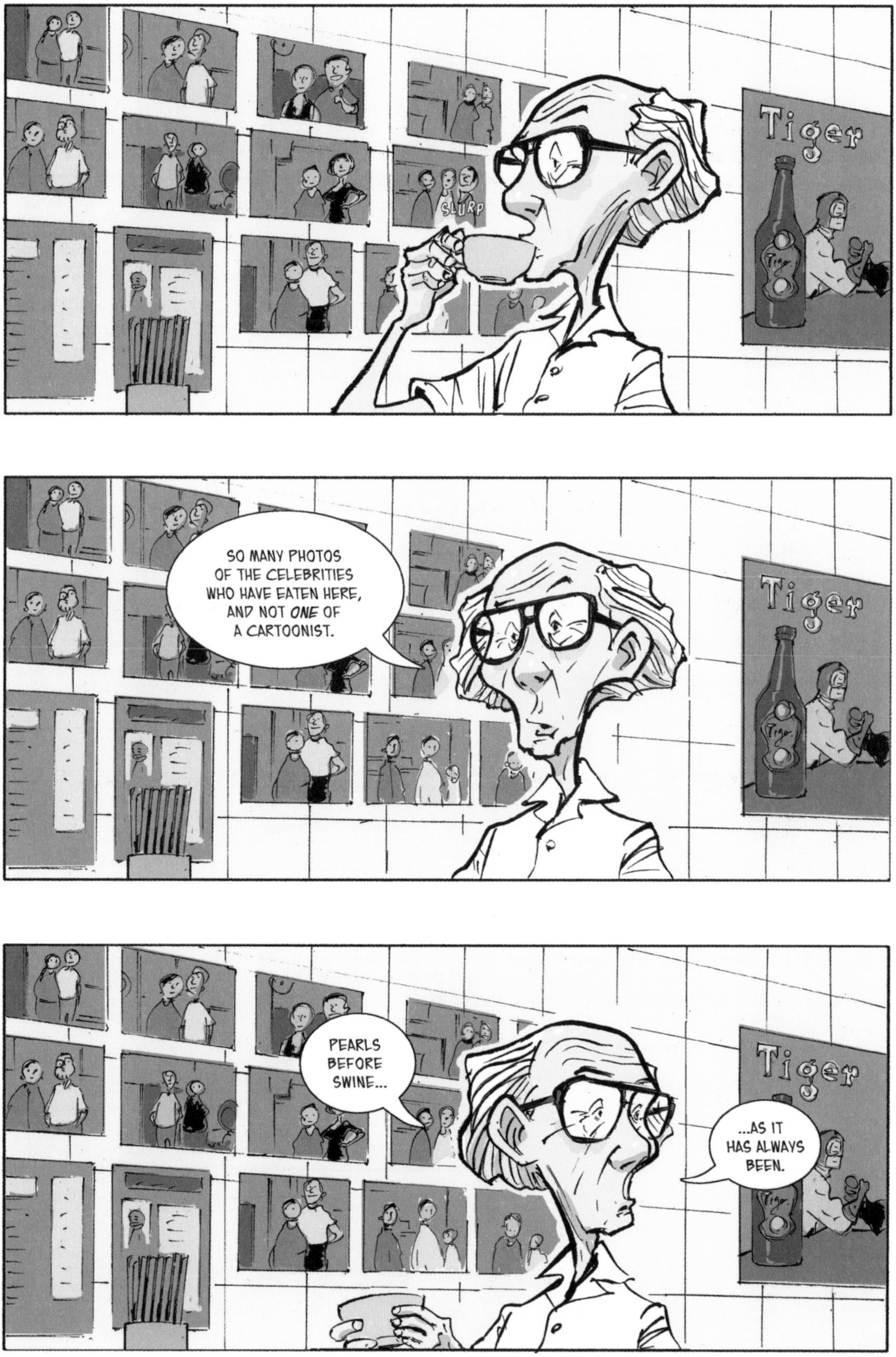
SLURP
Tiger
SO MANY PHOTOS OF THE CELEBRITIES WHO HAVE EATEN HERE, AND NOT *ONE* OF A CARTOONIST.
Tiger
PEARLS BEFORE SWINE...
...AS IT HAS ALWAYS BEEN.
Tiger

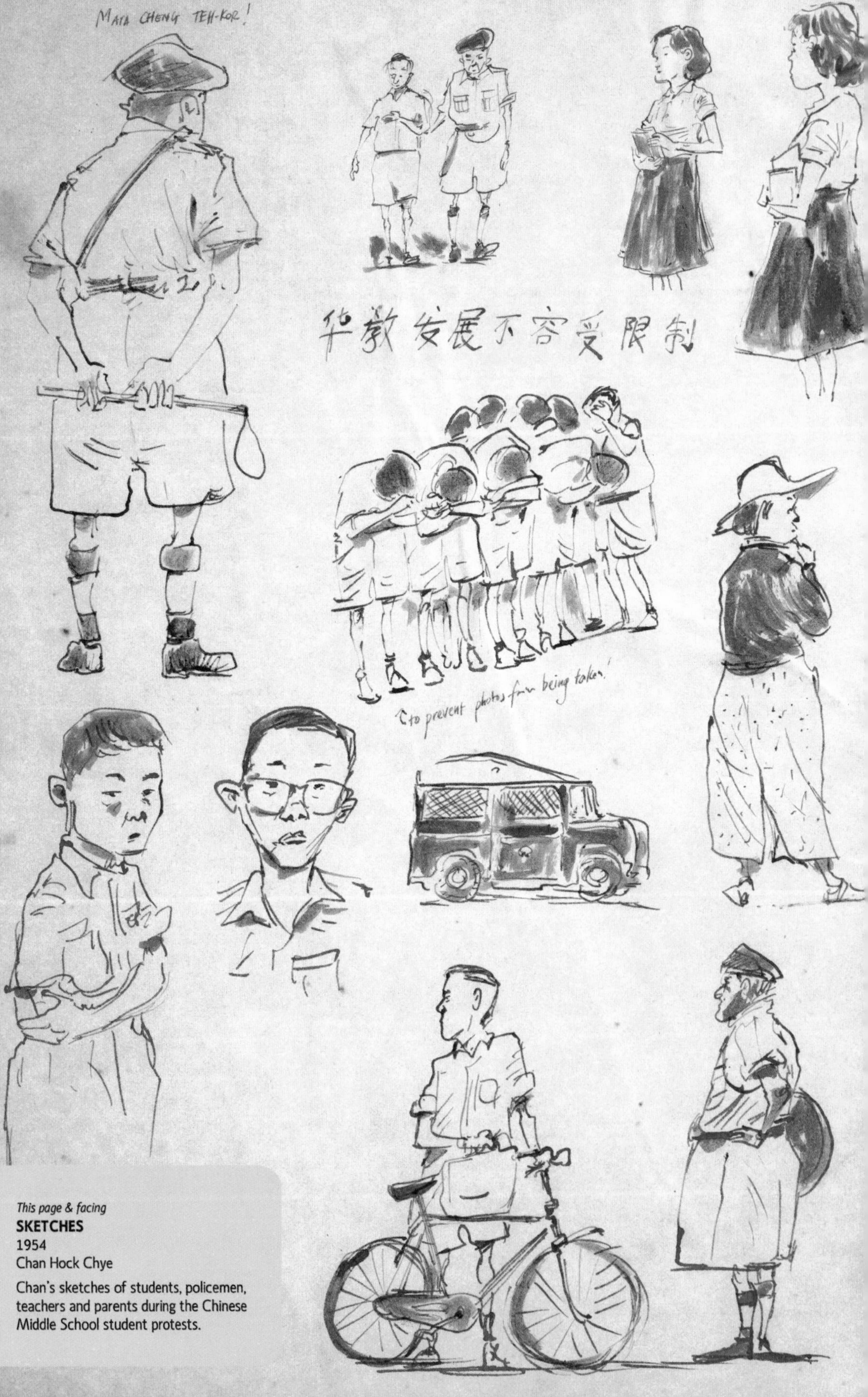
MATA CHENG TEH-KOR!
华教发展不容受限制
↑ to prevent photos from being taken!

This page & facing

SKETCHES

1954

Chan Hock Chye

Chan's sketches of students, policemen, teachers and parents during the Chinese Middle School student protests.

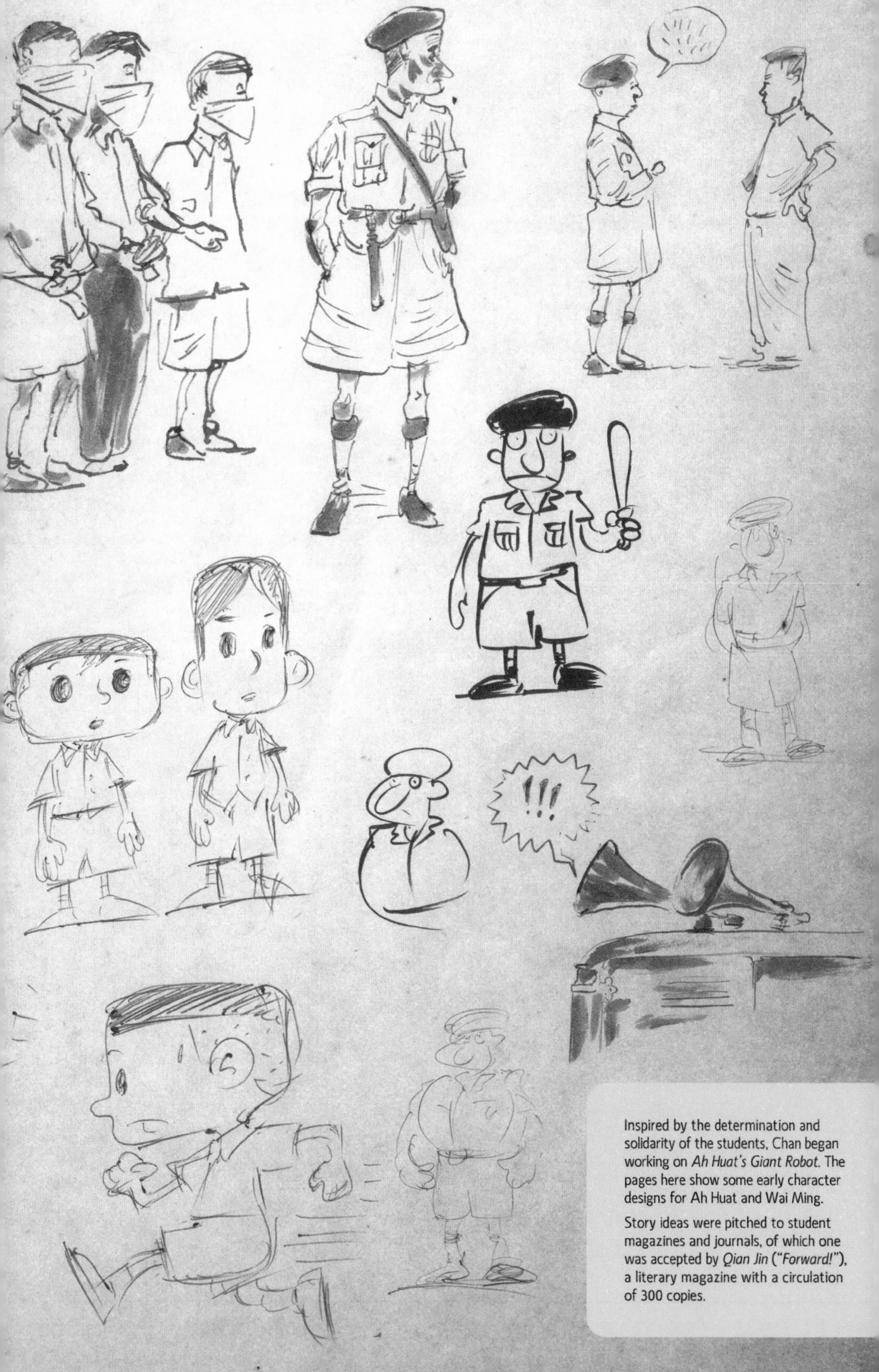
!!!

Inspired by the determination and solidarity of the students, Chan began working on *Ah Huat's Giant Robot*. The pages here show some early character designs for Ah Huat and Wai Ming.

Story ideas were pitched to student magazines and journals, of which one was accepted by *Qian Jin* ("*Forward!*"), a literary magazine with a circulation of 300 copies.

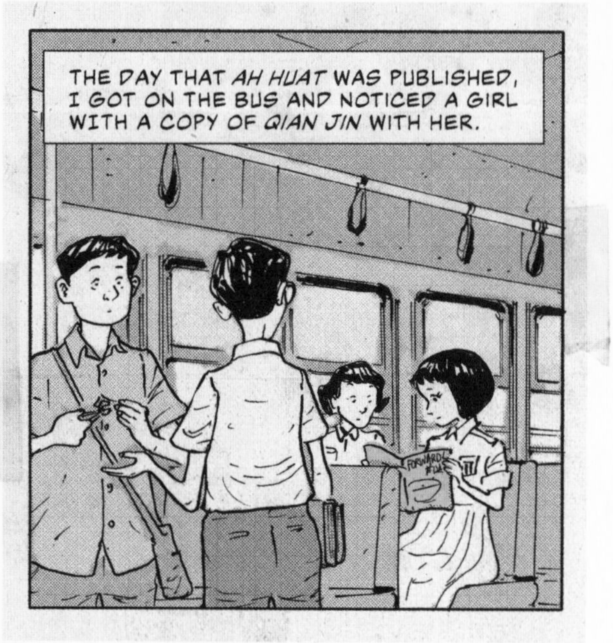
THE DAY THAT AH HUAT WAS PUBLISHED, I GOT ON THE BUS AND NOTICED A GIRL WITH A COPY OF QIAN JIN WITH HER.

Above & following

THE GIRL ON THE BUS

1988

Chan Hock Chye

Self-published

An excerpt from a short story that laid the ground for the art style that Chan would subsequently adopt for his autobiographical comics.

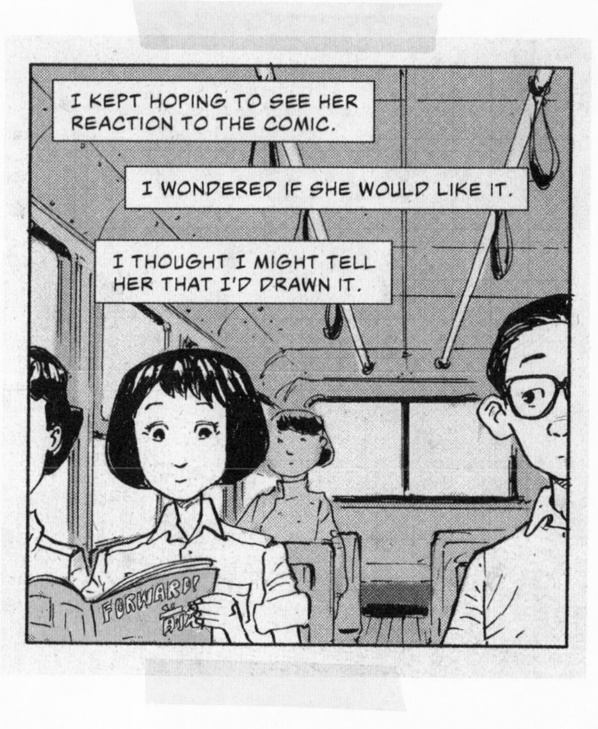
I KEPT HOPING TO SEE HER REACTION TO THE COMIC.
I WONDERED IF SHE WOULD LIKE IT.
I THOUGHT I MIGHT TELL HER THAT I'D DRAWN IT.
FORWARD!

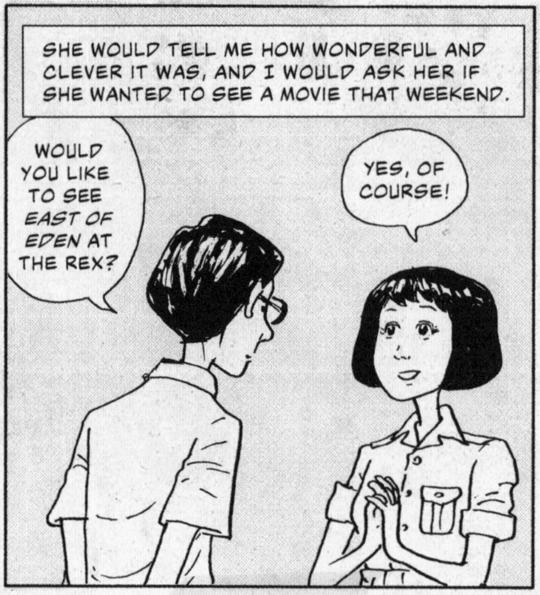
SHE WOULD TELL ME HOW WONDERFUL AND CLEVER IT WAS, AND I WOULD ASK HER IF SHE WANTED TO SEE A MOVIE THAT WEEKEND.
WOULD YOU LIKE TO SEE *EAST OF EDEN* AT THE REX?
YES, OF COURSE!

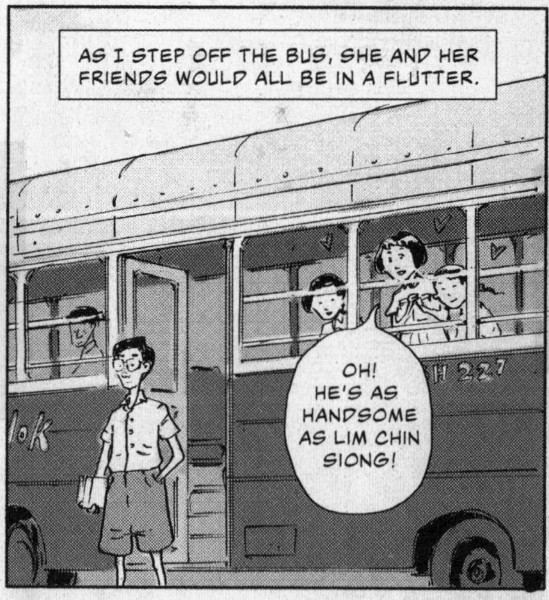
AS I STEP OFF THE BUS, SHE AND HER FRIENDS WOULD ALL BE IN A FLUTTER.
OH! HE'S AS HANDSOME AS LIM CHIN SIONG!

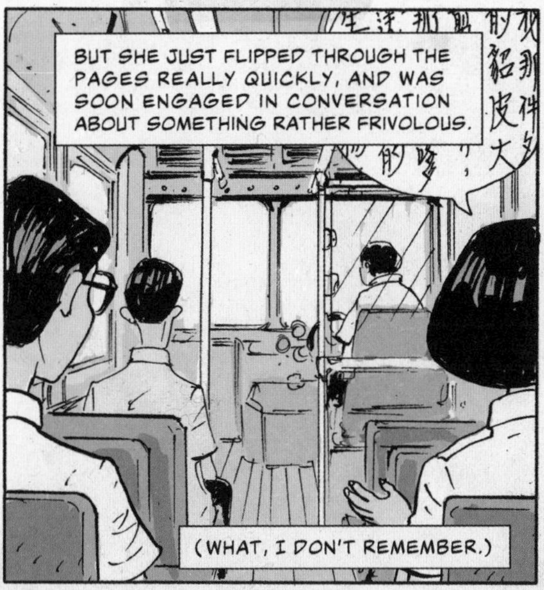
BUT SHE JUST FLIPPED THROUGH THE PAGES REALLY QUICKLY, AND WAS SOON ENGAGED IN CONVERSATION ABOUT SOMETHING RATHER FRIVOLOUS.
(WHAT, I DON'T REMEMBER.)

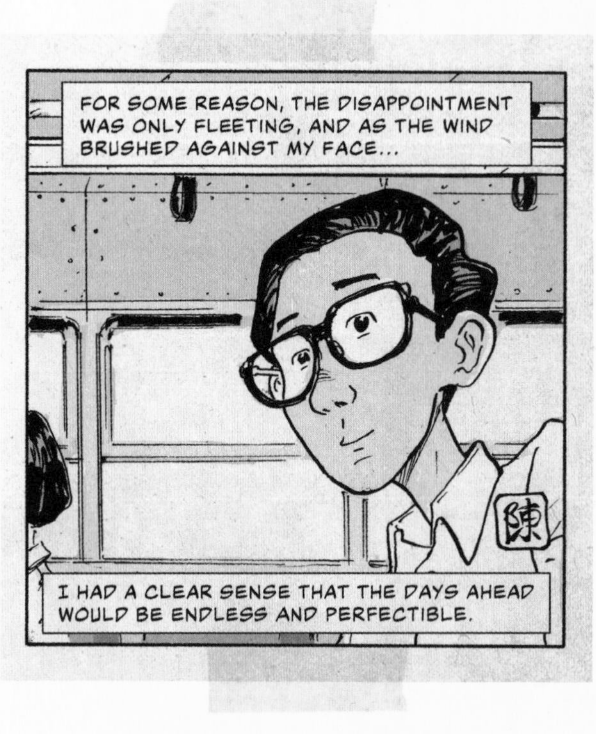
FOR SOME REASON, THE DISAPPOINTMENT WAS ONLY FLEETING, AND AS THE WIND BRUSHED AGAINST MY FACE...
陳
I HAD A CLEAR SENSE THAT THE DAYS AHEAD WOULD BE ENDLESS AND PERFECTIBLE.

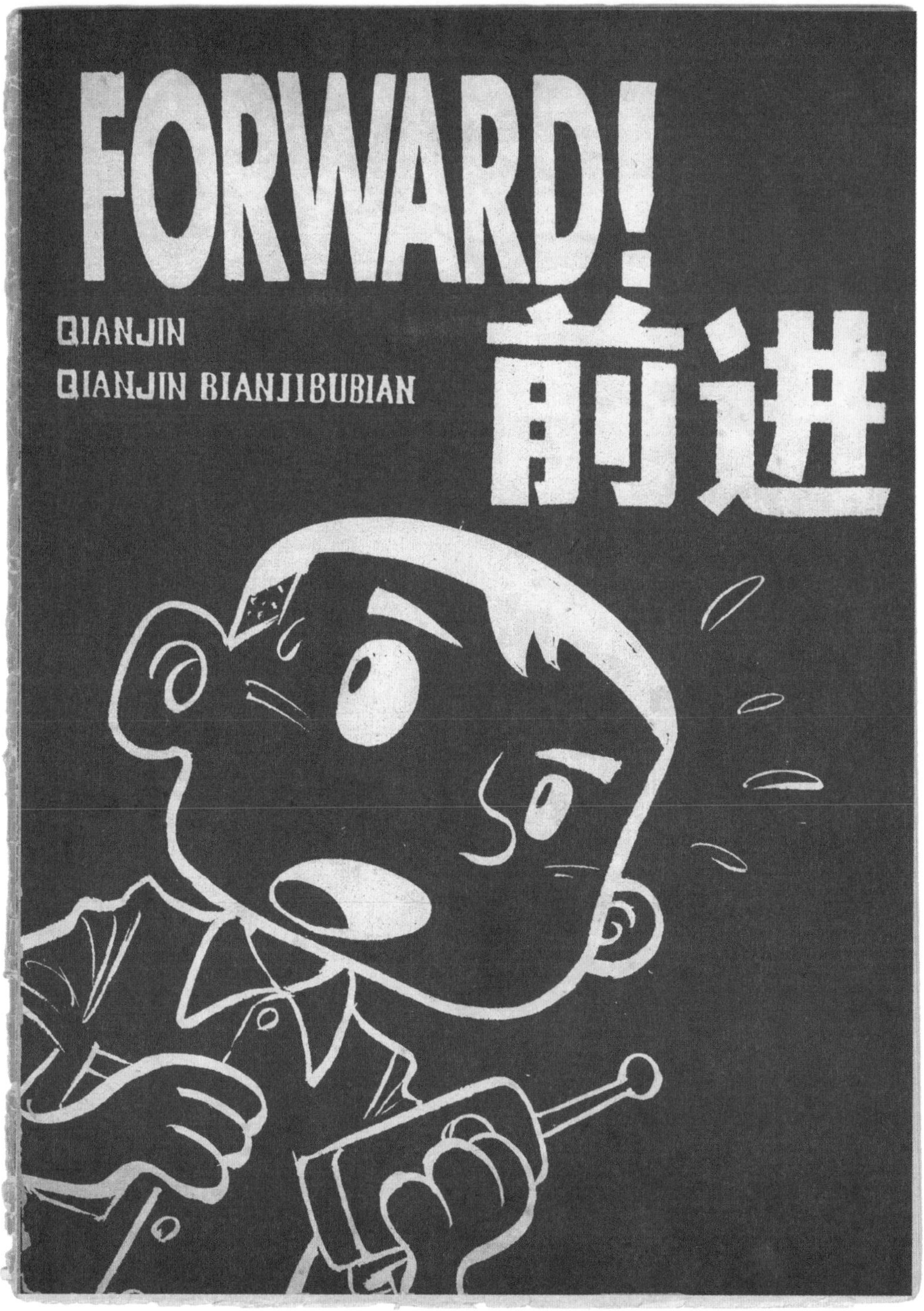
FORWARD!
QIANJIN
QIANJIN BIANJIBUBIAN
前进

Above
FORWARD! (QIAN JIN) Cover
1954
Chan Hock Chye
Tiger Press

Following
AH HUAT'S GIANT ROBOT Vol. 2: THE HOCK LEE BUS INCIDENT
1956
Chan Hock Chye
Stones Throw Press

Selected excerpts from Chan's response to the Hock Lee bus strike of May 12, 1955.

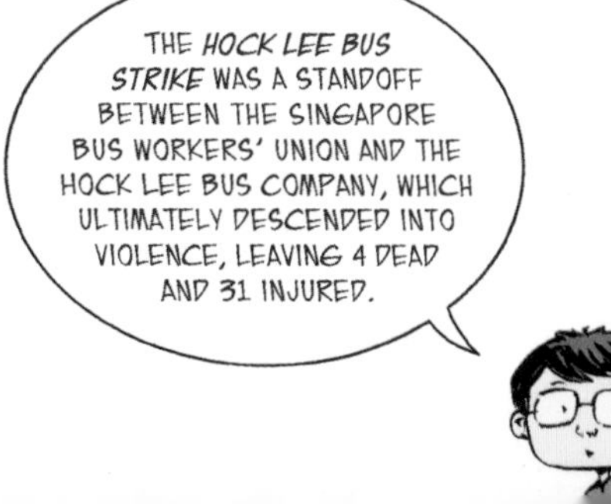
THE *HOCK LEE BUS STRIKE* WAS A STANDOFF BETWEEN THE SINGAPORE BUS WORKERS' UNION AND THE HOCK LEE BUS COMPANY, WHICH ULTIMATELY DESCENDED INTO VIOLENCE, LEAVING 4 DEAD AND 31 INJURED.

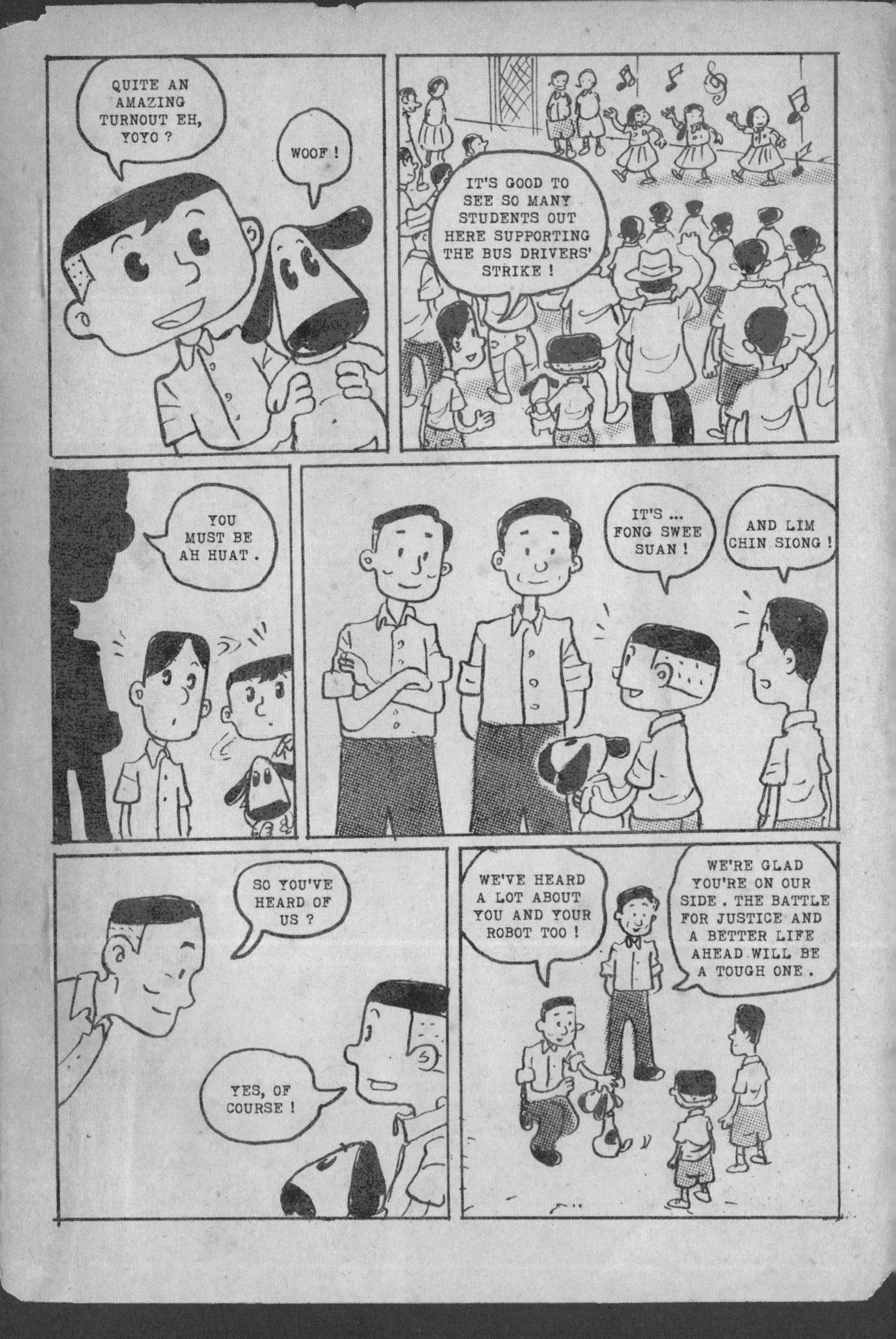

QUITE AN AMAZING TURNOUT EH, YOYO ?
WOOF !
IT'S GOOD TO SEE SO MANY STUDENTS OUT HERE SUPPORTING THE BUS DRIVERS' STRIKE !
YOU MUST BE AH HUAT .
IT'S ... FONG SWEE SUAN !
AND LIM CHIN SIONG !
SO YOU'VE HEARD OF US ?
YES, OF COURSE !
WE'VE HEARD A LOT ABOUT YOU AND YOUR ROBOT TOO !
WE'RE GLAD YOU'RE ON OUR SIDE . THE BATTLE FOR JUSTICE AND A BETTER LIFE AHEAD WILL BE A TOUGH ONE .

Chan imagines a meeting between his fictional characters Ah Huat, Wai Ming and Yoyo the Dog, and real-life trade union leaders **Fong Swee Suan** and **Lim Chin Siong** during the standoff.

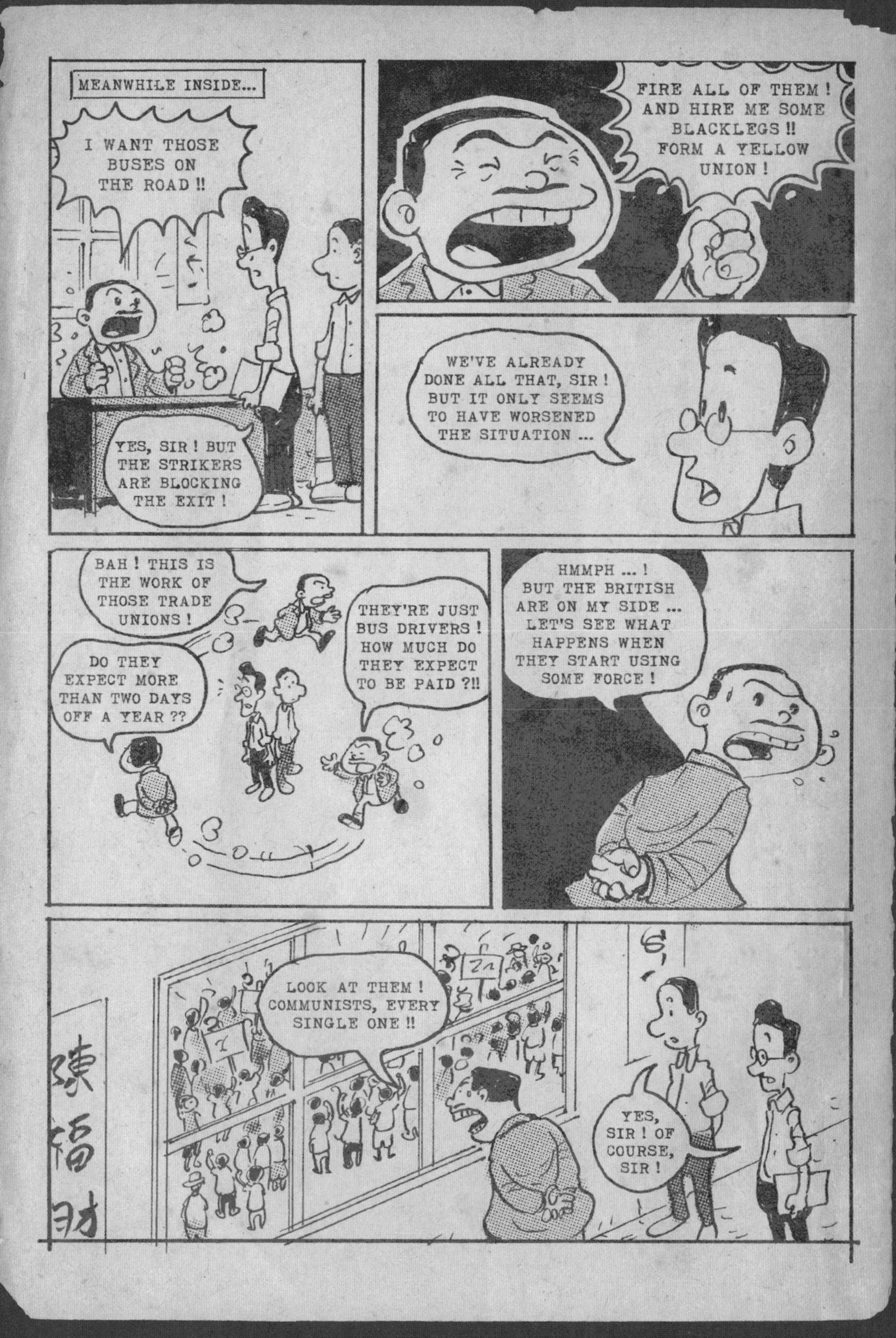
MEANWHILE INSIDE...
I WANT THOSE BUSES ON THE ROAD !!
YES, SIR ! BUT THE STRIKERS ARE BLOCKING THE EXIT !
FIRE ALL OF THEM ! AND HIRE ME SOME BLACKLEGS !! FORM A YELLOW UNION !
WE'VE ALREADY DONE ALL THAT, SIR ! BUT IT ONLY SEEMS TO HAVE WORSENED THE SITUATION ...
BAH ! THIS IS THE WORK OF THOSE TRADE UNIONS !
DO THEY EXPECT MORE THAN TWO DAYS OFF A YEAR ??
THEY'RE JUST BUS DRIVERS ! HOW MUCH DO THEY EXPECT TO BE PAID ?!!
HMMPH ... ! BUT THE BRITISH ARE ON MY SIDE ... LET'S SEE WHAT HAPPENS WHEN THEY START USING SOME FORCE !
陳福財
LOOK AT THEM ! COMMUNISTS, EVERY SINGLE ONE !!
YES, SIR ! OF COURSE, SIR !

Chan had little sympathy for the **Hock Lee Bus Company** bosses. In the story, they are seen as callous and exploitative, with scant regard for employee welfare. "**Blacklegs**" refer to men hired by companies to break up strikes by replacing uncooperative workers, whilst "**yellow unions**" was a generally derogatory term used to describe pliant trade unions set up by the employers themselves.

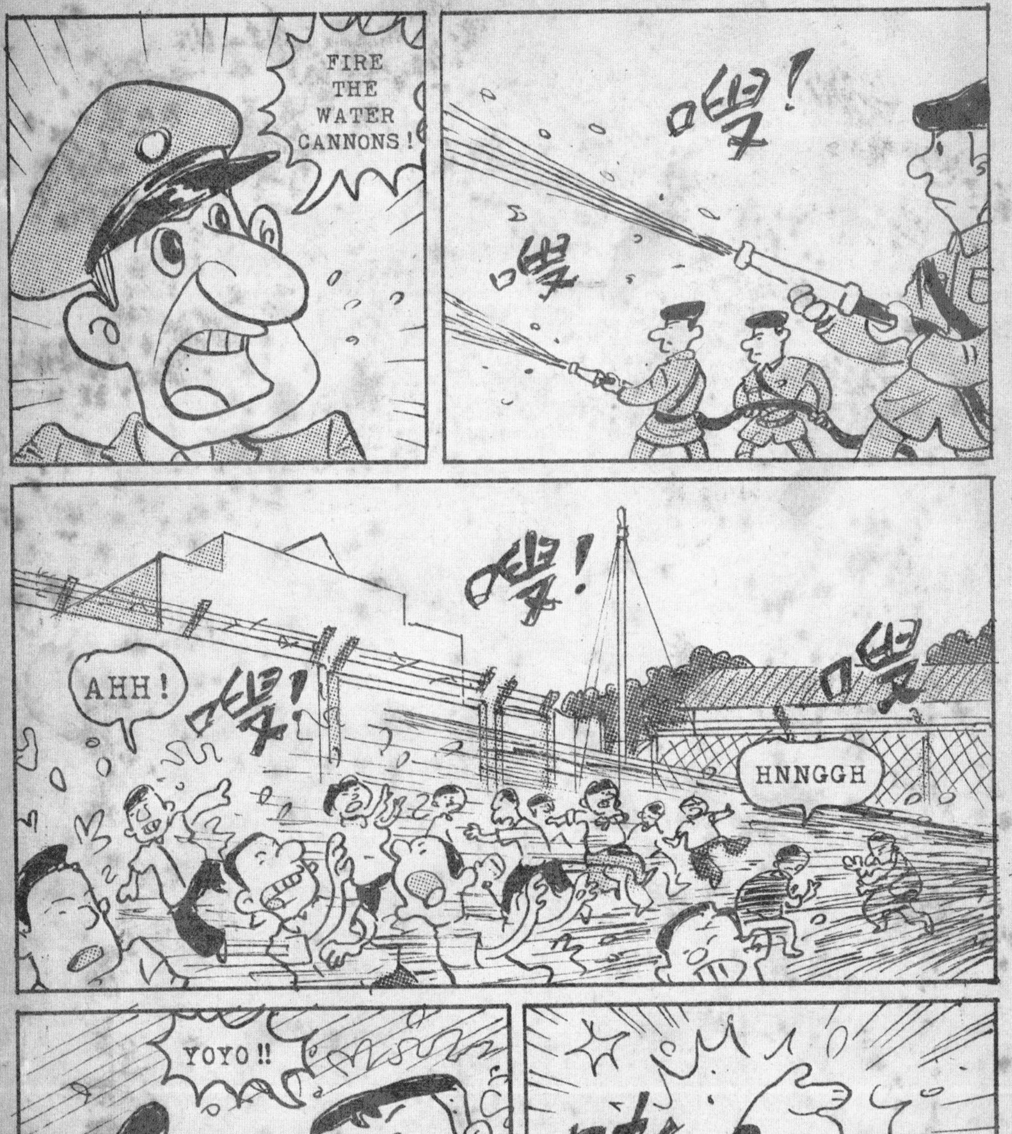
FIRE THE WATER CANNONS!
嘍!
嘍
嘍!
AHH!
嘍!
嘍
HNNGGH
YOYO!!
啪

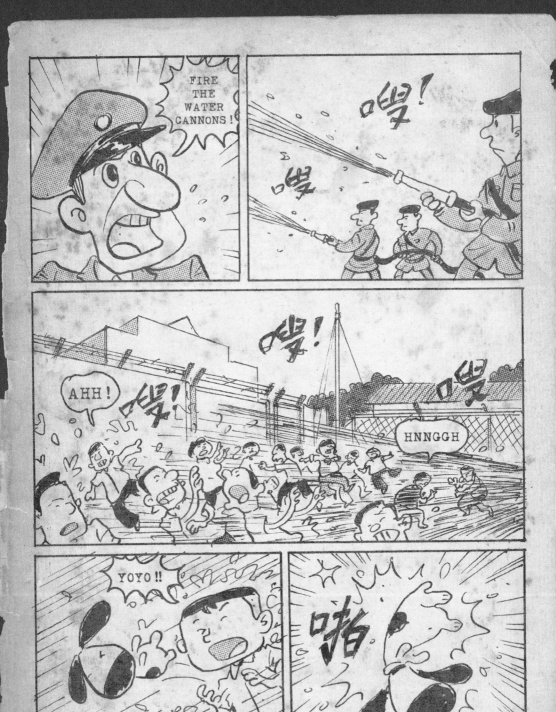

Official accounts of the Hock Lee Bus Riots have often blamed communist agitators for the strike and the subsequent outbreak of violence, but union leaders involved have always maintained that they had only been concerned with improving workers' welfare. Eyewitness accounts further suggest that the rioting had been sparked by aggressive police tactics, which had unleashed the pent-up anger and frustration of the picketers.

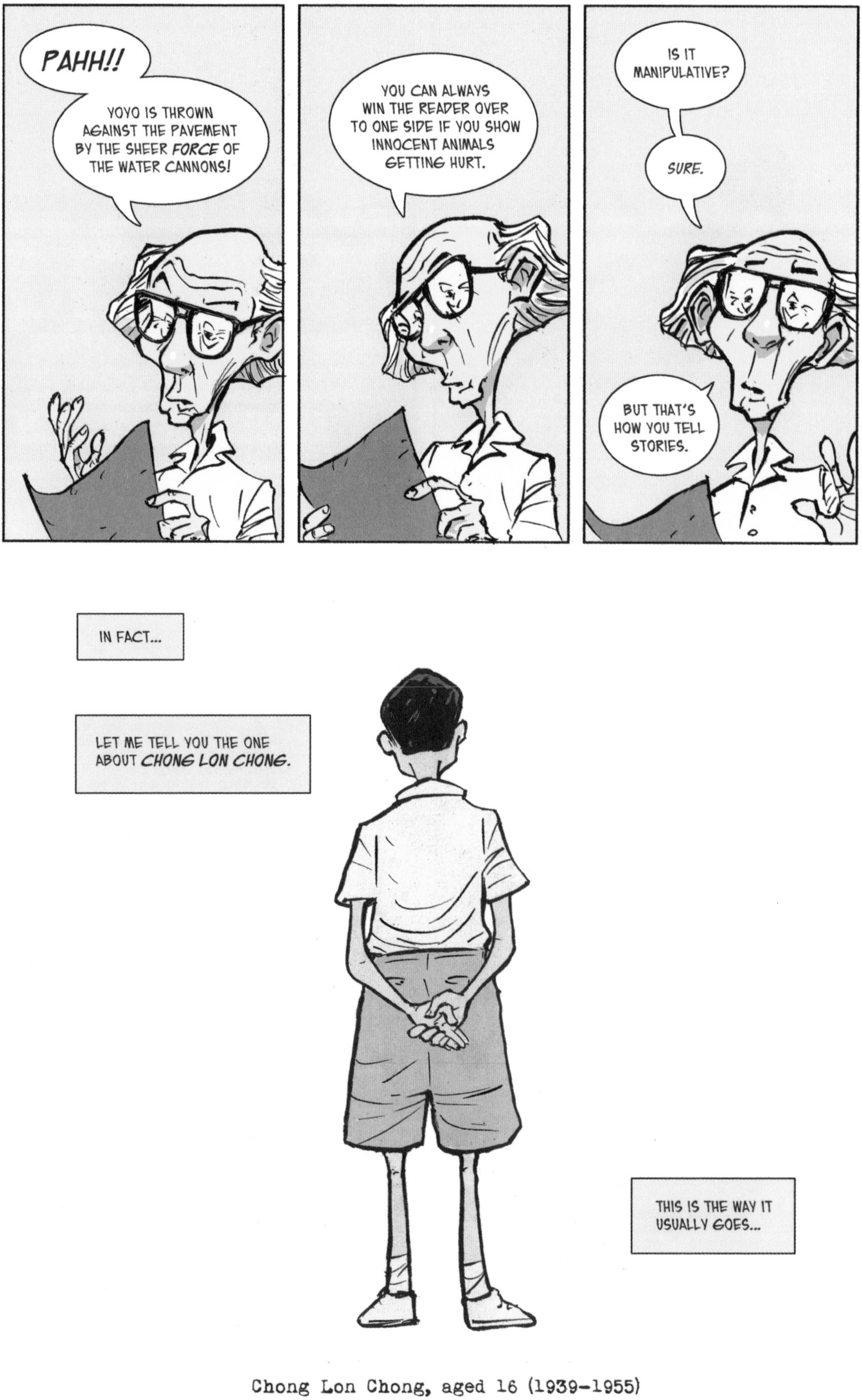
PAHH!!
YOYO IS THROWN AGAINST THE PAVEMENT BY THE SHEER FORCE OF THE WATER CANNONS!
YOU CAN ALWAYS WIN THE READER OVER TO ONE SIDE IF YOU SHOW INNOCENT ANIMALS GETTING HURT.
IS IT MANIPULATIVE?
SURE.
BUT THAT'S HOW YOU TELL STORIES.
IN FACT...
LET ME TELL YOU THE ONE ABOUT CHONG LON CHONG.
THIS IS THE WAY IT USUALLY GOES...
Chong Lon Chong, aged 16 (1939-1955)

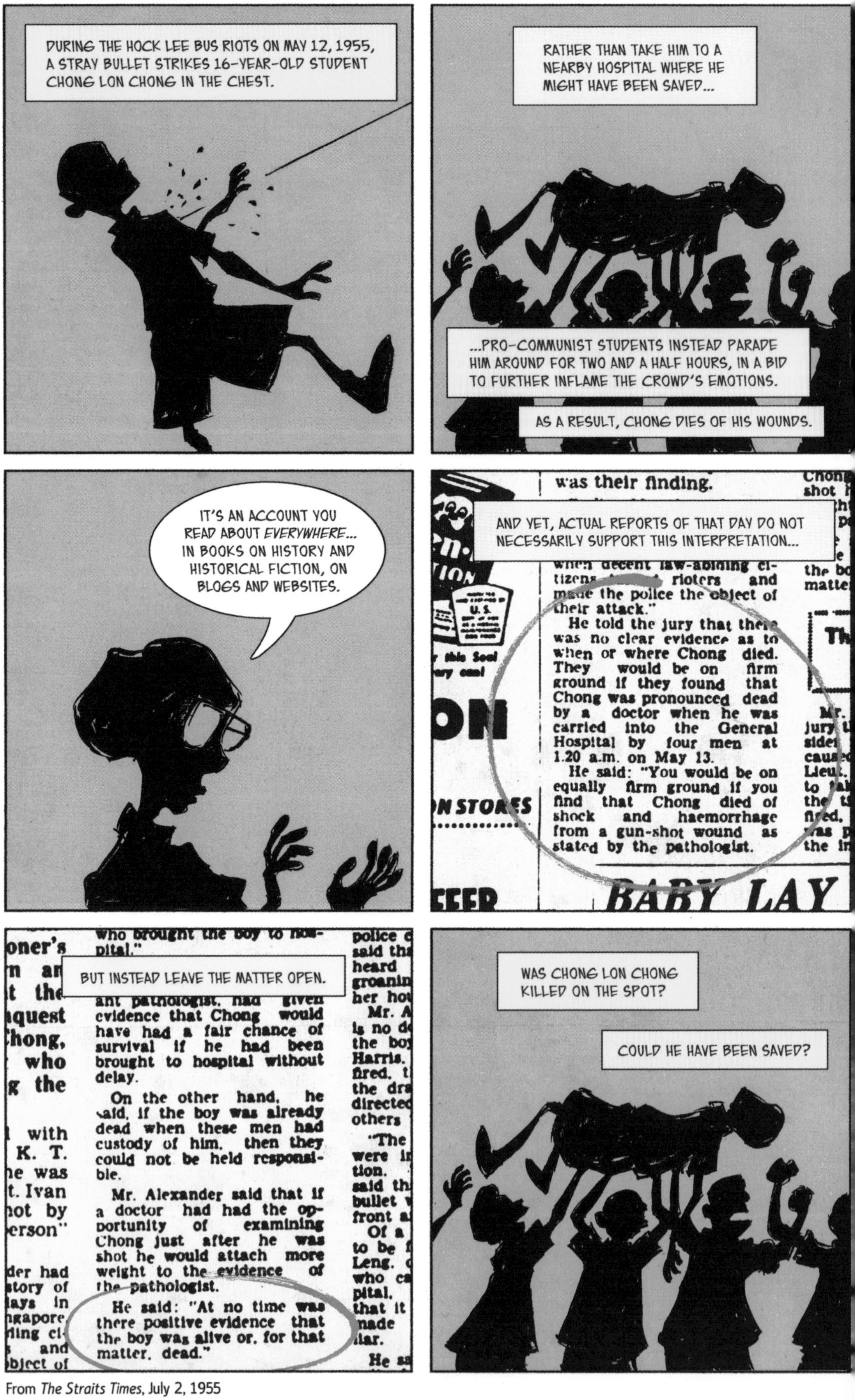
DURING THE HOCK LEE BUS RIOTS ON MAY 12, 1955, A STRAY BULLET STRIKES 16-YEAR-OLD STUDENT CHONG LON CHONG IN THE CHEST.
RATHER THAN TAKE HIM TO A NEARBY HOSPITAL WHERE HE MIGHT HAVE BEEN SAVED...
...PRO-COMMUNIST STUDENTS INSTEAD PARADE HIM AROUND FOR TWO AND A HALF HOURS, IN A BID TO FURTHER INFLAME THE CROWD'S EMOTIONS.
AS A RESULT, CHONG DIES OF HIS WOUNDS.
IT'S AN ACCOUNT YOU READ ABOUT *EVERYWHERE*... IN BOOKS ON HISTORY AND HISTORICAL FICTION, ON BLOGS AND WEBSITES.
was their finding.
AND YET, ACTUAL REPORTS OF THAT DAY DO NOT NECESSARILY SUPPORT THIS INTERPRETATION...
rioters and made the police the object of their attack."
He told the jury that there was no clear evidence as to when or where Chong died. They would be on firm ground if they found that Chong was pronounced dead by a doctor when he was carried into the General Hospital by four men at 1.20 a.m. on May 13.
He said: "You would be on equally firm ground if you find that Chong died of shock and haemorrhage from a gun-shot wound as stated by the pathologist.
BABY LAY
who brought the boy to hospital."
BUT INSTEAD LEAVE THE MATTER OPEN.
evidence that Chong would have had a fair chance of survival if he had been brought to hospital without delay.
On the other hand, he said, if the boy was already dead when these men had custody of him, then they could not be held responsible.
Mr. Alexander said that if a doctor had had the opportunity of examining Chong just after he was shot he would attach more weight to the evidence of the pathologist.
He said: "At no time was there positive evidence that the boy was alive or, for that matter, dead."
WAS CHONG LON CHONG KILLED ON THE SPOT?
COULD HE HAVE BEEN SAVED?

From *The Straits Times*, July 2, 1955

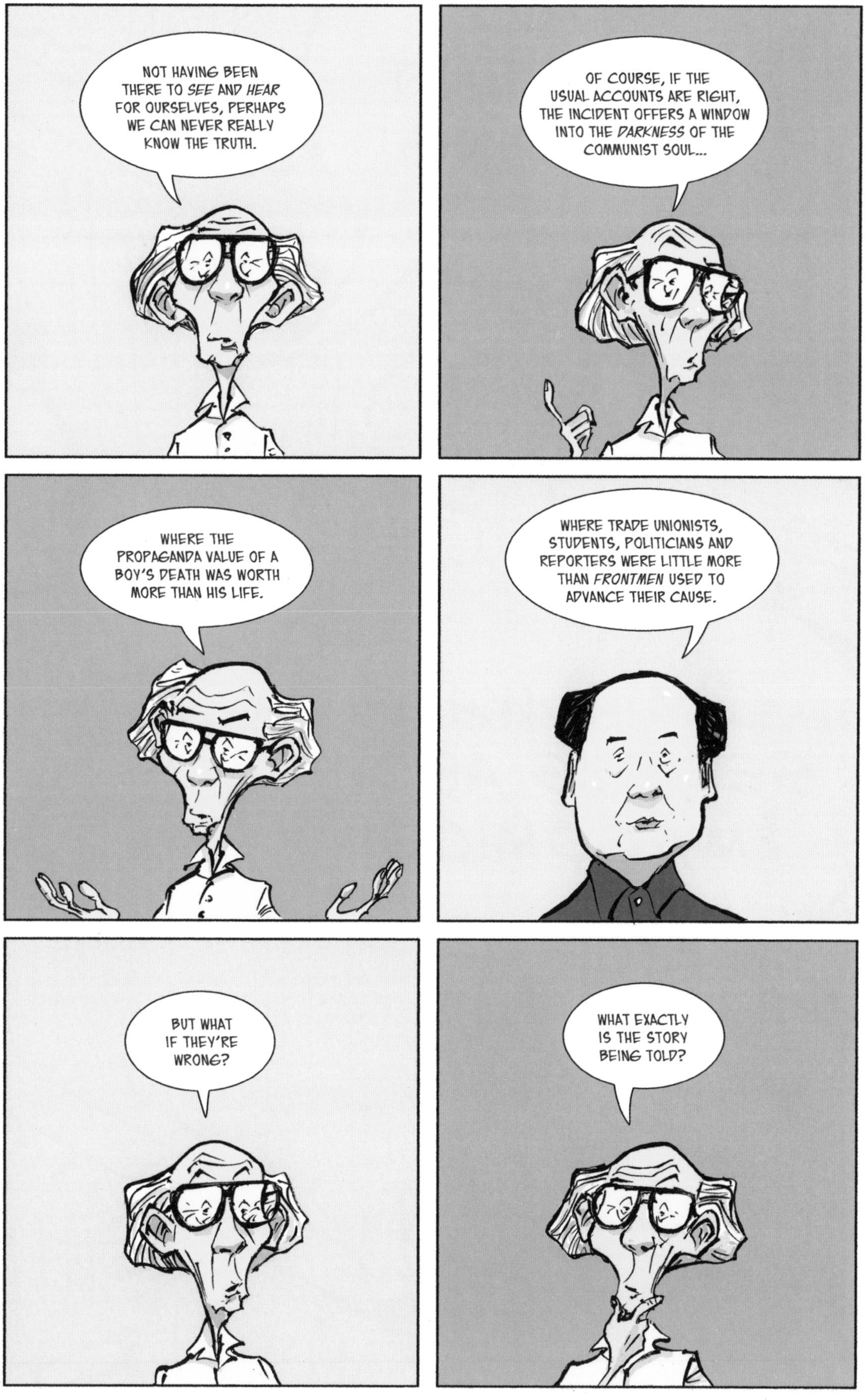
NOT HAVING BEEN THERE TO *SEE* AND *HEAR* FOR OURSELVES, PERHAPS WE CAN NEVER REALLY KNOW THE TRUTH.
OF COURSE, IF THE USUAL ACCOUNTS ARE RIGHT, THE INCIDENT OFFERS A WINDOW INTO THE *DARKNESS* OF THE COMMUNIST SOUL...
WHERE THE PROPAGANDA VALUE OF A BOY'S DEATH WAS WORTH MORE THAN HIS LIFE.
WHERE TRADE UNIONISTS, STUDENTS, POLITICIANS AND REPORTERS WERE LITTLE MORE THAN *FRONTMEN* USED TO ADVANCE THEIR CAUSE.
BUT WHAT IF THEY'RE WRONG?
WHAT EXACTLY IS THE STORY BEING TOLD?

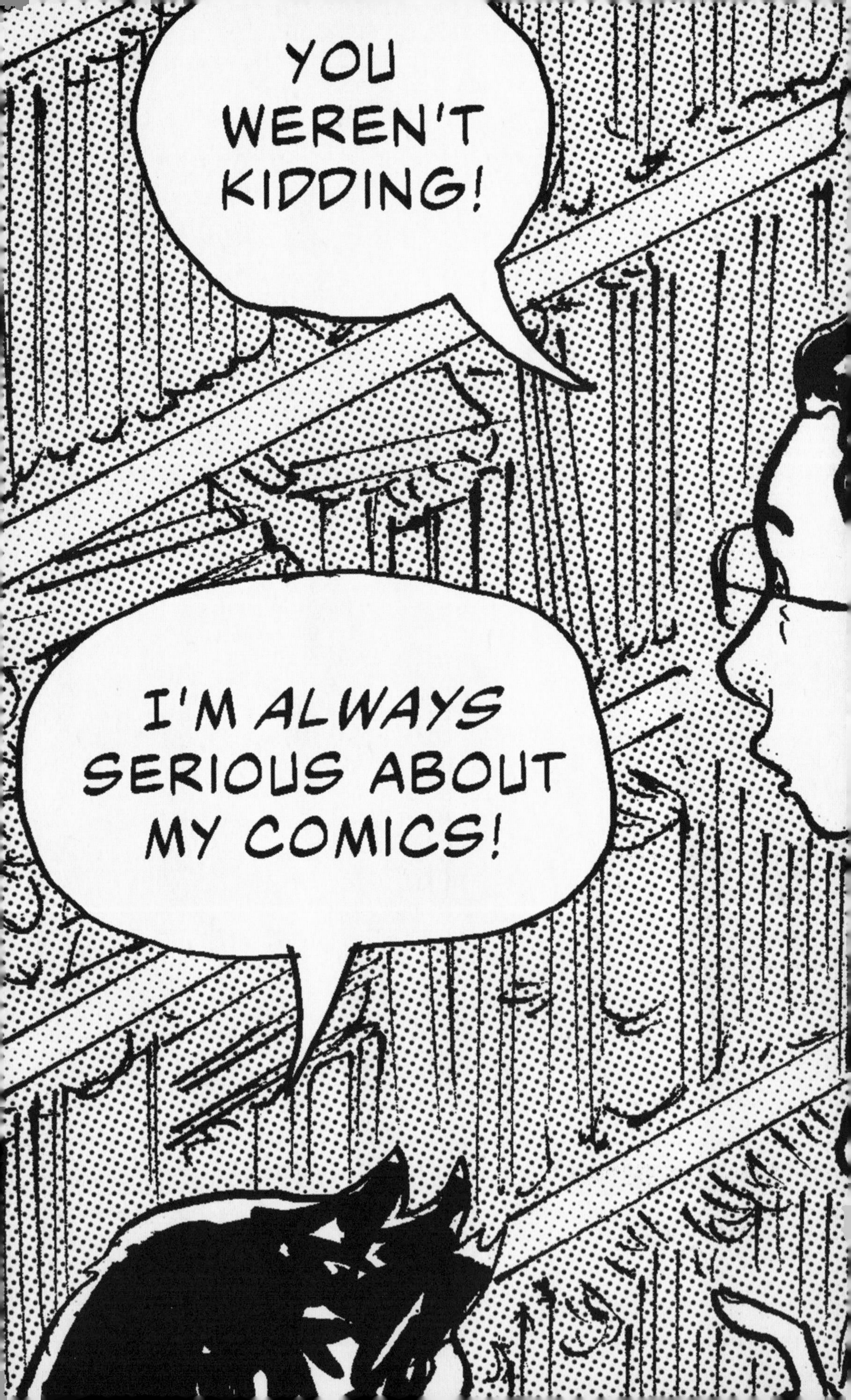
YOU WEREN'T KIDDING!
I'M *ALWAYS* SERIOUS ABOUT MY COMICS!

Chapter Three

STANDING ON OUR OWN TWO FEET

站
起
来

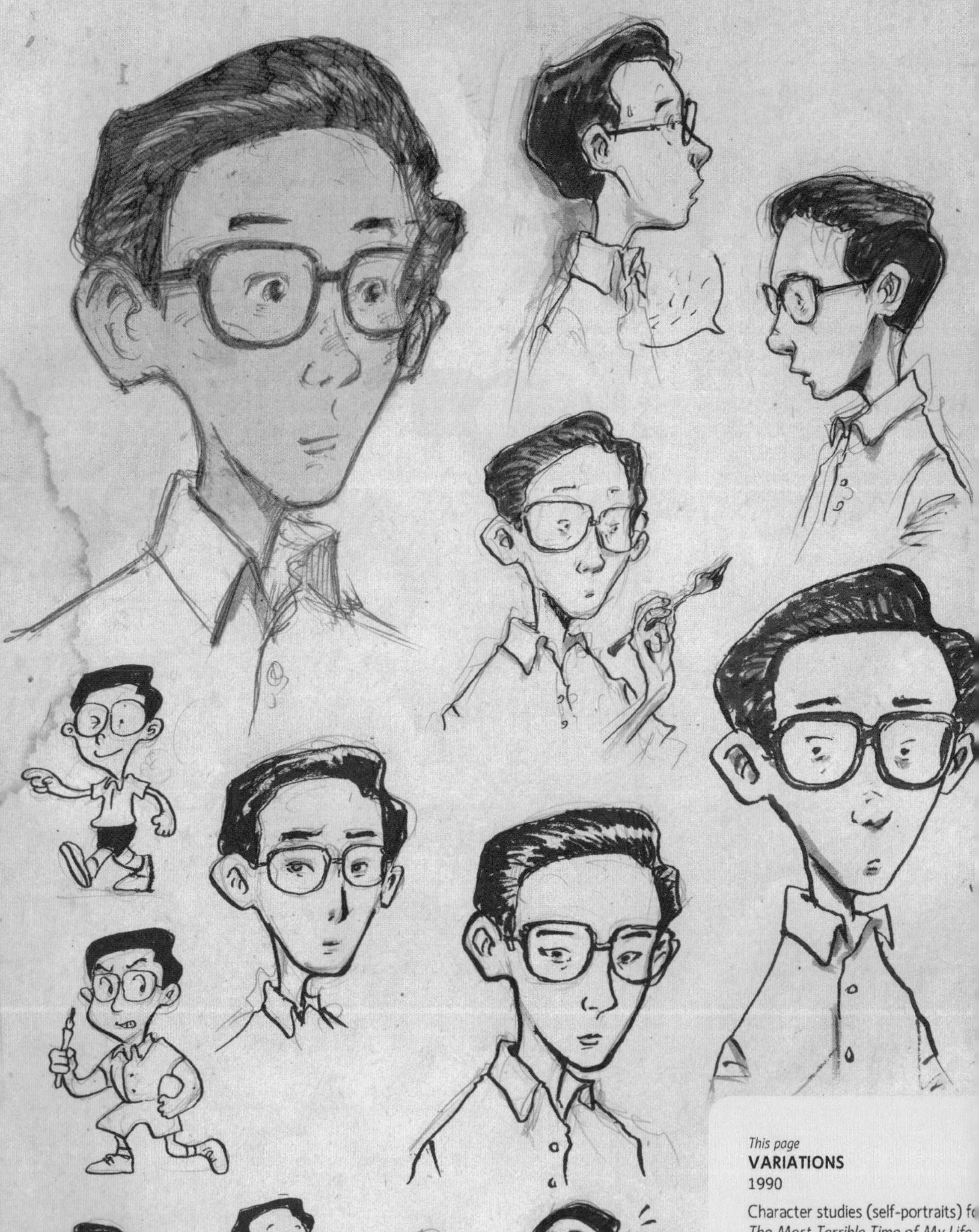

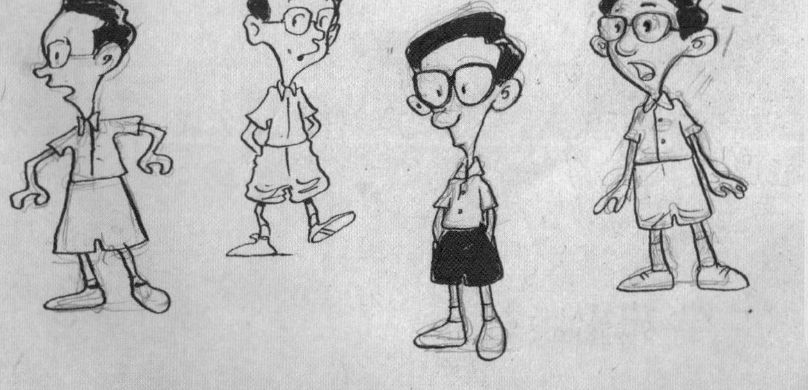

This page

VARIATIONS

1990

Character studies (self-portraits) fo

The Most Terrible Time of My Life.

Opposite & following

THE MOST TERRIBLE TIME OF MY LIFE

1991

Self-published

At the age of 53, Chan began working on what was meant to be a multi-volume autobiographical comic. Only one volume was ever completed, however, covering the period 1955–1963.

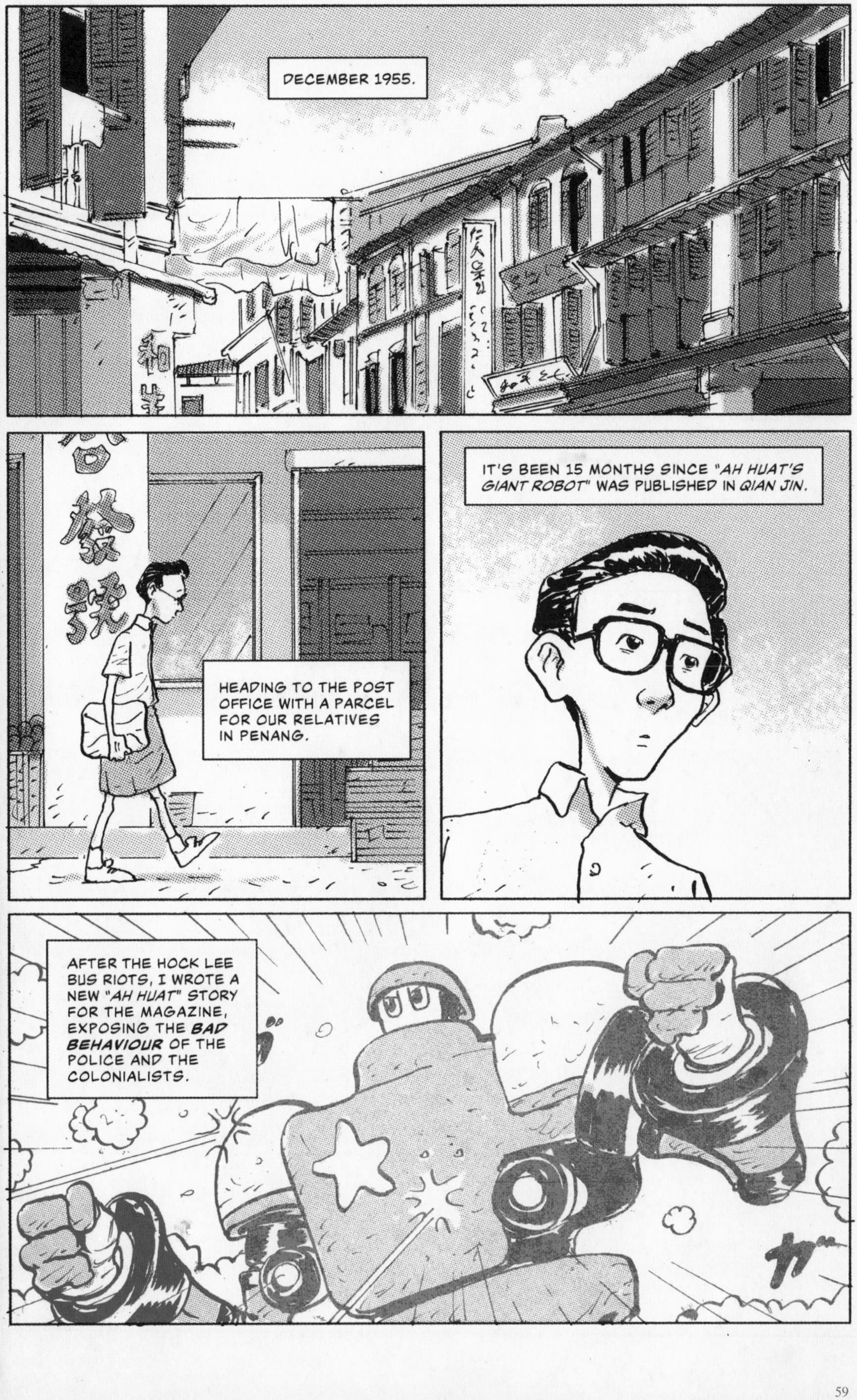
DECEMBER 1955.
HEADING TO THE POST OFFICE WITH A PARCEL FOR OUR RELATIVES IN PENANG.
IT'S BEEN 15 MONTHS SINCE "AH HUAT'S GIANT ROBOT" WAS PUBLISHED IN QIAN JIN.
AFTER THE HOCK LEE BUS RIOTS, I WROTE A NEW "AH HUAT" STORY FOR THE MAGAZINE, EXPOSING THE BAD BEHAVIOUR OF THE POLICE AND THE COLONIALISTS.

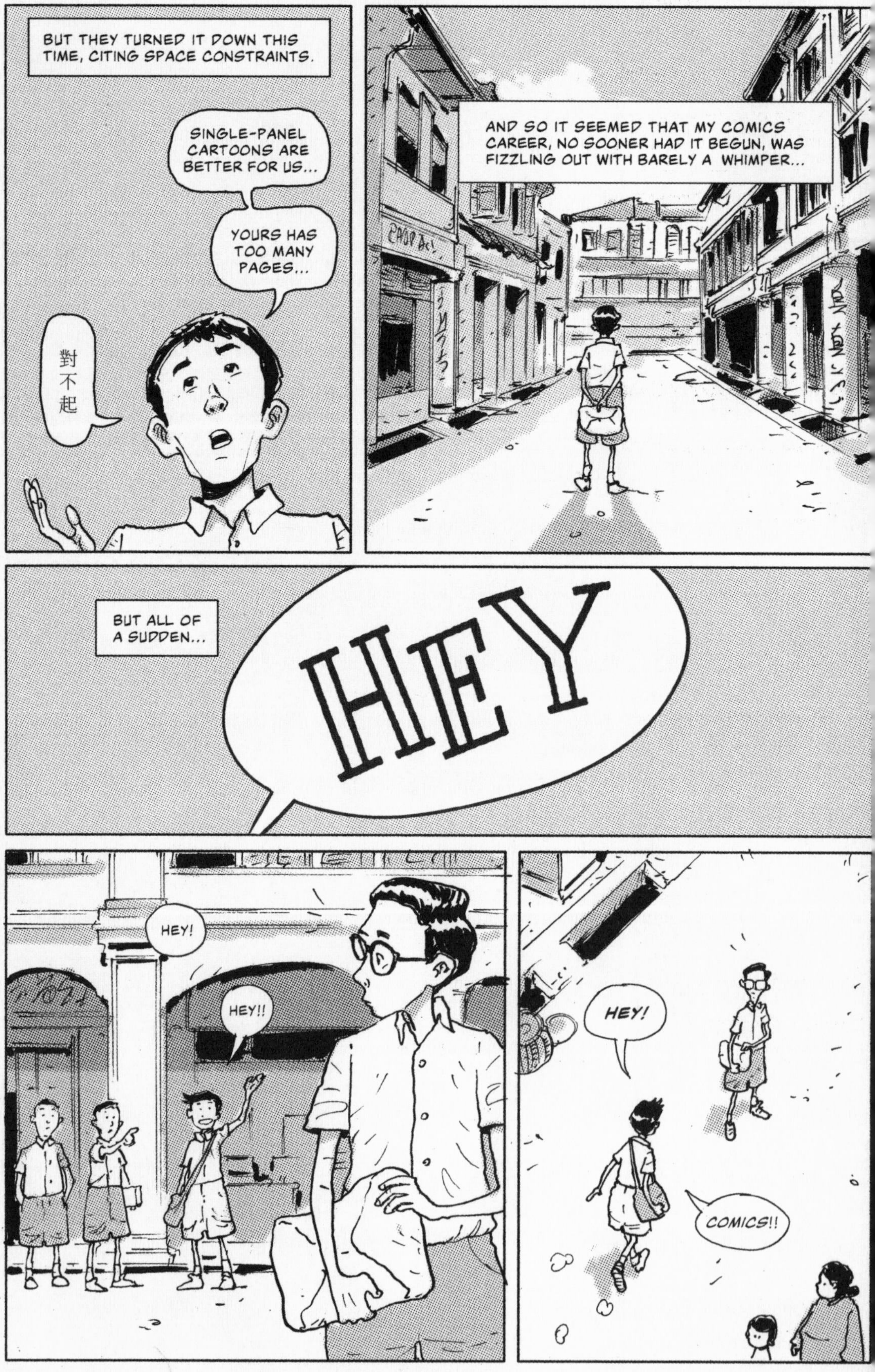
BUT THEY TURNED IT DOWN THIS TIME, CITING SPACE CONSTRAINTS.
SINGLE-PANEL CARTOONS ARE BETTER FOR US...
YOURS HAS TOO MANY PAGES...
對不起
AND SO IT SEEMED THAT MY COMICS CAREER, NO SOONER HAD IT BEGUN, WAS FIZZLING OUT WITH BARELY A WHIMPER...
BUT ALL OF A SUDDEN...
HEY
HEY!
HEY!!
HEY!
COMICS!!

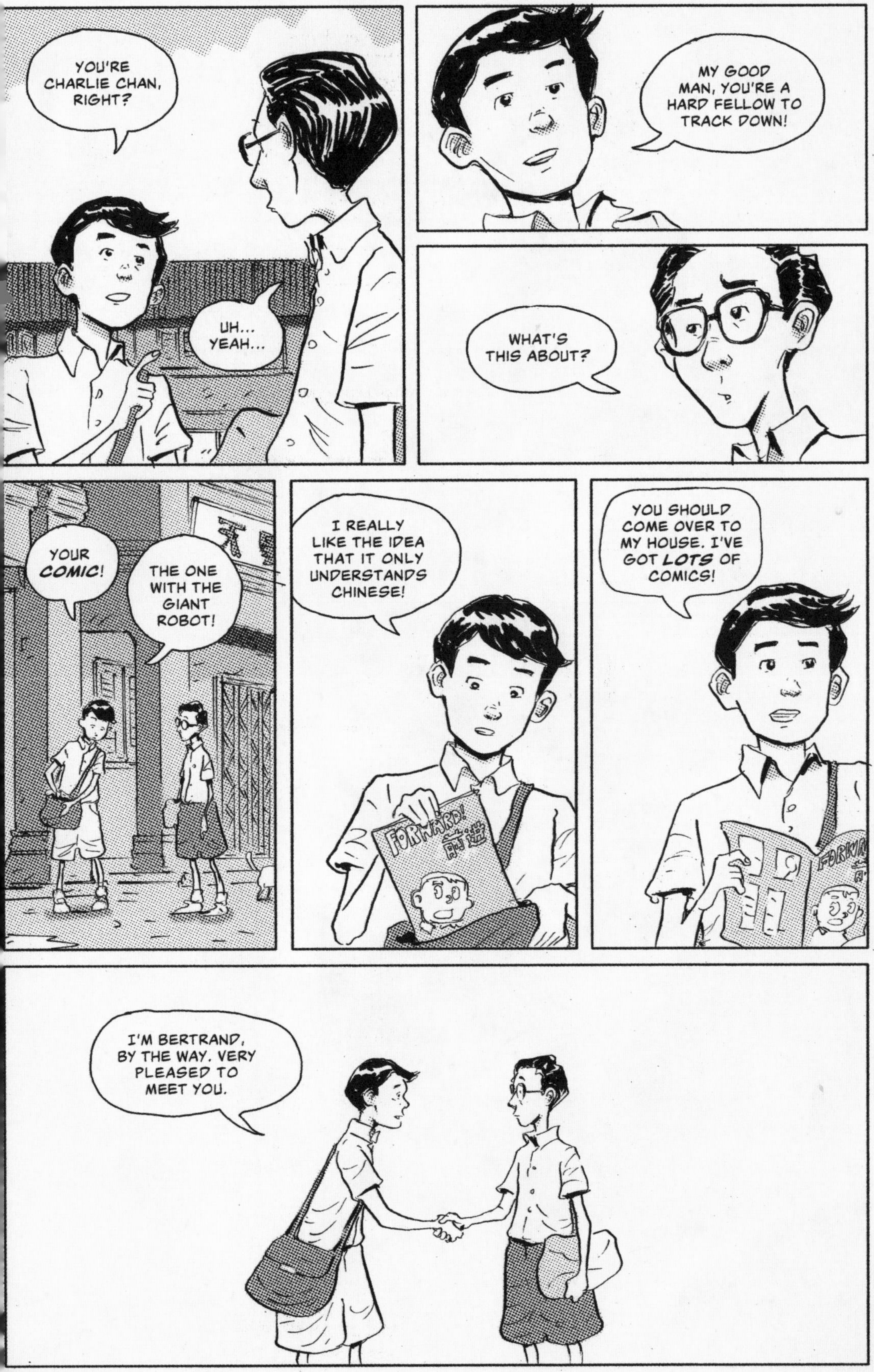
YOU'RE CHARLIE CHAN, RIGHT?
UH... YEAH...
MY GOOD MAN, YOU'RE A HARD FELLOW TO TRACK DOWN!
WHAT'S THIS ABOUT?
YOUR COMIC!
THE ONE WITH THE GIANT ROBOT!
I REALLY LIKE THE IDEA THAT IT ONLY UNDERSTANDS CHINESE!
FORWARD! 前进
YOU SHOULD COME OVER TO MY HOUSE. I'VE GOT LOTS OF COMICS!
I'M BERTRAND, BY THE WAY. VERY PLEASED TO MEET YOU.

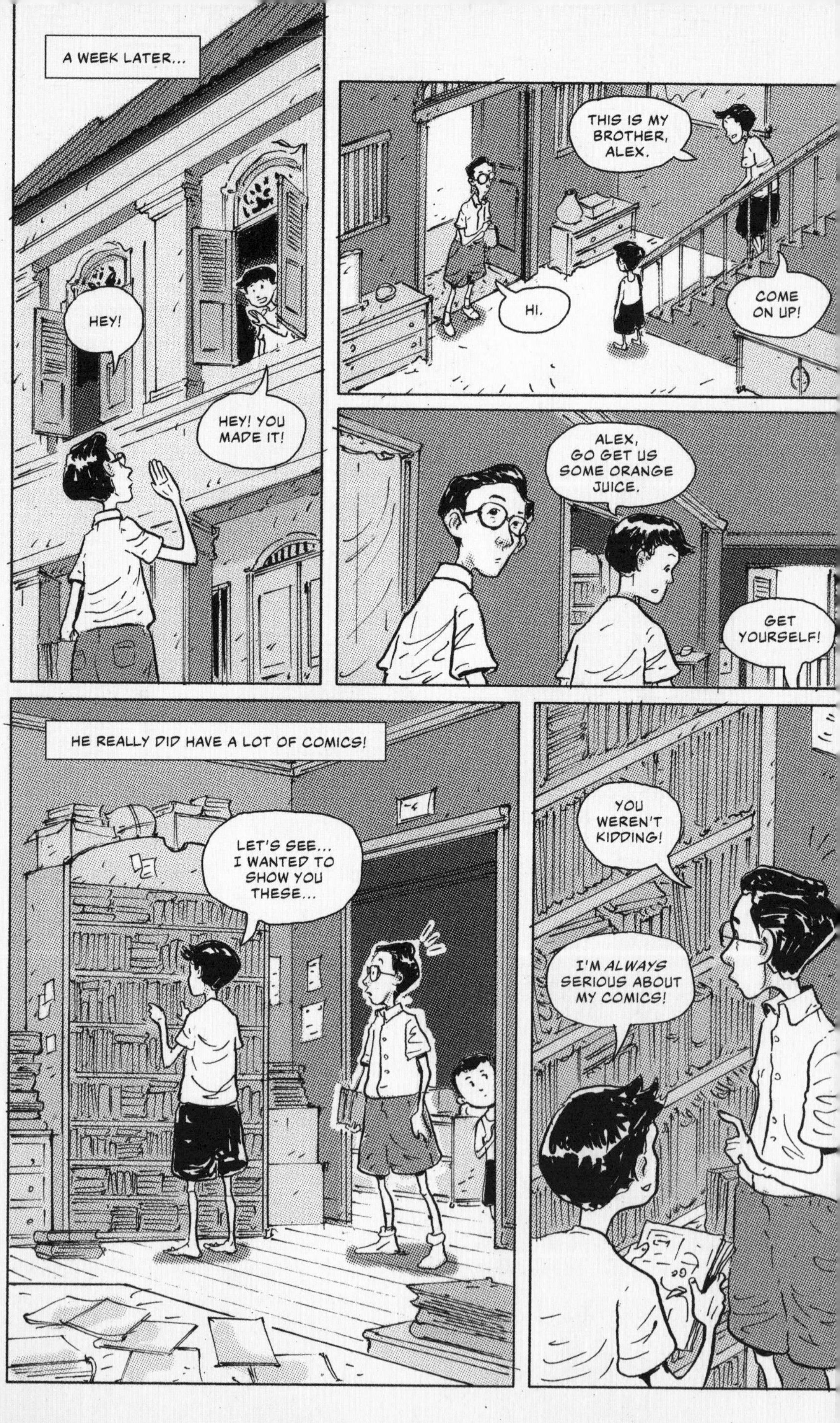
A WEEK LATER...
HEY!
HEY! YOU MADE IT!
THIS IS MY BROTHER, ALEX.
HI.
COME ON UP!
ALEX, GO GET US SOME ORANGE JUICE.
GET YOURSELF!
HE REALLY DID HAVE A LOT OF COMICS!
LET'S SEE... I WANTED TO SHOW YOU THESE...
YOU WEREN'T KIDDING!
I'M *ALWAYS* SERIOUS ABOUT MY COMICS!

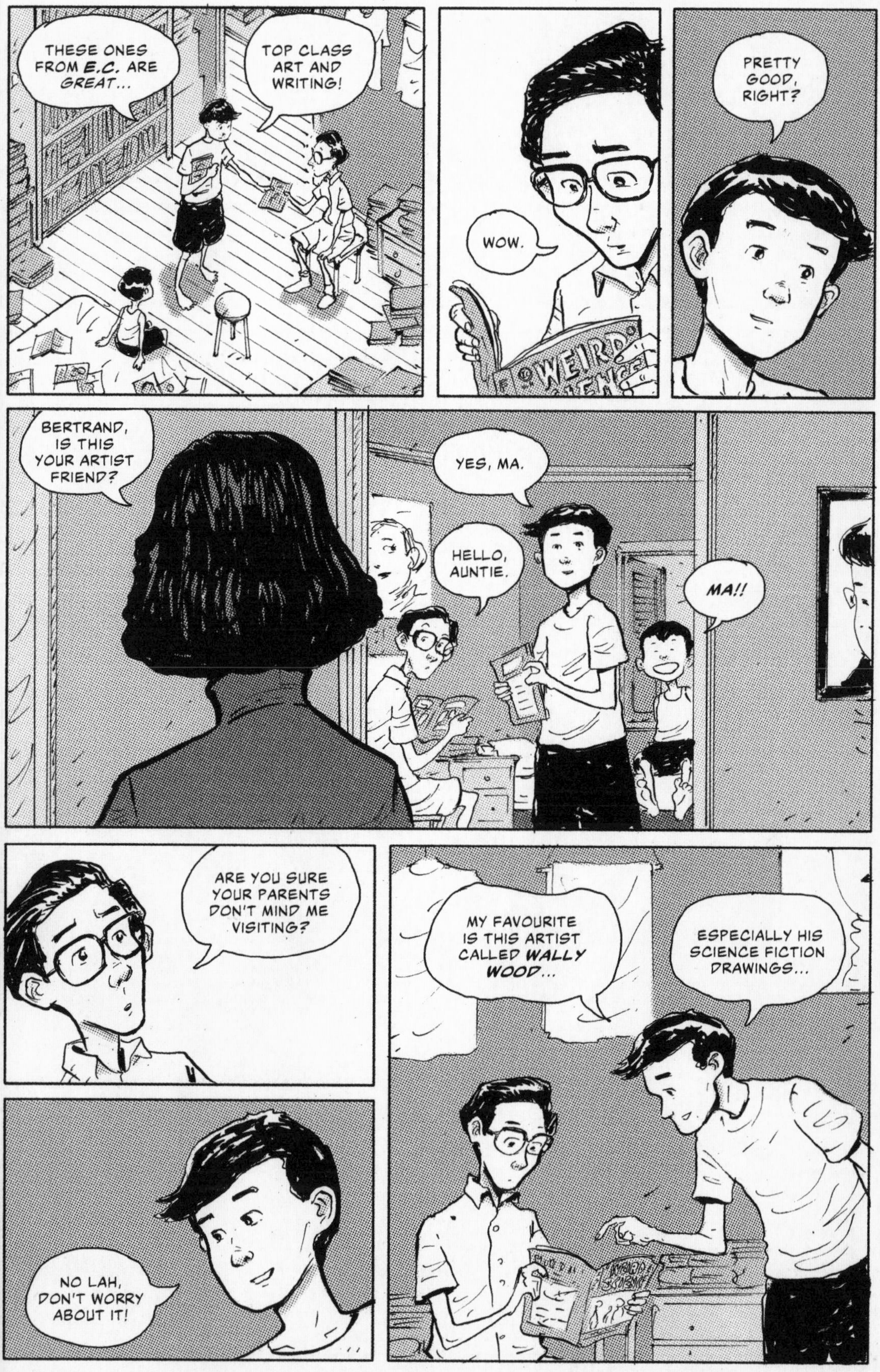

THESE ONES FROM E.C. ARE GREAT...
TOP CLASS ART AND WRITING!
WOW.
WEIRD SCIENCE
PRETTY GOOD, RIGHT?
BERTRAND, IS THIS YOUR ARTIST FRIEND?
YES, MA.
HELLO, AUNTIE.
MA!!
ARE YOU SURE YOUR PARENTS DON'T MIND ME VISITING?
NO LAH, DON'T WORRY ABOUT IT!
MY FAVOURITE IS THIS ARTIST CALLED WALLY WOOD...
ESPECIALLY HIS SCIENCE FICTION DRAWINGS...

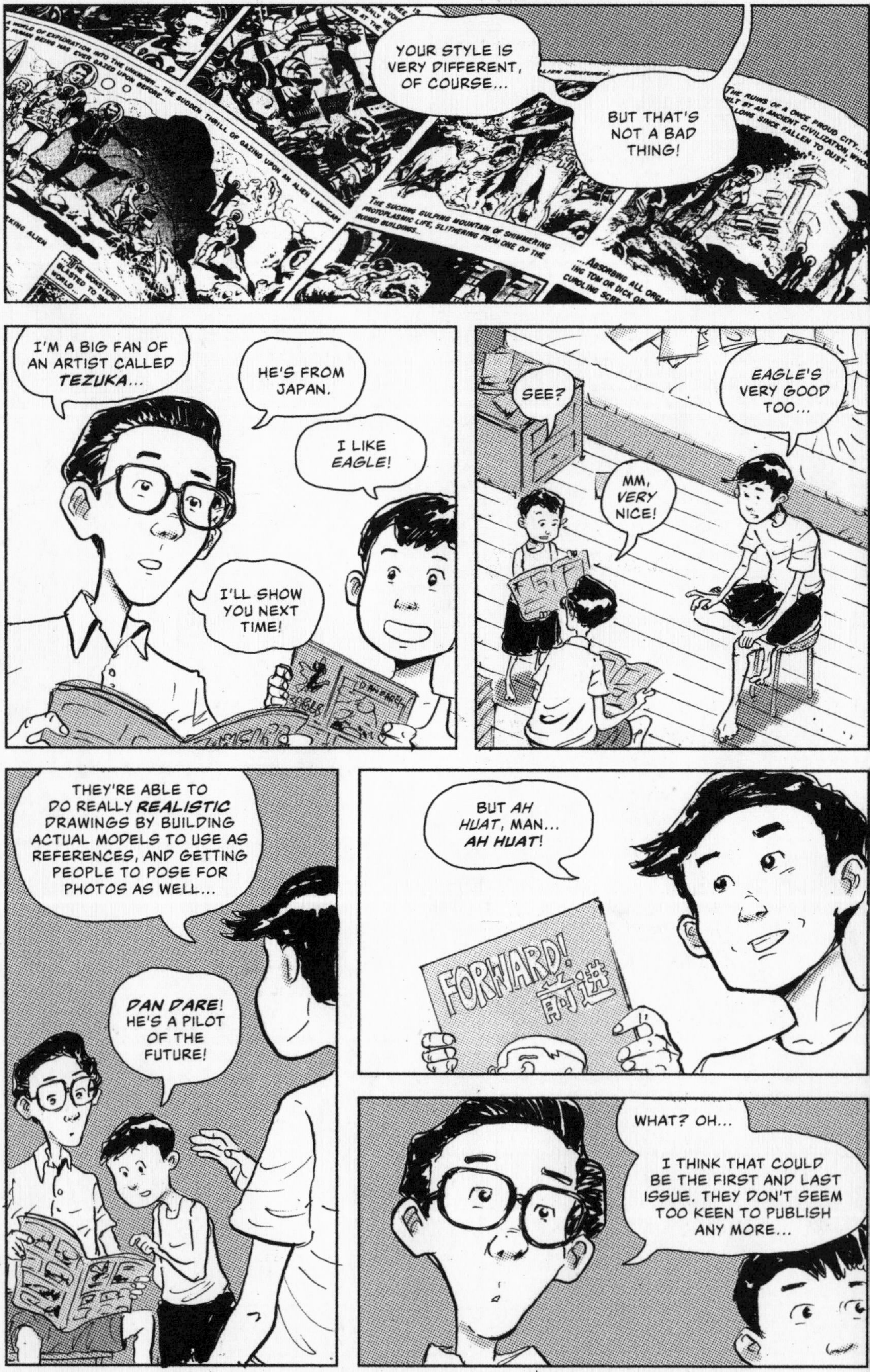
YOUR STYLE IS VERY DIFFERENT, OF COURSE...
BUT THAT'S NOT A BAD THING!
I'M A BIG FAN OF AN ARTIST CALLED *TEZUKA*...
HE'S FROM JAPAN.
I LIKE *EAGLE*!
I'LL SHOW YOU NEXT TIME!
SEE?
EAGLE'S VERY GOOD TOO...
MM, *VERY* NICE!
THEY'RE ABLE TO DO REALLY ***REALISTIC*** DRAWINGS BY BUILDING ACTUAL MODELS TO USE AS REFERENCES, AND GETTING PEOPLE TO POSE FOR PHOTOS AS WELL...
DAN DARE! HE'S A PILOT OF THE FUTURE!
BUT *AH HUAT*, MAN... ***AH HUAT***!
FORWARD! 前进
WHAT? OH...
I THINK THAT COULD BE THE FIRST AND LAST ISSUE. THEY DON'T SEEM TOO KEEN TO PUBLISH ANY MORE...

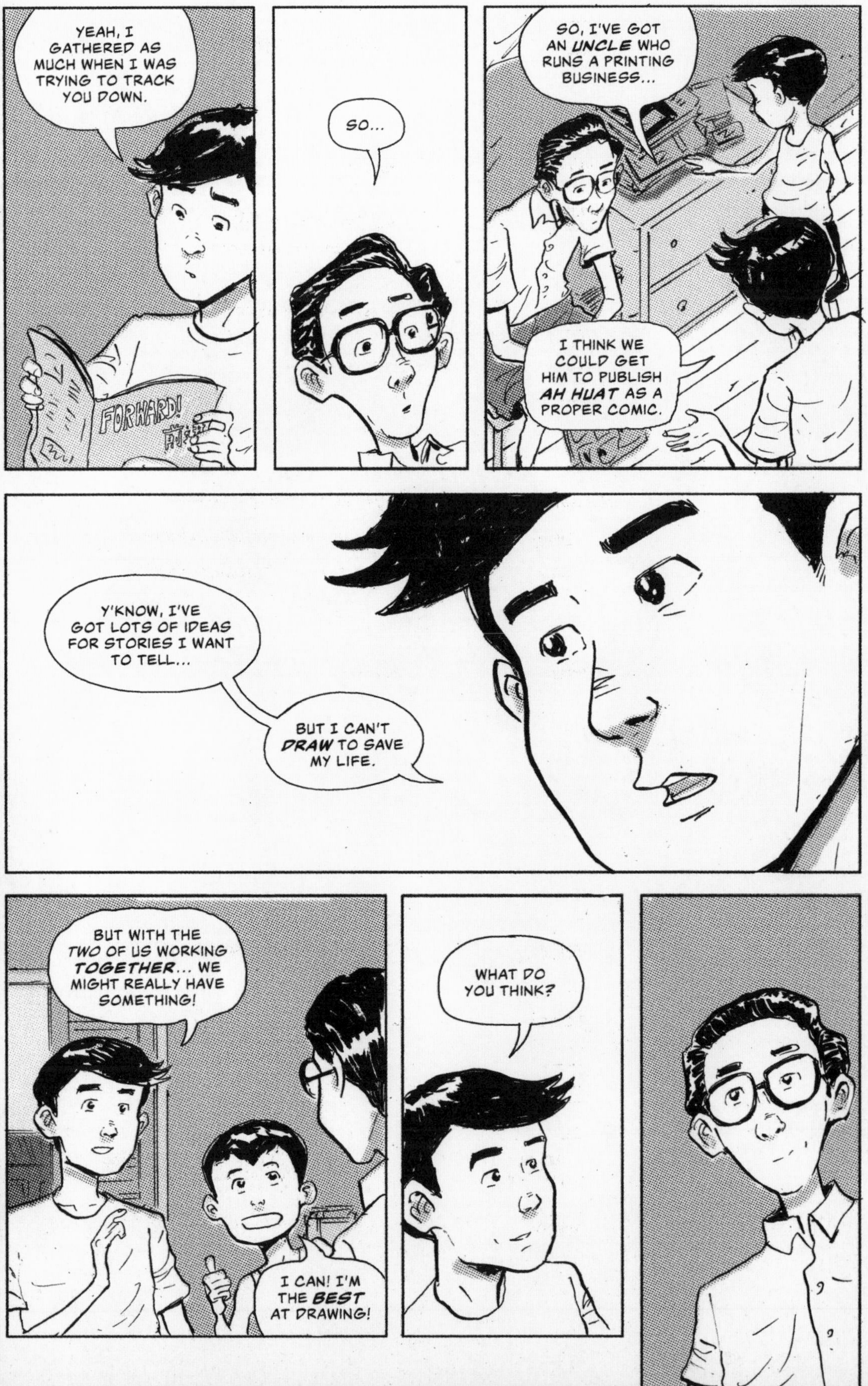
YEAH, I GATHERED AS MUCH WHEN I WAS TRYING TO TRACK YOU DOWN.
FORWARD! 前进
SO...
SO, I'VE GOT AN UNCLE WHO RUNS A PRINTING BUSINESS...
I THINK WE COULD GET HIM TO PUBLISH AH HUAT AS A PROPER COMIC.
Y'KNOW, I'VE GOT LOTS OF IDEAS FOR STORIES I WANT TO TELL...
BUT I CAN'T DRAW TO SAVE MY LIFE.
BUT WITH THE TWO OF US WORKING TOGETHER... WE MIGHT REALLY HAVE SOMETHING!
I CAN! I'M THE BEST AT DRAWING!
WHAT DO YOU THINK?

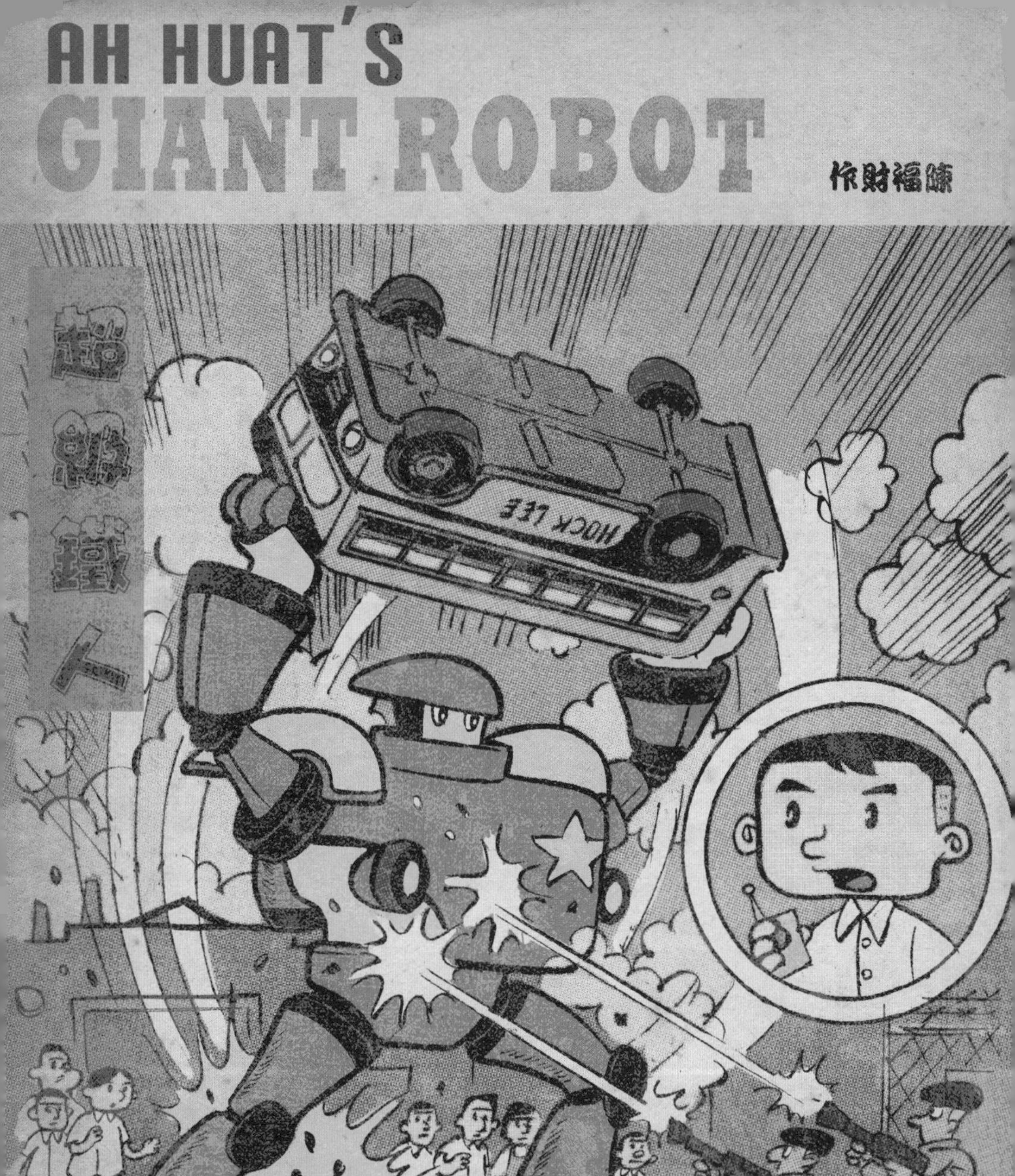
AH HUAT'S
GIANT ROBOT
陳福財作
超級鐵人
HOCK LEE

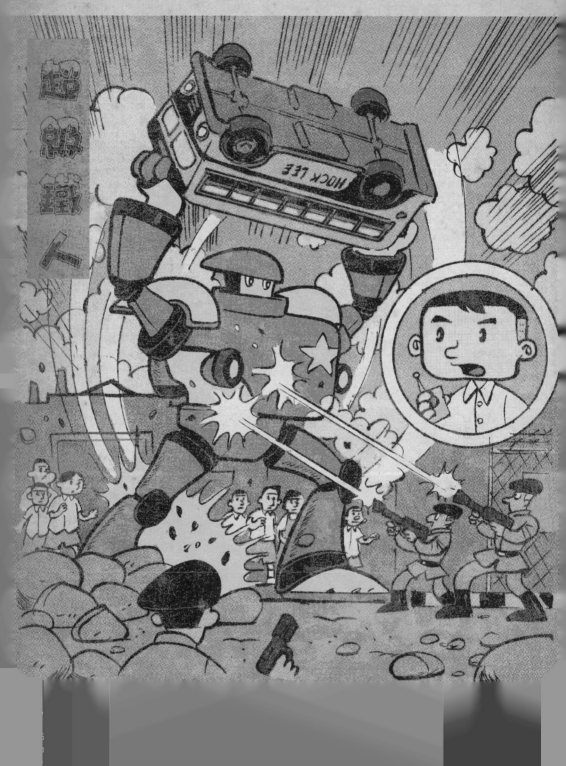

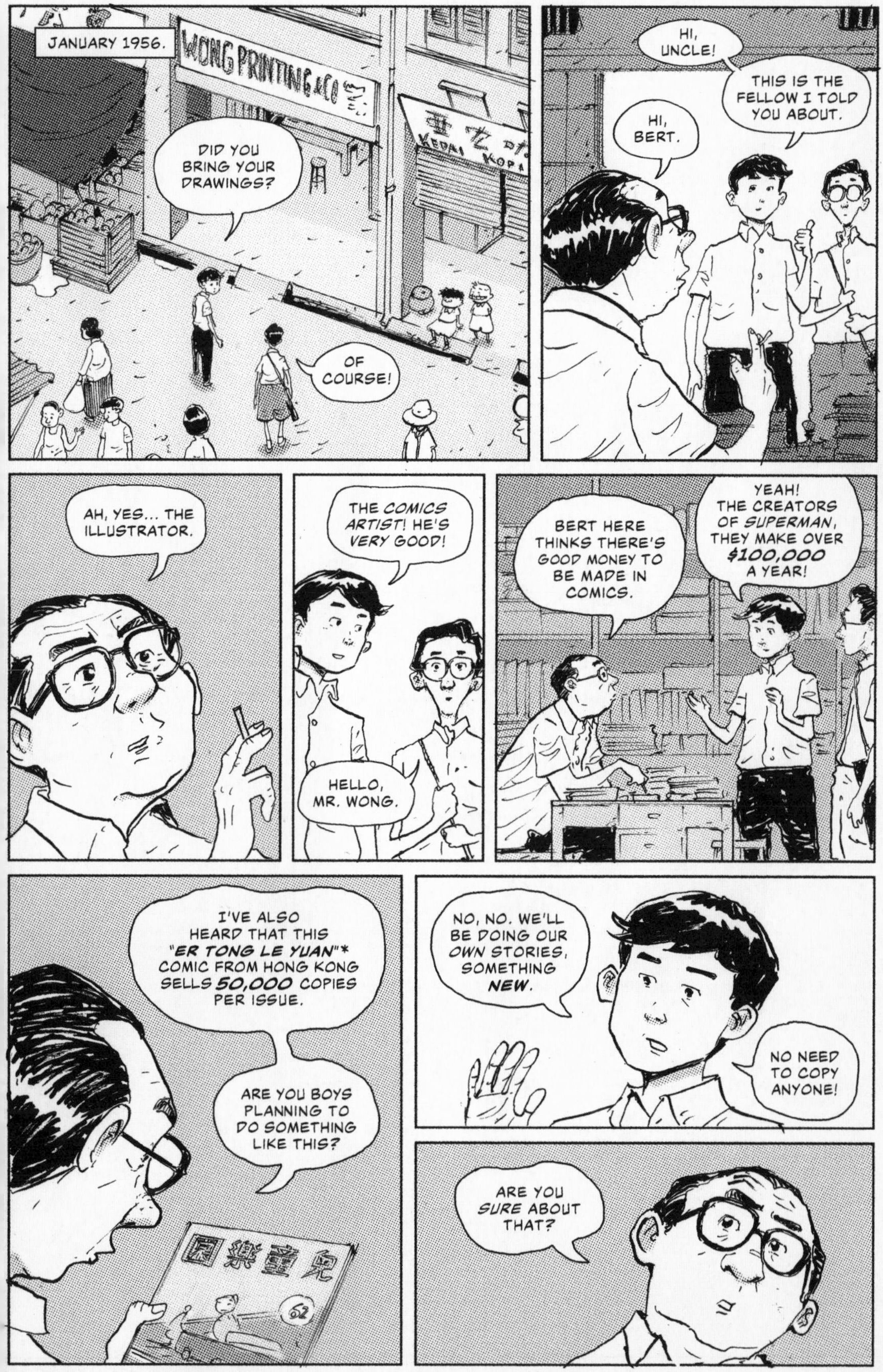
JANUARY 1956.
WONG PRINTING & CO
DID YOU BRING YOUR DRAWINGS?
OF COURSE!
HI, UNCLE!
THIS IS THE FELLOW I TOLD YOU ABOUT.
HI, BERT.
AH, YES... THE ILLUSTRATOR.
THE *COMICS ARTIST*! HE'S *VERY GOOD*!
HELLO, MR. WONG.
BERT HERE THINKS THERE'S GOOD MONEY TO BE MADE IN COMICS.
YEAH! THE CREATORS OF *SUPERMAN*, THEY MAKE OVER **$100,000** A YEAR!
I'VE ALSO HEARD THAT THIS "***ER TONG LE YUAN***"* COMIC FROM HONG KONG SELLS **50,000** COPIES PER ISSUE.
ARE YOU BOYS PLANNING TO DO SOMETHING LIKE THIS?
園樂童兒
62
NO, NO. WE'LL BE DOING OUR *OWN STORIES*, SOMETHING ***NEW***.
NO NEED TO COPY ANYONE!
ARE YOU *SURE* ABOUT THAT?

*儿童乐园 ("CHILDREN'S PARADISE")

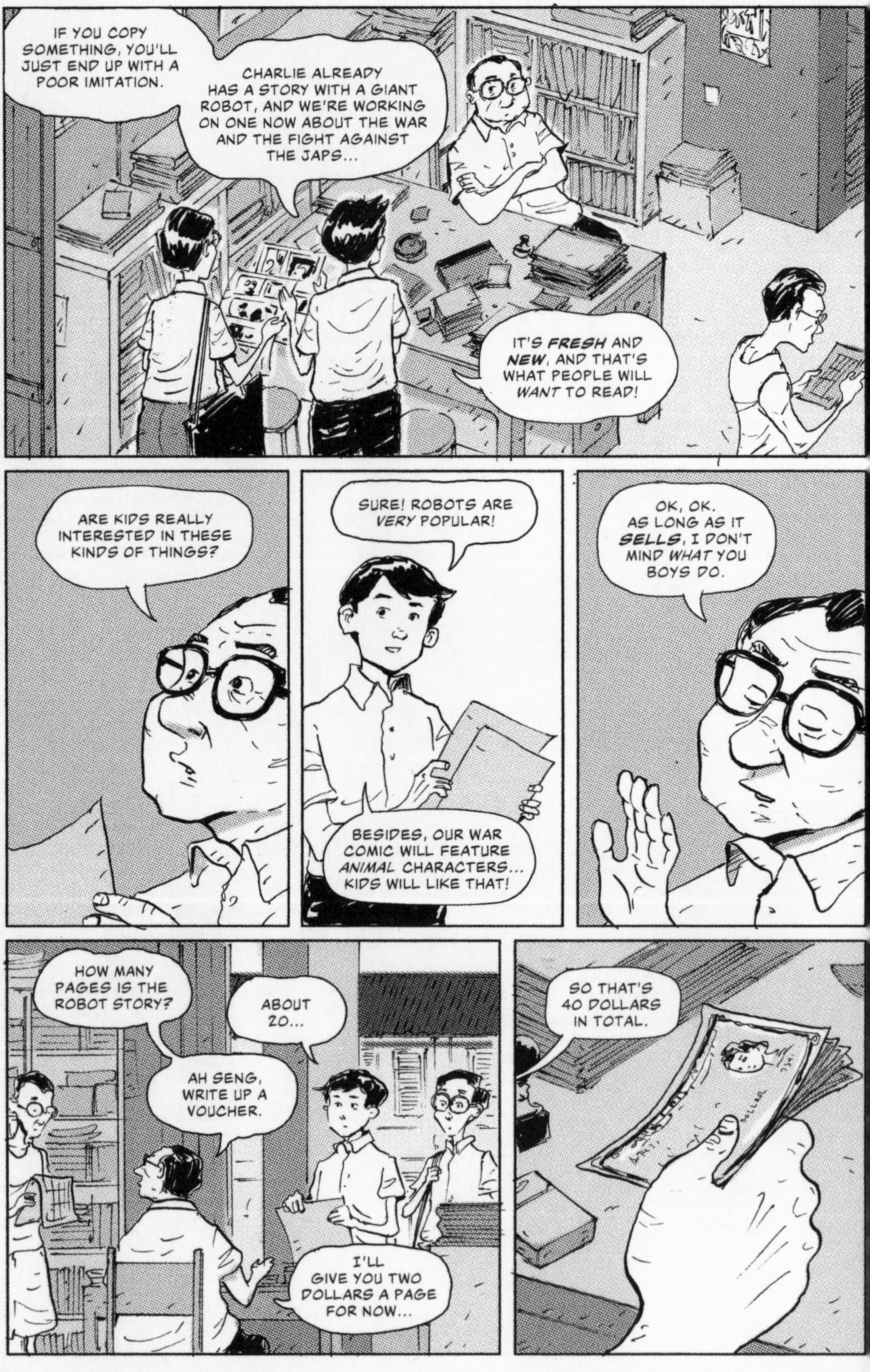
IF YOU COPY SOMETHING, YOU'LL JUST END UP WITH A POOR IMITATION.
CHARLIE ALREADY HAS A STORY WITH A GIANT ROBOT, AND WE'RE WORKING ON ONE NOW ABOUT THE WAR AND THE FIGHT AGAINST THE JAPS...
IT'S **FRESH** AND **NEW**, AND THAT'S WHAT PEOPLE WILL *WANT* TO READ!
ARE KIDS REALLY INTERESTED IN THESE KINDS OF THINGS?
SURE! ROBOTS ARE *VERY* POPULAR!
BESIDES, OUR WAR COMIC WILL FEATURE *ANIMAL* CHARACTERS... KIDS WILL LIKE THAT!
OK, OK. AS LONG AS IT **SELLS**, I DON'T MIND *WHAT* YOU BOYS DO.
HOW MANY PAGES IS THE ROBOT STORY?
ABOUT 20...
AH SENG, WRITE UP A VOUCHER.
I'LL GIVE YOU TWO DOLLARS A PAGE FOR NOW...
SO THAT'S 40 DOLLARS IN TOTAL.

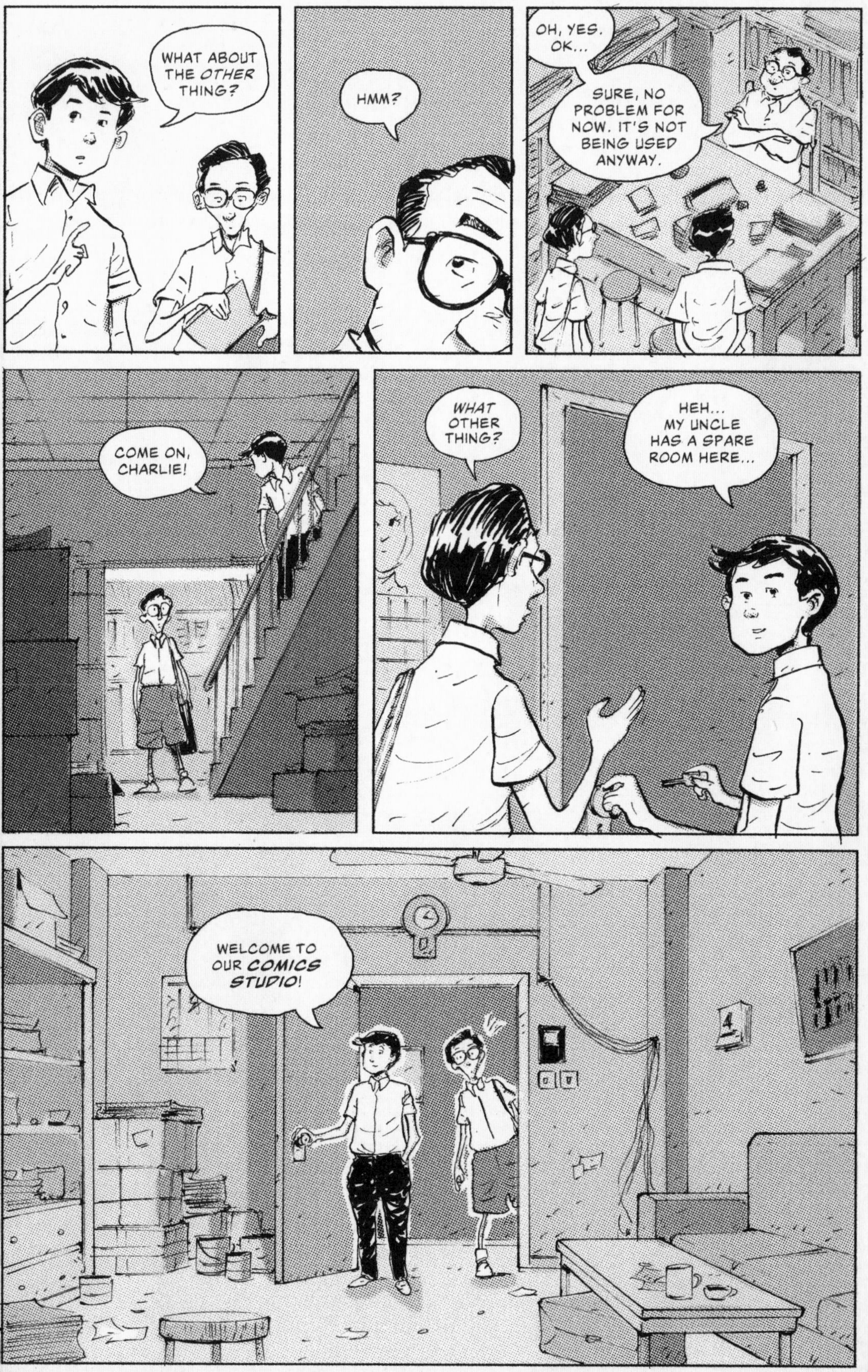
WHAT ABOUT THE OTHER THING?
HMM?
OH, YES. OK...
SURE, NO PROBLEM FOR NOW. IT'S NOT BEING USED ANYWAY.
COME ON, CHARLIE!
WHAT OTHER THING?
HEH... MY UNCLE HAS A SPARE ROOM HERE...
WELCOME TO OUR COMICS STUDIO!
4

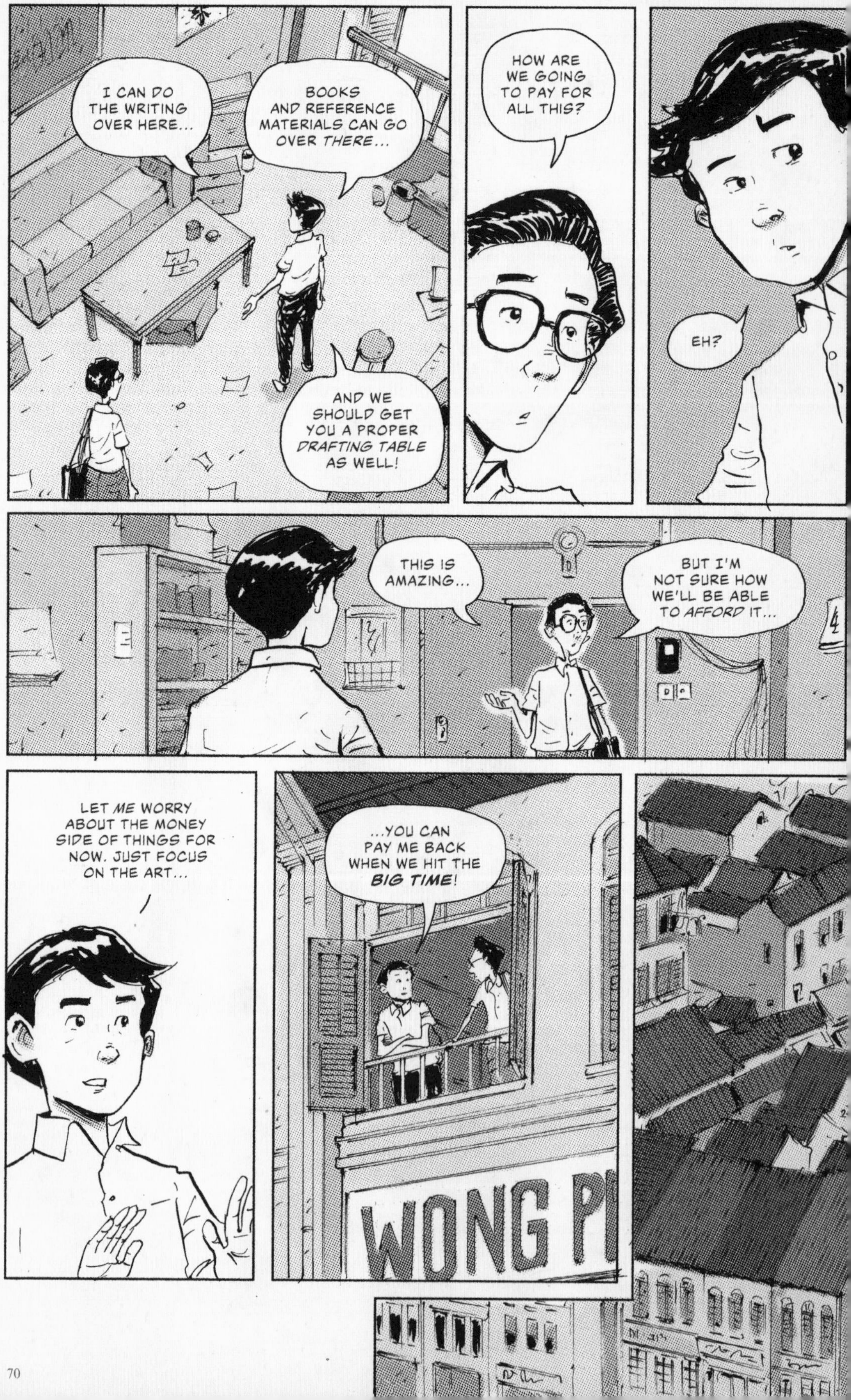
I CAN DO THE WRITING OVER HERE...
BOOKS AND REFERENCE MATERIALS CAN GO OVER *THERE*...
AND WE SHOULD GET YOU A PROPER *DRAFTING TABLE* AS WELL!
HOW ARE WE GOING TO PAY FOR ALL THIS?
EH?
THIS IS AMAZING...
BUT I'M NOT SURE HOW WE'LL BE ABLE TO *AFFORD* IT...
LET *ME* WORRY ABOUT THE MONEY SIDE OF THINGS FOR NOW. JUST FOCUS ON THE ART...
...YOU CAN PAY ME BACK WHEN WE HIT THE ***BIG TIME***!
WONG P

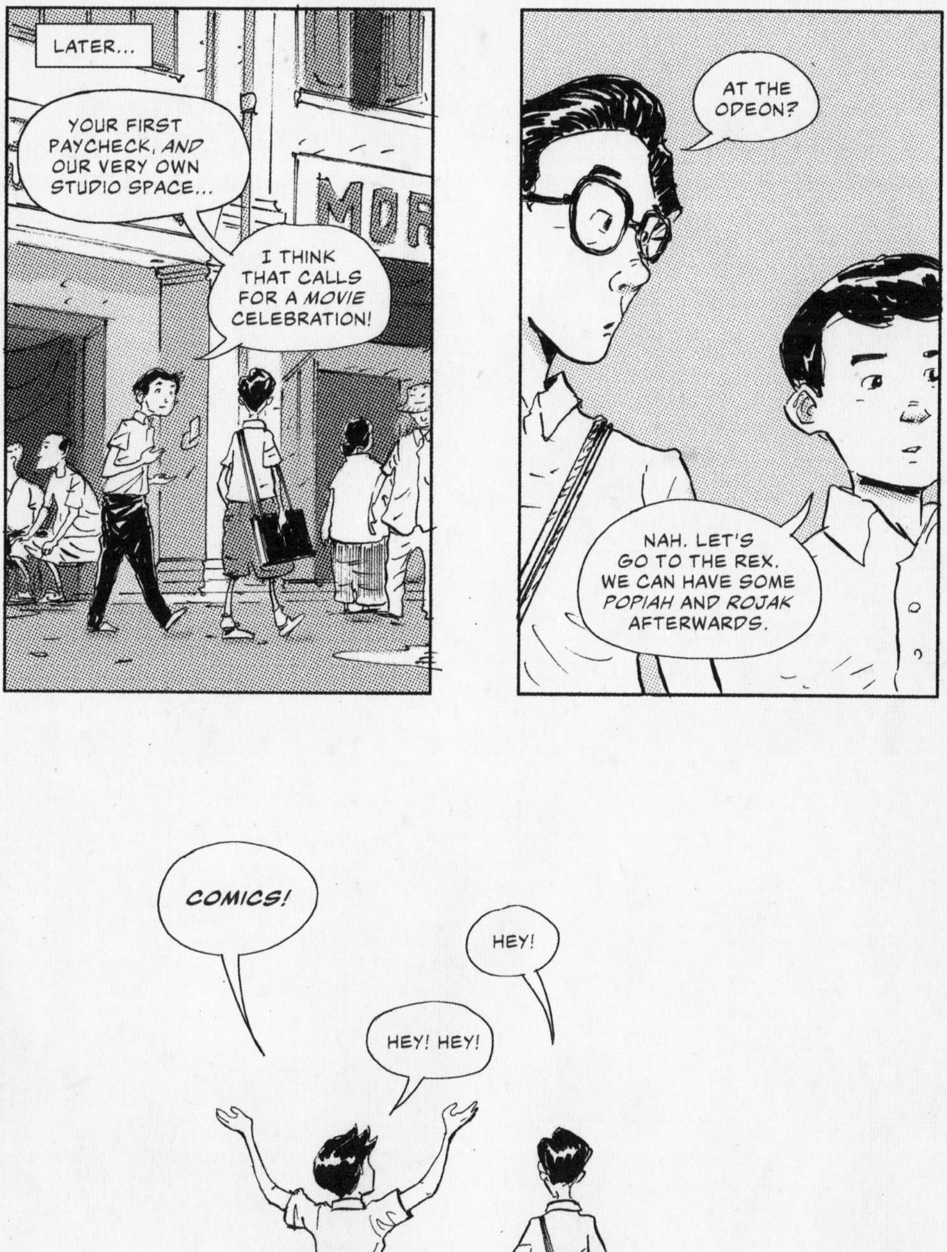
LATER...
YOUR FIRST PAYCHECK, *AND* OUR VERY OWN STUDIO SPACE...
I THINK THAT CALLS FOR A *MOVIE* CELEBRATION!
AT THE ODEON?
NAH. LET'S GO TO THE REX. WE CAN HAVE SOME *POPIAH* AND *ROJAK* AFTERWARDS.
COMICS!
HEY!
HEY! HEY!

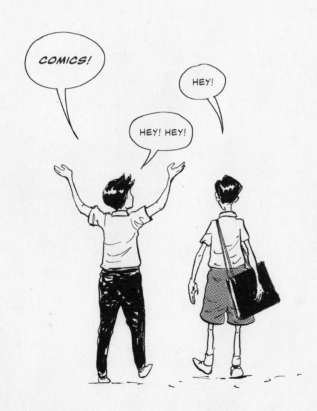

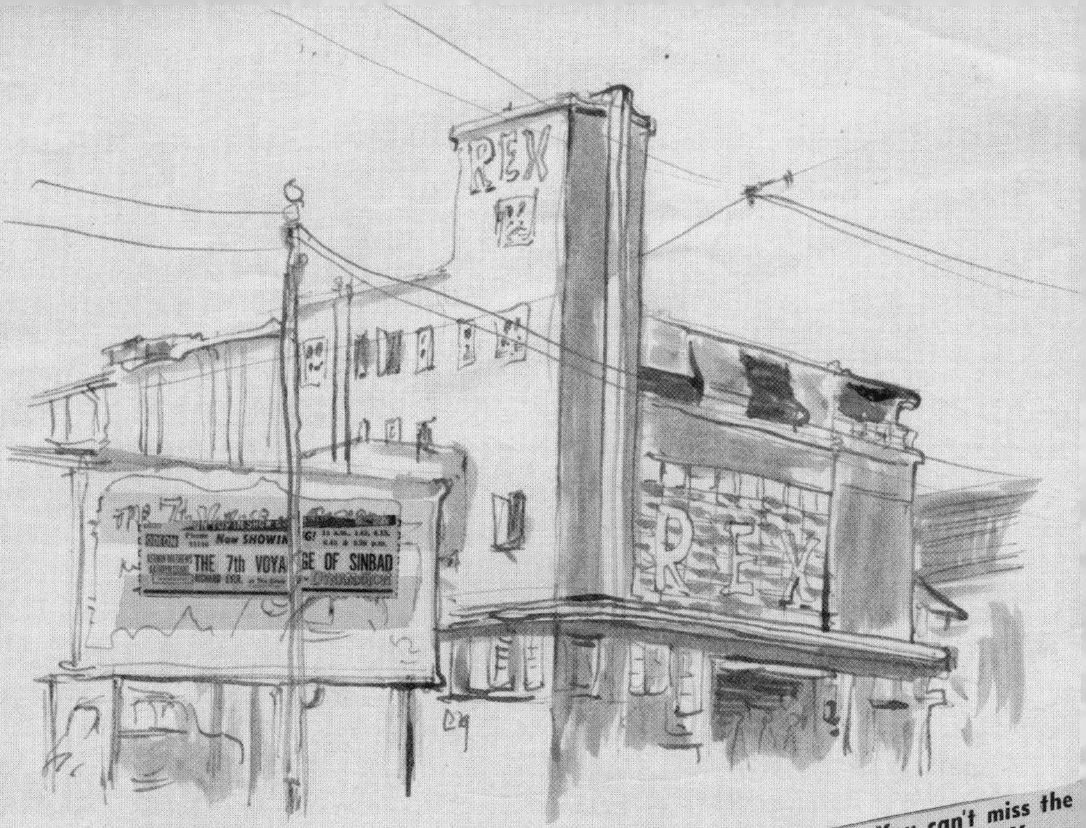
REX
ODEON
Now SHOWING!
THE 7th VOYAGE OF SINBAD
RICHARD EYER
REX

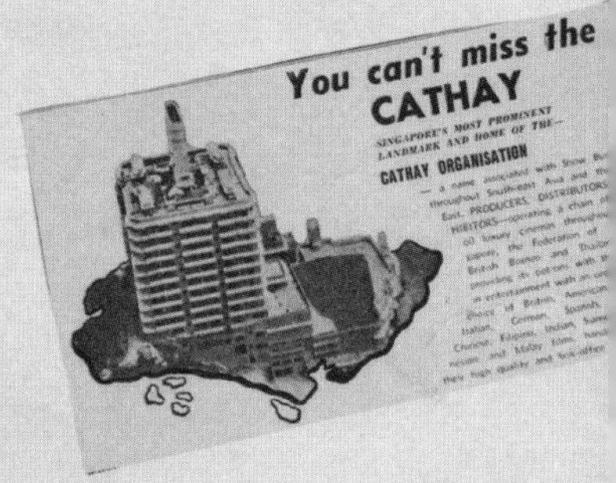
You can't miss the
CATHAY
SINGAPORE'S MOST PROMINENT LANDMARK AND HOME OF THE—
CATHAY ORGANISATION

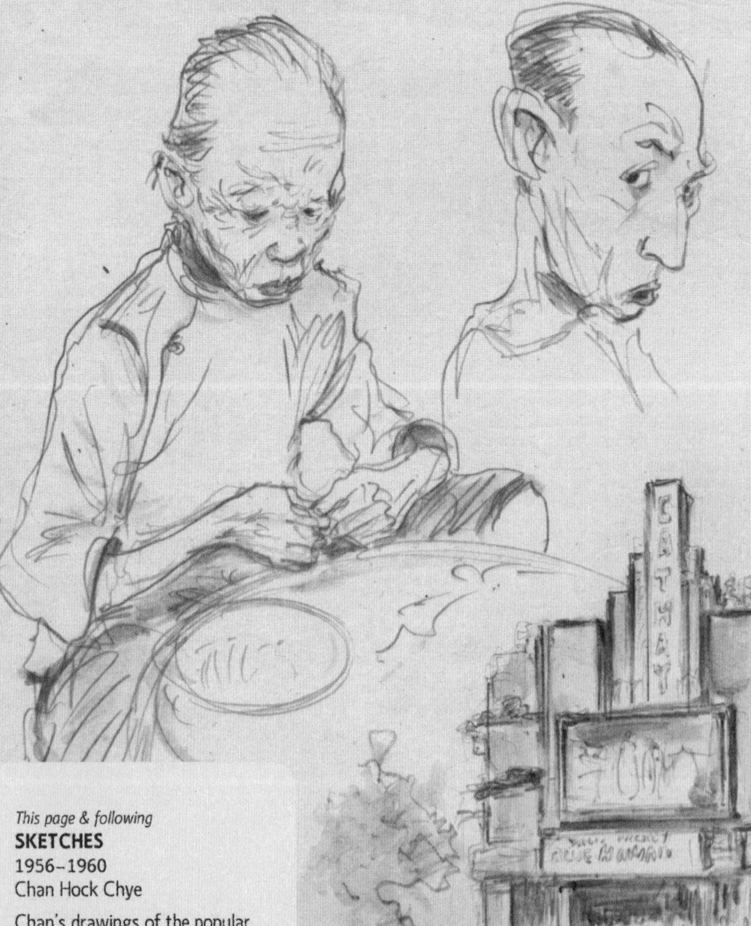

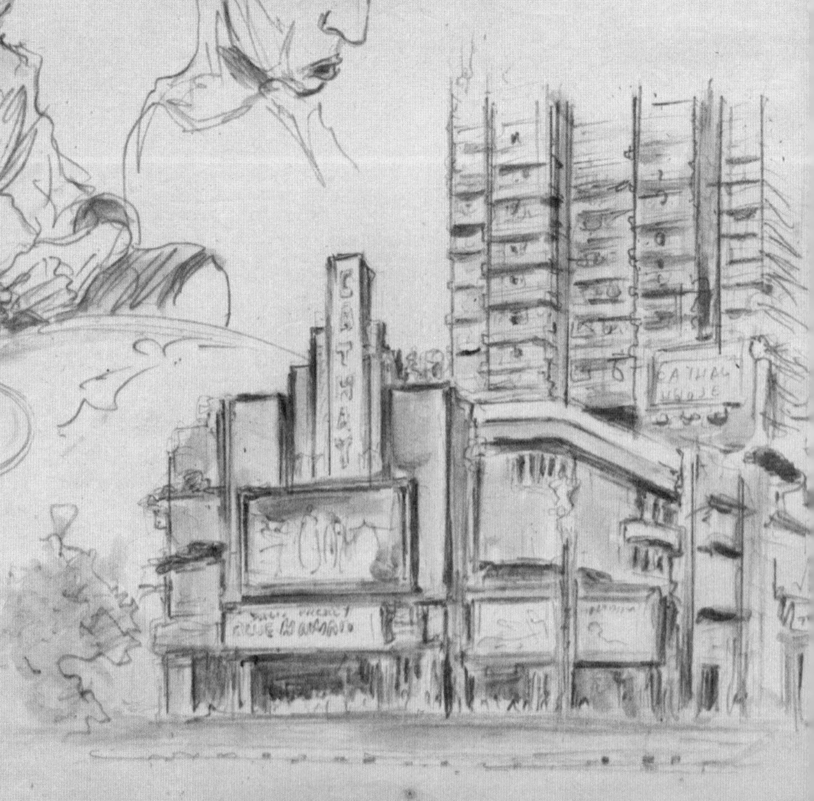
CATHAY

This page & following
SKETCHES
1956–1960
Chan Hock Chye

Chan's drawings of the popular Rex and Cathay cinemas.

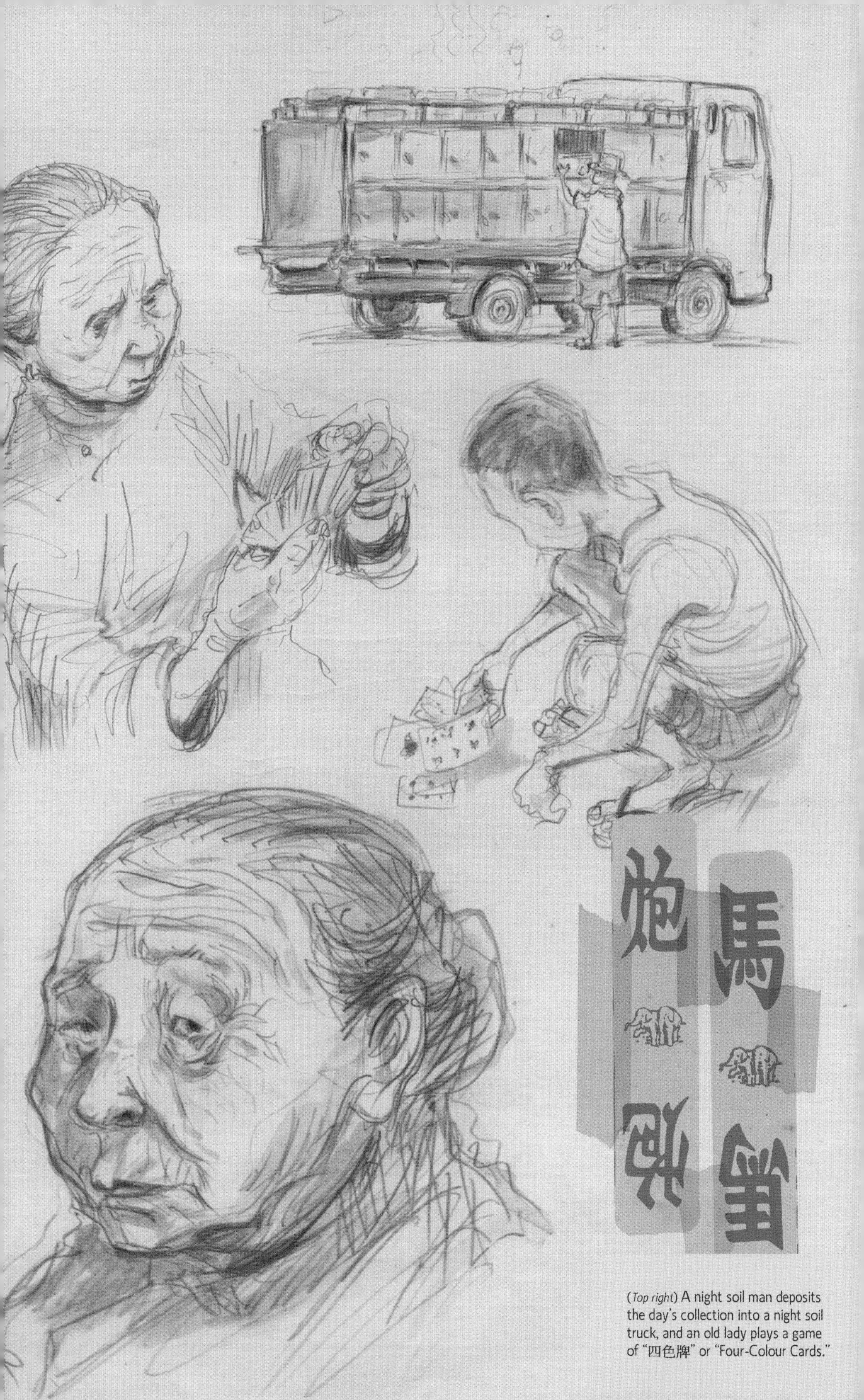
馬
炮

(*Top right*) A night soil man deposits the day's collection into a night soil truck, and an old lady plays a game of "四色牌" or "Four-Colour Cards."

Great World Amusement Park (*Tua Seh Kai*, or 大世界, *see bottom of page*), founded in 1929, was one of three popular amusement parks (along with New World and Happy World) offering affordable entertainment for the masses. Changing times and tastes led to their gradual decline, and Great World was closed for good in 1978.

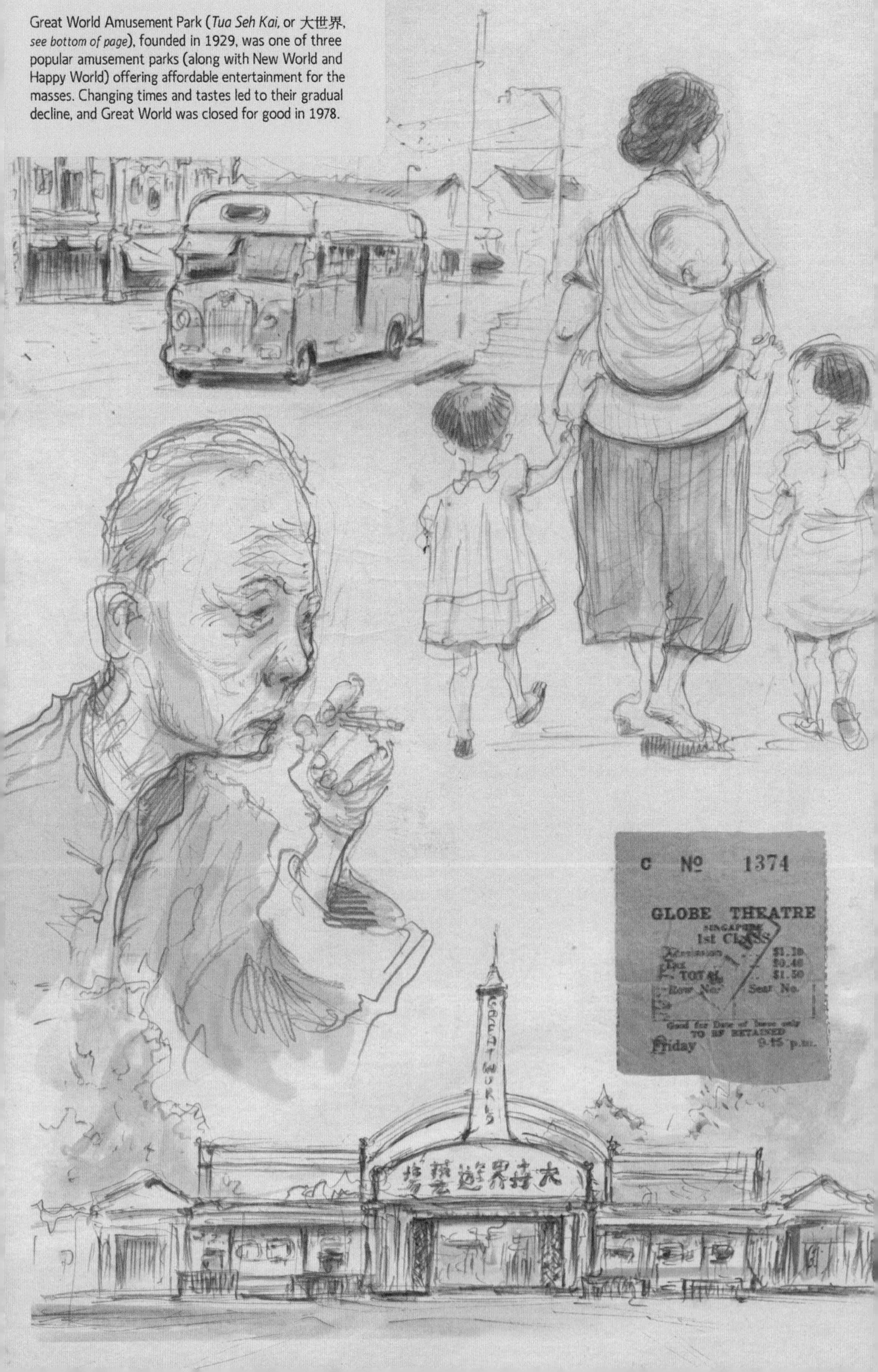
C No 1374
GLOBE THEATRE
SINGAPORE
1st CLASS
Admission $1.10
Tax $0.40
TOTal $1.50
Row No. Seat No.
Good for Date of Issue only
TO BE RETAINED
Friday 9.15 p.m.
GREAT WORLD
大世界遊藝場

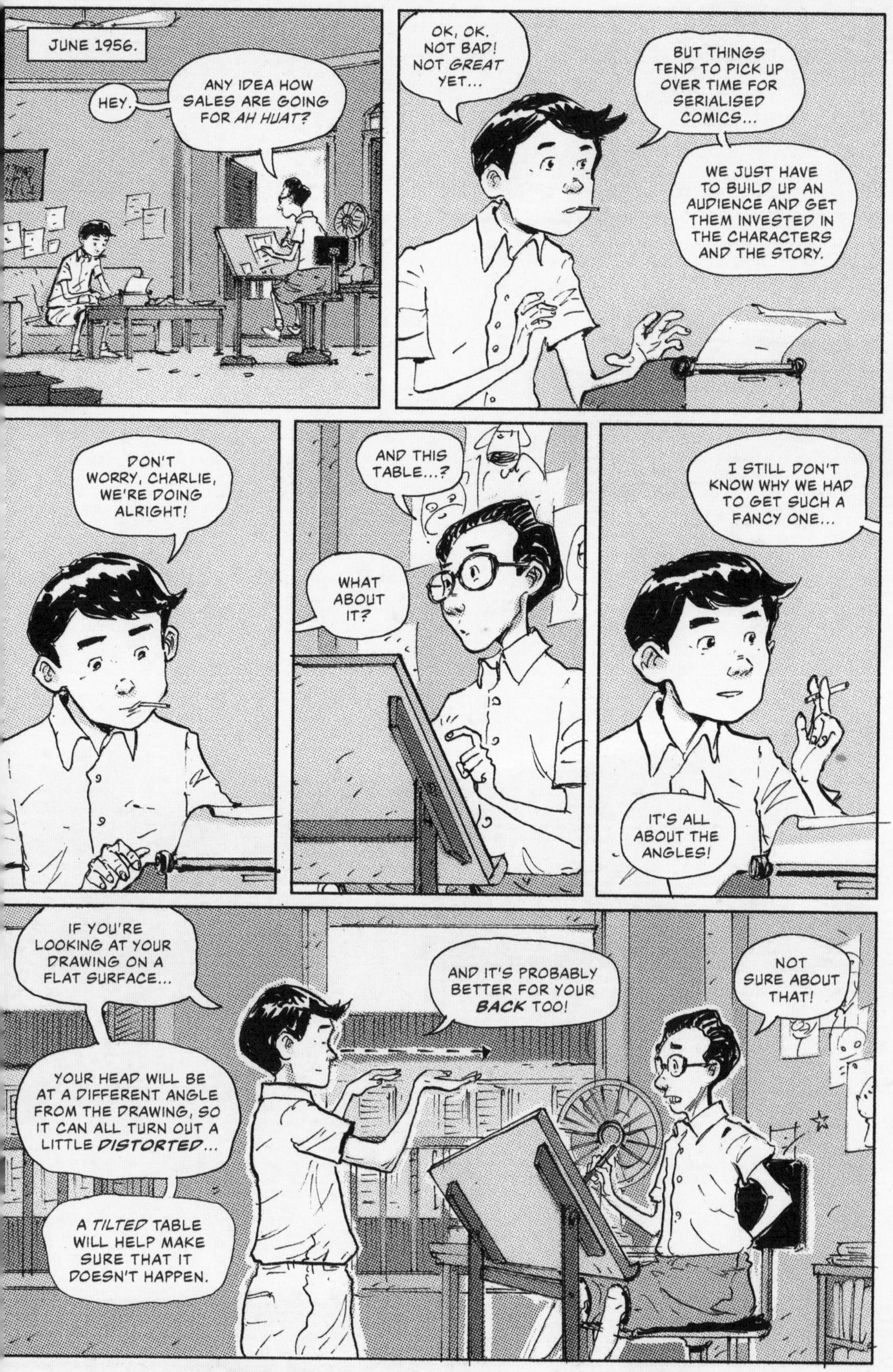
JUNE 1956.
HEY.
ANY IDEA HOW SALES ARE GOING FOR AH HUAT?
OK, OK. NOT BAD! NOT GREAT YET...
BUT THINGS TEND TO PICK UP OVER TIME FOR SERIALISED COMICS...
WE JUST HAVE TO BUILD UP AN AUDIENCE AND GET THEM INVESTED IN THE CHARACTERS AND THE STORY.
DON'T WORRY, CHARLIE, WE'RE DOING ALRIGHT!
AND THIS TABLE...?
WHAT ABOUT IT?
I STILL DON'T KNOW WHY WE HAD TO GET SUCH A FANCY ONE...
IT'S ALL ABOUT THE ANGLES!
IF YOU'RE LOOKING AT YOUR DRAWING ON A FLAT SURFACE...
YOUR HEAD WILL BE AT A DIFFERENT ANGLE FROM THE DRAWING, SO IT CAN ALL TURN OUT A LITTLE DISTORTED...
A TILTED TABLE WILL HELP MAKE SURE THAT IT DOESN'T HAPPEN.
AND IT'S PROBABLY BETTER FOR YOUR BACK TOO!
NOT SURE ABOUT THAT!

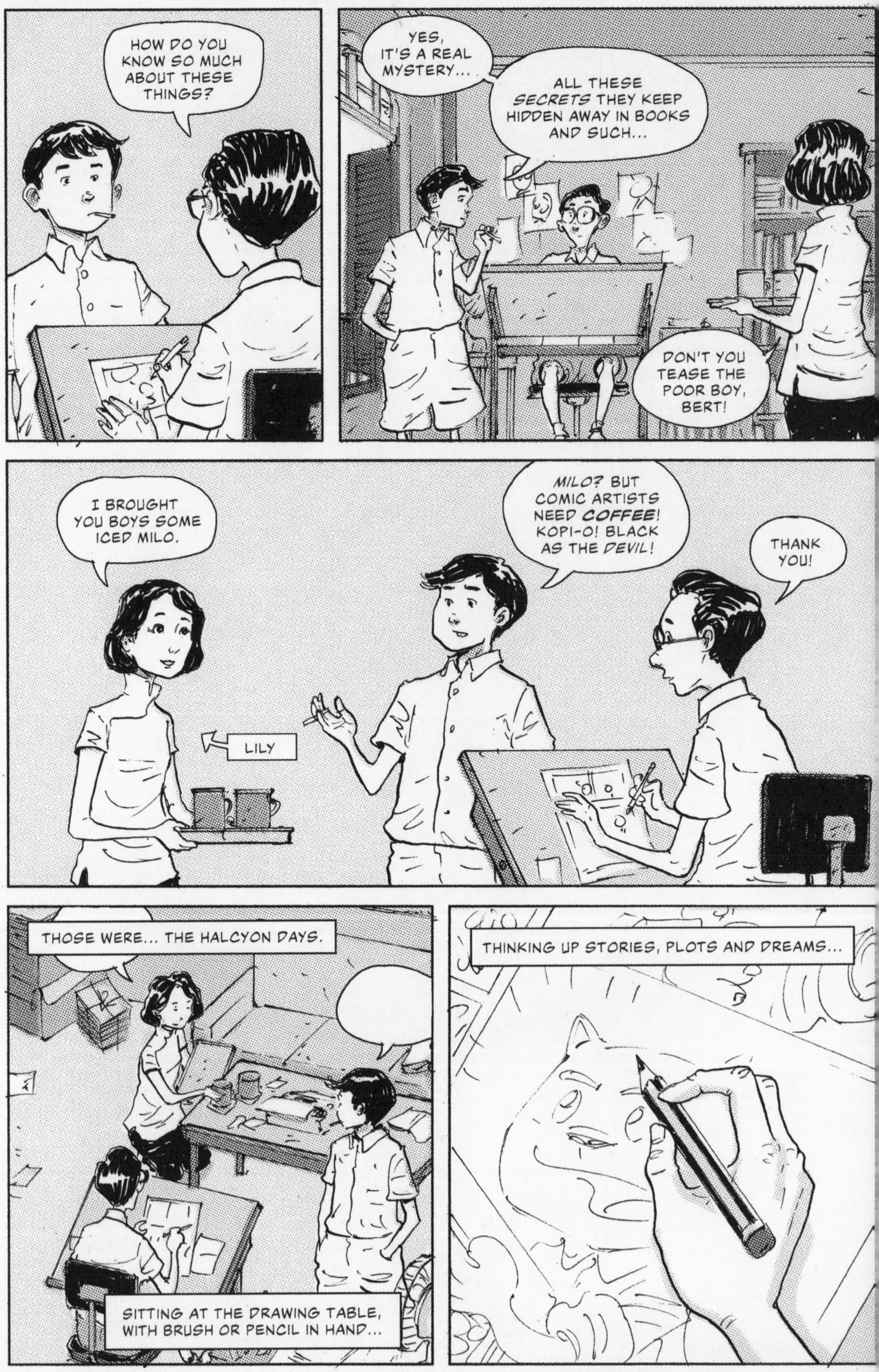
HOW DO YOU KNOW SO MUCH ABOUT THESE THINGS?
YES, IT'S A REAL MYSTERY...
ALL THESE *SECRETS* THEY KEEP HIDDEN AWAY IN BOOKS AND SUCH...
DON'T YOU TEASE THE POOR BOY, BERT!
I BROUGHT YOU BOYS SOME ICED MILO.
LILY
MILO? BUT COMIC ARTISTS NEED ***COFFEE***! KOPI-O! BLACK AS THE *DEVIL*!
THANK YOU!
THOSE WERE... THE HALCYON DAYS.
SITTING AT THE DRAWING TABLE, WITH BRUSH OR PENCIL IN HAND...
THINKING UP STORIES, PLOTS AND DREAMS...

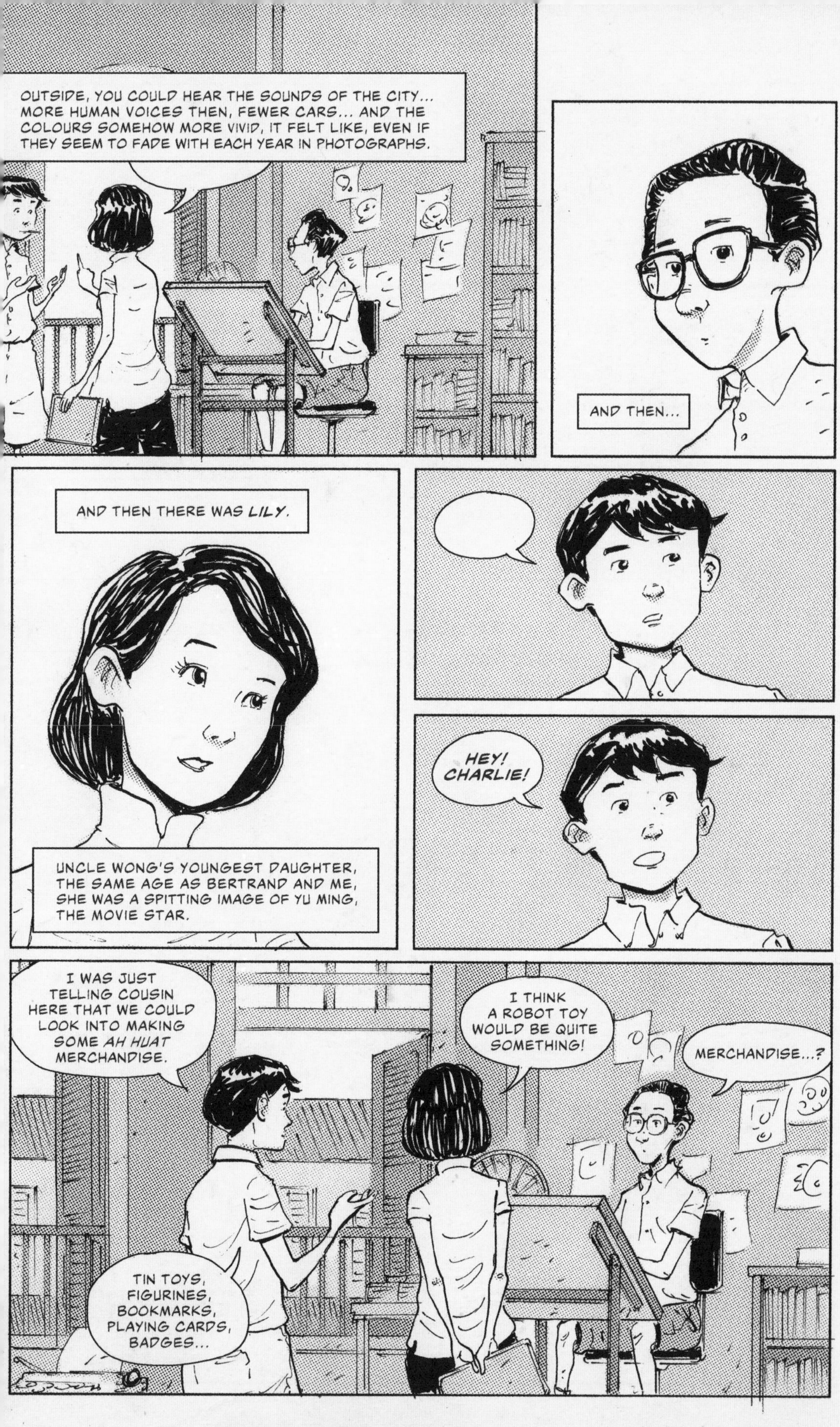
OUTSIDE, YOU COULD HEAR THE SOUNDS OF THE CITY... MORE HUMAN VOICES THEN, FEWER CARS... AND THE COLOURS SOMEHOW MORE VIVID, IT FELT LIKE, EVEN IF THEY SEEM TO FADE WITH EACH YEAR IN PHOTOGRAPHS.
AND THEN...
AND THEN THERE WAS *LILY*.
UNCLE WONG'S YOUNGEST DAUGHTER, THE SAME AGE AS BERTRAND AND ME, SHE WAS A SPITTING IMAGE OF YU MING, THE MOVIE STAR.
HEY! CHARLIE!
I WAS JUST TELLING COUSIN HERE THAT WE COULD LOOK INTO MAKING SOME *AH HUAT* MERCHANDISE.
TIN TOYS, FIGURINES, BOOKMARKS, PLAYING CARDS, BADGES...
I THINK A ROBOT TOY WOULD BE QUITE SOMETHING!
MERCHANDISE...?

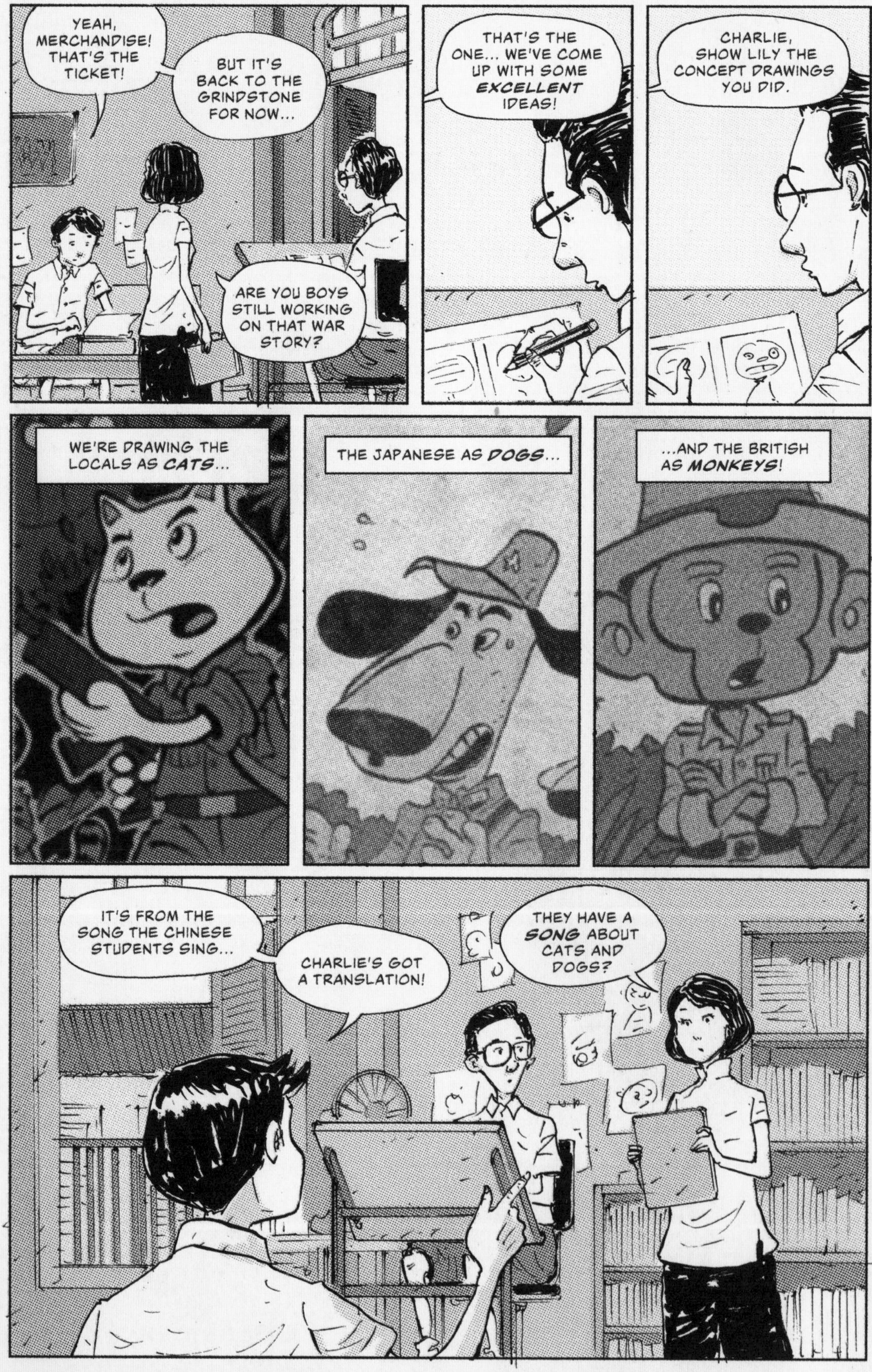

YEAH, MERCHANDISE! THAT'S THE TICKET!
BUT IT'S BACK TO THE GRINDSTONE FOR NOW...
ARE YOU BOYS STILL WORKING ON THAT WAR STORY?
THAT'S THE ONE... WE'VE COME UP WITH SOME EXCELLENT IDEAS!
CHARLIE, SHOW LILY THE CONCEPT DRAWINGS YOU DID.
WE'RE DRAWING THE LOCALS AS CATS...
THE JAPANESE AS DOGS...
...AND THE BRITISH AS MONKEYS!
IT'S FROM THE SONG THE CHINESE STUDENTS SING...
CHARLIE'S GOT A TRANSLATION!
THEY HAVE A SONG ABOUT CATS AND DOGS?

I LOVE MALAYA.
MALAYA IS MY HOME...
JAPANESE TIME, WE WERE NOT FREE...
NOW WE'RE IN GREATER MISERY...
AFTER THE DOGS HAVE GONE, THE MONKEYS HAVE RETURNED...
TURNING MALAYA INTO A BITTER SEA...
WELL, JUST SO YOU BOYS KNOW...

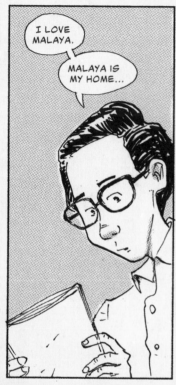

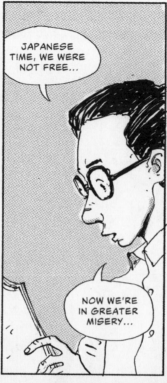

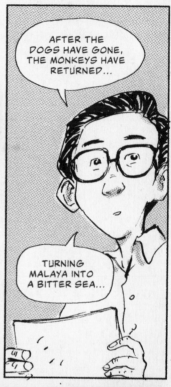

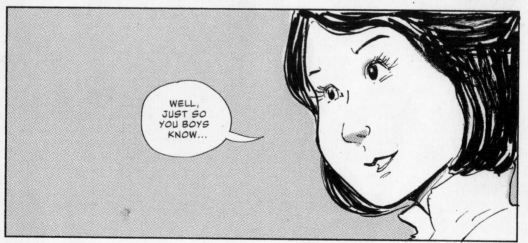

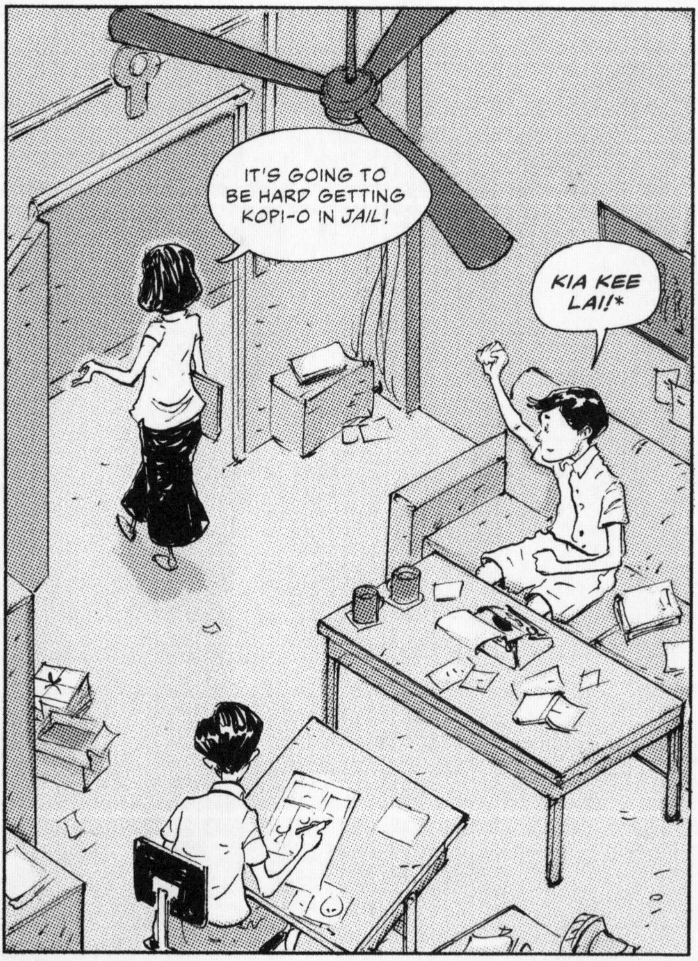
IT'S GOING TO BE HARD GETTING KOPI-O IN JAIL!
KIA KEE LAI!*

*"站起来!": HOKKIEN FOR "STAND ON YOUR OWN TWO FEET!"

我愛我的馬來亞
1=F 2/4
我愛我的馬來亞，馬來亞是我家鄉，日本時期不自由，
如今更苦難。誰知狗去猴子來馬來亞成苦海。
兄弟們呀，姐妹們，不能再等待。不能再等待。

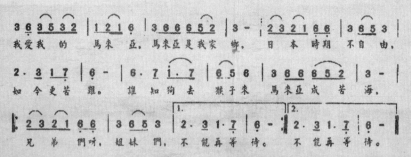

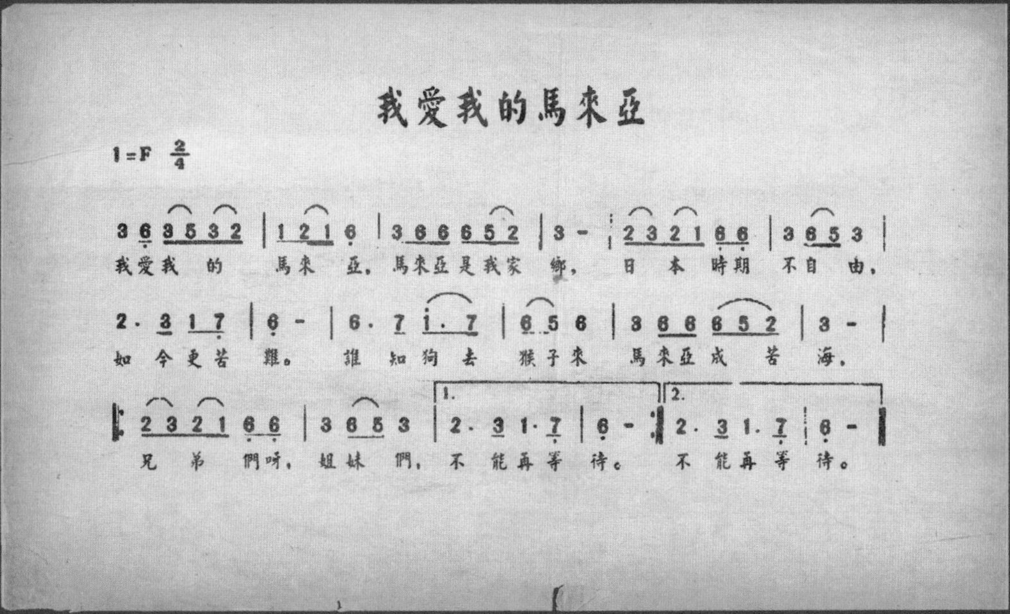

我爱我的马来亚
I love my Malaya

马来亚是我家乡
Malaya is my home

日本时期不自由
During the Japanese Occupation
We were not free

如今更苦愁
Now we are in greater misery

谁知狗去猴子来
Who knew when the dogs had gone
The monkeys would return

马来亚成苦海
And turn Malaya into a bitter sea

兄弟们呀姐妹们
Oh my brothers, my sisters

不能再等待
We can wait no more

同胞们呀快起来
Oh my compatriots
Let us all stand up

不能再等待
We can wait no more

Above
"I LOVE MY MALAYA"
Song sheet
c. 1956
Collection of Chan Hock Chye

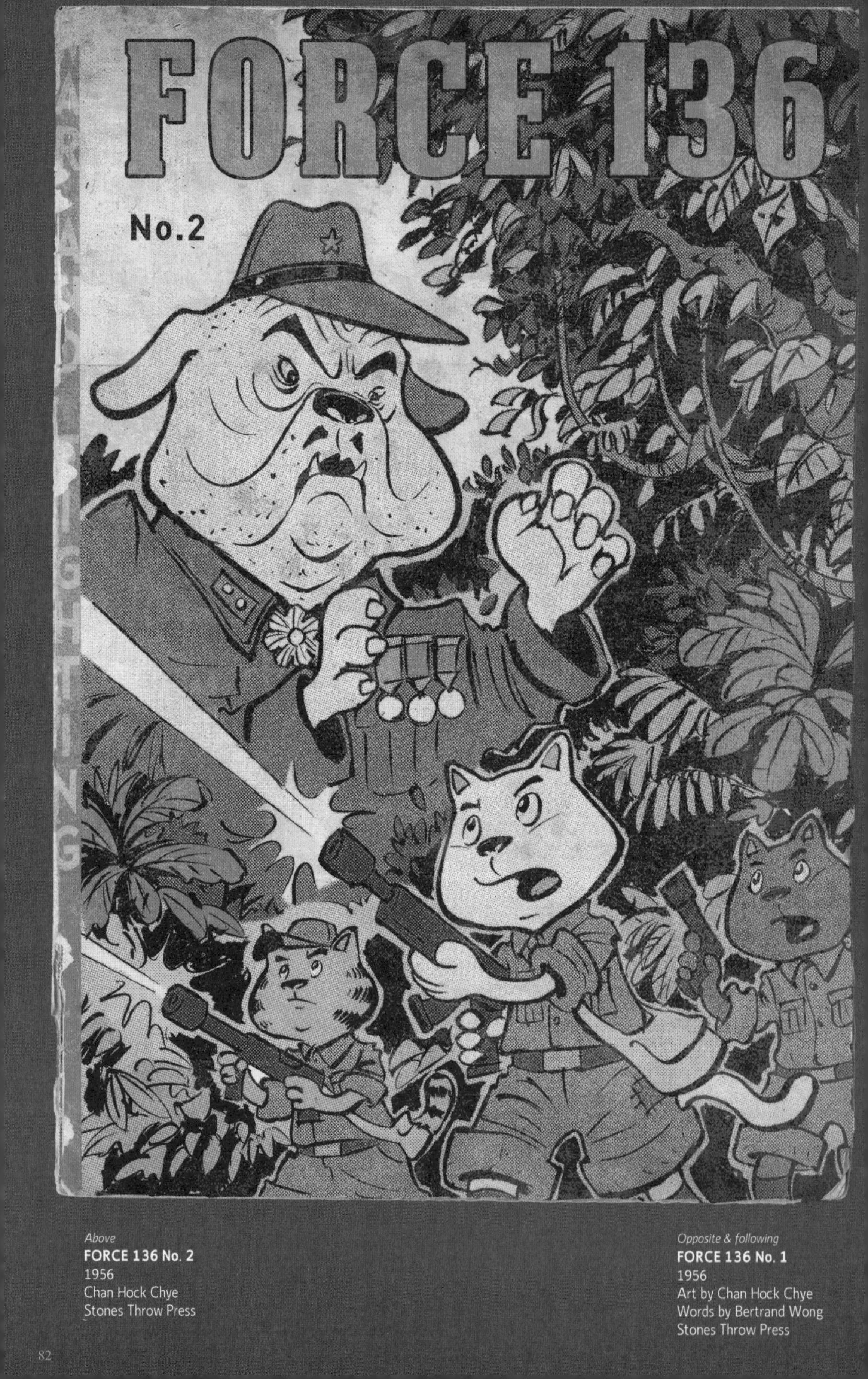
FORCE 136
No.2

Above
FORCE 136 No. 2
1956
Chan Hock Chye
Stones Throw Press

Opposite & following
FORCE 136 No. 1
1956
Art by Chan Hock Chye
Words by Bertrand Wong
Stones Throw Press

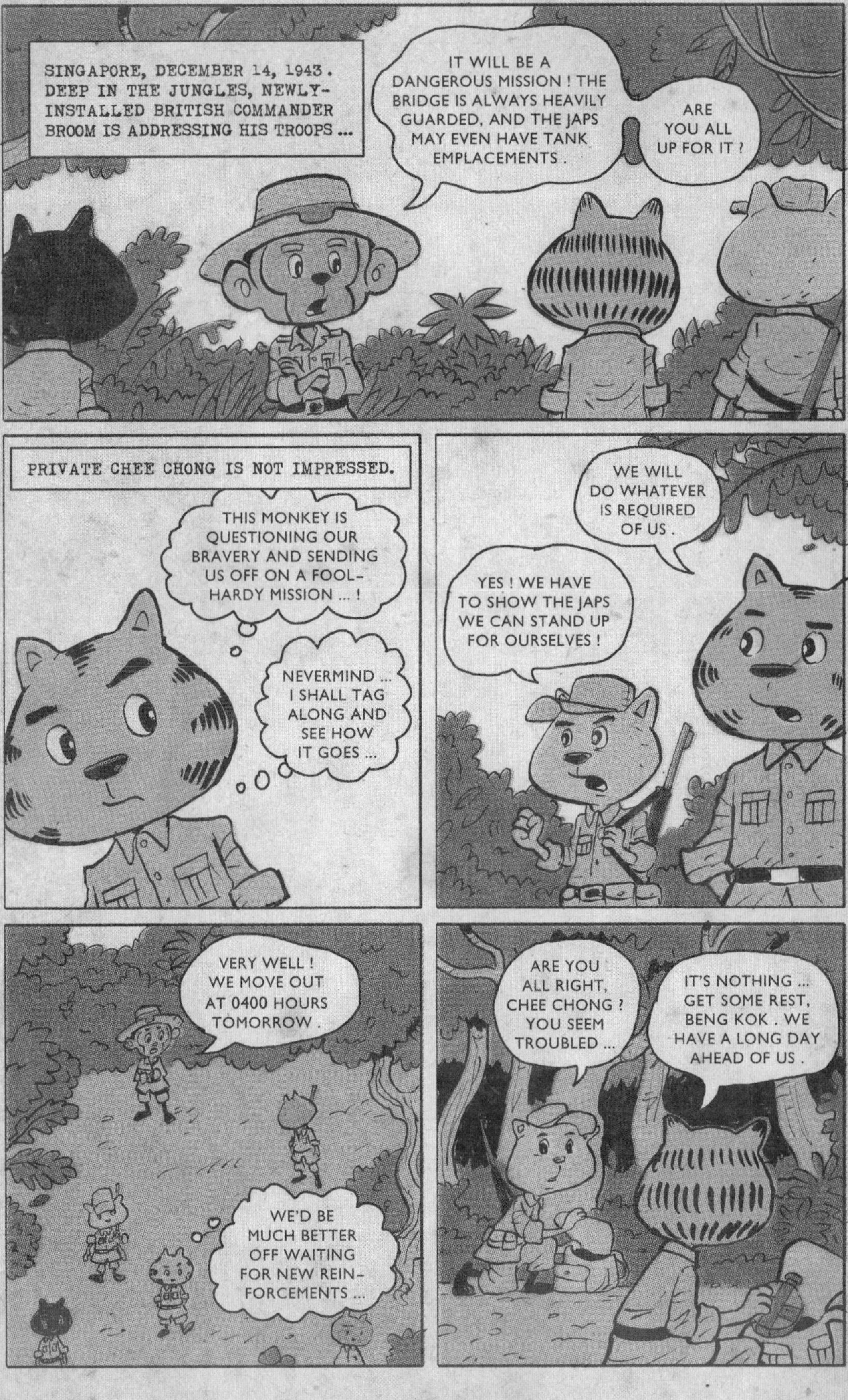
SINGAPORE, DECEMBER 14, 1943. DEEP IN THE JUNGLES, NEWLY-INSTALLED BRITISH COMMANDER BROOM IS ADDRESSING HIS TROOPS ...
IT WILL BE A DANGEROUS MISSION ! THE BRIDGE IS ALWAYS HEAVILY GUARDED, AND THE JAPS MAY EVEN HAVE TANK EMPLACEMENTS .
ARE YOU ALL UP FOR IT ?
PRIVATE CHEE CHONG IS NOT IMPRESSED.
THIS MONKEY IS QUESTIONING OUR BRAVERY AND SENDING US OFF ON A FOOL-HARDY MISSION ... !
NEVERMIND ... I SHALL TAG ALONG AND SEE HOW IT GOES ...
WE WILL DO WHATEVER IS REQUIRED OF US .
YES ! WE HAVE TO SHOW THE JAPS WE CAN STAND UP FOR OURSELVES !
VERY WELL ! WE MOVE OUT AT 0400 HOURS TOMORROW .
WE'D BE MUCH BETTER OFF WAITING FOR NEW REIN-FORCEMENTS ...
ARE YOU ALL RIGHT, CHEE CHONG ? YOU SEEM TROUBLED ...
IT'S NOTHING ... GET SOME REST, BENG KOK . WE HAVE A LONG DAY AHEAD OF US .

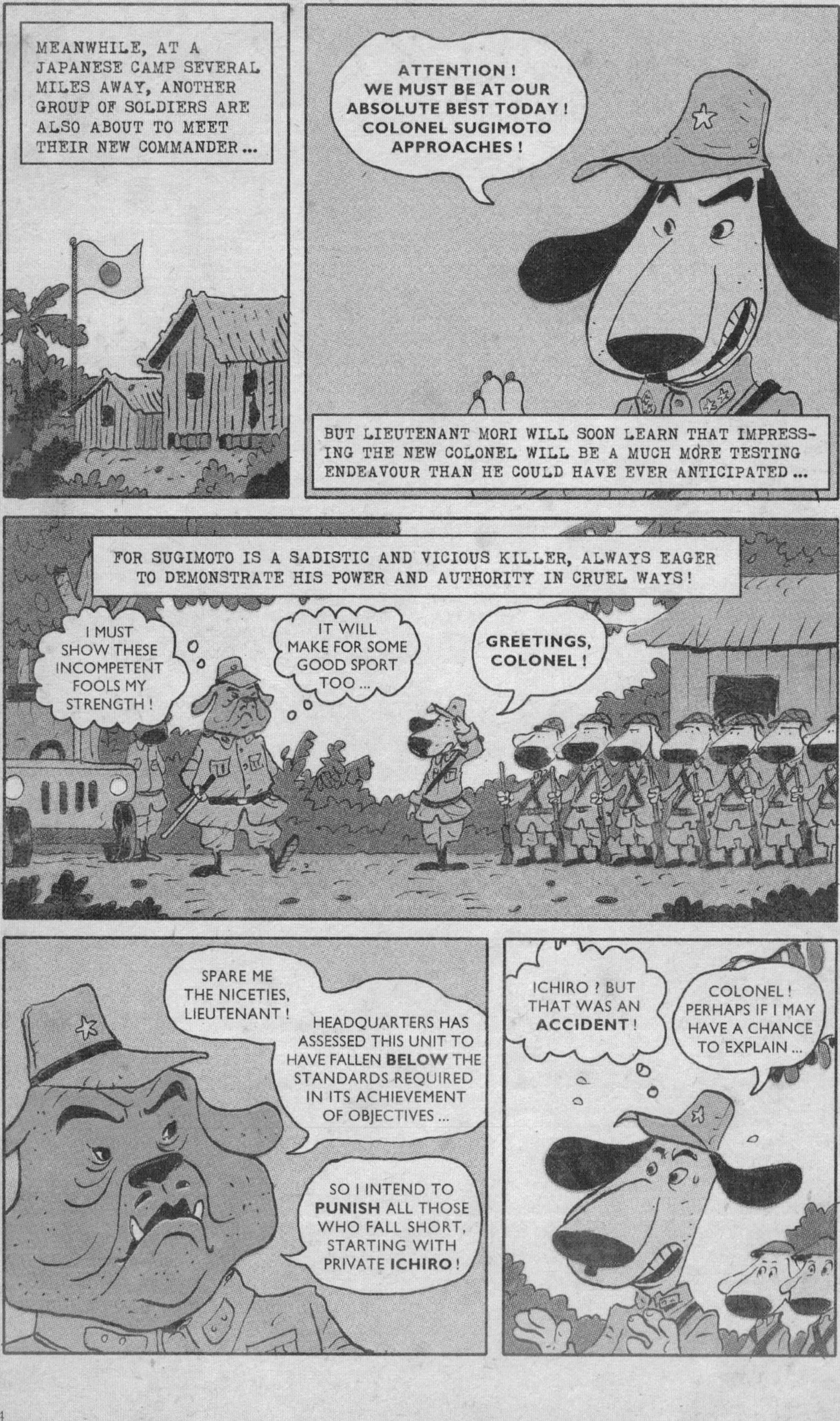

MEANWHILE, AT A JAPANESE CAMP SEVERAL MILES AWAY, ANOTHER GROUP OF SOLDIERS ARE ALSO ABOUT TO MEET THEIR NEW COMMANDER ...
ATTENTION ! WE MUST BE AT OUR ABSOLUTE BEST TODAY ! COLONEL SUGIMOTO APPROACHES !
BUT LIEUTENANT MORI WILL SOON LEARN THAT IMPRESSING THE NEW COLONEL WILL BE A MUCH MORE TESTING ENDEAVOUR THAN HE COULD HAVE EVER ANTICIPATED ...
FOR SUGIMOTO IS A SADISTIC AND VICIOUS KILLER, ALWAYS EAGER TO DEMONSTRATE HIS POWER AND AUTHORITY IN CRUEL WAYS !
I MUST SHOW THESE INCOMPETENT FOOLS MY STRENGTH !
IT WILL MAKE FOR SOME GOOD SPORT TOO ...
GREETINGS, COLONEL !
SPARE ME THE NICETIES, LIEUTENANT !
HEADQUARTERS HAS ASSESSED THIS UNIT TO HAVE FALLEN BELOW THE STANDARDS REQUIRED IN ITS ACHIEVEMENT OF OBJECTIVES ...
SO I INTEND TO PUNISH ALL THOSE WHO FALL SHORT, STARTING WITH PRIVATE ICHIRO !
ICHIRO ? BUT THAT WAS AN ACCIDENT !
COLONEL ! PERHAPS IF I MAY HAVE A CHANCE TO EXPLAIN ...

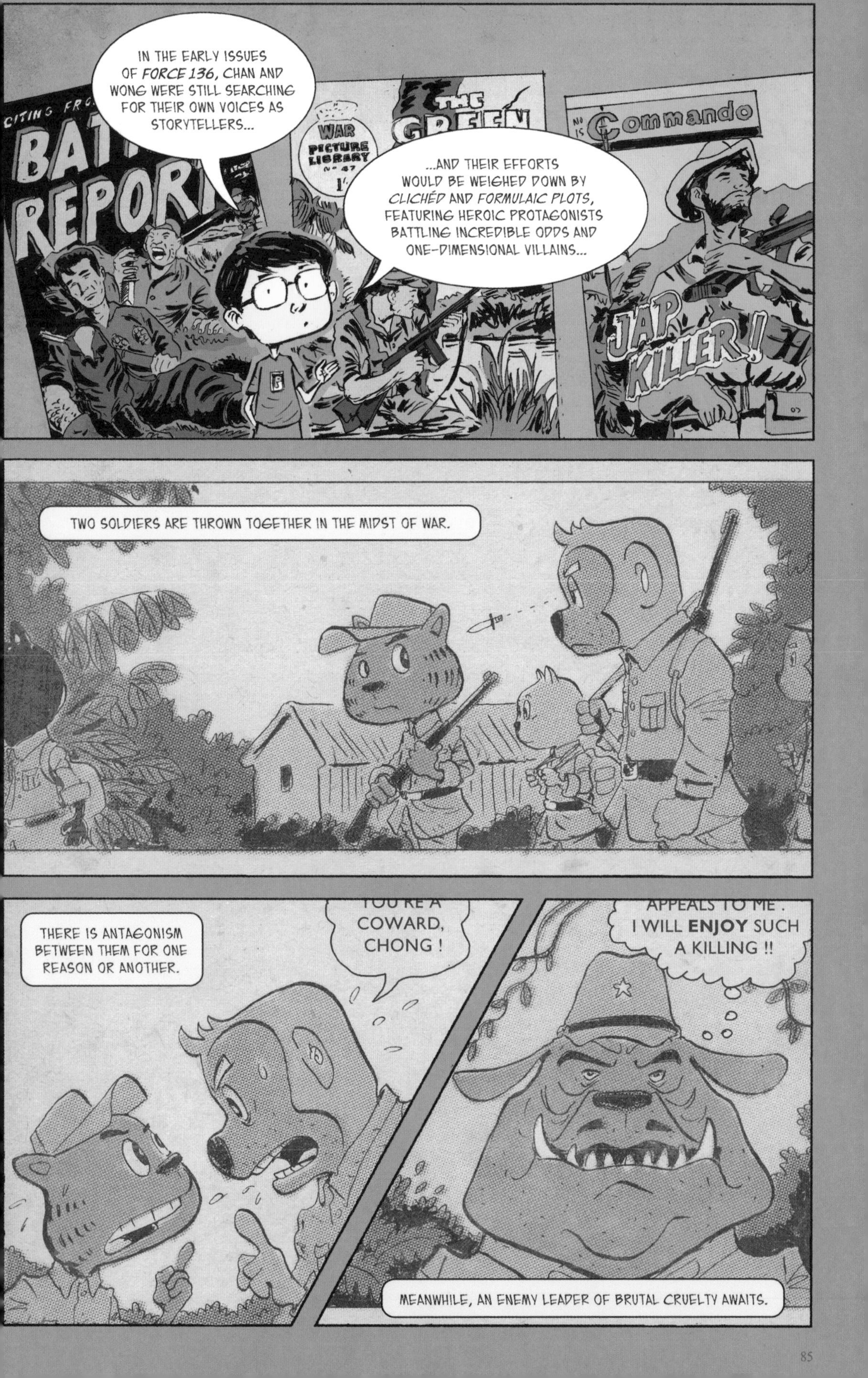
IN THE EARLY ISSUES OF *FORCE 136*, CHAN AND WONG WERE STILL SEARCHING FOR THEIR OWN VOICES AS STORYTELLERS...
WAR PICTURE LIBRARY
Commando
...AND THEIR EFFORTS WOULD BE WEIGHED DOWN BY *CLICHÉD* AND *FORMULAIC PLOTS*, FEATURING HEROIC PROTAGONISTS BATTLING INCREDIBLE ODDS AND ONE-DIMENSIONAL VILLAINS...
JAP KILLER!
TWO SOLDIERS ARE THROWN TOGETHER IN THE MIDST OF WAR.
THERE IS ANTAGONISM BETWEEN THEM FOR ONE REASON OR ANOTHER.
YOU'RE A COWARD, CHONG !
APPEALS TO ME . I WILL **ENJOY** SUCH A KILLING !!
MEANWHILE, AN ENEMY LEADER OF BRUTAL CRUELTY AWAITS.

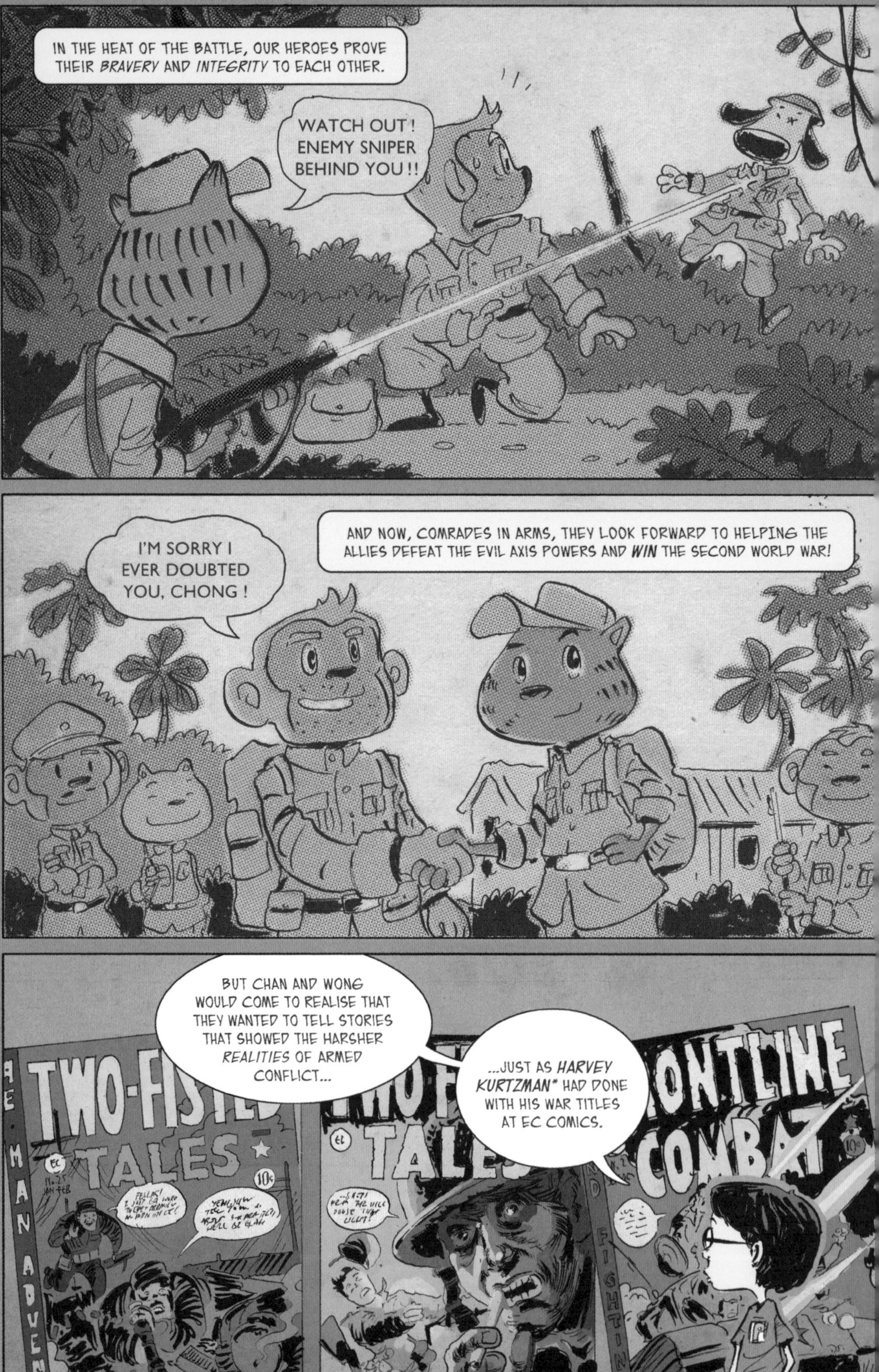
IN THE HEAT OF THE BATTLE, OUR HEROES PROVE THEIR *BRAVERY* AND *INTEGRITY* TO EACH OTHER.
WATCH OUT! ENEMY SNIPER BEHIND YOU!!
I'M SORRY I EVER DOUBTED YOU, CHONG!
AND NOW, COMRADES IN ARMS, THEY LOOK FORWARD TO HELPING THE ALLIES DEFEAT THE EVIL AXIS POWERS AND ***WIN*** THE SECOND WORLD WAR!
BUT CHAN AND WONG WOULD COME TO REALISE THAT THEY WANTED TO TELL STORIES THAT SHOWED THE HARSHER *REALITIES* OF ARMED CONFLICT...
...JUST AS *HARVEY KURTZMAN** HAD DONE WITH HIS WAR TITLES AT EC COMICS.
TWO-FISTED TALES
COMBAT

*ASIDE FROM *TWO-FISTED TALES* AND *FRONTLINE COMBAT*, KURTZMAN WAS ALSO THE DRIVING FORCE BEHIND THE INFLUENTIAL *MAD MAGAZINE* AT EC COMICS.

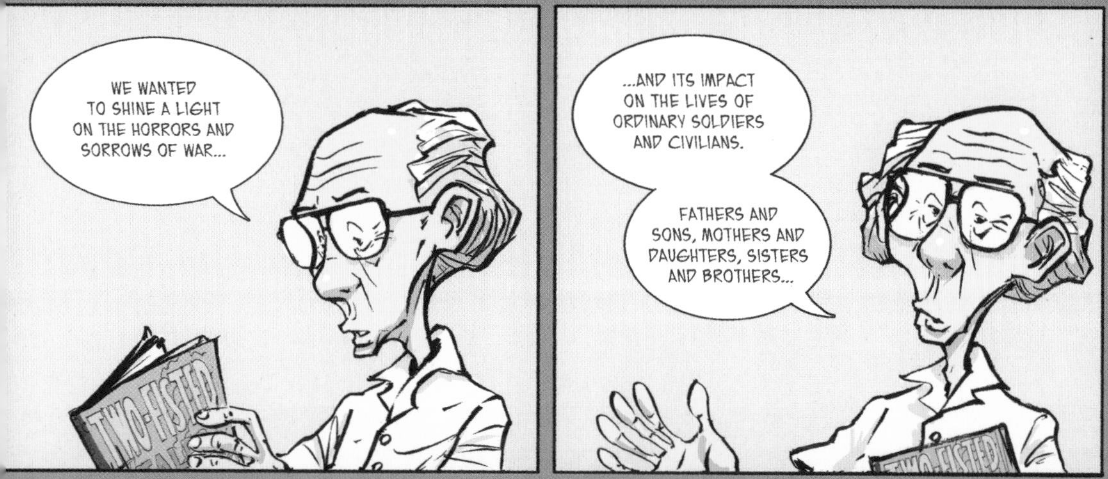
WE WANTED TO SHINE A LIGHT ON THE HORRORS AND SORROWS OF WAR...
TWO-FISTED
...AND ITS IMPACT ON THE LIVES OF ORDINARY SOLDIERS AND CIVILIANS.
FATHERS AND SONS, MOTHERS AND DAUGHTERS, SISTERS AND BROTHERS...
TWO-FISTED

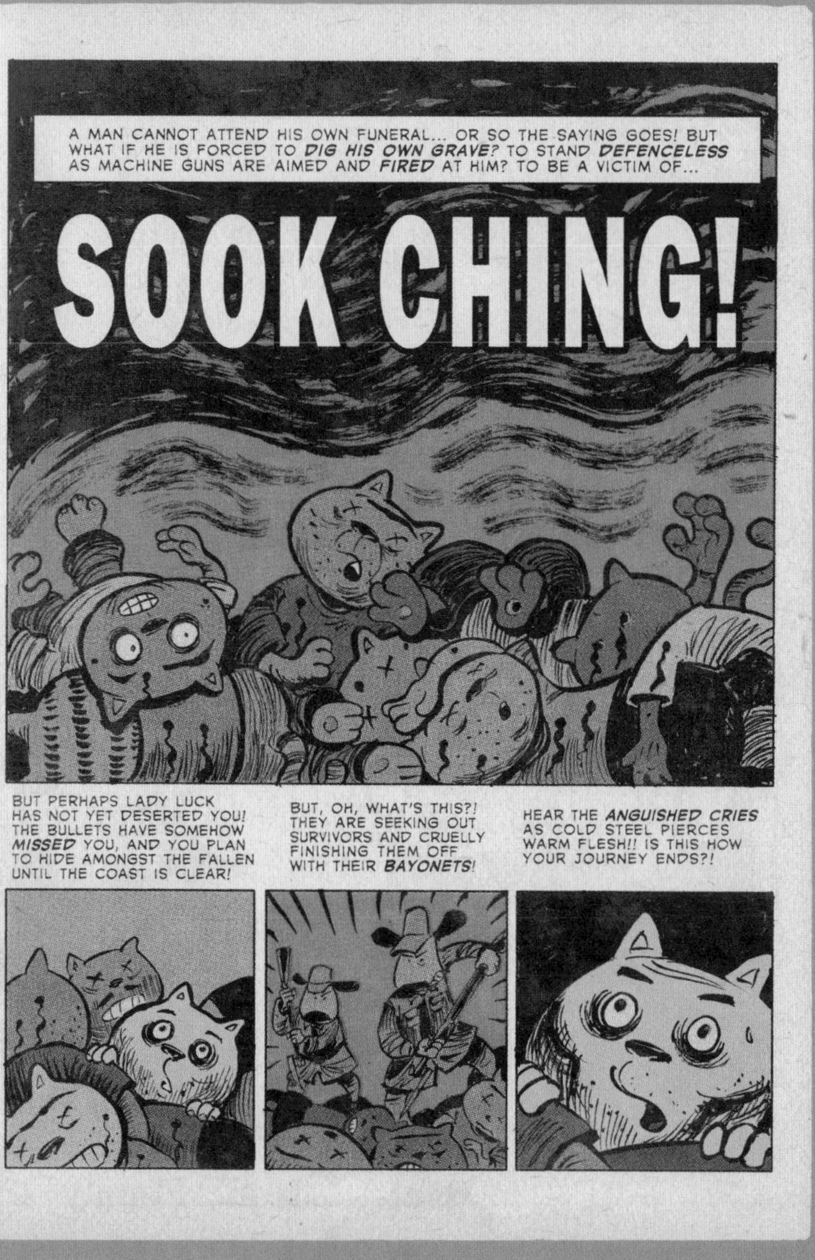
A MAN CANNOT ATTEND HIS OWN FUNERAL... OR SO THE SAYING GOES! BUT WHAT IF HE IS FORCED TO DIG HIS OWN GRAVE? TO STAND DEFENCELESS AS MACHINE GUNS ARE AIMED AND FIRED AT HIM? TO BE A VICTIM OF...
SOOK CHING!
BUT PERHAPS LADY LUCK HAS NOT YET DESERTED YOU! THE BULLETS HAVE SOMEHOW MISSED YOU, AND YOU PLAN TO HIDE AMONGST THE FALLEN UNTIL THE COAST IS CLEAR!
BUT, OH, WHAT'S THIS?! THEY ARE SEEKING OUT SURVIVORS AND CRUELLY FINISHING THEM OFF WITH THEIR BAYONETS!
HEAR THE ANGUISHED CRIES AS COLD STEEL PIERCES WARM FLESH!! IS THIS HOW YOUR JOURNEY ENDS?!

Left

FORCE 136 No. 4: SOOK CHING

1957

Art by Chan Hock Chye

Words by Bertrand Wong

Stones Throw Press

The story recalls the massacre of Chinese civilians under Operation Sook Ching ("purge through cleansing") after the Japanese conquest of Singapore in 1942.

To punish the Chinese community for its support of anti-Japanese war efforts in Manchuria and Malaya, as many as 50,000 Chinese males between the ages of 18 and 50 were singled out for execution using a largely arbitrary screening process.

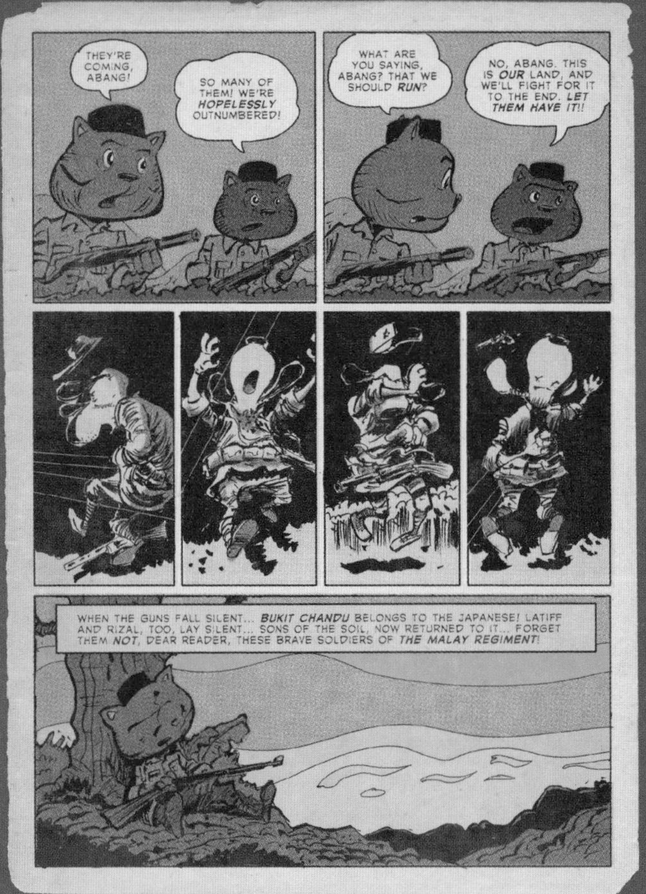
THEY'RE COMING, ABANG!
SO MANY OF THEM! WE'RE *HOPELESSLY* OUTNUMBERED!
WHAT ARE YOU SAYING, ABANG? THAT WE SHOULD *RUN*?
NO, ABANG. THIS IS *OUR* LAND, AND WE'LL FIGHT FOR IT TO THE END. *LET THEM HAVE IT!!*
WHEN THE GUNS FALL SILENT... *BUKIT CHANDU* BELONGS TO THE JAPANESE! LATIFF AND RIZAL, TOO, LAY SILENT... SONS OF THE SOIL, NOW RETURNED TO IT... FORGET THEM *NOT*, DEAR READER, THESE BRAVE SOLDIERS OF *THE MALAY REGIMENT*!

Left

FORCE 136 No. 5: OPIUM HILL
1957
Art by Chan Hock Chye
Words by Bertrand Wong
Stones Throw Press

A depiction of the Battle of Bukit Chandu ("Opium Hill" in Malay) on February 13–14, 1942, just before the fall of Singapore. Heavily outnumbered, Lieutenant Adnan Saidi and the men of the C Company of the 1st Malay Brigade valiantly held their ground for nearly two days before being overrun.

Right

FORCE 136 No. 6: SOLDIER'S TALE
1957
Art by Chan Hock Chye
Words by Bertrand Wong
Stones Throw Press

Told through the eyes of a Japanese infantryman, the story charts the changing fortunes of the Imperial Army as the tide of the war turns, forcing its soldiers to embark on an arduous retreat through the mountains and jungles of Burma, whilst battling starvation, malaria and dysentry.

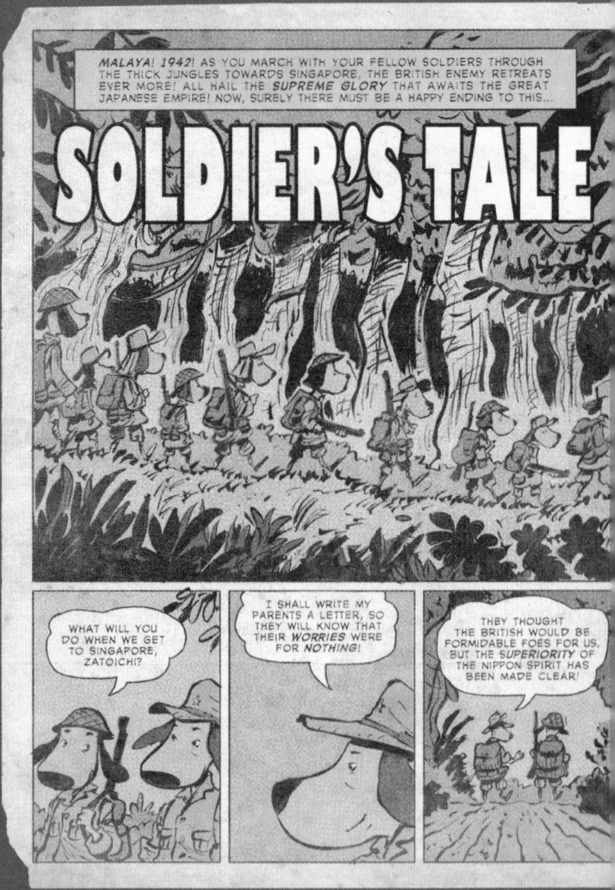
MALAYA! 1942! AS YOU MARCH WITH YOUR FELLOW SOLDIERS THROUGH THE THICK JUNGLES TOWARDS SINGAPORE, THE BRITISH ENEMY RETREATS EVER MORE! ALL HAIL THE *SUPREME GLORY* THAT AWAITS THE GREAT JAPANESE EMPIRE! NOW, SURELY THERE MUST BE A HAPPY ENDING TO THIS...
SOLDIER'S TALE
WHAT WILL YOU DO WHEN WE GET TO SINGAPORE, ZATOICHI?
I SHALL WRITE MY PARENTS A LETTER, SO THEY WILL KNOW THAT THEIR *WORRIES* WERE FOR *NOTHING*!
THEY THOUGHT THE BRITISH WOULD BE FORMIDABLE FOES FOR US, BUT THE *SUPERIORITY* OF THE NIPPON SPIRIT HAS BEEN MADE CLEAR!

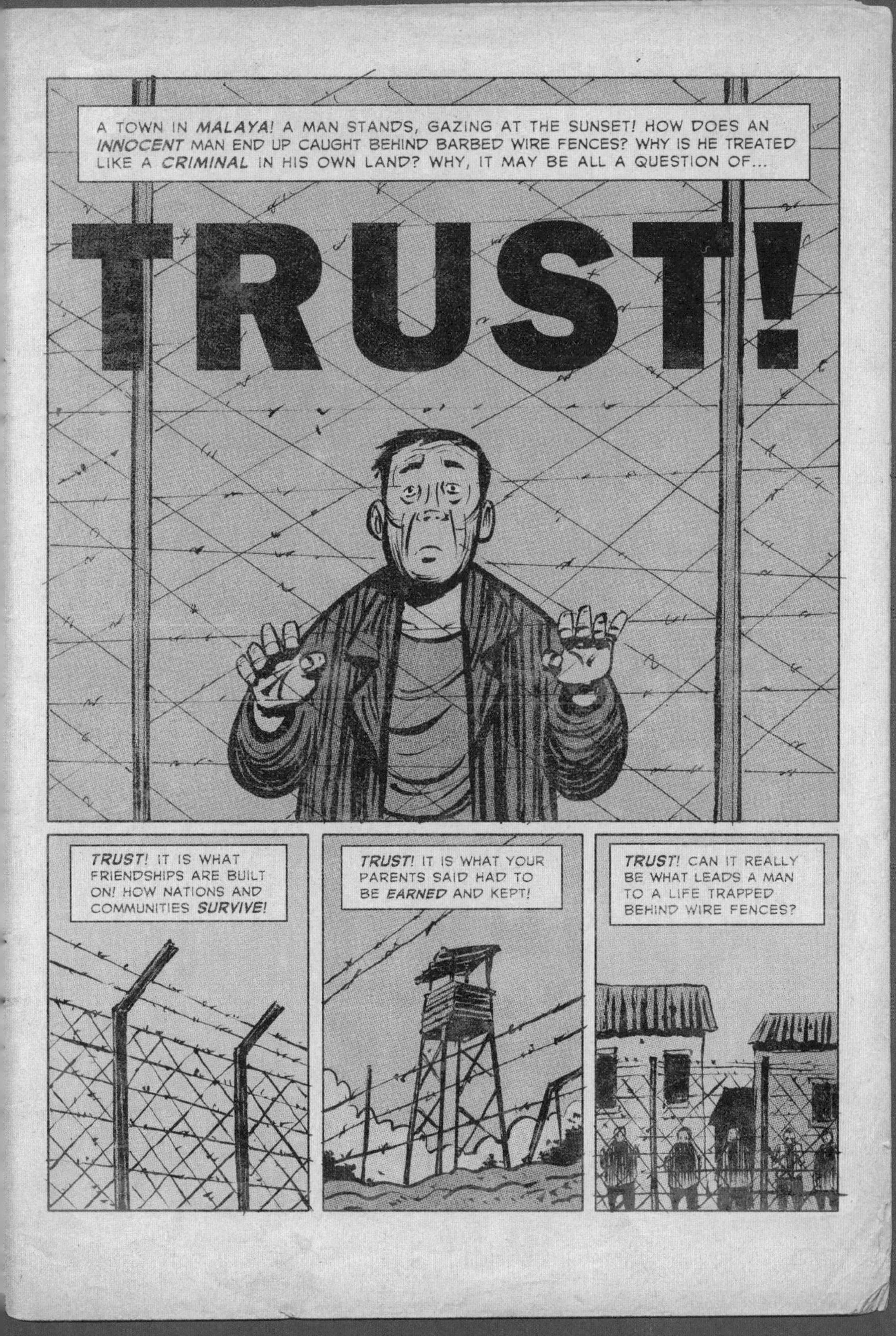
A TOWN IN MALAYA! A MAN STANDS, GAZING AT THE SUNSET! HOW DOES AN INNOCENT MAN END UP CAUGHT BEHIND BARBED WIRE FENCES? WHY IS HE TREATED LIKE A CRIMINAL IN HIS OWN LAND? WHY, IT MAY BE ALL A QUESTION OF...
TRUST!
TRUST! IT IS WHAT FRIENDSHIPS ARE BUILT ON! HOW NATIONS AND COMMUNITIES SURVIVE!
TRUST! IT IS WHAT YOUR PARENTS SAID HAD TO BE EARNED AND KEPT!
TRUST! CAN IT REALLY BE WHAT LEADS A MAN TO A LIFE TRAPPED BEHIND WIRE FENCES?

Above & following **FORCE 136 No. 7: TRUST!** (1957) | Art by Chan Hock Chye, Words by Bertrand Wong | Stones Throw Press

By the seventh and final issue of *Force 136*, Chan and Wong had abandoned the use of animal characters. The focus had also shifted from the Second World War to the **Malayan Emergency**, the battle fought between the Malayan Communist Party (MCP) and the British army from 1948 to 1960.

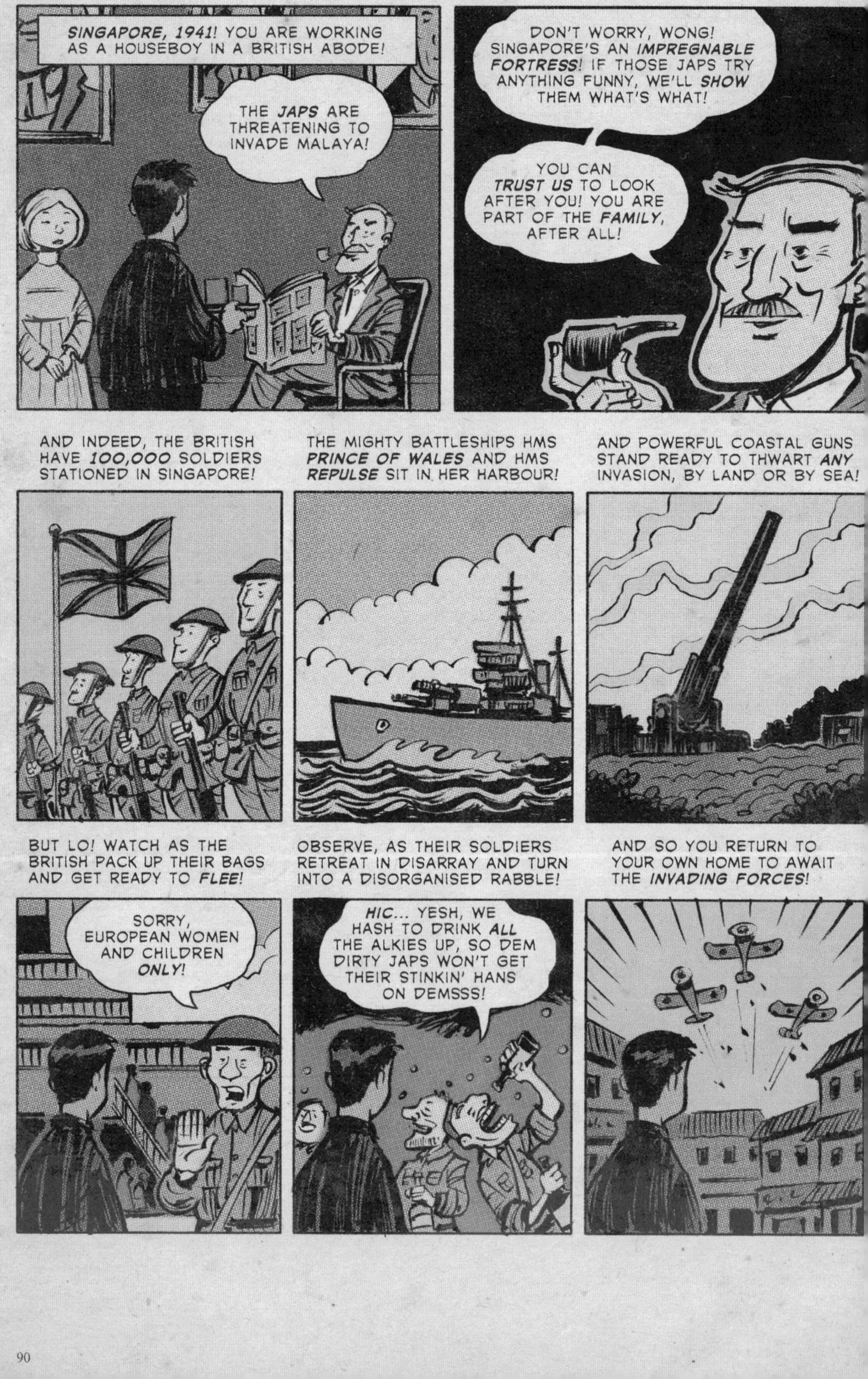
SINGAPORE, 1941! YOU ARE WORKING AS A HOUSEBOY IN A BRITISH ABODE!
THE JAPS ARE THREATENING TO INVADE MALAYA!
DON'T WORRY, WONG! SINGAPORE'S AN IMPREGNABLE FORTRESS! IF THOSE JAPS TRY ANYTHING FUNNY, WE'LL SHOW THEM WHAT'S WHAT!
YOU CAN TRUST US TO LOOK AFTER YOU! YOU ARE PART OF THE FAMILY, AFTER ALL!
AND INDEED, THE BRITISH HAVE 100,000 SOLDIERS STATIONED IN SINGAPORE!
THE MIGHTY BATTLESHIPS HMS PRINCE OF WALES AND HMS REPULSE SIT IN HER HARBOUR!
AND POWERFUL COASTAL GUNS STAND READY TO THWART ANY INVASION, BY LAND OR BY SEA!
BUT LO! WATCH AS THE BRITISH PACK UP THEIR BAGS AND GET READY TO FLEE!
SORRY, EUROPEAN WOMEN AND CHILDREN ONLY!
OBSERVE, AS THEIR SOLDIERS RETREAT IN DISARRAY AND TURN INTO A DISORGANISED RABBLE!
HIC... YESH, WE HASH TO DRINK ALL THE ALKIES UP, SO DEM DIRTY JAPS WON'T GET THEIR STINKIN' HANS ON DEMSSS!
AND SO YOU RETURN TO YOUR OWN HOME TO AWAIT THE INVADING FORCES!

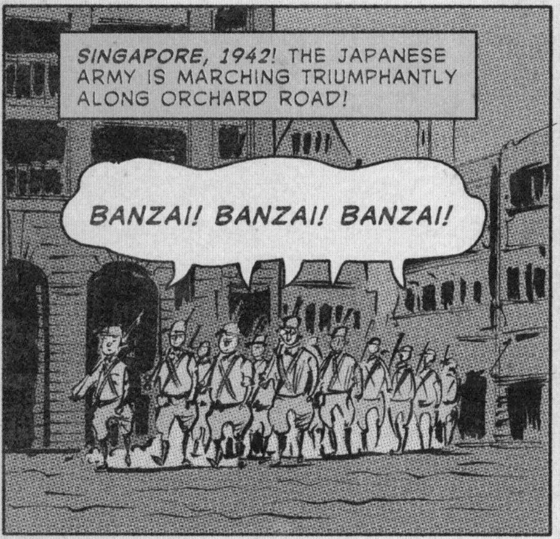
SINGAPORE, 1942! THE JAPANESE ARMY IS MARCHING TRIUMPHANTLY ALONG ORCHARD ROAD!
BANZAI! BANZAI! BANZAI!

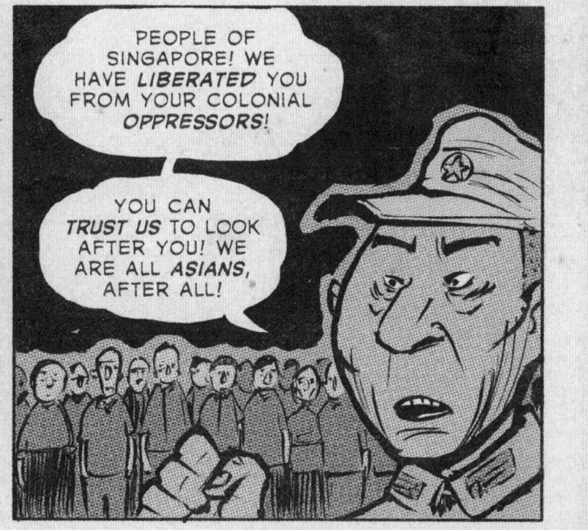
PEOPLE OF SINGAPORE! WE HAVE LIBERATED YOU FROM YOUR COLONIAL OPPRESSORS!
YOU CAN TRUST US TO LOOK AFTER YOU! WE ARE ALL ASIANS, AFTER ALL!

AND INDEED, YOU HAD BEEN BUT A MERE ***SECOND-CLASS CITIZEN*** UNDER BRITISH RULE!

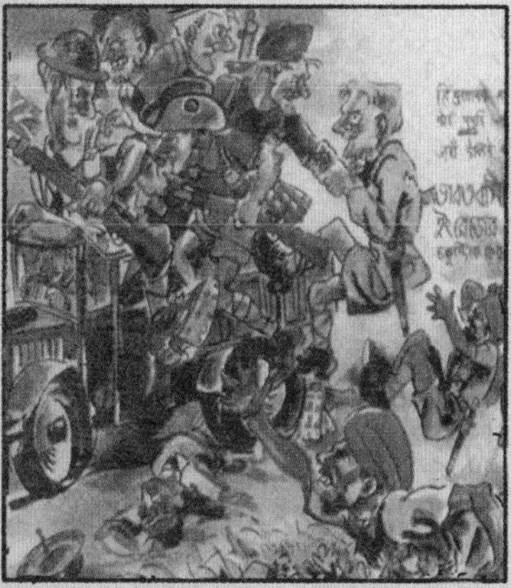

NOW THE JAPANESE PROMISE A ***GREATER EAST ASIA CO-PROSPERITY SPHERE***, FREE FROM COLONIAL SUBJUGATION!

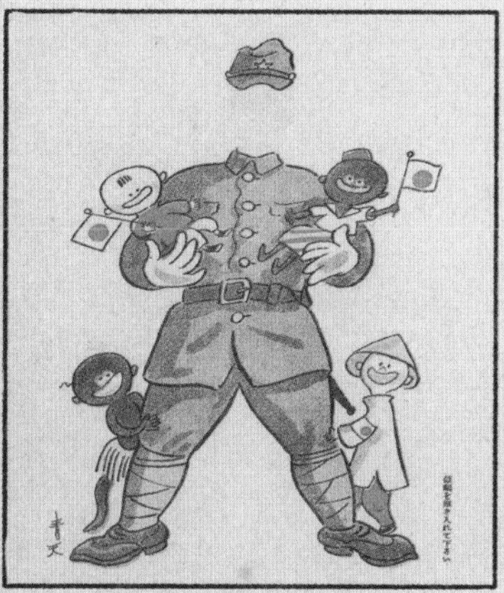

AND OFFER THE PROSPECT OF AN ***INDIAN NATIONAL ARMY*** TO HELP INDIA FIGHT FOR ITS ***INDEPENDENCE***!

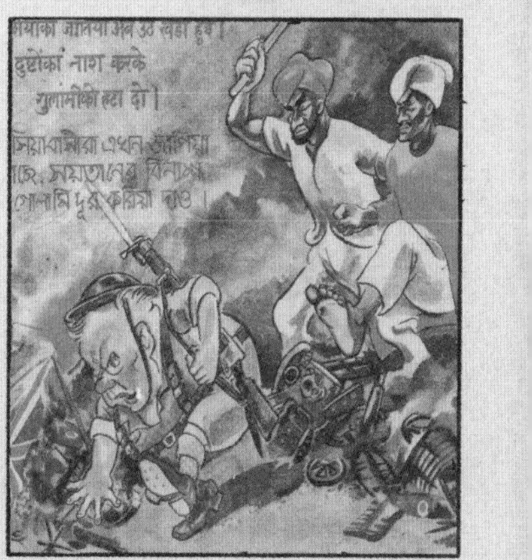

BUT LO! WATCH AS THEY ROUND UP MANY INNOCENTS, WHO WILL ***NEVER*** RETURN!

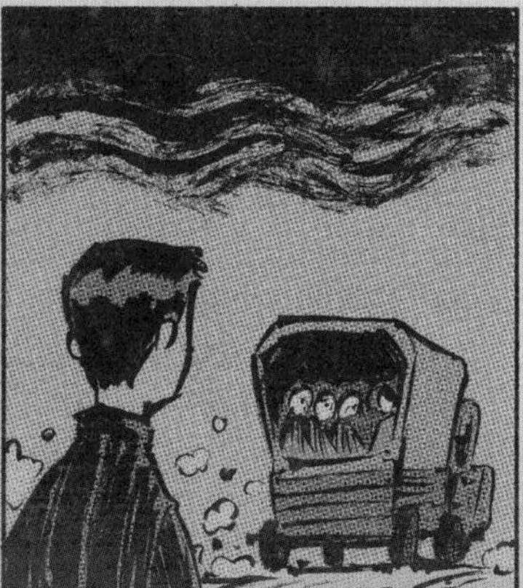

SHIVER, AS YOU LISTEN TO WHISPERED TALES ABOUT THEIR WANTON ACTS OF ***UNSPEAKABLE*** CRUELTY!

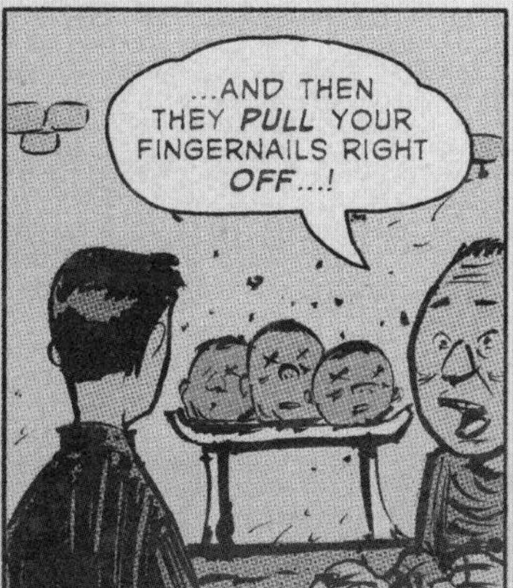
...AND THEN THEY PULL YOUR FINGERNAILS RIGHT OFF...!

AND SO YOU ***FLEE*** INTO THE JUNGLES OF MALAYA TO ESCAPE THE HORRORS!

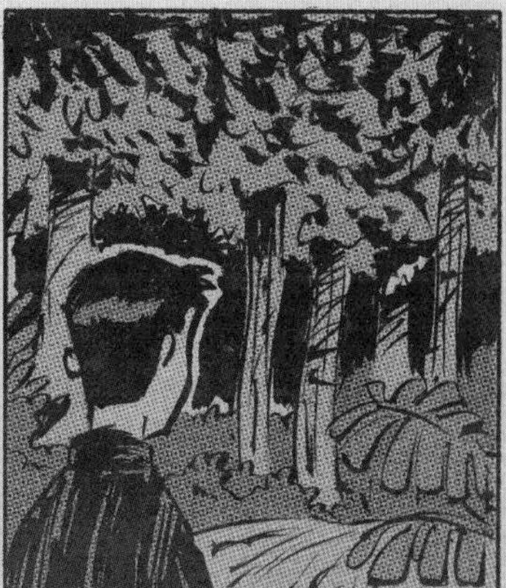

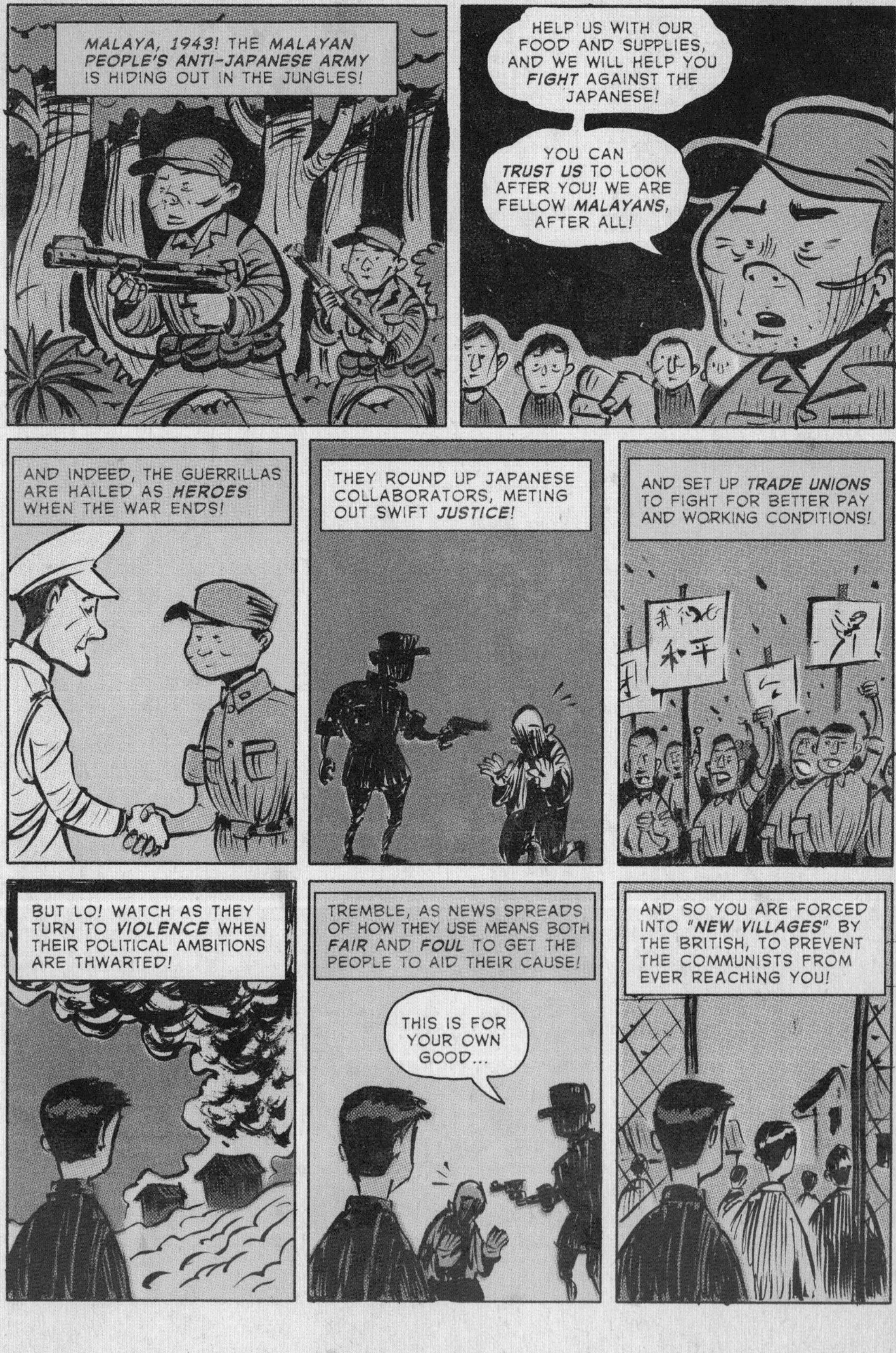
MALAYA, 1943! THE MALAYAN PEOPLE'S ANTI-JAPANESE ARMY IS HIDING OUT IN THE JUNGLES!
HELP US WITH OUR FOOD AND SUPPLIES, AND WE WILL HELP YOU FIGHT AGAINST THE JAPANESE!
YOU CAN TRUST US TO LOOK AFTER YOU! WE ARE FELLOW MALAYANS, AFTER ALL!
AND INDEED, THE GUERRILLAS ARE HAILED AS HEROES WHEN THE WAR ENDS!
THEY ROUND UP JAPANESE COLLABORATORS, METING OUT SWIFT JUSTICE!
AND SET UP TRADE UNIONS TO FIGHT FOR BETTER PAY AND WORKING CONDITIONS!
和平
BUT LO! WATCH AS THEY TURN TO VIOLENCE WHEN THEIR POLITICAL AMBITIONS ARE THWARTED!
TREMBLE, AS NEWS SPREADS OF HOW THEY USE MEANS BOTH FAIR AND FOUL TO GET THE PEOPLE TO AID THEIR CAUSE!
THIS IS FOR YOUR OWN GOOD...
AND SO YOU ARE FORCED INTO "NEW VILLAGES" BY THE BRITISH, TO PREVENT THE COMMUNISTS FROM EVER REACHING YOU!

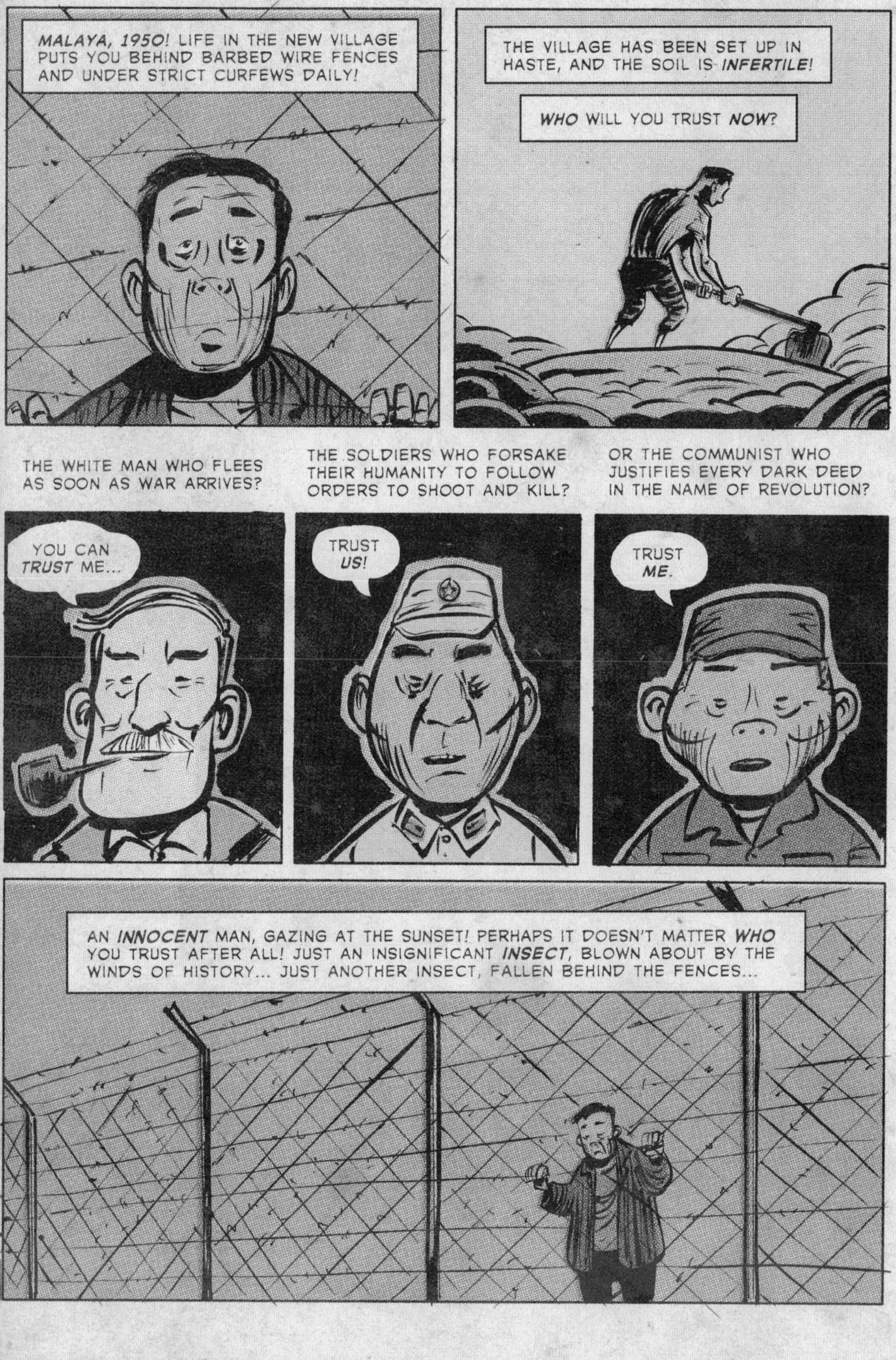
MALAYA, 1950! LIFE IN THE NEW VILLAGE PUTS YOU BEHIND BARBED WIRE FENCES AND UNDER STRICT CURFEWS DAILY!
THE VILLAGE HAS BEEN SET UP IN HASTE, AND THE SOIL IS INFERTILE!
WHO WILL YOU TRUST NOW?
THE WHITE MAN WHO FLEES AS SOON AS WAR ARRIVES?
YOU CAN TRUST ME...
THE SOLDIERS WHO FORSAKE THEIR HUMANITY TO FOLLOW ORDERS TO SHOOT AND KILL?
TRUST US!
OR THE COMMUNIST WHO JUSTIFIES EVERY DARK DEED IN THE NAME OF REVOLUTION?
TRUST ME.
AN INNOCENT MAN, GAZING AT THE SUNSET! PERHAPS IT DOESN'T MATTER WHO YOU TRUST AFTER ALL! JUST AN INSIGNIFICANT INSECT, BLOWN ABOUT BY THE WINDS OF HISTORY... JUST ANOTHER INSECT, FALLEN BEHIND THE FENCES...

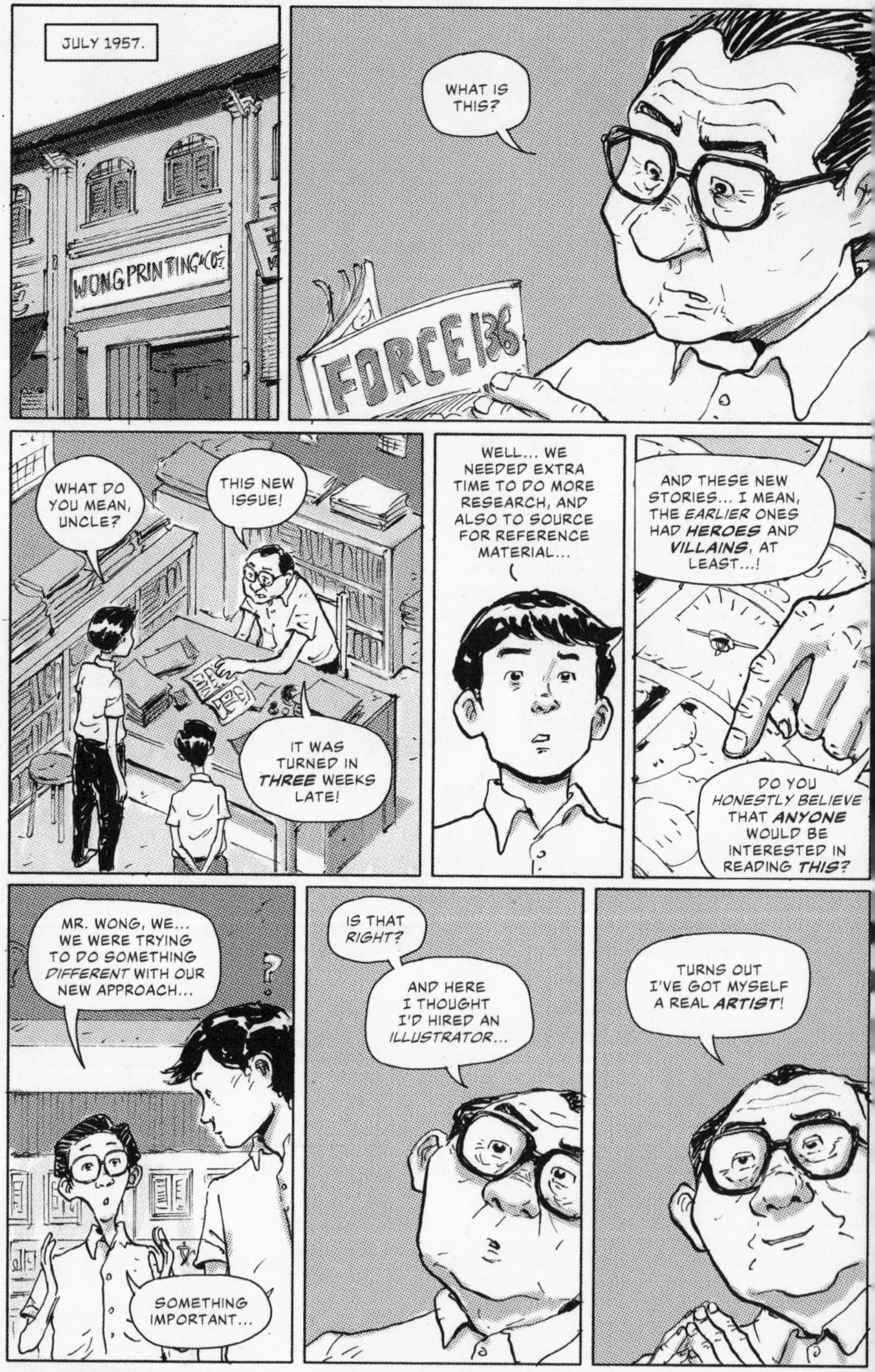
JULY 1957.
WONG PRINTING & CO.
WHAT IS THIS?
FORCE 136
WHAT DO YOU MEAN, UNCLE?
THIS NEW ISSUE!
IT WAS TURNED IN *THREE* WEEKS LATE!
WELL... WE NEEDED EXTRA TIME TO DO MORE RESEARCH, AND ALSO TO SOURCE FOR REFERENCE MATERIAL...
AND THESE NEW STORIES... I MEAN, THE *EARLIER* ONES HAD ***HEROES*** AND ***VILLAINS***, AT LEAST...!
DO YOU *HONESTLY BELIEVE* THAT ***ANYONE*** WOULD BE INTERESTED IN READING ***THIS?***
MR. WONG, WE... WE WERE TRYING TO DO SOMETHING *DIFFERENT* WITH OUR NEW APPROACH...
?
SOMETHING IMPORTANT...
IS THAT *RIGHT?*
AND HERE I THOUGHT I'D HIRED AN *ILLUSTRATOR*...
TURNS OUT I'VE GOT MYSELF A REAL ***ARTIST***!

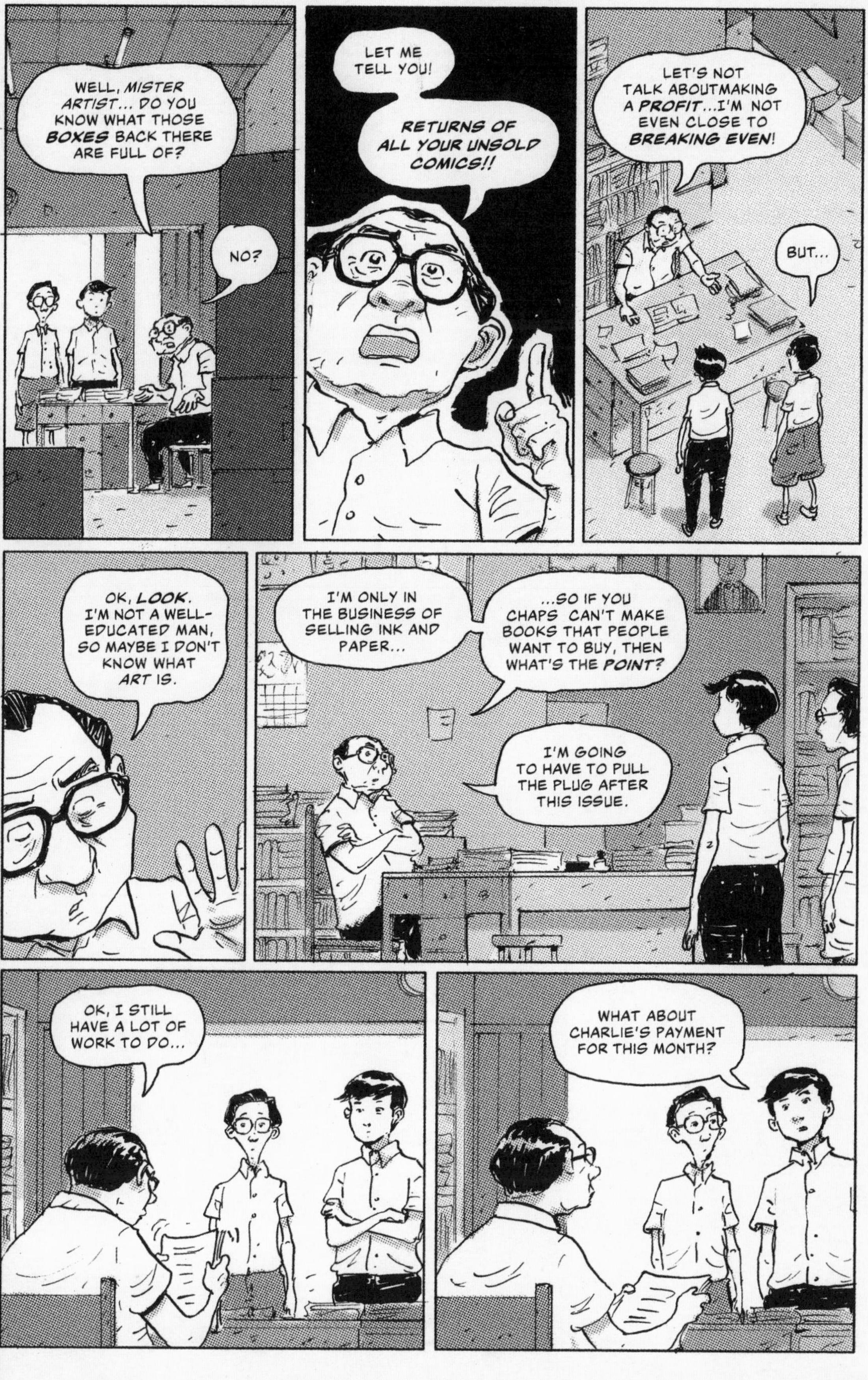
WELL, MISTER ARTIST... DO YOU KNOW WHAT THOSE BOXES BACK THERE ARE FULL OF?
NO?
LET ME TELL YOU!
RETURNS OF ALL YOUR UNSOLD COMICS!!
LET'S NOT TALK ABOUTMAKING A PROFIT...I'M NOT EVEN CLOSE TO BREAKING EVEN!
BUT...
OK, LOOK. I'M NOT A WELL-EDUCATED MAN, SO MAYBE I DON'T KNOW WHAT ART IS.
I'M ONLY IN THE BUSINESS OF SELLING INK AND PAPER...
...SO IF YOU CHAPS CAN'T MAKE BOOKS THAT PEOPLE WANT TO BUY, THEN WHAT'S THE POINT?
I'M GOING TO HAVE TO PULL THE PLUG AFTER THIS ISSUE.
OK, I STILL HAVE A LOT OF WORK TO DO...
WHAT ABOUT CHARLIE'S PAYMENT FOR THIS MONTH?

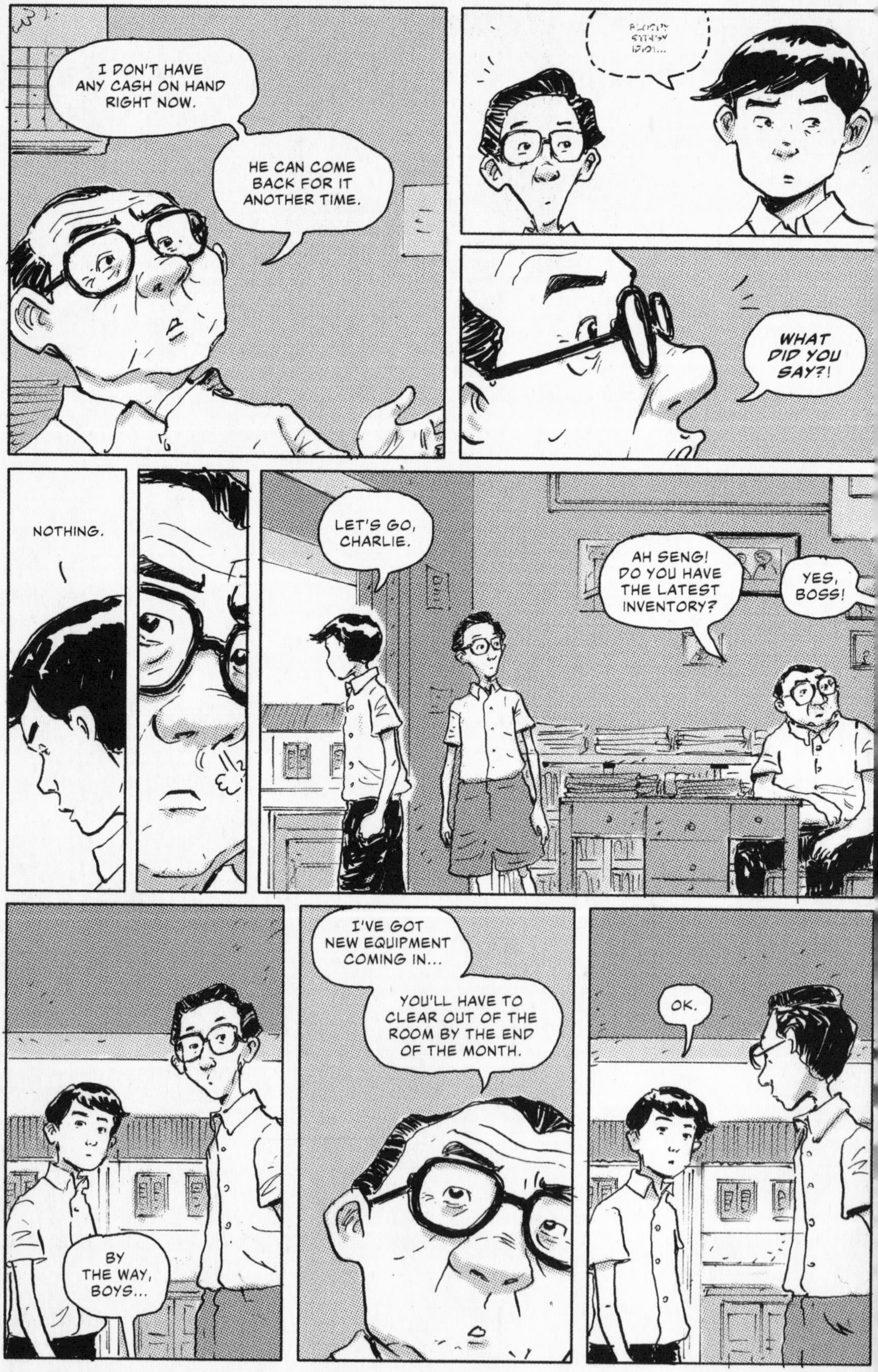

I DON'T HAVE ANY CASH ON HAND RIGHT NOW.
HE CAN COME BACK FOR IT ANOTHER TIME.
WHAT DID YOU SAY?!
NOTHING.
LET'S GO, CHARLIE.
AH SENG! DO YOU HAVE THE LATEST INVENTORY?
YES, BOSS!
BY THE WAY, BOYS...
I'VE GOT NEW EQUIPMENT COMING IN...
YOU'LL HAVE TO CLEAR OUT OF THE ROOM BY THE END OF THE MONTH.
OK.

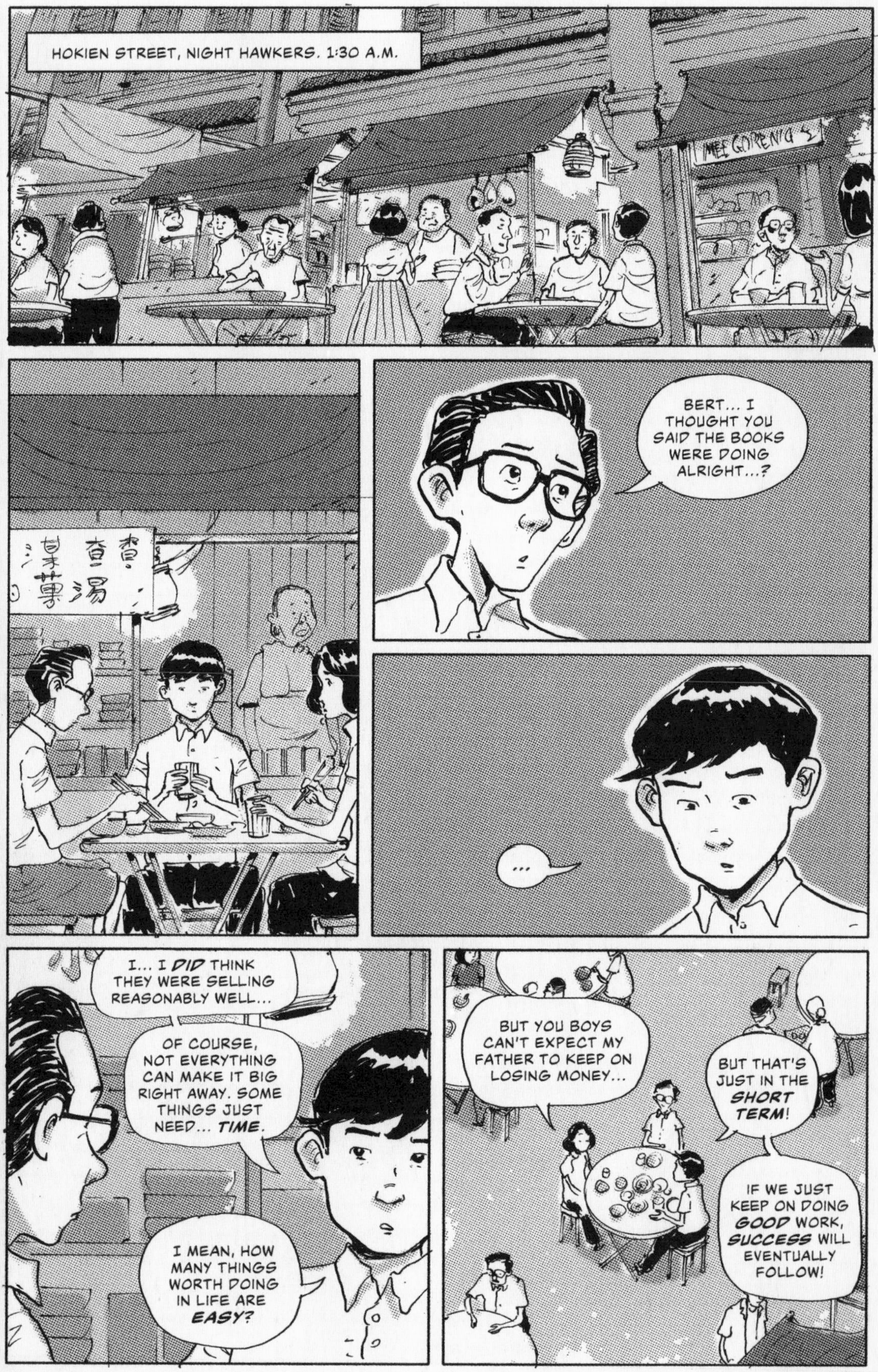
HOKIEN STREET, NIGHT HAWKERS. 1:30 A.M.
MEE GORENG
BERT... I THOUGHT YOU SAID THE BOOKS WERE DOING ALRIGHT...?
...
I... I *DID* THINK THEY WERE SELLING REASONABLY WELL...
OF COURSE, NOT EVERYTHING CAN MAKE IT BIG RIGHT AWAY. SOME THINGS JUST NEED... *TIME*.
I MEAN, HOW MANY THINGS WORTH DOING IN LIFE ARE *EASY*?
BUT YOU BOYS CAN'T EXPECT MY FATHER TO KEEP ON LOSING MONEY...
BUT THAT'S JUST IN THE *SHORT TERM*!
IF WE JUST KEEP ON DOING *GOOD* WORK, *SUCCESS* WILL EVENTUALLY FOLLOW!

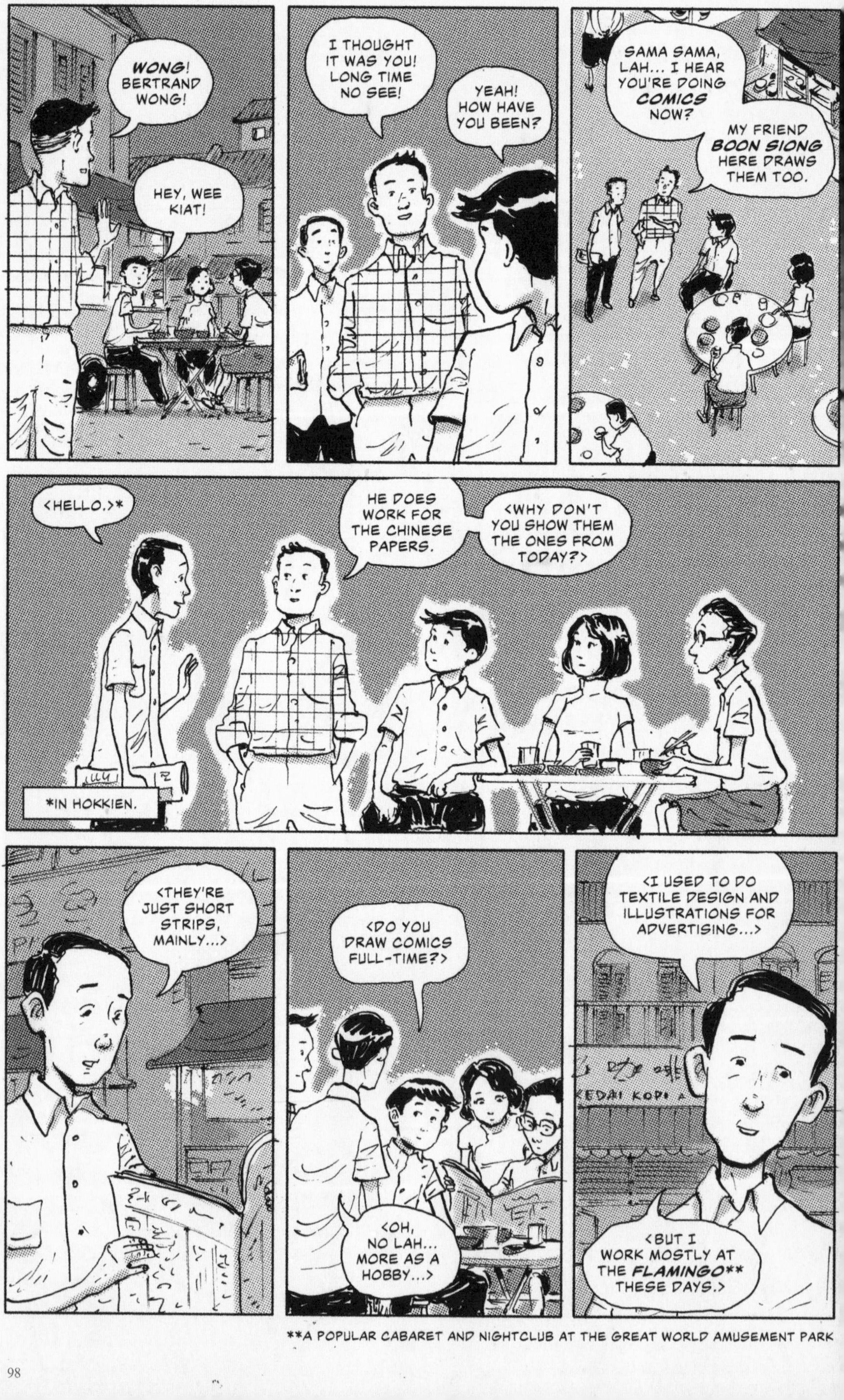
WONG! BERTRAND WONG!
HEY, WEE KIAT!
I THOUGHT IT WAS YOU! LONG TIME NO SEE!
YEAH! HOW HAVE YOU BEEN?
SAMA SAMA, LAH... I HEAR YOU'RE DOING COMICS NOW?
MY FRIEND BOON SIONG HERE DRAWS THEM TOO.
<HELLO.>*
HE DOES WORK FOR THE CHINESE PAPERS.
<WHY DON'T YOU SHOW THEM THE ONES FROM TODAY?>
*IN HOKKIEN.
<THEY'RE JUST SHORT STRIPS, MAINLY...>
<DO YOU DRAW COMICS FULL-TIME?>
<OH, NO LAH... MORE AS A HOBBY...>
<I USED TO DO TEXTILE DESIGN AND ILLUSTRATIONS FOR ADVERTISING...>
<BUT I WORK MOSTLY AT THE FLAMINGO** THESE DAYS.>

**A POPULAR CABARET AND NIGHTCLUB AT THE GREAT WORLD AMUSEMENT PARK

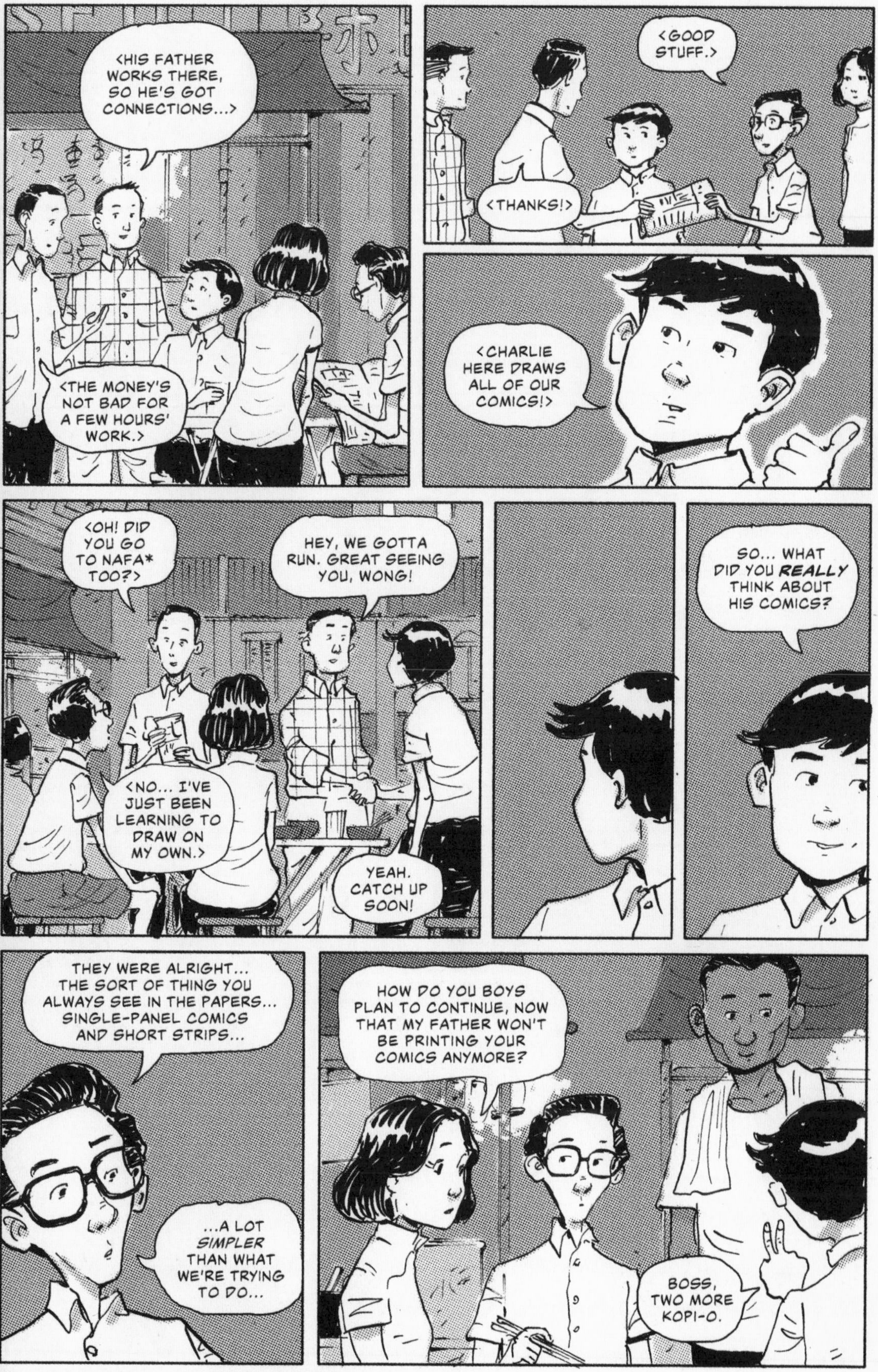
<HIS FATHER WORKS THERE, SO HE'S GOT CONNECTIONS...>
<THE MONEY'S NOT BAD FOR A FEW HOURS' WORK.>
<GOOD STUFF.>
<THANKS!>
<CHARLIE HERE DRAWS ALL OF OUR COMICS!>
<OH! DID YOU GO TO NAFA* TOO?>
HEY, WE GOTTA RUN. GREAT SEEING YOU, WONG!
<NO... I'VE JUST BEEN LEARNING TO DRAW ON MY OWN.>
YEAH. CATCH UP SOON!
SO... WHAT DID YOU REALLY THINK ABOUT HIS COMICS?
THEY WERE ALRIGHT... THE SORT OF THING YOU ALWAYS SEE IN THE PAPERS... SINGLE-PANEL COMICS AND SHORT STRIPS...
...A LOT SIMPLER THAN WHAT WE'RE TRYING TO DO...
HOW DO YOU BOYS PLAN TO CONTINUE, NOW THAT MY FATHER WON'T BE PRINTING YOUR COMICS ANYMORE?
BOSS, TWO MORE KOPI-O.

*NANYANG ACADEMY OF FINE ARTS, SINGAPORE

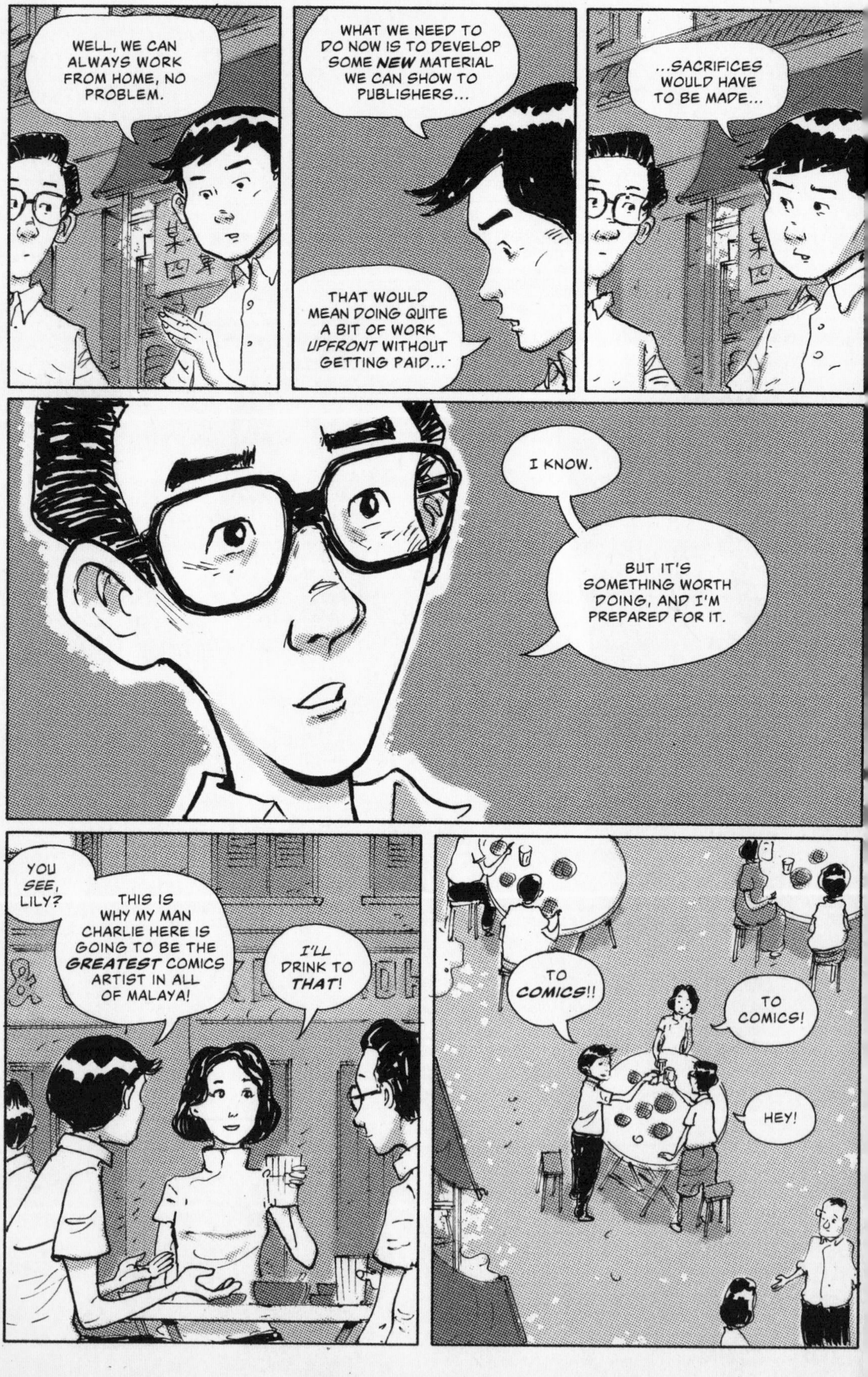
WELL, WE CAN ALWAYS WORK FROM HOME, NO PROBLEM.
WHAT WE NEED TO DO NOW IS TO DEVELOP SOME NEW MATERIAL WE CAN SHOW TO PUBLISHERS...
THAT WOULD MEAN DOING QUITE A BIT OF WORK UPFRONT WITHOUT GETTING PAID...
...SACRIFICES WOULD HAVE TO BE MADE...
I KNOW.
BUT IT'S SOMETHING WORTH DOING, AND I'M PREPARED FOR IT.
YOU SEE, LILY?
THIS IS WHY MY MAN CHARLIE HERE IS GOING TO BE THE GREATEST COMICS ARTIST IN ALL OF MALAYA!
I'LL DRINK TO THAT!
TO COMICS!!
TO COMICS!
HEY!

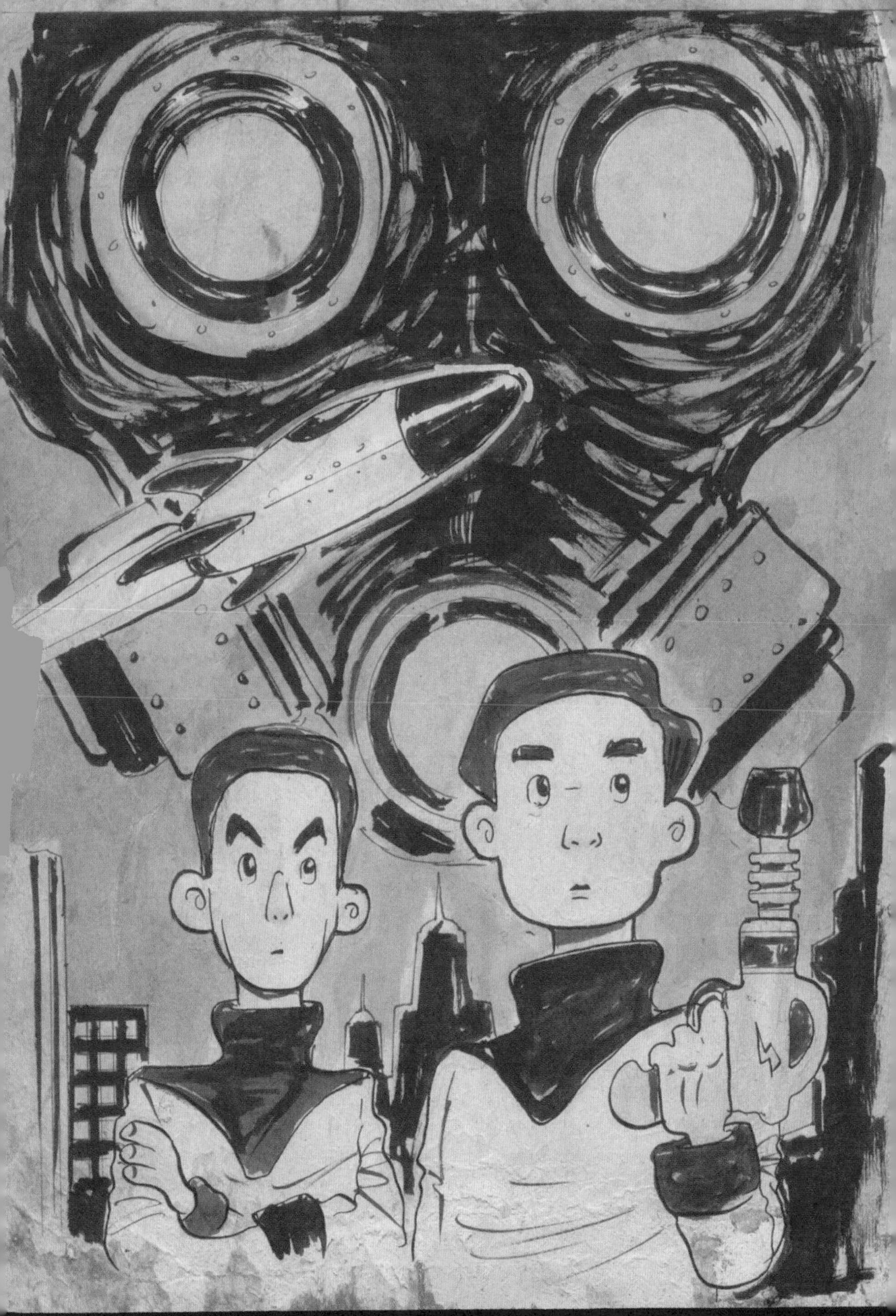

Above **INVASION Cover Sketch** (1957) | Chan Hock Chye | Unpublished

Chan and Wong's next project was to be a science fiction epic, with cartoon versions of Lim Chin Siong and Lee Kuan Yew as leaders of a resistance group fighting against an alien invasion. In its early stages of development, the comic featured a Tezuka-influenced art style and a battle for independence that was to be fought with laser guns and rocketships.

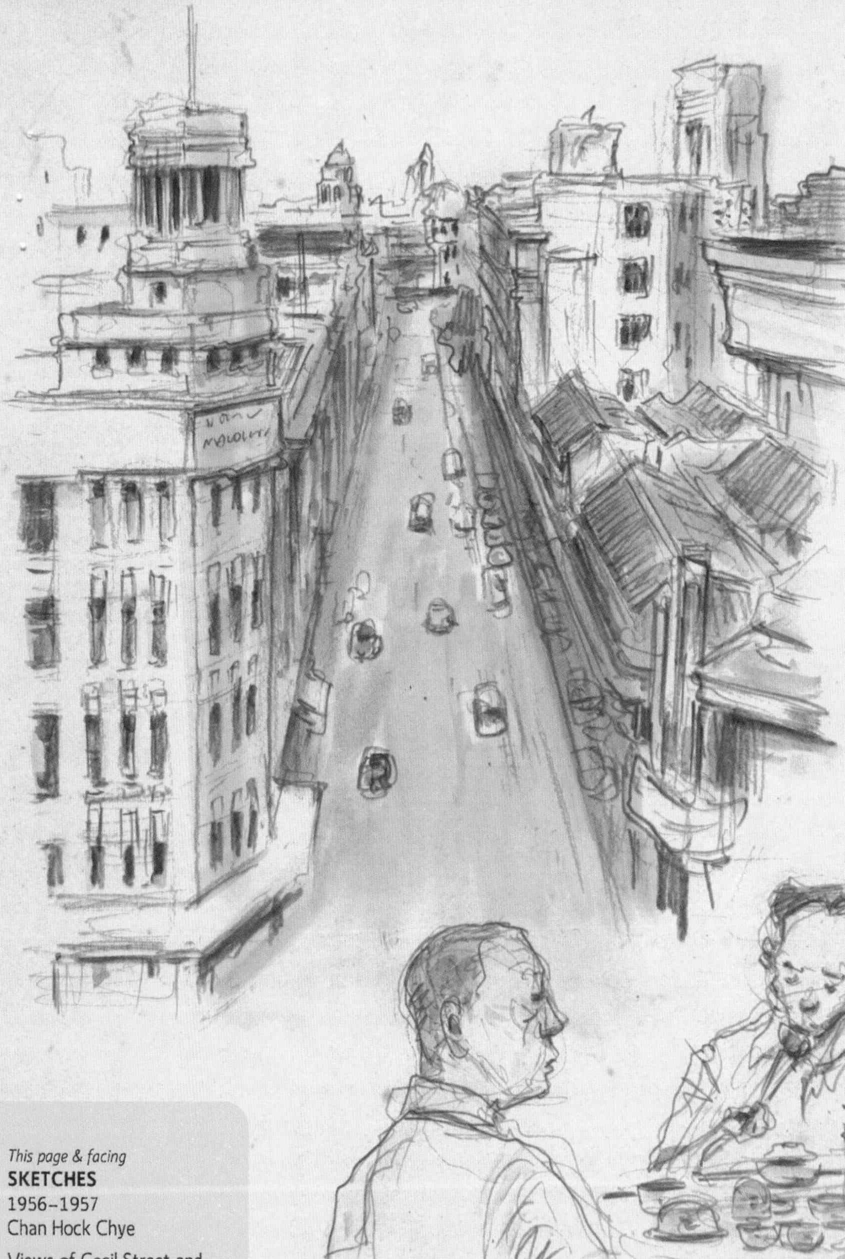

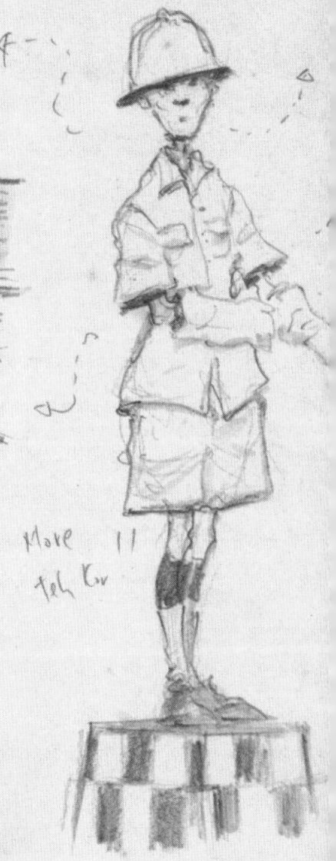

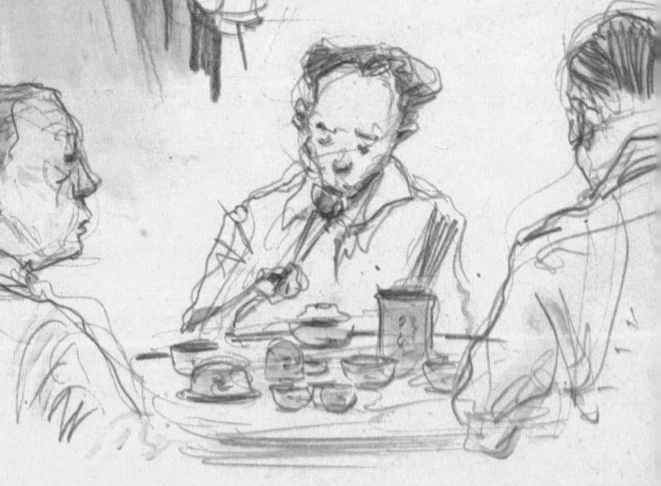

This page & facing
SKETCHES
1956–1957
Chan Hock Chye

Views of Cecil Street and the Fullerton Hotel along the Singapore River.

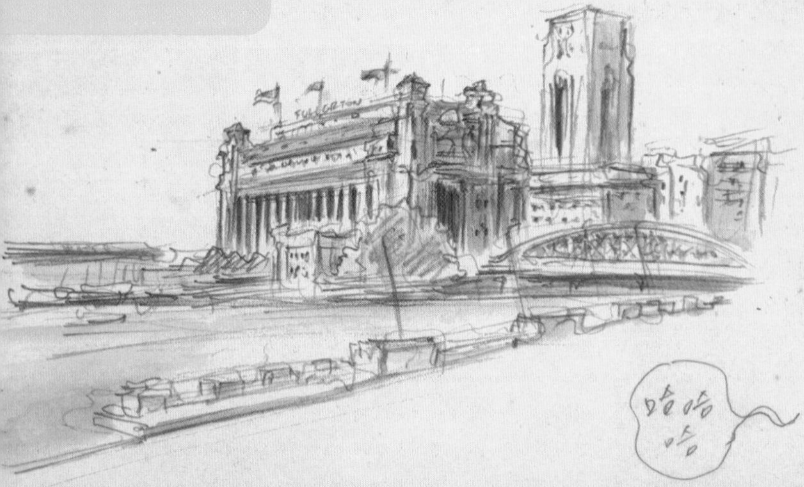

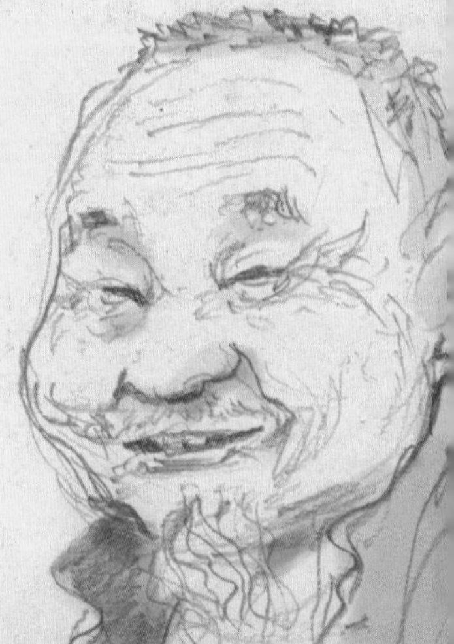
哈哈
哈

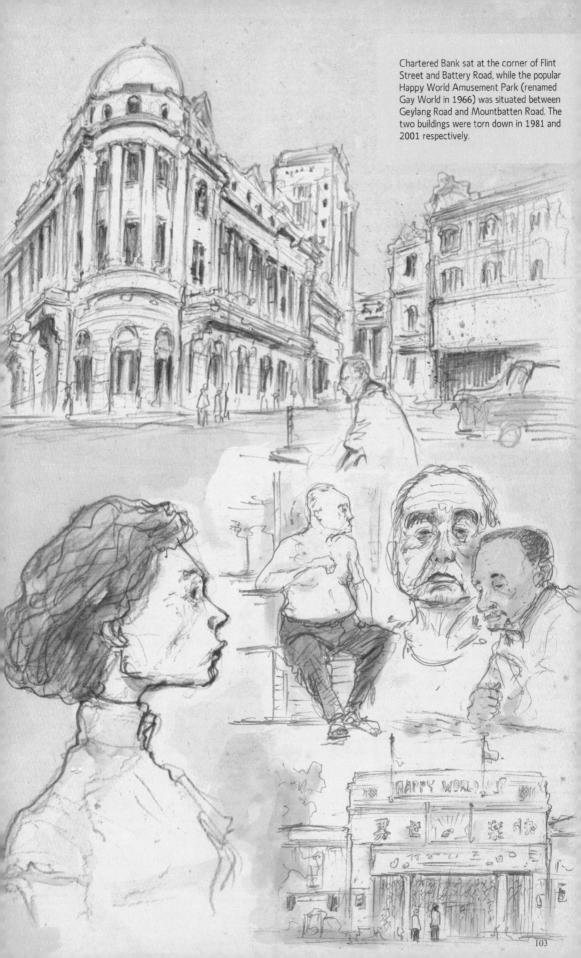

Chartered Bank sat at the corner of Flint Street and Battery Road, while the popular Happy World Amusement Park (renamed Gay World in 1966) was situated between Geylang Road and Mountbatten Road. The two buildings were torn down in 1981 and 2001 respectively.

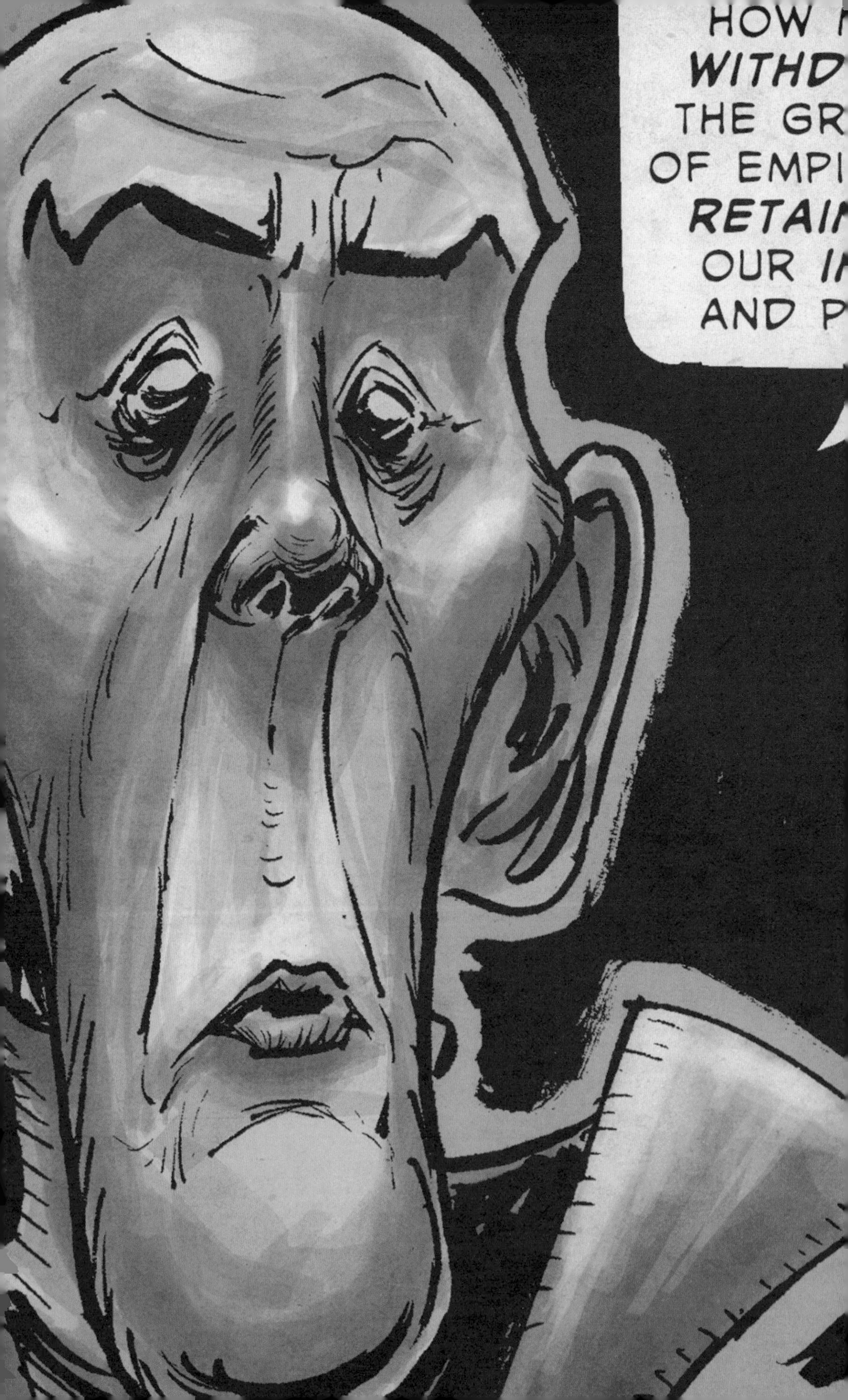
HOW
WITHD
THE GR
OF EMPI
RETAI
OUR
AND P

T WE
FROM
COSTS
AND YET
OME OF
UENCE
TIGE?)

Chapter Four

THE ALLEGORIES OF CHAN & WONG

陈黄寓言

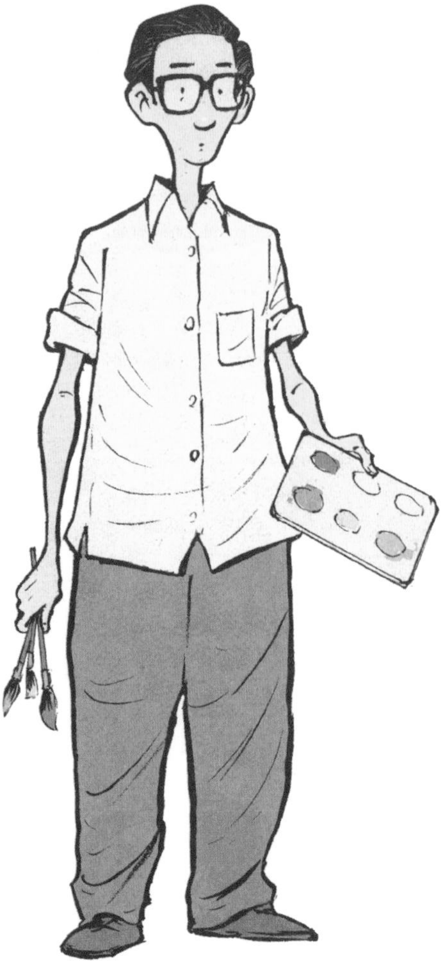

Charlie Chan Hock Chye, aged 19, 1957

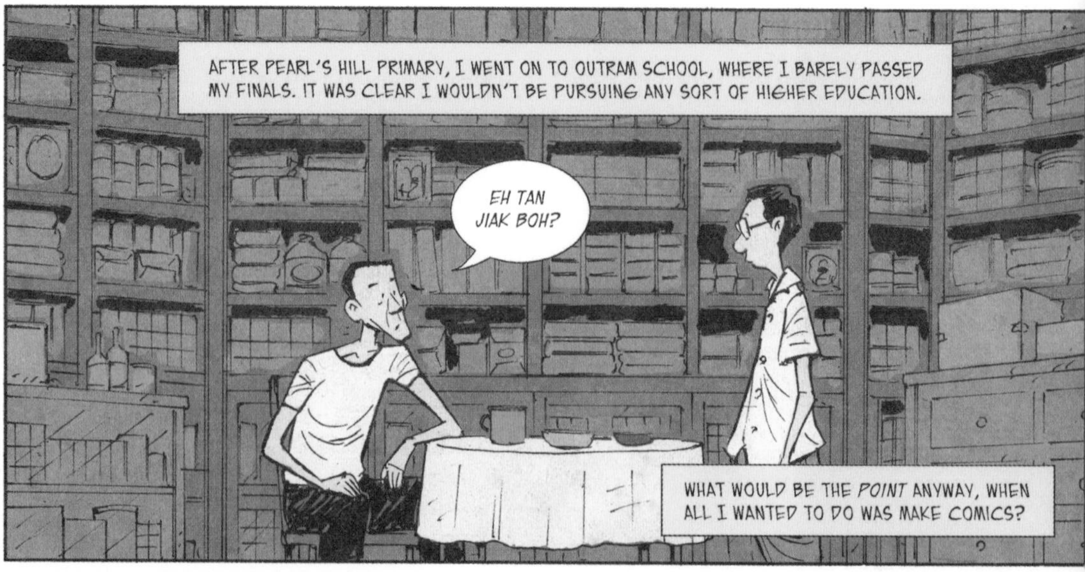
AFTER PEARL'S HILL PRIMARY, I WENT ON TO OUTRAM SCHOOL, WHERE I BARELY PASSED MY FINALS. IT WAS CLEAR I WOULDN'T BE PURSUING ANY SORT OF HIGHER EDUCATION.
EH TAN JIAK BOH?
WHAT WOULD BE THE *POINT* ANYWAY, WHEN ALL I WANTED TO DO WAS MAKE COMICS?

I WOULD RUN INTO BOON SIONG DURING LATE-NIGHT SUPPERS ALONG HOKIEN STREET. HE WAS USUALLY THERE TO ACCOMPANY THE GIRLS FROM THE FLAMINGO NIGHTCLUB AFTER WORK, AND WE'D GRADUALLY STRUCK UP A FRIENDSHIP OF SORTS.

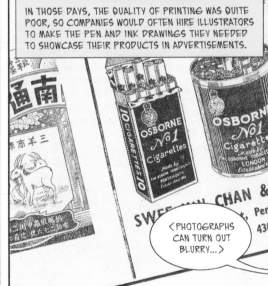

HE HAD STUDIED AT THE NANYANG ACADEMY OF FINE ARTS, AND WOULD SOMETIMES SHOW ME THE RUDIMENTS OF OIL PAINTING AND WATERCOLOUR...

< YOU HAVE TO WORK ON THE BIG SHAPES FIRST... >

...AS WELL AS SOME OF THE TRICKS OF THE TRADE FOR COMMERCIAL ILLUSTRATION.

< YOU CAN USE A SPECIAL RULER TO DRAW CURVES. >

IN THOSE DAYS, THE QUALITY OF PRINTING WAS QUITE POOR, SO COMPANIES WOULD OFTEN HIRE ILLUSTRATORS TO MAKE THE PEN AND INK DRAWINGS THEY NEEDED TO SHOWCASE THEIR PRODUCTS IN ADVERTISEMENTS.

OSBORNE Nº1 Cigarettes

OSBORN Nº1 Cigarette

SWEE MIN CHAN &

< PHOTOGRAPHS CAN TURN OUT BLURRY... >

I WAS ABLE TO MAKE SOME MONEY WITH SUCH WORK, WHILE MAKING NEW COMICS WITH BERTRAND.

TO BE REALLY HONEST, MY ATTITUDE TOWARDS BOON SIONG WAS ALWAYS ONE MORE OF *GRATITUDE* THAN ADMIRATION...

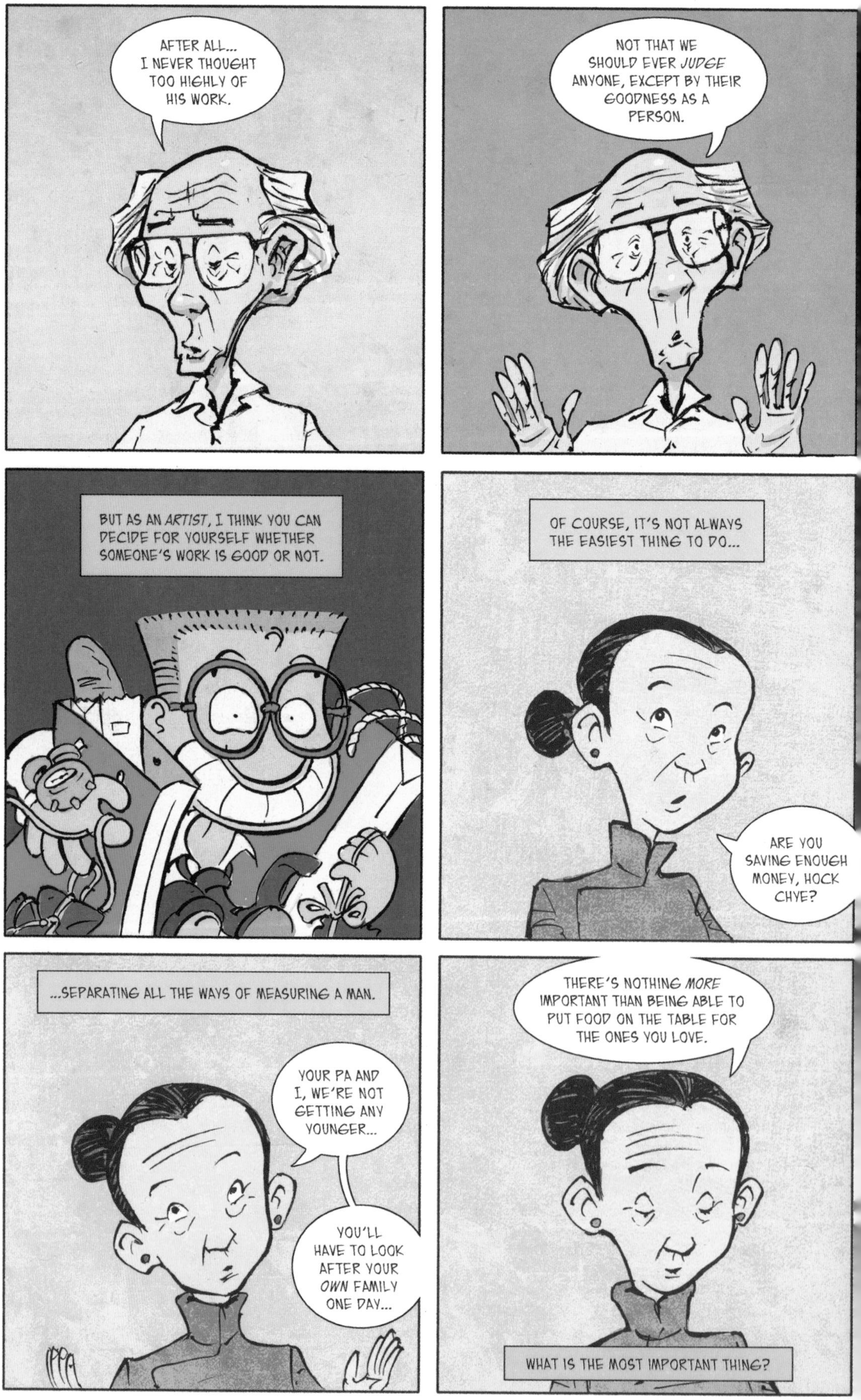
AFTER ALL... I NEVER THOUGHT TOO HIGHLY OF HIS WORK.
NOT THAT WE SHOULD EVER *JUDGE* ANYONE, EXCEPT BY THEIR GOODNESS AS A PERSON.
BUT AS AN *ARTIST*, I THINK YOU CAN DECIDE FOR YOURSELF WHETHER SOMEONE'S WORK IS GOOD OR NOT.
OF COURSE, IT'S NOT ALWAYS THE EASIEST THING TO DO...
ARE YOU SAVING ENOUGH MONEY, HOCK CHYE?
...SEPARATING ALL THE WAYS OF MEASURING A MAN.
YOUR PA AND I, WE'RE NOT GETTING ANY YOUNGER...
YOU'LL HAVE TO LOOK AFTER YOUR *OWN* FAMILY ONE DAY...
THERE'S NOTHING *MORE* IMPORTANT THAN BEING ABLE TO PUT FOOD ON THE TABLE FOR THE ONES YOU LOVE.
WHAT IS THE MOST IMPORTANT THING?

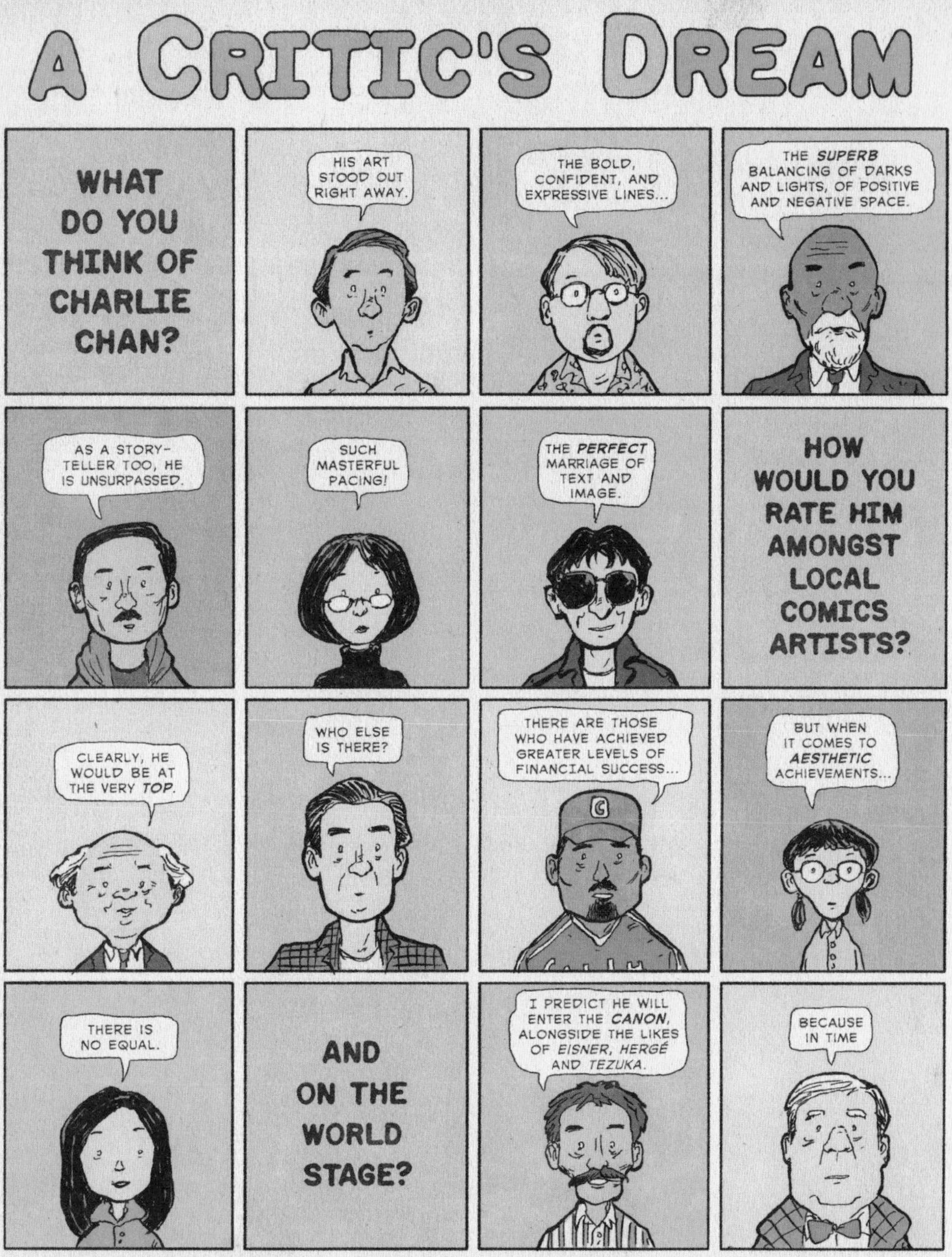
A CRITIC'S DREAM
WHAT DO YOU THINK OF CHARLIE CHAN?
HIS ART STOOD OUT RIGHT AWAY.
THE BOLD, CONFIDENT, AND EXPRESSIVE LINES...
THE SUPERB BALANCING OF DARKS AND LIGHTS, OF POSITIVE AND NEGATIVE SPACE.
AS A STORY-TELLER TOO, HE IS UNSURPASSED.
SUCH MASTERFUL PACING!
THE PERFECT MARRIAGE OF TEXT AND IMAGE.
HOW WOULD YOU RATE HIM AMONGST LOCAL COMICS ARTISTS?
CLEARLY, HE WOULD BE AT THE VERY TOP.
WHO ELSE IS THERE?
THERE ARE THOSE WHO HAVE ACHIEVED GREATER LEVELS OF FINANCIAL SUCCESS...
BUT WHEN IT COMES TO AESTHETIC ACHIEVEMENTS...
THERE IS NO EQUAL.
AND ON THE WORLD STAGE?
I PREDICT HE WILL ENTER THE CANON, ALONGSIDE THE LIKES OF EISNER, HERGÉ AND TEZUKA.
BECAUSE IN TIME
GREAT ART WILL ALWAYS BE RECOGNISED
THE CREAM ALWAYS RISES
TO THE TOP!
OH, MY! WHAT A DREAM! I MUST HAVE MORE DELICIOUS RAREBIT FOR MY SUPPERS!

Above **A CRITIC'S DREAM** (1984) | Chan Hock Chye | Unpublished

Inspired by Winsor McCay's newspaper comic strip *Dream of the Rarebit Fiend*, in which strange and fantastical dreams would always be attributed to a meal of Welsh rarebit, Chan offers a glimpse into his own psyche and aspirations.

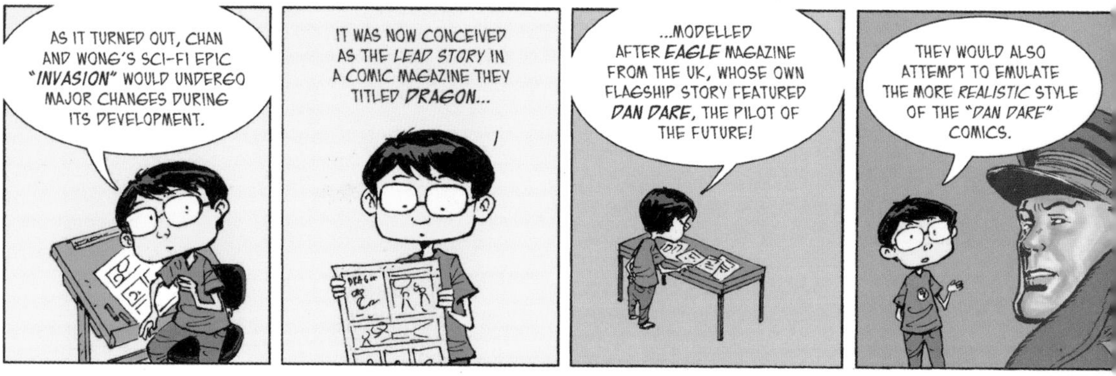
AS IT TURNED OUT, CHAN AND WONG'S SCI-FI EPIC "INVASION" WOULD UNDERGO MAJOR CHANGES DURING ITS DEVELOPMENT.
IT WAS NOW CONCEIVED AS THE LEAD STORY IN A COMIC MAGAZINE THEY TITLED DRAGON...
...MODELLED AFTER EAGLE MAGAZINE FROM THE UK, WHOSE OWN FLAGSHIP STORY FEATURED DAN DARE, THE PILOT OF THE FUTURE!
THEY WOULD ALSO ATTEMPT TO EMULATE THE MORE REALISTIC STYLE OF THE "DAN DARE" COMICS.

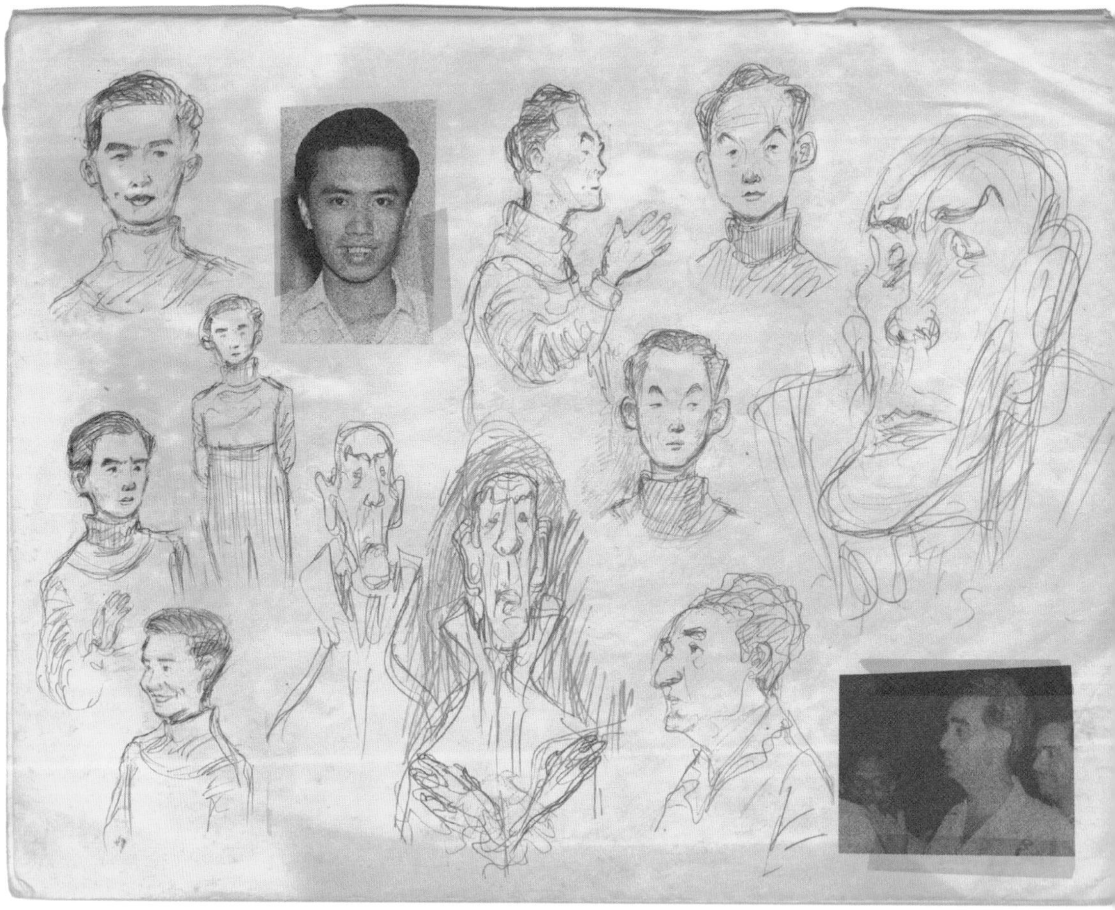

Above **INVASION Character Sketches** (1957) | Chan Hock Chye

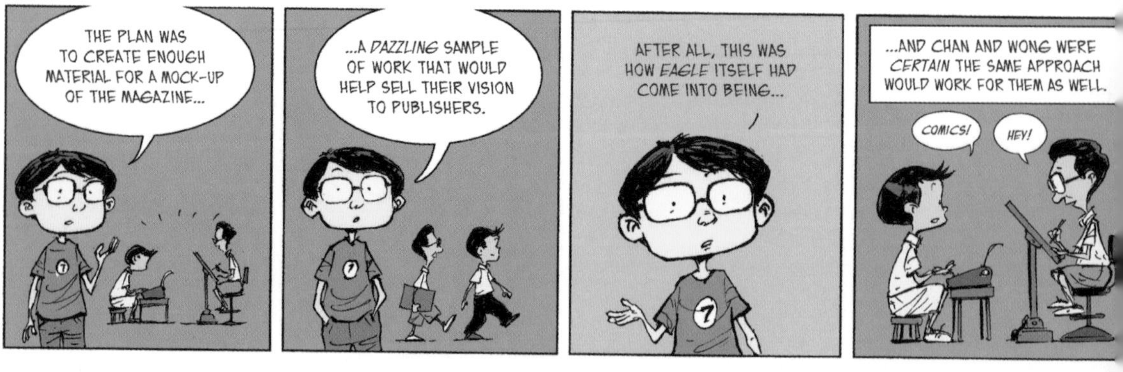
THE PLAN WAS TO CREATE ENOUGH MATERIAL FOR A MOCK-UP OF THE MAGAZINE...
...A DAZZLING SAMPLE OF WORK THAT WOULD HELP SELL THEIR VISION TO PUBLISHERS.
AFTER ALL, THIS WAS HOW EAGLE ITSELF HAD COME INTO BEING...
...AND CHAN AND WONG WERE CERTAIN THE SAME APPROACH WOULD WORK FOR THEM AS WELL.
COMICS!
HEY!

SINGAPORE'S NATIONAL STRIP CARTOON WEEKLY

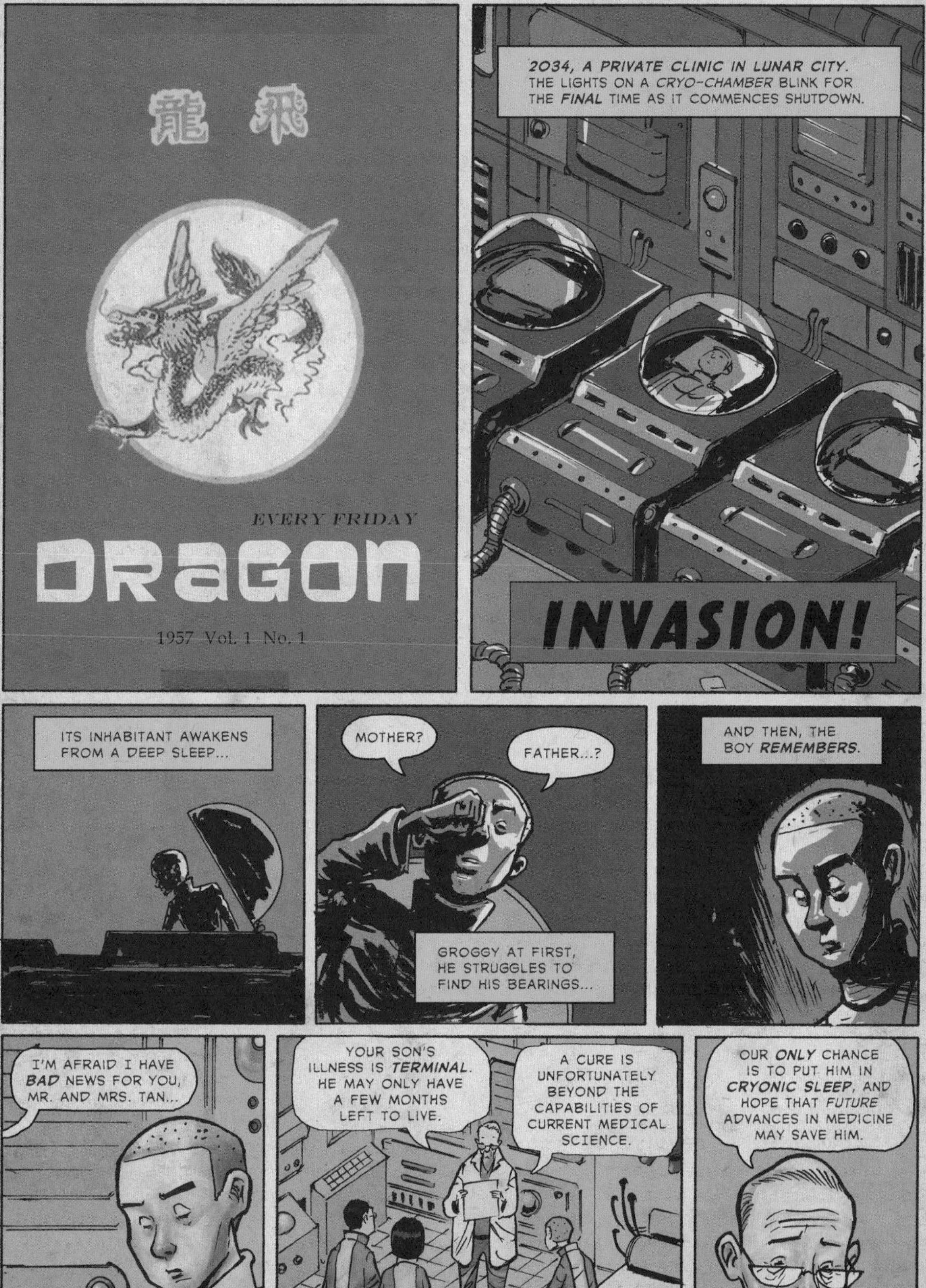
飛龍
EVERY FRIDAY
DRAGON
1957 Vol. 1 No. 1
2034, A PRIVATE CLINIC IN LUNAR CITY. THE LIGHTS ON A CRYO-CHAMBER BLINK FOR THE FINAL TIME AS IT COMMENCES SHUTDOWN.
INVASION!
ITS INHABITANT AWAKENS FROM A DEEP SLEEP...
MOTHER?
FATHER...?
GROGGY AT FIRST, HE STRUGGLES TO FIND HIS BEARINGS...
AND THEN, THE BOY REMEMBERS.
I'M AFRAID I HAVE BAD NEWS FOR YOU, MR. AND MRS. TAN...
YOUR SON'S ILLNESS IS TERMINAL. HE MAY ONLY HAVE A FEW MONTHS LEFT TO LIVE.
A CURE IS UNFORTUNATELY BEYOND THE CAPABILITIES OF CURRENT MEDICAL SCIENCE.
OUR ONLY CHANCE IS TO PUT HIM IN CRYONIC SLEEP, AND HOPE THAT FUTURE ADVANCES IN MEDICINE MAY SAVE HIM.

Above & following **INVASION Vol. 1 Nos. 1 & 2** (1957) | Art by Chan Hock Chye, Words by Bertrand Wong

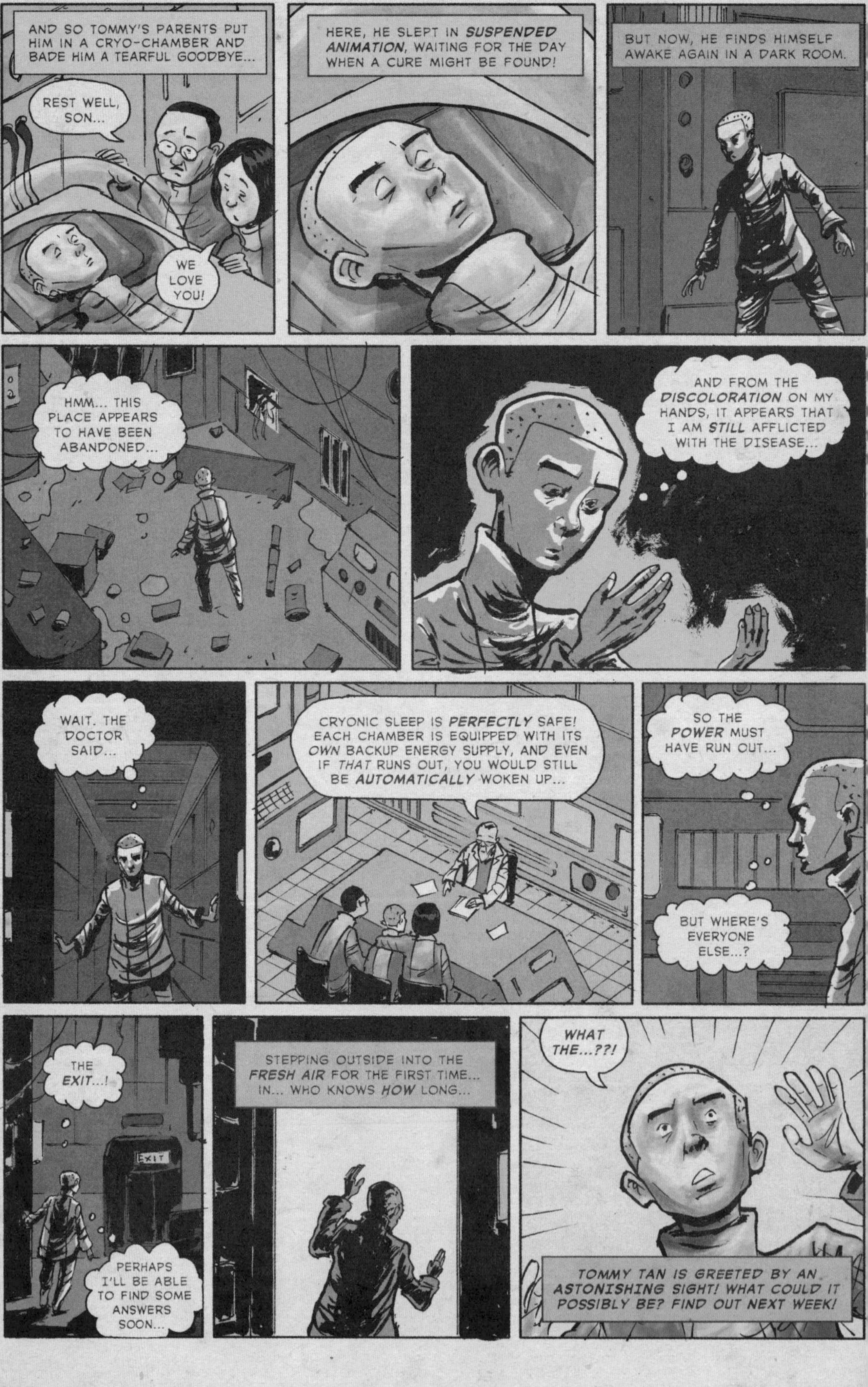
AND SO TOMMY'S PARENTS PUT HIM IN A CRYO-CHAMBER AND BADE HIM A TEARFUL GOODBYE...
REST WELL, SON...
WE LOVE YOU!
HERE, HE SLEPT IN SUSPENDED ANIMATION, WAITING FOR THE DAY WHEN A CURE MIGHT BE FOUND!
BUT NOW, HE FINDS HIMSELF AWAKE AGAIN IN A DARK ROOM.
HMM... THIS PLACE APPEARS TO HAVE BEEN ABANDONED...
AND FROM THE DISCOLORATION ON MY HANDS, IT APPEARS THAT I AM STILL AFFLICTED WITH THE DISEASE...
WAIT. THE DOCTOR SAID...
CRYONIC SLEEP IS PERFECTLY SAFE! EACH CHAMBER IS EQUIPPED WITH ITS OWN BACKUP ENERGY SUPPLY, AND EVEN IF THAT RUNS OUT, YOU WOULD STILL BE AUTOMATICALLY WOKEN UP...
SO THE POWER MUST HAVE RUN OUT...
BUT WHERE'S EVERYONE ELSE...?
THE EXIT...!
EXIT
PERHAPS I'LL BE ABLE TO FIND SOME ANSWERS SOON...
STEPPING OUTSIDE INTO THE FRESH AIR FOR THE FIRST TIME... IN... WHO KNOWS HOW LONG...
WHAT THE...??!
TOMMY TAN IS GREETED BY AN ASTONISHING SIGHT! WHAT COULD IT POSSIBLY BE? FIND OUT NEXT WEEK!

SINGAPORE'S NATIONAL STRIP CARTOON WEEKLY

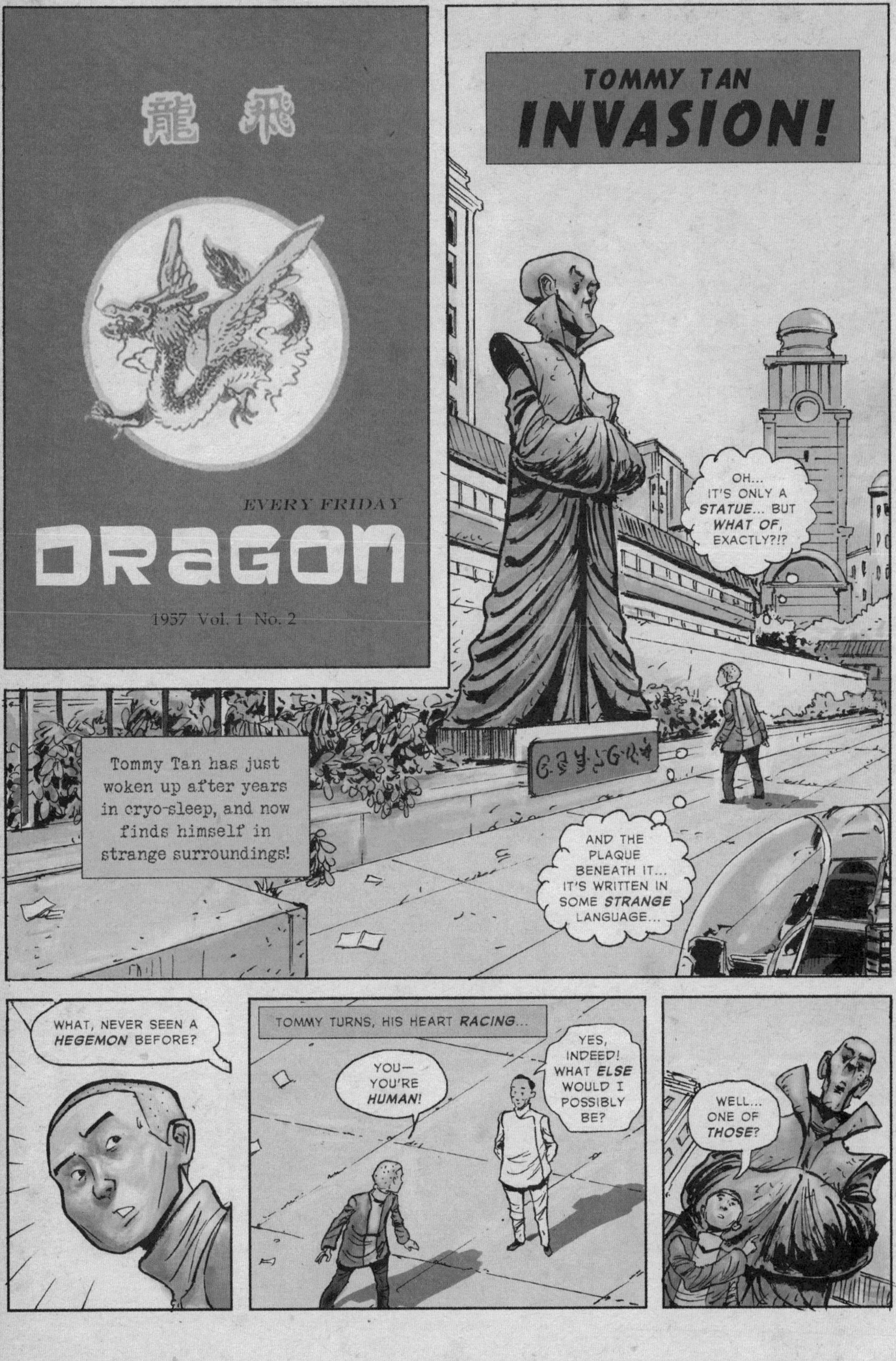

飛龍
EVERY FRIDAY
DRAGON
1957 Vol. 1 No. 2
TOMMY TAN
INVASION!
OH... IT'S ONLY A STATUE... BUT WHAT OF, EXACTLY?!?
Tommy Tan has just woken up after years in cryo-sleep, and now finds himself in strange surroundings!
AND THE PLAQUE BENEATH IT... IT'S WRITTEN IN SOME STRANGE LANGUAGE...
WHAT, NEVER SEEN A HEGEMON BEFORE?
TOMMY TURNS, HIS HEART RACING...
YOU— YOU'RE HUMAN!
YES, INDEED! WHAT ELSE WOULD I POSSIBLY BE?
WELL... ONE OF THOSE?

INVASION! A BEGINNER'S

Co-Creator Charlie Chan's Guide

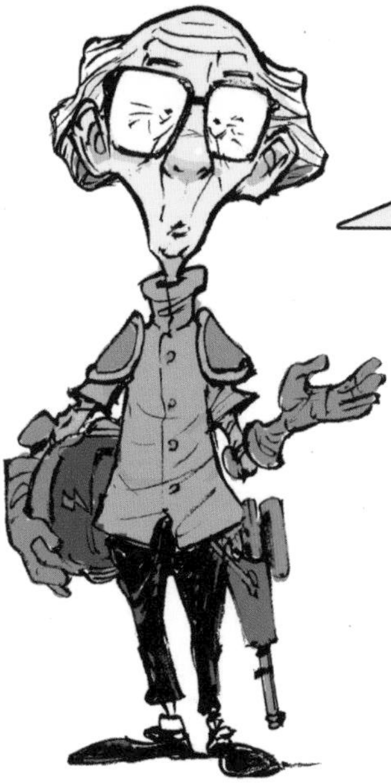

Our main character is **Tommy Tan**, a young boy who wakes up to find from his new acquaintance **Mr. Wei** that **120 years** have passed since he was put in cryo-sleep.

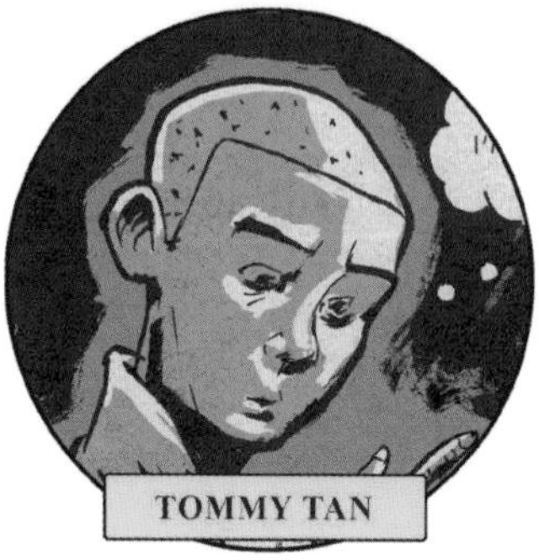

TOMMY TAN

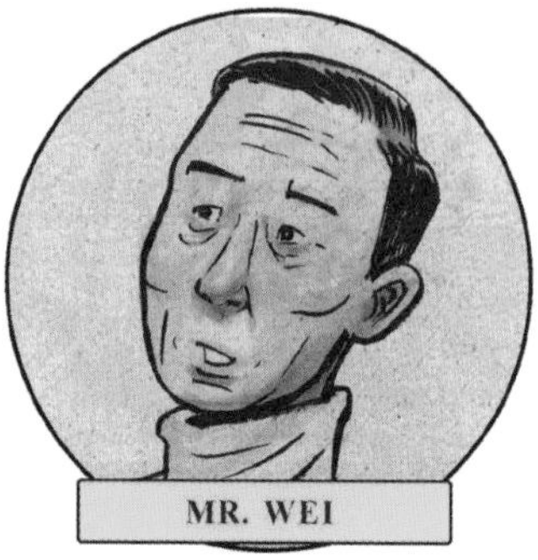

MR. WEI

Tommy is appalled to learn that the human race had allowed itself to be thus **subjugated**, and is determined to help **free** Lunar City from its alien shackles...

But after seeing the fluent Hegemonese speaker and legal counsel **Harry Lee Kuan Yew** successfully defend workers' rights at a court hearing...

Compounded with th knowledge that he ha but a **short time** left before his illness catches up with him..

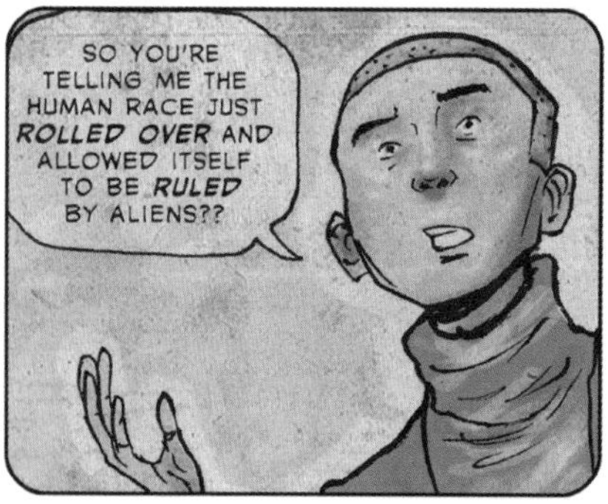
SO YOU'RE TELLING ME THE HUMAN RACE JUST *ROLLED OVER* AND ALLOWED ITSELF TO BE *RULED* BY ALIENS??

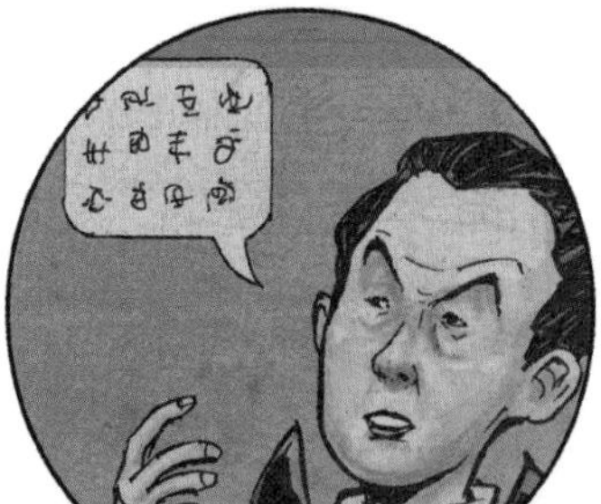

HARRY LEE KUAN YEW

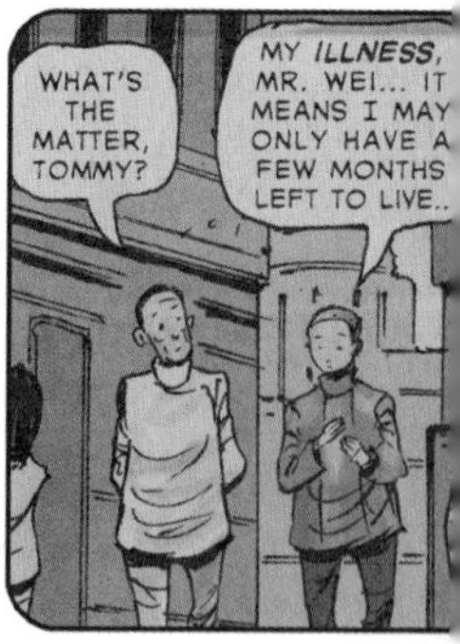
WHAT'S THE MATTER, TOMMY?
MY *ILLNESS*, MR. WEI... IT MEANS I MAY ONLY HAVE A FEW MONTHS LEFT TO LIVE..

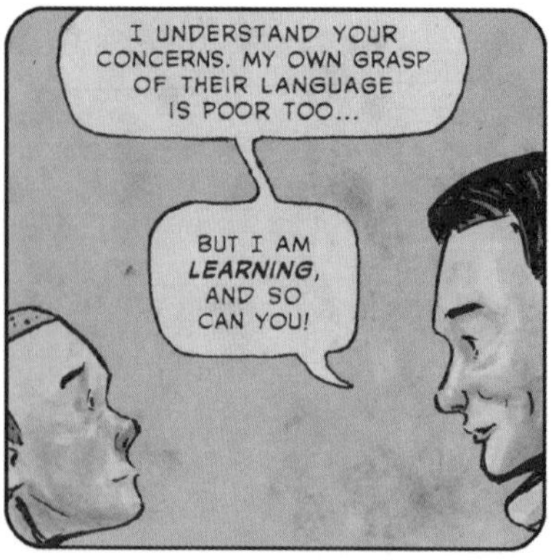
I UNDERSTAND YOUR CONCERNS. MY OWN GRASP OF THEIR LANGUAGE IS POOR TOO...
BUT I AM *LEARNING*, AND SO CAN YOU!

Lim Chin Siong and Harry Lee eventually come to realise that each needs the other's talents and resources to win the support of the people and **take on** the alien occupiers.

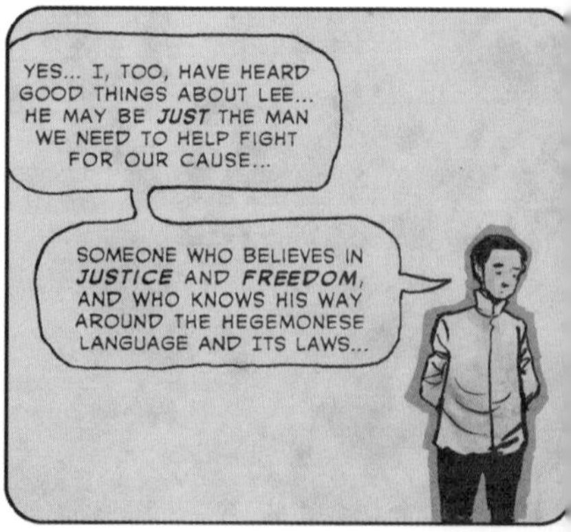
YES... I, TOO, HAVE HEARD GOOD THINGS ABOUT LEE... HE MAY BE *JUST* THE MAN WE NEED TO HELP FIGHT FOR OUR CAUSE...
SOMEONE WHO BELIEVES IN *JUSTICE* AND *FREEDOM*, AND WHO KNOWS HIS WAY AROUND THE HEGEMONESE LANGUAGE AND ITS LAWS...

GUIDE

From an interview transcript dated July 14, 2012.

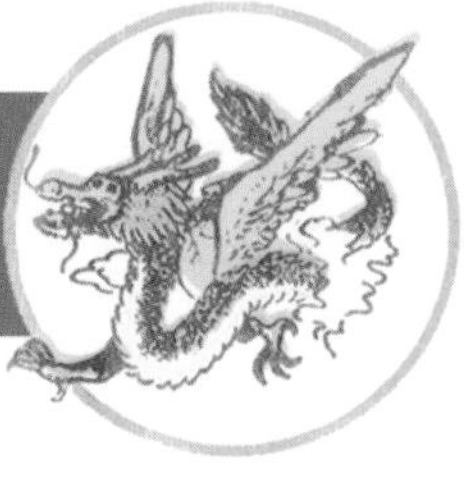

to the Science Fiction Epic!

During this time, his homeworld of **Lunar City** has been conquered by an **alien** race known as the **Hegemons**...

...and his people forced to adopt the alien language, **Hegemonese**, for all official matters.

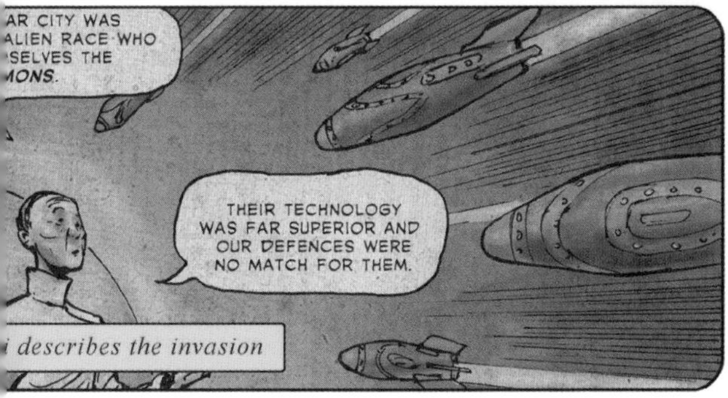
AR CITY WAS ALIEN RACE WHO SELVES THE MONS.
THEIR TECHNOLOGY WAS FAR SUPERIOR AND OUR DEFENCES WERE NO MATCH FOR THEM.

describes the invasion

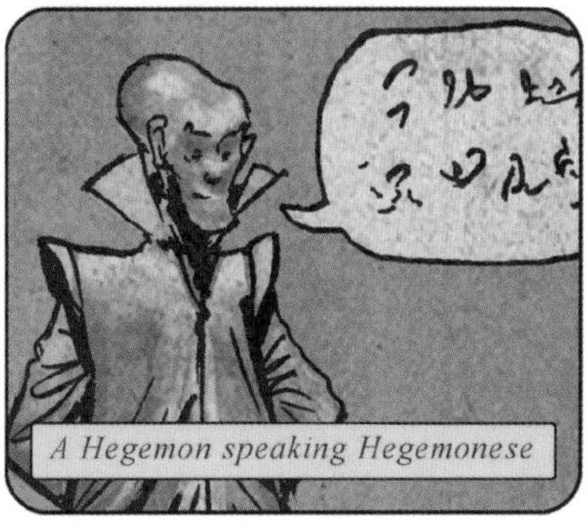

A Hegemon speaking Hegemonese

Tommy worries that his inability to speak Hegemonese will render him **worthless** in the fight for independence.

Mr. Wei decides to take him to meet the famous freedom fighter **Lim Chin Siong**...

...who swiftly allays Tommy's fears, and inspires in him a new sense of **hope** and **purpose.**

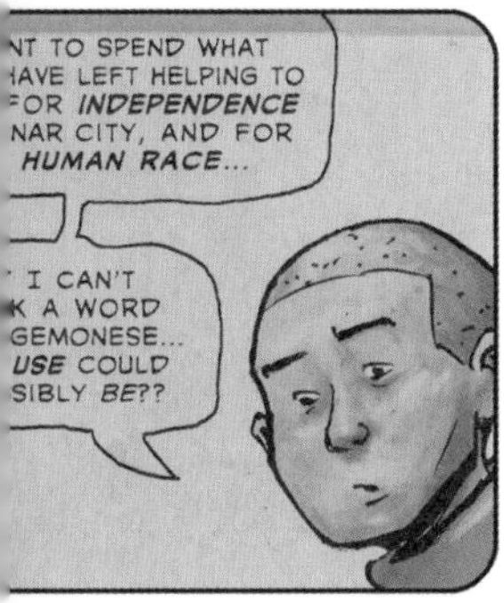
NT TO SPEND WHAT HAVE LEFT HELPING TO FOR *INDEPENDENCE* NAR CITY, AND FOR *HUMAN RACE*...
I CAN'T A WORD GEMONESE... *USE* COULD SIBLY *BE*??

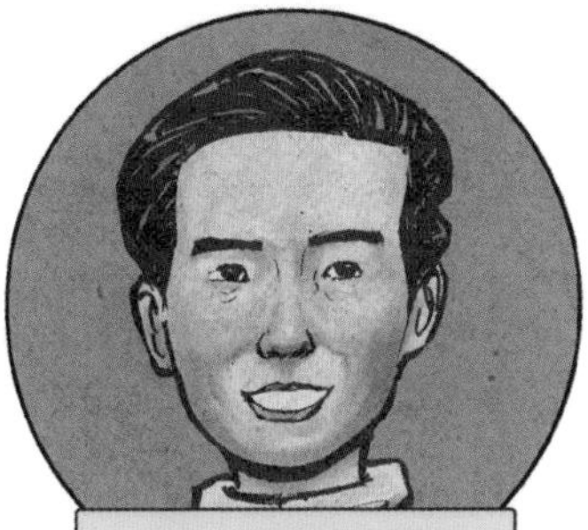

LIM CHIN SIONG

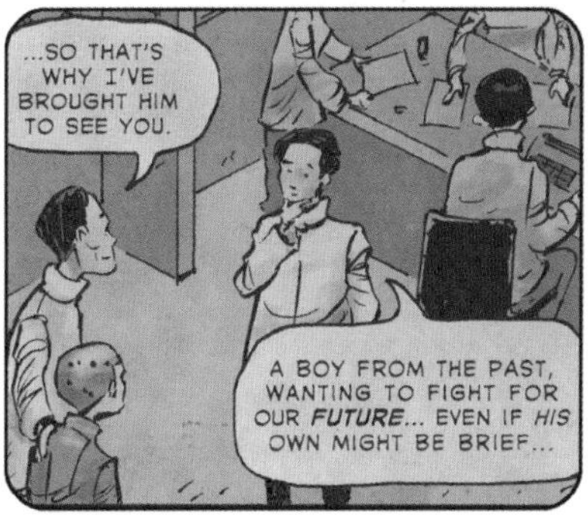
...SO THAT'S WHY I'VE BROUGHT HIM TO SEE YOU.
A BOY FROM THE PAST, WANTING TO FIGHT FOR OUR *FUTURE*... EVEN IF *HIS* OWN MIGHT BE BRIEF...

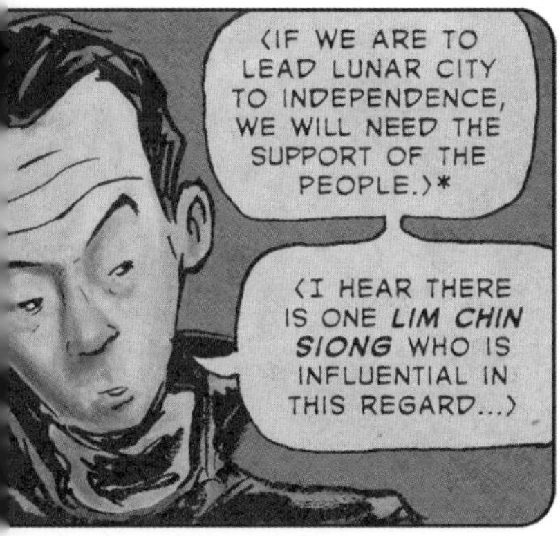
<IF WE ARE TO LEAD LUNAR CITY TO INDEPENDENCE, WE WILL NEED THE SUPPORT OF THE PEOPLE.>*
<I HEAR THERE IS ONE *LIM CHIN SIONG* WHO IS INFLUENTIAL IN THIS REGARD...>

And so they **join forces** in their quest to overthrow the Hegemons and help Lunar City regain its **independence**!

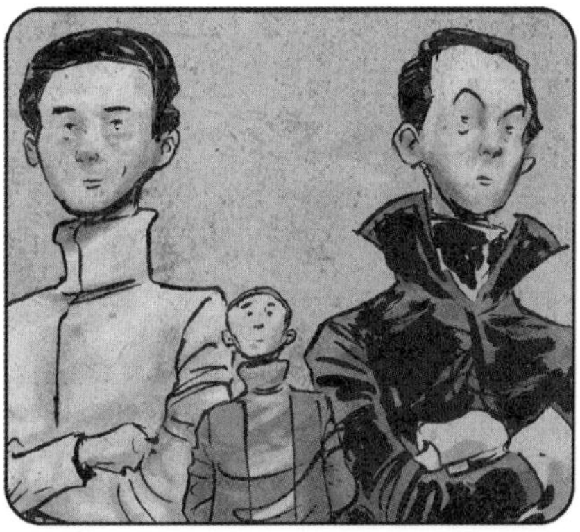

INVASION! A BEGINNER'S

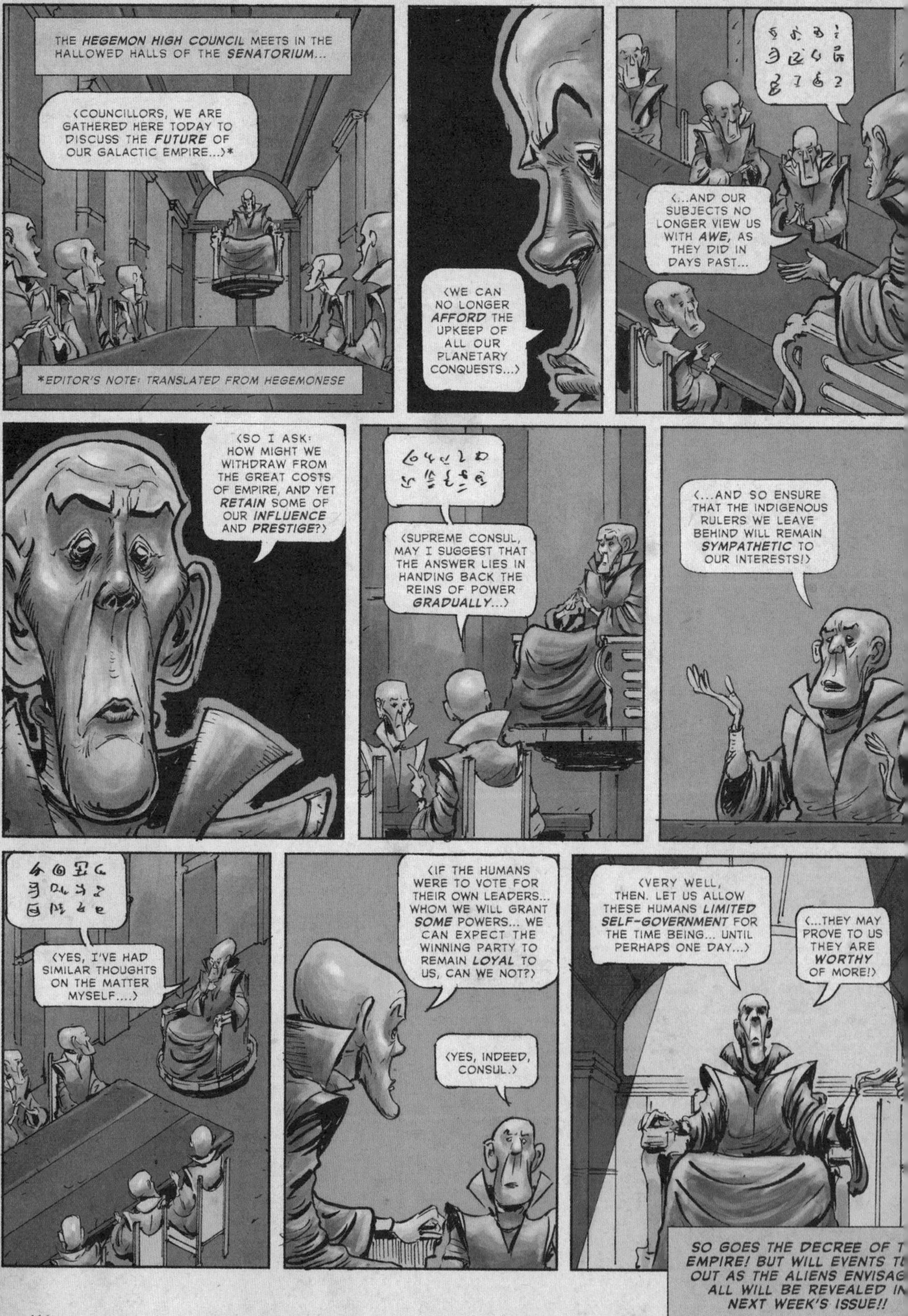
THE HEGEMON HIGH COUNCIL MEETS IN THE HALLOWED HALLS OF THE SENATORIUM...
‹COUNCILLORS, WE ARE GATHERED HERE TODAY TO DISCUSS THE FUTURE OF OUR GALACTIC EMPIRE...›*
*EDITOR'S NOTE: TRANSLATED FROM HEGEMONESE
‹WE CAN NO LONGER AFFORD THE UPKEEP OF ALL OUR PLANETARY CONQUESTS...›
‹...AND OUR SUBJECTS NO LONGER VIEW US WITH AWE, AS THEY DID IN DAYS PAST...
‹SO I ASK: HOW MIGHT WE WITHDRAW FROM THE GREAT COSTS OF EMPIRE, AND YET RETAIN SOME OF OUR INFLUENCE AND PRESTIGE?›
‹SUPREME CONSUL, MAY I SUGGEST THAT THE ANSWER LIES IN HANDING BACK THE REINS OF POWER GRADUALLY...›
‹...AND SO ENSURE THAT THE INDIGENOUS RULERS WE LEAVE BEHIND WILL REMAIN SYMPATHETIC TO OUR INTERESTS!›
‹YES, I'VE HAD SIMILAR THOUGHTS ON THE MATTER MYSELF....›
‹IF THE HUMANS WERE TO VOTE FOR THEIR OWN LEADERS... WHOM WE WILL GRANT SOME POWERS... WE CAN EXPECT THE WINNING PARTY TO REMAIN LOYAL TO US, CAN WE NOT?›
‹YES, INDEED, CONSUL.›
‹VERY WELL, THEN. LET US ALLOW THESE HUMANS LIMITED SELF-GOVERNMENT FOR THE TIME BEING... UNTIL PERHAPS ONE DAY...›
‹...THEY MAY PROVE TO US THEY ARE WORTHY OF MORE!›
SO GOES THE DECREE OF T EMPIRE! BUT WILL EVENTS T OUT AS THE ALIENS ENVISAG ALL WILL BE REVEALED IN NEXT WEEK'S ISSUE!!

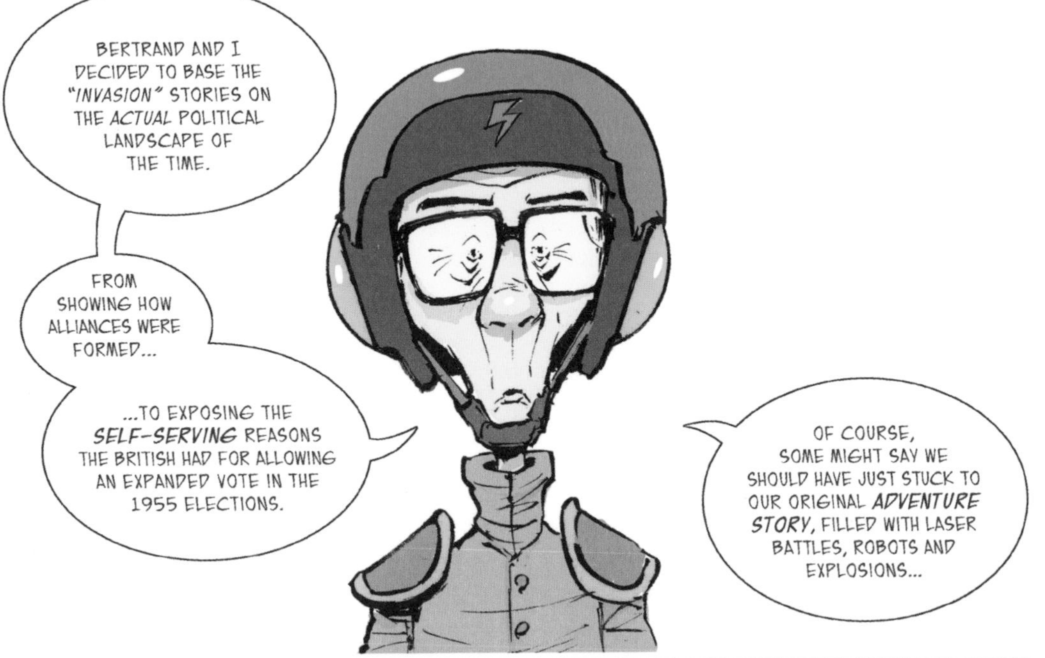
BERTRAND AND I DECIDED TO BASE THE "*INVASION*" STORIES ON THE *ACTUAL* POLITICAL LANDSCAPE OF THE TIME.
FROM SHOWING HOW ALLIANCES WERE FORMED...
...TO EXPOSING THE ***SELF-SERVING*** REASONS THE BRITISH HAD FOR ALLOWING AN EXPANDED VOTE IN THE 1955 ELECTIONS.
OF COURSE, SOME MIGHT SAY WE SHOULD HAVE JUST STUCK TO OUR ORIGINAL ***ADVENTURE STORY***, FILLED WITH LASER BATTLES, ROBOTS AND EXPLOSIONS...

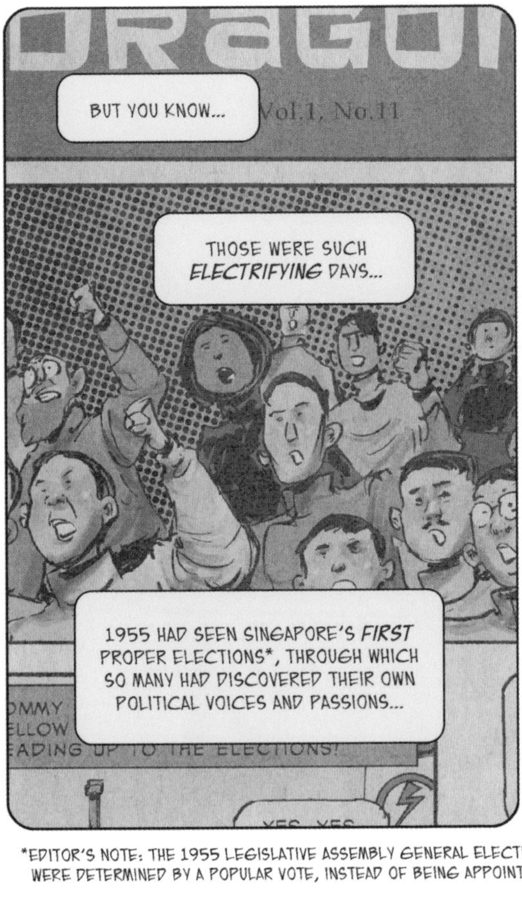
BUT YOU KNOW...
Vol.1, No.11
THOSE WERE SUCH ***ELECTRIFYING*** DAYS...
1955 HAD SEEN SINGAPORE'S *FIRST* PROPER ELECTIONS*, THROUGH WHICH SO MANY HAD DISCOVERED THEIR OWN POLITICAL VOICES AND PASSIONS...

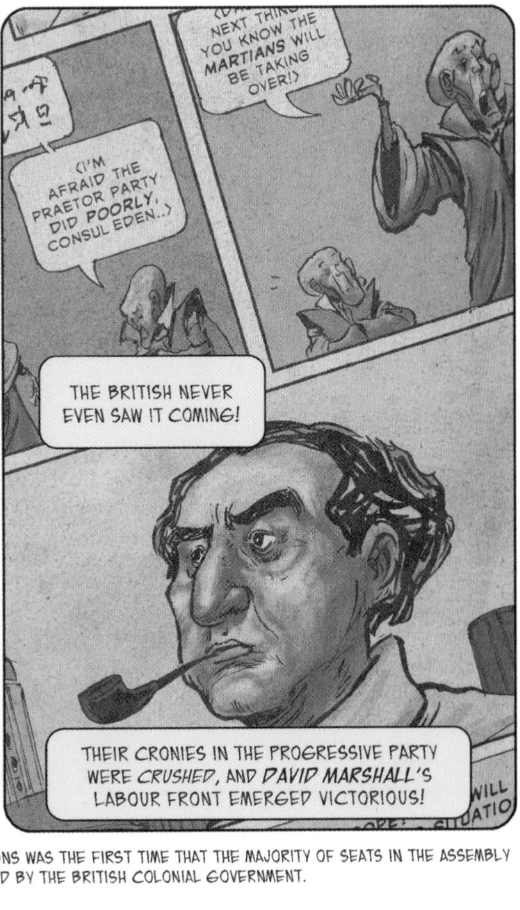
NEXT THING YOU KNOW THE **MARTIANS** WILL BE TAKING OVER!)
(I'M AFRAID THE PRAETOR PARTY DID **POORLY**, CONSUL EDEN..)
THE BRITISH NEVER EVEN SAW IT COMING!
THEIR CRONIES IN THE PROGRESSIVE PARTY WERE *CRUSHED*, AND ***DAVID MARSHALL***'S LABOUR FRONT EMERGED VICTORIOUS!

*EDITOR'S NOTE: THE 1955 LEGISLATIVE ASSEMBLY GENERAL ELECTIONS WAS THE FIRST TIME THAT THE MAJORITY OF SEATS IN THE ASSEMBLY WERE DETERMINED BY A POPULAR VOTE, INSTEAD OF BEING APPOINTED BY THE BRITISH COLONIAL GOVERNMENT.

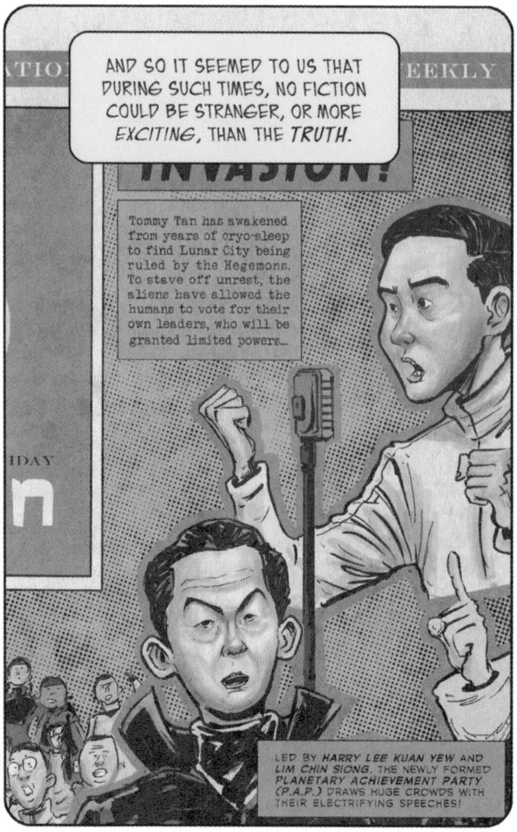
AND SO IT SEEMED TO US THAT DURING SUCH TIMES, NO FICTION COULD BE STRANGER, OR MORE *EXCITING*, THAN THE ***TRUTH***.
INVASION!
Tommy Tan has awakened from years of cryo-sleep to find Lunar City being ruled by the Hegemons. To stave off unrest, the aliens have allowed the humans to vote for their own leaders, who will be granted limited powers...
LED BY ***HARRY LEE KUAN YEW*** AND ***LIM CHIN SIONG***, THE NEWLY FORMED ***PLANETARY ACHIEVEMENT PARTY (P.A.P.)*** DRAWS HUGE CROWDS WITH THEIR ELECTRIFYING SPEECHES!

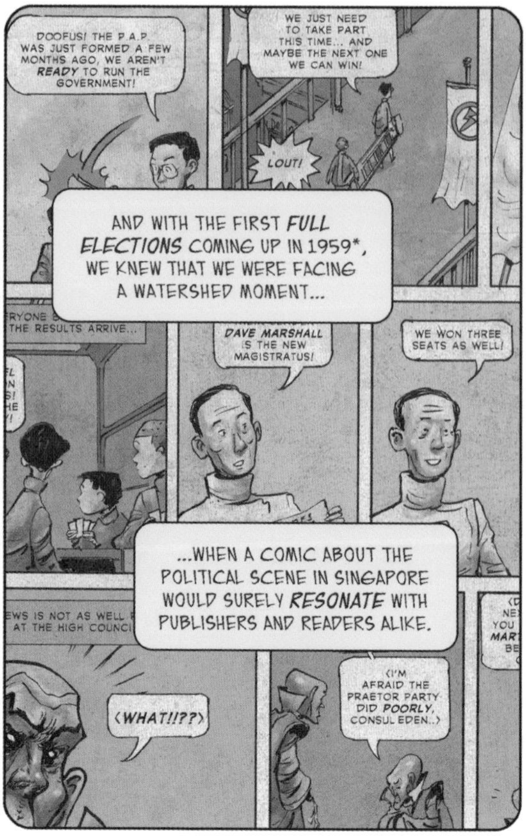
DOOFUS! THE P.A.P. WAS JUST FORMED A FEW MONTHS AGO, WE AREN'T ***READY*** TO RUN THE GOVERNMENT!
WE JUST NEED TO TAKE PART THIS TIME... AND MAYBE THE NEXT ONE WE CAN WIN!
LOUT!
AND WITH THE FIRST ***FULL ELECTIONS*** COMING UP IN 1959*, WE KNEW THAT WE WERE FACING A WATERSHED MOMENT...
DAVE MARSHALL IS THE NEW MAGISTRATUS!
WE WON THREE SEATS AS WELL!
...WHEN A COMIC ABOUT THE POLITICAL SCENE IN SINGAPORE WOULD SURELY ***RESONATE*** WITH PUBLISHERS AND READERS ALIKE.
<***WHAT!!??***>
<I'M AFRAID THE PRAETOR PARTY DID ***POORLY***, CONSUL EDEN..>

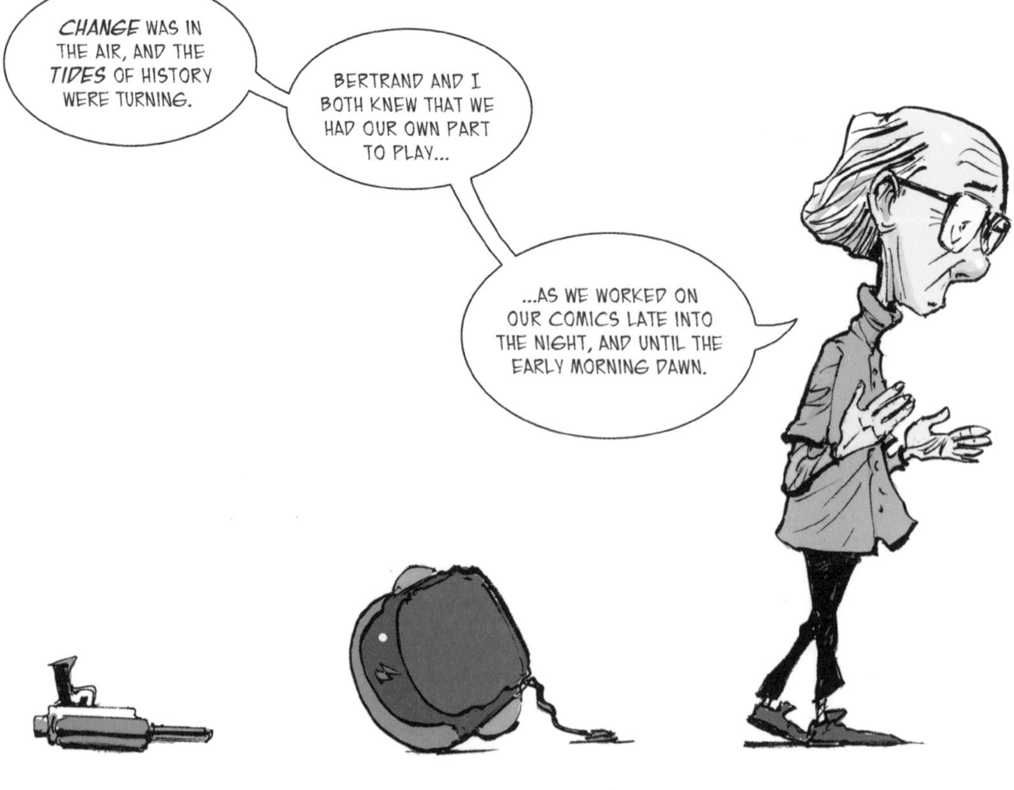
CHANGE WAS IN THE AIR, AND THE ***TIDES*** OF HISTORY WERE TURNING.
BERTRAND AND I BOTH KNEW THAT WE HAD OUR OWN PART TO PLAY...
...AS WE WORKED ON OUR COMICS LATE INTO THE NIGHT, AND UNTIL THE EARLY MORNING DAWN.

*EDITOR'S NOTE: WITH THE 1959 GENERAL ELECTIONS, ***ALL*** THE SEATS IN THE LEGISLATIVE ASSEMBLY WOULD BE PUT TO A POPULAR VOTE. FOR THE FIRST TIME, THE WINNING PARTY WOULD BE GRANTED POWERS OVER FULL INTERNAL SELF-GOVERNMENT.

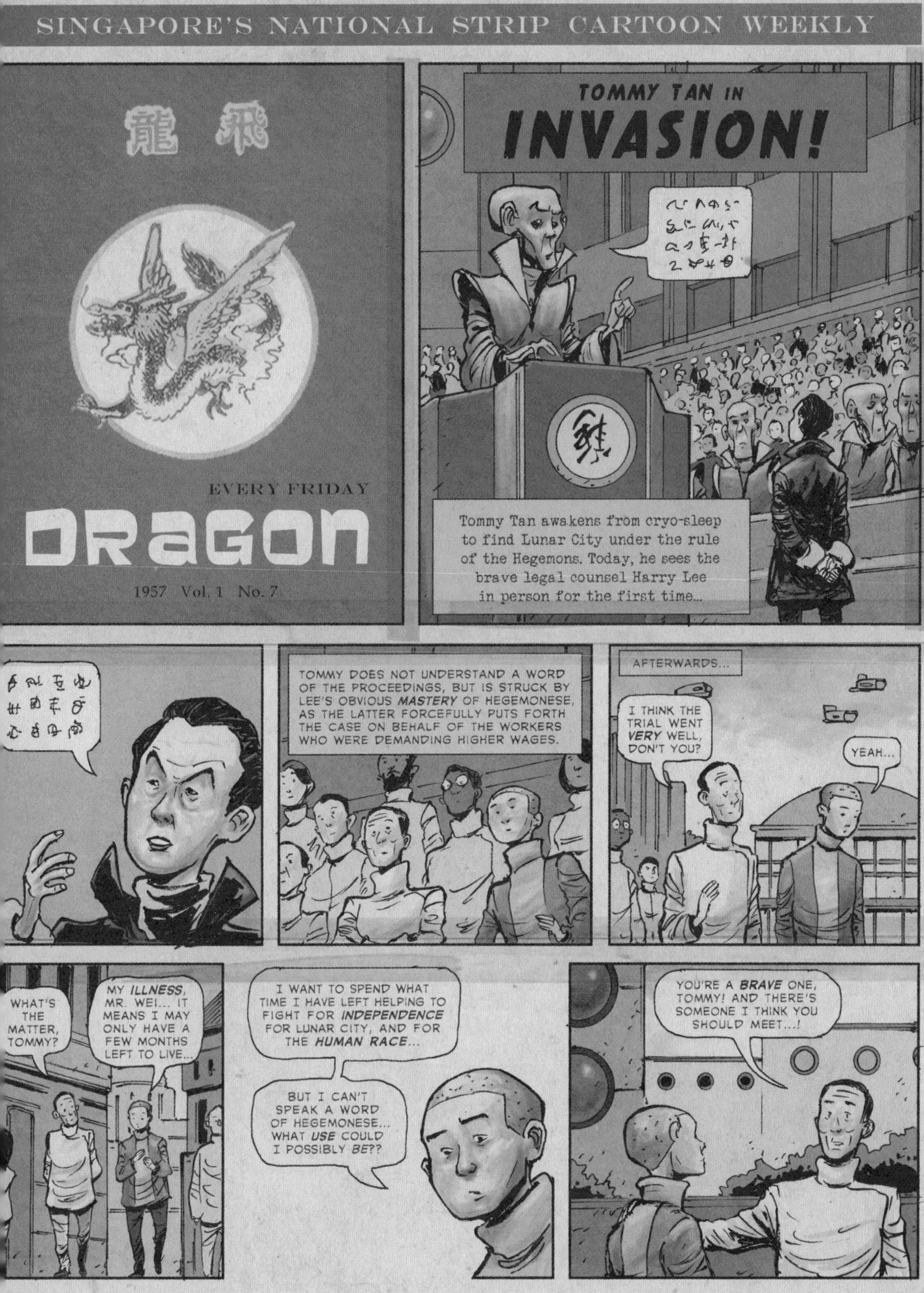
SINGAPORE'S NATIONAL STRIP CARTOON WEEKLY
龍 飛
EVERY FRIDAY
DRAGON
1957 Vol. 1 No. 7
TOMMY TAN IN
INVASION!
Tommy Tan awakens from cryo-sleep to find Lunar City under the rule of the Hegemons. Today, he sees the brave legal counsel Harry Lee in person for the first time...
TOMMY DOES NOT UNDERSTAND A WORD OF THE PROCEEDINGS, BUT IS STRUCK BY LEE'S OBVIOUS MASTERY OF HEGEMONESE, AS THE LATTER FORCEFULLY PUTS FORTH THE CASE ON BEHALF OF THE WORKERS WHO WERE DEMANDING HIGHER WAGES.
AFTERWARDS...
I THINK THE TRIAL WENT VERY WELL, DON'T YOU?
YEAH...
WHAT'S THE MATTER, TOMMY?
MY ILLNESS, MR. WEI... IT MEANS I MAY ONLY HAVE A FEW MONTHS LEFT TO LIVE...
I WANT TO SPEND WHAT TIME I HAVE LEFT HELPING TO FIGHT FOR INDEPENDENCE FOR LUNAR CITY, AND FOR THE HUMAN RACE...
BUT I CAN'T SPEAK A WORD OF HEGEMONESE... WHAT USE COULD I POSSIBLY BE??
YOU'RE A BRAVE ONE, TOMMY! AND THERE'S SOMEONE I THINK YOU SHOULD MEET...!

Above & following **INVASION Vol. 1 No. 7** (1958) | Art by Chan Hock Chye, Words by Bertrand Wong

TOMMY FOLLOWS MR. WEI TO A CRUMBLING BUILDING IN THE OLD QUARTERS OF LUNAR CITY...

THIS IS THE PLACE!

AND MEETS THE INDEPENDENCE FIGHTER *LIM CHIN SIONG!*

MR. WEI HELPS TO EXPLAIN TOMMY'S PREDICAMENT...

...SO THAT'S WHY I'VE BROUGHT HIM TO SEE YOU.

A BOY FROM THE PAST, WANTING TO FIGHT FOR OUR *FUTURE*... EVEN IF H OWN MIGHT BE BRIEF...

IT WOULD BE AN *HONOUR* TO HAVE YOU JOIN US IN OUR STRUGGLE, TOMMY.

BUT... I CAN'T SPEAK HEGEMONESE...

I UNDERSTAND YOUR CONCERNS. MY OWN GRASP OF THEIR LANGUAGE IS POOR TOO...

BUT I AM *LEARNING*, AND SO CAN YOU!

HOW DID THE TRIAL GO, BY THE WAY?

VERY GOOD, I THINK! THAT LEGAL COUNSEL *HARRY LEE* REALLY SEEMS TO KNOW HIS STUFF!

I BELIEVE THE WORKERS WILL RECEIVE THE WAC RAISE THEY SEEM

YES... I, TOO, HAVE HEARD GOOD THINGS ABOUT LEE... HE MAY BE *JUST* THE MAN WE NEED TO HELP FIGHT FOR OUR CAUSE...

SOMEONE WHO BELIEVES IN *JUSTICE* AND *FREEDOM*, AND WHO KNOWS HIS WAY AROUND THE HEGEMONESE LANGUAGE AND ITS LAWS...

PERHAPS WE SHOULD TRY TO MEET UP WITH HIM...

WHAT DO YOU THINK, TOMMY?

I... I THINK THAT WOULD BE *GREAT!*

MEANWHILE, UNBEKNOWNST TO OUR FRIENDS, LEGAL COUNSEL LEE IS ENGAGED IN A *VERY SIMILAR* DISCUSSION WITH HIS COLLEAGUES...

〈IF WE ARE TO LEAD LUNAR CITY TO INDEPENDENCE, WE WILL NEED THE SUPPORT OF THE PEOPLE.〉*

〈I HEAR THERE IS ONE *LIM CHIN SIONG* WHO IS INFLUENTIAL IN THIS REGARD...〉

〈PERHAPS IT IS TIME WE MET UP WITH THIS MAN...〉

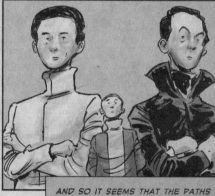

AND SO IT SEEMS THAT THE PATHS THE TWO MEN ARE DESTINED TO CR WILL THEY TURN OUT TO BE FRIEN OR FOES? FIND OUT NEXT WEEK

*EDITOR'S NOTE: TRANSLATED FROM HEGEMONESE

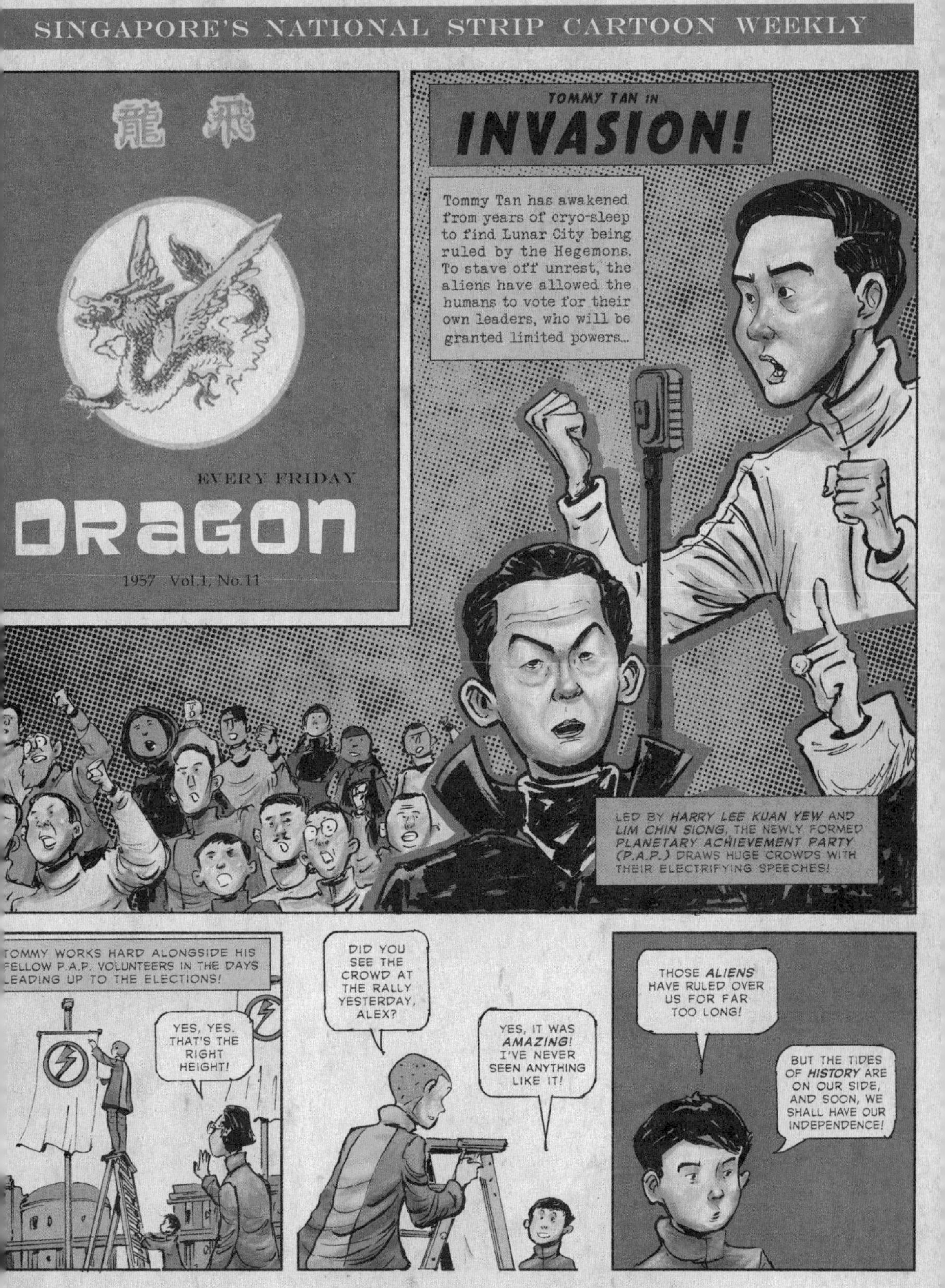
SINGAPORE'S NATIONAL STRIP CARTOON WEEKLY
龍飛
EVERY FRIDAY
DRAGON
1957 Vol.1, No.11
TOMMY TAN IN
INVASION!
Tommy Tan has awakened from years of cryo-sleep to find Lunar City being ruled by the Hegemons. To stave off unrest, the aliens have allowed the humans to vote for their own leaders, who will be granted limited powers...
LED BY HARRY LEE KUAN YEW AND LIM CHIN SIONG, THE NEWLY FORMED PLANETARY ACHIEVEMENT PARTY (P.A.P.) DRAWS HUGE CROWDS WITH THEIR ELECTRIFYING SPEECHES!
TOMMY WORKS HARD ALONGSIDE HIS FELLOW P.A.P. VOLUNTEERS IN THE DAYS LEADING UP TO THE ELECTIONS!
YES, YES. THAT'S THE RIGHT HEIGHT!
DID YOU SEE THE CROWD AT THE RALLY YESTERDAY, ALEX?
YES, IT WAS AMAZING! I'VE NEVER SEEN ANYTHING LIKE IT!
THOSE ALIENS HAVE RULED OVER US FOR FAR TOO LONG!
BUT THE TIDES OF HISTORY ARE ON OUR SIDE, AND SOON, WE SHALL HAVE OUR INDEPENDENCE!

Above **INVASION Vol. 1 No. 11** (1958) | Art by Chan Hock Chye, Words by Bertrand Wong

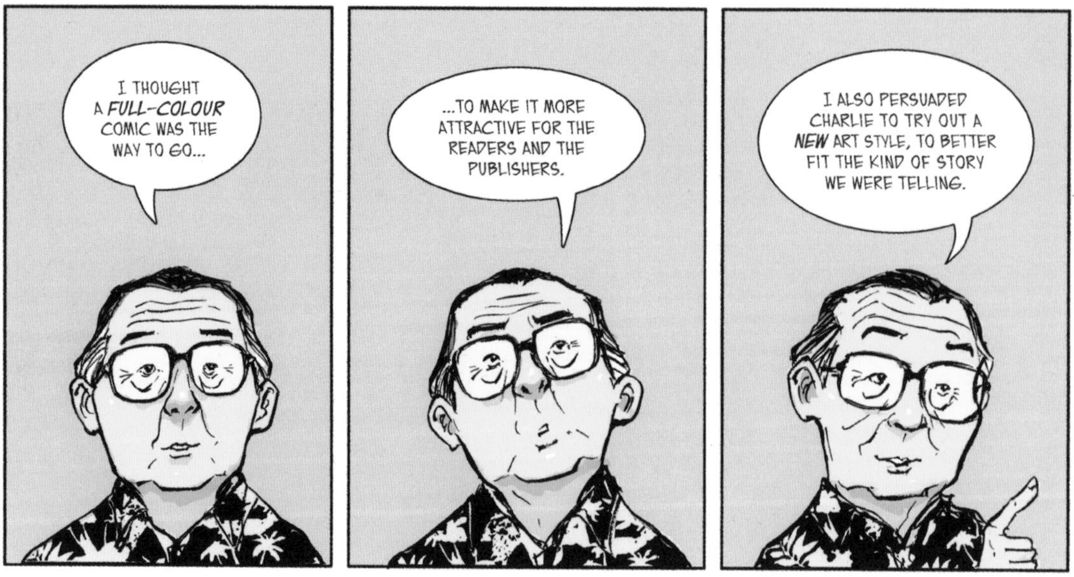
I THOUGHT A *FULL-COLOUR* COMIC WAS THE WAY TO GO...
...TO MAKE IT MORE ATTRACTIVE FOR THE READERS AND THE PUBLISHERS.
I ALSO PERSUADED CHARLIE TO TRY OUT A *NEW* ART STYLE, TO BETTER FIT THE KIND OF STORY WE WERE TELLING.

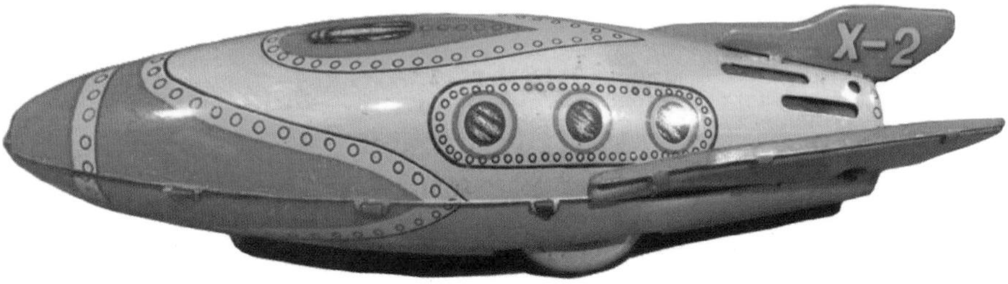
X-2

Above
X-2 Sparkling Friction Rocket Space Ship
1953
Masudaya Modern Toys

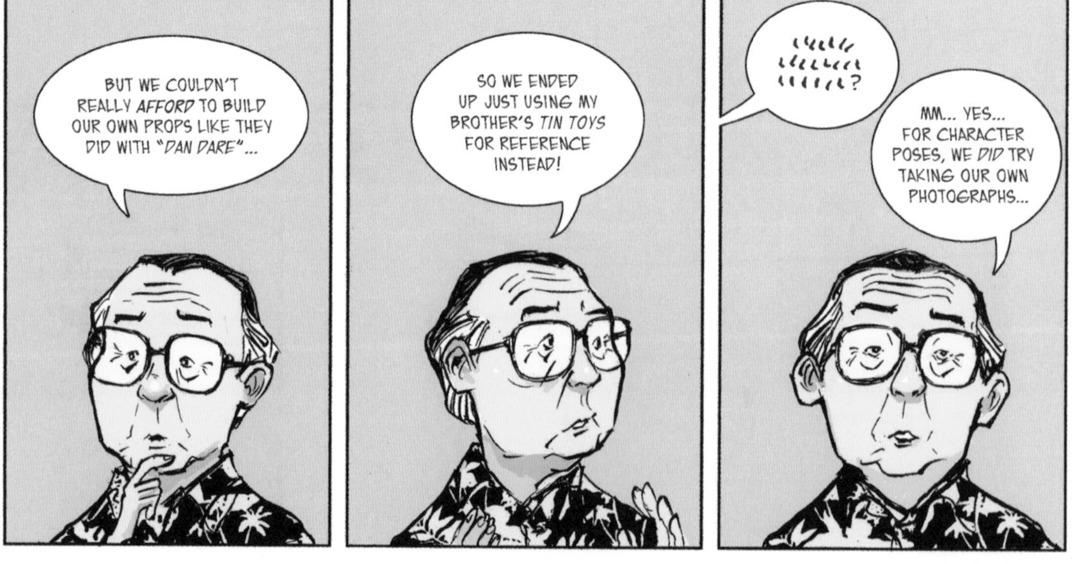
BUT WE COULDN'T REALLY *AFFORD* TO BUILD OUR OWN PROPS LIKE THEY DID WITH "*DAN DARE*"...
SO WE ENDED UP JUST USING MY BROTHER'S *TIN TOYS* FOR REFERENCE INSTEAD!
MM... YES... FOR CHARACTER POSES, WE *DID* TRY TAKING OUR OWN PHOTOGRAPHS...

BUT YOU MUST UNDERSTAND, IT WAS A MUCH MORE *DIFFICULT* PROCESS BACK IN THOSE DAYS...

WE CERTAINLY DIDN'T HAVE THE EASE AND LUXURY OF *DIGITAL* CAMERAS!

YOU WOULD NEVER KNOW HOW YOUR SHOTS WOULD TURN OUT, UNTIL THE *NEGATIVES* HAD ACTUALLY BEEN DEVELOPED!

FOR *PUBLIC* FIGURES, WE HAD TO RELY MAINLY ON NEWSPAPER PHOTOGRAPHS...

THOUGH WE *DID* SEE SOME OF THEM IN PERSON A FEW TIMES, USUALLY DURING ELECTION RALLIES.

LIM CHIN SIONG, JUST THE ONCE, AT THE SINGAPORE BADMINTON HALL...

YOU COULD SEE HE'D PUT IN THE EFFORT TO LEARN MALAY, AS WELL AS ENGLISH.

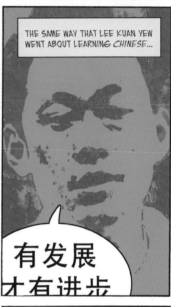

THE SAME WAY THAT LEE KUAN YEW WENT ABOUT LEARNING *CHINESE*...

有发展
才有进步

DID YOU KNOW THAT HE ONCE INTRODUCED LIM CHIN SIONG AS THE *NEXT PRIME MINISTER* OF SINGAPORE?

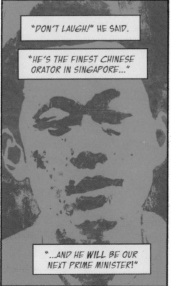

"*DON'T LAUGH!*" HE SAID.

"*HE'S THE FINEST CHINESE ORATOR IN SINGAPORE...*"

"*...AND HE WILL BE OUR NEXT PRIME MINISTER!*"

HEH.

FUNNY HOW THINGS TURNED OUT, I SUPPOSE!

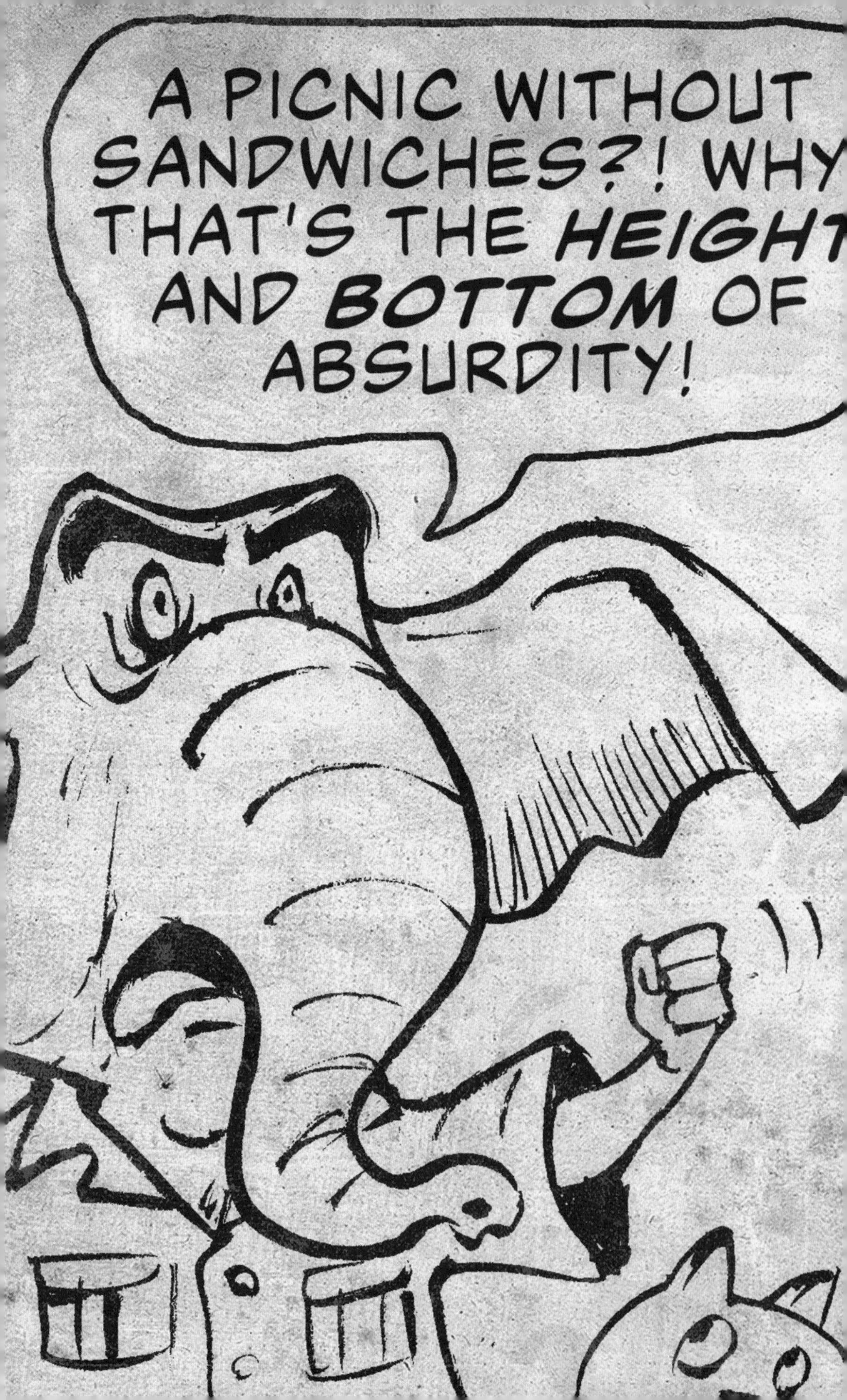
A PICNIC WITHOUT SANDWICHES?! WHY THAT'S THE *HEIGHT* AND *BOTTOM* OF ABSURDITY!

ASIDE FROM HIS WORK WITH BERTRAND ON *"INVASION,"* CHAN ALSO CREATED OTHER COMICS FOR THE PLANNED MOCK-UP OF *DRAGON*.

AMONGST THESE WAS A STRIP CALLED *"BUKIT CHAPALANG."*

BUKIT MEANING "HILL" IN MALAY, AND *CHAPALANG* MEANING "A HODGEPODGE OF DIFFERENT THINGS"!

IT STARTED OUT AS A STRAIGHTFORWARD RETELLING OF A SERIES OF POPULAR *MALAYAN FOLKTALES* KNOWN AS THE *"SANG KANCIL"* STORIES....

MEOW.

...ABOUT A VERY *CLEVER MOUSE-DEER* OR *"KANCIL,"* WHO USES HIS *WITS* TO OUTSMART OTHER ANIMALS AND TO SURVIVE THE PERILS OF THE JUNGLE.

Opposite
BUKIT CHAPALANG
Detail
1958
Chan Hock Chye

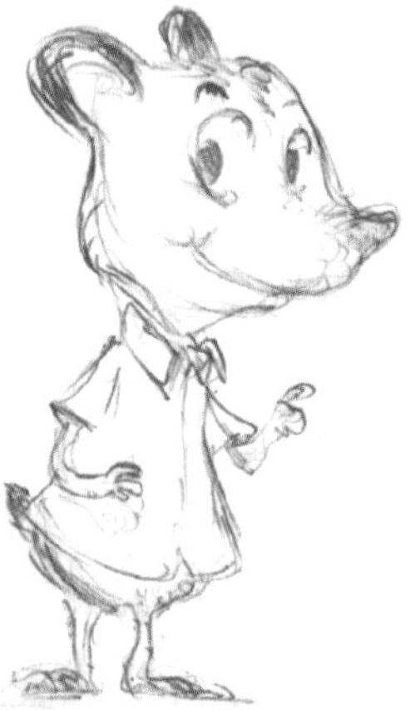

Right
DRAGON Editorial Mock-up
1958
Unpublished

Wong and Chan pasted their own materials over an existing *Eagle* page to create this mock-up. "*Bukit Chapalang*" appears in the bottom tier.

Above & below
SANG KANCIL Sketches
1957
Chan Hock Chye

Opposite
BUKIT CHAPALANG: SANG KANCIL & THE CROCODILE
1958
Chan Hock Chye

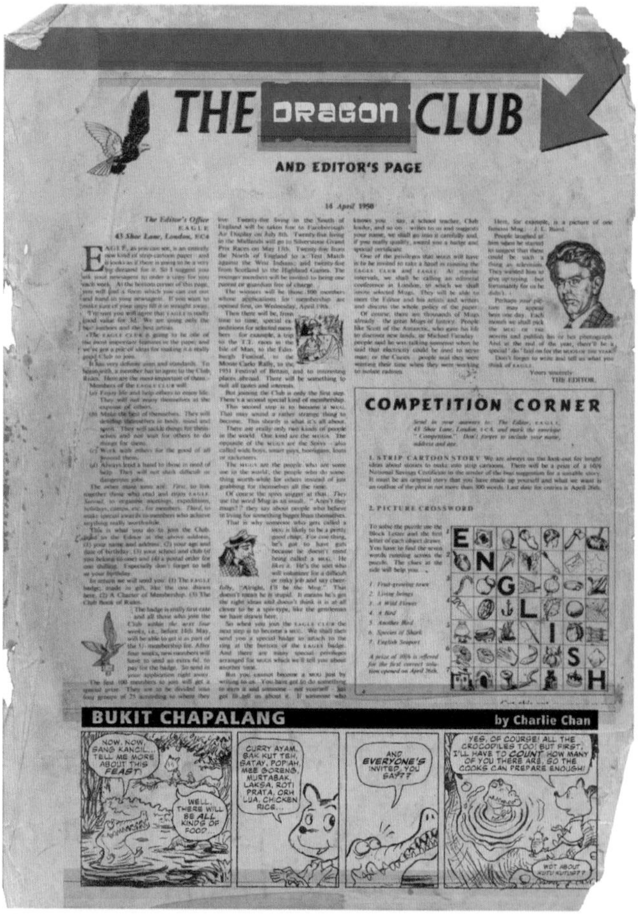
THE DRAGON CLUB
AND EDITOR'S PAGE
COMPETITION CORNER
1. STRIP CARTOON STORY
2. PICTURE CROSSWORD
E N G L I S H
BUKIT CHAPALANG
by Charlie Chan
NOW, NOW, SANG KANCIL... TELL ME MORE ABOUT THIS FEAST!
WELL, THERE WILL BE ALL KINDS OF FOOD...
CURRY AYAM, BAK KUT TEH, SATAY, POPIAH, MEE GORENG, MURTABAK, LAKSA, ROTI PRATA, ORH LUA, CHICKEN RICE...
AND EVERYONE'S INVITED, YOU SAY??
YES, OF COURSE! ALL THE CROCODILES TOO! BUT FIRST, I'LL HAVE TO COUNT HOW MANY OF YOU THERE ARE, SO THE COOKS CAN PREPARE ENOUGH!

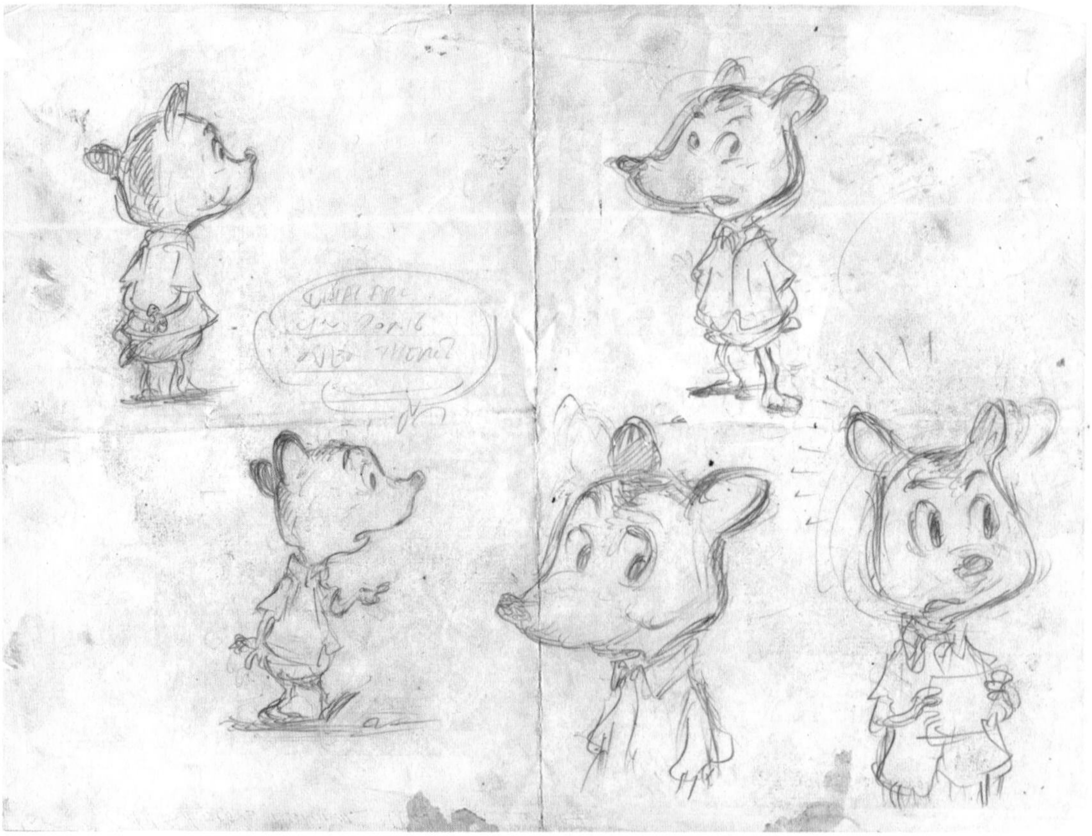

BUKIT CHAPALANG by Charlie Chan

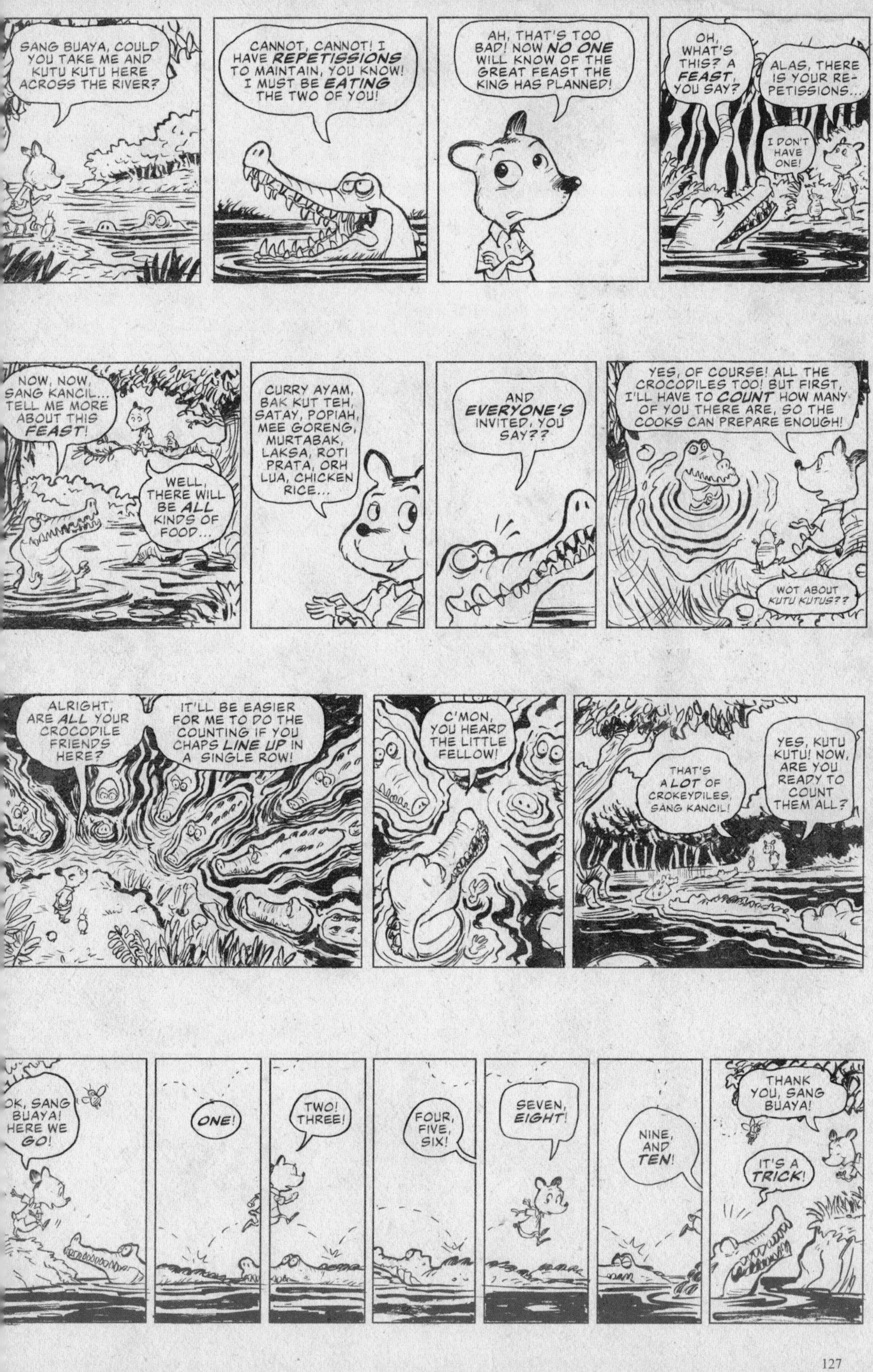
SANG BUAYA, COULD YOU TAKE ME AND KUTU KUTU HERE ACROSS THE RIVER?
CANNOT, CANNOT! I HAVE REPETISSIONS TO MAINTAIN, YOU KNOW! I MUST BE EATING THE TWO OF YOU!
AH, THAT'S TOO BAD! NOW NO ONE WILL KNOW OF THE GREAT FEAST THE KING HAS PLANNED!
OH, WHAT'S THIS? A FEAST, YOU SAY?
ALAS, THERE IS YOUR REPETISSIONS...
I DON'T HAVE ONE!
NOW, NOW, SANG KANCIL... TELL ME MORE ABOUT THIS FEAST!
WELL, THERE WILL BE ALL KINDS OF FOOD...
CURRY AYAM, BAK KUT TEH, SATAY, POPIAH, MEE GORENG, MURTABAK, LAKSA, ROTI PRATA, ORH LUA, CHICKEN RICE...
AND EVERYONE'S INVITED, YOU SAY??
YES, OF COURSE! ALL THE CROCODILES TOO! BUT FIRST, I'LL HAVE TO COUNT HOW MANY OF YOU THERE ARE, SO THE COOKS CAN PREPARE ENOUGH!
WOT ABOUT KUTU KUTUS??
ALRIGHT, ARE ALL YOUR CROCODILE FRIENDS HERE?
IT'LL BE EASIER FOR ME TO DO THE COUNTING IF YOU CHAPS LINE UP IN A SINGLE ROW!
C'MON, YOU HEARD THE LITTLE FELLOW!
THAT'S A LOT OF CROKEYDILES, SANG KANCIL!
YES, KUTU KUTU! NOW, ARE YOU READY TO COUNT THEM ALL?
OK, SANG BUAYA! HERE WE GO!
ONE!
TWO! THREE!
FOUR, FIVE, SIX!
SEVEN, EIGHT!
NINE, AND TEN!
THANK YOU, SANG BUAYA!
IT'S A TRICK!

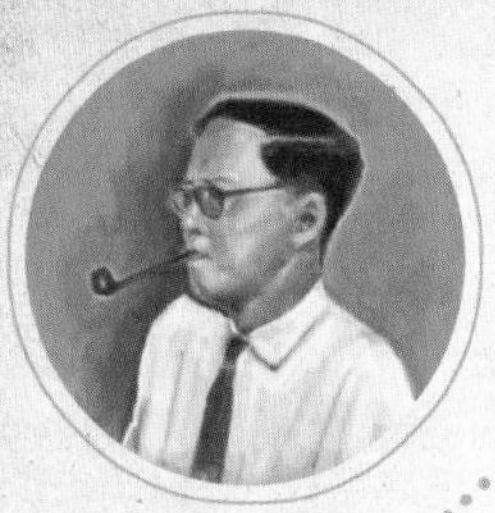

LIM YEW HOCK
Kingfisher
(Sang Pekaka)

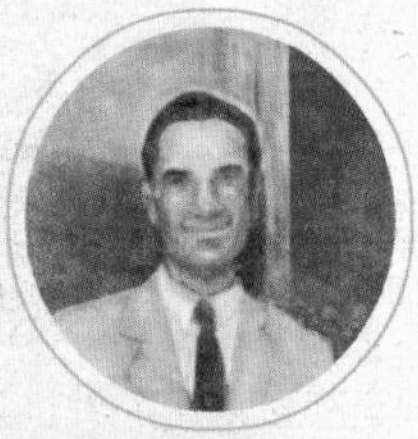

SIR WILLIAM GOODE
Lion (Sir Lion)

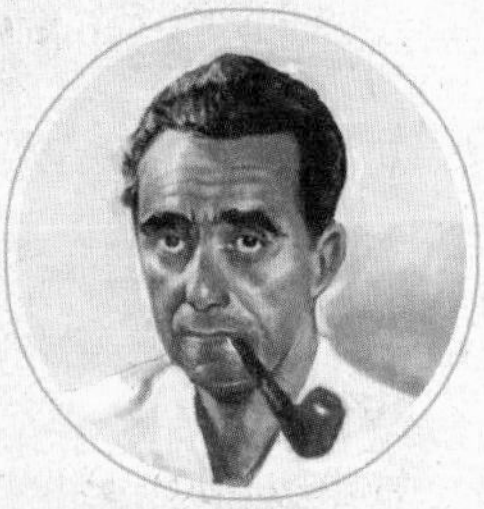

DAVID MARSHALL
Elephant (Sang Gajah)

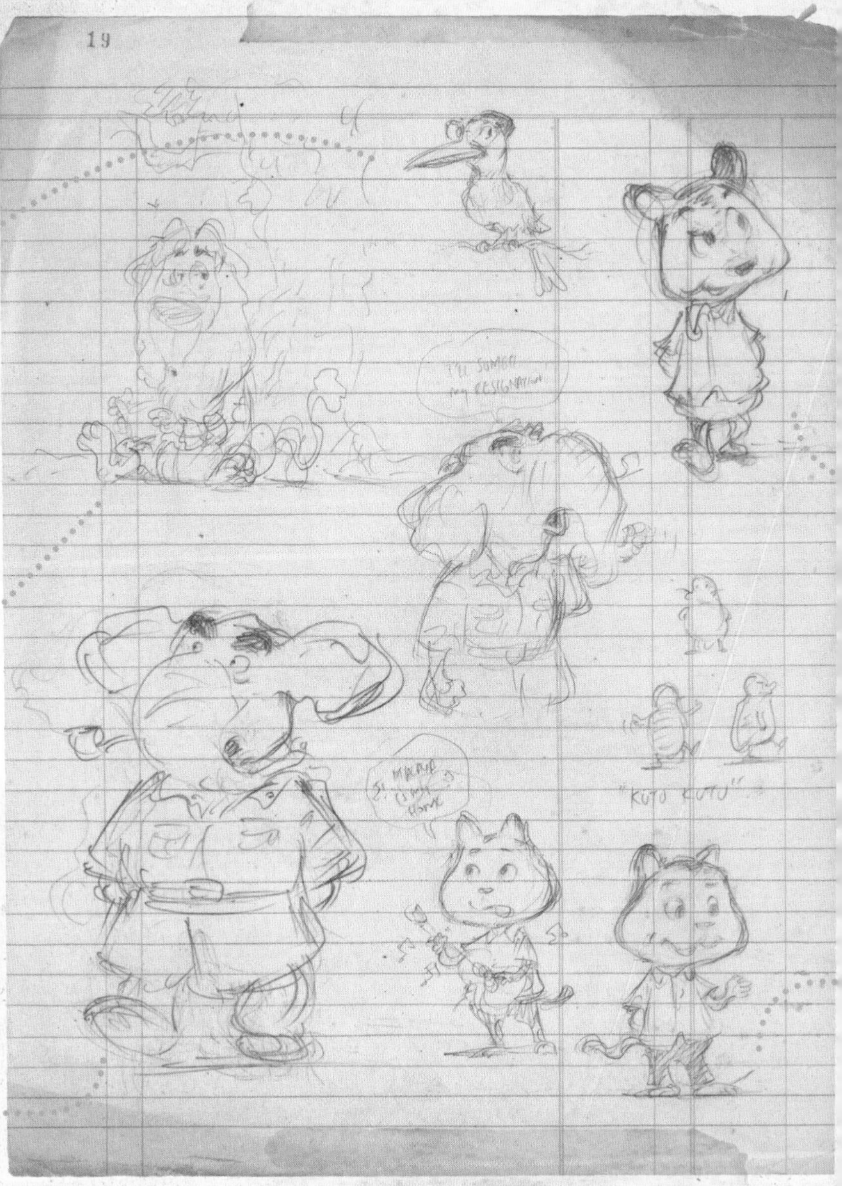
19
"KUTU KUTU"

Above **CHARACTER SKETCHES & COUNTERPARTS** (1958) | Chan Hock Chye

Below **BUKIT CHAPALANG: THE PICNIC** (1958) | Chan Hock Chye | Unpublished

Sang Gajah (David Marshall) begins his tenure as Chief Minister, forcing concessions from the British by threatening to resign.

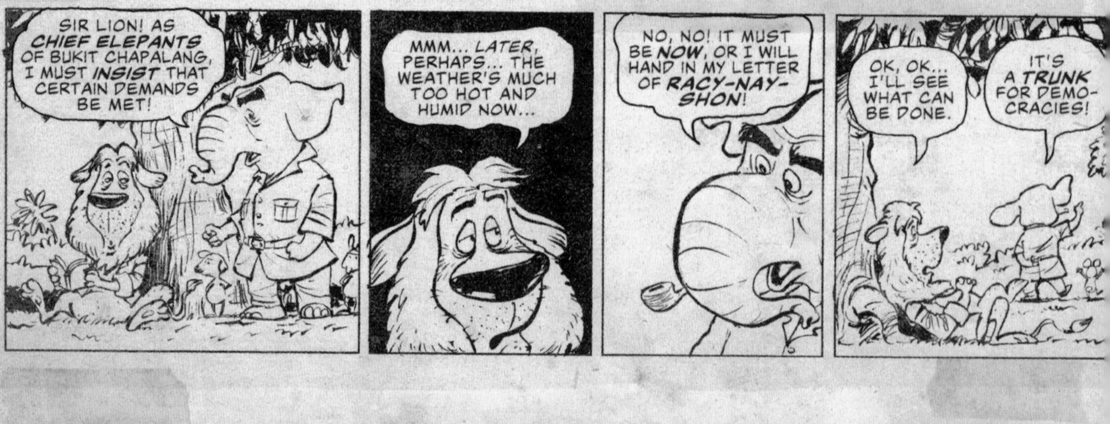
SIR LION! AS CHIEF ELEPANTS OF BUKIT CHAPALANG, I MUST INSIST THAT CERTAIN DEMANDS BE MET!
MMM... LATER, PERHAPS... THE WEATHER'S MUCH TOO HOT AND HUMID NOW...
NO, NO! IT MUST BE NOW, OR I WILL HAND IN MY LETTER OF RACY-NAY-SHON!
OK, OK... I'LL SEE WHAT CAN BE DONE.
IT'S A TRUNK FOR DEMO-CRACIES!

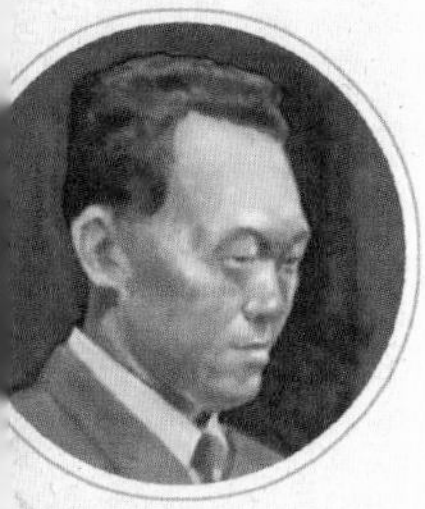

LEE KUAN YEW
Mouse-deer
(Sang Kancil)

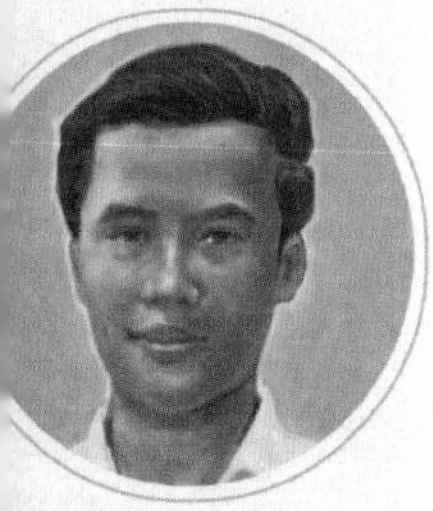

LIM CHIN SIONG
Cat (Sang Kucing)

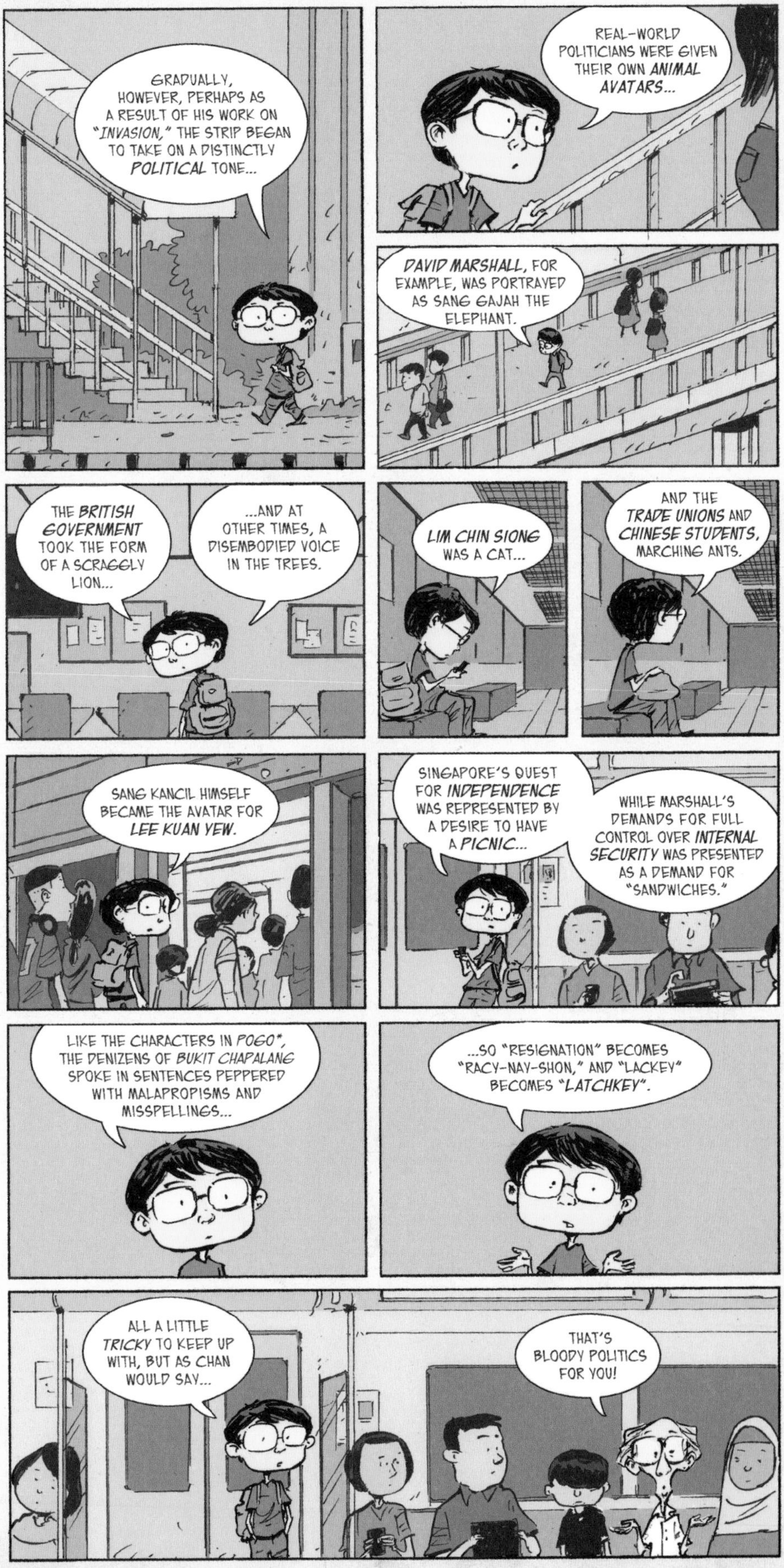
GRADUALLY, HOWEVER, PERHAPS AS A RESULT OF HIS WORK ON "INVASION," THE STRIP BEGAN TO TAKE ON A DISTINCTLY POLITICAL TONE...
REAL-WORLD POLITICIANS WERE GIVEN THEIR OWN ANIMAL AVATARS...
DAVID MARSHALL, FOR EXAMPLE, WAS PORTRAYED AS SANG GAJAH THE ELEPHANT.
THE BRITISH GOVERNMENT TOOK THE FORM OF A SCRAGGLY LION...
...AND AT OTHER TIMES, A DISEMBODIED VOICE IN THE TREES.
LIM CHIN SIONG WAS A CAT...
AND THE TRADE UNIONS AND CHINESE STUDENTS, MARCHING ANTS.
SANG KANCIL HIMSELF BECAME THE AVATAR FOR LEE KUAN YEW.
SINGAPORE'S QUEST FOR INDEPENDENCE WAS REPRESENTED BY A DESIRE TO HAVE A PICNIC...
WHILE MARSHALL'S DEMANDS FOR FULL CONTROL OVER INTERNAL SECURITY WAS PRESENTED AS A DEMAND FOR "SANDWICHES."
LIKE THE CHARACTERS IN POGO*, THE DENIZENS OF BUKIT CHAPALANG SPOKE IN SENTENCES PEPPERED WITH MALAPROPISMS AND MISSPELLINGS...
...SO "RESIGNATION" BECOMES "RACY-NAY-SHON," AND "LACKEY" BECOMES "LATCHKEY".
ALL A LITTLE TRICKY TO KEEP UP WITH, BUT AS CHAN WOULD SAY...
THAT'S BLOODY POLITICS FOR YOU!

*AN AMERICAN COMIC STRIP BY WALT KELLY

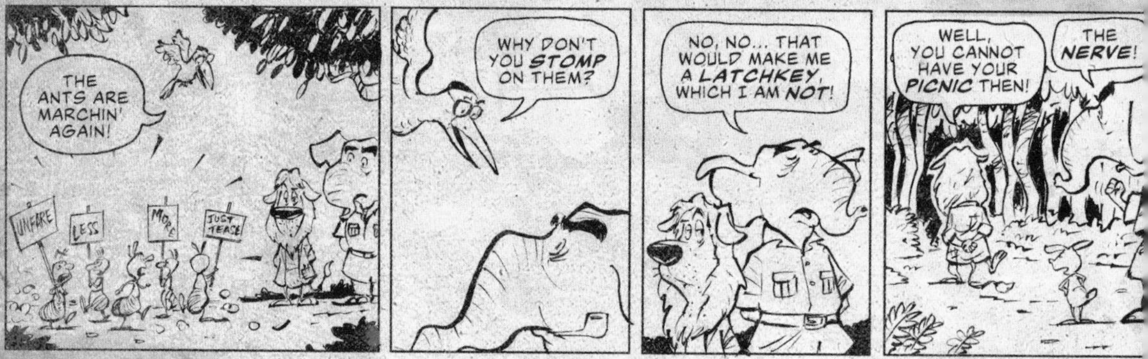
THE ANTS ARE MARCHIN' AGAIN!
UNFARE
LESS
MORE
JUST TEASE
WHY DON'T YOU STOMP ON THEM?
NO, NO... THAT WOULD MAKE ME A LATCHKEY, WHICH I AM NOT!
WELL, YOU CANNOT HAVE YOUR PICNIC THEN!
THE NERVE!

David Marshall's reluctance to use force to curb trade union and student protests left the British with little confidence that economic and political stability would be maintained if independence was to be granted to Singapore.

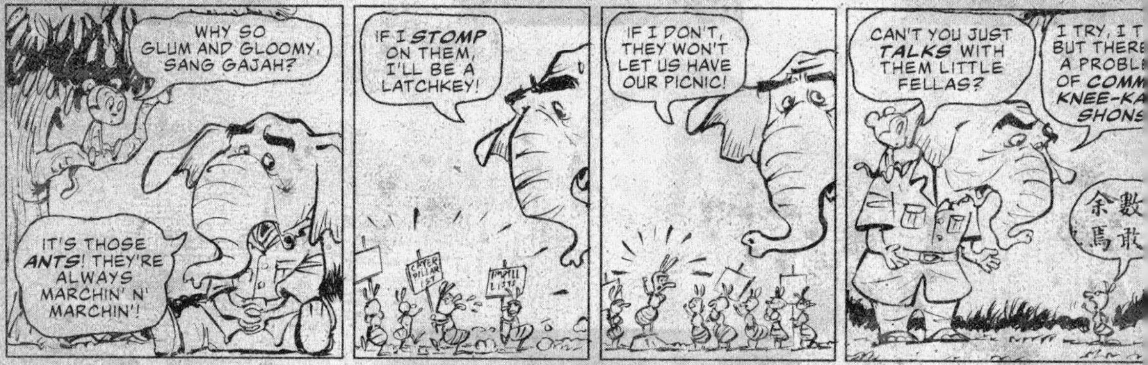
WHY SO GLUM AND GLOOMY, SANG GAJAH?
IT'S THOSE ANTS! THEY'RE ALWAYS MARCHIN' N' MARCHIN'!
IF I STOMP ON THEM, I'LL BE A LATCHKEY!
CATER PILLAR IST
IF I DON'T, THEY WON'T LET US HAVE OUR PICNIC!
CAN'T YOU JUST TALKS WITH THEM LITTLE FELLAS?
I TRY, I T BUT THERE A PROBL OF COMM KNEE-KA SHONS

Marshall was caught in a bind. Taking tougher measures might help to assuage the colonial authorities, but he would also be accused of being a stooge and lackey.

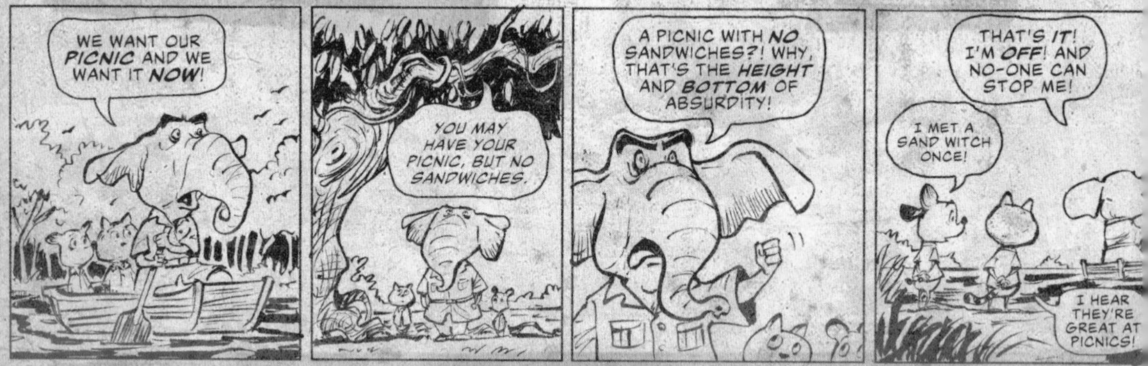
WE WANT OUR PICNIC AND WE WANT IT NOW!
YOU MAY HAVE YOUR PICNIC, BUT NO SANDWICHES.
A PICNIC WITH NO SANDWICHES?! WHY, THAT'S THE HEIGHT AND BOTTOM OF ABSURDITY!
THAT'S IT! I'M OFF! AND NO-ONE CAN STOP ME!
I MET A SAND WITCH ONCE!
I HEAR THEY'RE GREAT AT PICNICS!

Regardless, Marshall continued to press for immediate and complete internal self-government, and once again threatened to resign as Chief Minister unless his demands were met. But the British remained unwilling to relinquish their control over matters of internal security, and would not be swayed by his threats this time.

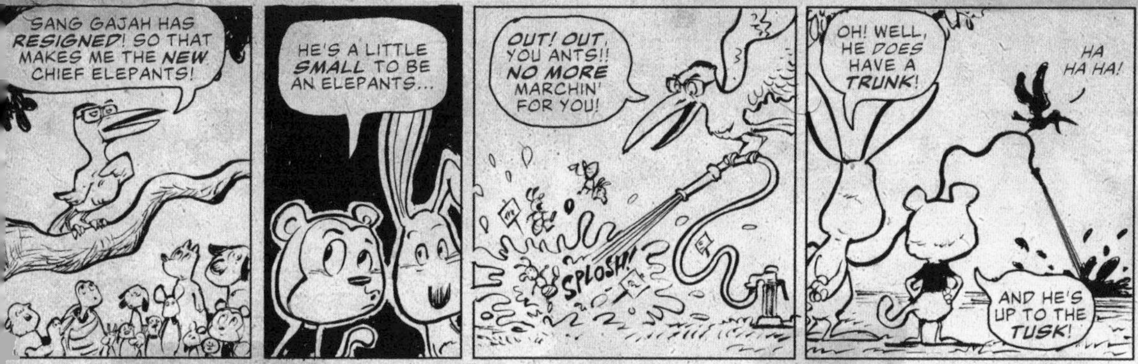
SANG GAJAH HAS RESIGNED! SO THAT MAKES ME THE NEW CHIEF ELEPANTS!
HE'S A LITTLE SMALL TO BE AN ELEPANTS...
OUT! OUT, YOU ANTS!! NO MORE MARCHIN' FOR YOU!
SPLOSH!
OH! WELL, HE DOES HAVE A TRUNK!
HA HA HA!
AND HE'S UP TO THE TUSK!

Taking over as the new Chief Minister was Lim Yew Hock, who had fewer reservations about using tear gas and water cannons to put down the student and worker protests. He would also go on to order the arrest of Lim Chin Siong and other leaders of the radical left in October 1956.

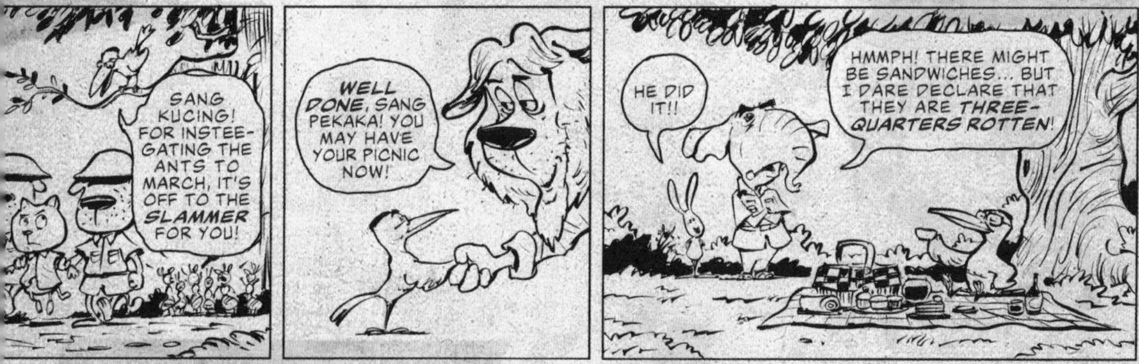
SANG KUCING! FOR INSTEE-GATING THE ANTS TO MARCH, IT'S OFF TO THE SLAMMER FOR YOU!
WELL DONE, SANG PEKAKA! YOU MAY HAVE YOUR PICNIC NOW!
HE DID IT!!
HMMPH! THERE MIGHT BE SANDWICHES... BUT I DARE DECLARE THAT THEY ARE THREE-QUARTERS ROTTEN!

The new Chief Minister's willingness to take action gave the British enough peace of mind to grant Singapore internal self-rule. The issue of internal security was resolved by the formation of a council, whereby a representative from the Federation of Malaya, rather than Britain, had the casting vote. This had the advantage of removing the appearance of colonial control, whilst maintaining powers in the hands of conservative forces. It was a deal Marshall would describe as granting "*tiga suku busuk merdeka*," Malay for "three-quarters rotten independence."

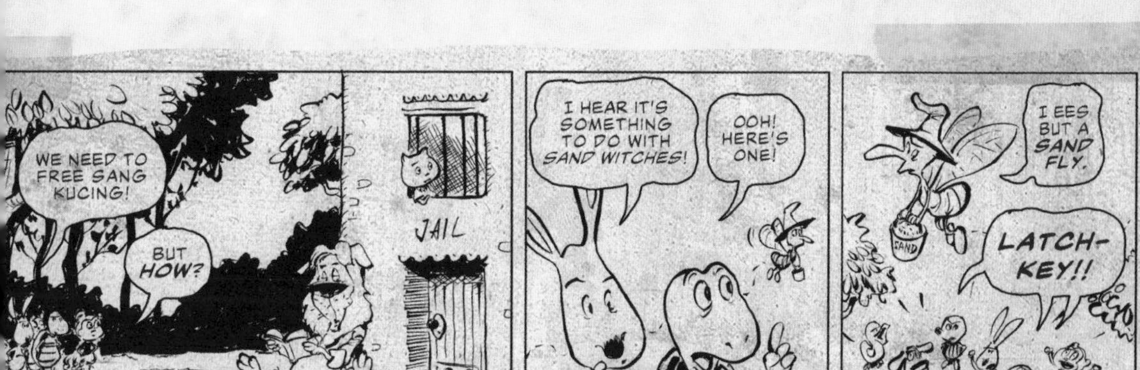
WE NEED TO FREE SANG KUCING!
BUT HOW?
JAIL
I HEAR IT'S SOMETHING TO DO WITH SAND WITCHES!
OOH! HERE'S ONE!
I EES BUT A SAND FLY.
SAND
LATCH-KEY!!

Meanwhile, Lim Chin Siong and the other political detainees languished in prison. Their continued incarceration highlighted the significance of having internal security powers, which granted the right to arrest and detain individuals indefinitely without trial.

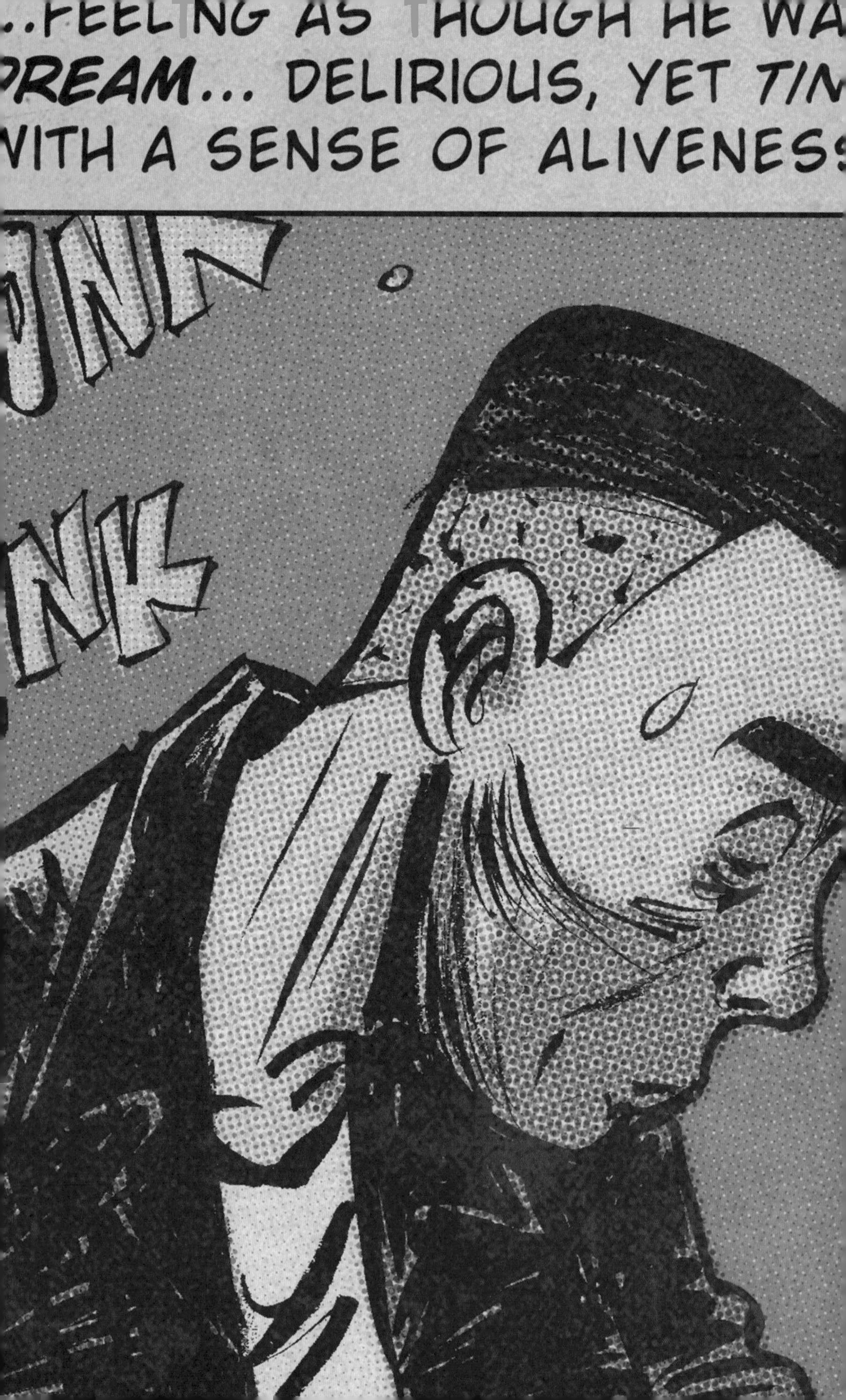
..FEELING AS THOUGH HE WA
DREAM... DELIRIOUS, YET TIN
WITH A SENSE OF ALIVENESS

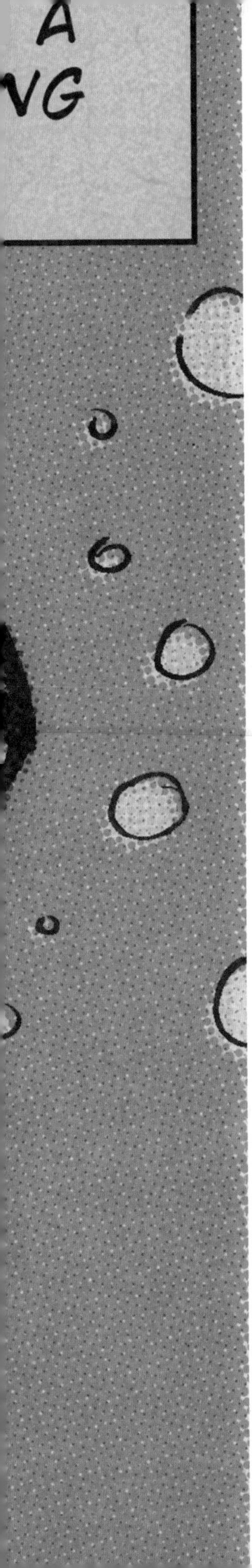

Chapter Five

SUPERHERO

时势造英雄

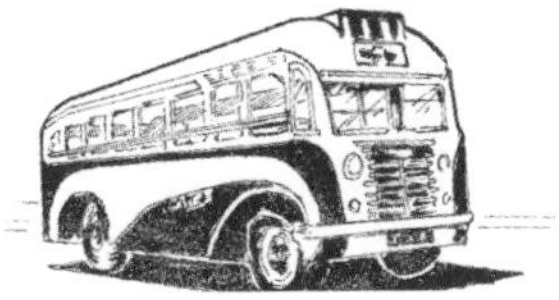

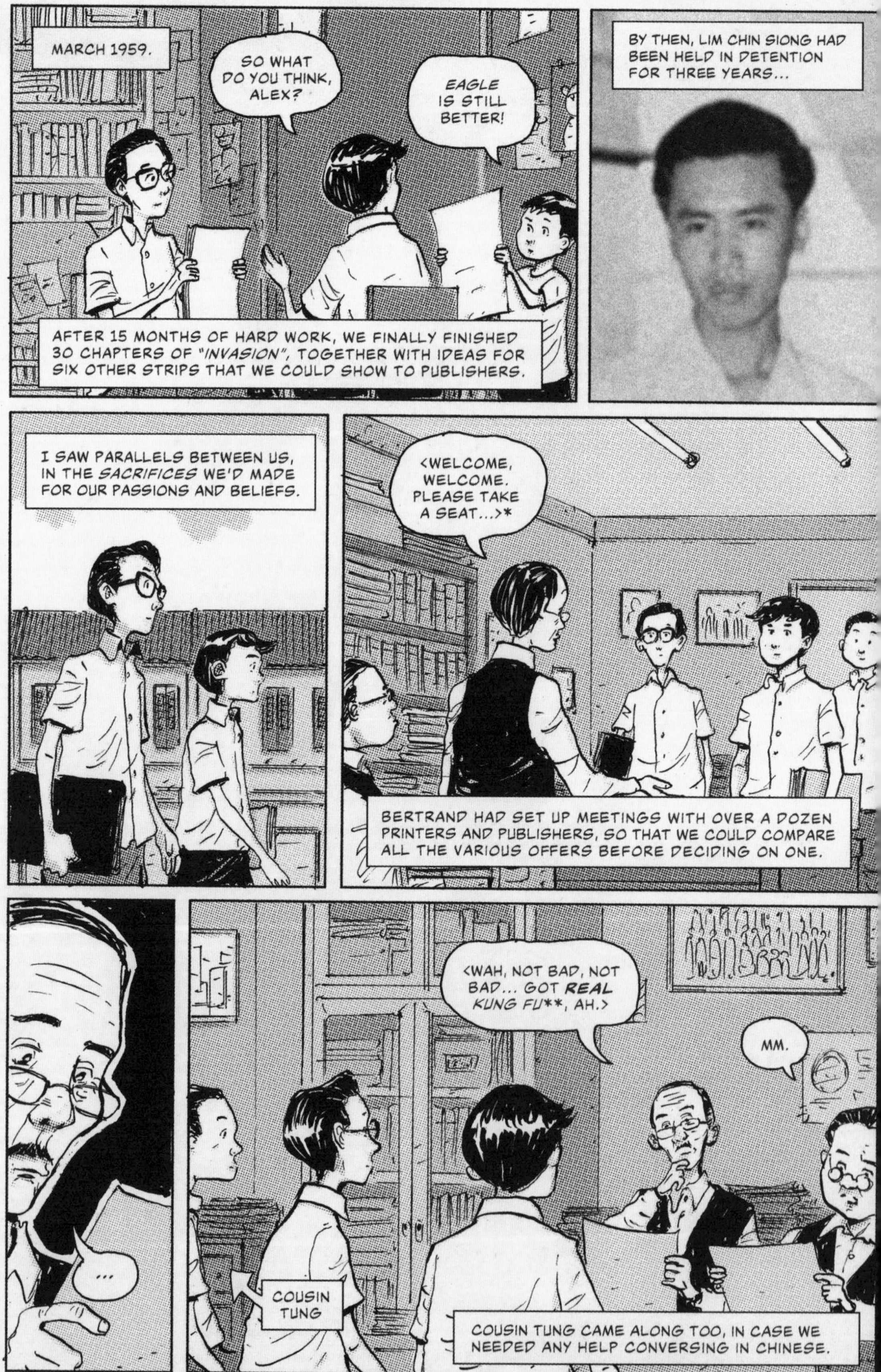
MARCH 1959.
SO WHAT DO YOU THINK, ALEX?
EAGLE IS STILL BETTER!
AFTER 15 MONTHS OF HARD WORK, WE FINALLY FINISHED 30 CHAPTERS OF "*INVASION*", TOGETHER WITH IDEAS FOR SIX OTHER STRIPS THAT WE COULD SHOW TO PUBLISHERS.
BY THEN, LIM CHIN SIONG HAD BEEN HELD IN DETENTION FOR THREE YEARS...
I SAW PARALLELS BETWEEN US, IN THE *SACRIFICES* WE'D MADE FOR OUR PASSIONS AND BELIEFS.
<WELCOME, WELCOME. PLEASE TAKE A SEAT...>*
BERTRAND HAD SET UP MEETINGS WITH OVER A DOZEN PRINTERS AND PUBLISHERS, SO THAT WE COULD COMPARE ALL THE VARIOUS OFFERS BEFORE DECIDING ON ONE.
...
<WAH, NOT BAD, NOT BAD... GOT ***REAL*** *KUNG FU***, AH.>
MM.
COUSIN TUNG
COUSIN TUNG CAME ALONG TOO, IN CASE WE NEEDED ANY HELP CONVERSING IN CHINESE.

*IN HOKKIEN.

**AN EXPRESSION CONVEYING ADMIRATION FOR A DISPLAY OF GENUINE SKILL.

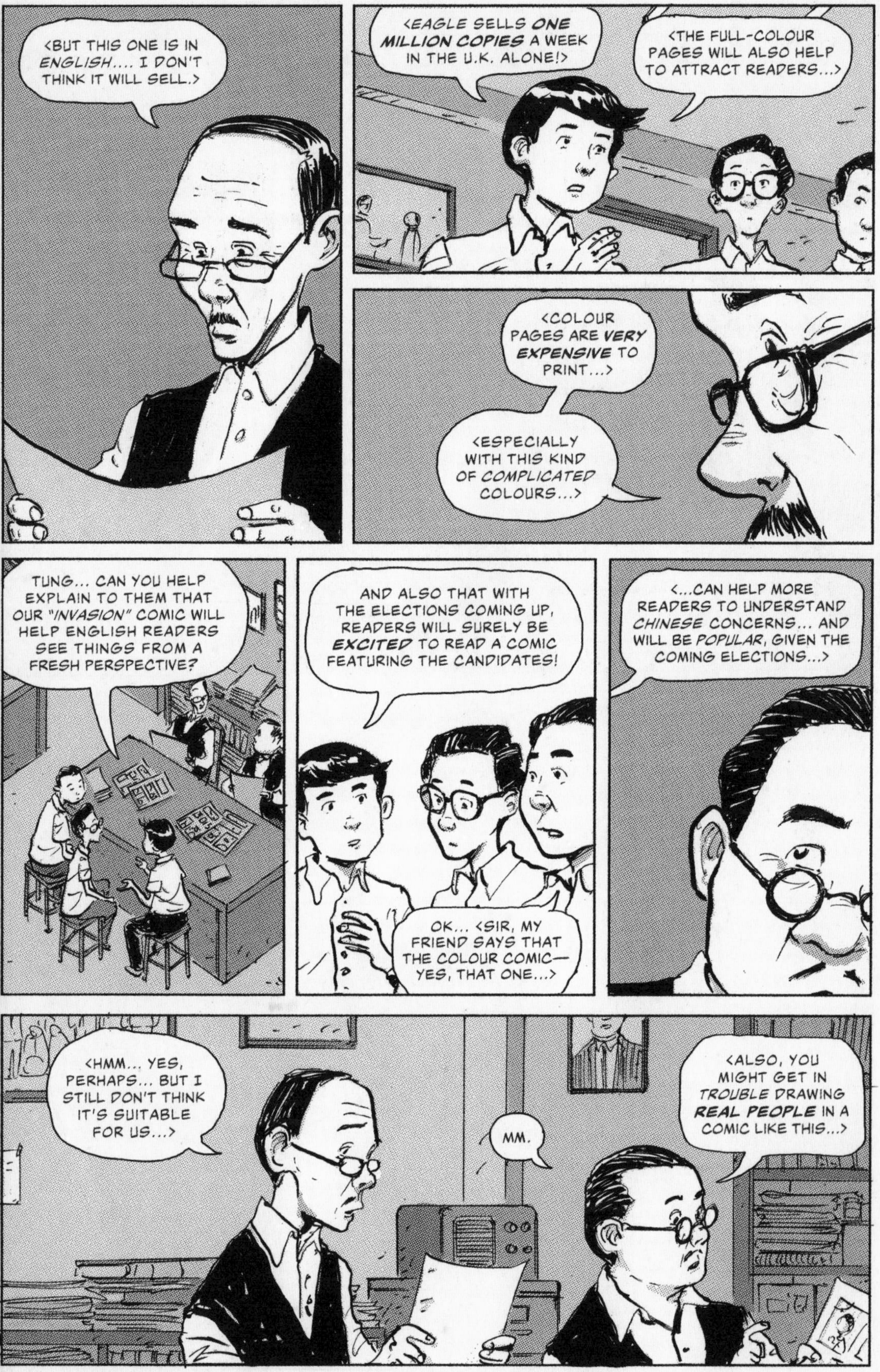
<BUT THIS ONE IS IN ENGLISH.... I DON'T THINK IT WILL SELL.>
<EAGLE SELLS ONE MILLION COPIES A WEEK IN THE U.K. ALONE!>
<THE FULL-COLOUR PAGES WILL ALSO HELP TO ATTRACT READERS...>
<COLOUR PAGES ARE VERY EXPENSIVE TO PRINT...>
<ESPECIALLY WITH THIS KIND OF COMPLICATED COLOURS...>
TUNG... CAN YOU HELP EXPLAIN TO THEM THAT OUR "INVASION" COMIC WILL HELP ENGLISH READERS SEE THINGS FROM A FRESH PERSPECTIVE?
AND ALSO THAT WITH THE ELECTIONS COMING UP, READERS WILL SURELY BE EXCITED TO READ A COMIC FEATURING THE CANDIDATES!
OK... <SIR, MY FRIEND SAYS THAT THE COLOUR COMIC— YES, THAT ONE...>
<...CAN HELP MORE READERS TO UNDERSTAND CHINESE CONCERNS... AND WILL BE POPULAR, GIVEN THE COMING ELECTIONS...>
<HMM... YES, PERHAPS... BUT I STILL DON'T THINK IT'S SUITABLE FOR US...>
MM.
<ALSO, YOU MIGHT GET IN TROUBLE DRAWING REAL PEOPLE IN A COMIC LIKE THIS...>

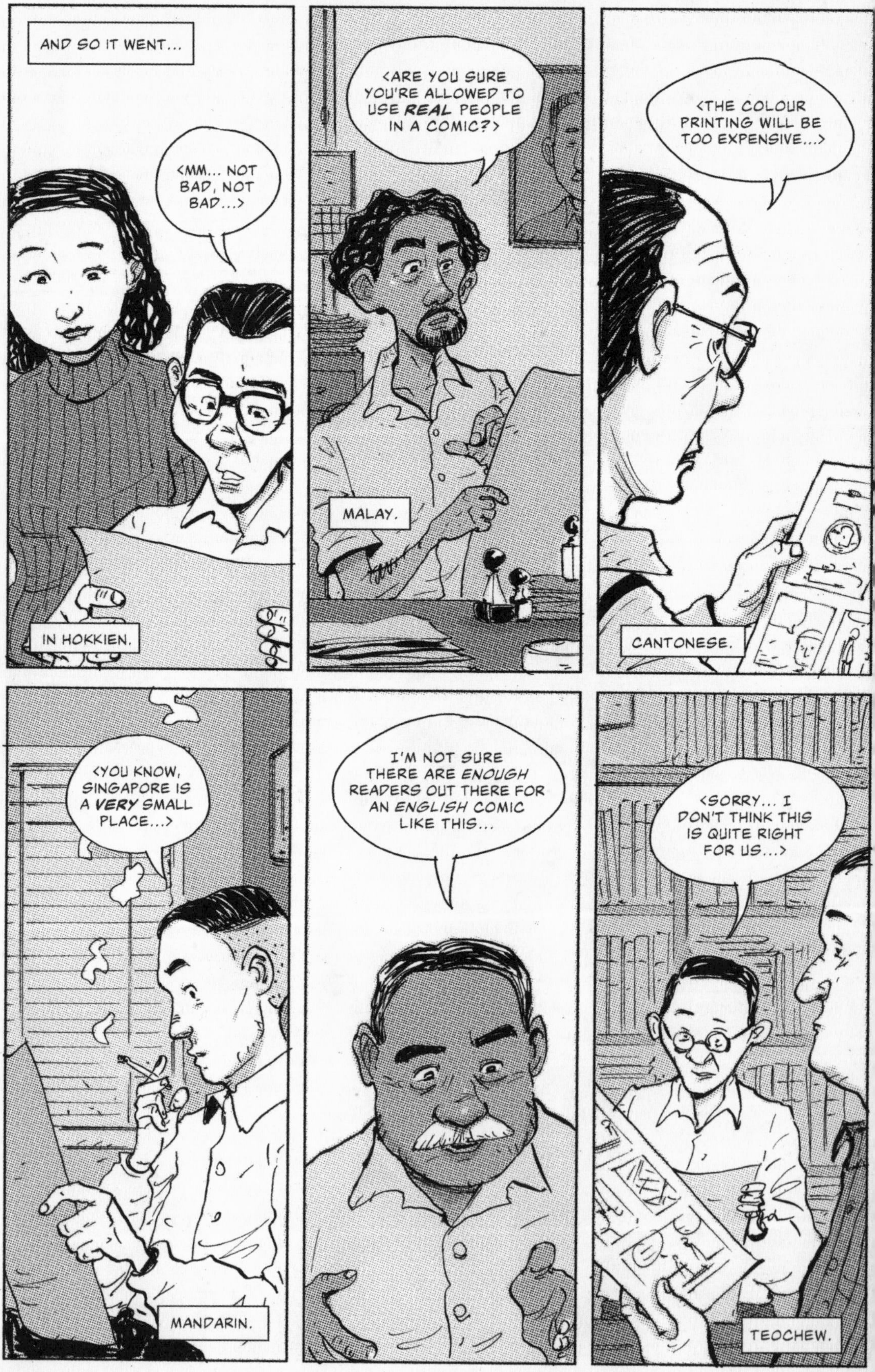
AND SO IT WENT...
<MM... NOT BAD, NOT BAD...>
IN HOKKIEN.
<ARE YOU SURE YOU'RE ALLOWED TO USE REAL PEOPLE IN A COMIC?>
MALAY.
<THE COLOUR PRINTING WILL BE TOO EXPENSIVE...>
CANTONESE.
<YOU KNOW, SINGAPORE IS A VERY SMALL PLACE...>
MANDARIN.
I'M NOT SURE THERE ARE ENOUGH READERS OUT THERE FOR AN ENGLISH COMIC LIKE THIS...
<SORRY... I DON'T THINK THIS IS QUITE RIGHT FOR US...>
TEOCHEW.

AND SO IT WENT.

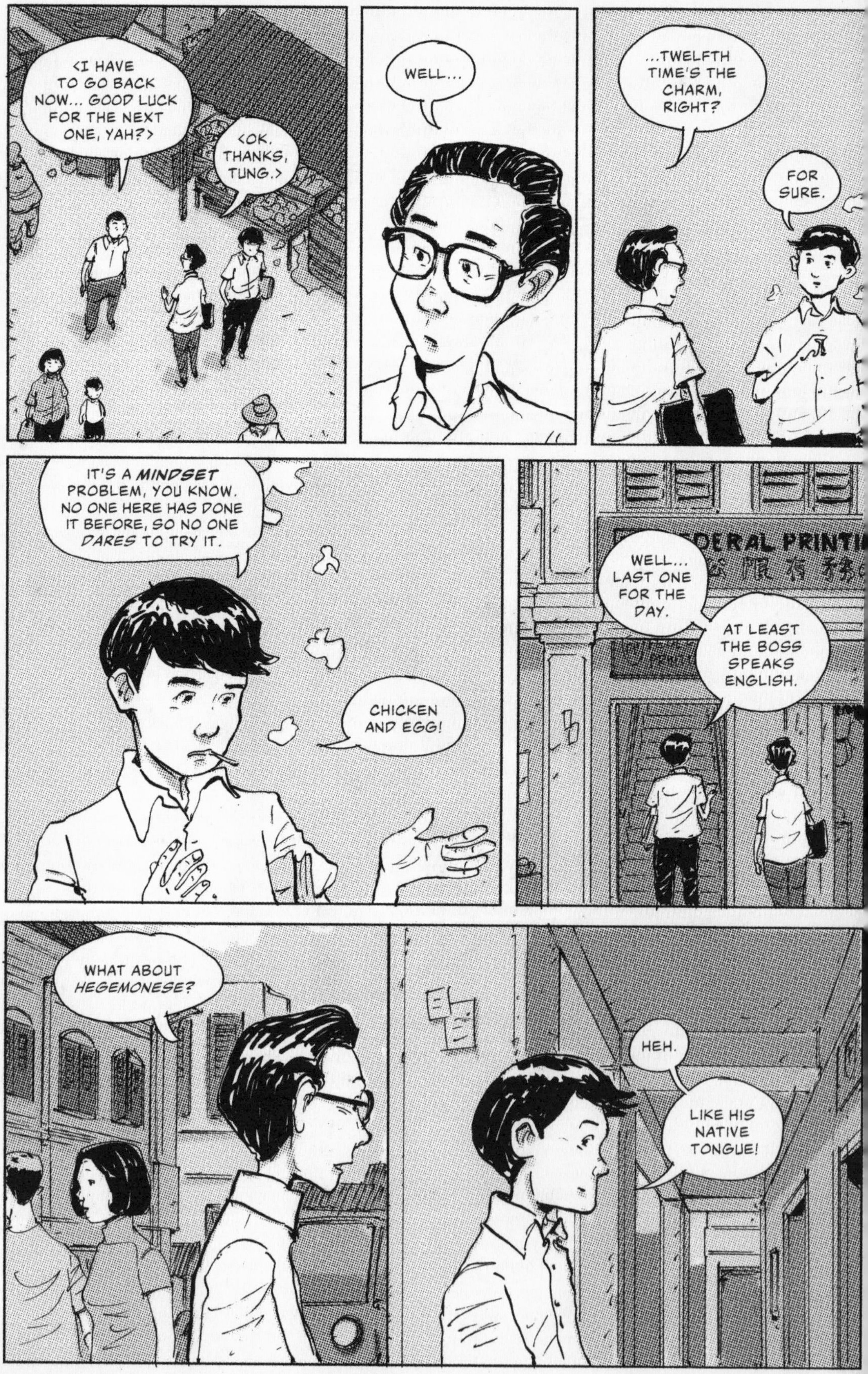
<I HAVE TO GO BACK NOW... GOOD LUCK FOR THE NEXT ONE, YAH?>
<OK. THANKS, TUNG.>
WELL...
...TWELFTH TIME'S THE CHARM, RIGHT?
FOR SURE.
IT'S A *MINDSET* PROBLEM, YOU KNOW. NO ONE HERE HAS DONE IT BEFORE, SO NO ONE *DARES* TO TRY IT.
CHICKEN AND EGG!
WELL... LAST ONE FOR THE DAY.
AT LEAST THE BOSS SPEAKS ENGLISH.
WHAT ABOUT *HEGEMONESE?*
HEH.
LIKE HIS NATIVE TONGUE!

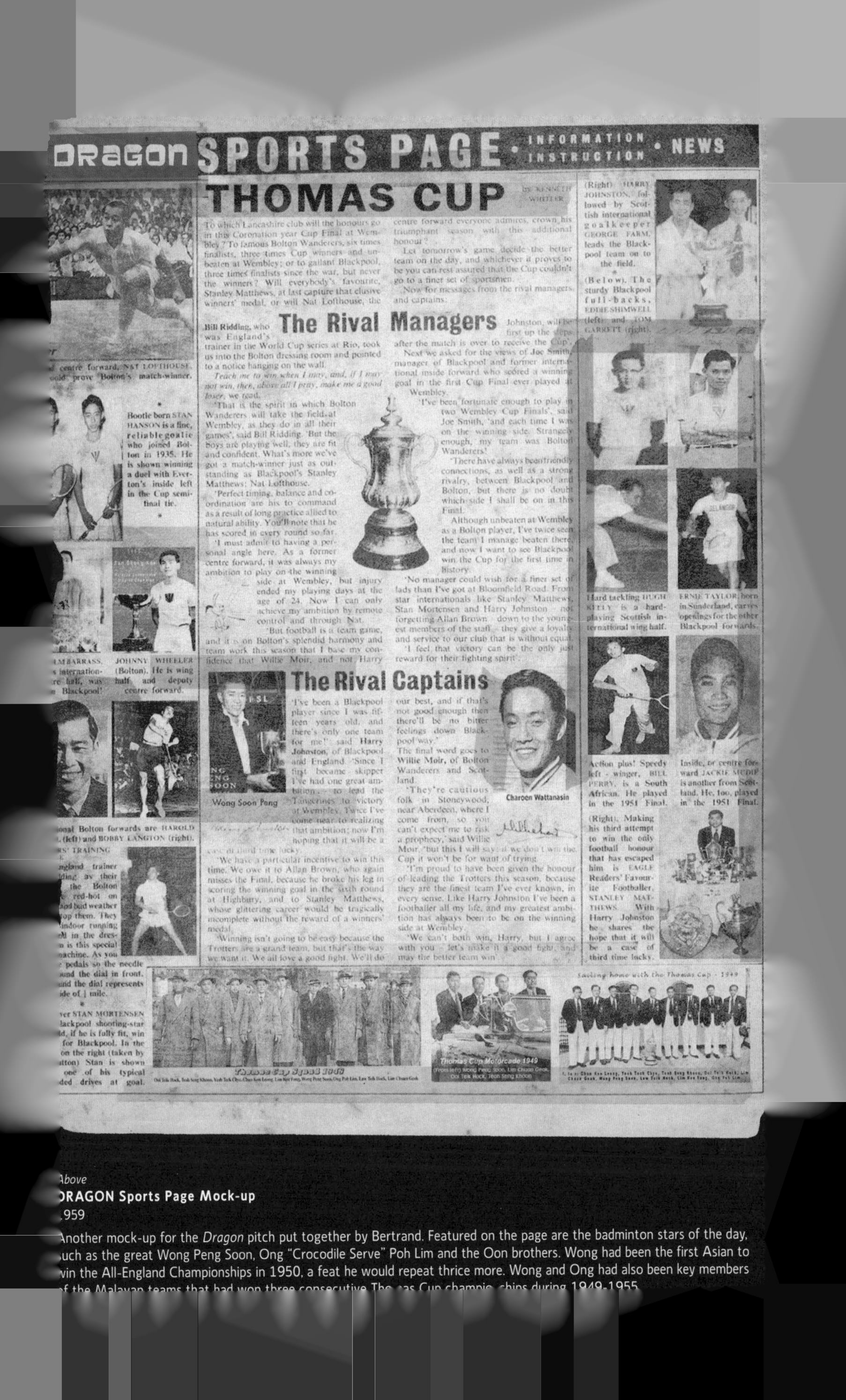

DRAGON SPORTS PAGE • INFORMATION INSTRUCTION • NEWS

THOMAS CUP

BY KENNETH WHITTER

To which Lancashire club will the honours go in this Coronation year Cup Final at Wembley? To famous Bolton Wanderers, six times finalists, three times Cup winners and unbeaten at Wembley; or to gallant Blackpool, three times finalists since the war, but never the winners? Will everybody's favourite, Stanley Matthews, at last capture that elusive winners' medal, or will Nat Lofthouse, the centre forward everyone admires, crown his triumphant season with this additional honour?

Let tomorrow's game decide the better team on the day, and whichever it proves to be you can rest assured that the Cup couldn't go to a finer set of sportsmen.

Now for messages from the rival managers and captains.

The Rival Managers

Bill Ridding, who was England's trainer in the World Cup series at Rio, took us into the Bolton dressing room and pointed to a notice hanging on the wall.

Teach me to win when I may, and, if I may not win, then, above all I pray, make me a good loser, we read.

'That is the spirit in which Bolton Wanderers will take the field at Wembley, as they do in all their games', said Bill Ridding. 'But the boys are playing well, they are fit and confident. What's more we've got a match-winner just as outstanding as Blackpool's Stanley Matthews: Nat Lofthouse.

'Perfect timing, balance and co-ordination are his to command as a result of long practice allied to natural ability. You'll note that he has scored in every round so far.

'I must admit to having a personal angle here. As a former centre forward, it was always my ambition to play on the winning side at Wembley, but injury ended my playing days at the age of 24. Now I can only achieve my ambition by remote control and through Nat.

'But football is a team game, and it is on Bolton's splendid harmony and team work this season that I base my confidence that Willie Moir, and not Harry Johnston, will be first up the steps after the match is over to receive the Cup'.

Next we asked for the views of **Joe Smith**, manager of Blackpool and former international inside forward who scored a winning goal in the first Cup Final ever played at Wembley.

'I've been fortunate enough to play in two Wembley Cup Finals', said Joe Smith, 'and each time I was on the winning side. Strangely enough, my team was Bolton Wanderers!

'There have always been friendly connections, as well as a strong rivalry, between Blackpool and Bolton, but there is no doubt which side I shall be on in this Final.

Although unbeaten at Wembley as a Bolton player, I've twice seen the team I manage beaten there, and now I want to see Blackpool win the Cup for the first time in history.

'No manager could wish for a finer set of lads than I've got at Bloomfield Road. From star internationals like Stanley Matthews, Stan Mortensen and Harry Johnston – not forgetting Allan Brown – down to the youngest members of the staff – they give a loyalty and service to our club that is without equal.

'I feel that victory can be the only just reward for their fighting spirit'.

The Rival Captains

Wong Soon Peng

'I've been a Blackpool player since I was fifteen years old, and there's only one team for me!' said **Harry Johnston**, of Blackpool and England. 'Since I first became skipper I've had one great ambition – to lead the Tangerines to victory at Wembley. Twice I've come near to realizing that ambition; now I'm hoping that it will be a case of third time lucky.

'We have a particular incentive to win this time. We owe it to Allan Brown, who again misses the Final, because he broke his leg in scoring the winning goal in the sixth round at Highbury, and to Stanley Matthews, whose glittering career would be tragically incomplete without the reward of a winners' medal.

'Winning isn't going to be easy because the Trotters are a grand team, but that's the way we want it. We all love a good fight. We'll do our best, and if that's not good enough then there'll be no bitter feelings down Blackpool way.'

The final word goes to **Willie Moir, of Bolton** Wanderers and Scotland.

'They're cautious folk in Stoneywood, near Aberdeen, where I come from, so you can't expect me to risk a prophecy,' said Willie Moir, 'but this I will say: if we don't win the Cup it won't be for want of trying.

'I'm proud to have been given the honour of leading the Trotters this season, because they are the finest team I've ever known, in every sense. Like Harry Johnston I've been a footballer all my life, and my greatest ambition has always been to be on the winning side at Wembley.

'We can't both win, Harry, but I agree with you – let's make it a good fight, and may the better team win'.

Charoen Wattanasin

centre forward, NAT LOFTHOUSE, would prove Bolton's match-winner.

Bootle born STAN HANSON is a fine, reliable goalie who joined Bolton in 1935. He is shown winning a duel with Everton's inside left in the Cup semi-final tie.

...M BARRASS, ...s international... ...re half, was ... Blackpool!

JOHNNY WHEELER (Bolton). He is wing half and deputy centre forward.

...onal Bolton forwards are HAROLD ... (left) and BOBBY LANGTON (right).

...RS' TRAINING

...ngland trainer ...dding as their ... the Bolton ... red-hot on ...and bad weather ...top them. They ...indoor running ...m in the dres... ...n is this special ...machine. As you ... pedals so the needle ...ound the dial in front, ...and the dial represents ...ide of ¼ mile.

...ver STAN MORTENSEN ...lackpool shooting-star ...ld, if he is fully fit, win ... for Blackpool. In the ... on the right (taken by ...tton) Stan is shown ... one of his typical ...ded drives at goal.

(Right) HARRY JOHNSTON, followed by Scottish international goalkeeper GEORGE FARM, leads the Blackpool team on to the field.

(Below). The sturdy Blackpool full-backs, EDDIE SHIMWELL (left) and TOM GARRETT (right).

Hard tackling HUGH KELLY is a hard-playing Scottish international wing half.

ERNIE TAYLOR, born in Sunderland, carves openings for the other Blackpool forwards.

Action plus! Speedy left-winger, BILL PERRY, is a South African. He played in the 1951 Final.

Inside, or centre forward JACKIE MUDIE is another from Scotland. He, too, played in the 1951 Final.

(Right). Making his third attempt to win the only football honour that has escaped him is EAGLE Readers' Favourite Footballer, STANLEY MATTHEWS. With Harry Johnston he shares the hope that it will be a case of third time lucky.

Thomas Cup Squad 1949

Thomas Cup Motorcade 1949
(From left) Wong Peng Soon, Lim Chuan Geok, Ooi Teik Hock, Teoh Seng Khoon

Sailing home with the Thomas Cup · 1949

Above

DRAGON Sports Page Mock-up

1959

Another mock-up for the *Dragon* pitch put together by Bertrand. Featured on the page are the badminton stars of the day, such as the great Wong Peng Soon, Ong "Crocodile Serve" Poh Lim and the Oon brothers. Wong had been the first Asian to win the All-England Championships in 1950, a feat he would repeat thrice more. Wong and Ong had also been key members of the Malayan teams that had won three consecutive Thomas Cup championships during 1949-1955.

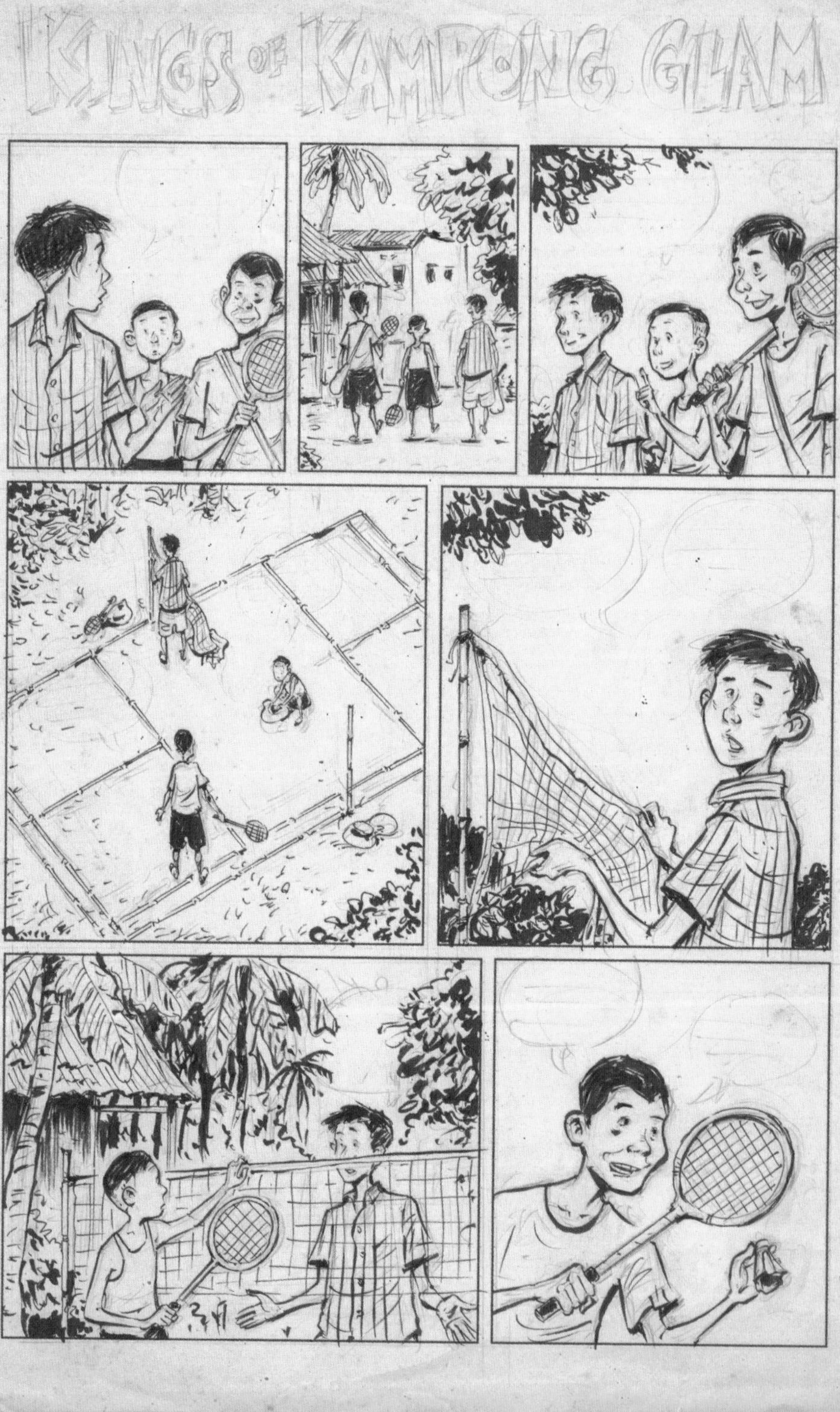
KINGS OF KAMPONG GLAM

Above **KINGS OF KAMPONG GLAM** (1959) | Chan Hock Chye | Unpublished

A comic for the *Dragon* pitch, featuring a trio of young boys with dreams of emulating their Thomas Cup-winning badminton heroes. The dialogue for these pages, meant to be filled in at a later stage, was never written.

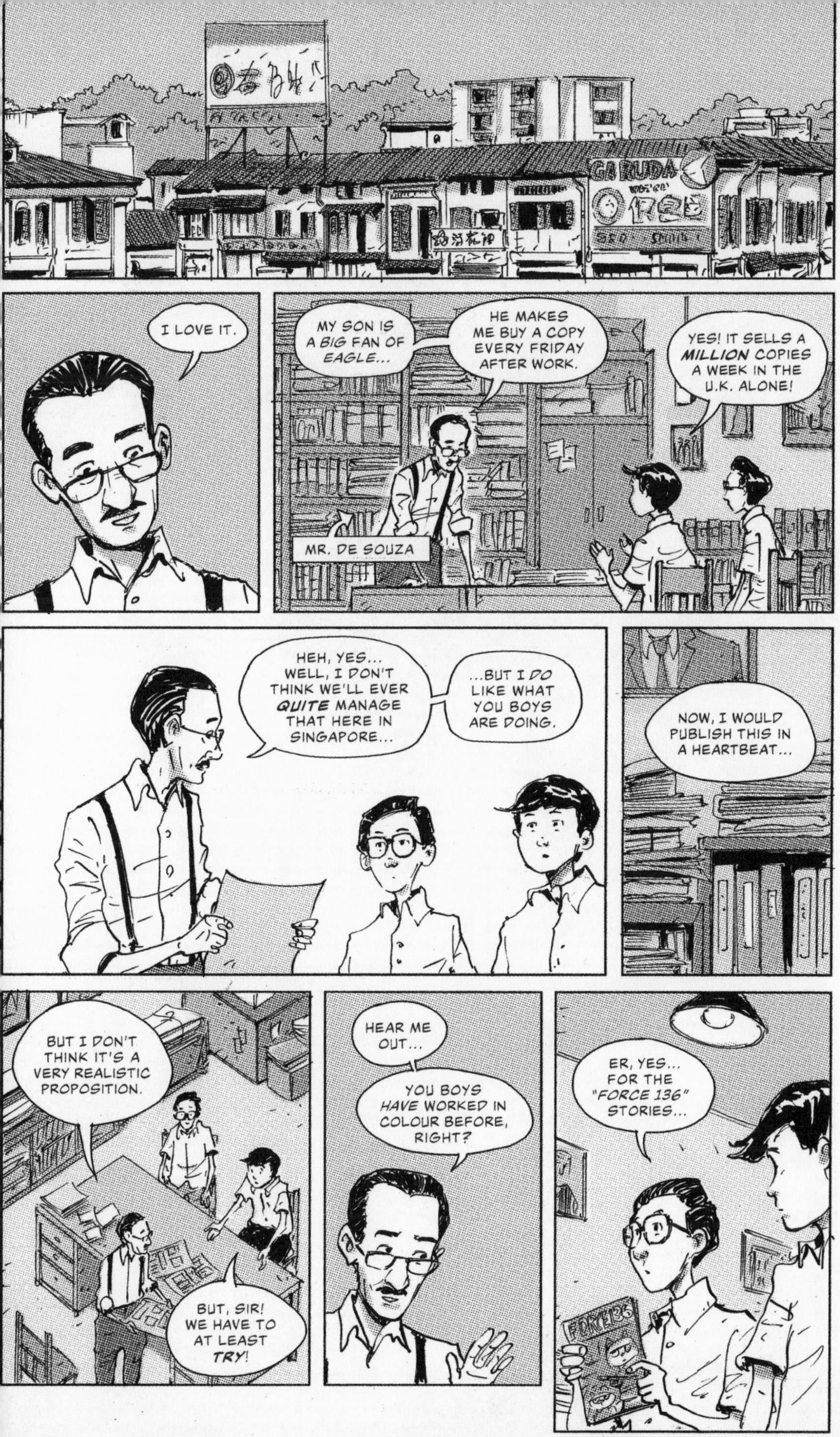
I LOVE IT.
MY SON IS A *BIG* FAN OF *EAGLE*...
HE MAKES ME BUY A COPY EVERY FRIDAY AFTER WORK.
MR. DE SOUZA
YES! IT SELLS A **MILLION** COPIES A WEEK IN THE U.K. ALONE!
HEH, YES... WELL, I DON'T THINK WE'LL EVER ***QUITE*** MANAGE THAT HERE IN SINGAPORE...
...BUT I *DO* LIKE WHAT YOU BOYS ARE DOING.
NOW, I WOULD PUBLISH THIS IN A HEARTBEAT...
BUT I DON'T THINK IT'S A VERY REALISTIC PROPOSITION.
BUT, SIR! WE HAVE TO AT LEAST ***TRY***!
HEAR ME OUT...
YOU BOYS *HAVE* WORKED IN COLOUR BEFORE, RIGHT?
ER, YES... FOR THE "*FORCE 136*" STORIES...

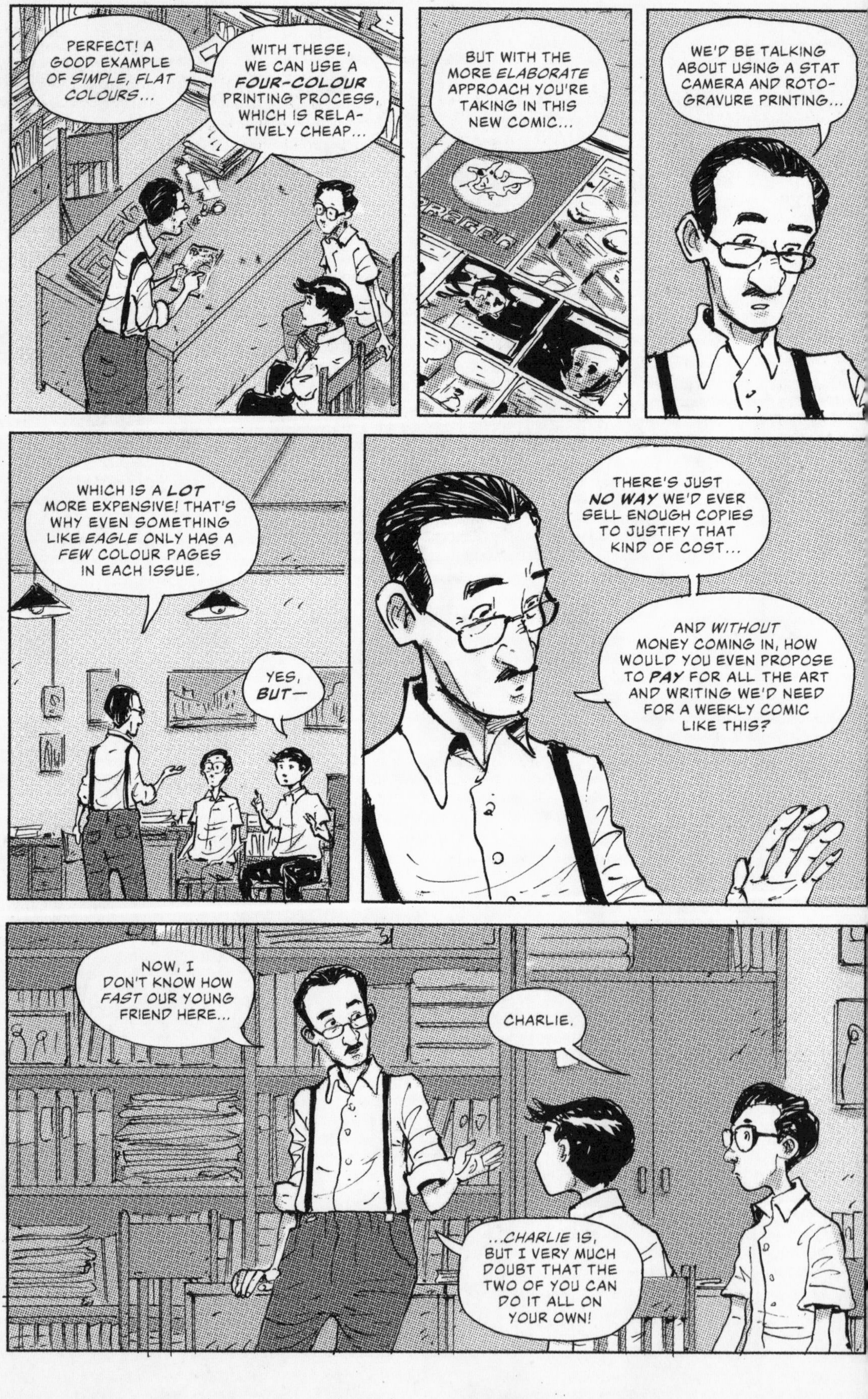
PERFECT! A GOOD EXAMPLE OF *SIMPLE, FLAT COLOURS*...
WITH THESE, WE CAN USE A **FOUR-COLOUR** PRINTING PROCESS, WHICH IS RELATIVELY CHEAP...
BUT WITH THE MORE *ELABORATE* APPROACH YOU'RE TAKING IN THIS NEW COMIC...
WE'D BE TALKING ABOUT USING A STAT CAMERA AND ROTOGRAVURE PRINTING...
WHICH IS A ***LOT*** MORE EXPENSIVE! THAT'S WHY EVEN SOMETHING LIKE *EAGLE* ONLY HAS A *FEW* COLOUR PAGES IN EACH ISSUE.
YES, ***BUT***—
THERE'S JUST ***NO WAY*** WE'D EVER SELL ENOUGH COPIES TO JUSTIFY THAT KIND OF COST...
AND *WITHOUT* MONEY COMING IN, HOW WOULD YOU EVEN PROPOSE TO ***PAY*** FOR ALL THE ART AND WRITING WE'D NEED FOR A WEEKLY COMIC LIKE THIS?
NOW, I DON'T KNOW HOW *FAST* OUR YOUNG FRIEND HERE...
CHARLIE.
...*CHARLIE* IS, BUT I VERY MUCH DOUBT THAT THE TWO OF YOU CAN DO IT ALL ON YOUR OWN!

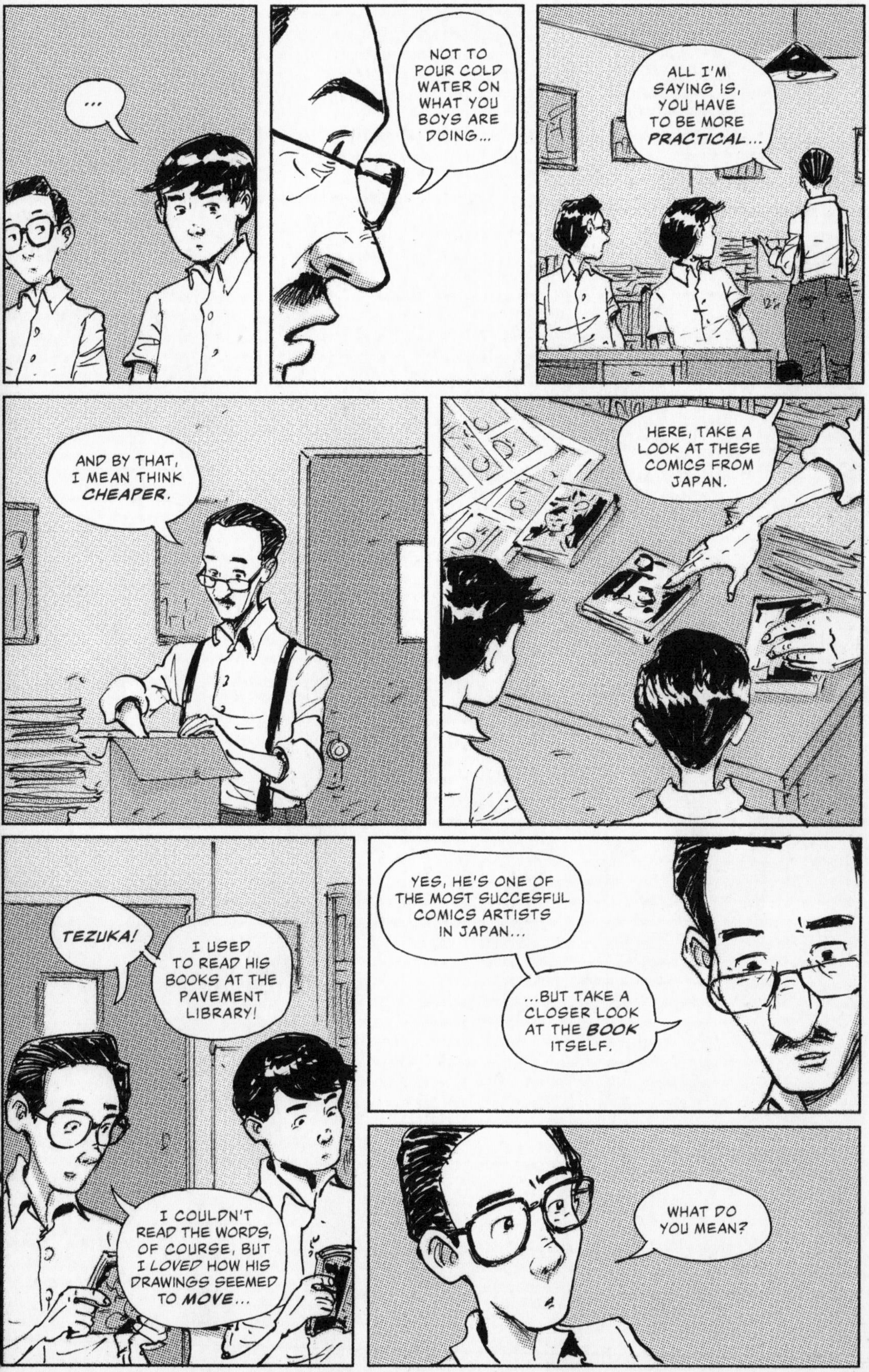
...
NOT TO POUR COLD WATER ON WHAT YOU BOYS ARE DOING...
ALL I'M SAYING IS, YOU HAVE TO BE MORE PRACTICAL...
AND BY THAT, I MEAN THINK CHEAPER.
HERE, TAKE A LOOK AT THESE COMICS FROM JAPAN.
TEZUKA!
I USED TO READ HIS BOOKS AT THE PAVEMENT LIBRARY!
I COULDN'T READ THE WORDS, OF COURSE, BUT I LOVED HOW HIS DRAWINGS SEEMED TO MOVE...
YES, HE'S ONE OF THE MOST SUCCESFUL COMICS ARTISTS IN JAPAN...
...BUT TAKE A CLOSER LOOK AT THE BOOK ITSELF.
WHAT DO YOU MEAN?

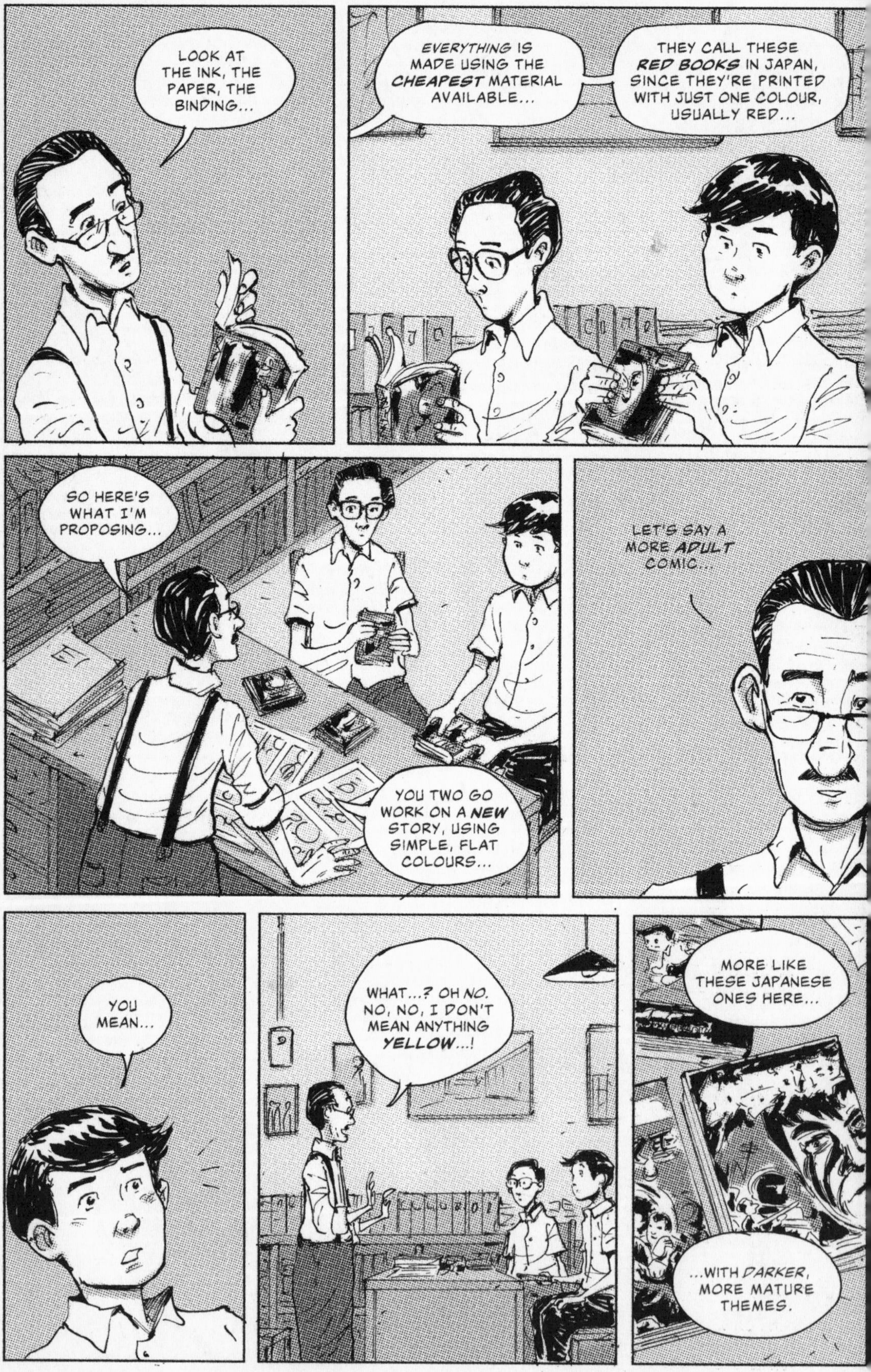
LOOK AT THE INK, THE PAPER, THE BINDING...
EVERYTHING IS MADE USING THE ***CHEAPEST*** MATERIAL AVAILABLE...
THEY CALL THESE ***RED BOOKS*** IN JAPAN, SINCE THEY'RE PRINTED WITH JUST ONE COLOUR, USUALLY RED...
SO HERE'S WHAT I'M PROPOSING...
YOU TWO GO WORK ON A ***NEW*** STORY, USING SIMPLE, FLAT COLOURS...
LET'S SAY A MORE ***ADULT*** COMIC...
YOU MEAN...
WHAT...? OH *NO.* NO, NO, I DON'T MEAN ANYTHING ***YELLOW***...!
MORE LIKE THESE JAPANESE ONES HERE...
...WITH *DARKER*, MORE MATURE THEMES.

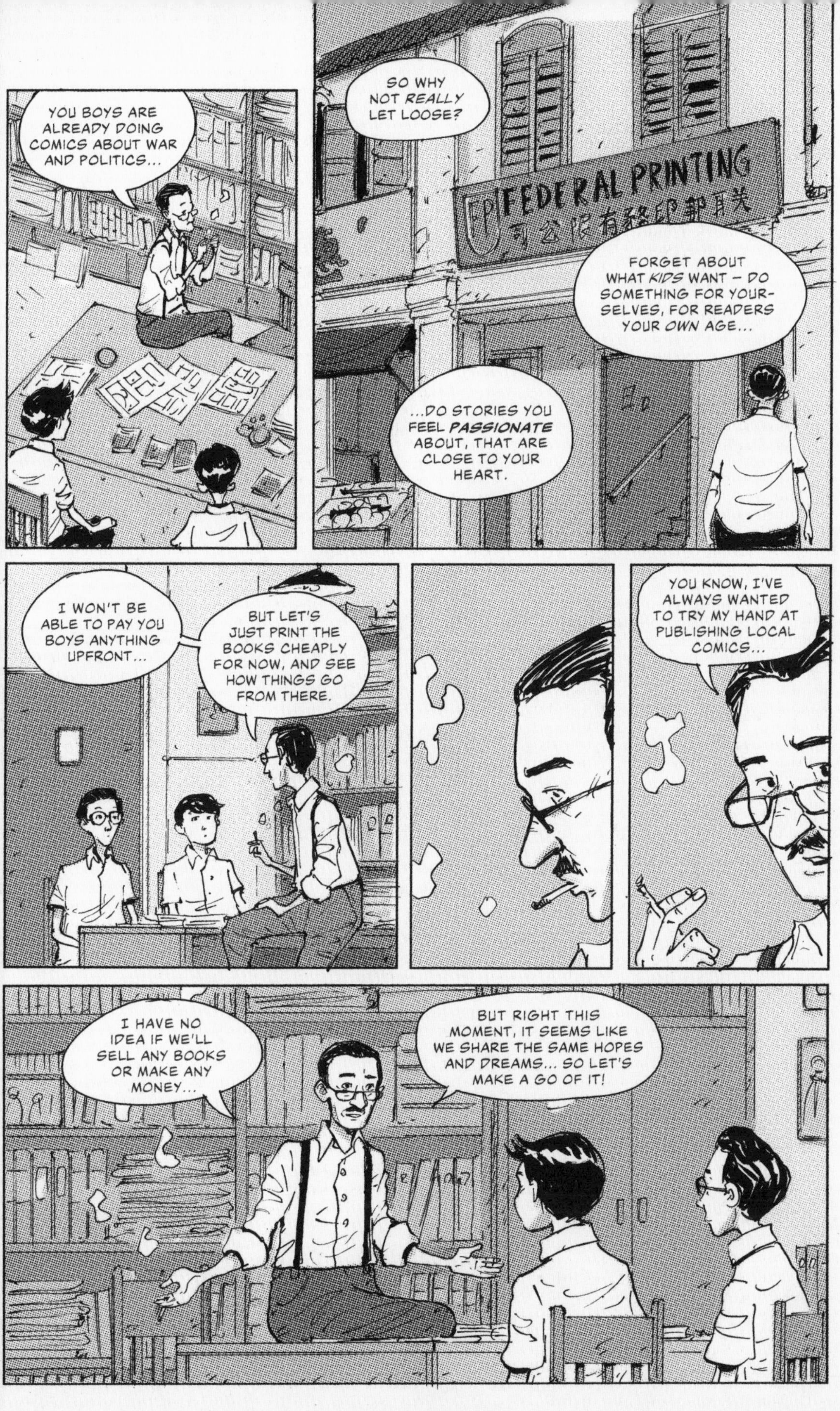
YOU BOYS ARE ALREADY DOING COMICS ABOUT WAR AND POLITICS...
SO WHY NOT *REALLY* LET LOOSE?
FEDERAL PRINTING
FORGET ABOUT WHAT *KIDS* WANT – DO SOMETHING FOR YOURSELVES, FOR READERS YOUR *OWN* AGE...
...DO STORIES YOU FEEL ***PASSIONATE*** ABOUT, THAT ARE CLOSE TO YOUR HEART.
I WON'T BE ABLE TO PAY YOU BOYS ANYTHING UPFRONT...
BUT LET'S JUST PRINT THE BOOKS CHEAPLY FOR NOW, AND SEE HOW THINGS GO FROM THERE.
YOU KNOW, I'VE ALWAYS WANTED TO TRY MY HAND AT PUBLISHING LOCAL COMICS...
I HAVE NO IDEA IF WE'LL SELL ANY BOOKS OR MAKE ANY MONEY...
BUT RIGHT THIS MOMENT, IT SEEMS LIKE WE SHARE THE SAME HOPES AND DREAMS... SO LET'S MAKE A GO OF IT!

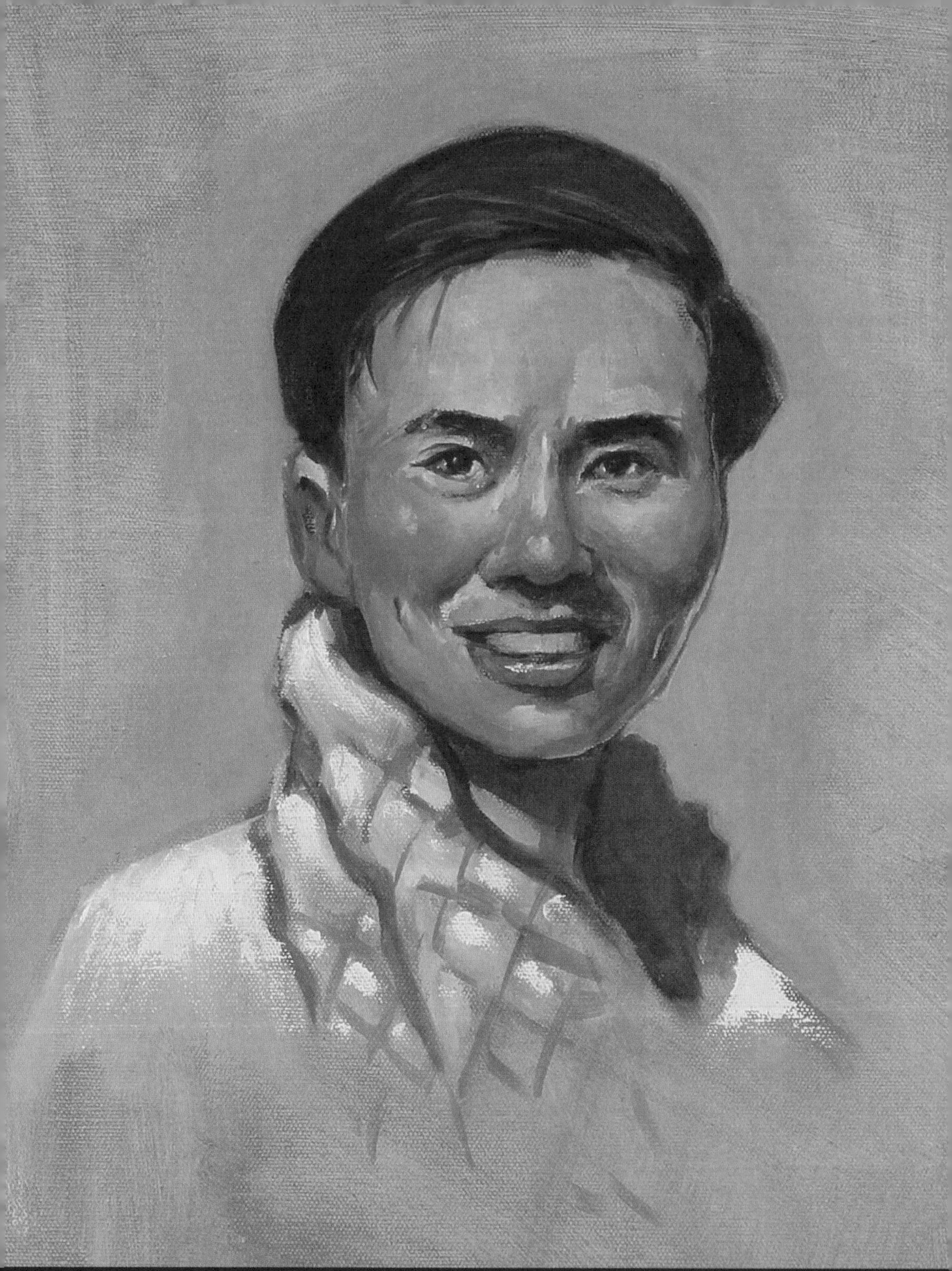

Above
LIM CHIN SIONG
1959
Chan Hock Chye
Oil on canvas

A painting based on a photograph, taken during Lim Chin Siong's release from his first period of detention (1956-1959) following the People's Action Party's (PAP) victory in the 1959 elections. He was freed alongside other union leaders, including Fong S[illegible] Suan

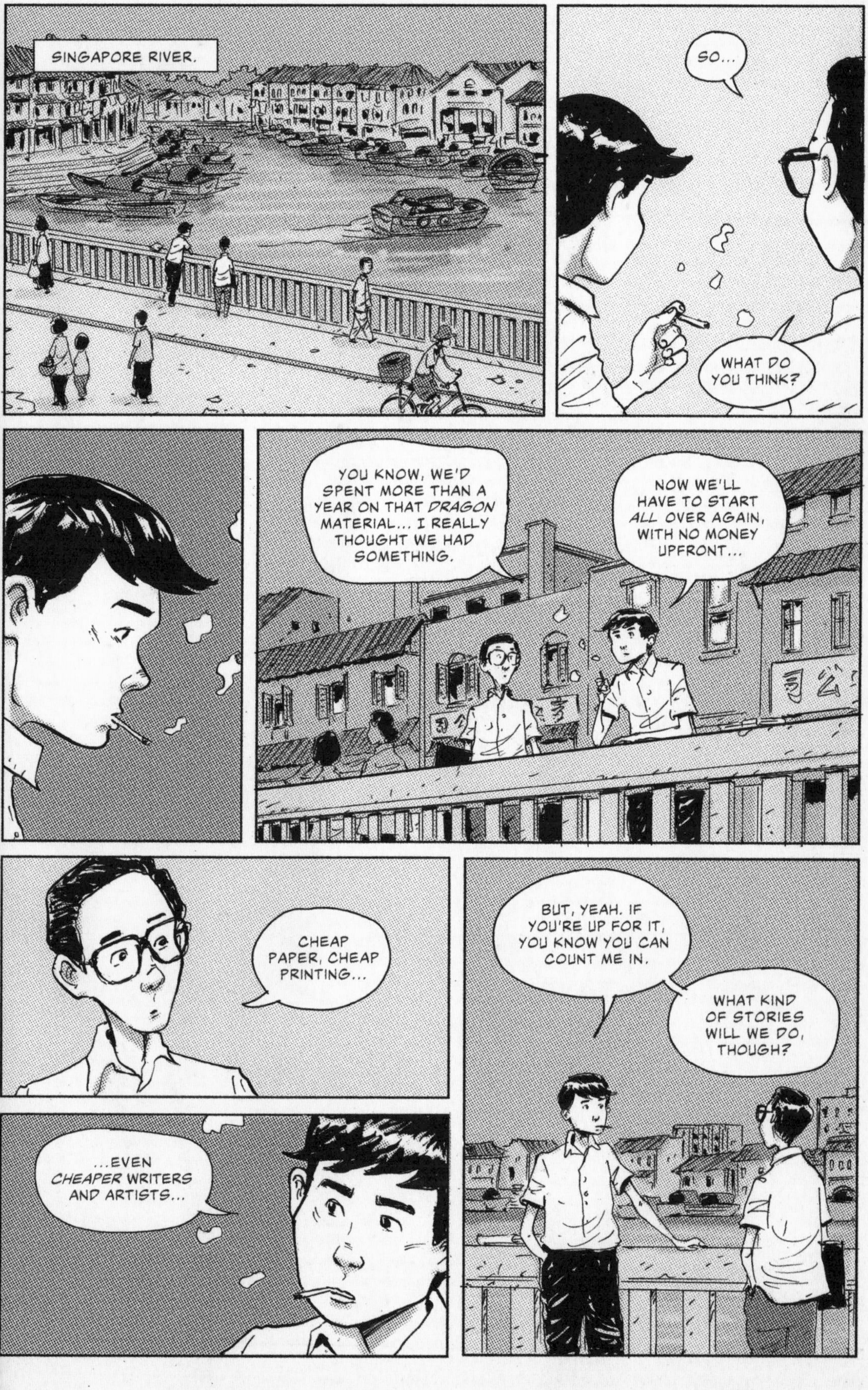
SINGAPORE RIVER.
SO...
WHAT DO YOU THINK?
YOU KNOW, WE'D SPENT MORE THAN A YEAR ON THAT *DRAGON* MATERIAL... I REALLY THOUGHT WE HAD SOMETHING.
NOW WE'LL HAVE TO START *ALL* OVER AGAIN, WITH NO MONEY UPFRONT...
CHEAP PAPER, CHEAP PRINTING...
BUT, YEAH. IF YOU'RE UP FOR IT, YOU KNOW YOU CAN COUNT ME IN.
WHAT KIND OF STORIES WILL WE DO, THOUGH?
...EVEN *CHEAPER* WRITERS AND ARTISTS...

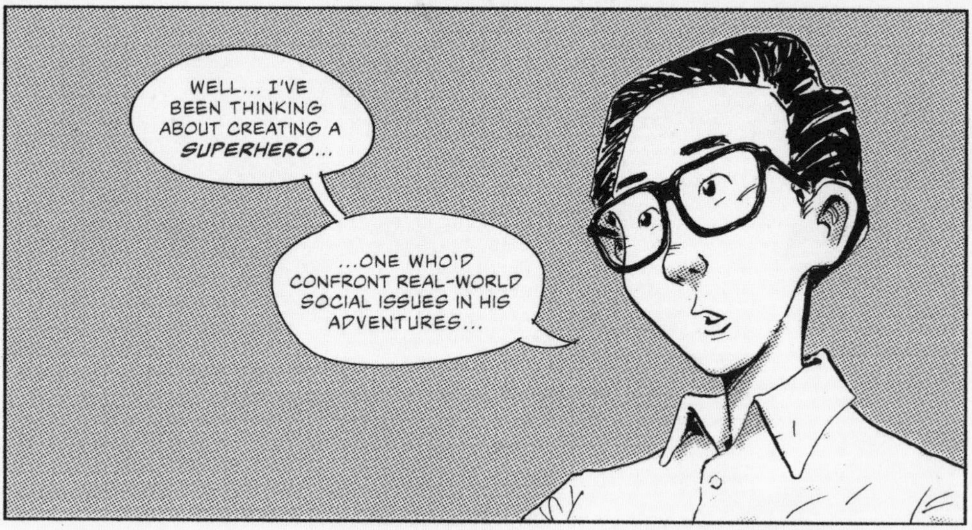
WELL... I'VE BEEN THINKING ABOUT CREATING A SUPERHERO...
...ONE WHO'D CONFRONT REAL-WORLD SOCIAL ISSUES IN HIS ADVENTURES...

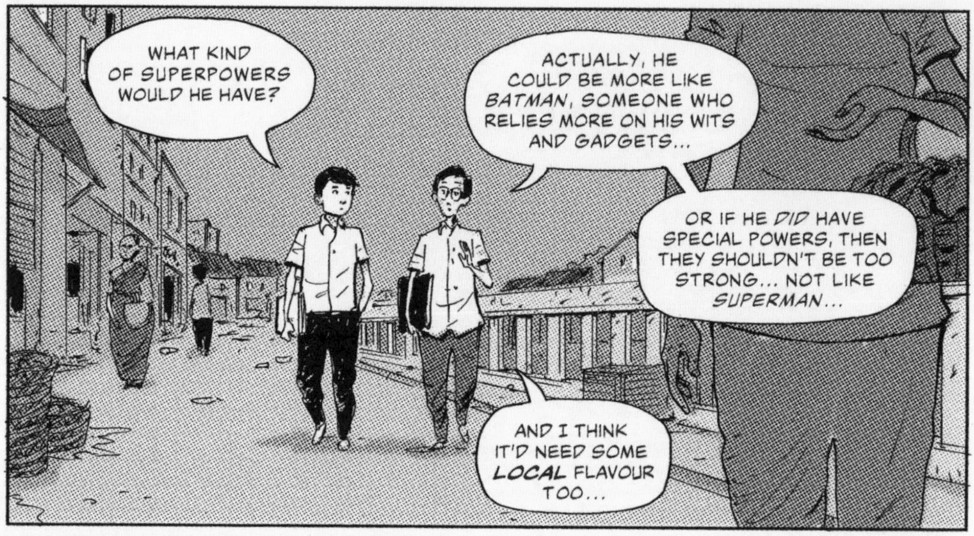
WHAT KIND OF SUPERPOWERS WOULD HE HAVE?
ACTUALLY, HE COULD BE MORE LIKE BATMAN, SOMEONE WHO RELIES MORE ON HIS WITS AND GADGETS...
OR IF HE DID HAVE SPECIAL POWERS, THEN THEY SHOULDN'T BE TOO STRONG... NOT LIKE SUPERMAN...
AND I THINK IT'D NEED SOME LOCAL FLAVOUR TOO...

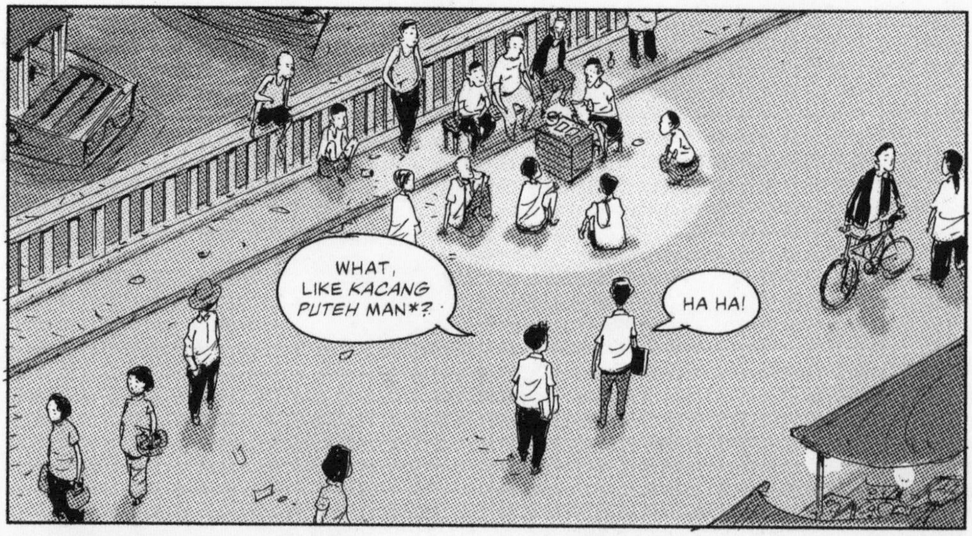
WHAT, LIKE KACANG PUTEH MAN*?
HA HA!

* A STREET HAWKER SELLING SUGARED PEANUTS AND OTHER SNACKS IN PAPER CONES.
KACANG PUTEH: MALAY FOR "WHITE BEANS AND NUTS"

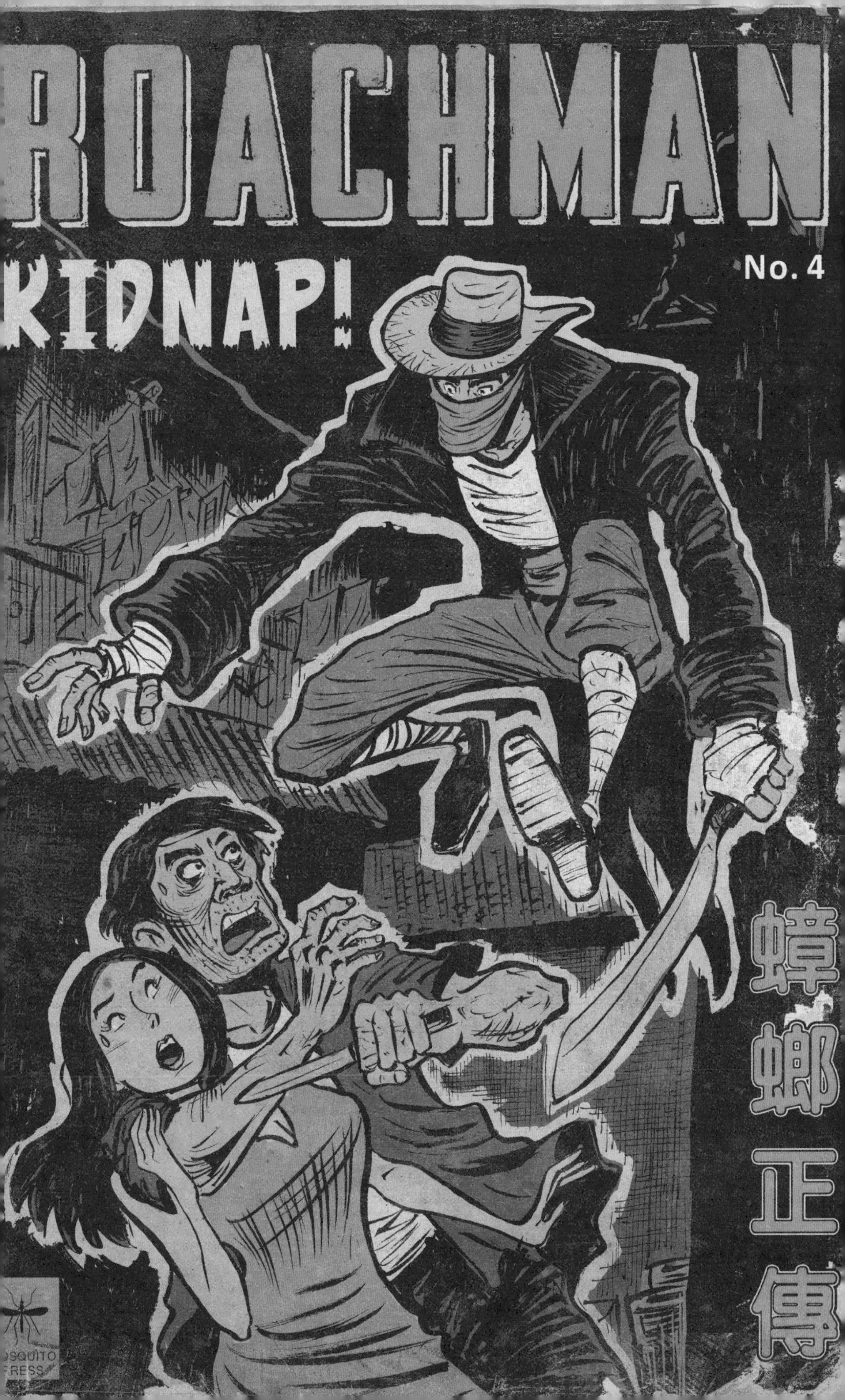

ROACHMAN
KIDNAP!
No. 4
蟑螂正傳
OSQUITO
PRESS

Previous
ROACHMAN No. 4: KIDNAP!
1960
Art by Chan Hock Chye
Words by Bertrand Wong
Mosquito Press

Roachman was a hybrid of pulp and superhero comics, with stories that often drew on sensationalist newspaper headlines of the day involving murders, kidnappings, suicides, animal attacks and the like.

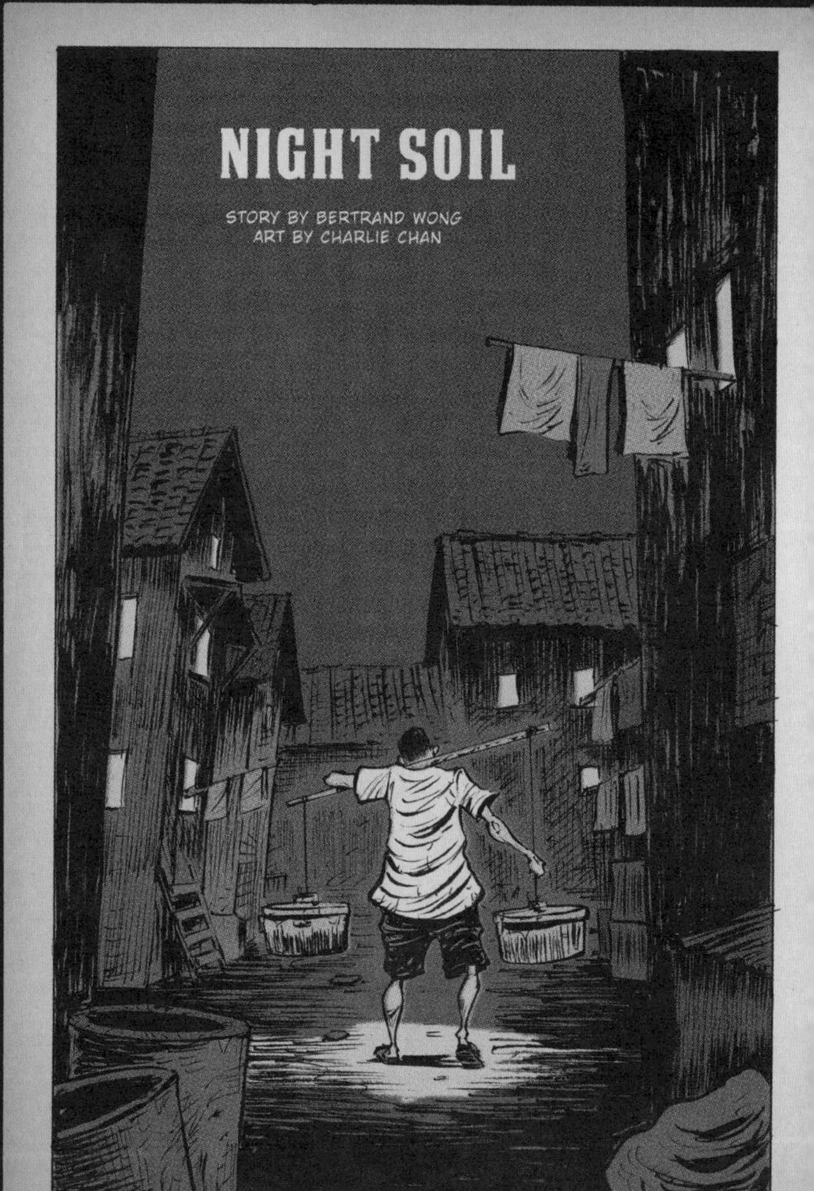
NIGHT SOIL
STORY BY BERTRAND WONG
ART BY CHARLIE CHAN

Above & following
ROACHMAN No. 1: NIGHT SOIL
1959
Art by Chan Hock Chye
Words by Bertrand Wong
Mosquito Press

The first issue of the series tells the origin story of the Roachman.

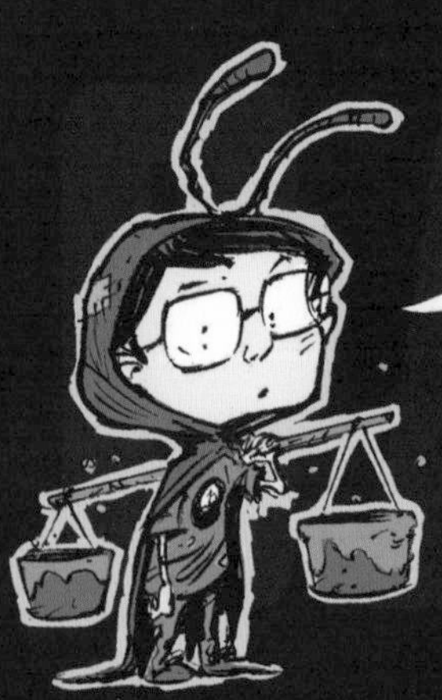
THE STORY'S HERO, ***AH GUAN***, WORKS AS A "***NIGHT SOIL***" MAN, A EUPHEMISM FOR WORKERS WHO COLLECTED AND DISPOSED OF HUMAN EXCRETA.
NIGHT SOIL PAILS AND THEIR COLLECTORS WERE A COMMON SIGHT IN SINGAPOREAN LIFE BEFORE THE INTRODUCTION OF MODERN WASTE FACILITIES IN THE 1960S...
...AND IT WASN'T UNTIL 1987 THAT THE LAST REMNANTS OF THE PRACTICE WERE PHASED OUT FOR GOOD.

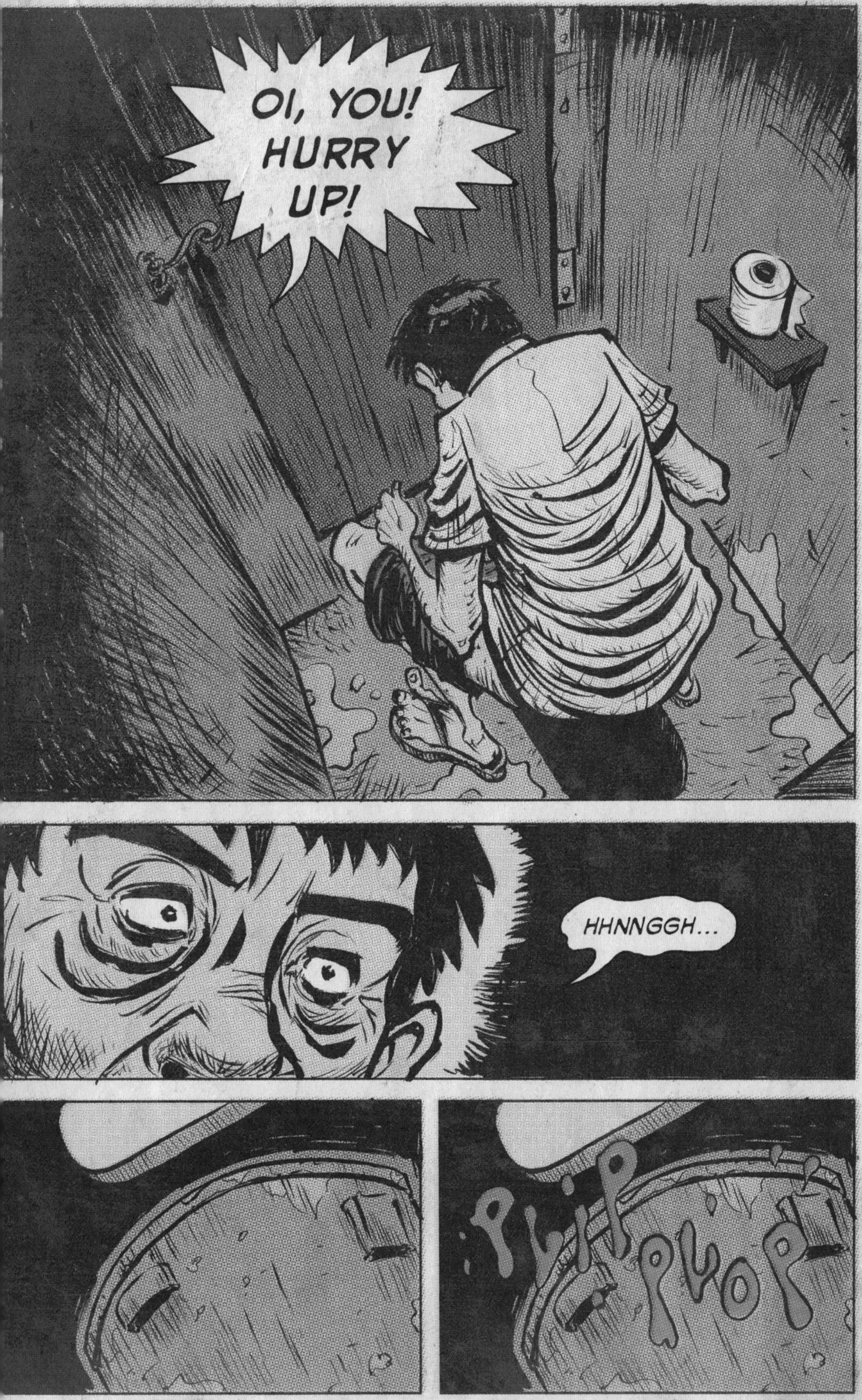
OI, YOU! HURRY UP!
HHNNGGH...
PLIP
PLOP

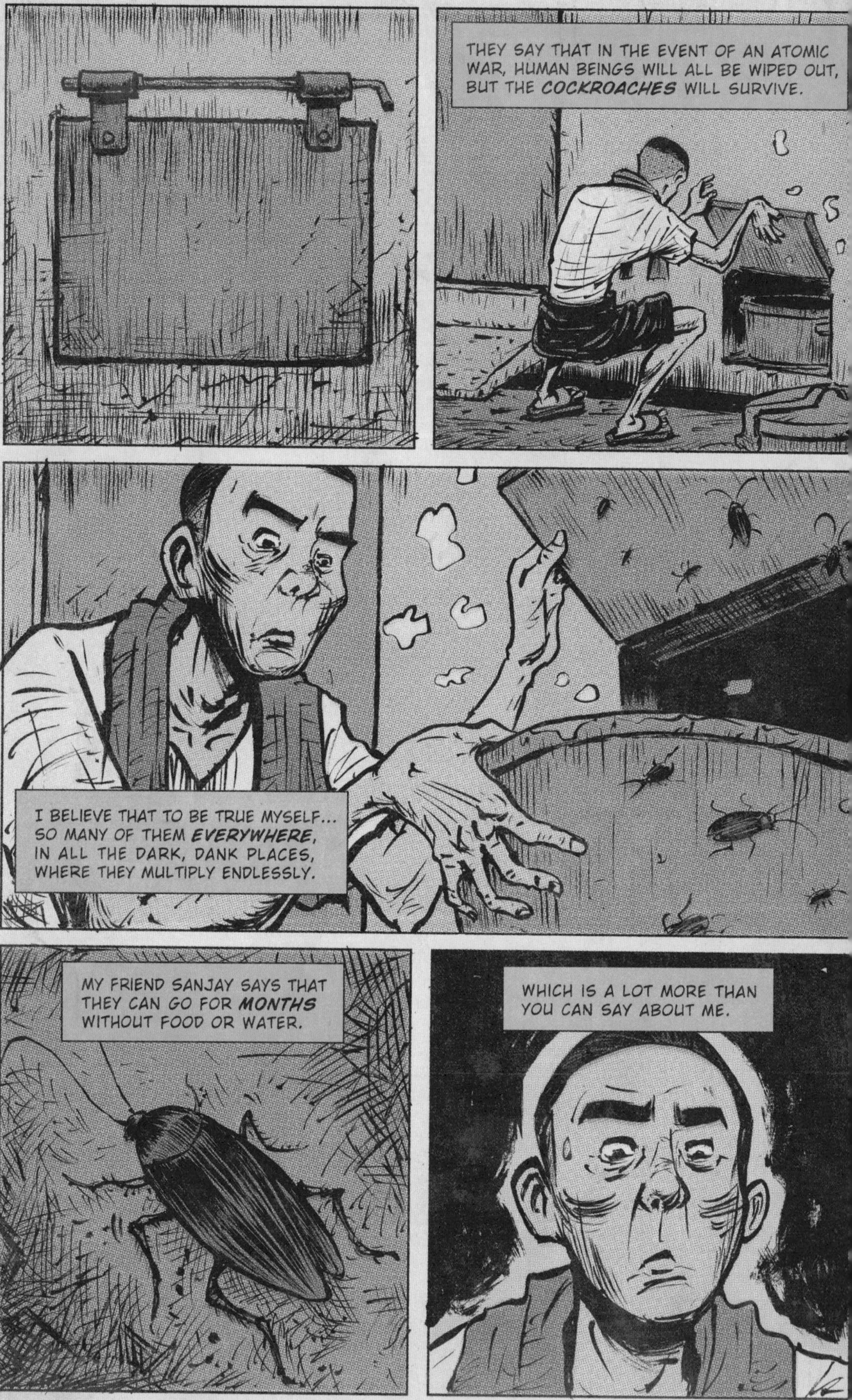
THEY SAY THAT IN THE EVENT OF AN ATOMIC WAR, HUMAN BEINGS WILL ALL BE WIPED OUT, BUT THE ***COCKROACHES*** WILL SURVIVE.
I BELIEVE THAT TO BE TRUE MYSELF... SO MANY OF THEM ***EVERYWHERE***, IN ALL THE DARK, DANK PLACES, WHERE THEY MULTIPLY ENDLESSLY.
MY FRIEND SANJAY SAYS THAT THEY CAN GO FOR ***MONTHS*** WITHOUT FOOD OR WATER.
WHICH IS A LOT MORE THAN YOU CAN SAY ABOUT ME.

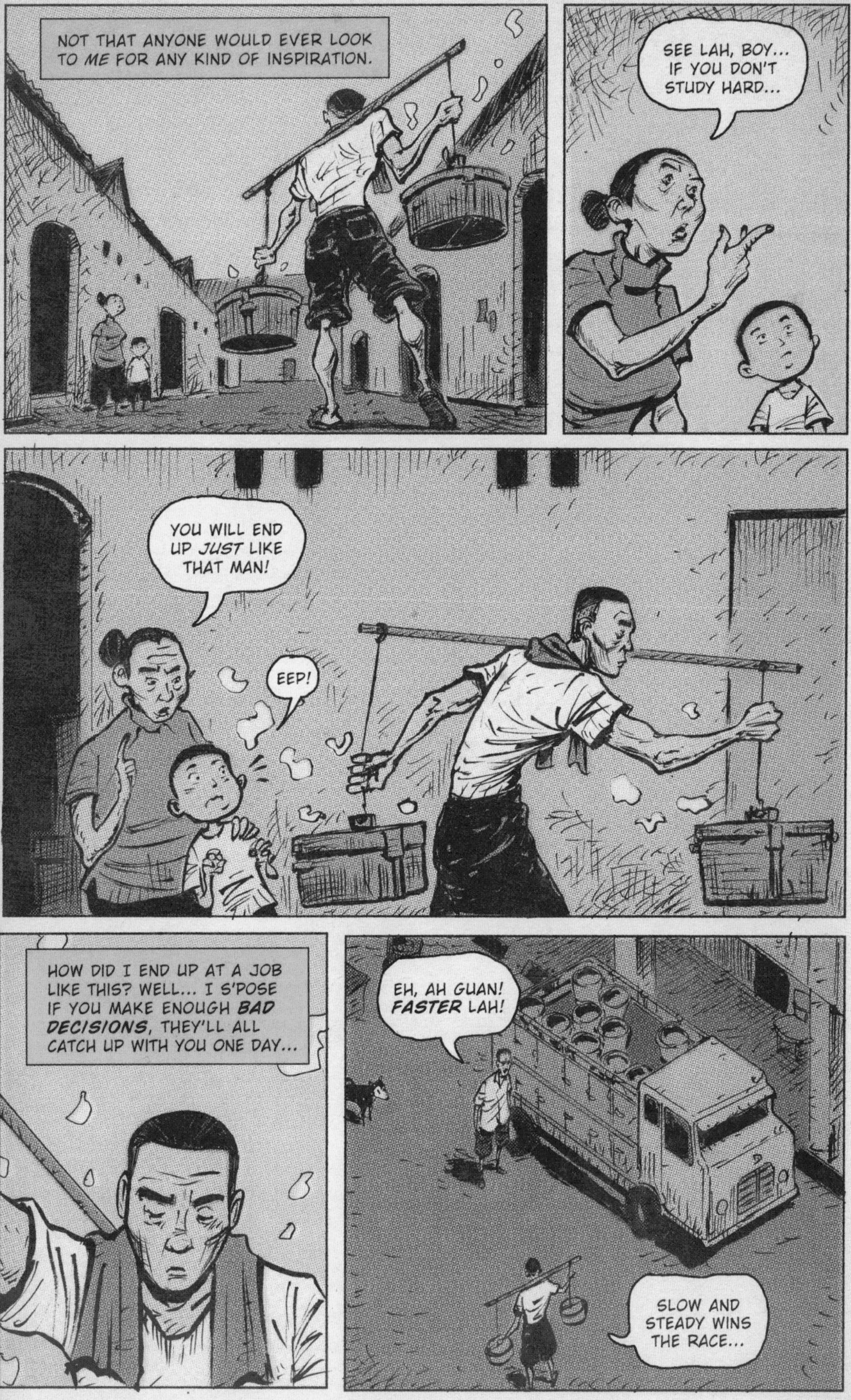
NOT THAT ANYONE WOULD EVER LOOK TO *ME* FOR ANY KIND OF INSPIRATION.
SEE LAH, BOY... IF YOU DON'T STUDY HARD...
YOU WILL END UP *JUST* LIKE THAT MAN!
EEP!
HOW DID I END UP AT A JOB LIKE THIS? WELL... I S'POSE IF YOU MAKE ENOUGH *BAD DECISIONS*, THEY'LL ALL CATCH UP WITH YOU ONE DAY...
EH, AH GUAN! *FASTER* LAH!
SLOW AND STEADY WINS THE RACE...

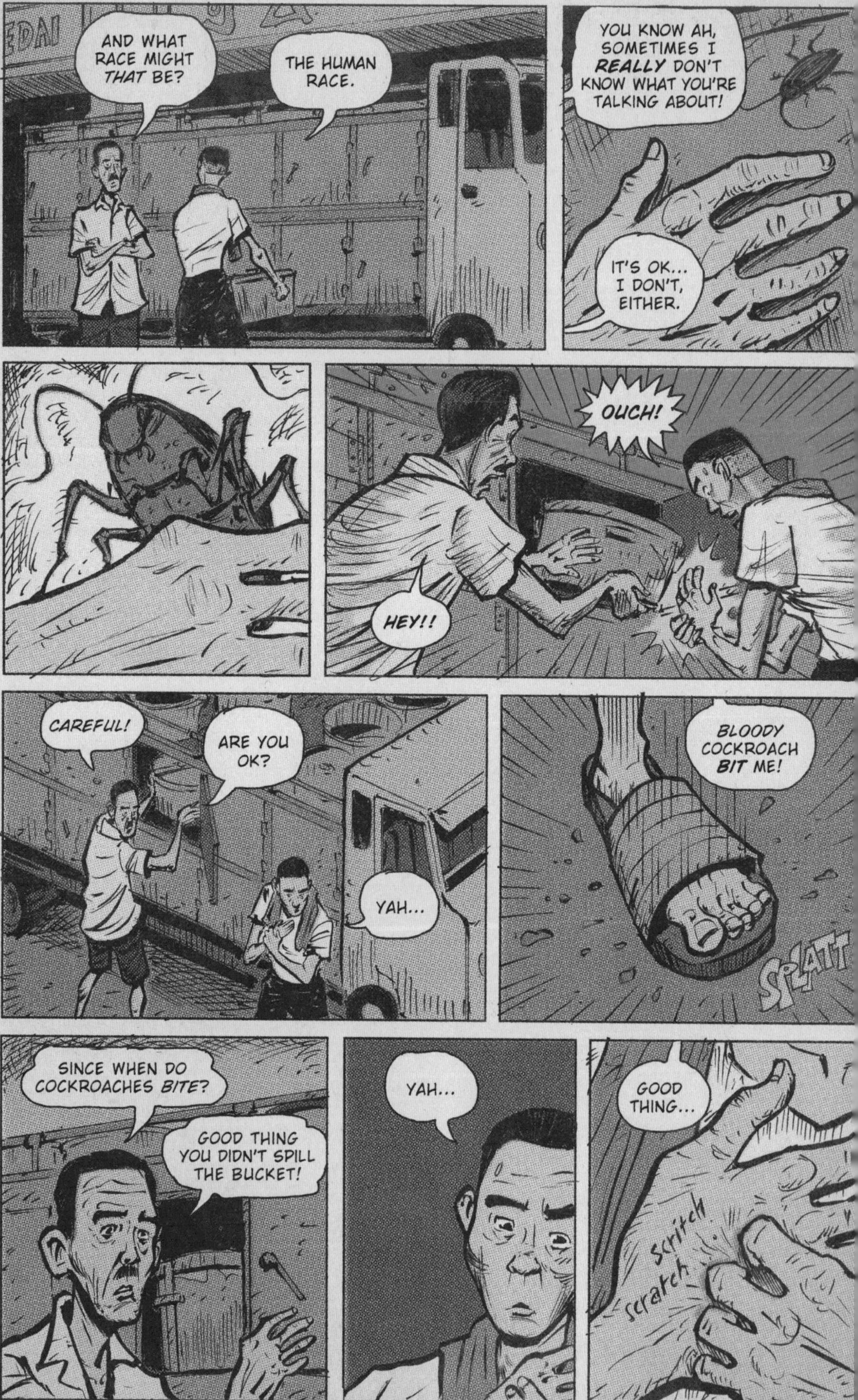
AND WHAT RACE MIGHT *THAT* BE?
THE HUMAN RACE.
YOU KNOW AH, SOMETIMES I ***REALLY*** DON'T KNOW WHAT YOU'RE TALKING ABOUT!
IT'S OK... I DON'T, EITHER.
OUCH!
HEY!!
CAREFUL!
ARE YOU OK?
YAH...
BLOODY COCKROACH ***BIT*** ME!
SPLATT
SINCE WHEN DO COCKROACHES *BITE*?
GOOD THING YOU DIDN'T SPILL THE BUCKET!
YAH...
GOOD THING...
scritch scratch

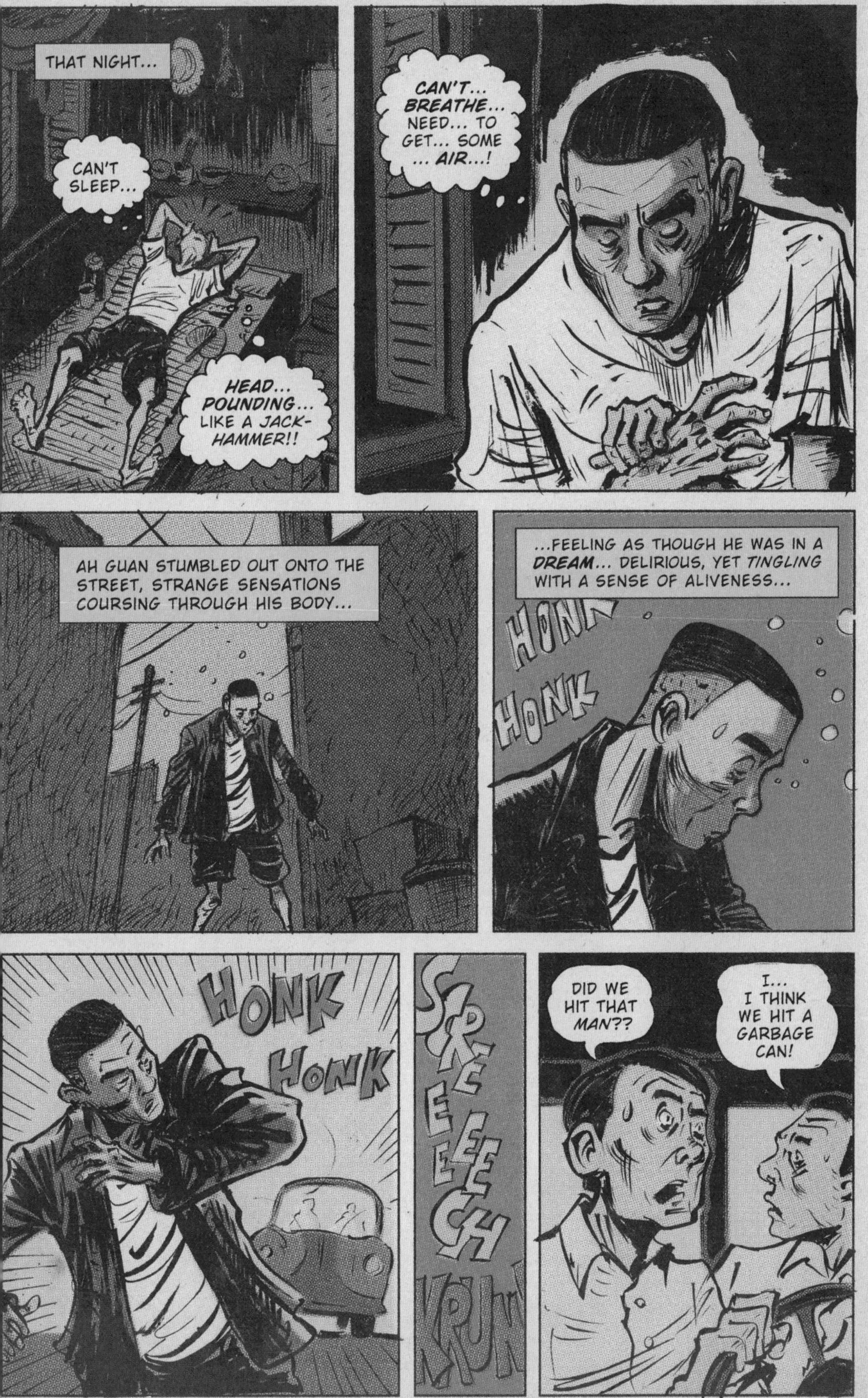
THAT NIGHT...
CAN'T SLEEP...
HEAD... POUNDING... LIKE A JACK-HAMMER!!
CAN'T... BREATHE... NEED... TO GET... SOME ... AIR...!
AH GUAN STUMBLED OUT ONTO THE STREET, STRANGE SENSATIONS COURSING THROUGH HIS BODY...
...FEELING AS THOUGH HE WAS IN A DREAM... DELIRIOUS, YET TINGLING WITH A SENSE OF ALIVENESS...
HONK
HONK
HONK
HONK
SKREEEECH
KRUN
DID WE HIT THAT MAN??
I... I THINK WE HIT A GARBAGE CAN!

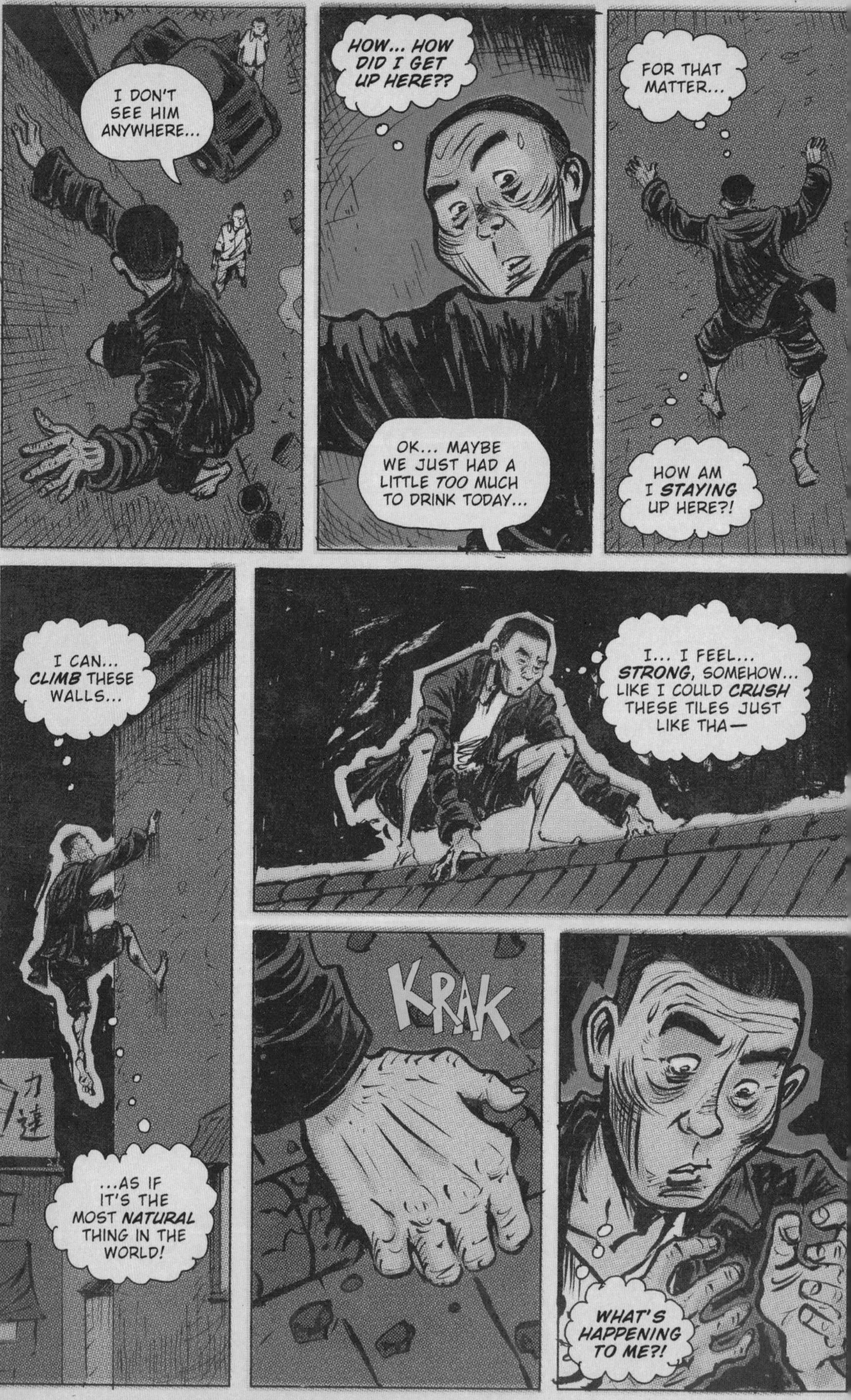
I DON'T SEE HIM ANYWHERE...
HOW... HOW DID I GET UP HERE??
OK... MAYBE WE JUST HAD A LITTLE TOO MUCH TO DRINK TODAY...
FOR THAT MATTER...
HOW AM I STAYING UP HERE?!
I CAN... CLIMB THESE WALLS...
...AS IF IT'S THE MOST NATURAL THING IN THE WORLD!
I... I FEEL... STRONG, SOMEHOW... LIKE I COULD CRUSH THESE TILES JUST LIKE THA—
KRAK
WHAT'S HAPPENING TO ME?!

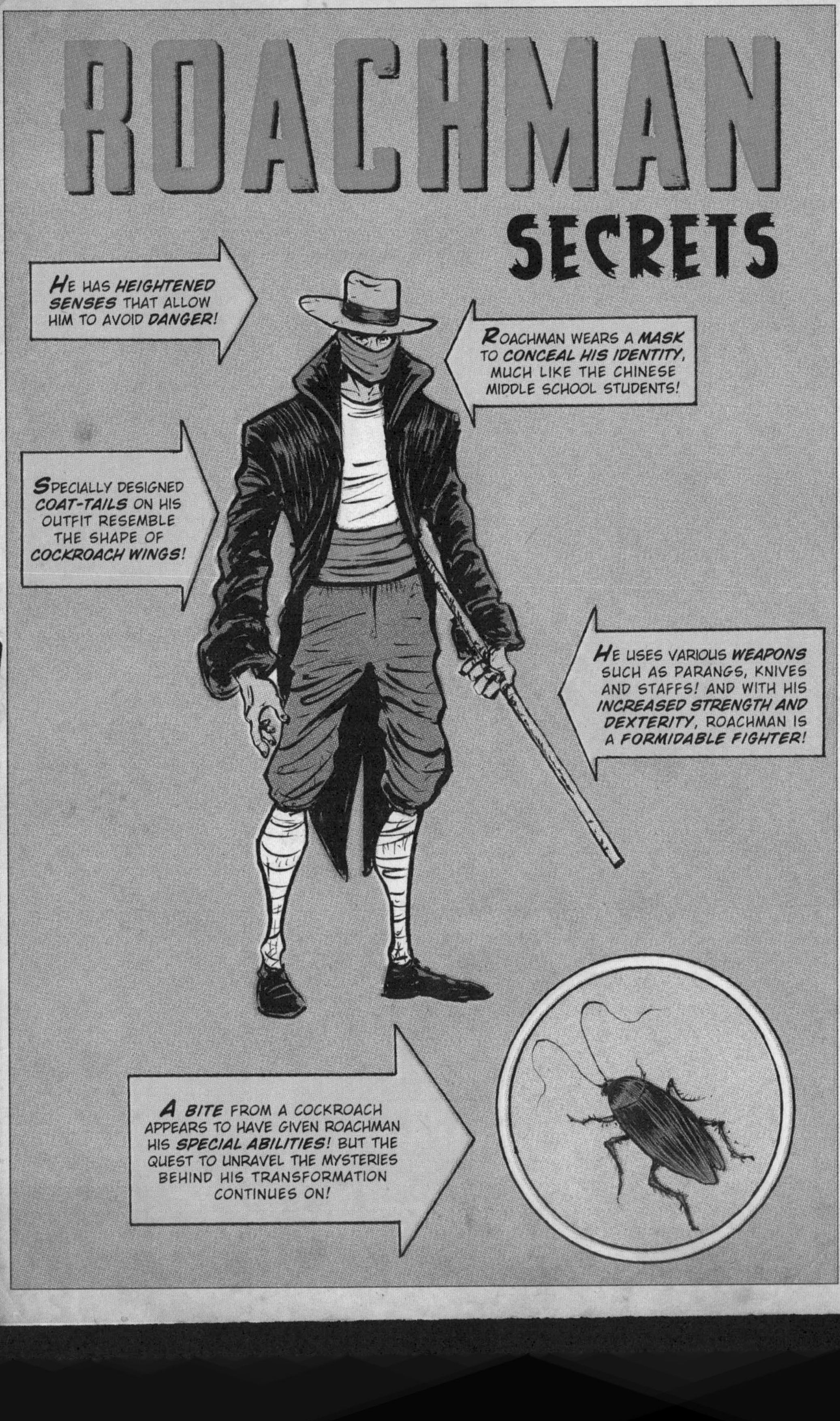
ROACHMAN
SECRETS
HE HAS HEIGHTENED SENSES THAT ALLOW HIM TO AVOID DANGER!
ROACHMAN WEARS A MASK TO CONCEAL HIS IDENTITY, MUCH LIKE THE CHINESE MIDDLE SCHOOL STUDENTS!
SPECIALLY DESIGNED COAT-TAILS ON HIS OUTFIT RESEMBLE THE SHAPE OF COCKROACH WINGS!
HE USES VARIOUS WEAPONS SUCH AS PARANGS, KNIVES AND STAFFS! AND WITH HIS INCREASED STRENGTH AND DEXTERITY, ROACHMAN IS A FORMIDABLE FIGHTER!
A BITE FROM A COCKROACH APPEARS TO HAVE GIVEN ROACHMAN HIS SPECIAL ABILITIES! BUT THE QUEST TO UNRAVEL THE MYSTERIES BEHIND HIS TRANSFORMATION CONTINUES ON!

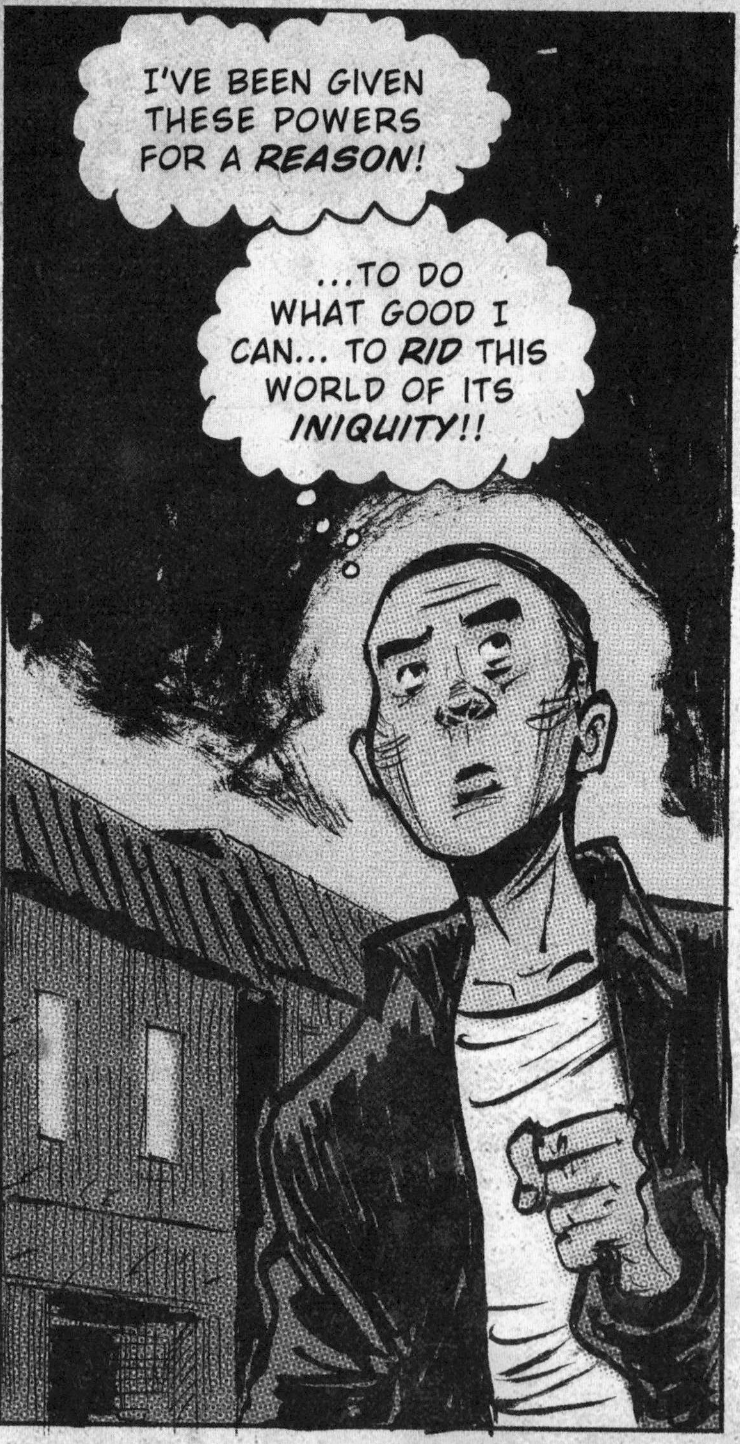
I'VE BEEN GIVEN THESE POWERS FOR A *REASON*!
...TO DO WHAT GOOD I CAN... TO *RID* THIS WORLD OF ITS *INIQUITY*!!

Above **ROACHMAN No. 1 Detail** (1960)

Ah Guan decides to use his newfound powers to help the downtrodden fight for a better life. He dons a homemade costume and adopts the guise of "Roachman" as his vigilante identity.

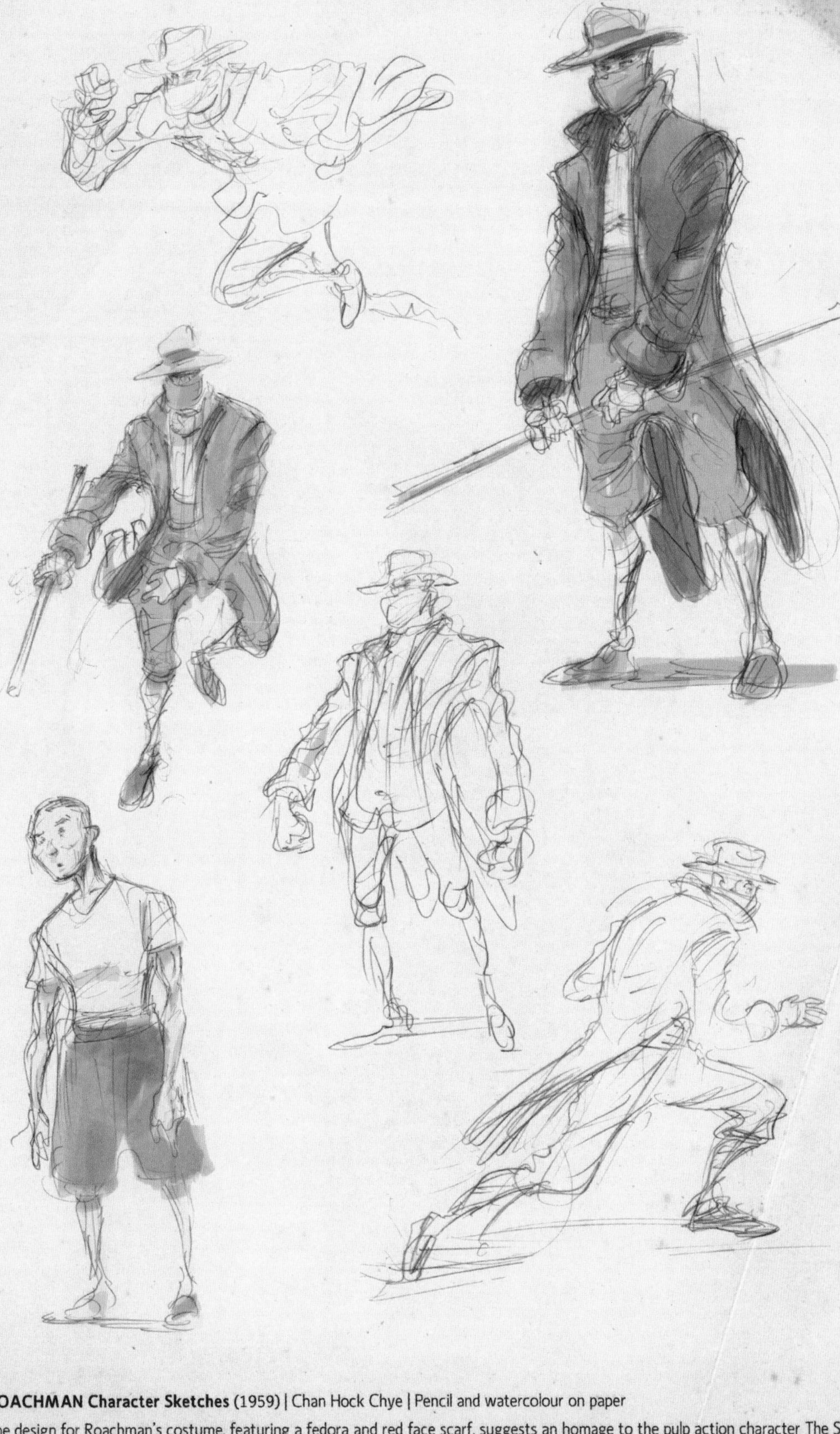

ROACHMAN Character Sketches (1959) | Chan Hock Chye | Pencil and watercolour on paper

The design for Roachman's costume, featuring a fedora and red face scarf, suggests an homage to the pulp action character The Shadow. According to Chan, however, his inspirations were the actual clothing worn by workers in Singapore at the time, as well as the handkerchiefs donned by the Chinese Middle School students during their protests to avoid indentification by the authorities.

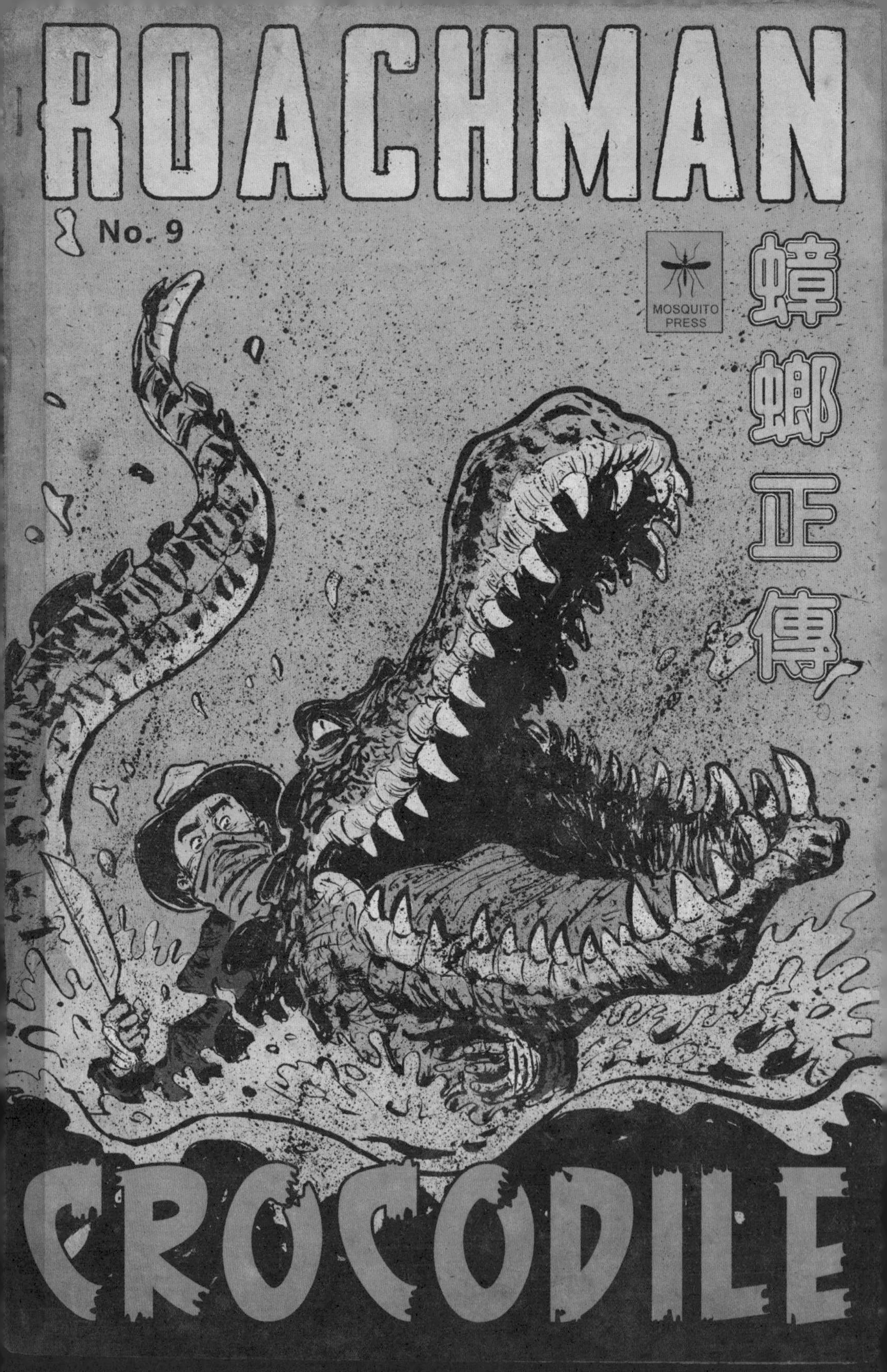
ROACHMAN
No. 9
MOSQUITO PRESS
蟑螂正傳
CROCODILE

Above **ROACHMAN No. 9: CROCODILE** (1960) | Mosquito Press

Top left **ROACHMAN No. 8: THE SERGEANT'S WIFE** (1960) Mosquito Press

Bottom left **ROACHMAN No. 14: THE SCRATCHER** (1961) Mosquito Press

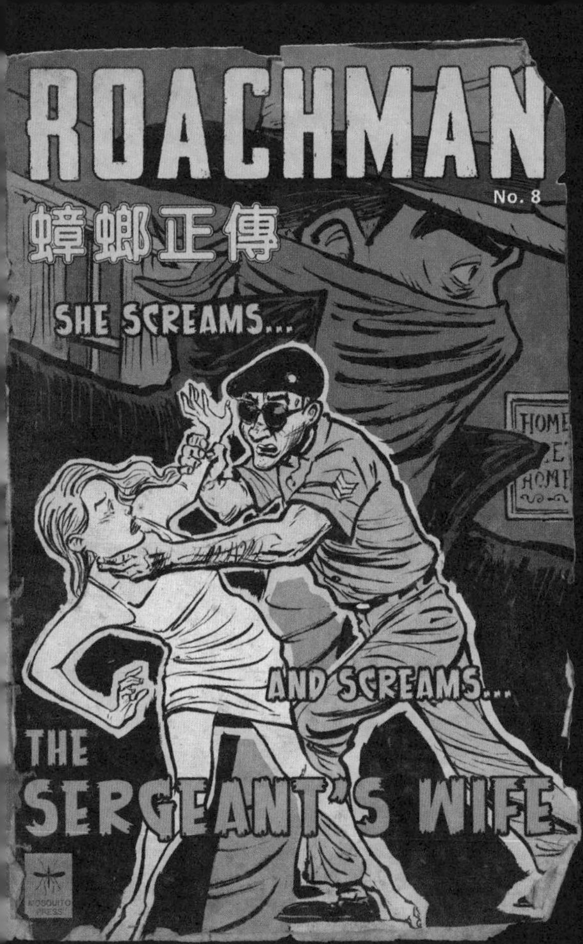
ROACHMAN
No. 8
蟑螂正傳
SHE SCREAMS...
AND SCREAMS...
THE SERGEANT'S WIFE
MOSQUITO PRESS

DESPITE THEIR SENSATIONALISTIC COVERS, THE "*ROACHMAN*" STORIES WERE OFTEN SERIOUS MEDITATIONS ON THE ISSUES OF THE DAY. THE *LUCIEN HICKS* CASE, FOR EXAMPLE, WHERE A BRITISH ARMY OFFICER WAS CHARGED WITH KILLING HIS WIFE IN 1959, WAS USED AS A LENS TO EXAMINE THE NATURE OF JUSTICE IN COLONIAL SOCIETY IN "*THE SERGEANT'S WIFE.*"

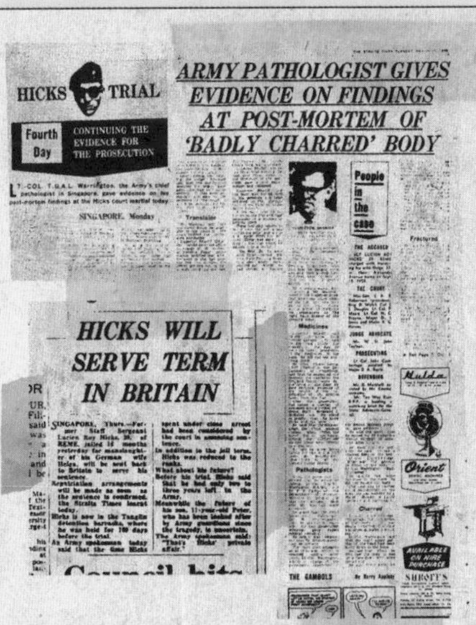
HICKS TRIAL

Fourth Day

CONTINUING THE EVIDENCE FOR THE PROSECUTION

ARMY PATHOLOGIST GIVES EVIDENCE ON FINDINGS AT POST-MORTEM OF 'BADLY CHARRED' BODY

SINGAPORE, Monday

People in the case

HICKS WILL SERVE TERM IN BRITAIN

THE GAMBOLS

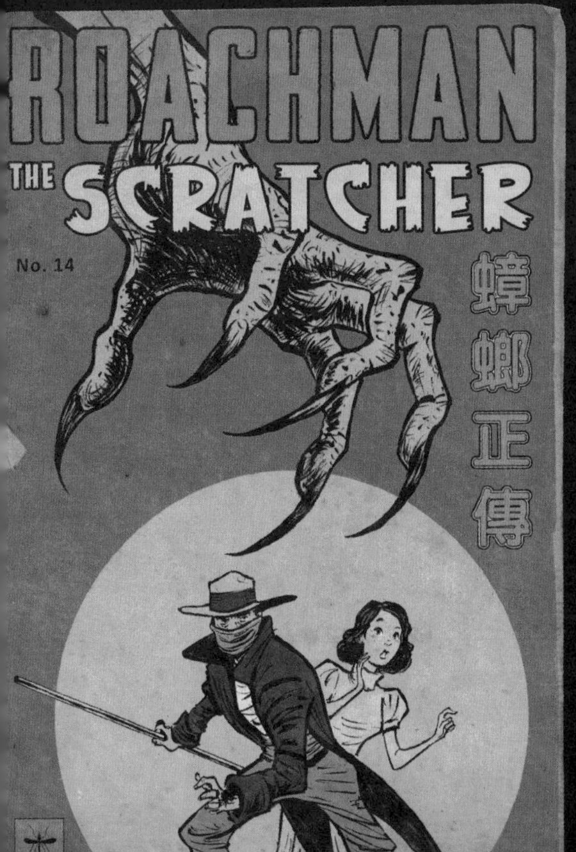
ROACHMAN
THE SCRATCHER
No. 14
蟑螂正傳
MOSQUITO PRESS

"*CROCODILE,*" MEANWHILE, STARTS OUT AS AN ACTION-ADVENTURE YARN, AS ROACHMAN IS TASKED WITH HUNTING DOWN A CROCODILE THAT HAS BEEN SOWING TERROR AMONG THE VILLAGERS. THE FINAL PANELS, HOWEVER, FEATURING SHOTS OF ROW UPON ROW OF CROCODILE SKIN MERCHANDISE, TURNS THE IDEA OF MAN-AS-VICTIM ON ITS HEAD.

THERE WERE LIGHT-HEARTED STORIES TOO, SUCH AS THE POLICE PROCEDURAL FARCE, "*THE SCRATCHER.*"

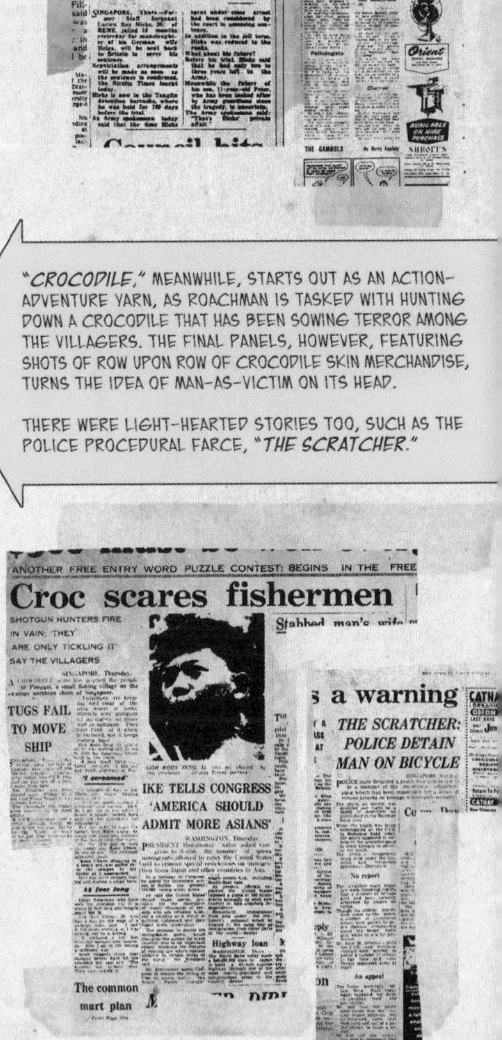
ANOTHER FREE ENTRY WORD PUZZLE CONTEST: BEGINS IN THE FREE

Croc scares fishermen

SHOTGUN HUNTERS FIRE IN VAIN: 'THEY ARE ONLY TICKLING IT' SAY THE VILLAGERS

TUGS FAIL TO MOVE SHIP

IKE TELLS CONGRESS 'AMERICA SHOULD ADMIT MORE ASIANS'

WASHINGTON, Thursday

Highway loan

The common mart plan

THE SCRATCHER: POLICE DETAIN MAN ON BICYCLE

No report

ODEON

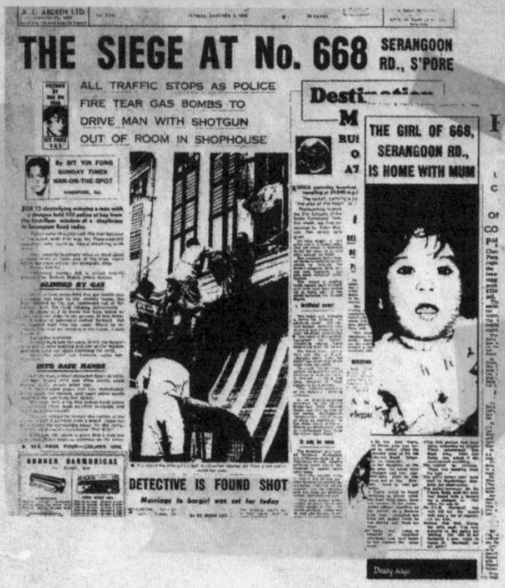

THE SIEGE AT No. 668 SERANGOON RD., S'PORE

ALL TRAFFIC STOPS AS POLICE FIRE TEAR GAS BOMBS TO DRIVE MAN WITH SHOTGUN OUT OF ROOM IN SHOPHOUSE

THE GIRL OF 668, SERANGOON RD., IS HOME WITH MUM

DETECTIVE IS FOUND SHOT

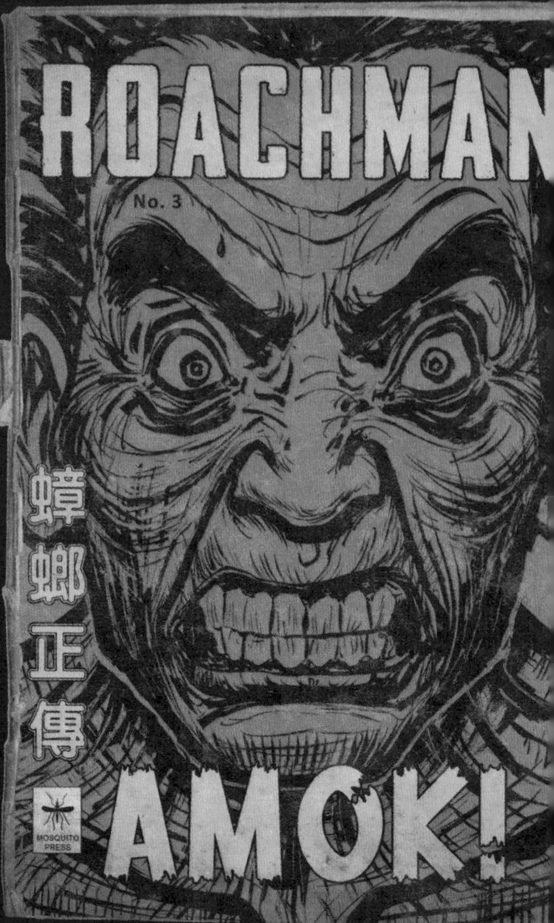

ROACHMAN
No. 3
蟑螂正傳
AMOK!
MOSQUITO PRESS

"*AMOK!*" EXPLORES THE AFTERMATH OF A FATHER'S VIOLENT PSYCHOLOGICAL BREAKDOWN, AND HIS FAMILY'S STRUGGLES TO COPE WITHOUT HIM FOLLOWING HIS ARREST AND INCARCERATION.

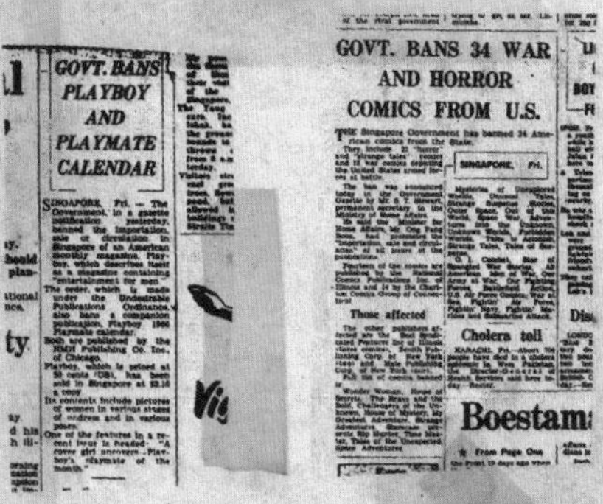

GOVT. BANS PLAYBOY AND PLAYMATE CALENDAR

GOVT. BANS 34 WAR AND HORROR COMICS FROM U.S.

Cholera toll

Boestama

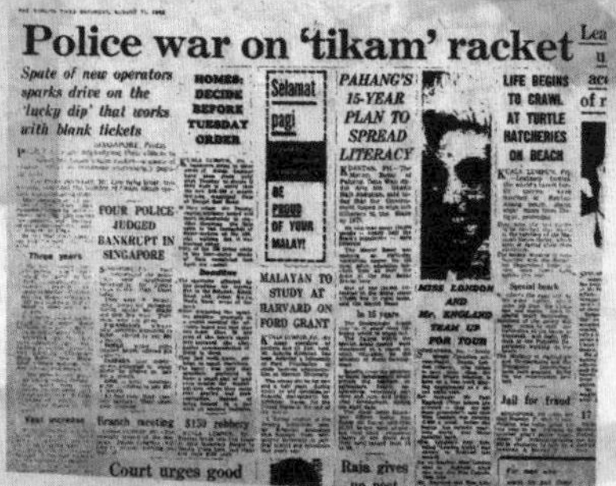

Police war on 'tikam' racket

Spate of new operators sparks drive on the 'lucky dip' that works with blank tickets

HOMES: DECIDE BEFORE TUESDAY ORDER

PAHANG'S 15-YEAR PLAN TO SPREAD LITERACY

LIFE BEGINS TO CRAWL AT TURTLE HATCHERIES ON BEACH

FOUR POLICE JUDGED BANKRUPT IN SINGAPORE

MALAYAN TO STUDY AT HARVARD ON FORD GRANT

Court urges good

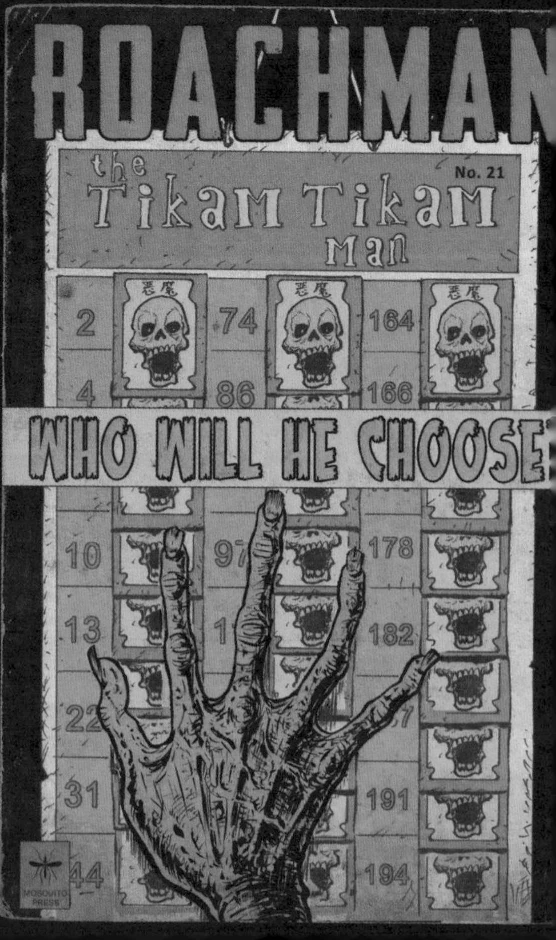

ROACHMAN
the Tikam Tikam man
No. 21
WHO WILL HE CHOOSE
MOSQUITO PRESS

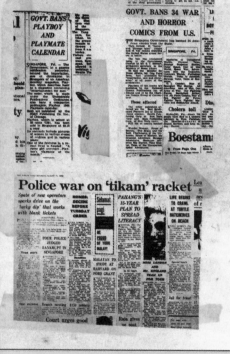

THE PAP'S WAR ON THE SUPPOSEDLY HARMFUL INFLUENCES OF WESTERN OR "YELLOW" CULTURE WAS ALSO FEATURED. GOVERNMENTAL BANS ON ADULT MAGAZINES AND GAMES OF CHANCE FOR CHILDREN (KNOWN AS "*TIKAM TIKAM*") WERE GIVEN A TONGUE-IN-CHEEK TREATMENT IN STORIES SUCH AS "*THE LAST PLAYBOY*" (1960), WHICH DEPICTS ONE MAN'S INCREASINGLY DESPERATE ATTEMPTS TO BUY UP EVERY LAST COPY OF THE RISQUÉ MAGAZINE BEFORE THE *UNDESIRABLE PUBLICATIONS ORDINANCE* CAME INTO EFFECT.

Top right **ROACHMAN No. 3: AMOK!** (1959) Mosquito Press

Bottom right **ROACHMAN No. 21: TIKAM TIKAM MAN** (1962) Mosquito Press

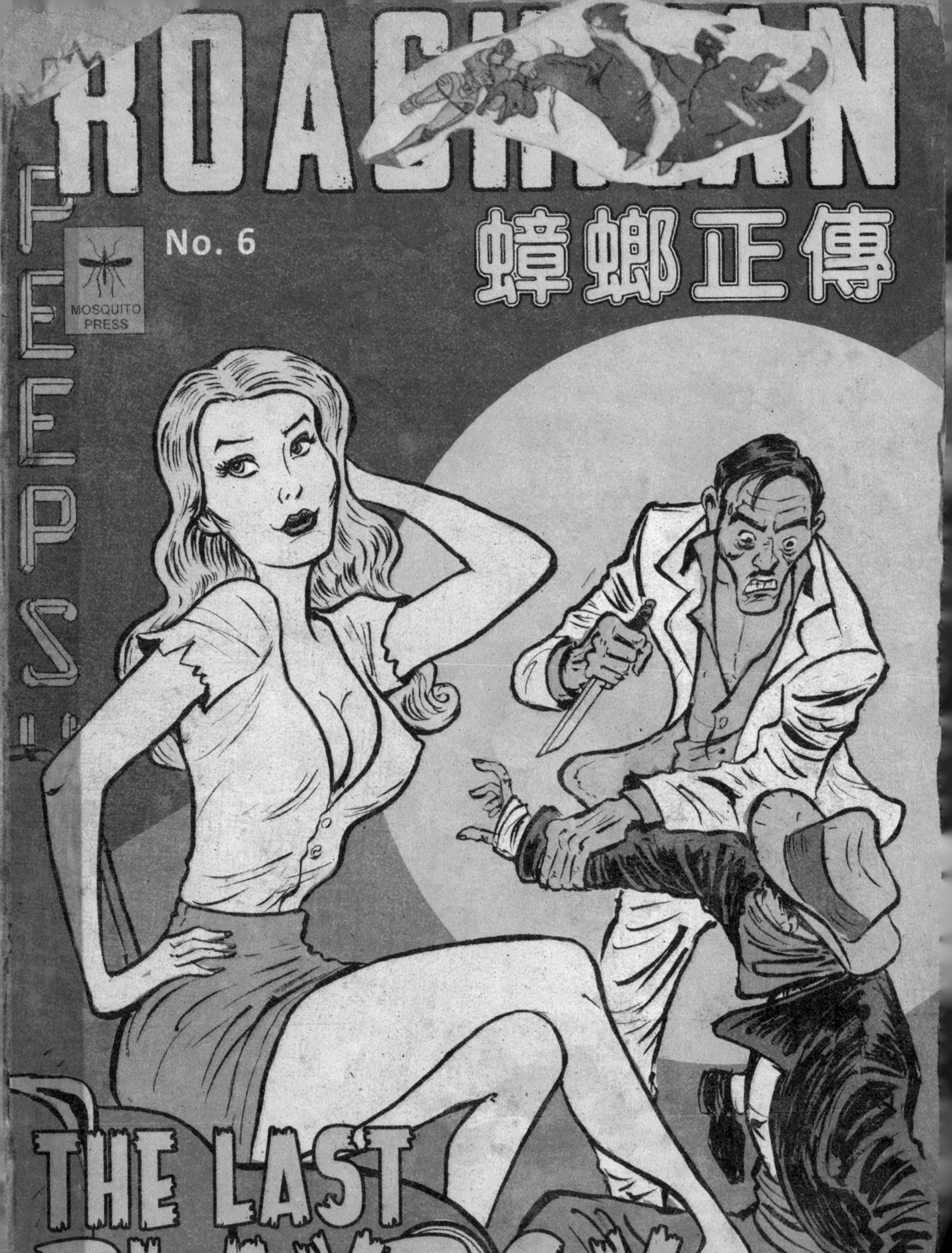
ROACHMAN
PEEPS
No. 6
MOSQUITO
PRESS
蟑螂正傳
THE LAST
PLAYBOY

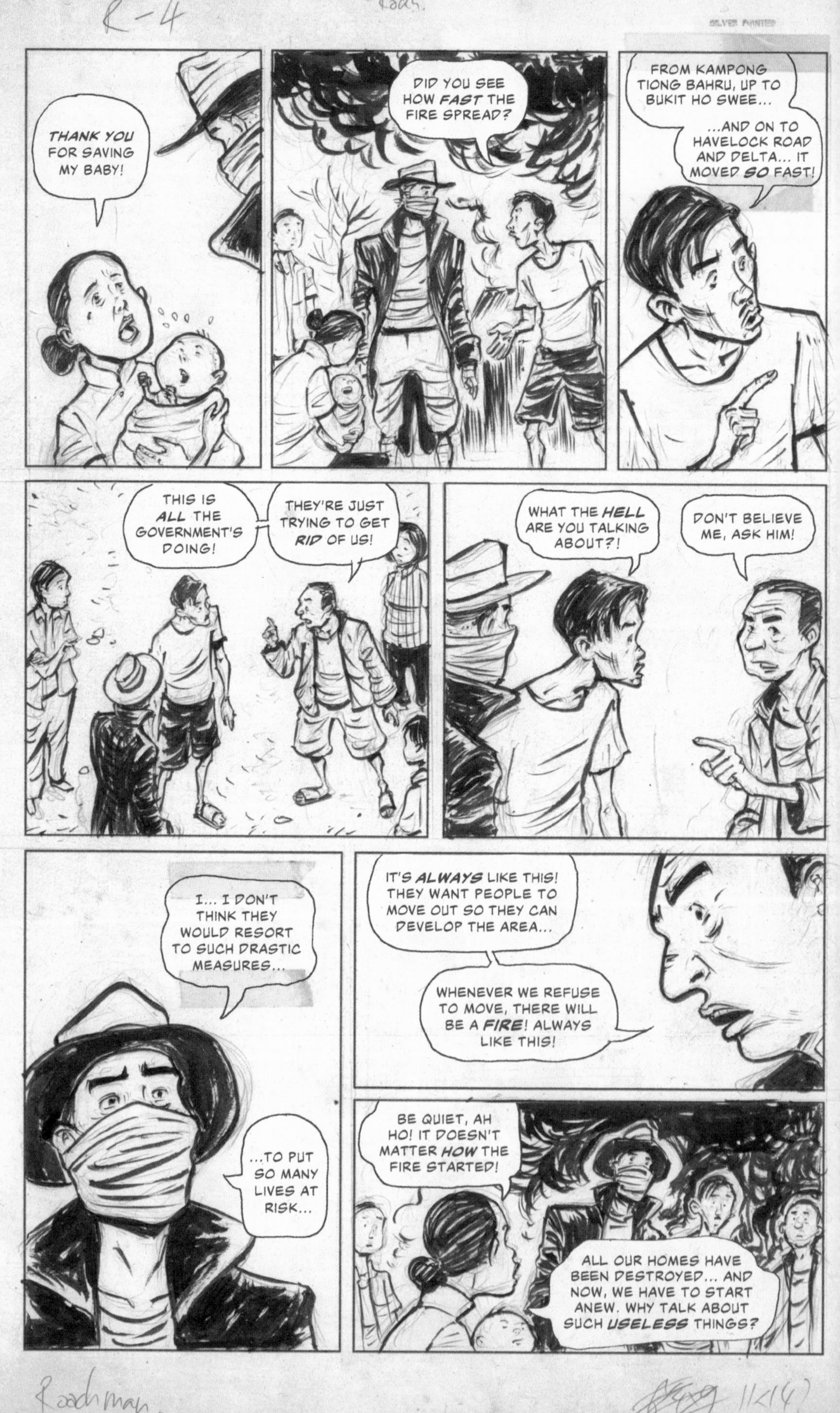
R-4
Roach.
THANK YOU FOR SAVING MY BABY!
DID YOU SEE HOW FAST THE FIRE SPREAD?
FROM KAMPONG TIONG BAHRU, UP TO BUKIT HO SWEE...
...AND ON TO HAVELOCK ROAD AND DELTA... IT MOVED SO FAST!
THIS IS ALL THE GOVERNMENT'S DOING!
THEY'RE JUST TRYING TO GET RID OF US!
WHAT THE HELL ARE YOU TALKING ABOUT?!
DON'T BELIEVE ME, ASK HIM!
I... I DON'T THINK THEY WOULD RESORT TO SUCH DRASTIC MEASURES...
...TO PUT SO MANY LIVES AT RISK...
IT'S ALWAYS LIKE THIS! THEY WANT PEOPLE TO MOVE OUT SO THEY CAN DEVELOP THE AREA...
WHENEVER WE REFUSE TO MOVE, THERE WILL BE A FIRE! ALWAYS LIKE THIS!
BE QUIET, AH HO! IT DOESN'T MATTER HOW THE FIRE STARTED!
ALL OUR HOMES HAVE BEEN DESTROYED... AND NOW, WE HAVE TO START ANEW. WHY TALK ABOUT SUCH USELESS THINGS?
Roachman

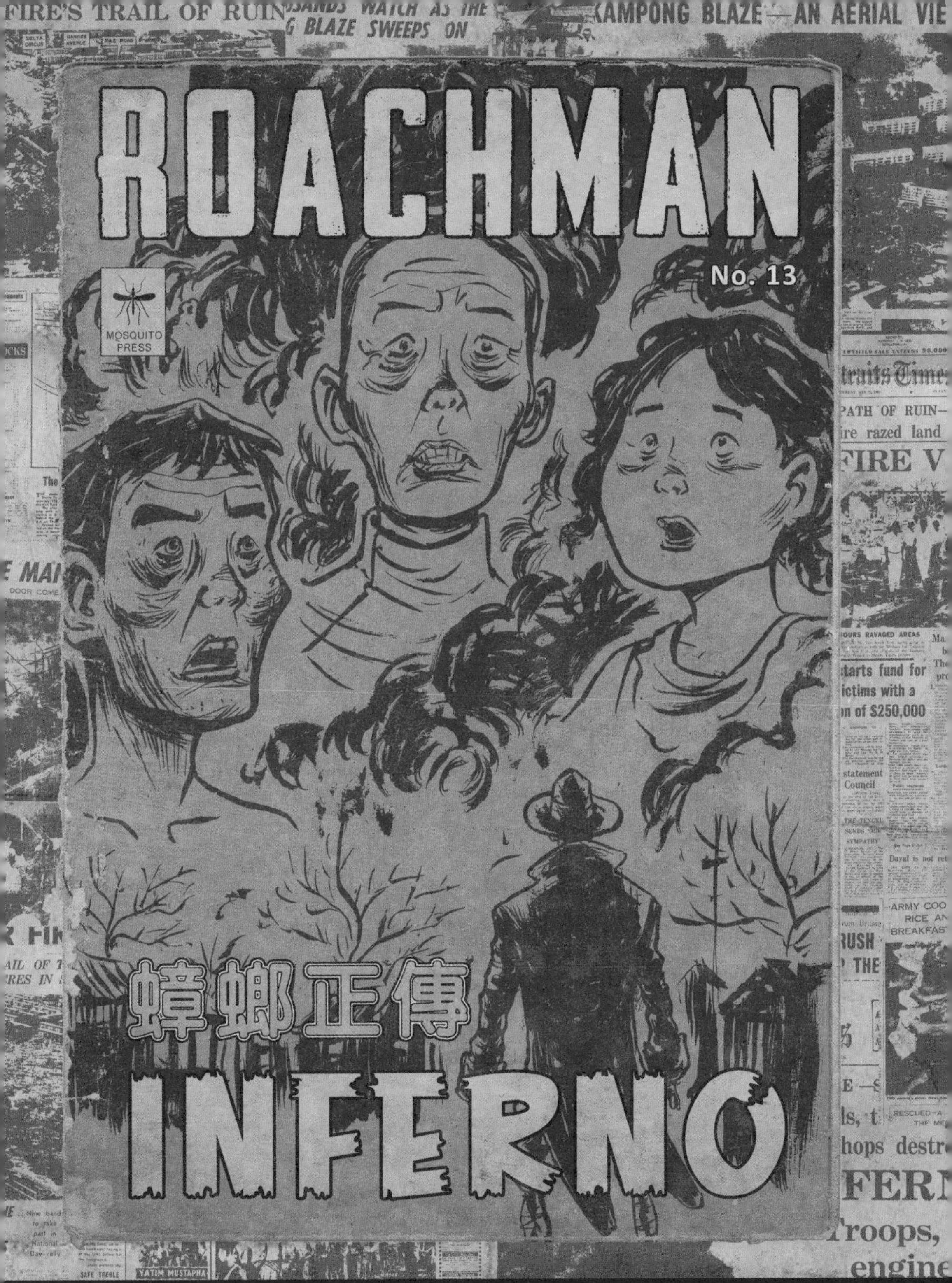
ROACHMAN
MOSQUITO PRESS
No. 13
蟑螂正傳
INFERNO

Opposite & above **ROACHMAN No. 13: INFERNO** (1961) | Art by Chan Hock Chye, Words by Bertrand Wong | Mosquito Press

ROACHMAN FINDS HIMSELF FACING DOWN FLAMES AND CONSPIRACY THEORIES DURING THE *BUKIT HO SWEE FIRE* IN "*INFERNO.*" THE INFAMOUS 100-ACRE FIRE DESTROYED THE HOMES OF SOME 16,000 SQUATTER KAMPONG DWELLERS, AND MARKED THE BEGINNING OF LARGE-SCALE PUBLIC HOUSING BUILDING AND RELOCATION BY THE PAP, WHICH WOULD IRREVOCABLY TRANSFORM THE URBAN AND SOCIAL LANDSCAPE OF SINGAPORE.

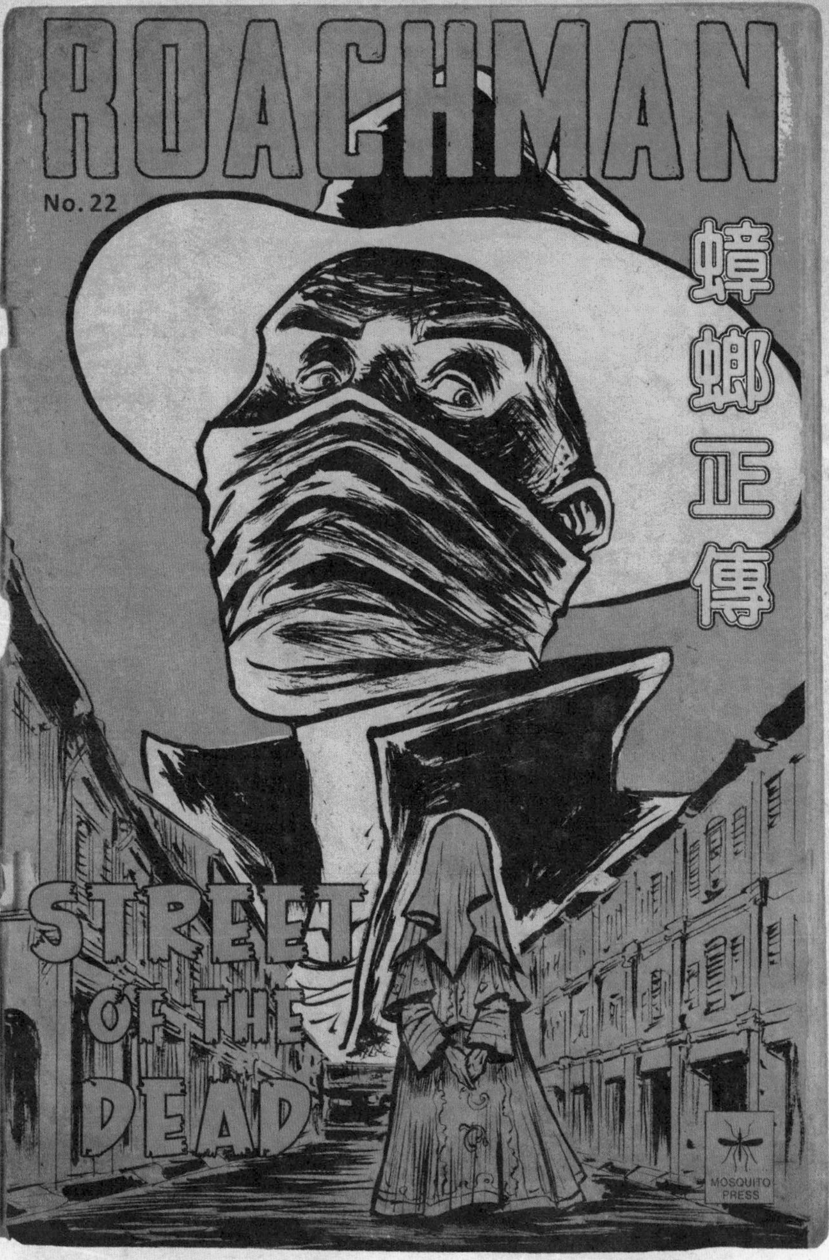

ROACHMAN
No. 22
蟑螂正傳
STREET OF THE DEAD
MOSQUITO PRESS

"STREET OF THE DEAD" WAS A COLLECTION OF SHORT STORIES SET IN *SAGO LANE*, INFAMOUS THEN FOR ITS "DEATH HOUSES" — FUNERAL HOMES THAT DOUBLED AS HOSPICES FOR THE ELDERLY TO SPEND THEIR FINAL DAYS.

THE MAIN STORY CENTRED ON A TEENAGE COUPLE WHO HAD COMMITTED SUICIDE TOGETHER AFTER APPARENT PARENTAL OBJECTIONS TO THEIR RELATIONSHIP, AND THE SUBSEQUENT "MARRIAGE" RITES HELD AT SAGO LANE TO "REUNITE" THE STAR-CROSSED LOVERS IN THE AFTERLIFE.

Left
ROACHMAN No. 22: STREET OF THE DEAD
1962
Mosquito Press

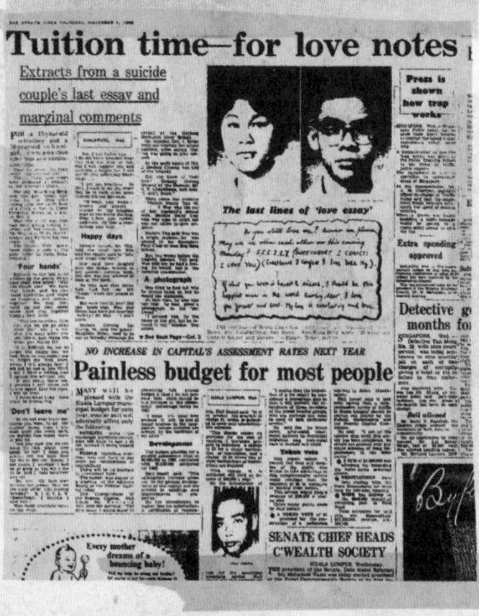

Tuition time—for love notes
Extracts from a suicide couple's last essay and marginal comments
Press is shown how trap works
The last lines of 'love essay'
Happy days
'Four hands'
A photograph
Extra spending approved
Detective gets months for
NO INCREASE IN CAPITAL'S ASSESSMENT RATES NEXT YEAR
Painless budget for most people
'Don't leave me'
SENATE CHIEF HEADS C'WEALTH SOCIETY
Every mother dreams of a bouncing baby!

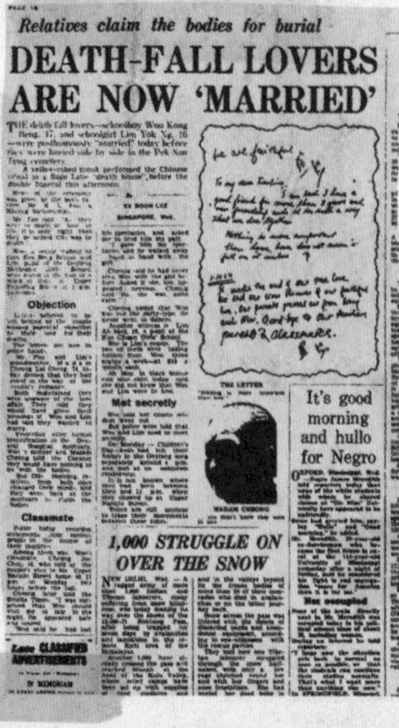

Relatives claim the bodies for burial
DEATH-FALL LOVERS ARE NOW 'MARRIED'
Objection
Not secretly
Classmate
It's good morning and hullo for Negro
1,000 STRUGGLE ON OVER THE SNOW
Low CLASSIFIED ADVERTISEMENTS

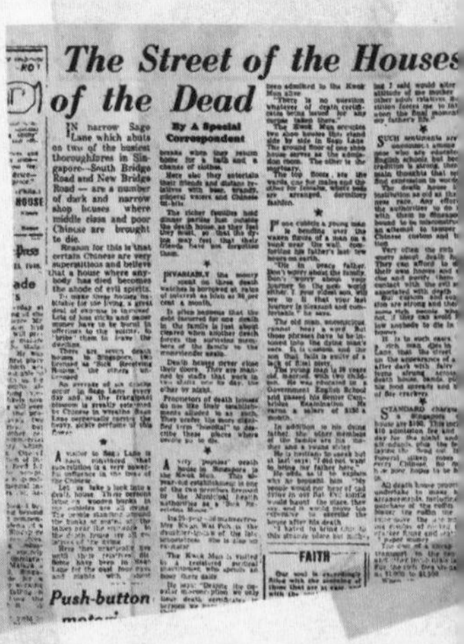

The Street of the Houses of the Dead
By A Special Correspondent
FAITH
Push-button

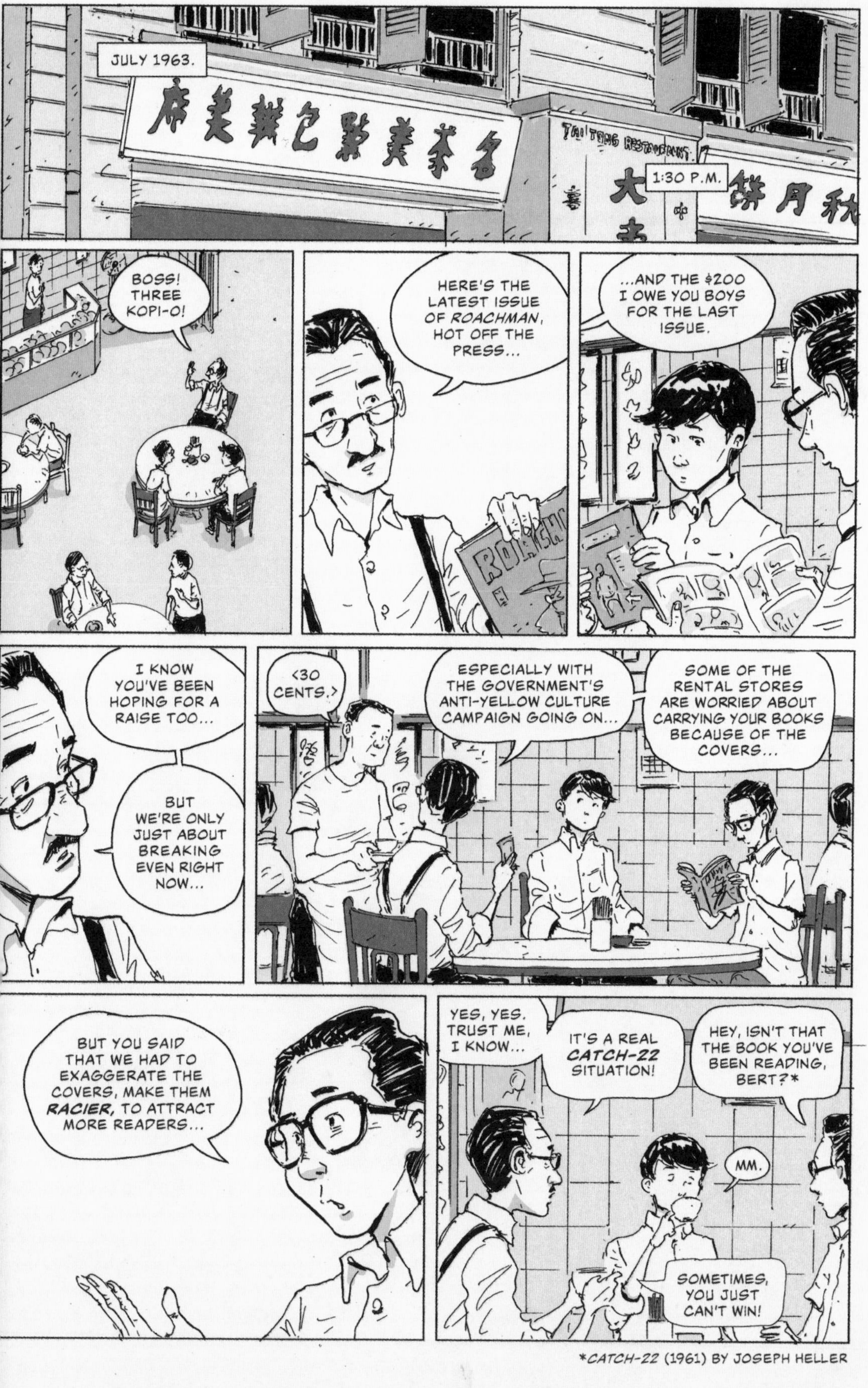

JULY 1963.
TAI TONG RESTAURANT
1:30 P.M.
BOSS! THREE KOPI-O!
HERE'S THE LATEST ISSUE OF *ROACHMAN*, HOT OFF THE PRESS...
...AND THE $200 I OWE YOU BOYS FOR THE LAST ISSUE.
I KNOW YOU'VE BEEN HOPING FOR A RAISE TOO...
BUT WE'RE ONLY JUST ABOUT BREAKING EVEN RIGHT NOW...
<30 CENTS.>
ESPECIALLY WITH THE GOVERNMENT'S ANTI-YELLOW CULTURE CAMPAIGN GOING ON...
SOME OF THE RENTAL STORES ARE WORRIED ABOUT CARRYING YOUR BOOKS BECAUSE OF THE COVERS...
BUT YOU SAID THAT WE HAD TO EXAGGERATE THE COVERS, MAKE THEM ***RACIER,*** TO ATTRACT MORE READERS...
YES, YES. TRUST ME, I KNOW...
IT'S A REAL ***CATCH-22*** SITUATION!
HEY, ISN'T THAT THE BOOK YOU'VE BEEN READING, BERT?*
MM.
SOMETIMES, YOU JUST CAN'T WIN!

**CATCH-22* (1961) BY JOSEPH HELLER

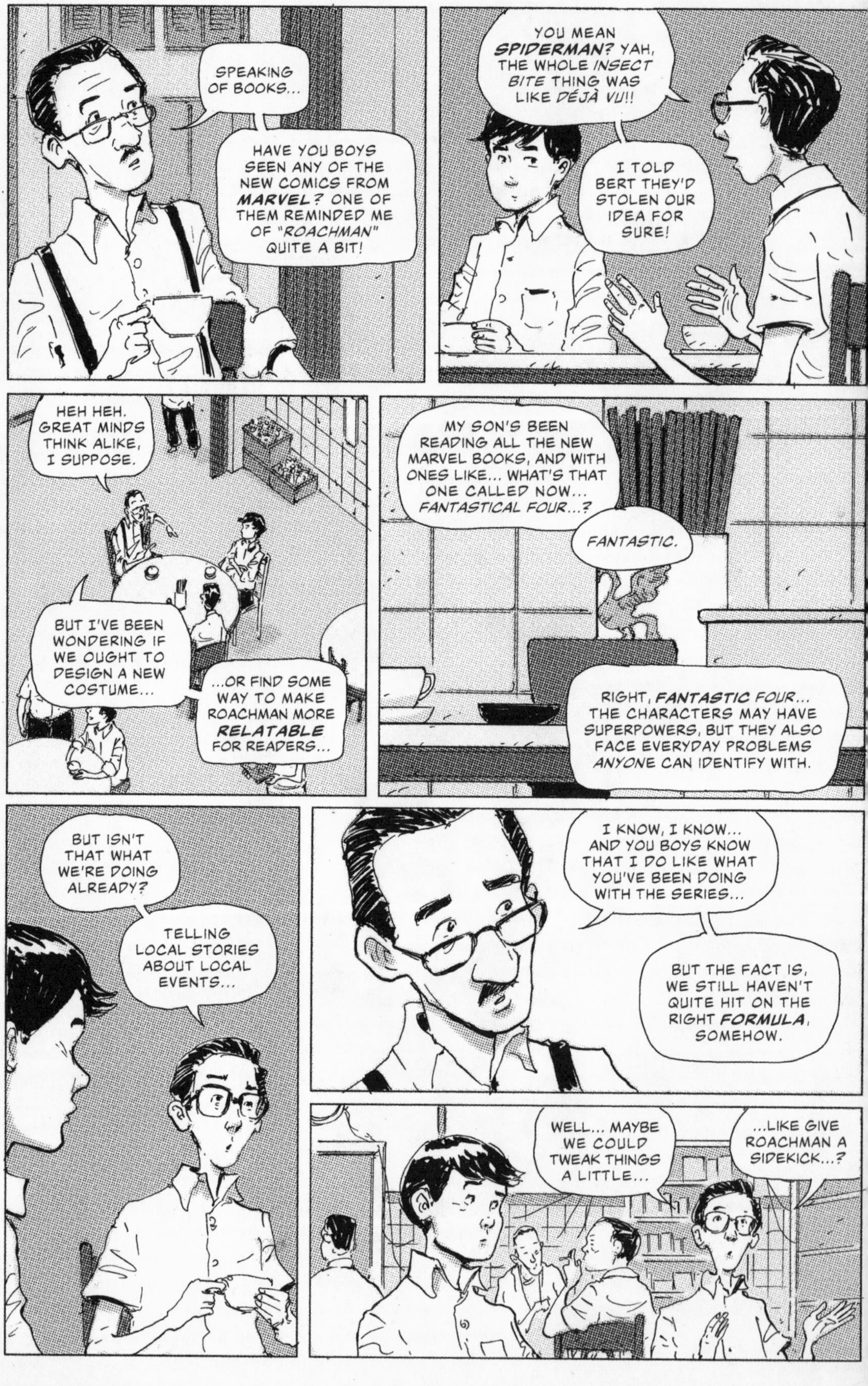
SPEAKING OF BOOKS...
HAVE YOU BOYS SEEN ANY OF THE NEW COMICS FROM **MARVEL**? ONE OF THEM REMINDED ME OF "*ROACHMAN*" QUITE A BIT!
YOU MEAN ***SPIDERMAN***? YAH, THE WHOLE *INSECT BITE* THING WAS LIKE *DÉJÀ VU*!!
I TOLD BERT THEY'D STOLEN OUR IDEA FOR SURE!
HEH HEH. GREAT MINDS THINK ALIKE, I SUPPOSE.
BUT I'VE BEEN WONDERING IF WE OUGHT TO DESIGN A NEW COSTUME...
...OR FIND SOME WAY TO MAKE ROACHMAN MORE ***RELATABLE*** FOR READERS...
MY SON'S BEEN READING ALL THE NEW MARVEL BOOKS, AND WITH ONES LIKE... WHAT'S THAT ONE CALLED NOW... *FANTASTICAL FOUR*...?
FANTASTIC.
RIGHT, ***FANTASTIC*** *FOUR*... THE CHARACTERS MAY HAVE SUPERPOWERS, BUT THEY ALSO FACE EVERYDAY PROBLEMS *ANYONE* CAN IDENTIFY WITH.
BUT ISN'T THAT WHAT WE'RE DOING ALREADY?
TELLING LOCAL STORIES ABOUT LOCAL EVENTS...
I KNOW, I KNOW... AND YOU BOYS KNOW THAT I DO LIKE WHAT YOU'VE BEEN DOING WITH THE SERIES...
BUT THE FACT IS, WE STILL HAVEN'T QUITE HIT ON THE RIGHT ***FORMULA***, SOMEHOW.
WELL... MAYBE WE COULD TWEAK THINGS A LITTLE...
...LIKE GIVE ROACHMAN A SIDEKICK...?

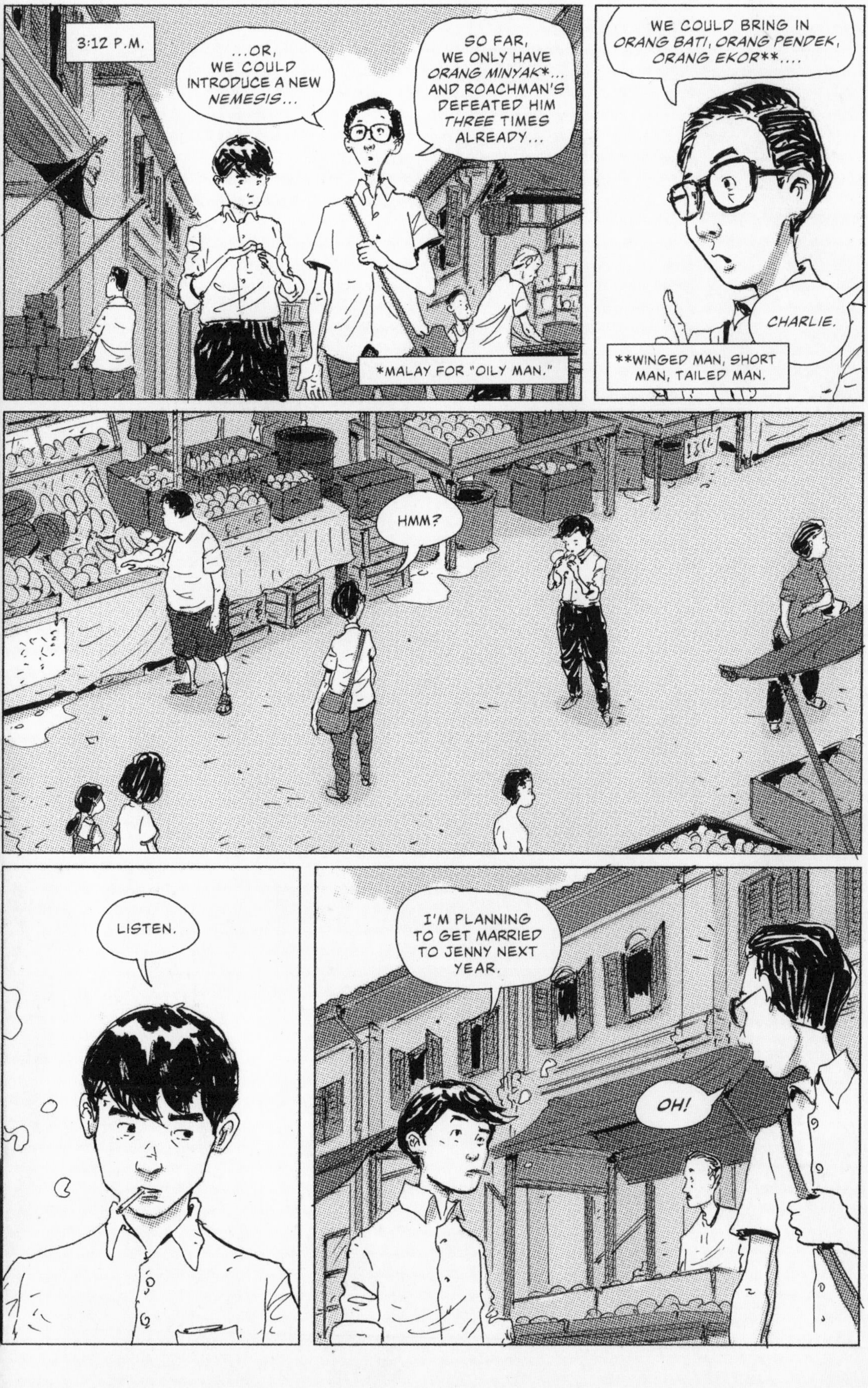
3:12 P.M.
...OR, WE COULD INTRODUCE A NEW *NEMESIS*...
SO FAR, WE ONLY HAVE *ORANG MINYAK**... AND ROACHMAN'S DEFEATED HIM *THREE TIMES* ALREADY...
*MALAY FOR "OILY MAN."
WE COULD BRING IN *ORANG BATI, ORANG PENDEK, ORANG EKOR***....
CHARLIE.
**WINGED MAN, SHORT MAN, TAILED MAN.
HMM?
LISTEN.
I'M PLANNING TO GET MARRIED TO JENNY NEXT YEAR.
OH!

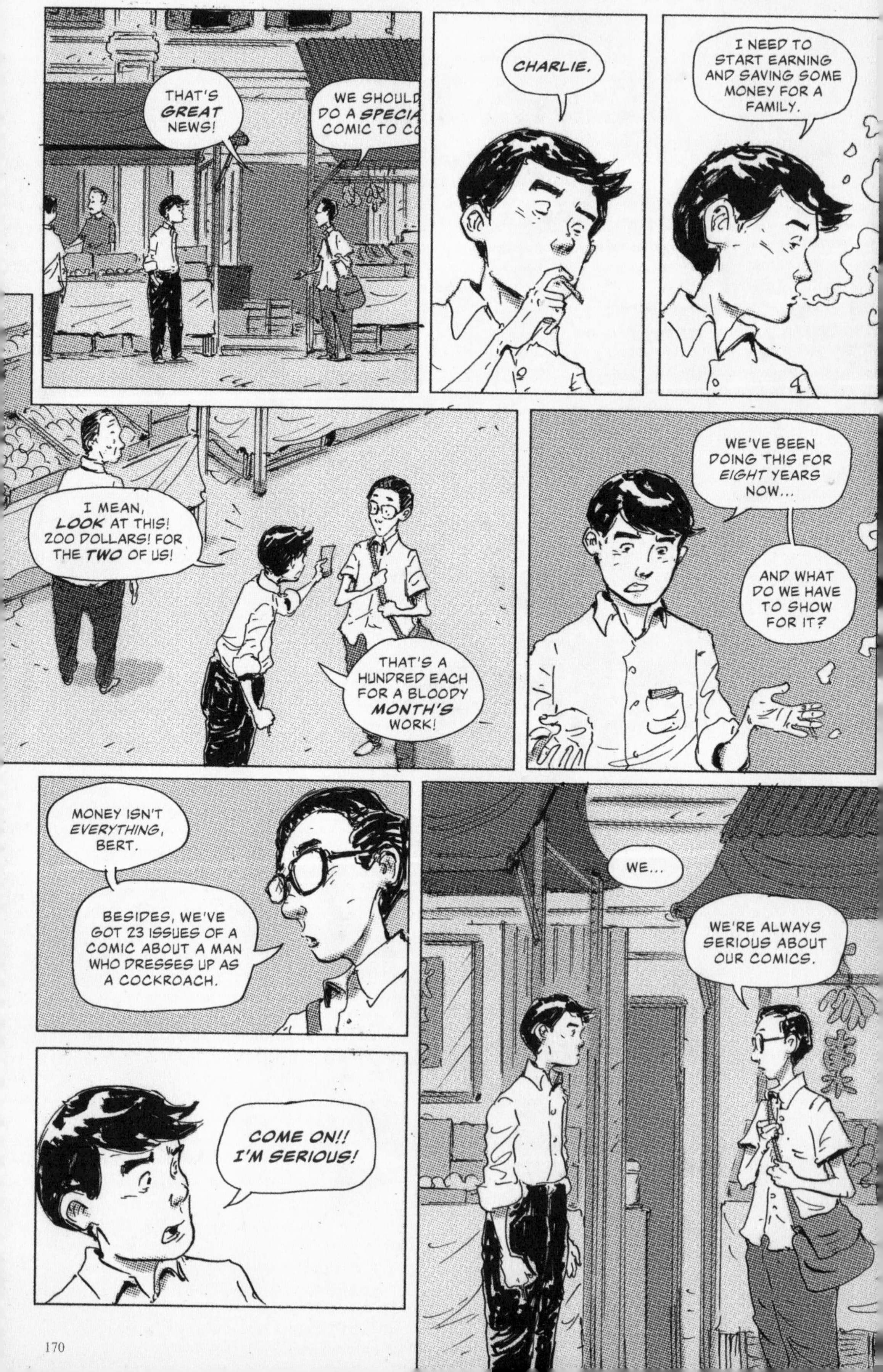
THAT'S GREAT NEWS!
WE SHOULD DO A SPECIA COMIC TO CO
CHARLIE.
I NEED TO START EARNING AND SAVING SOME MONEY FOR A FAMILY.
I MEAN, LOOK AT THIS! 200 DOLLARS! FOR THE TWO OF US!
THAT'S A HUNDRED EACH FOR A BLOODY MONTH'S WORK!
WE'VE BEEN DOING THIS FOR EIGHT YEARS NOW...
AND WHAT DO WE HAVE TO SHOW FOR IT?
MONEY ISN'T EVERYTHING, BERT.
BESIDES, WE'VE GOT 23 ISSUES OF A COMIC ABOUT A MAN WHO DRESSES UP AS A COCKROACH.
COME ON!! I'M SERIOUS!
WE...
WE'RE ALWAYS SERIOUS ABOUT OUR COMICS.

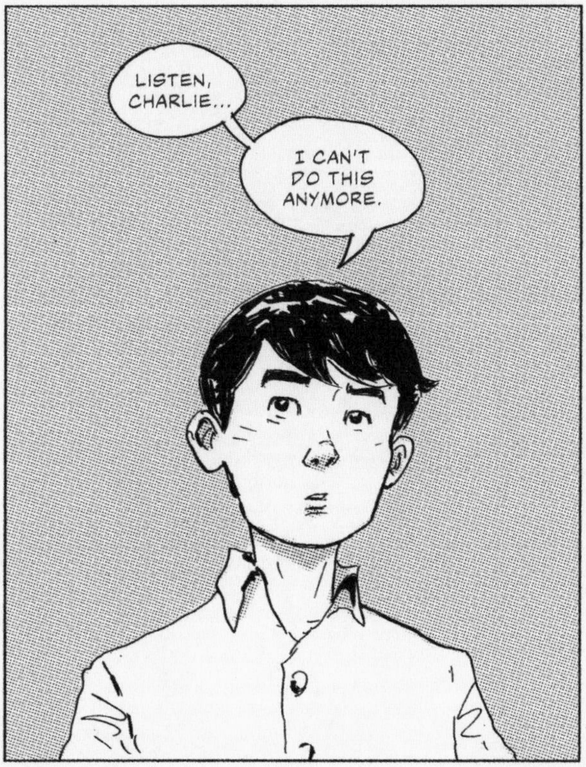
LISTEN, CHARLIE...
I CAN'T DO THIS ANYMORE.

Lim Chin Siong was freed from detention after the
People's Action Party's victory in the 1959 elections.

But divisions within the Party would lead to a split between the radical left led by Lim and the moderates under Lee Kuan Yew in 1961.

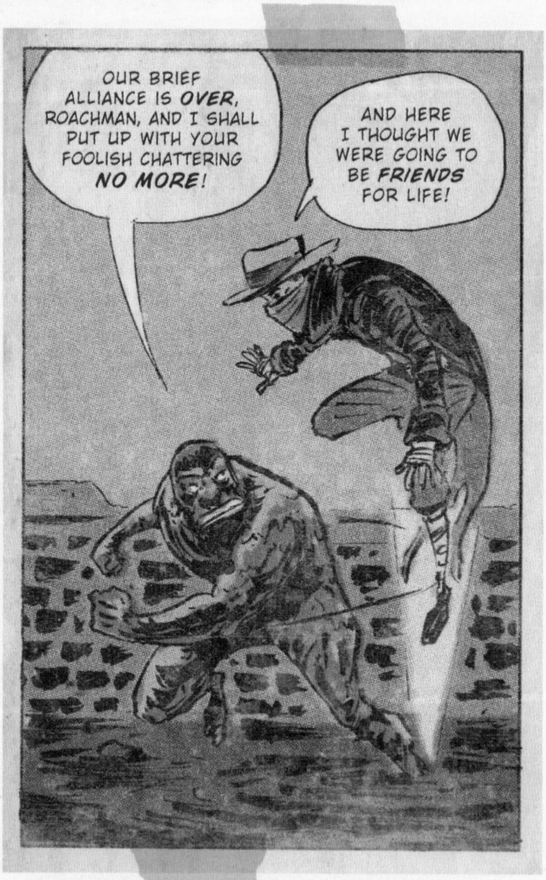
OUR BRIEF ALLIANCE IS OVER, ROACHMAN, AND I SHALL PUT UP WITH YOUR FOOLISH CHATTERING NO MORE!
AND HERE I THOUGHT WE WERE GOING TO BE FRIENDS FOR LIFE!

Lee and the PAP feared that the new splinter party, the **Barisan Sosialis**, would triumph in the next elections.

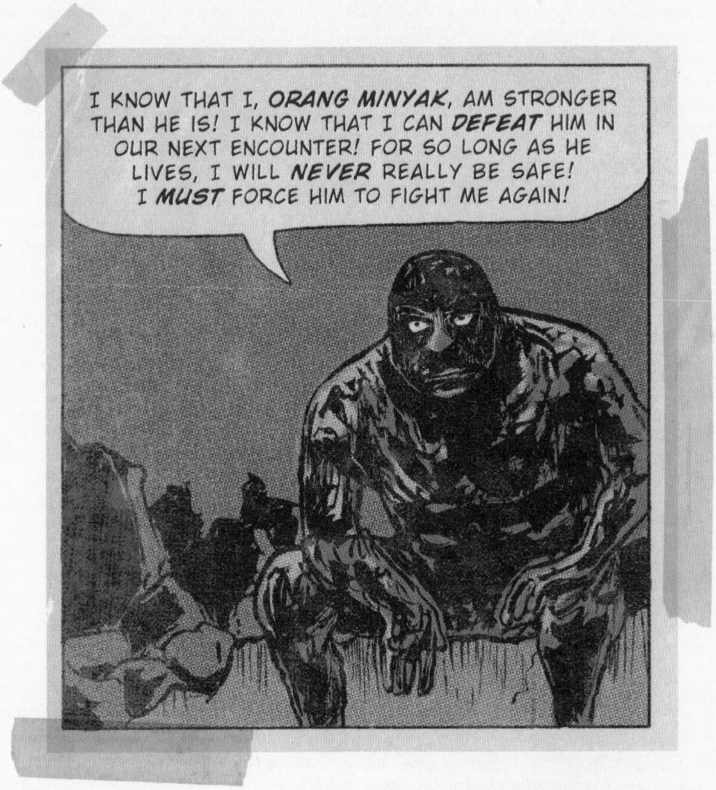
I KNOW THAT I, ORANG MINYAK, AM STRONGER THAN HE IS! I KNOW THAT I CAN DEFEAT HIM IN OUR NEXT ENCOUNTER! FOR SO LONG AS HE LIVES, I WILL NEVER REALLY BE SAFE! I MUST FORCE HIM TO FIGHT ME AGAIN!

Meanwhile, the Prime Minister of Malaya, Tunku Abdul Rahman, was deeply concerned about the prospect of having a communist-led Singapore right at his doorstep.

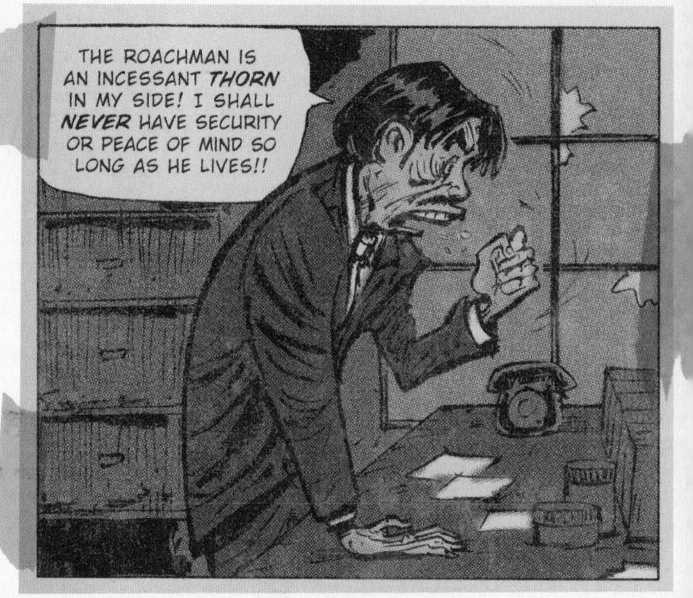
THE ROACHMAN IS AN INCESSANT ***THORN*** IN MY SIDE! I SHALL ***NEVER*** HAVE SECURITY OR PEACE OF MIND SO LONG AS HE LIVES!!

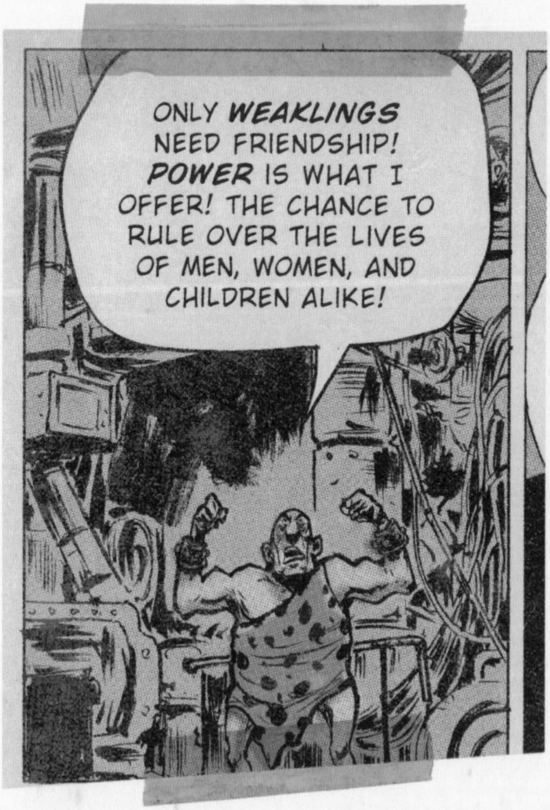
ONLY ***WEAKLINGS*** NEED FRIENDSHIP! ***POWER*** IS WHAT I OFFER! THE CHANCE TO RULE OVER THE LIVES OF MEN, WOMEN, AND CHILDREN ALIKE!

And the British certainly had no wish for an independent Singapore with a radical left-wing, anti-colonial government in charge.

On February 2, 1963, the Singapore, Malayan and British governments jointly launched **Operation Coldstore**, arresting Lim Chin Siong alongside more than a hundred other left-wing leaders and activists, placing them in indefinite detention without trial.

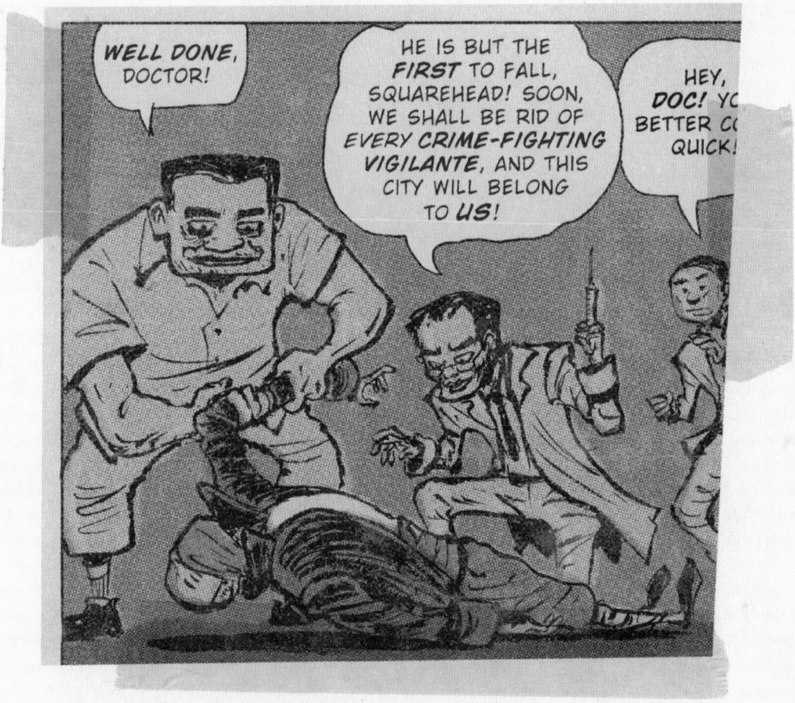
WELL DONE, DOCTOR!
HE IS BUT THE FIRST TO FALL, SQUAREHEAD! SOON, WE SHALL BE RID OF EVERY CRIME-FIGHTING VIGILANTE, AND THIS CITY WILL BELONG TO US!
HEY, DOC! YO BETTER CO QUICK!

During this second period of incarceration, Lim reportedly struggled with depression. After an attempted suicide, he was released on July 28, 1969, after agreeing to renounce politics and to go into exile in London.

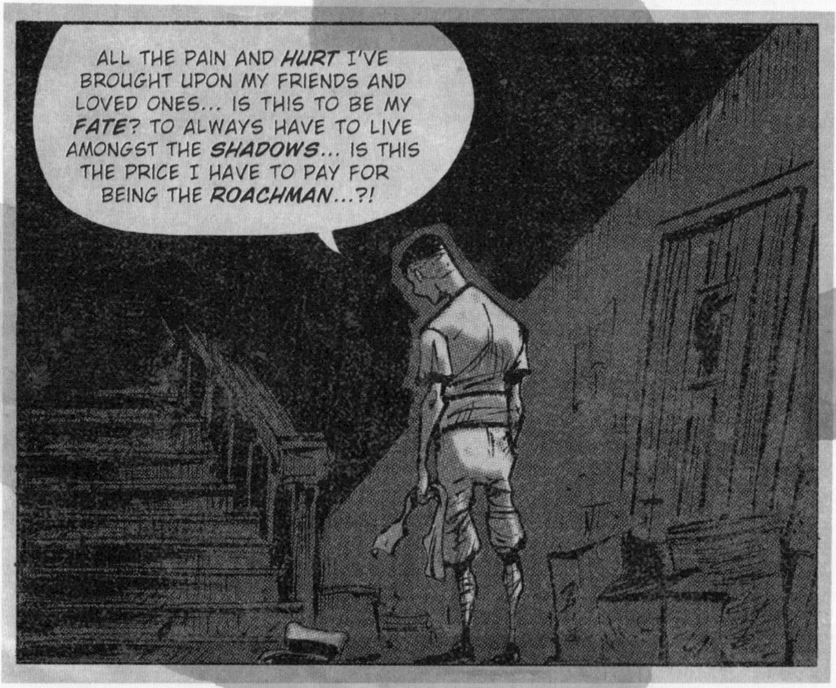
ALL THE PAIN AND HURT I'VE BROUGHT UPON MY FRIENDS AND LOVED ONES... IS THIS TO BE MY FATE? TO ALWAYS HAVE TO LIVE AMONGST THE SHADOWS... IS THIS THE PRICE I HAVE TO PAY FOR BEING THE ROACHMAN...?!

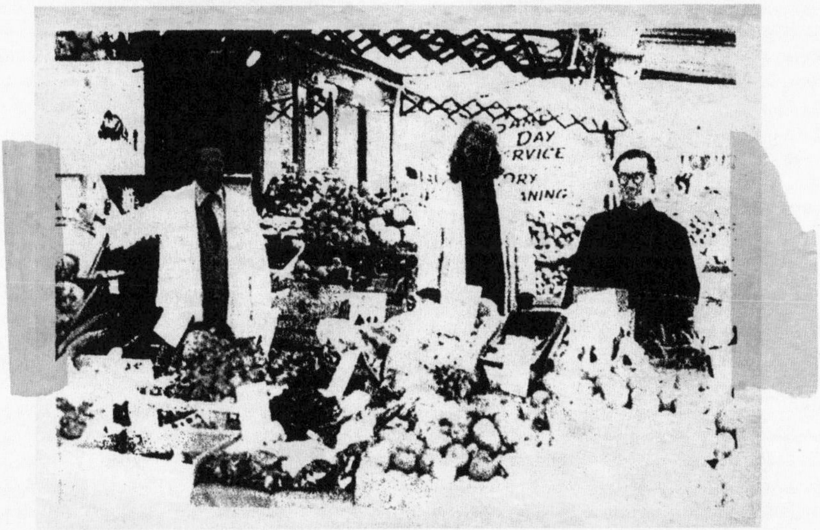
DAY
RVICE

He would work there as a fruit and vegetable seller for the next decade.

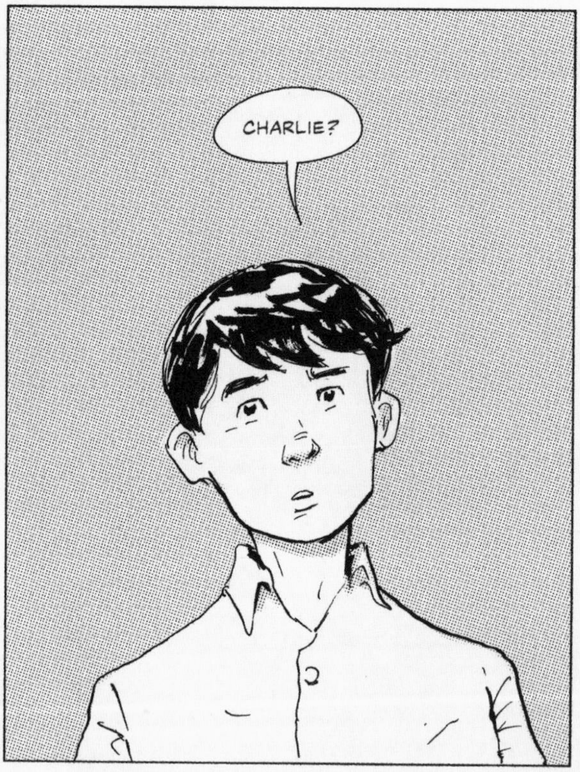
CHARLIE?

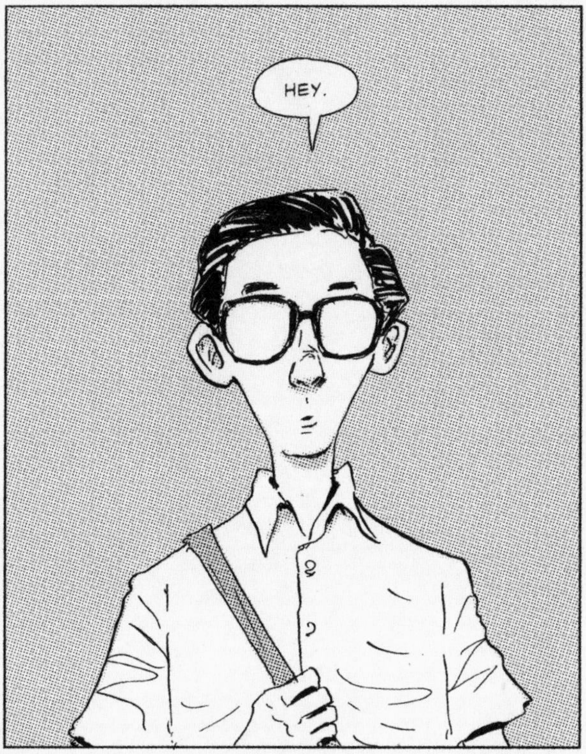
HEY.

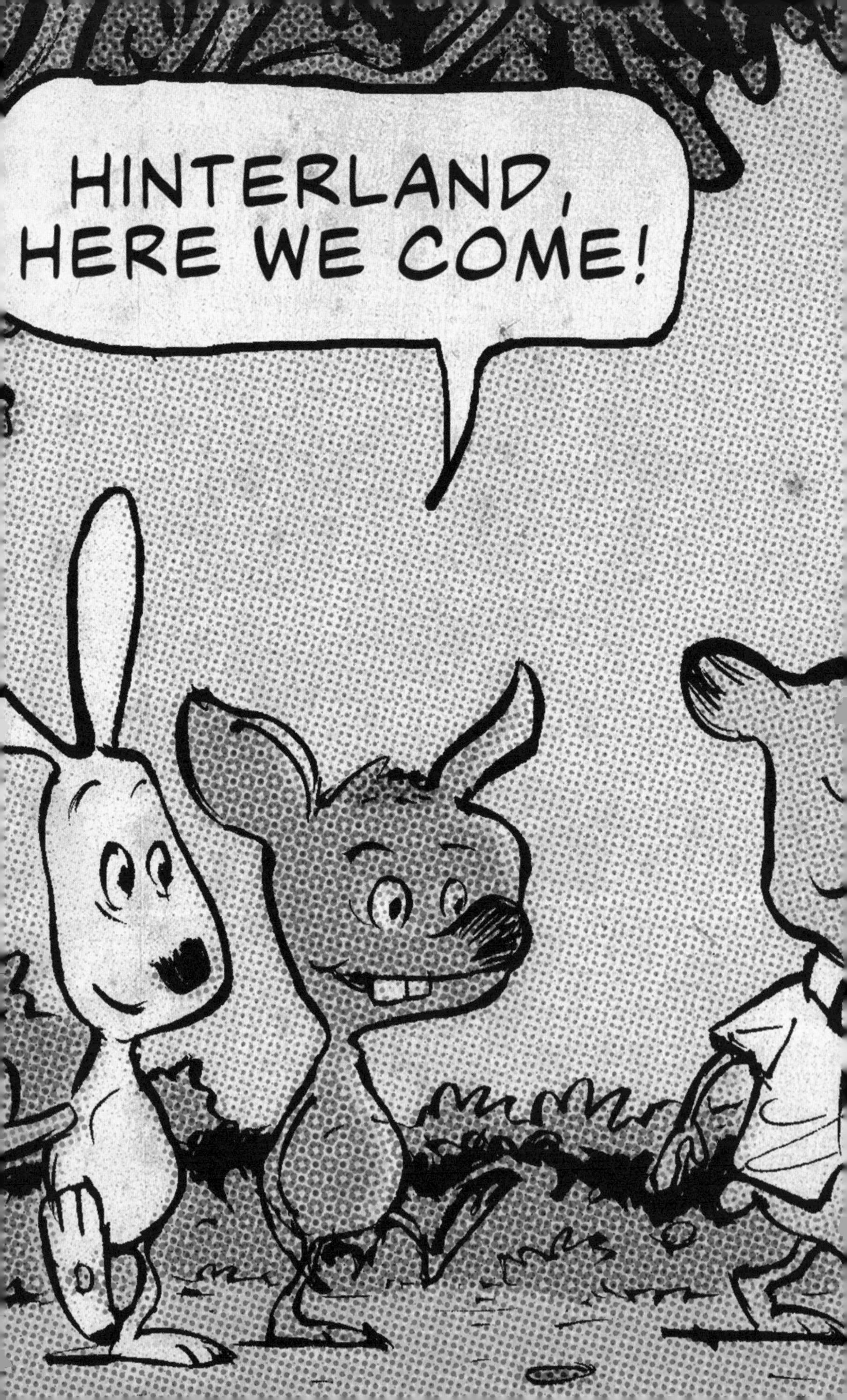
HINTERLAND, HERE WE COME!

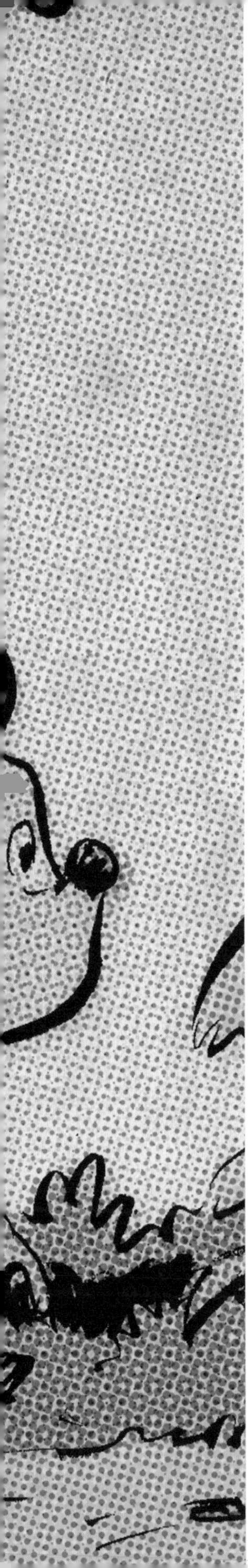

Chapter Six

SANG KUCING & THE ANTS

猫先生与小红蚁

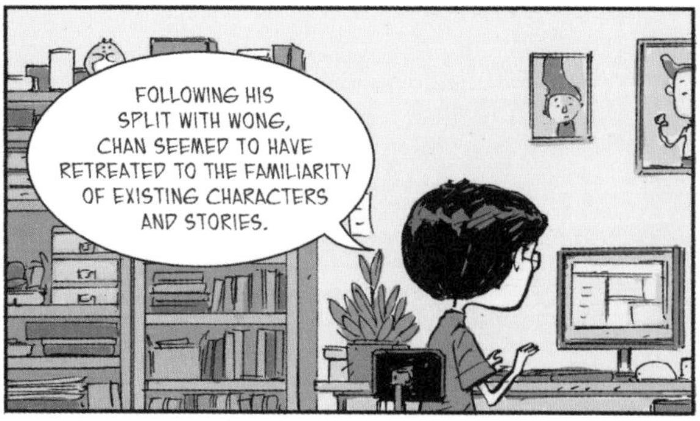
FOLLOWING HIS SPLIT WITH WONG, CHAN SEEMED TO HAVE RETREATED TO THE FAMILIARITY OF EXISTING CHARACTERS AND STORIES.

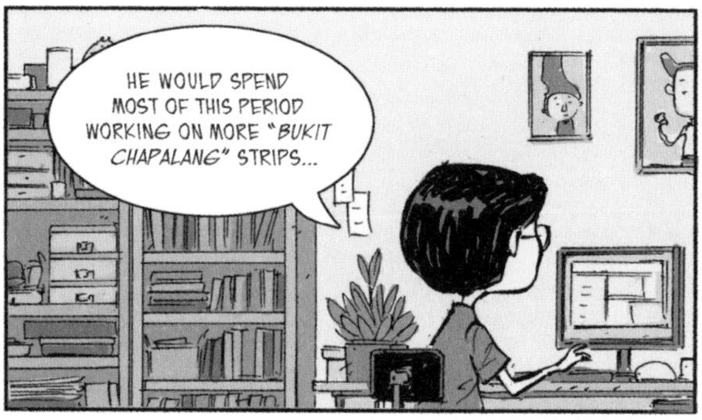
HE WOULD SPEND MOST OF THIS PERIOD WORKING ON MORE "*BUKIT CHAPALANG*" STRIPS...

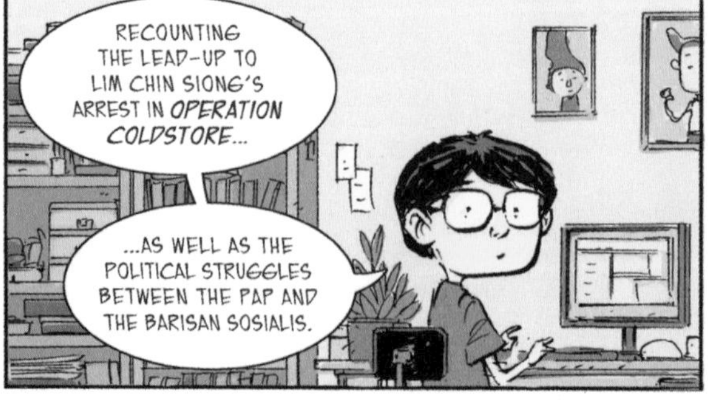
RECOUNTING THE LEAD-UP TO LIM CHIN SIONG'S ARREST IN *OPERATION COLDSTORE*...
...AS WELL AS THE POLITICAL STRUGGLES BETWEEN THE PAP AND THE BARISAN SOSIALIS.

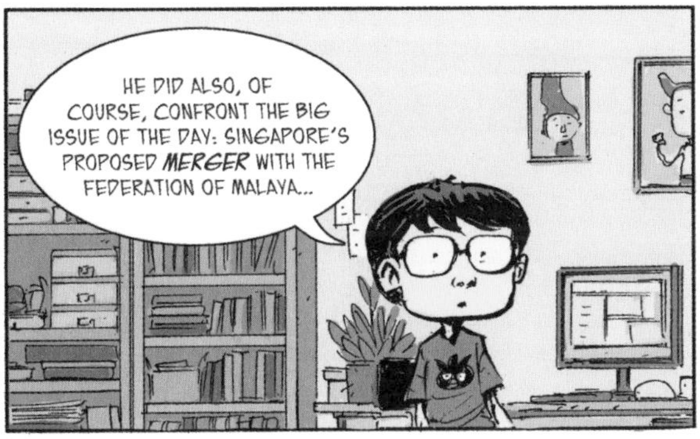
HE DID ALSO, OF COURSE, CONFRONT THE BIG ISSUE OF THE DAY: SINGAPORE'S PROPOSED *MERGER* WITH THE FEDERATION OF MALAYA...

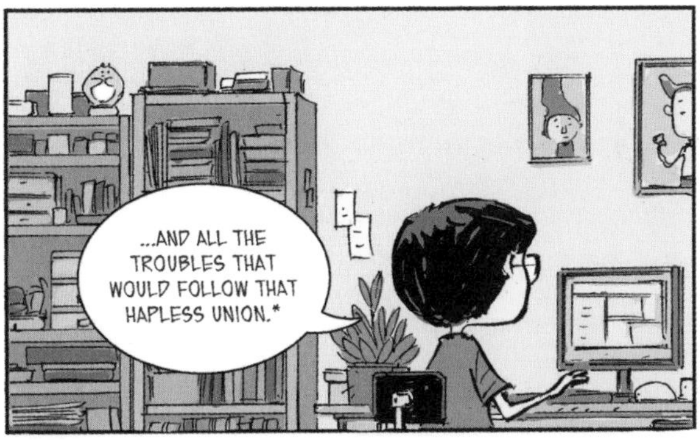
...AND ALL THE TROUBLES THAT WOULD FOLLOW THAT HAPLESS UNION.*

*MALAYSIA WAS FORMED ON SEPTEMBER 16, 1963, WITH THE MERGER OF THE FEDERATION OF MALAYA WITH SINGAPORE, NORTH BORNEO (SABAH) AND SARAWAK.

Following
BUKIT CHAPALANG
c. 1963–1965
Chan Hock Chye
Unpublished

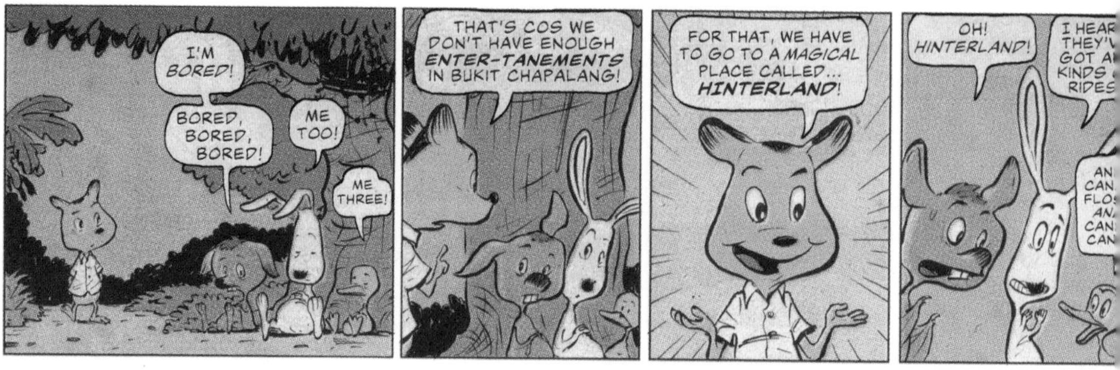

I'M BORED!
BORED, BORED, BORED!
ME TOO!
ME THREE!
THAT'S COS WE DON'T HAVE ENOUGH ENTER-TANEMENTS IN BUKIT CHAPALANG!
FOR THAT, WE HAVE TO GO TO A MAGICAL PLACE CALLED... HINTERLAND!
OH! HINTERLAND!

At the time, almost everyone believed that a merger with the Federation of Malaya would be necessary for Singapore's survival once full independence had been granted by the British. The Malayan mainland could serve as a hinterland for the fledgling island state, providing both natural resources and a larger common market.

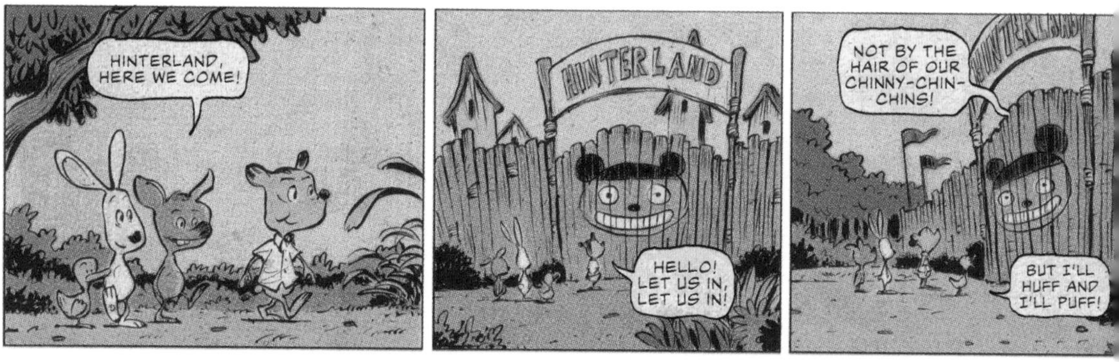

HINTERLAND, HERE WE COME!
HINTERLAND
HELLO! LET US IN, LET US IN!
NOT BY THE HAIR OF OUR CHINNY-CHIN-CHINS!
BUT I'LL HUFF AND I'LL PUFF!

The leaders of Malaya, however, were not exactly keen on the idea.

Absorbing Singapore's large Chinese population of 1.3 million would mean altering Malaya's "racial arithmetic": the Malay population would be outnumbered by the Chinese, thereby transforming the electoral landscape.

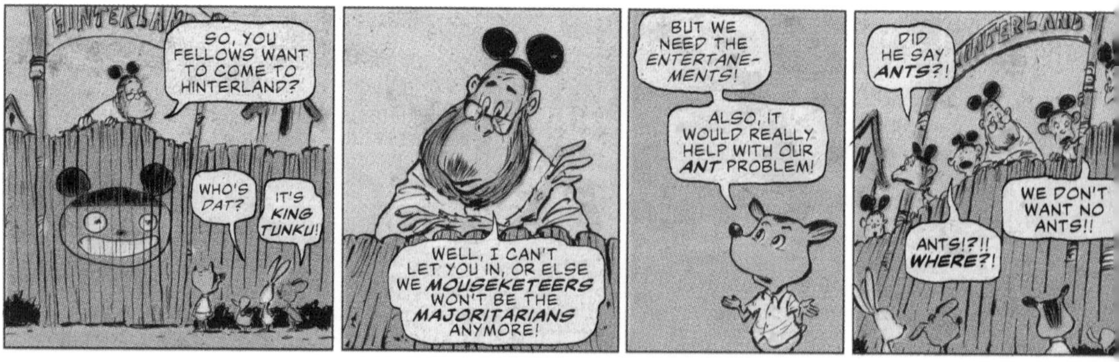

SO, YOU FELLOWS WANT TO COME TO HINTERLAND?
WHO'S DAT?
IT'S KING TUNKU!
WELL, I CAN'T LET YOU IN, OR ELSE WE MOUSEKETEERS WON'T BE THE MAJORITARIANS ANYMORE!
BUT WE NEED THE ENTERTANE-MENTS!
ALSO, IT WOULD REALLY HELP WITH OUR ANT PROBLEM!
DID HE SAY ANTS?!
ANTS!?!! WHERE?!
WE DON'T WANT NO ANTS!!

Such a change would threaten the political dominance of the Malay ruling elite. Attitudes towards merger shifted only after PAP candidates were defeated in two successive by-elections in 1961, sparking fears that a more radical party might ultimately prevail in Singapore.

In Chan's comic, "Mouseketeers" were used to represent the Malays, while Malayan Prime Minister Tunku Abdul Rahman was depicted as a benevolent orangutan.

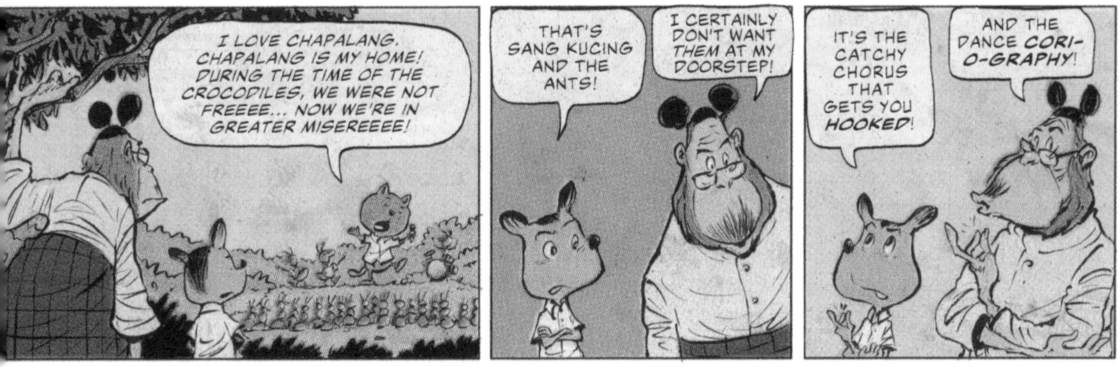
I LOVE CHAPALANG. CHAPALANG IS MY HOME! DURING THE TIME OF THE CROCODILES, WE WERE NOT FREEEE... NOW WE'RE IN GREATER MISEREEEE!
THAT'S SANG KUCING AND THE ANTS!
I CERTAINLY DON'T WANT THEM AT MY DOORSTEP!
IT'S THE CATCHY CHORUS THAT GETS YOU **HOOKED**!
AND THE DANCE **CORI-O-GRAPHY**!

The Tunku's fears were heightened after Lim Chin Siong and his supporters formed the Barisan Sosialis following their expulsion from the PAP in 1961. Believing the Barisan to be a communist party, he was concerned that Singapore might become a "Little China" under Lim, a base and stepping stone from which communism could be propagated to Malaya.

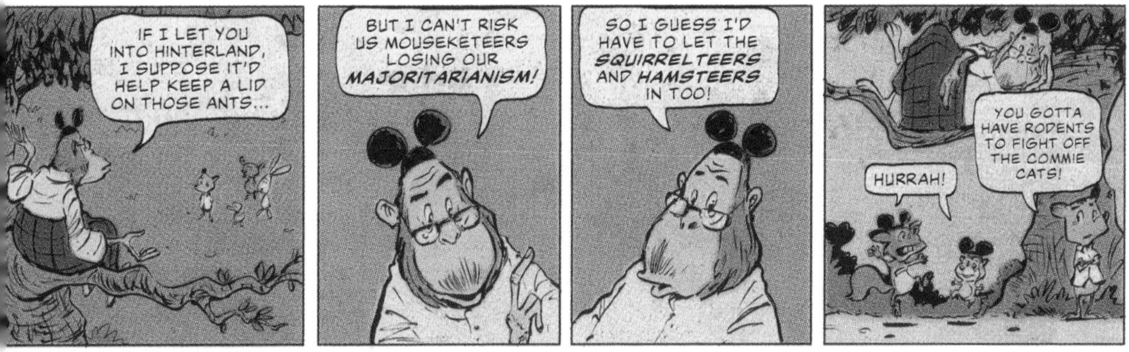
IF I LET YOU INTO HINTERLAND, I SUPPOSE IT'D HELP KEEP A LID ON THOSE ANTS...
BUT I CAN'T RISK US MOUSEKETEERS LOSING OUR **MAJORITARIANISM!**
SO I GUESS I'D HAVE TO LET THE **SQUIRRELTEERS** AND **HAMSTEERS** IN TOO!
YOU GOTTA HAVE RODENTS TO FIGHT OFF THE COMMIE CATS!
HURRAH!

Both the Tunku and Lee Kuan Yew saw the merger as a means of preventing such a scenario, since the conservative Malayan government would be able to crack down on any left-wing ambitions.

In order to preserve the existing balance of races, the British Borneo territories of Sabah and Sarawak, with their large non-Chinese populations, were subsequently incorporated into the plans for the union.

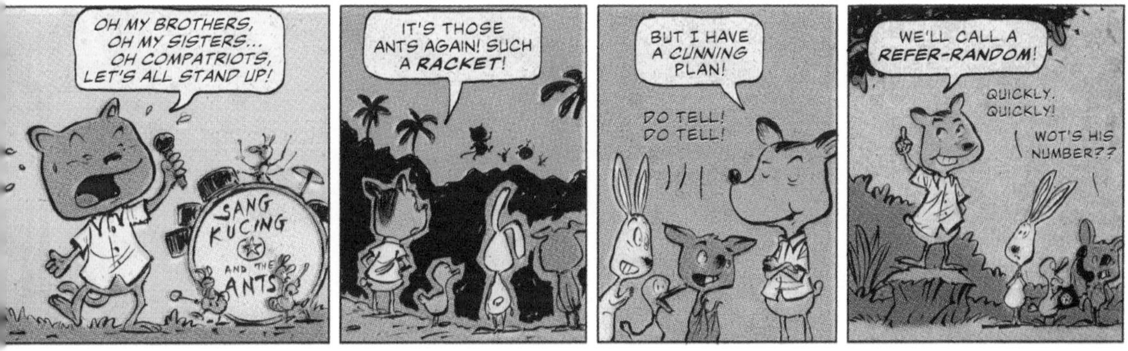
OH MY BROTHERS, OH MY SISTERS... OH COMPATRIOTS, LET'S ALL STAND UP!
SANG KUCING AND THE ANTS
IT'S THOSE ANTS AGAIN! SUCH A **RACKET**!
BUT I HAVE A CUNNING PLAN!
DO TELL! DO TELL!
WE'LL CALL A **REFER-RANDOM**!
QUICKLY. QUICKLY!
WOT'S HIS NUMBER??

The Barisan Sosialis strongly objected to the proposal, fearing for their political survival if merger was to go through, while questioning whether the terms of the merger were ideal for Singapore.

In response, Lee Kuan Yew decided to hold a Referendum on Merger.

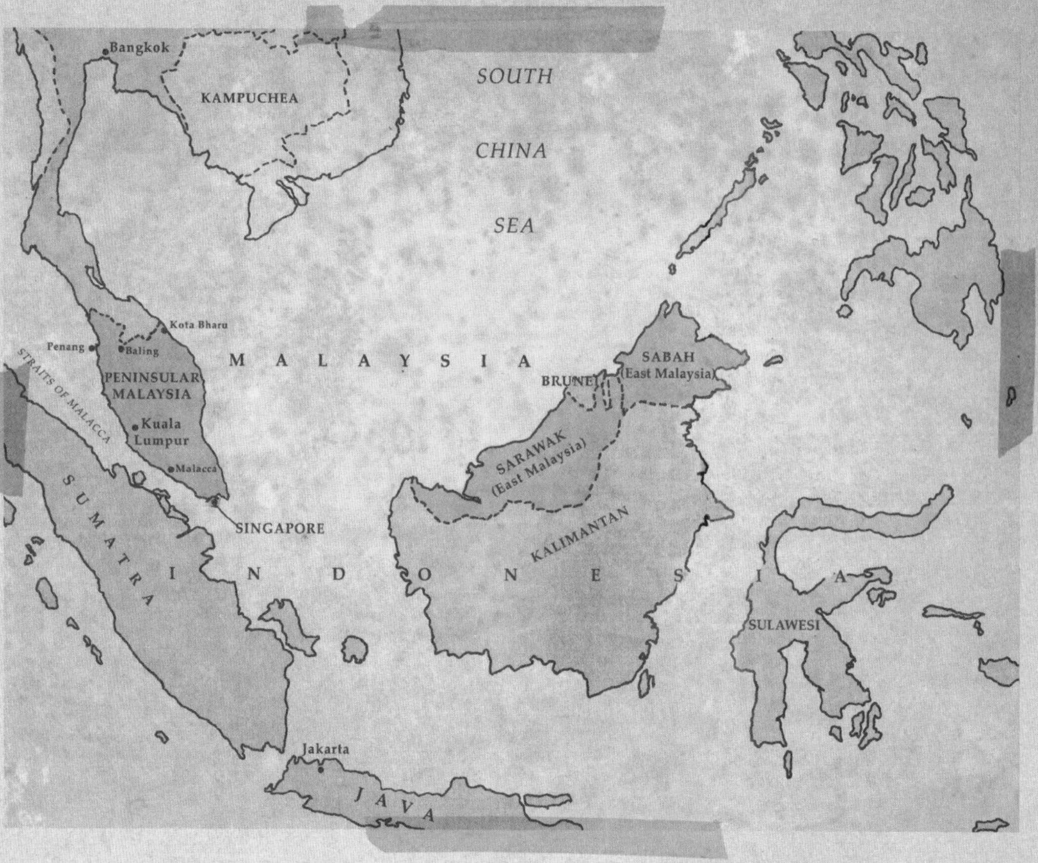
Bangkok
KAMPUCHEA
SOUTH
CHINA
SEA
Kota Bharu
Penang
Baling
M A L A Y S I A
PENINSULAR
MALAYSIA
STRAITS OF MALACCA
Kuala
Lumpur
Malacca
SINGAPORE
SUMATRA
BRUNEI
SABAH
(East Malaysia)
SARAWAK
(East Malaysia)
KALIMANTAN
I N D O N E S I A
SULAWESI
Jakarta
JAVA

Above

MAP OF MALAYSIA

1963

The coloured areas on the map highlight the former British territories making up the new Federation of Malaysia: Peninsular Malaysia, Singapore, Sarawak and Sabah.

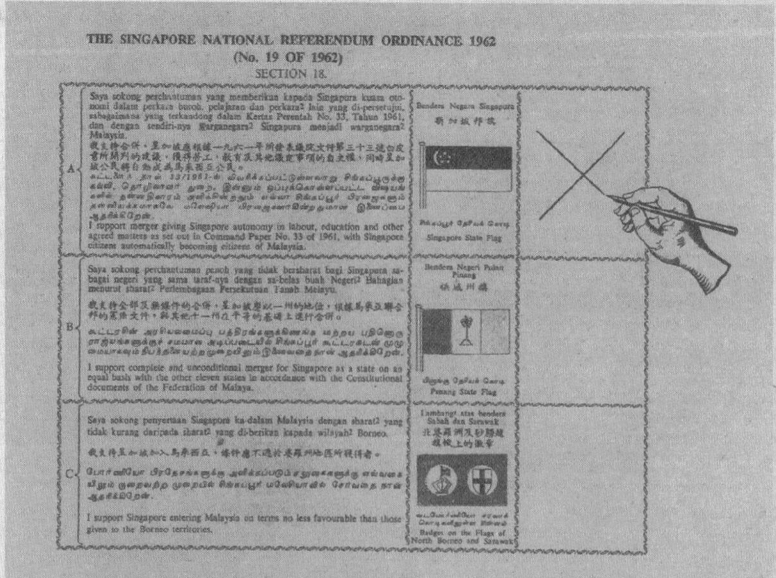

THE SINGAPORE NATIONAL REFERENDUM ORDINANCE 1962

(No. 19 OF 1962)

SECTION 18.

A

Saya sokong perchantuman yang memberikan kapada Singapura kuasa otonomi dalam perkara buroh, pelajaran dan perkara2 lain yang di-persetujui, sabagaimana yang terkandong dalam Kertas Perentah No. 33, Tahun 1961, dan dengan sendiri-nya warganegara2 Singapura menjadi warganegara2 Malaysia.

I support merger giving Singapore autonomy in labour, education and other agreed matters as set out in Command Paper No. 33 of 1961, with Singapore citizens automatically becoming citizens of Malaysia.

Bendera Negara Singapura

Singapore State Flag

B

Saya sokong perchantuman penoh yang tidak bersharat bagi Singapura sabagai negeri yang sama taraf-nya dengan sa-belas buah Negeri2 Bahagian menurut sharat2 Perlembagaan Persekutuan Tanah Melayu.

I support complete and unconditional merger for Singapore as a state on an equal basis with the other eleven states in accordance with the Constitutional documents of the Federation of Malaya.

Bendera Negeri Pulau Pinang

Penang State Flag

C

Saya sokong penyertaan Singapura ka-dalam Malaysia dengan sharat2 yang tidak kurang daripada sharat2 yang di-berikan kapada wilayah2 Borneo.

I support Singapore entering Malaysia on terms no less favourable than those given to the Borneo territories.

Lambang2 atas bendera Sabah dan Sarawak

Badges on the Flags of North Borneo and Sarawak

Right

REFERENDUM DAY INFORMATION FLYER

1962

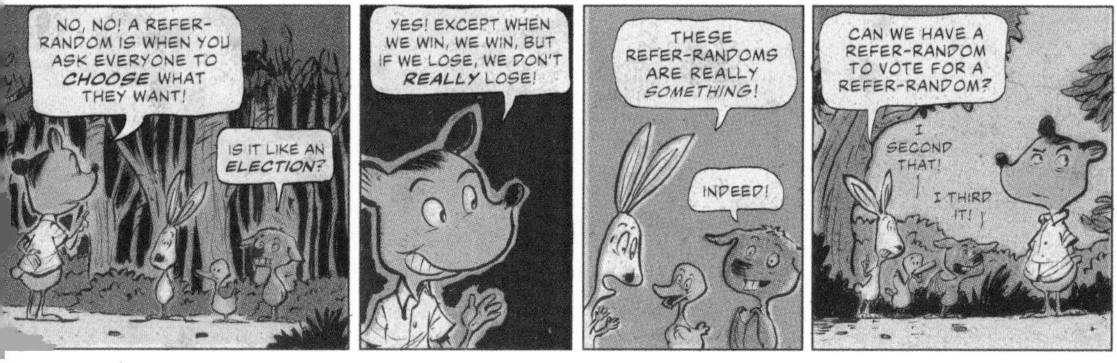
NO, NO! A REFER-RANDOM IS WHEN YOU ASK EVERYONE TO **CHOOSE** WHAT THEY WANT!
IS IT LIKE AN **ELECTION?**
YES! EXCEPT WHEN WE WIN, WE WIN, BUT IF WE LOSE, WE DON'T **REALLY** LOSE!
THESE REFER-RANDOMS ARE REALLY *SOMETHING!*
INDEED!
CAN WE HAVE A REFER-RANDOM TO VOTE FOR A REFER-RANDOM?
I SECOND THAT!
I THIRD IT!

The referendum ostensibly offered voters three choices. But as then Deputy Prime Minister and PAP stalwart Toh Chin Chye would later admit, "*[T]he ballot paper was crafted by Lee Kuan Yew... frankly, they were all votes for merger... Few understood [it]. Few even knew where Sabah was... But we got away with it... It was a win-win situation for the government.*"

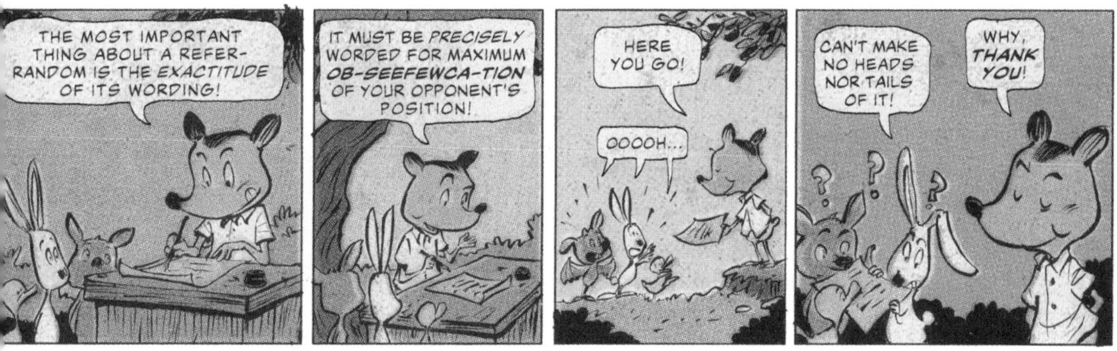
THE MOST IMPORTANT THING ABOUT A REFER-RANDOM IS THE *EXACTITUDE* OF ITS WORDING!
IT MUST BE *PRECISELY* WORDED FOR MAXIMUM **OB-SEEFEWCA-TION** OF YOUR OPPONENT'S POSITION!
HERE YOU GO!
OOOOH...
CAN'T MAKE NO HEADS NOR TAILS OF IT!
WHY, **THANK YOU!**

The PAP's strategy and tactics during the lead-up to the Merger Referendum would be described as acts of "Machiavellian brilliance," while the Barisan's reactions were muddled at best, often playing right into their opponent's hands.

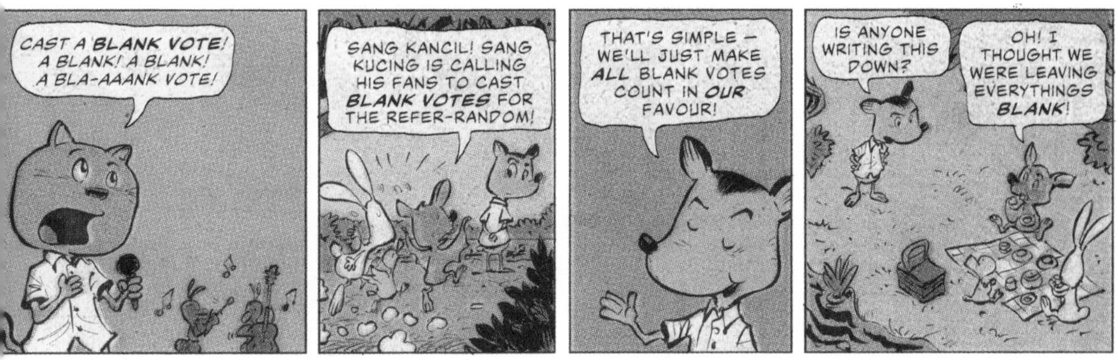
CAST A **BLANK VOTE!** A BLANK! A BLANK! A BLA-AAANK VOTE!
SANG KANCIL! SANG KUCING IS CALLING HIS FANS TO CAST **BLANK VOTES** FOR THE REFER-RANDOM!
THAT'S SIMPLE — WE'LL JUST MAKE **ALL** BLANK VOTES COUNT IN **OUR** FAVOUR!
IS ANYONE WRITING THIS DOWN?
OH! I THOUGHT WE WERE LEAVING EVERYTHINGS **BLANK!**

When the Barisan called for supporters to cast blank votes in protest, for example, they found that the PAP had already included a clause in the Referendum bill, which allowed for blank and uncertain votes to be counted towards merger.

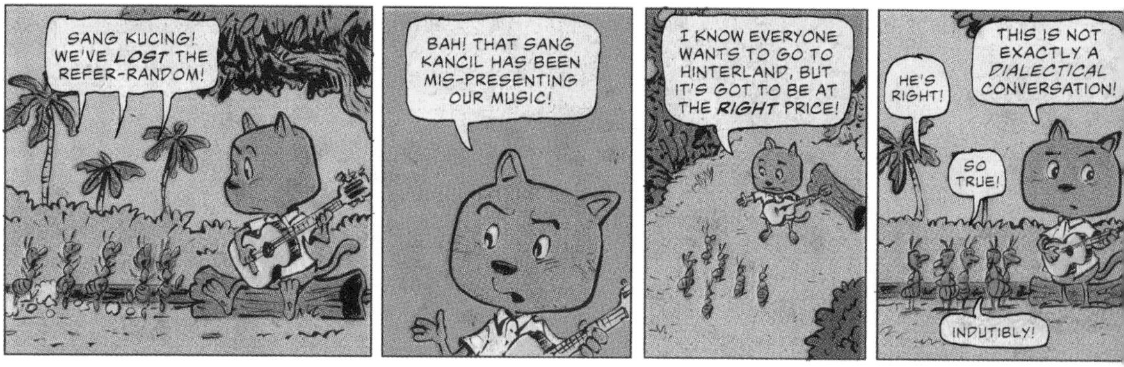
SANG KUCING! WE'VE *LOST* THE REFER-RANDOM!
BAH! THAT SANG KANCIL HAS BEEN MIS-PRESENTING OUR MUSIC!
I KNOW EVERYONE WANTS TO GO TO HINTERLAND, BUT IT'S GOT TO BE AT THE *RIGHT* PRICE!
THIS IS NOT EXACTLY A *DIALECTICAL* CONVERSATION!
HE'S RIGHT!
SO TRUE!
INDUTIBLY!

As it turned out, 71% of the votes were cast in favour of the PAP's option "A," whilst only 25% had cast a blank vote. The PAP had demonstrated their political mettle, and the Barisan Sosialis had been thoroughly outmanoeuvred.

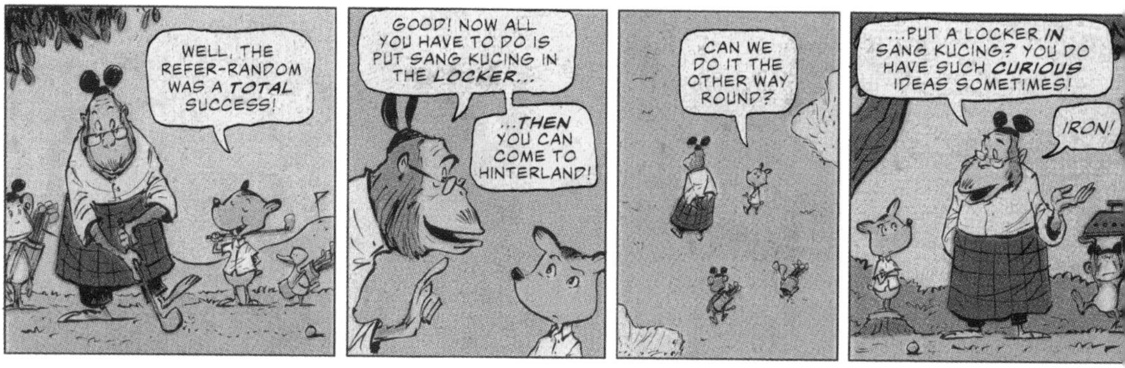
WELL, THE REFER-RANDOM WAS A *TOTAL* SUCCESS!
GOOD! NOW ALL YOU HAVE TO DO IS PUT SANG KUCING IN THE *LOCKER...*
...THEN YOU CAN COME TO HINTERLAND!
CAN WE DO IT THE OTHER WAY ROUND?
...PUT A LOCKER *IN* SANG KUCING? YOU DO HAVE SUCH *CURIOUS* IDEAS SOMETIMES!
IRON!

Meanwhile, the governments of Britain, Malaya and Singapore all believed that it would be in their best interests to have the leaders of the Barisan Sosialis arrested. None of them wanted to shoulder the blame for such an unpopular action though, and there was a period of hand-wringing as each side jostled to have another assume the responsibility.

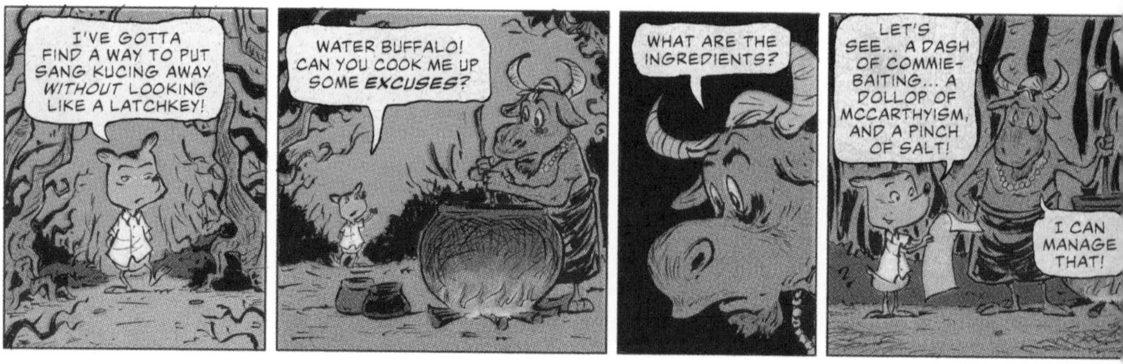
I'VE GOTTA FIND A WAY TO PUT SANG KUCING AWAY *WITHOUT* LOOKING LIKE A LATCHKEY!
WATER BUFFALO! CAN YOU COOK ME UP SOME *EXCUSES?*
WHAT ARE THE INGREDIENTS?
LET'S SEE... A DASH OF COMMIE-BAITING... A DOLLOP OF MCCARTHYISM, AND A PINCH OF SALT!
I CAN MANAGE THAT!

An attempted leftist revolution in Brunei led by Sheik A.M. Azahari in December 1962 finally provided a pretext for arresting Lim Chin Siong and more than a hundred other alleged subversives. Lim's lunch meeting with Azahari in Singapore days before the revolt, together with the Barisan's declaration of solidarity with the uprising, were held up as evidence that the radical party was ready and willing to resort to armed insurrection.

APART FROM *"BUKIT CHAPALANG,"* CHAN ALSO WROTE AND DREW A TWO-PAGE *"INVASION"* STORY ON HIS OWN, FEATURING THE DEATH OF TOMMY TAN.

PERHAPS HE'D WANTED TO BRING SOME *CLOSURE* TO TOMMY'S TALE, WHICH HAD BEEN LEFT UNRESOLVED FOLLOWING THE FAILURE OF THE *DRAGON* PROJECT TO SECURE A PUBLISHER.

ACKNOWLEDGED IN THE STORY WERE THE *INROADS* MADE BY THE PAP, SUCH AS THEIR EXTRAORDINARY SUCCESS IN REPLACING OVERCROWDED SLUMS WITH AFFORDABLE PUBLIC HOUSING.

THEIR TREMENDOUS EFFORTS IN IMPROVING HEALTHCARE, EDUCATION AND THE ECONOMY HAD ALSO GENERATED A LOT OF GOODWILL AND CONFIDENCE.

AND WITH ALL THE BEST LEADERS OF THE BARISAN SOSIALIS OUT OF THE PICTURE...

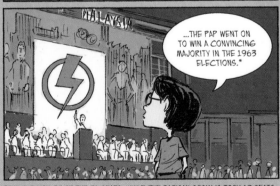

...THE PAP WENT ON TO WIN A *CONVINCING* MAJORITY IN THE 1963 ELECTIONS.*

*THE PAP WON 37 OF THE 51 SEATS, WHILE THE BARISAN SOSIALIS TOOK 13 SEATS. THE UNITED PEOPLE'S PARTY WON THE SOLE REMAINING SEAT.

Following
INVASION: THE DEATH OF TOMMY TAN
1963
Chan Hock Chye
Unpublished

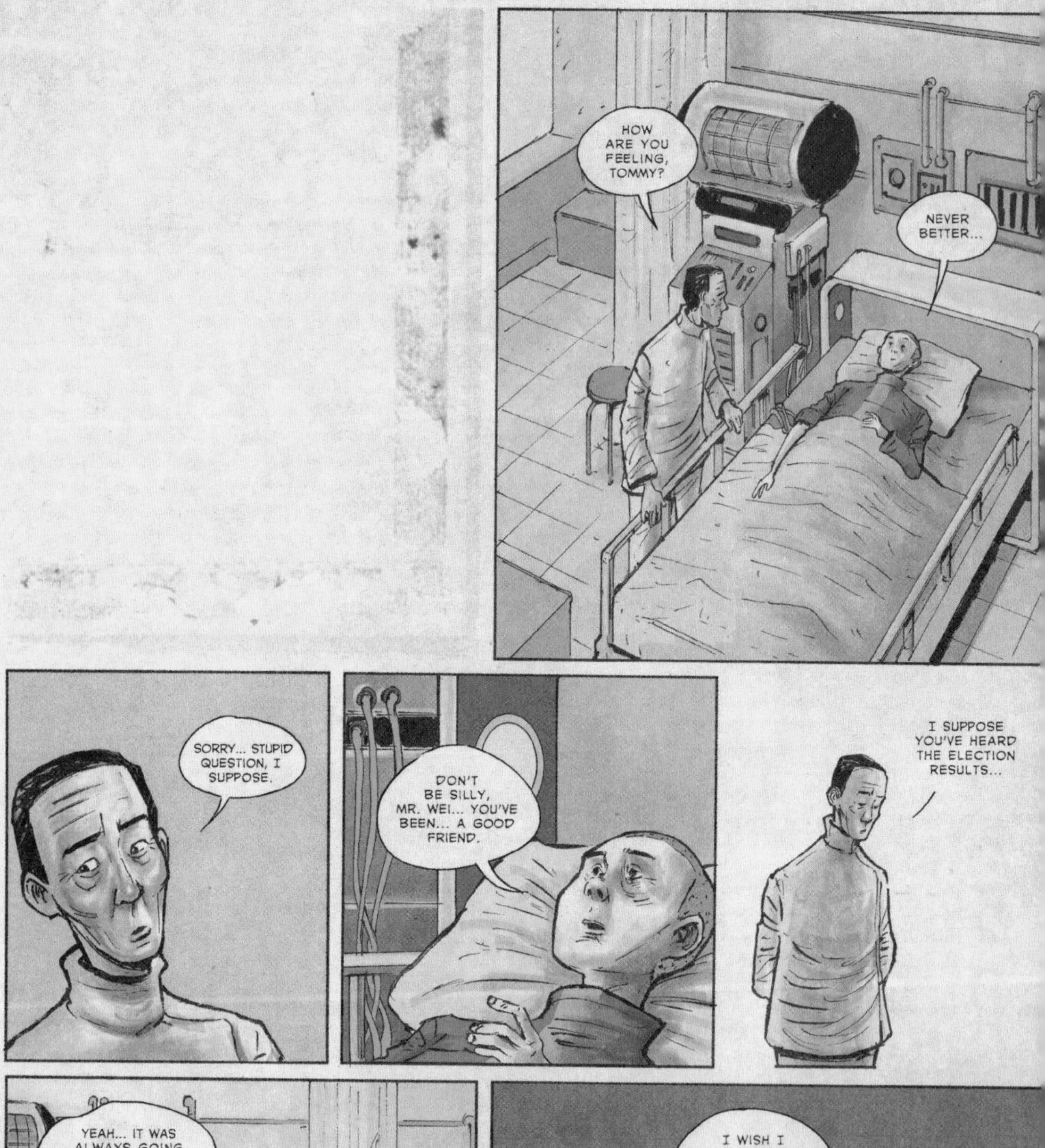
HOW ARE YOU FEELING, TOMMY?
NEVER BETTER...
SORRY... STUPID QUESTION, I SUPPOSE.
DON'T BE SILLY, MR. WEI... YOU'VE BEEN... A GOOD FRIEND.
I SUPPOSE YOU'VE HEARD THE ELECTION RESULTS...
YEAH... IT WAS ALWAYS GOING TO BE... TOUGH... WHAT WITH EVERYONE LOCKED UP...
I WISH I COULD HAVE... HELPED OUT... AT THE RALLIES...
THOUGH I GUESS IT WOULDN'T... HAVE MADE... MUCH OF A DIFFERENCE...

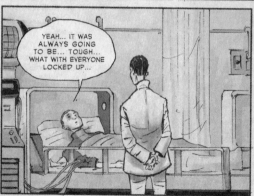

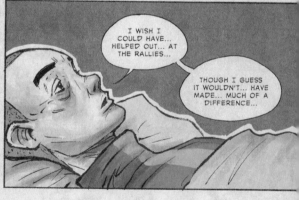

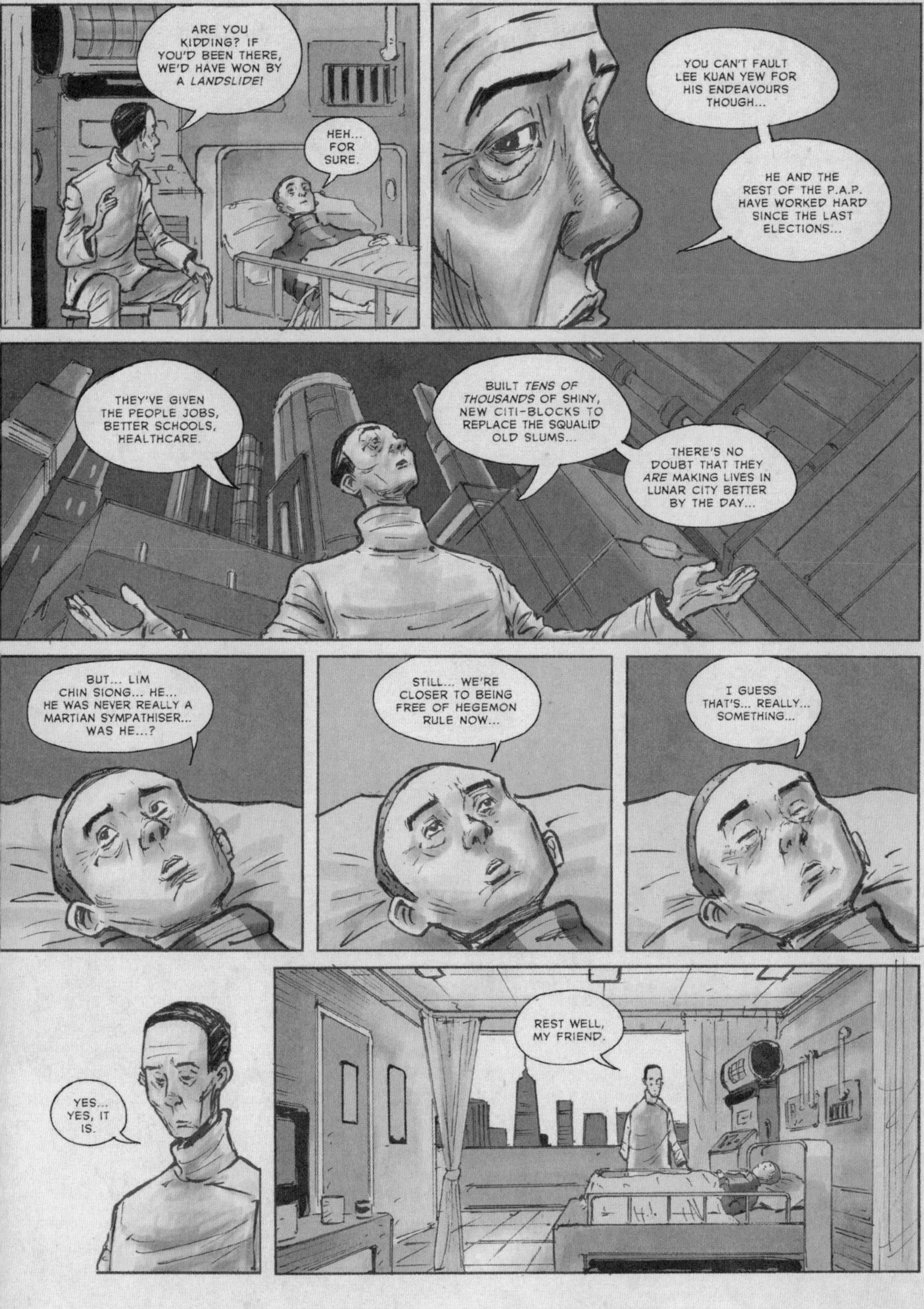
ARE YOU KIDDING? IF YOU'D BEEN THERE, WE'D HAVE WON BY A *LANDSLIDE!*
HEH... FOR SURE.
YOU CAN'T FAULT LEE KUAN YEW FOR HIS ENDEAVOURS THOUGH...
HE AND THE REST OF THE P.A.P. HAVE WORKED HARD SINCE THE LAST ELECTIONS...
THEY'VE GIVEN THE PEOPLE JOBS, BETTER SCHOOLS, HEALTHCARE.
BUILT *TENS OF THOUSANDS* OF SHINY, NEW CITI-BLOCKS TO REPLACE THE SQUALID OLD SLUMS...
THERE'S NO DOUBT THAT THEY *ARE* MAKING LIVES IN LUNAR CITY BETTER BY THE DAY...
BUT... LIM CHIN SIONG... HE... HE WAS NEVER REALLY A MARTIAN SYMPATHISER... WAS HE...?
STILL... WE'RE CLOSER TO BEING FREE OF HEGEMON RULE NOW...
I GUESS THAT'S... REALLY... SOMETHING...
YES... YES, IT IS.
REST WELL, MY FRIEND.

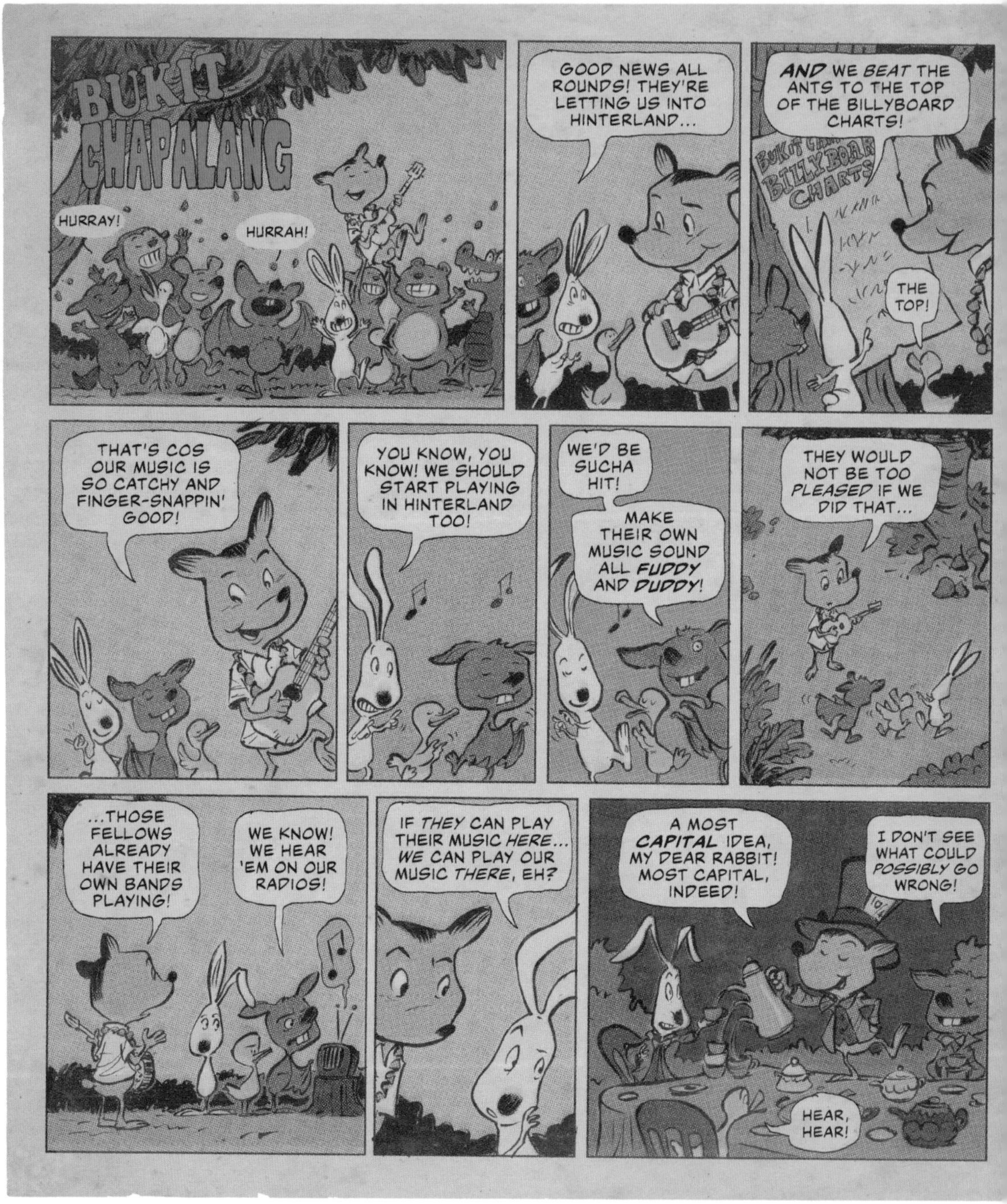
BUKIT CHAPALANG
HURRAY!
HURRAH!
GOOD NEWS ALL ROUNDS! THEY'RE LETTING US INTO HINTERLAND...
AND WE BEAT THE ANTS TO THE TOP OF THE BILLYBOARD CHARTS!
THE TOP!
THAT'S COS OUR MUSIC IS SO CATCHY AND FINGER-SNAPPIN' GOOD!
YOU KNOW, YOU KNOW! WE SHOULD START PLAYING IN HINTERLAND TOO!
WE'D BE SUCHA HIT!
MAKE THEIR OWN MUSIC SOUND ALL FUDDY AND DUDDY!
THEY WOULD NOT BE TOO PLEASED IF WE DID THAT...
...THOSE FELLOWS ALREADY HAVE THEIR OWN BANDS PLAYING!
WE KNOW! WE HEAR 'EM ON OUR RADIOS!
IF THEY CAN PLAY THEIR MUSIC HERE... WE CAN PLAY OUR MUSIC THERE, EH?
A MOST CAPITAL IDEA, MY DEAR RABBIT! MOST CAPITAL, INDEED!
I DON'T SEE WHAT COULD POSSIBLY GO WRONG!
HEAR, HEAR!

With the formation of Malaysia on September 16, 1963, the PAP had achieved their goal of merger. A convincing victory in the Singapore elections followed that same month. The party now felt emboldened enough to contest the 1964 federal general elections in the Malaysian mainland, despite assurances by Lee Kuan Yew that they would not do so.

Above & following
BUKIT CHAPALANG
1963–1964
Chan Hock Chye
Self-published

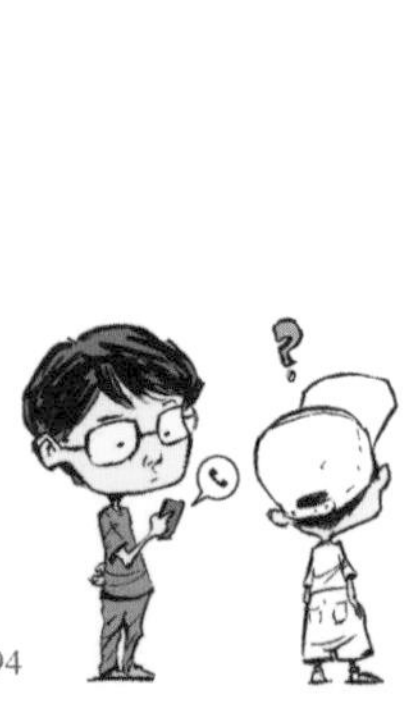

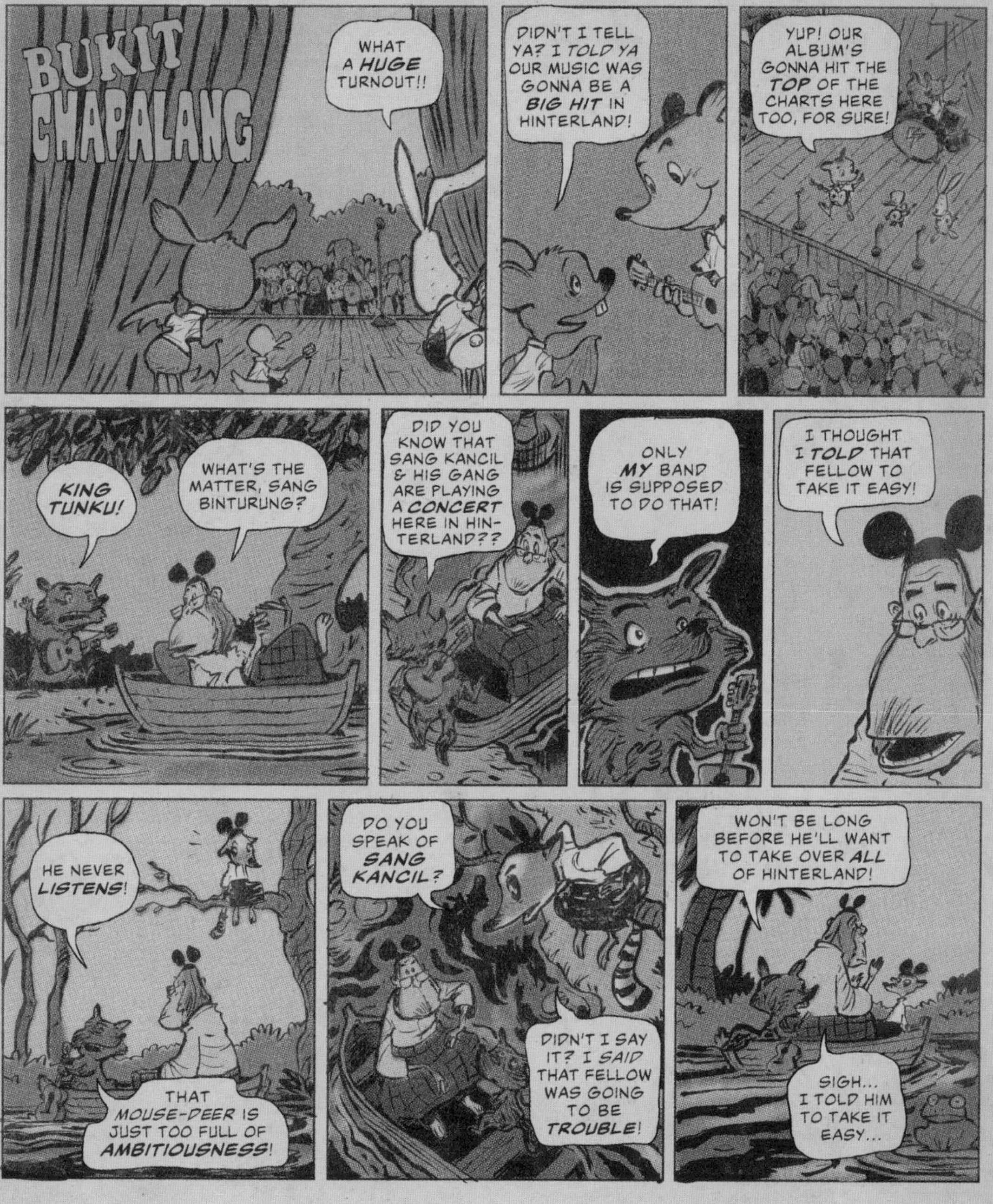
BUKIT CHAPALANG
WHAT A HUGE TURNOUT!!
DIDN'T I TELL YA? I TOLD YA OUR MUSIC WAS GONNA BE A BIG HIT IN HINTERLAND!
YUP! OUR ALBUM'S GONNA HIT THE TOP OF THE CHARTS HERE TOO, FOR SURE!
KING TUNKU!
WHAT'S THE MATTER, SANG BINTURUNG?
DID YOU KNOW THAT SANG KANCIL & HIS GANG ARE PLAYING A CONCERT HERE IN HINTERLAND??
ONLY MY BAND IS SUPPOSED TO DO THAT!
I THOUGHT I TOLD THAT FELLOW TO TAKE IT EASY!
HE NEVER LISTENS!
THAT MOUSE-DEER IS JUST TOO FULL OF AMBITIOUSNESS!
DO YOU SPEAK OF SANG KANCIL?
DIDN'T I SAY IT? I SAID THAT FELLOW WAS GOING TO BE TROUBLE!
WON'T BE LONG BEFORE HE'LL WANT TO TAKE OVER ALL OF HINTERLAND!
SIGH... I TOLD HIM TO TAKE IT EASY...

The **Malaysian Chinese Association** (MCA) was one of three political parties that made up the ruling coalition, and the appointed representative of Chinese interests in the Federation. The PAP had hoped that a show of strength in the federal elections would demonstrate their appeal to Chinese voters, thereby convincing the Tunku that they could replace the MCA as a worthy coalition partner. This move, however, antagonised the MCA and its leader, **Tan Siew Sin**, and further fuelled fears amongst conservative Malay leaders like the **United Malays National Organisation** (UMNO) Secretary-General **Dato Syed Ja'afar Albar** that Lee Kuan Yew's ultimate ambitions lay in becoming the Prime Minister of all Malaysia.

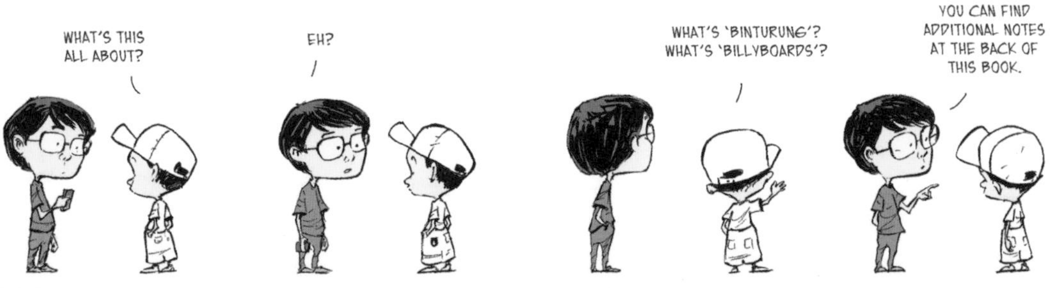
WHAT'S THIS ALL ABOUT?
EH?
WHAT'S 'BINTURUNG'? WHAT'S 'BILLYBOARDS'?
YOU CAN FIND ADDITIONAL NOTES AT THE BACK OF THIS BOOK.

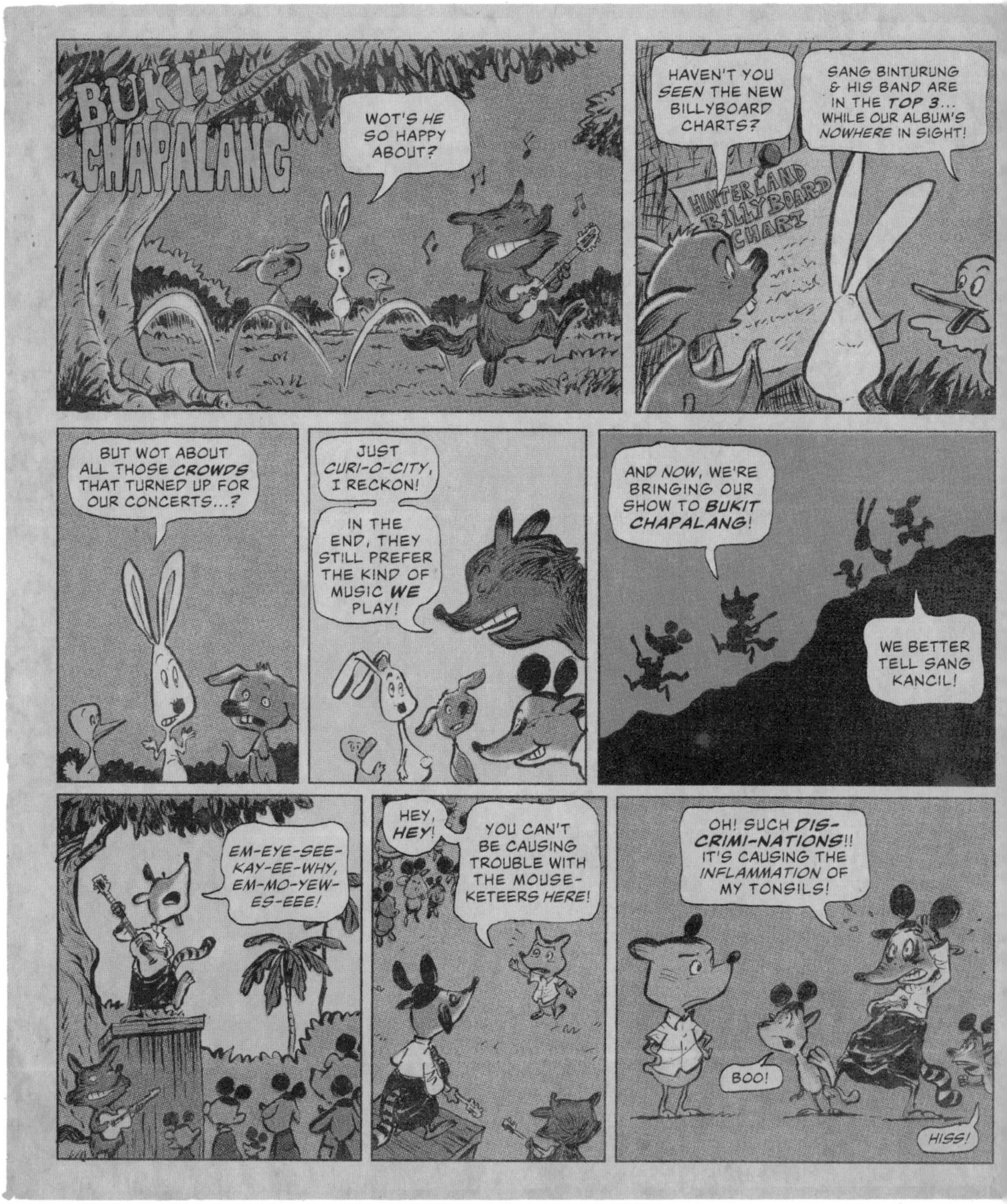

BUKIT CHAPALANG
WOT'S HE SO HAPPY ABOUT?
HAVEN'T YOU SEEN THE NEW BILLYBOARD CHARTS?
SANG BINTURUNG & HIS BAND ARE IN THE TOP 3... WHILE OUR ALBUM'S NOWHERE IN SIGHT!
HINTERLAND BILLYBOARD CHART
BUT WOT ABOUT ALL THOSE CROWDS THAT TURNED UP FOR OUR CONCERTS...?
JUST CURI-O-CITY, I RECKON!
IN THE END, THEY STILL PREFER THE KIND OF MUSIC WE PLAY!
AND NOW, WE'RE BRINGING OUR SHOW TO BUKIT CHAPALANG!
WE BETTER TELL SANG KANCIL!
EM-EYE-SEE-KAY-EE-WHY, EM-MO-YEW-ES-EEE!
HEY, HEY!
YOU CAN'T BE CAUSING TROUBLE WITH THE MOUSE-KETEERS HERE!
OH! SUCH DIS-CRIMI-NATIONS!! IT'S CAUSING THE INFLAMMATION OF MY TONSILS!
BOO!
HISS!

Despite large turnouts for their election rallies, the PAP performed dismally, winning only one of nine seats contested, whilst the MCA made significant gains. Incensed by what they saw as broken promises, and the overreaching ambition and impatience on the part of the PAP, the ruling coalition in Malaysia now sought to crush them in Singapore itself, with Syed Ja'afar Albar leading a virulent campaign to discredit the PAP and Lee Kuan Yew amongst Malay voters in Singapore.

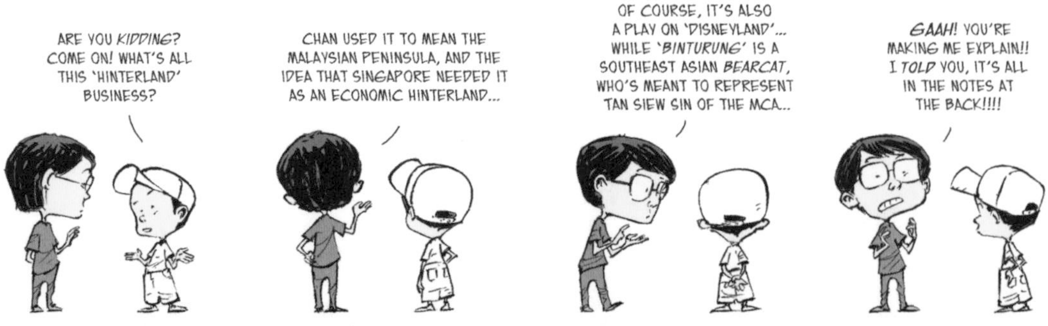

ARE YOU KIDDING? COME ON! WHAT'S ALL THIS 'HINTERLAND' BUSINESS?
CHAN USED IT TO MEAN THE MALAYSIAN PENINSULA, AND THE IDEA THAT SINGAPORE NEEDED IT AS AN ECONOMIC HINTERLAND...
OF COURSE, IT'S ALSO A PLAY ON 'DISNEYLAND'... WHILE 'BINTURUNG' IS A SOUTHEAST ASIAN BEARCAT, WHO'S MEANT TO REPRESENT TAN SIEW SIN OF THE MCA...
GAAH! YOU'RE MAKING ME EXPLAIN!! I TOLD YOU, IT'S ALL IN THE NOTES AT THE BACK!!!!

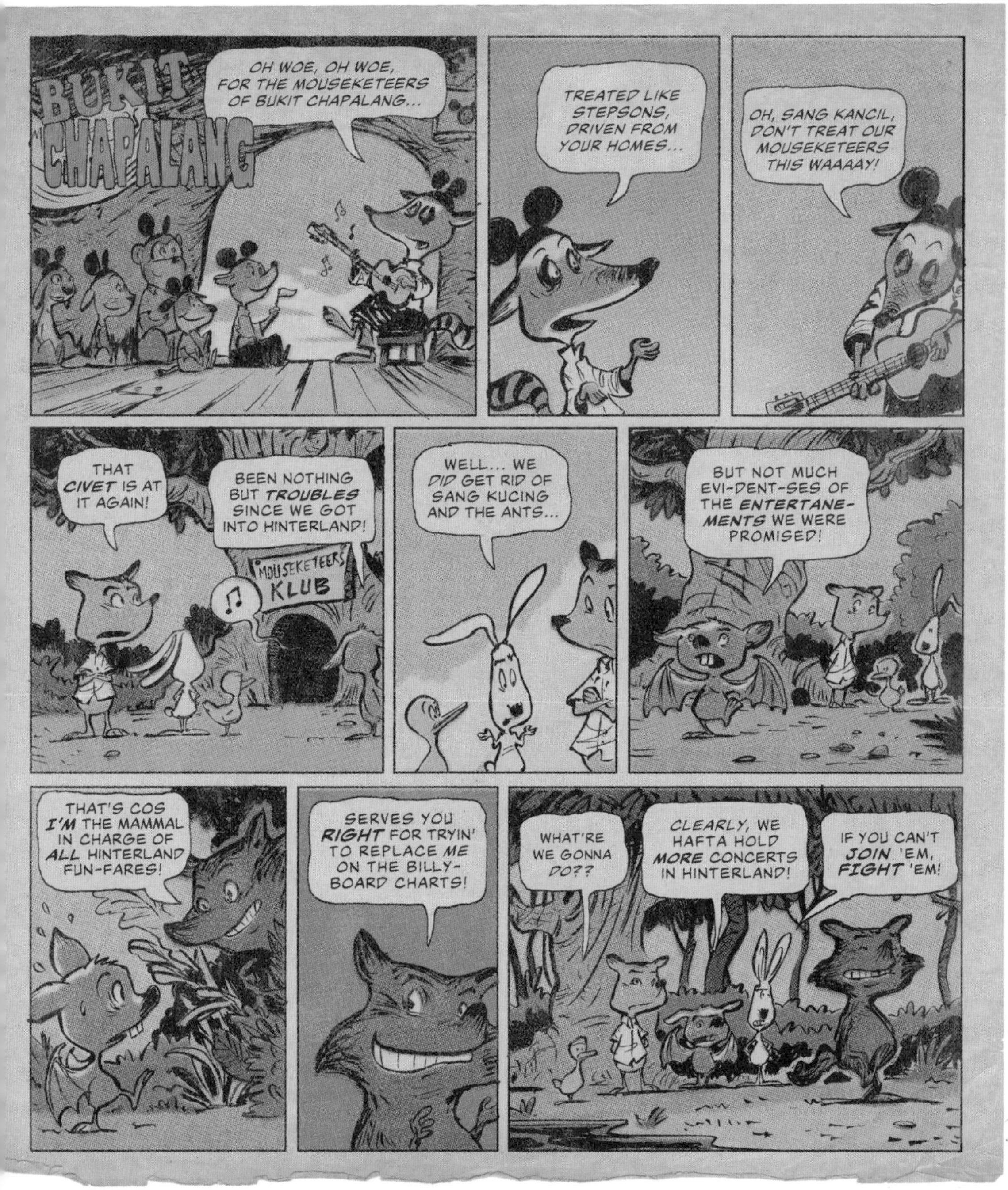
BUKIT CHAPALANG
OH WOE, OH WOE, FOR THE MOUSEKETEERS OF BUKIT CHAPALANG...
TREATED LIKE STEPSONS, DRIVEN FROM YOUR HOMES...
OH, SANG KANCIL, DON'T TREAT OUR MOUSEKETEERS THIS WAAAAY!
THAT *CIVET* IS AT IT AGAIN!
BEEN NOTHING BUT *TROUBLES* SINCE WE GOT INTO HINTERLAND!
MOUSEKETEERS KLUB
WELL... WE *DID* GET RID OF SANG KUCING AND THE ANTS...
BUT NOT MUCH EVI-DENT-SES OF THE *ENTERTANE-MENTS* WE WERE PROMISED!
THAT'S COS *I'M* THE MAMMAL IN CHARGE OF *ALL* HINTERLAND FUN-FARES!
SERVES YOU *RIGHT* FOR TRYIN' TO REPLACE *ME* ON THE BILLY-BOARD CHARTS!
WHAT'RE WE GONNA *DO*??
CLEARLY, WE HAFTA HOLD *MORE* CONCERTS IN HINTERLAND!
IF YOU CAN'T *JOIN* 'EM, *FIGHT* 'EM!

There was to be more trouble on other fronts. The Malaysian Minister of Finance was none other than MCA leader Tan Siew Sin, who now used his power and influence to make it difficult for Singapore to receive the financial and economic benefits it had hoped would come with merger. Meanwhile, Syed Ja'afar Albar and Lee Kuan Yew continued their war of words.

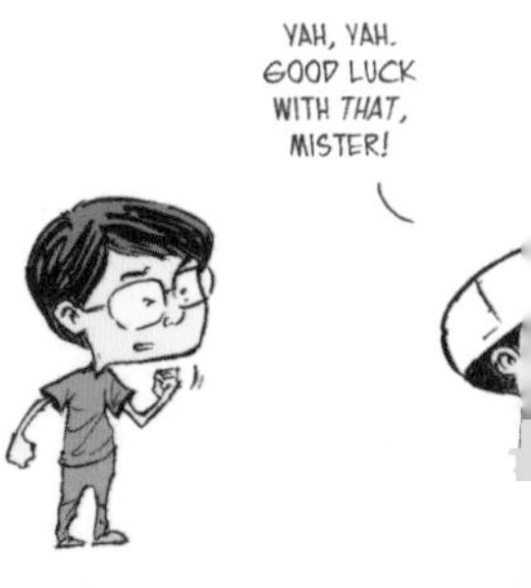
YAH, YAH. GOOD LUCK WITH *THAT*, MISTER!

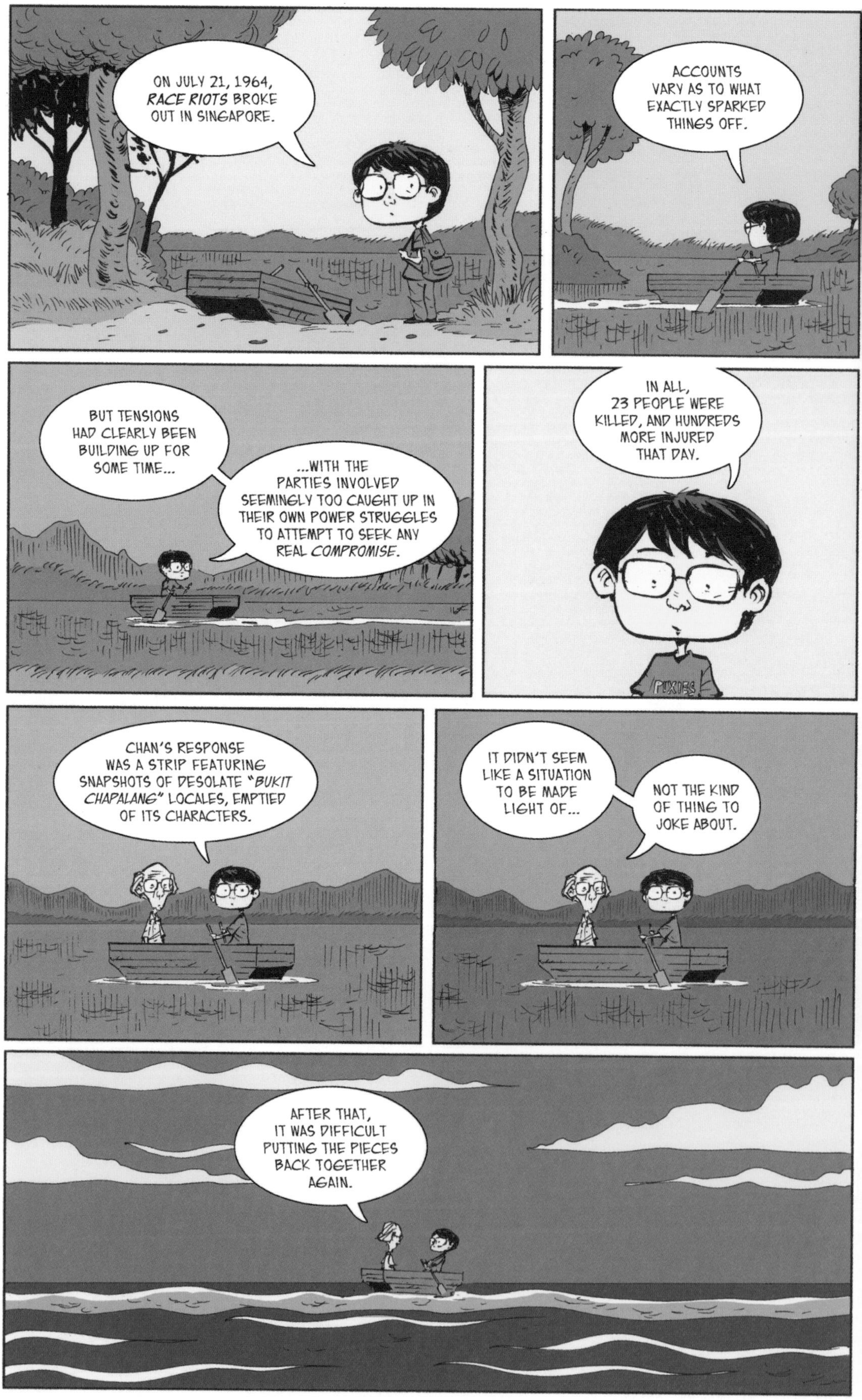

ON JULY 21, 1964, *RACE RIOTS* BROKE OUT IN SINGAPORE.
ACCOUNTS VARY AS TO WHAT EXACTLY SPARKED THINGS OFF.
BUT TENSIONS HAD CLEARLY BEEN BUILDING UP FOR SOME TIME...
...WITH THE PARTIES INVOLVED SEEMINGLY TOO CAUGHT UP IN THEIR OWN POWER STRUGGLES TO ATTEMPT TO SEEK ANY REAL *COMPROMISE*.
IN ALL, 23 PEOPLE WERE KILLED, AND HUNDREDS MORE INJURED THAT DAY.
PIXIES
CHAN'S RESPONSE WAS A STRIP FEATURING SNAPSHOTS OF DESOLATE "*BUKIT CHAPALANG*" LOCALES, EMPTIED OF ITS CHARACTERS.
IT DIDN'T SEEM LIKE A SITUATION TO BE MADE LIGHT OF...
NOT THE KIND OF THING TO JOKE ABOUT.
AFTER THAT, IT WAS DIFFICULT PUTTING THE PIECES BACK TOGETHER AGAIN.

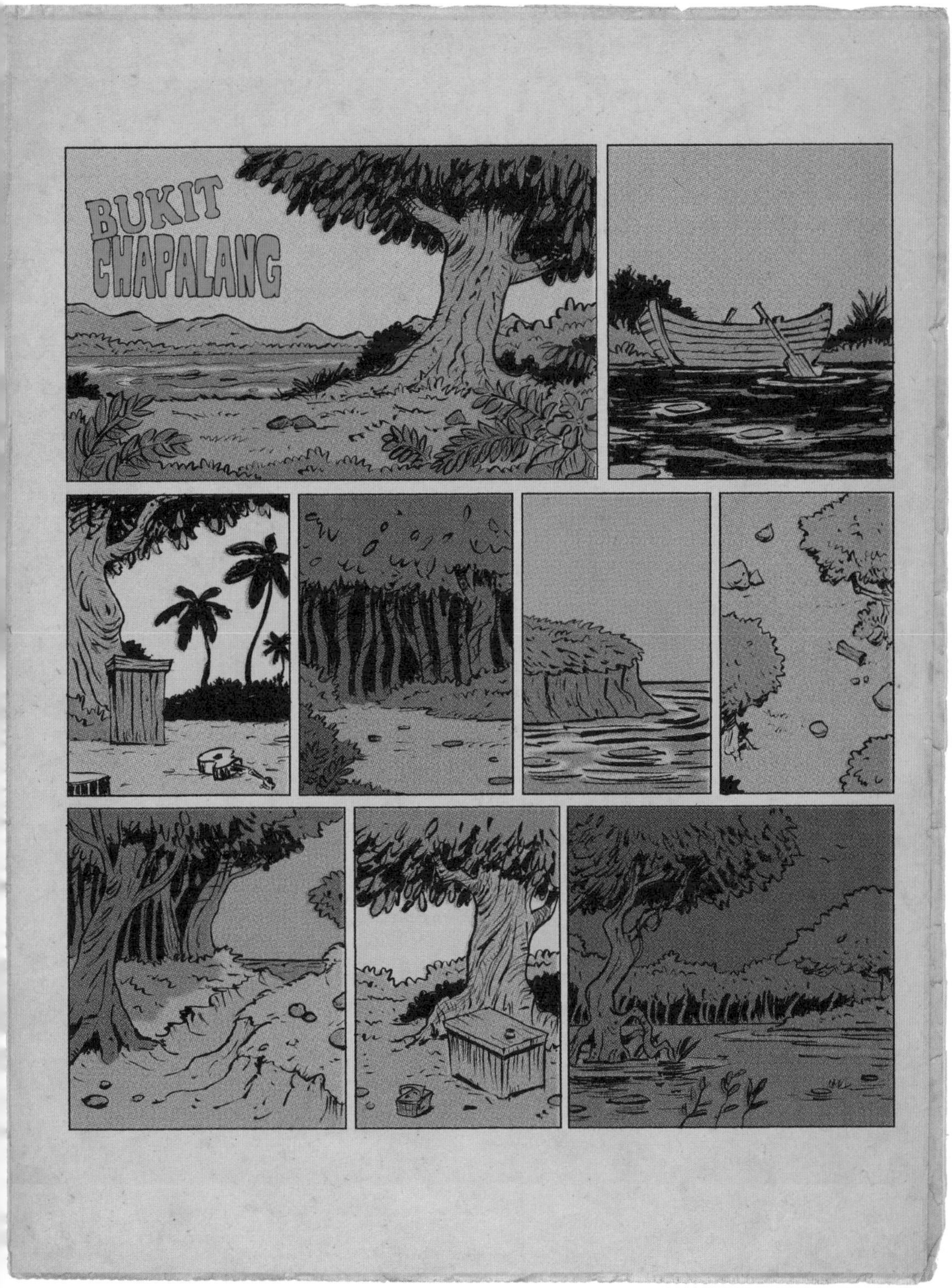
BUKIT
CHAPALANG

Above
BUKIT CHAPALANG
1965
Chan Hock Chye
Self-published

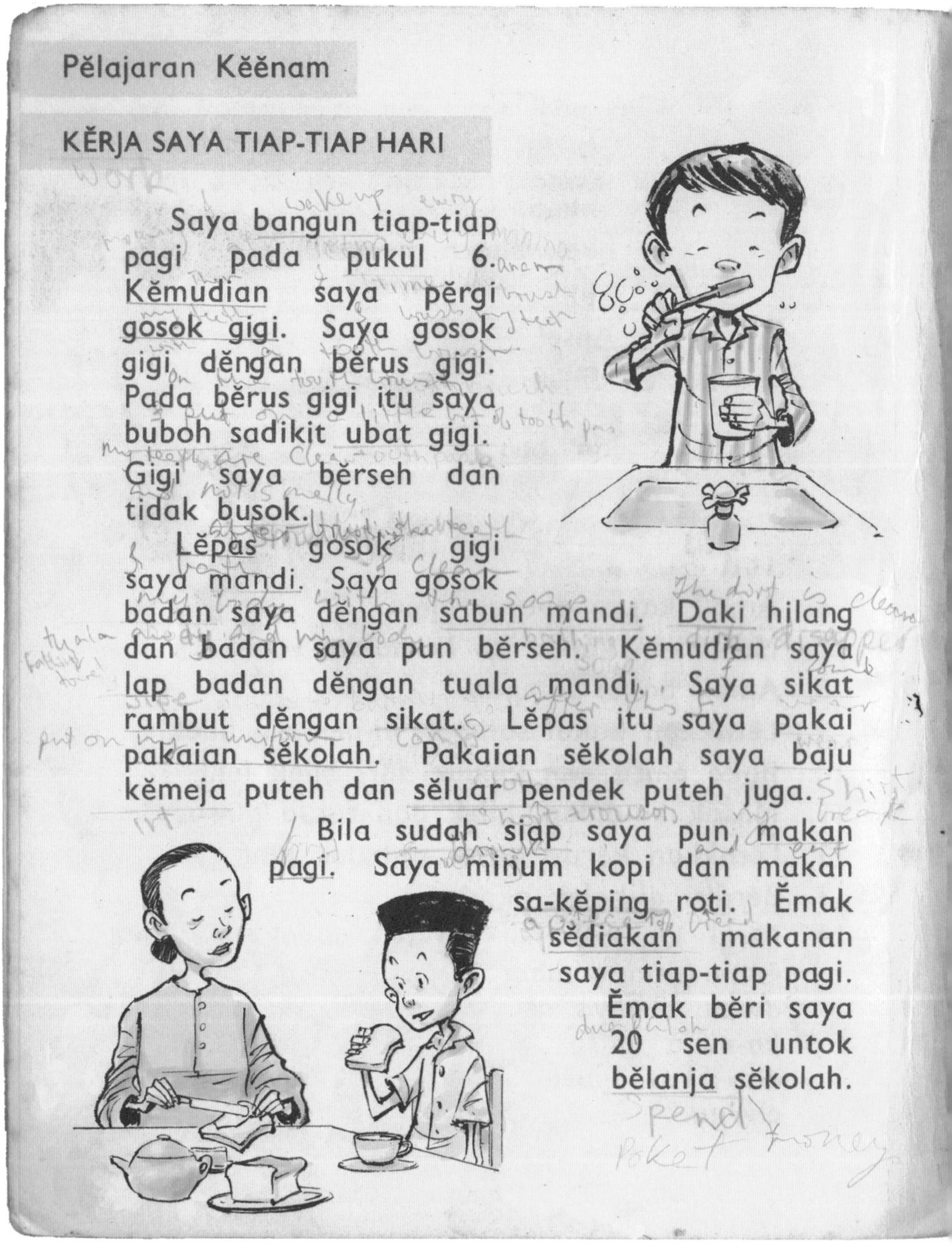

Pĕlajaran Kĕĕnam

KĔRJA SAYA TIAP-TIAP HARI

Saya bangun tiap-tiap pagi pada pukul 6. Kĕmudian saya pĕrgi gosok gigi. Saya gosok gigi dĕngan bĕrus gigi. Pada bĕrus gigi itu saya buboh sadikit ubat gigi. Gigi saya bĕrseh dan tidak busok.

Lĕpas gosok gigi saya mandi. Saya gosok badan saya dĕngan sabun mandi. Daki hilang dan badan saya pun bĕrseh. Kĕmudian saya lap badan dĕngan tuala mandi. Saya sikat rambut dĕngan sikat. Lĕpas itu saya pakai pakaian sĕkolah. Pakaian sĕkolah saya baju kĕmeja puteh dan sĕluar pendek puteh juga.

Bila sudah siap saya pun makan pagi. Saya minum kopi dan makan sa-kĕping roti. Ĕmak sĕdiakan makanan saya tiap-tiap pagi. Ĕmak bĕri saya 20 sen untok bĕlanja sĕkolah.

Above & opposite

PELAJARAN BAHASA KEBANGSAAN: BUKU SATU (NATIONAL LANGUAGE EDUCATION: BOOK ONE)

1965

Art by Chan Hock Chye

Words by Syed Nasir Bin Ismail

Illustrations from a proof copy of a book teaching basic Bahasa Melayu (Malay language), which was to be adopted as Singapore's national language after it joined Malaysia. Race riots and political tensions, however, would lead to Singapore's separation from the Federation on August 9, 1965. The book's publication was cancelled shortly after, and Chan would never receive payment for this work.

HARI HUJAN

Pagi semalam hujan lebat. Saya dan kawan-kawan pergi ka-sekolah pakai payong. Bapa pun pergi bekerja pakai payong. Di-sekolah tidak ada senaman. Semua murid berkumpul di-dalam dewan. Mereka mendengar uchapan Guru Besar.

Murid-murid tidak suka kalau hari hujan sebab mereka tidak dapat main bola. Itek sangat suka kalau hari hujan sebab ia dapat mandi. Kalau hujan terlalu lebat boleh menjadi bah. Kalau bah besar, pokok-pokok tanaman banyak yang rosak dan ayam itek pun banyak yang mati. Rumah-rumah ada yang hanyut dan kadang-kadang orang pun ada yang mati lemas.

27

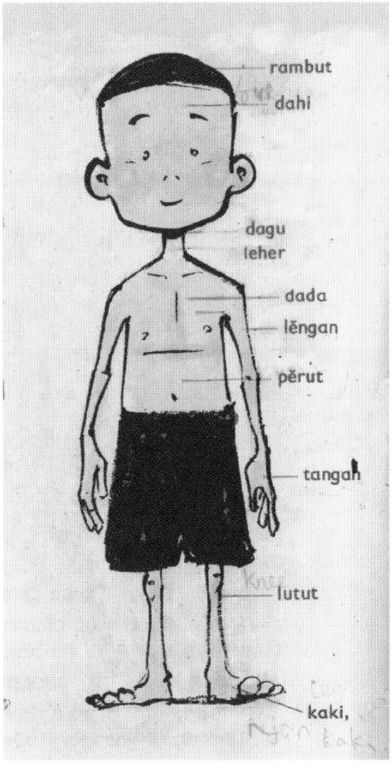

Pelajaran Kedua Belas

PERBUALAN | **BABAK I** | **DI-GERAI IKAN**

Penjual ikan:	Che' hendak ikan apa?
Mak Midah:	Berapa harga ikan tenggiri ini sa-kati?
Penjual ikan:	Sa-ringgit sa-kati.

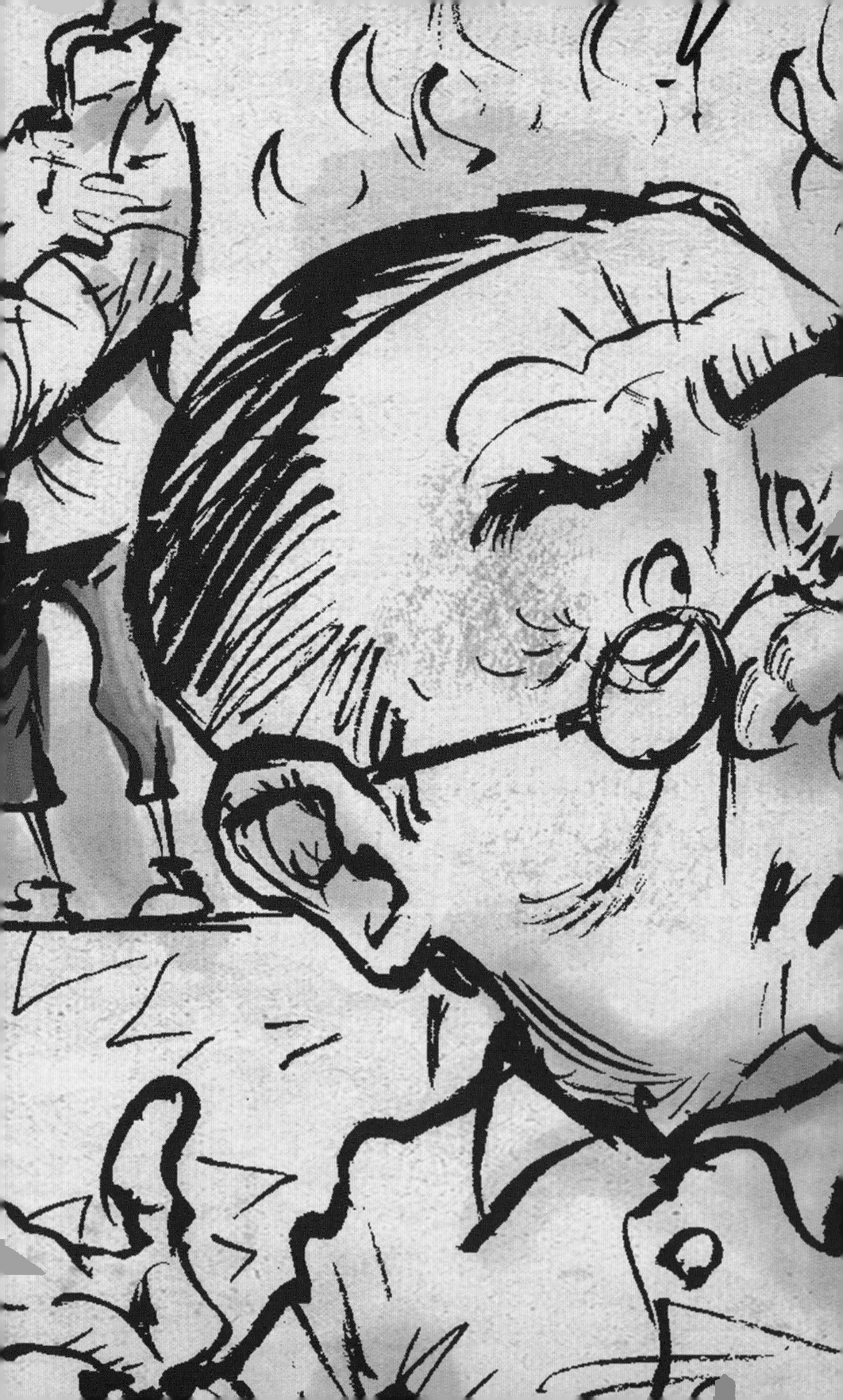

Chapter Seven

IT'S ALL ABOUT BEING PRACTICAL

脚踏实地

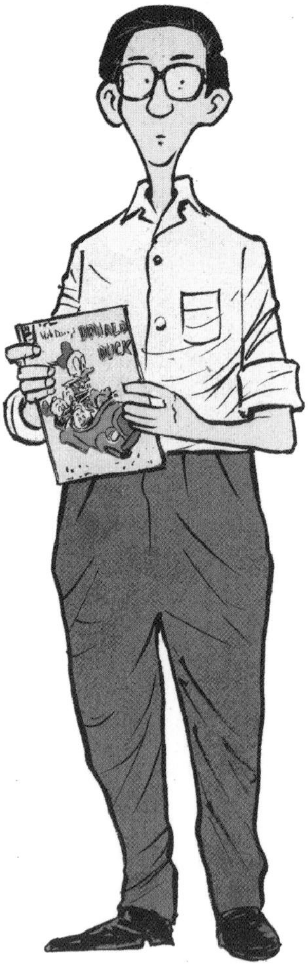
DONALD DUCK

Charlie Chan Hock Chye, aged 27, 1965

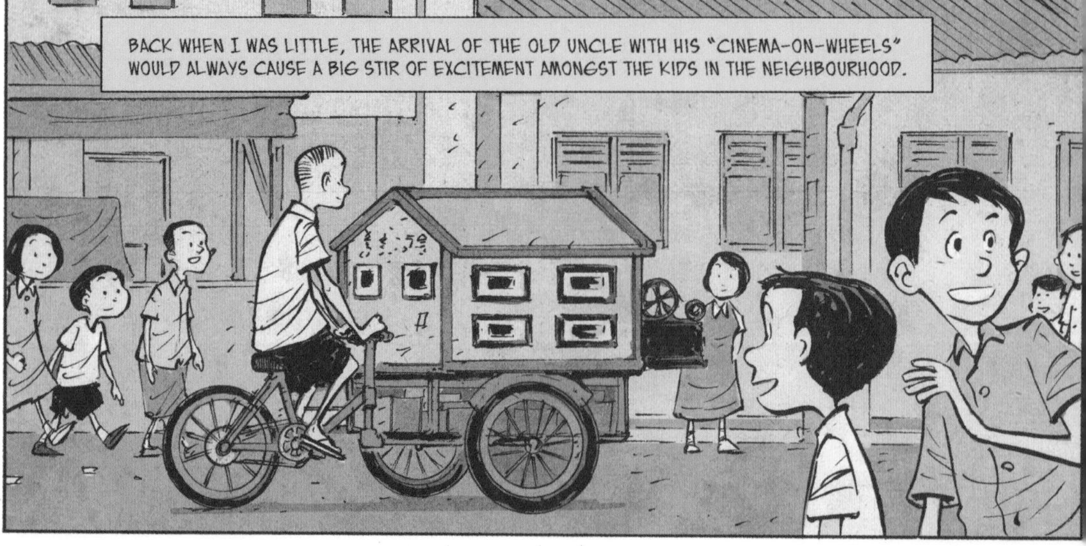
BACK WHEN I WAS LITTLE, THE ARRIVAL OF THE OLD UNCLE WITH HIS "CINEMA-ON-WHEELS" WOULD ALWAYS CAUSE A BIG STIR OF EXCITEMENT AMONGST THE KIDS IN THE NEIGHBOURHOOD.

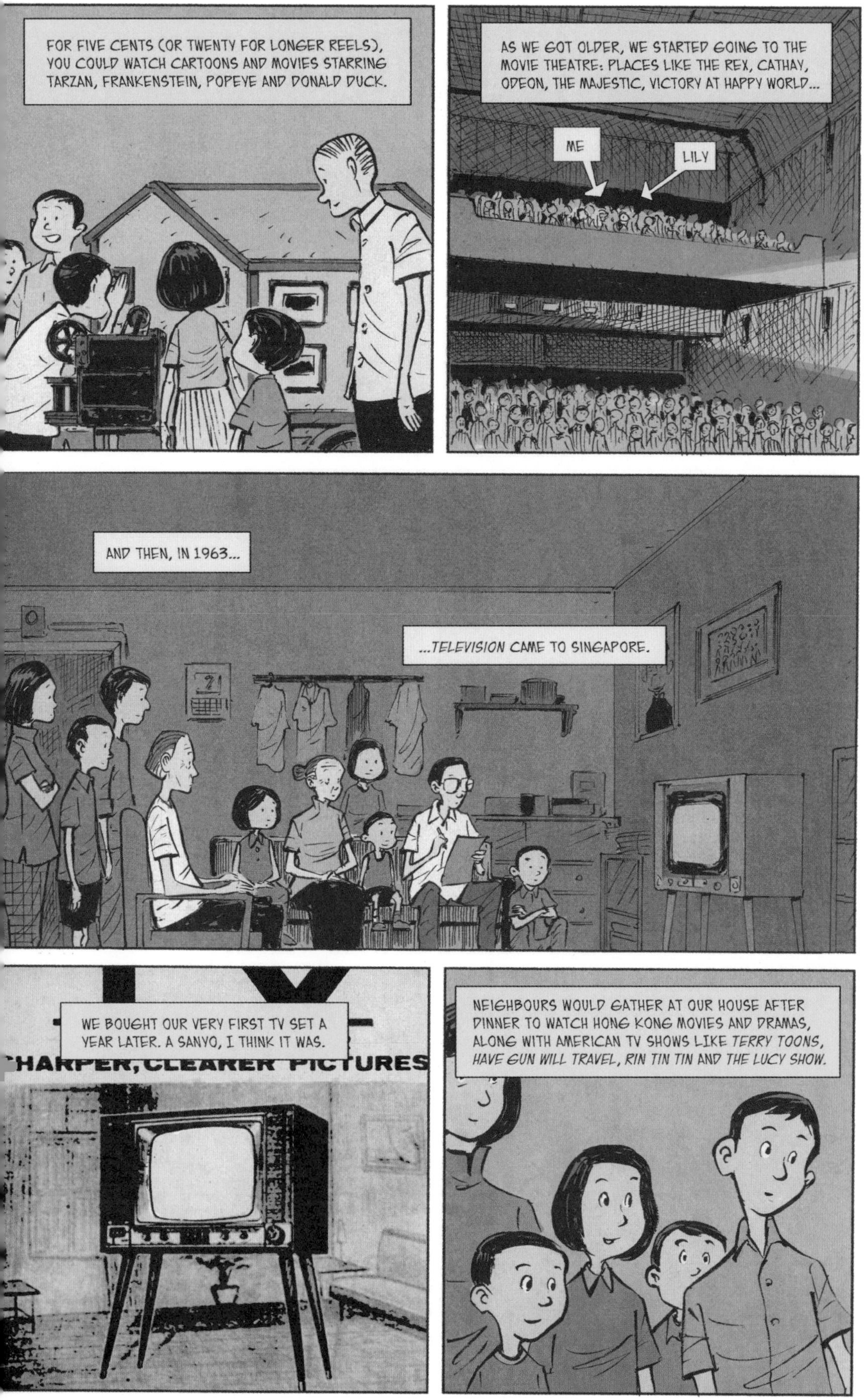
FOR FIVE CENTS (OR TWENTY FOR LONGER REELS), YOU COULD WATCH CARTOONS AND MOVIES STARRING TARZAN, FRANKENSTEIN, POPEYE AND DONALD DUCK.
AS WE GOT OLDER, WE STARTED GOING TO THE MOVIE THEATRE: PLACES LIKE THE REX, CATHAY, ODEON, THE MAJESTIC, VICTORY AT HAPPY WORLD...
ME
LILY
AND THEN, IN 1963...
...*TELEVISION* CAME TO SINGAPORE.
WE BOUGHT OUR VERY FIRST TV SET A YEAR LATER. A SANYO, I THINK IT WAS.
HARPER, CLEARER PICTURES
NEIGHBOURS WOULD GATHER AT OUR HOUSE AFTER DINNER TO WATCH HONG KONG MOVIES AND DRAMAS, ALONG WITH AMERICAN TV SHOWS LIKE *TERRY TOONS*, *HAVE GUN WILL TRAVEL*, *RIN TIN TIN* AND *THE LUCY SHOW*.

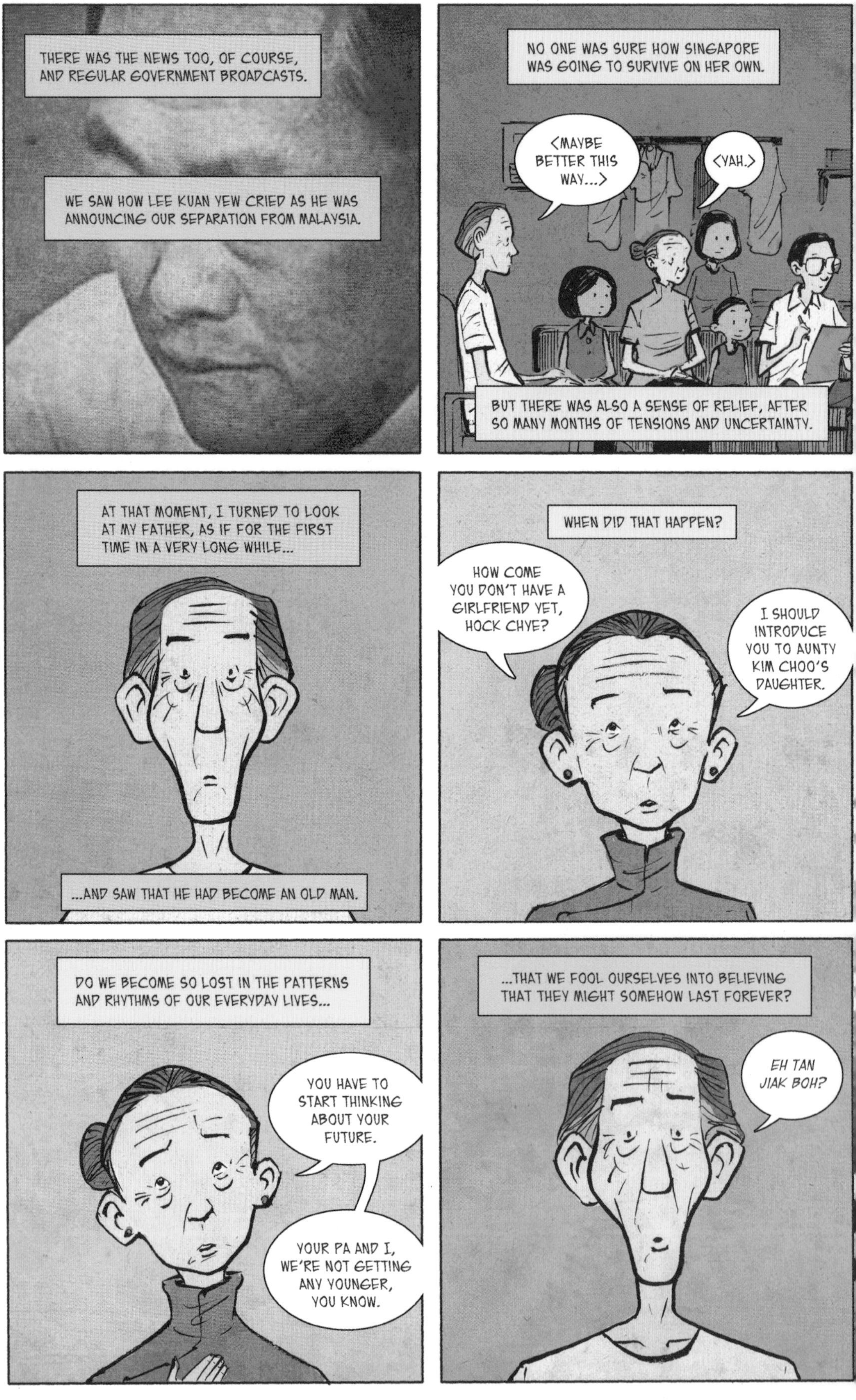
THERE WAS THE NEWS TOO, OF COURSE, AND REGULAR GOVERNMENT BROADCASTS.
WE SAW HOW LEE KUAN YEW CRIED AS HE WAS ANNOUNCING OUR SEPARATION FROM MALAYSIA.
NO ONE WAS SURE HOW SINGAPORE WAS GOING TO SURVIVE ON HER OWN.
<MAYBE BETTER THIS WAY...>
<YAH.>
BUT THERE WAS ALSO A SENSE OF RELIEF, AFTER SO MANY MONTHS OF TENSIONS AND UNCERTAINTY.
AT THAT MOMENT, I TURNED TO LOOK AT MY FATHER, AS IF FOR THE FIRST TIME IN A VERY LONG WHILE...
...AND SAW THAT HE HAD BECOME AN OLD MAN.
WHEN DID THAT HAPPEN?
HOW COME YOU DON'T HAVE A GIRLFRIEND YET, HOCK CHYE?
I SHOULD INTRODUCE YOU TO AUNTY KIM CHOO'S DAUGHTER.
DO WE BECOME SO LOST IN THE PATTERNS AND RHYTHMS OF OUR EVERYDAY LIVES...
YOU HAVE TO START THINKING ABOUT YOUR FUTURE.
YOUR PA AND I, WE'RE NOT GETTING ANY YOUNGER, YOU KNOW.
...THAT WE FOOL OURSELVES INTO BELIEVING THAT THEY MIGHT SOMEHOW LAST FOREVER?
EH TAN JIAK BOH?

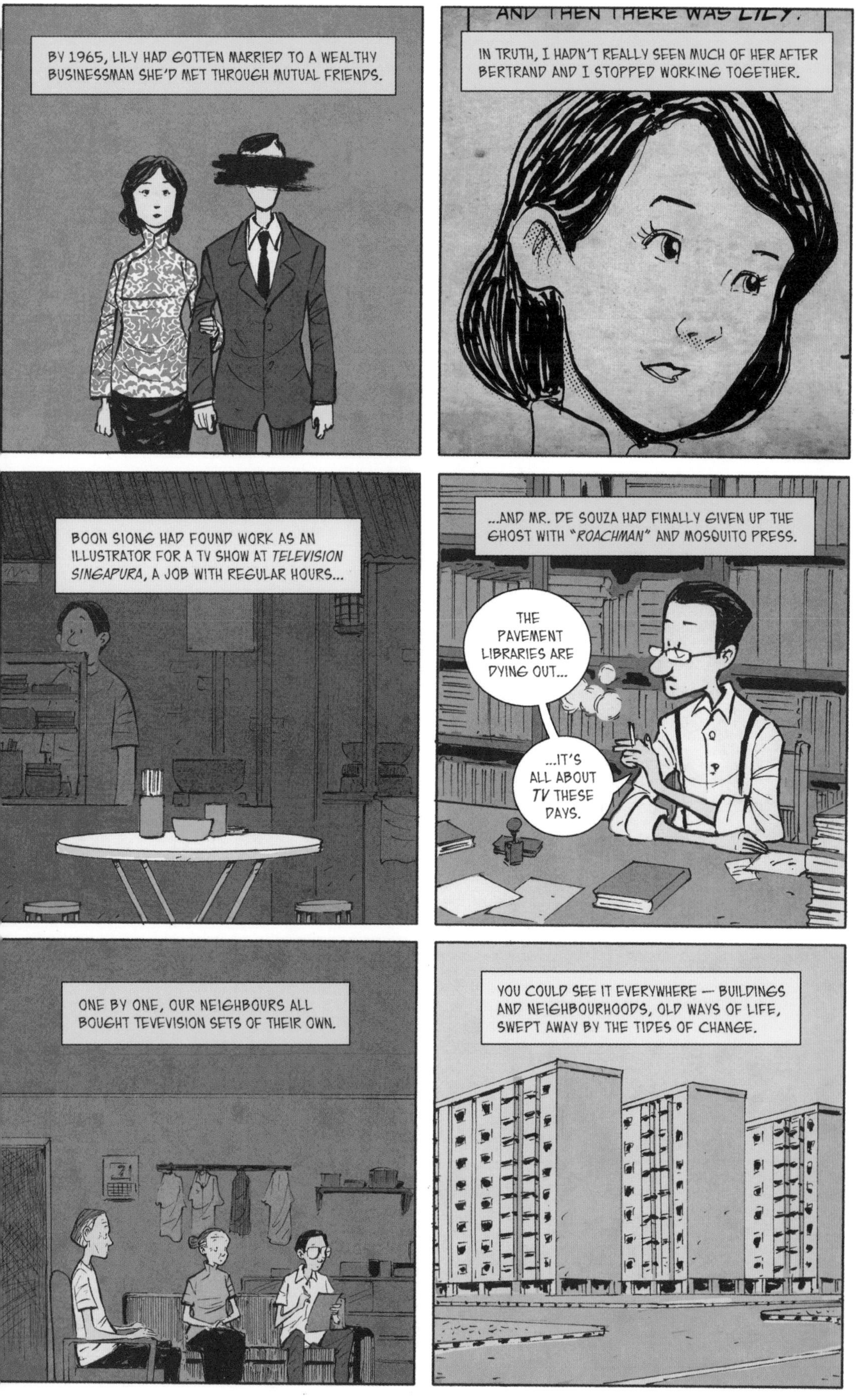
BY 1965, LILY HAD GOTTEN MARRIED TO A WEALTHY BUSINESSMAN SHE'D MET THROUGH MUTUAL FRIENDS.
AND THEN THERE WAS LILY.
IN TRUTH, I HADN'T REALLY SEEN MUCH OF HER AFTER BERTRAND AND I STOPPED WORKING TOGETHER.
BOON SIONG HAD FOUND WORK AS AN ILLUSTRATOR FOR A TV SHOW AT *TELEVISION SINGAPURA*, A JOB WITH REGULAR HOURS...
...AND MR. DE SOUZA HAD FINALLY GIVEN UP THE GHOST WITH "*ROACHMAN*" AND MOSQUITO PRESS.
THE PAVEMENT LIBRARIES ARE DYING OUT...
...IT'S ALL ABOUT *TV* THESE DAYS.
ONE BY ONE, OUR NEIGHBOURS ALL BOUGHT TEVEVISION SETS OF THEIR OWN.
YOU COULD SEE IT EVERYWHERE — BUILDINGS AND NEIGHBOURHOODS, OLD WAYS OF LIFE, SWEPT AWAY BY THE TIDES OF CHANGE.

THE UNCLE AND HIS PORTABLE CINEMA WOULD STILL COME BY, BUT THE KIDS JUST DIDN'T SEEM TO GET AS EXCITED ABOUT HIS APPEARANCE ANYMORE.

AS THE YEARS WENT BY, YOU'D SEE HIM LESS AND LESS OFTEN...

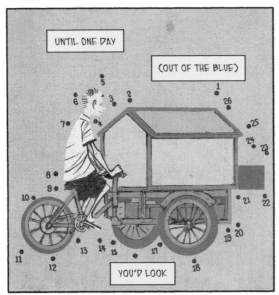

UNTIL ONE DAY

(OUT OF THE BLUE)

YOU'D LOOK

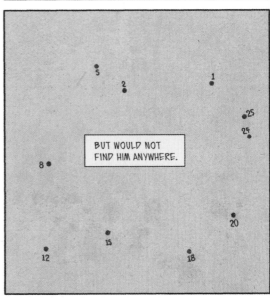

BUT WOULD NOT FIND HIM ANYWHERE.

CHARLIE CHAN HOCK CHYE.

SINGAPORE'S GREATEST COMICS ARTIST.

WELL ON THE WAY.

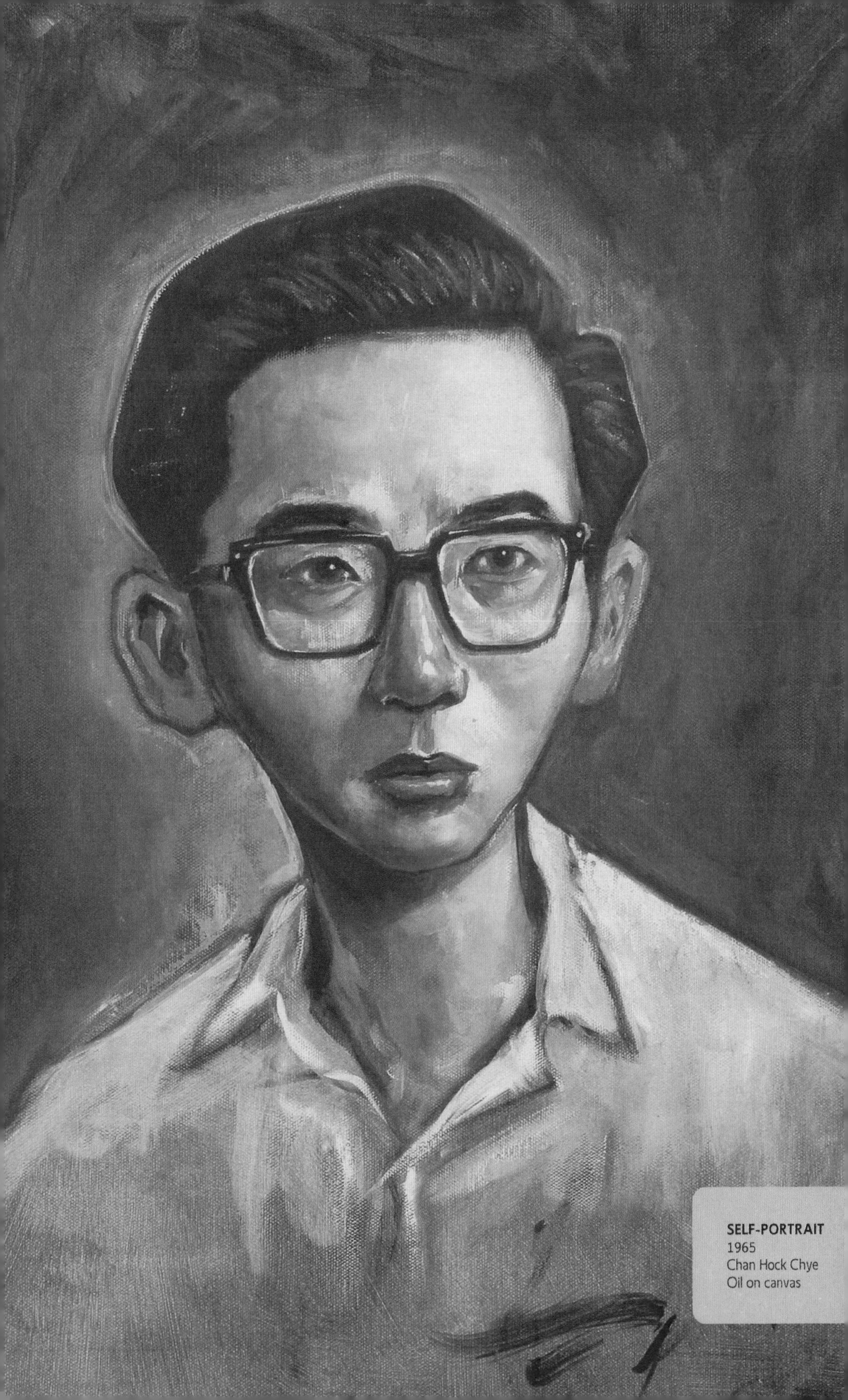

SELF-PORTRAIT
1965
Chan Hock Chye
Oil on canvas

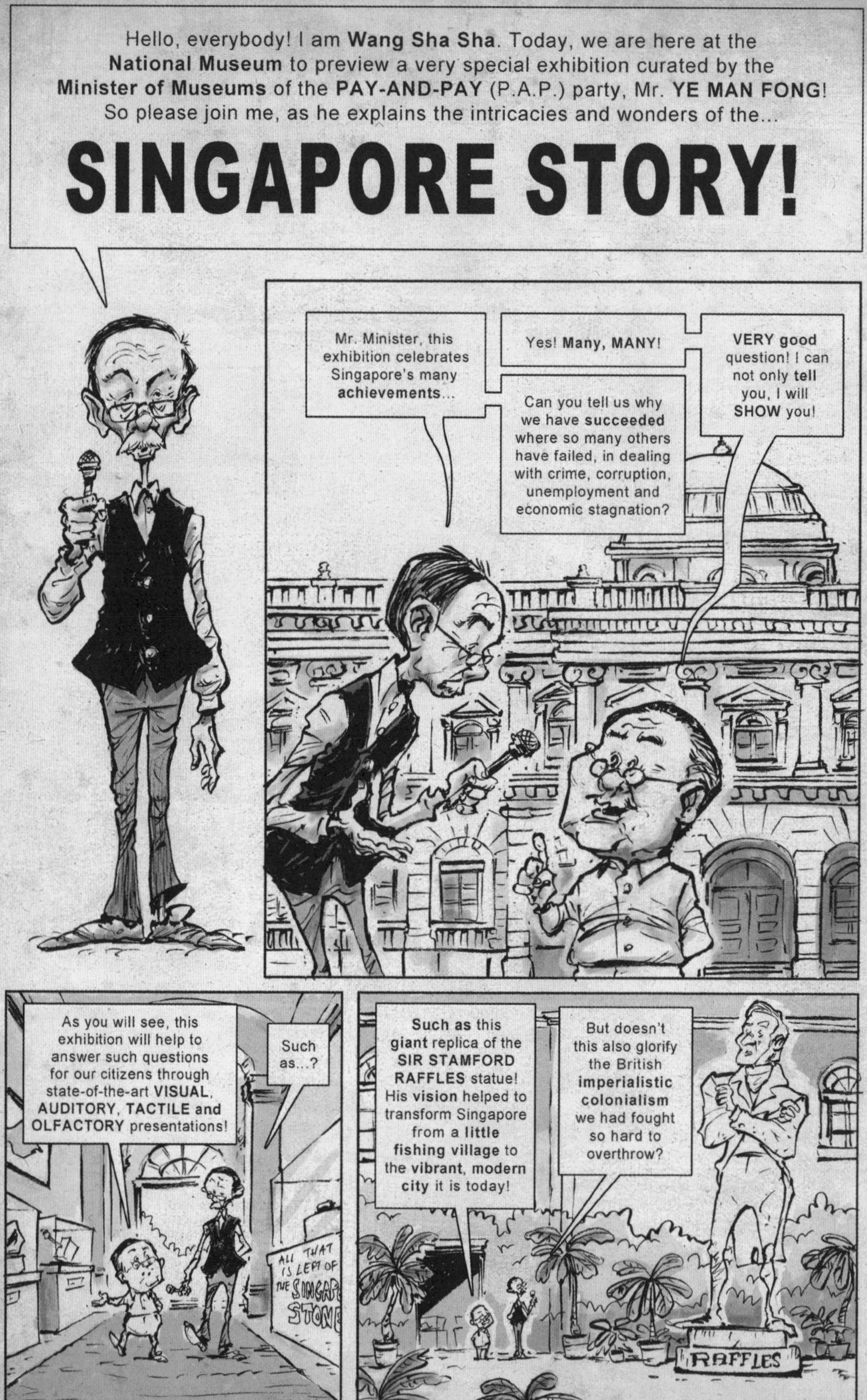
Hello, everybody! I am Wang Sha Sha. Today, we are here at the National Museum to preview a very special exhibition curated by the Minister of Museums of the PAY-AND-PAY (P.A.P.) party, Mr. YE MAN FONG! So please join me, as he explains the intricacies and wonders of the...
SINGAPORE STORY!
Mr. Minister, this exhibition celebrates Singapore's many achievements...
Yes! Many, MANY!
Can you tell us why we have succeeded where so many others have failed, in dealing with crime, corruption, unemployment and economic stagnation?
VERY good question! I can not only tell you, I will SHOW you!
As you will see, this exhibition will help to answer such questions for our citizens through state-of-the-art VISUAL, AUDITORY, TACTILE and OLFACTORY presentations!
Such as...?
ALL THAT IS LEFT OF
STONE
Such as this giant replica of the SIR STAMFORD RAFFLES statue! His vision helped to transform Singapore from a little fishing village to the vibrant, modern city it is today!
But doesn't this also glorify the British imperialistic colonialism we had fought so hard to overthrow?
RAFFLES

Above **SINGAPORE STORY** (1991) | Chan Hock Chye | Unpublished

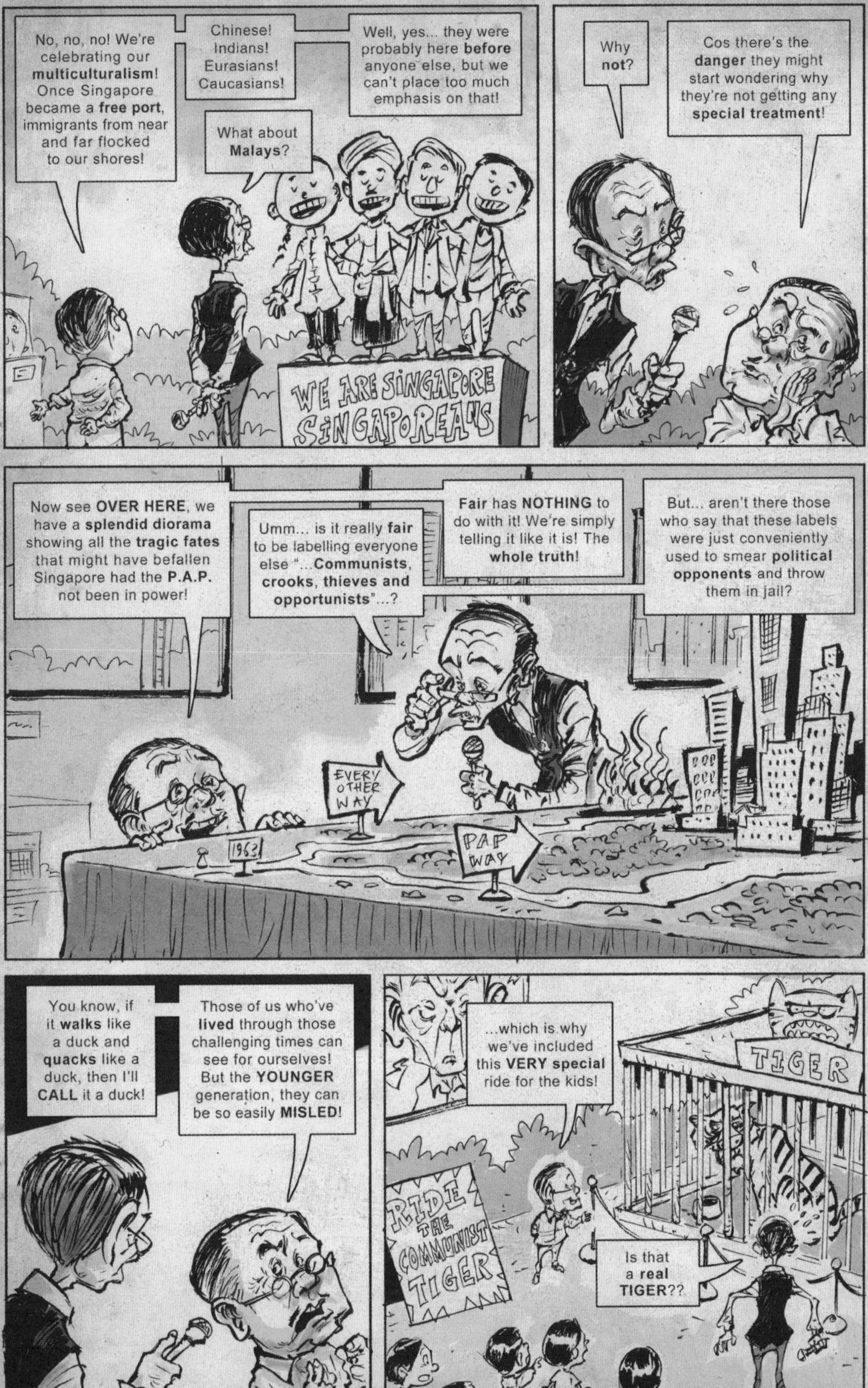
No, no, no! We're celebrating our **multiculturalism**! Once Singapore became a **free port**, immigrants from near and far flocked to our shores!
Chinese! Indians! Eurasians! Caucasians!
What about **Malays**?
Well, yes... they were probably here **before** anyone else, but we can't place too much emphasis on that!
WE ARE SINGAPORE SINGAPOREANS
Why **not**?
Cos there's the **danger** they might start wondering why they're not getting any **special treatment**!
Now see **OVER HERE**, we have a **splendid diorama** showing all the **tragic fates** that might have befallen Singapore had the **P.A.P.** not been in power!
Umm... is it really **fair** to be labelling everyone else "...**Communists, crooks, thieves and opportunists**"...?
Fair has **NOTHING** to do with it! We're simply telling it like it is! The **whole truth**!
But... aren't there those who say that these labels were just conveniently used to smear **political opponents** and throw them in jail?
EVERY OTHER WAY
1963
PAP WAY
You know, if it **walks** like a duck and **quacks** like a duck, then I'll **CALL** it a duck!
Those of us who've **lived** through those challenging times can see for ourselves! But the **YOUNGER** generation, they can be so easily **MISLED**!
...which is why we've included this **VERY special** ride for the kids!
TIGER
RIDE THE COMMUNIST TIGER
Is that a **real TIGER**??

The two characters featured were based on popular local stand-up comedians **Wang Sha** and **Ye Fong**. Initially a live theatre act, the duo became staples on the airwaves when Television Singapura began broadcasting in 1963. With skits that mashed Chinese dialects, Mandarin, Malay and English with playful satires on social campaigns, the duo became the grand old masters of Singapore comedy, and bade goodbye to local audiences with a final performance in 1994. Ye Feng died a year later, and Wang Sha passed away in 1998.

Why, YES! We'd ridden the **Communist Tiger** to independence, and now, kids can get to experience something similar for themselves!

Isn't it... a bit **dangerous**?

But **of course!** Just ask little Boon Teck here!

He's lost a bit of blood today, but he'll **never** underestimate the Communists again! Isn't that right, Boon Teck?

Pain! Pain!!

And of course, we also need to teach the people about the dangers of **racial** and **religious** discord!

Here, visitors can not only dress up in traditional costumes and enact a **mock riot**, they can also have a **commemorative photo** taken to remind them of the need to shun all politics based on race and religion!

Say **cheese!**

RACE RIO

Which is, of course, why we had to leave Malaysia! We simply **couldn't** accept a society in which any one race would be given **special treatment**, as this chart so clearly illustrates!

SPECIAL RIGHTS ↓

MERITOCRACY! ↗

But... when we joined Malaysia, didn't we already **know** and **accept** their policy of preferential treatment for Malays?

I'm SHOCKED! **Shocked** that you would even **SAY** that! Are you implying that we should be totally **rigid** and **doctrinaire**, and not **adapt** to changing circumstances??!

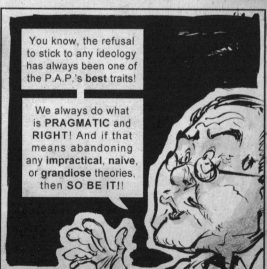

You know, the refusal to stick to any ideology has always been one of the P.A.P.'s **best** traits!

We always do what is PRAGMATIC and RIGHT! And if that means abandoning any **impractical**, **naive**, or **grandiose** theories, then SO BE IT!!

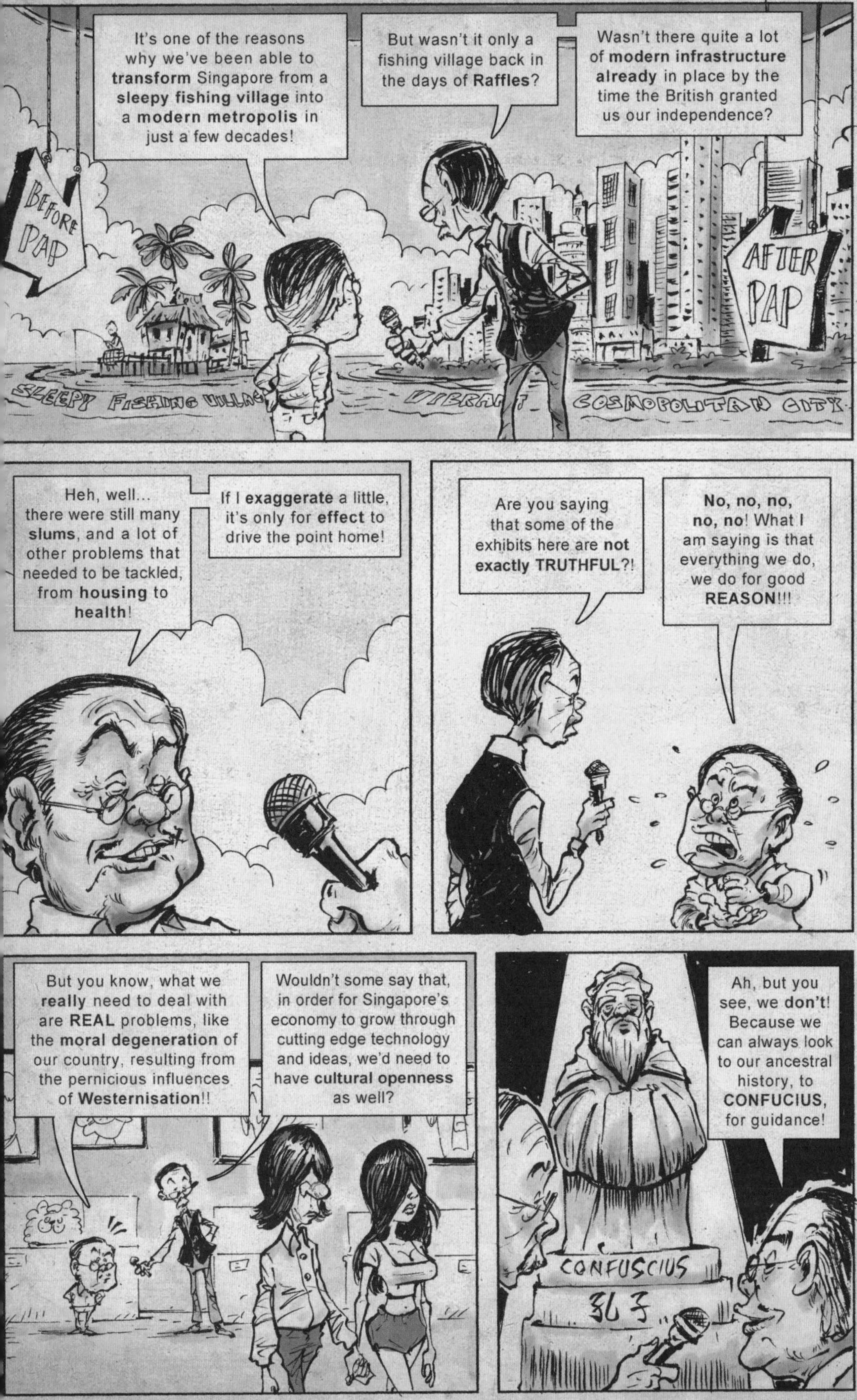

It's one of the reasons why we've been able to **transform** Singapore from a **sleepy fishing village** into a **modern metropolis** in just a few decades!
BEFORE PAP
SLEEPY FISHING VILLAG
But wasn't it only a fishing village back in the days of **Raffles**?
Wasn't there quite a lot of **modern infrastructure already** in place by the time the British granted us our independence?
AFTER PAP
VIBRA
COSMOPOLITAN CITY
Heh, well... there were still many **slums**, and a lot of other problems that needed to be tackled, from **housing** to **health**!
If I **exaggerate** a little, it's only for **effect** to drive the point home!
Are you saying that some of the exhibits here are **not exactly TRUTHFUL**?!
No, no, no, no, no! What I am saying is that everything we do, we do for good **REASON**!!!
But you know, what we **really** need to deal with are **REAL** problems, like the **moral degeneration** of our country, resulting from the pernicious influences of **Westernisation**!!
Wouldn't some say that, in order for Singapore's economy to grow through cutting edge technology and ideas, we'd need to have **cultural openness** as well?
Ah, but you see, we **don't**! Because we can always look to our ancestral history, to **CONFUCIUS**, for guidance!
CONFUSCIUS
孔子

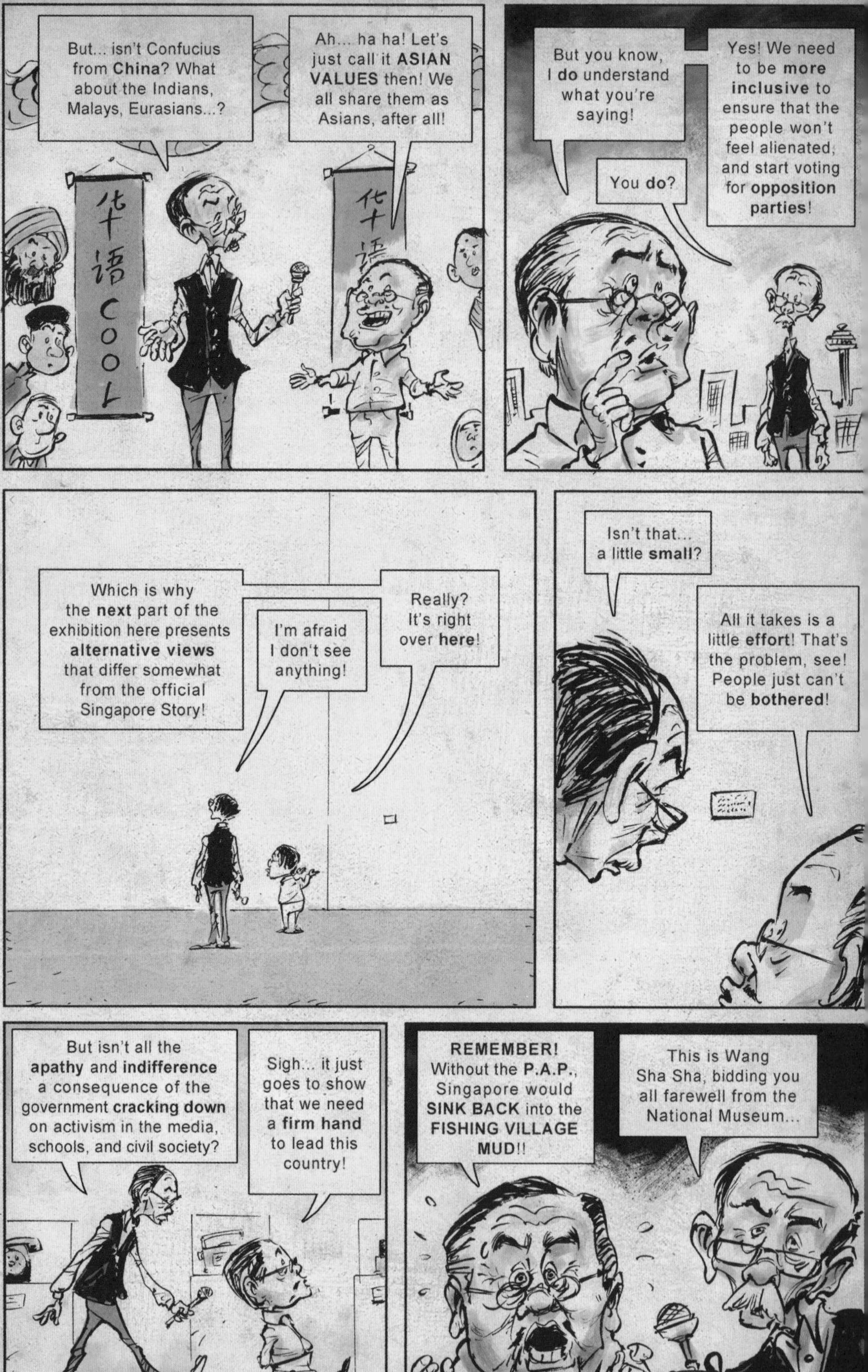
But... isn't Confucius from **China**? What about the Indians, Malays, Eurasians...?
Ah... ha ha! Let's just call it **ASIAN VALUES** then! We all share them as Asians, after all!
华语 COOL
But you know, I **do** understand what you're saying!
You **do**?
Yes! We need to be **more inclusive** to ensure that the people won't feel alienated, and start voting for **opposition parties**!
Which is why the **next** part of the exhibition here presents **alternative views** that differ somewhat from the official Singapore Story!
I'm afraid I don't see anything!
Really? It's right over **here**!
Isn't that... a little **small**?
All it takes is a little **effort**! That's the problem, see! People just can't be **bothered**!
But isn't all the **apathy** and **indifference** a consequence of the government **cracking down** on activism in the media, schools, and civil society?
Sigh... it just goes to show that we need a **firm hand** to lead this country!
REMEMBER! Without the **P.A.P.**, Singapore would **SINK BACK** into the **FISHING VILLAGE MUD**!!
This is Wang Sha Sha, bidding you all farewell from the National Museum...

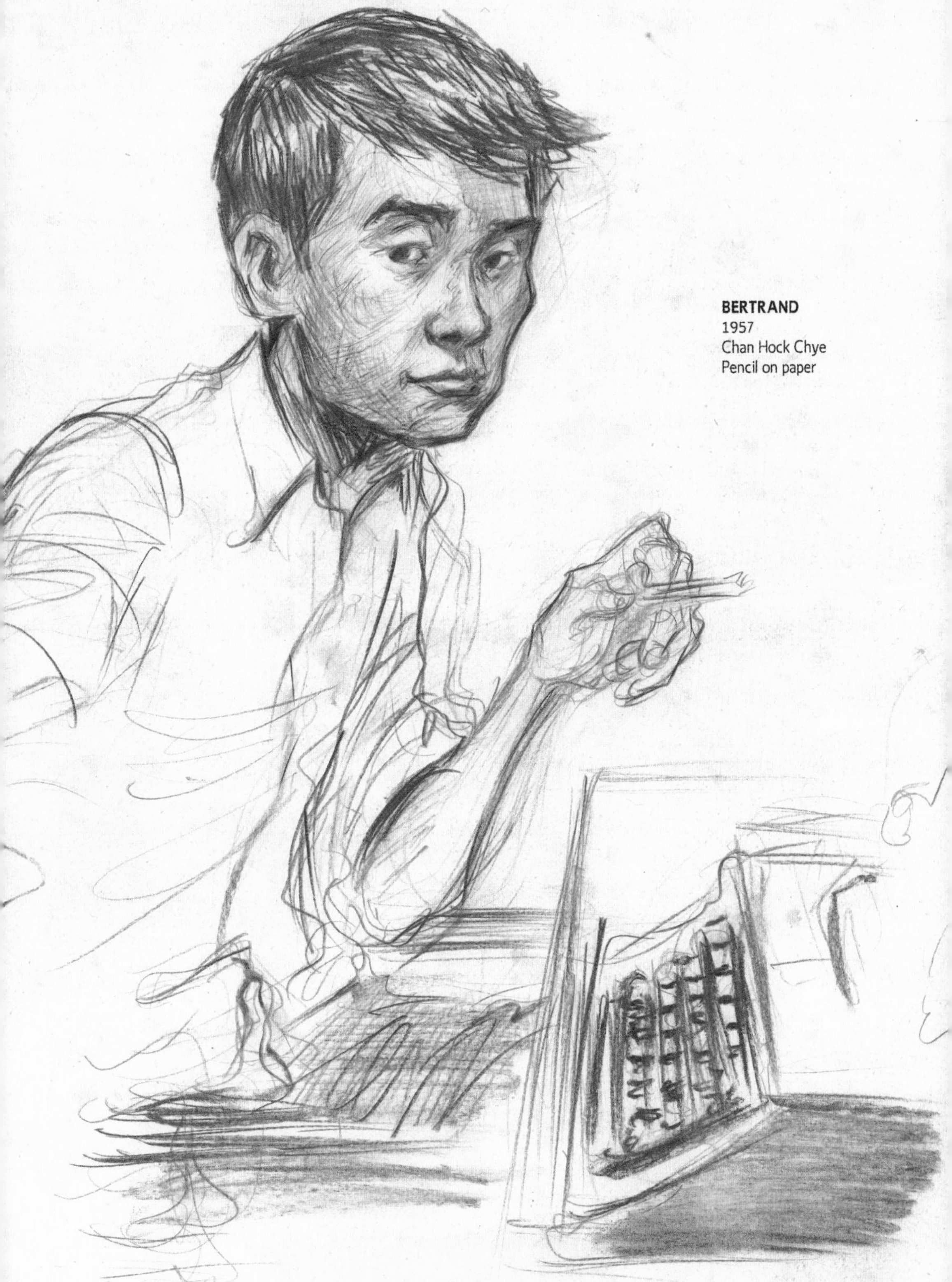

BERTRAND
1957
Chan Hock Chye
Pencil on paper

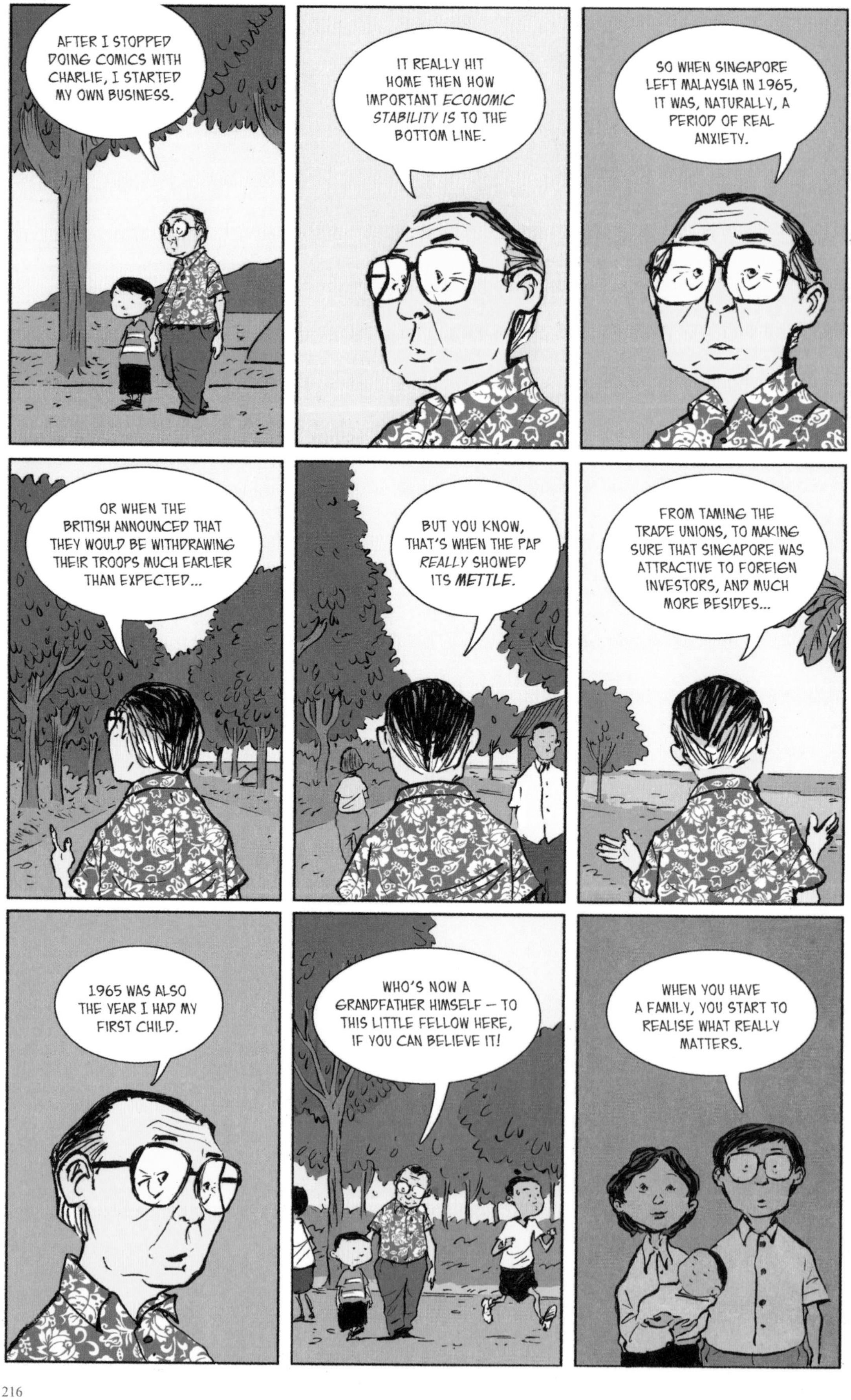
AFTER I STOPPED DOING COMICS WITH CHARLIE, I STARTED MY OWN BUSINESS.
IT REALLY HIT HOME THEN HOW IMPORTANT *ECONOMIC STABILITY IS* TO THE BOTTOM LINE.
SO WHEN SINGAPORE LEFT MALAYSIA IN 1965, IT WAS, NATURALLY, A PERIOD OF REAL ANXIETY.
OR WHEN THE BRITISH ANNOUNCED THAT THEY WOULD BE WITHDRAWING THEIR TROOPS MUCH EARLIER THAN EXPECTED...
BUT YOU KNOW, THAT'S WHEN THE PAP *REALLY* SHOWED ITS ***METTLE.***
FROM TAMING THE TRADE UNIONS, TO MAKING SURE THAT SINGAPORE WAS ATTRACTIVE TO FOREIGN INVESTORS, AND MUCH MORE BESIDES...
1965 WAS ALSO THE YEAR I HAD MY FIRST CHILD.
WHO'S NOW A GRANDFATHER HIMSELF — TO THIS LITTLE FELLOW HERE, IF YOU CAN BELIEVE IT!
WHEN YOU HAVE A FAMILY, YOU START TO REALISE WHAT REALLY MATTERS.

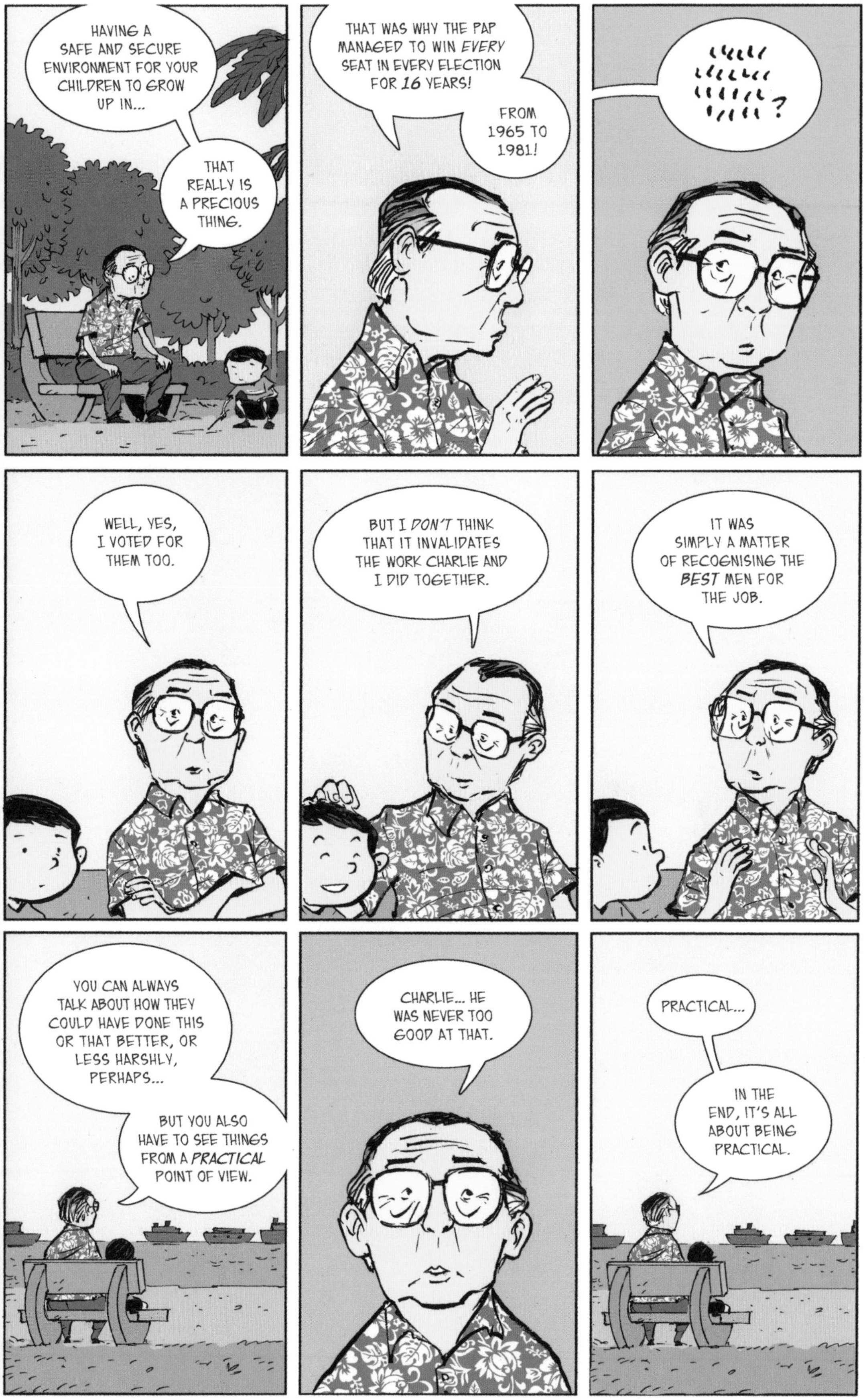

HAVING A SAFE AND SECURE ENVIRONMENT FOR YOUR CHILDREN TO GROW UP IN...
THAT REALLY IS A PRECIOUS THING.
THAT WAS WHY THE PAP MANAGED TO WIN EVERY SEAT IN EVERY ELECTION FOR 16 YEARS!
FROM 1965 TO 1981!
?
WELL, YES, I VOTED FOR THEM TOO.
BUT I DON'T THINK THAT IT INVALIDATES THE WORK CHARLIE AND I DID TOGETHER.
IT WAS SIMPLY A MATTER OF RECOGNISING THE BEST MEN FOR THE JOB.
YOU CAN ALWAYS TALK ABOUT HOW THEY COULD HAVE DONE THIS OR THAT BETTER, OR LESS HARSHLY, PERHAPS...
BUT YOU ALSO HAVE TO SEE THINGS FROM A PRACTICAL POINT OF VIEW.
CHARLIE... HE WAS NEVER TOO GOOD AT THAT.
PRACTICAL...
IN THE END, IT'S ALL ABOUT BEING PRACTICAL.

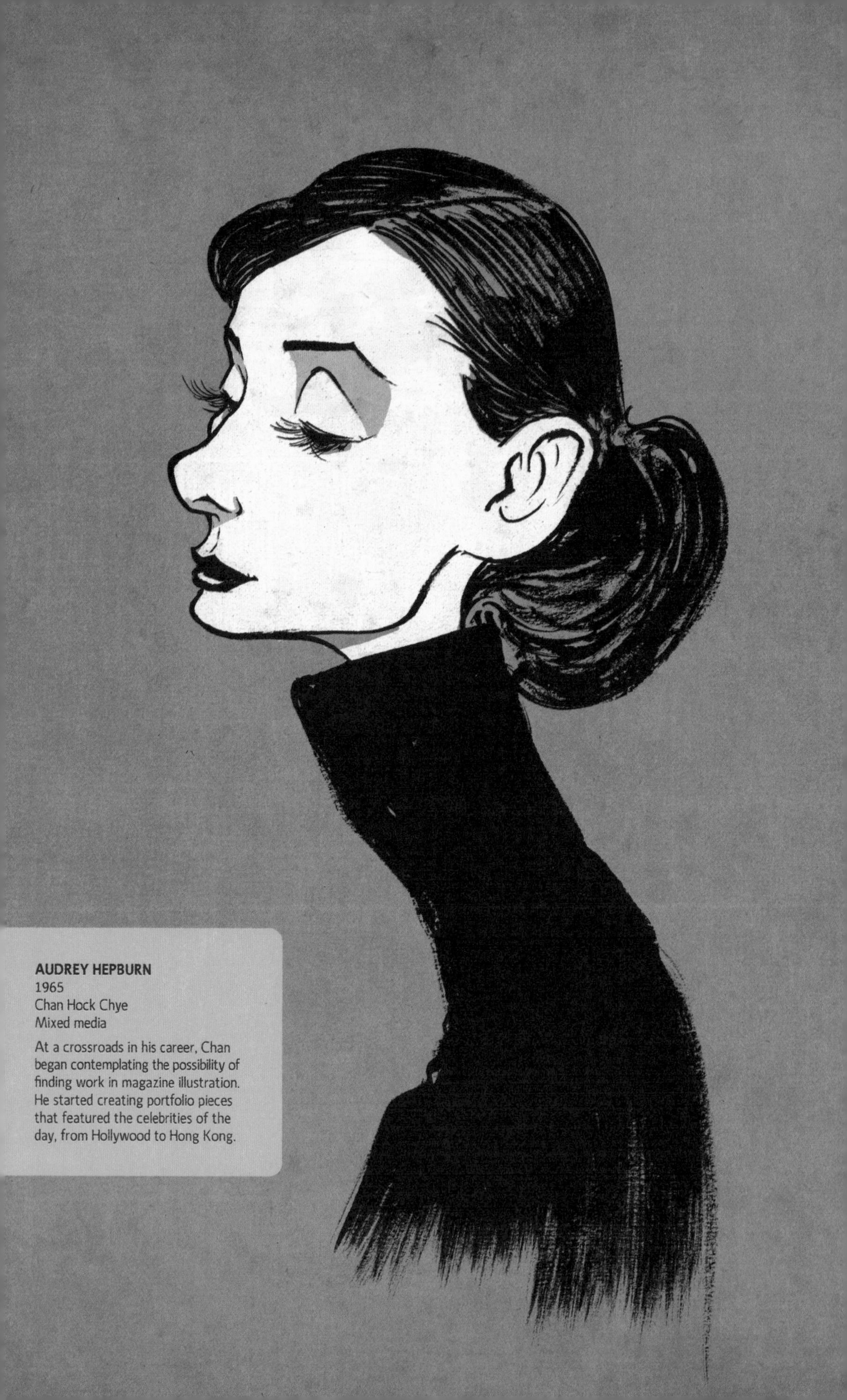

AUDREY HEPBURN
1965
Chan Hock Chye
Mixed media

At a crossroads in his career, Chan began contemplating the possibility of finding work in magazine illustration. He started creating portfolio pieces that featured the celebrities of the day, from Hollywood to Hong Kong.

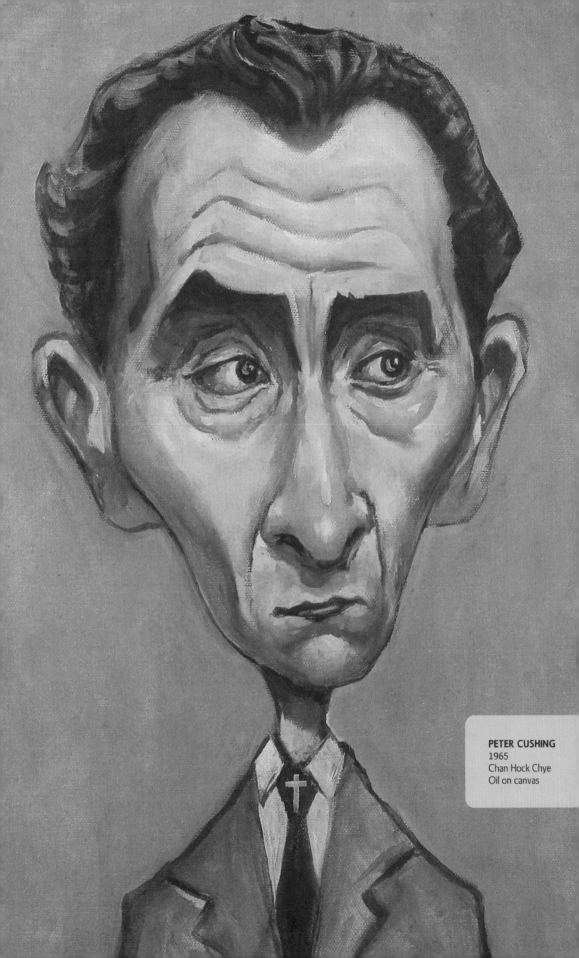

PETER CUSHING
1965
Chan Hock Chye
Oil on canvas

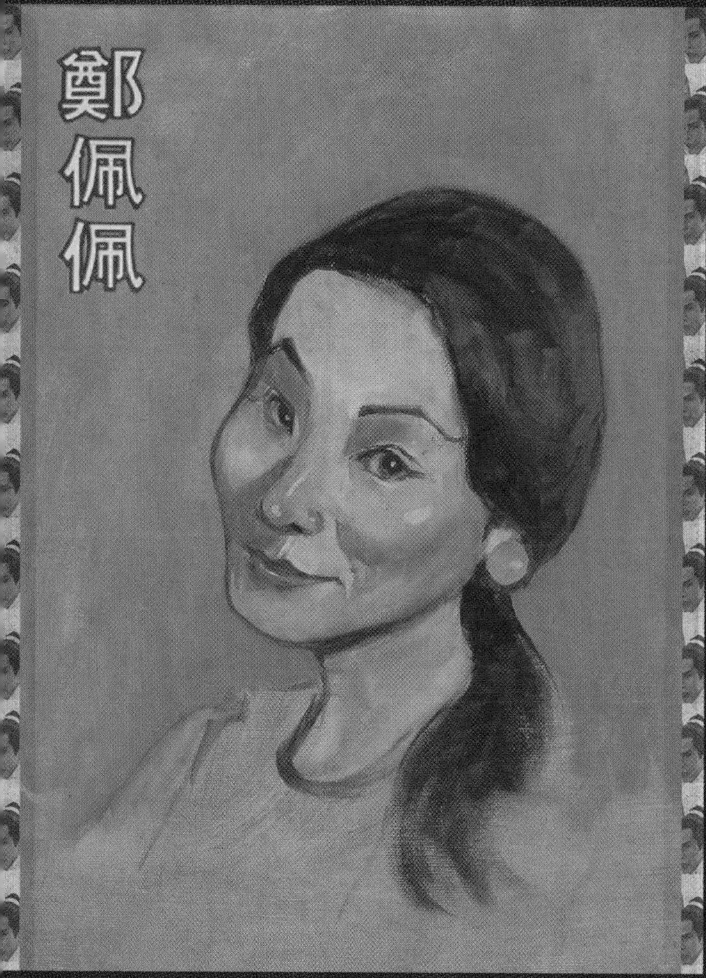
鄭佩佩

This page (clockwise from top left)
CHENG PEI-PEI, PAUL NEWMAN & JACKIE GLEASON, ROY CHIAO AND GREGORY PECK
1965
Chan Hock Chye
Various media

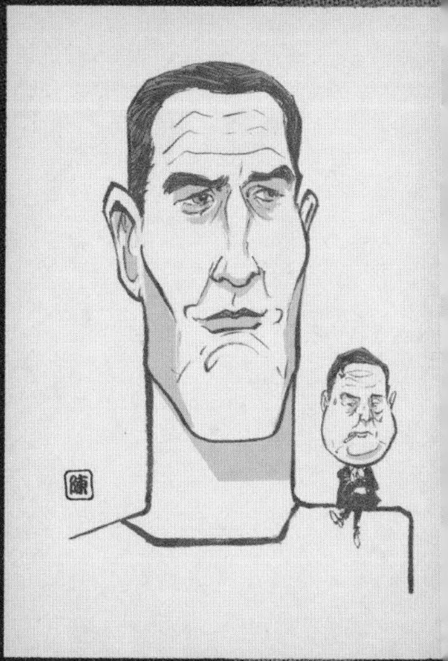

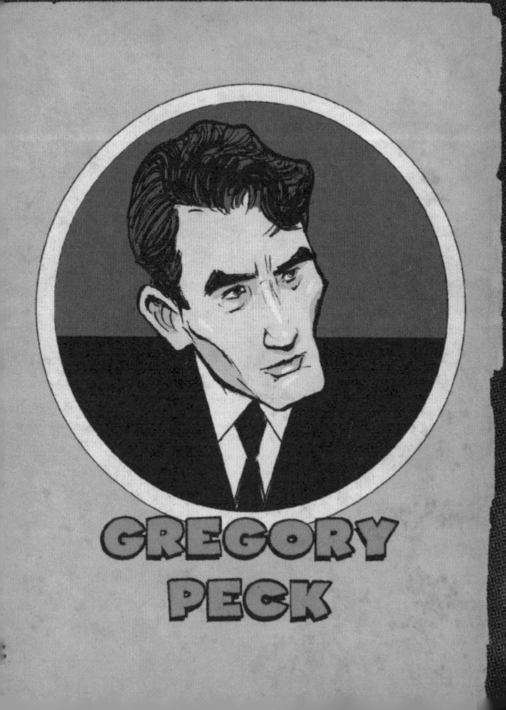
GREGORY
PECK

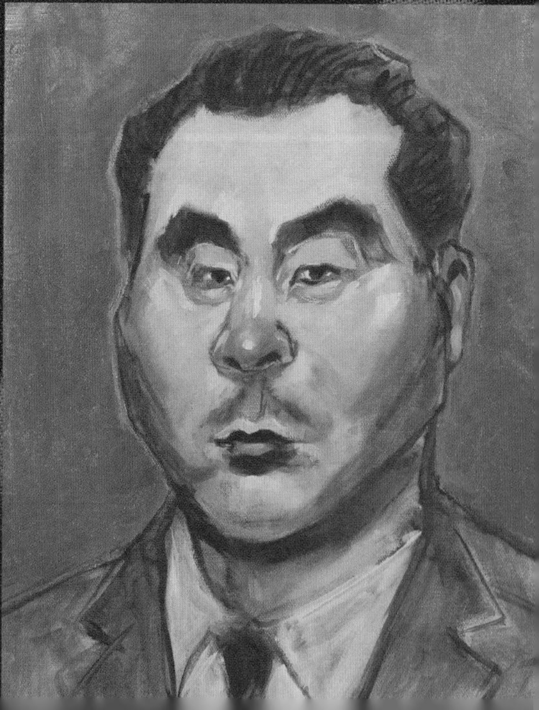

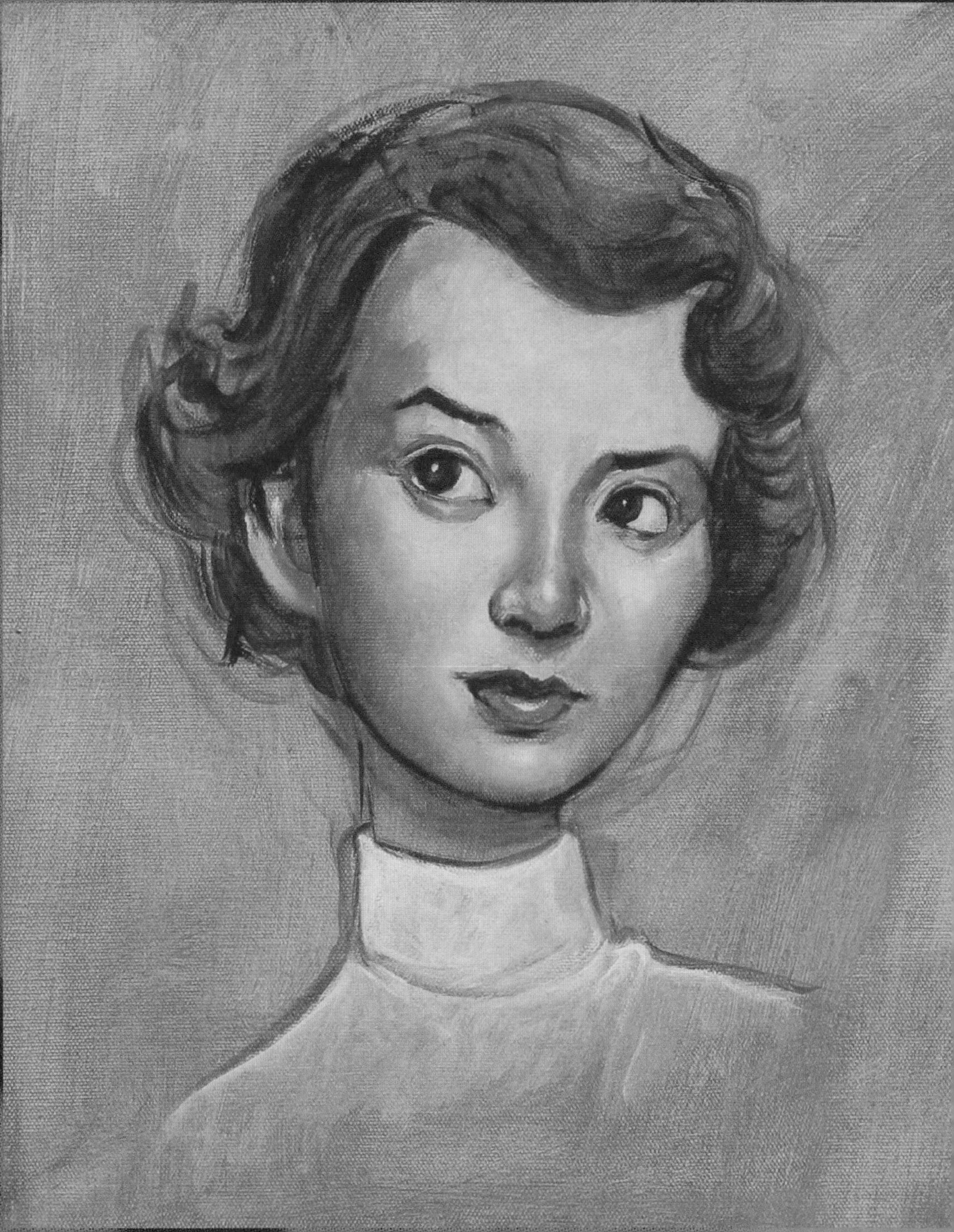

Above

YU MING

1965

Chan Hock Chye

Oil on canvas

Lucilla Yu Ming was a Hong Kong film star from the 1950s to 1960s, whose visits to Singapore would always attract huge, rapturous crowds. Chan says that he was often struck by how much the actress reminded him of Lily.

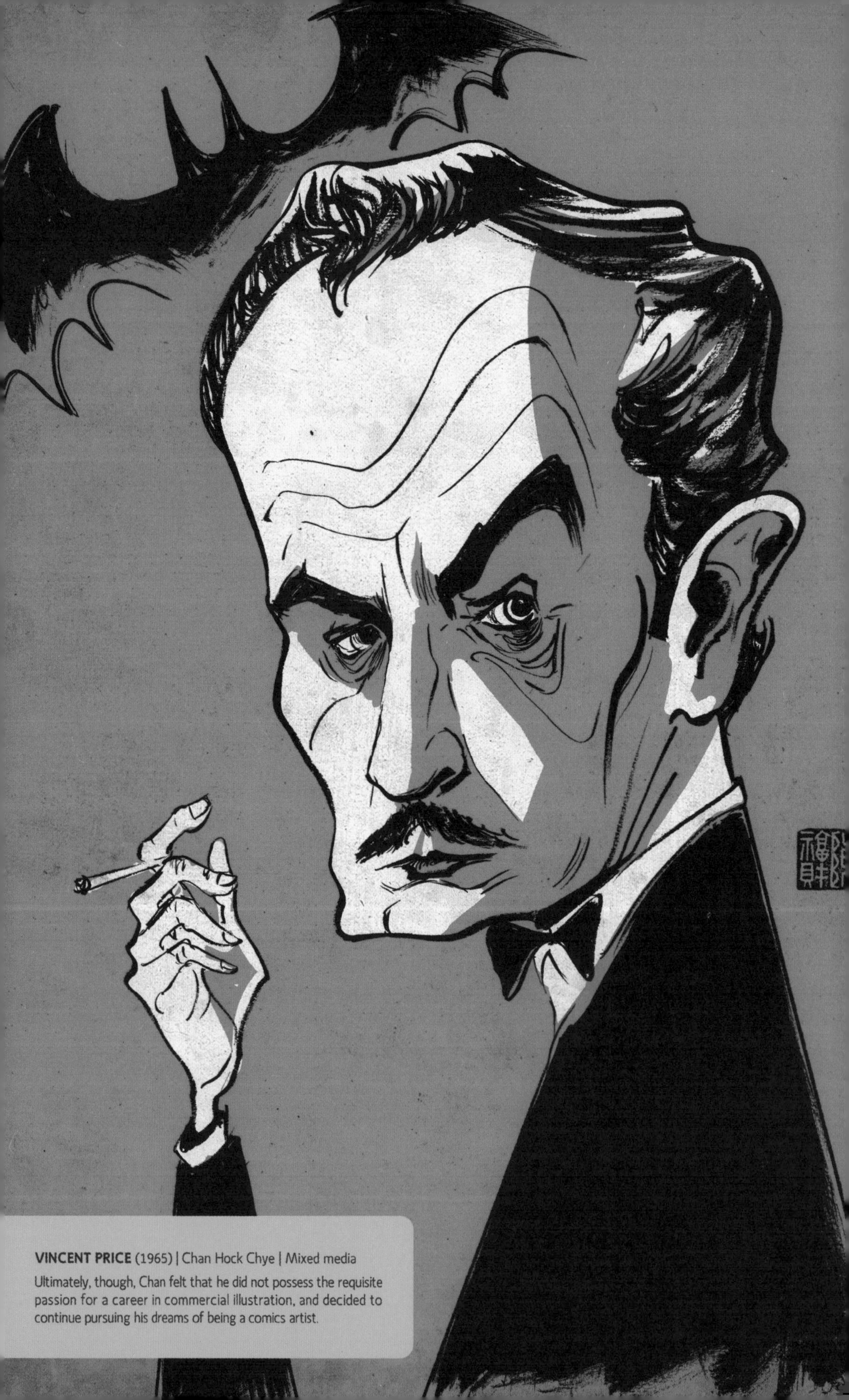

VINCENT PRICE (1965) | Chan Hock Chye | Mixed media

Ultimately, though, Chan felt that he did not possess the requisite passion for a career in commercial illustration, and decided to continue pursuing his dreams of being a comics artist.

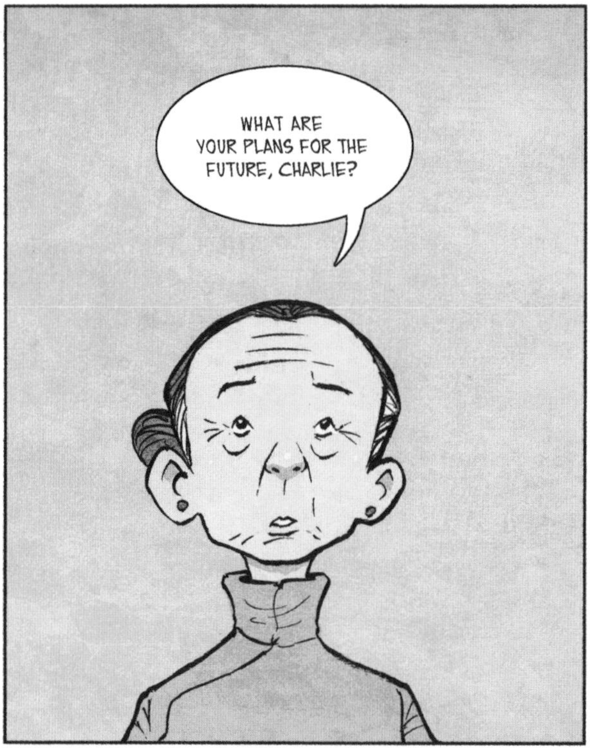
WHAT ARE YOUR PLANS FOR THE FUTURE, CHARLIE?

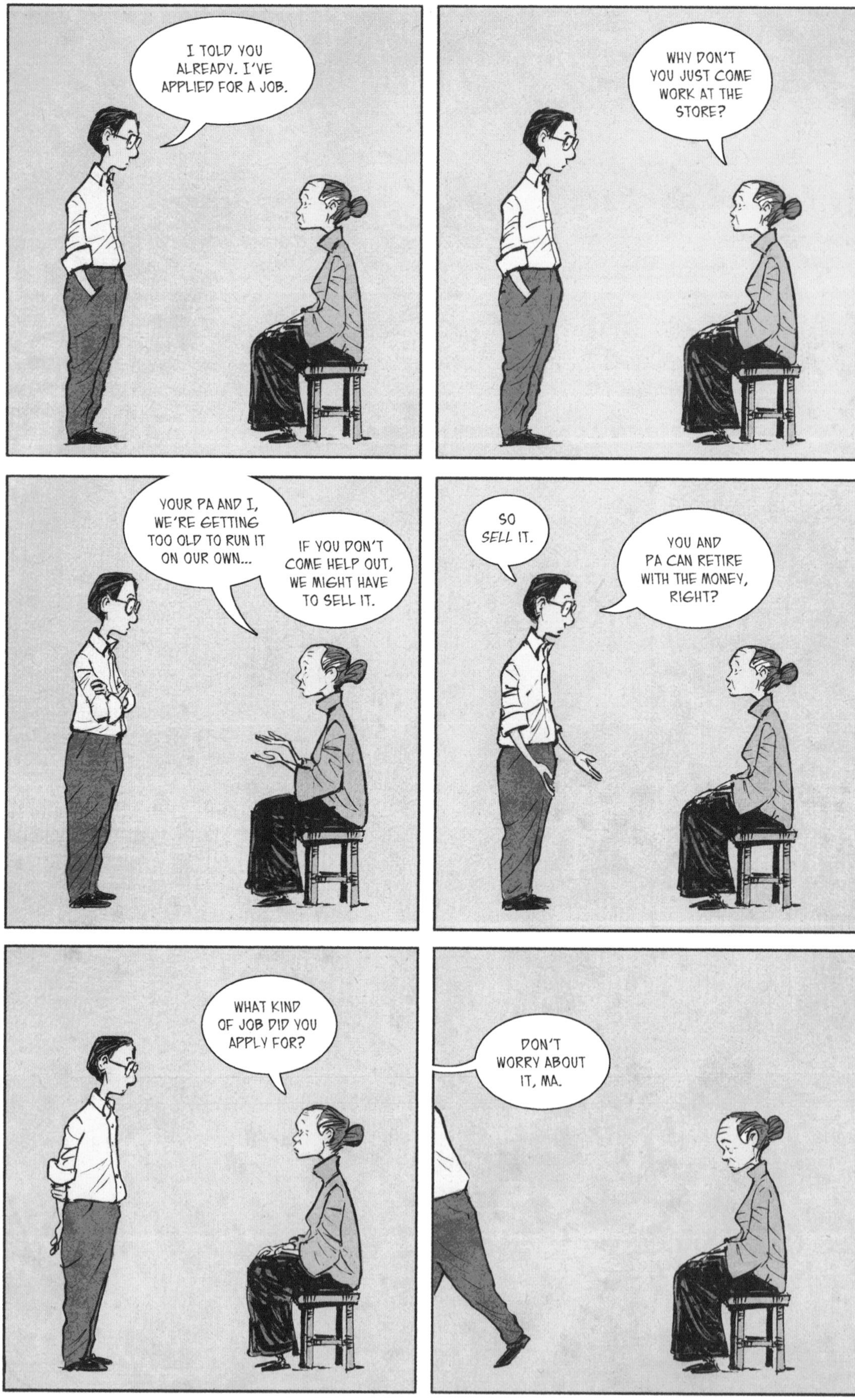
I TOLD YOU ALREADY. I'VE APPLIED FOR A JOB.
WHY DON'T YOU JUST COME WORK AT THE STORE?
YOUR PA AND I, WE'RE GETTING TOO OLD TO RUN IT ON OUR OWN...
IF YOU DON'T COME HELP OUT, WE MIGHT HAVE TO SELL IT.
SO SELL IT.
YOU AND PA CAN RETIRE WITH THE MONEY, RIGHT?
WHAT KIND OF JOB DID YOU APPLY FOR?
DON'T WORRY ABOUT IT, MA.

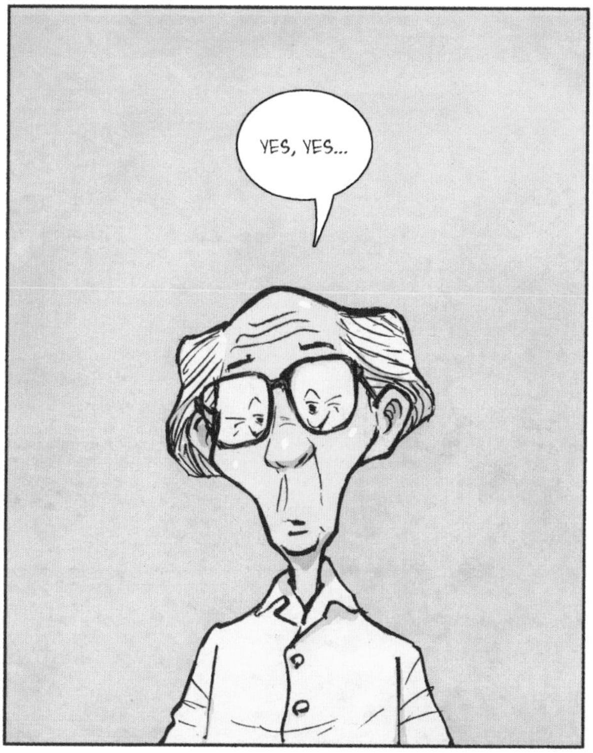
YES, YES...

The Night Watchman

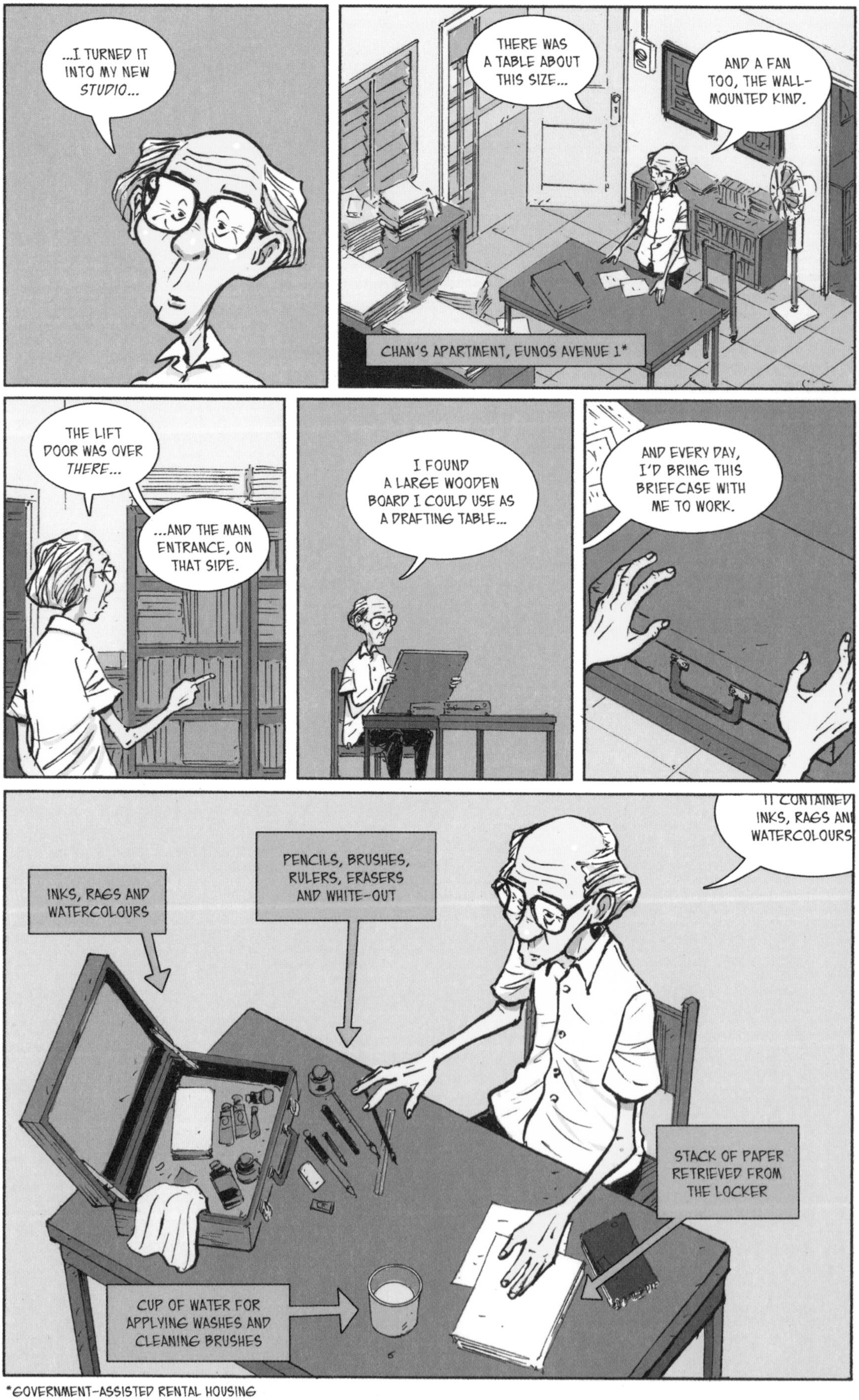
...I TURNED IT INTO MY NEW STUDIO...
THERE WAS A TABLE ABOUT THIS SIZE...
AND A FAN TOO, THE WALL-MOUNTED KIND.
CHAN'S APARTMENT, EUNOS AVENUE 1*
THE LIFT DOOR WAS OVER THERE...
...AND THE MAIN ENTRANCE, ON THAT SIDE.
I FOUND A LARGE WOODEN BOARD I COULD USE AS A DRAFTING TABLE...
AND EVERY DAY, I'D BRING THIS BRIEFCASE WITH ME TO WORK.
IT CONTAINED INKS, RAGS AN WATERCOLOURS
INKS, RAGS AND WATERCOLOURS
PENCILS, BRUSHES, RULERS, ERASERS AND WHITE-OUT
STACK OF PAPER RETRIEVED FROM THE LOCKER
CUP OF WATER FOR APPLYING WASHES AND CLEANING BRUSHES

*GOVERNMENT-ASSISTED RENTAL HOUSING

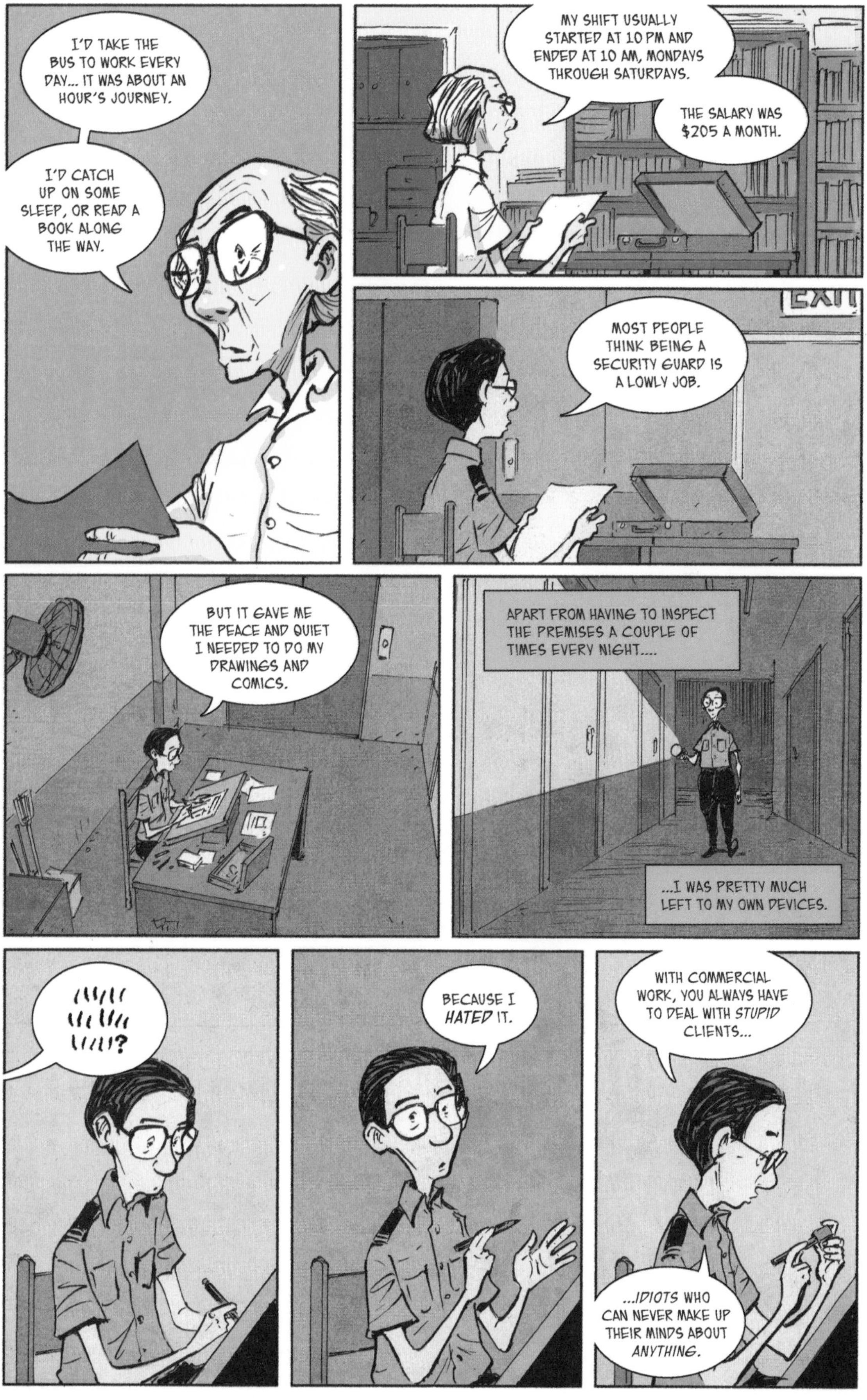
I'D TAKE THE BUS TO WORK EVERY DAY... IT WAS ABOUT AN HOUR'S JOURNEY.
I'D CATCH UP ON SOME SLEEP, OR READ A BOOK ALONG THE WAY.
MY SHIFT USUALLY STARTED AT 10 PM AND ENDED AT 10 AM, MONDAYS THROUGH SATURDAYS.
THE SALARY WAS $205 A MONTH.
EXIT
MOST PEOPLE THINK BEING A SECURITY GUARD IS A LOWLY JOB.
BUT IT GAVE ME THE PEACE AND QUIET I NEEDED TO DO MY DRAWINGS AND COMICS.
APART FROM HAVING TO INSPECT THE PREMISES A COUPLE OF TIMES EVERY NIGHT....
...I WAS PRETTY MUCH LEFT TO MY OWN DEVICES.
BECAUSE I *HATED* IT.
WITH COMMERCIAL WORK, YOU ALWAYS HAVE TO DEAL WITH *STUPID* CLIENTS...
...*IDIOTS* WHO CAN NEVER MAKE UP THEIR MINDS ABOUT *ANYTHING*.

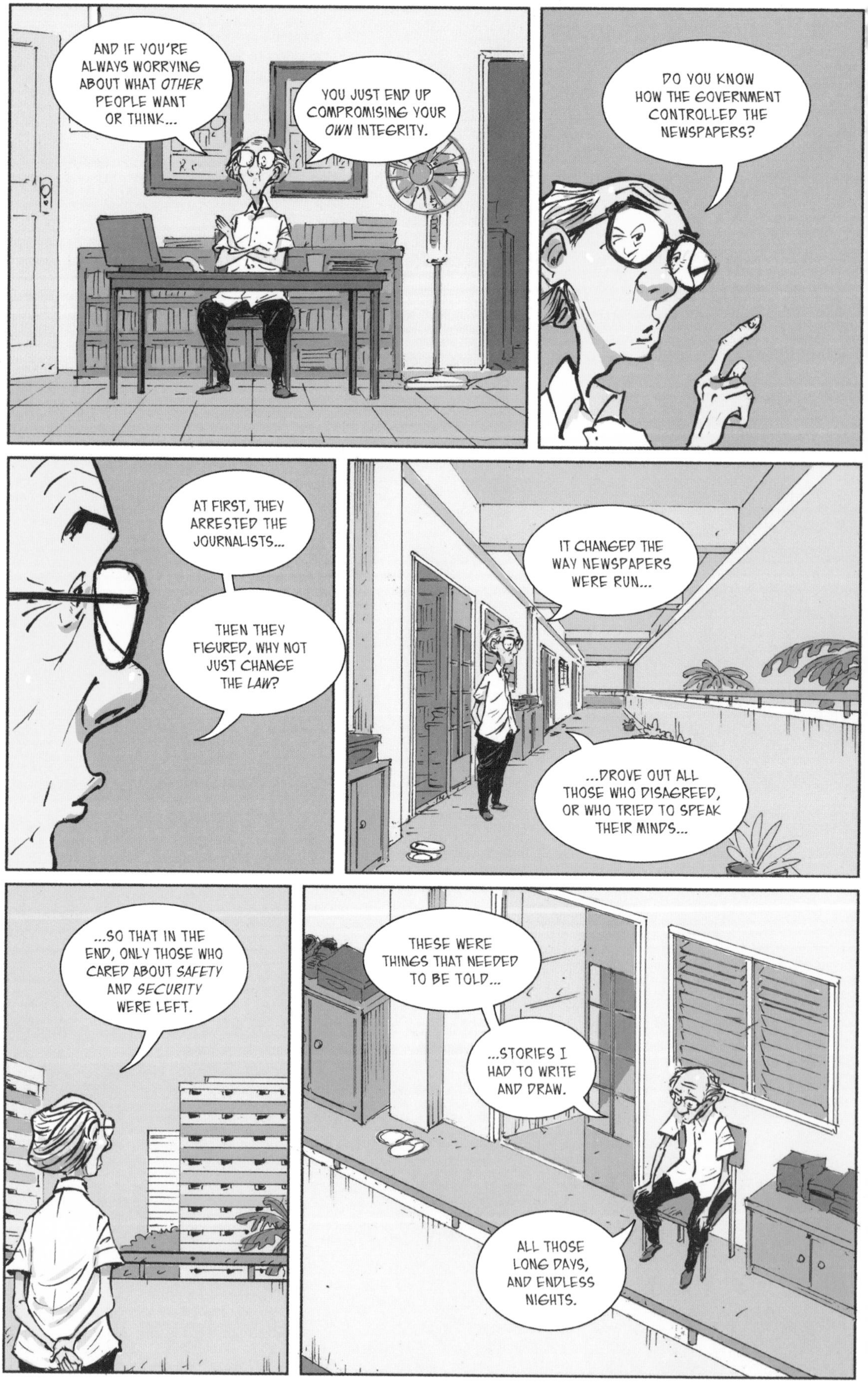
AND IF YOU'RE ALWAYS WORRYING ABOUT WHAT *OTHER* PEOPLE WANT OR THINK...
YOU JUST END UP COMPROMISING YOUR *OWN* INTEGRITY.
DO YOU KNOW HOW THE GOVERNMENT CONTROLLED THE NEWSPAPERS?
AT FIRST, THEY ARRESTED THE JOURNALISTS...
THEN THEY FIGURED, WHY NOT JUST CHANGE THE *LAW*?
IT CHANGED THE WAY NEWSPAPERS WERE RUN...
...DROVE OUT ALL THOSE WHO DISAGREED, OR WHO TRIED TO SPEAK THEIR MINDS...
...SO THAT IN THE END, ONLY THOSE WHO CARED ABOUT *SAFETY* AND *SECURITY* WERE LEFT.
THESE WERE THINGS THAT NEEDED TO BE TOLD...
...STORIES I HAD TO WRITE AND DRAW.
ALL THOSE LONG DAYS, AND ENDLESS NIGHTS.

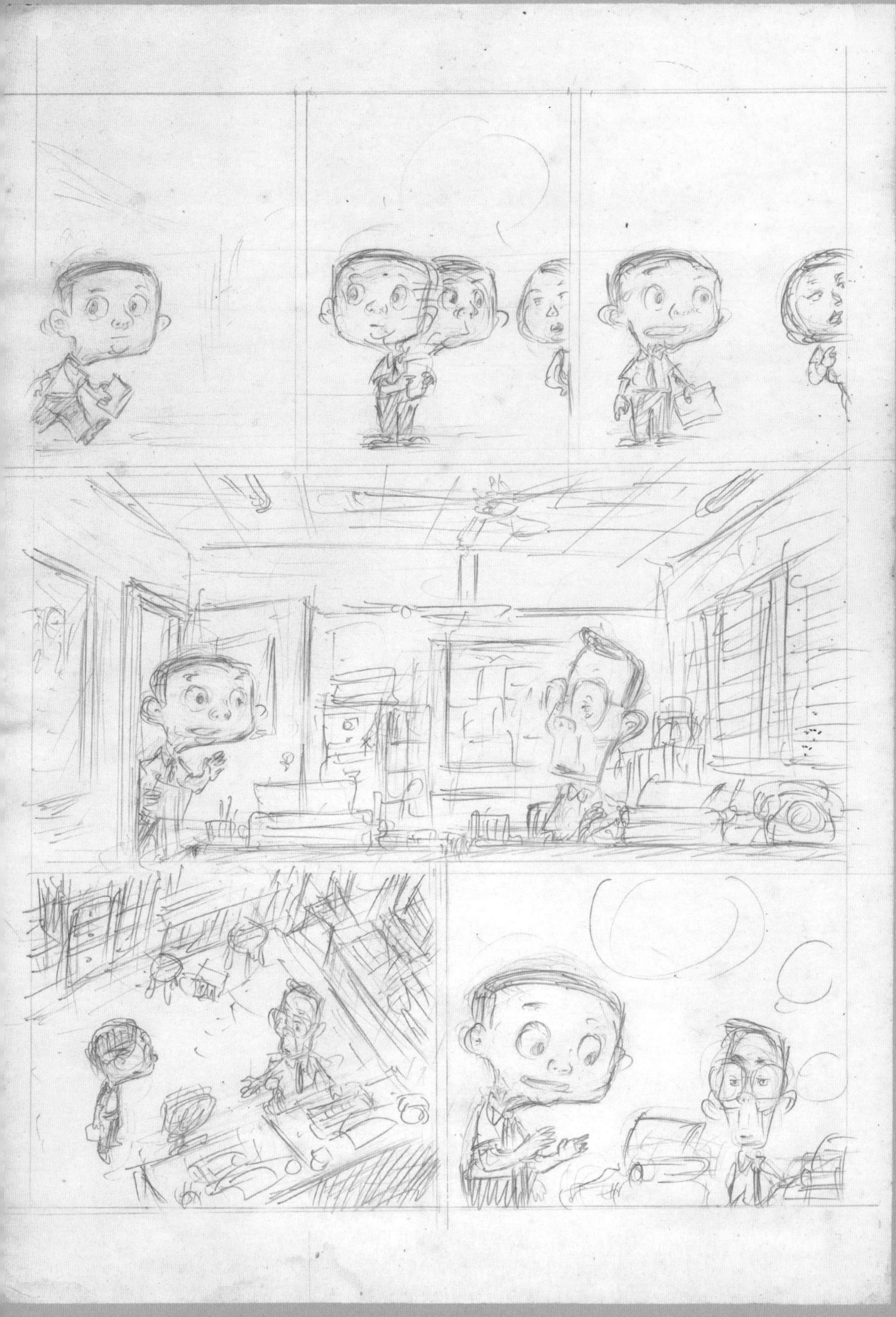

Above **SINKAPOR INKS Pencilled Page** (1988) | Chan Hock Chye

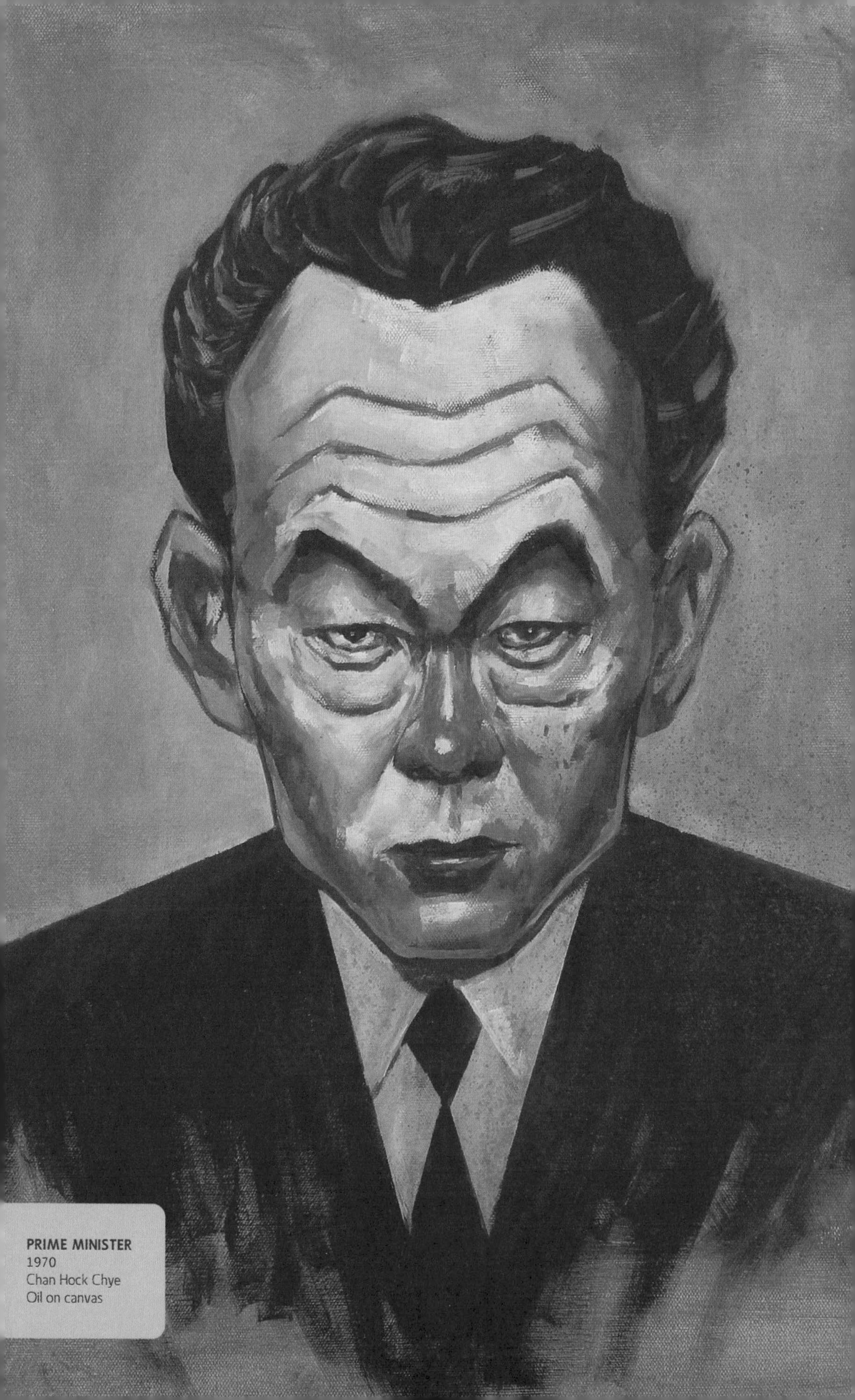

PRIME MINISTER
1970
Chan Hock Chye
Oil on canvas

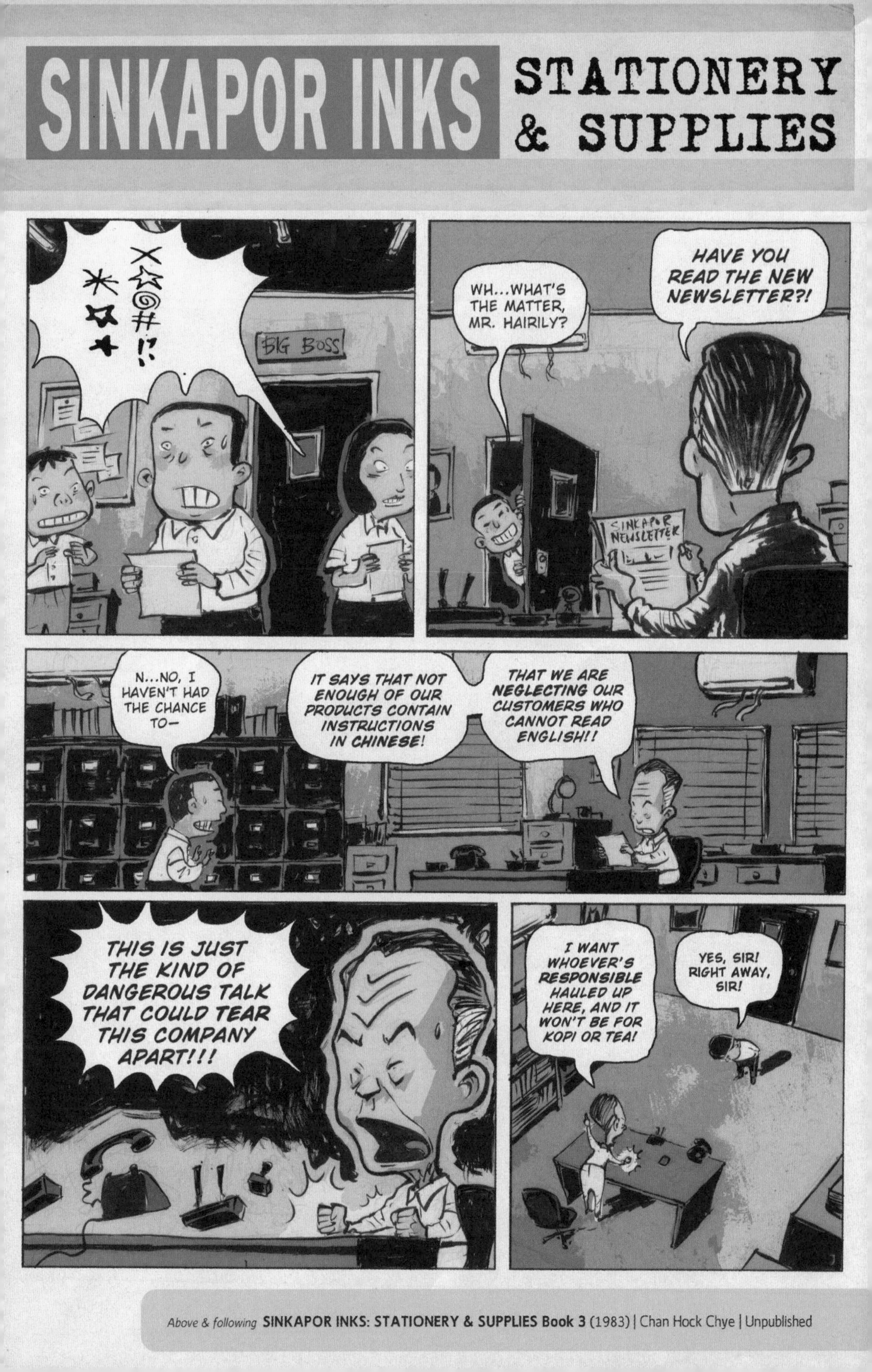
SINKAPOR INKS
STATIONERY & SUPPLIES
BIG BOSS
WH...WHAT'S THE MATTER, MR. HAIRILY?
HAVE YOU READ THE NEW NEWSLETTER?!
SINKAPOR NEWSLETTER
N...NO, I HAVEN'T HAD THE CHANCE TO—
IT SAYS THAT NOT ENOUGH OF OUR PRODUCTS CONTAIN INSTRUCTIONS IN CHINESE!
THAT WE ARE NEGLECTING OUR CUSTOMERS WHO CANNOT READ ENGLISH!!
THIS IS JUST THE KIND OF DANGEROUS TALK THAT COULD TEAR THIS COMPANY APART!!!
I WANT WHOEVER'S RESPONSIBLE HAULED UP HERE, AND IT WON'T BE FOR KOPI OR TEA!
YES, SIR! RIGHT AWAY, SIR!

Above & following **SINKAPOR INKS: STATIONERY & SUPPLIES Book 3** (1983) | Chan Hock Chye | Unpublished

ERASER by Sonny Liew (After "Talking Heads" by Chan Hock Chye)

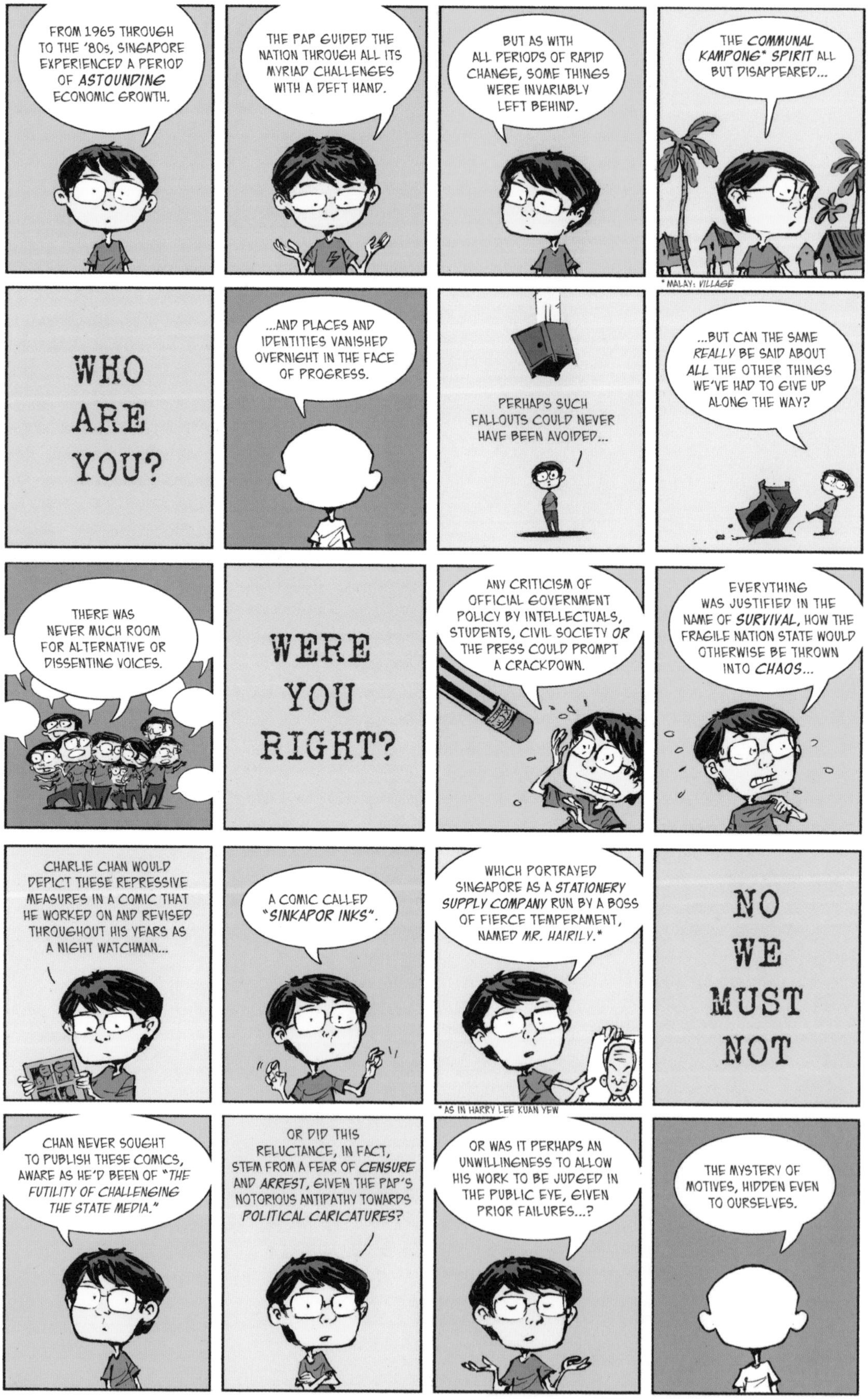

FROM 1965 THROUGH TO THE '80s, SINGAPORE EXPERIENCED A PERIOD OF *ASTOUNDING* ECONOMIC GROWTH.
THE PAP GUIDED THE NATION THROUGH ALL ITS MYRIAD CHALLENGES WITH A DEFT HAND.
BUT AS WITH ALL PERIODS OF RAPID CHANGE, SOME THINGS WERE INVARIABLY LEFT BEHIND.
THE *COMMUNAL KAMPONG* SPIRIT* ALL BUT DISAPPEARED...
*MALAY: *VILLAGE*
WHO ARE YOU?
...AND PLACES AND IDENTITIES VANISHED OVERNIGHT IN THE FACE OF PROGRESS.
PERHAPS SUCH FALLOUTS COULD NEVER HAVE BEEN AVOIDED...
...BUT CAN THE SAME *REALLY* BE SAID ABOUT *ALL* THE OTHER THINGS WE'VE HAD TO GIVE UP ALONG THE WAY?
THERE WAS NEVER MUCH ROOM FOR ALTERNATIVE OR DISSENTING VOICES.
WERE YOU RIGHT?
ANY CRITICISM OF OFFICIAL GOVERNMENT POLICY BY INTELLECTUALS, STUDENTS, CIVIL SOCIETY *OR* THE PRESS COULD PROMPT A CRACKDOWN.
EVERYTHING WAS JUSTIFIED IN THE NAME OF *SURVIVAL*, HOW THE FRAGILE NATION STATE WOULD OTHERWISE BE THROWN INTO *CHAOS*...
CHARLIE CHAN WOULD DEPICT THESE REPRESSIVE MEASURES IN A COMIC THAT HE WORKED ON AND REVISED THROUGHOUT HIS YEARS AS A NIGHT WATCHMAN...
A COMIC CALLED "*SINKAPOR INKS*".
WHICH PORTRAYED SINGAPORE AS A *STATIONERY SUPPLY COMPANY* RUN BY A BOSS OF FIERCE TEMPERAMENT, NAMED *MR. HAIRILY.**
*AS IN HARRY LEE KUAN YEW
NO WE MUST NOT
CHAN NEVER SOUGHT TO PUBLISH THESE COMICS, AWARE AS HE'D BEEN OF "*THE FUTILITY OF CHALLENGING THE STATE MEDIA.*"
OR DID THIS RELUCTANCE, IN FACT, STEM FROM A FEAR OF *CENSURE* AND *ARREST*, GIVEN THE PAP'S NOTORIOUS ANTIPATHY TOWARDS *POLITICAL CARICATURES*?
OR WAS IT PERHAPS AN UNWILLINGNESS TO ALLOW HIS WORK TO BE JUDGED IN THE PUBLIC EYE, GIVEN PRIOR FAILURES...?
THE MYSTERY OF MOTIVES, HIDDEN EVEN TO OURSELVES.

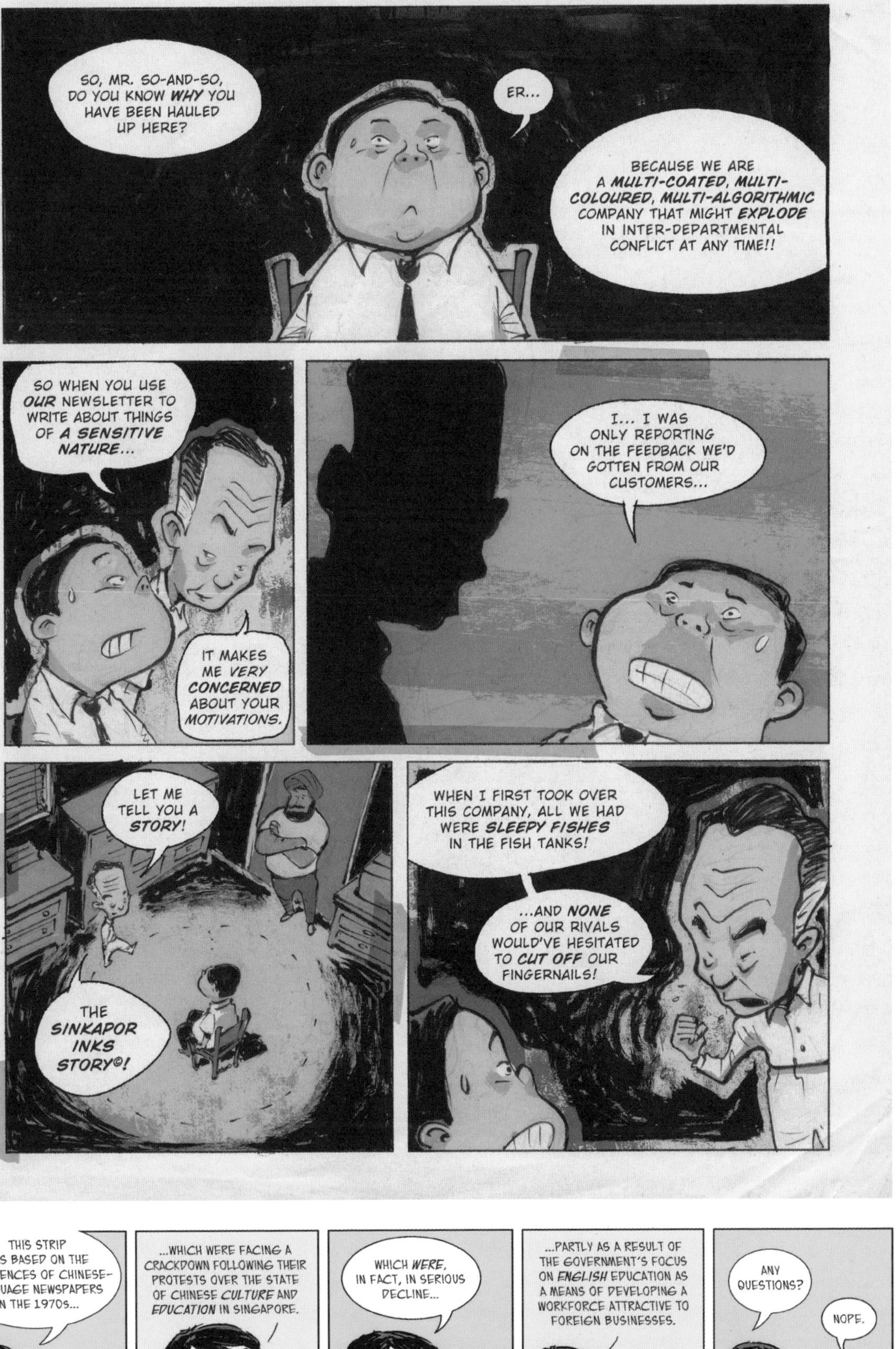
SO, MR. SO-AND-SO, DO YOU KNOW WHY YOU HAVE BEEN HAULED UP HERE?
ER...
BECAUSE WE ARE A MULTI-COATED, MULTI-COLOURED, MULTI-ALGORITHMIC COMPANY THAT MIGHT EXPLODE IN INTER-DEPARTMENTAL CONFLICT AT ANY TIME!!
SO WHEN YOU USE OUR NEWSLETTER TO WRITE ABOUT THINGS OF A SENSITIVE NATURE...
IT MAKES ME VERY CONCERNED ABOUT YOUR MOTIVATIONS.
I... I WAS ONLY REPORTING ON THE FEEDBACK WE'D GOTTEN FROM OUR CUSTOMERS...
LET ME TELL YOU A STORY!
THE SINKAPOR INKS STORY©!
WHEN I FIRST TOOK OVER THIS COMPANY, ALL WE HAD WERE SLEEPY FISHES IN THE FISH TANKS!
...AND NONE OF OUR RIVALS WOULD'VE HESITATED TO CUT OFF OUR FINGERNAILS!

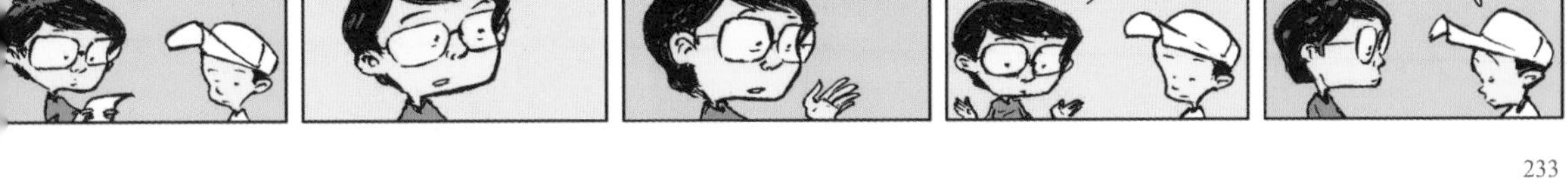
THIS STRIP WAS BASED ON THE EXPERIENCES OF CHINESE-LANGUAGE NEWSPAPERS IN THE 1970s...
...WHICH WERE FACING A CRACKDOWN FOLLOWING THEIR PROTESTS OVER THE STATE OF CHINESE CULTURE AND EDUCATION IN SINGAPORE.
WHICH WERE, IN FACT, IN SERIOUS DECLINE...
...PARTLY AS A RESULT OF THE GOVERNMENT'S FOCUS ON ENGLISH EDUCATION AS A MEANS OF DEVELOPING A WORKFORCE ATTRACTIVE TO FOREIGN BUSINESSES.
ANY QUESTIONS?
NOPE.

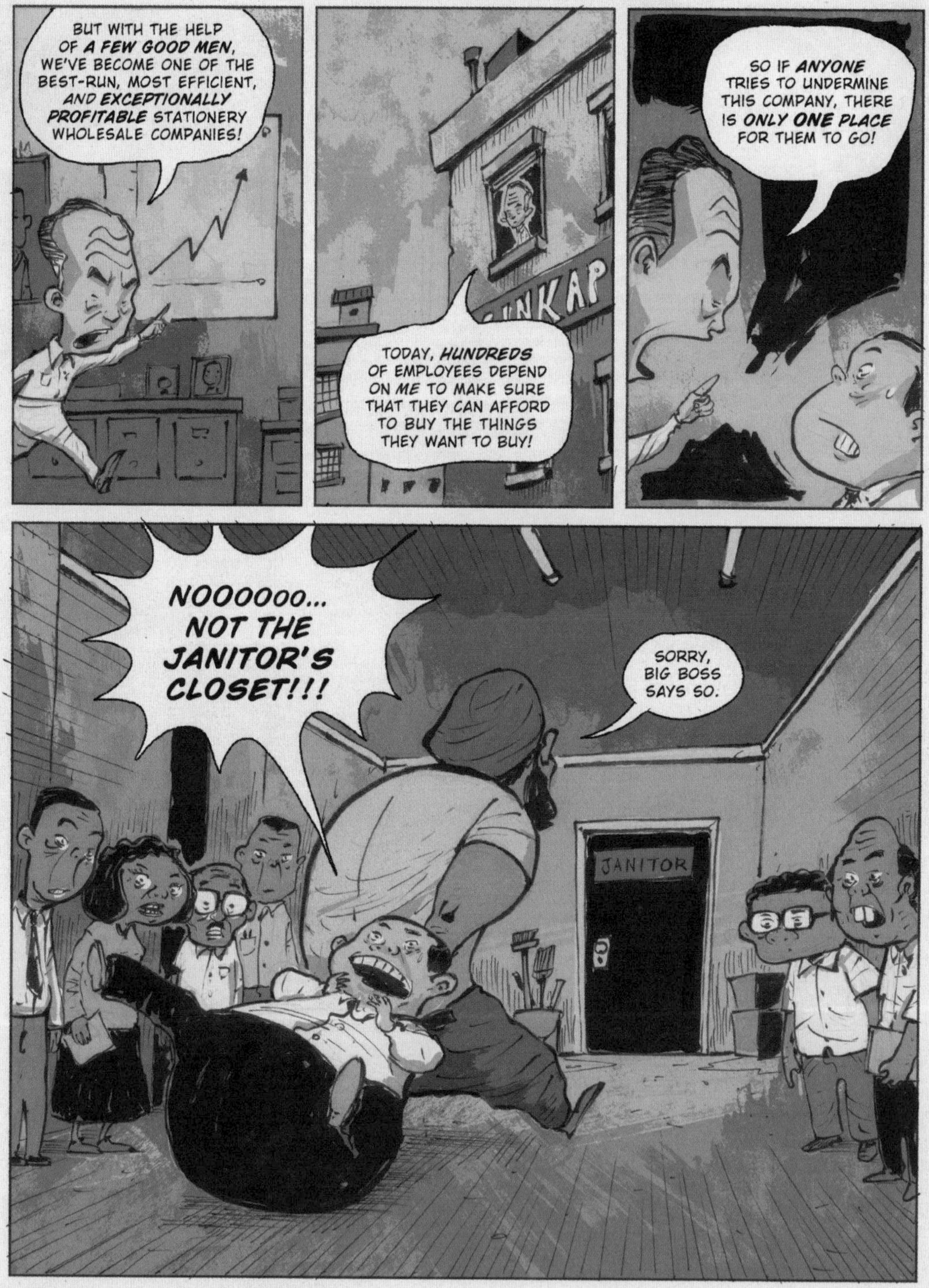
BUT WITH THE HELP OF A FEW GOOD MEN, WE'VE BECOME ONE OF THE BEST-RUN, MOST EFFICIENT, AND EXCEPTIONALLY PROFITABLE STATIONERY WHOLESALE COMPANIES!
TODAY, HUNDREDS OF EMPLOYEES DEPEND ON ME TO MAKE SURE THAT THEY CAN AFFORD TO BUY THE THINGS THEY WANT TO BUY!
SO IF ANYONE TRIES TO UNDERMINE THIS COMPANY, THERE IS ONLY ONE PLACE FOR THEM TO GO!
NOOOOOO... NOT THE JANITOR'S CLOSET!!!
SORRY, BIG BOSS SAYS SO.
JANITOR

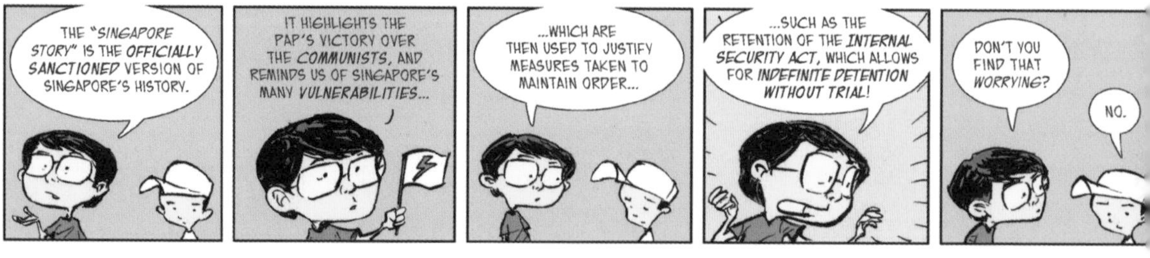
THE "SINGAPORE STORY" IS THE OFFICIALLY SANCTIONED VERSION OF SINGAPORE'S HISTORY.
IT HIGHLIGHTS THE PAP'S VICTORY OVER THE COMMUNISTS, AND REMINDS US OF SINGAPORE'S MANY VULNERABILITIES...
...WHICH ARE THEN USED TO JUSTIFY MEASURES TAKEN TO MAINTAIN ORDER...
...SUCH AS THE RETENTION OF THE INTERNAL SECURITY ACT, WHICH ALLOWS FOR INDEFINITE DETENTION WITHOUT TRIAL!
DON'T YOU FIND THAT WORRYING?
NO.

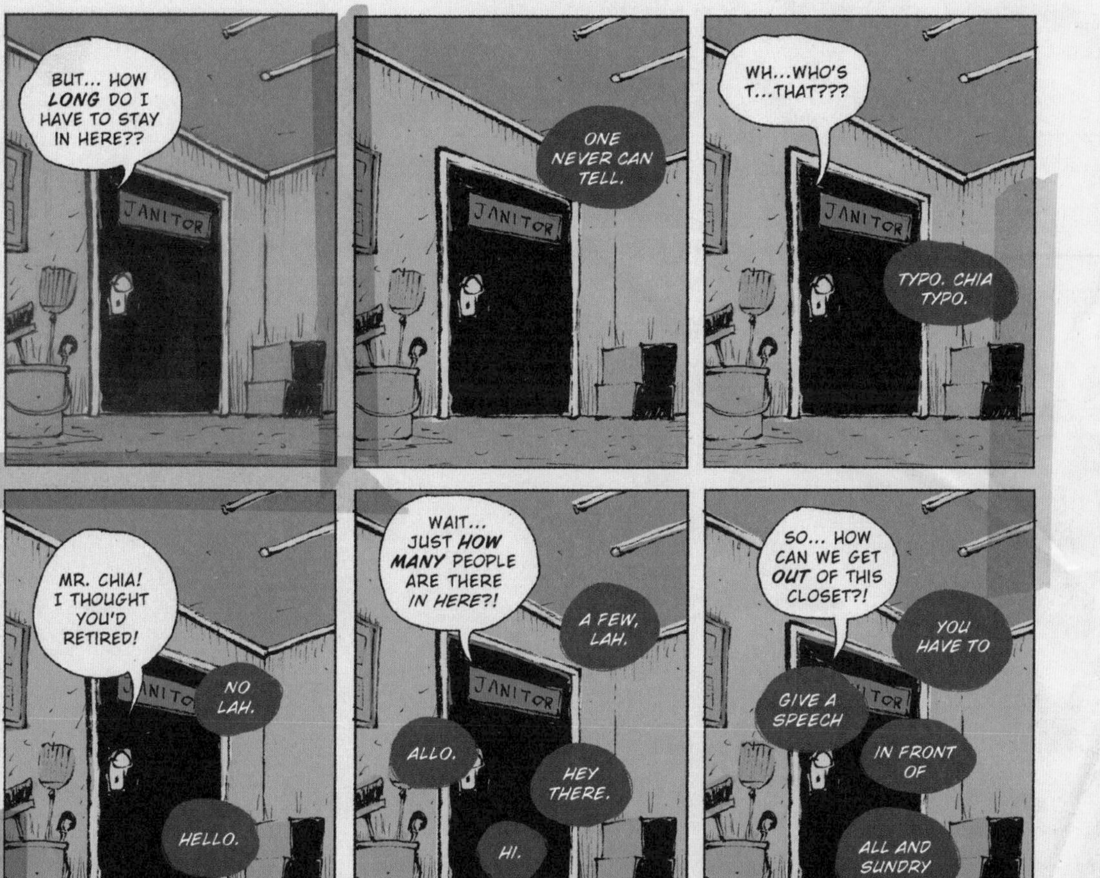
BUT... HOW LONG DO I HAVE TO STAY IN HERE??
JANITOR
ONE NEVER CAN TELL.
WH...WHO'S T...THAT???
TYPO. CHIA TYPO.
MR. CHIA! I THOUGHT YOU'D RETIRED!
NO LAH.
HELLO.
WAIT... JUST HOW MANY PEOPLE ARE THERE IN HERE?!
A FEW, LAH.
ALLO.
HEY THERE.
HI.
SO... HOW CAN WE GET OUT OF THIS CLOSET?!
YOU HAVE TO
GIVE A SPEECH
IN FRONT OF
ALL AND SUNDRY
ADMIT THAT
YOU'VE BEEN WORKING
FOR COMPETITORS
TO UNDERMINE AND TAKE OVER
THE COMPANY
BUT I WAS JUST REPORTING ON GENUINE CONSUMER FEEDBACK!
HA-HAHA
HA
AH, SWEET
SWEET
NAIVETY

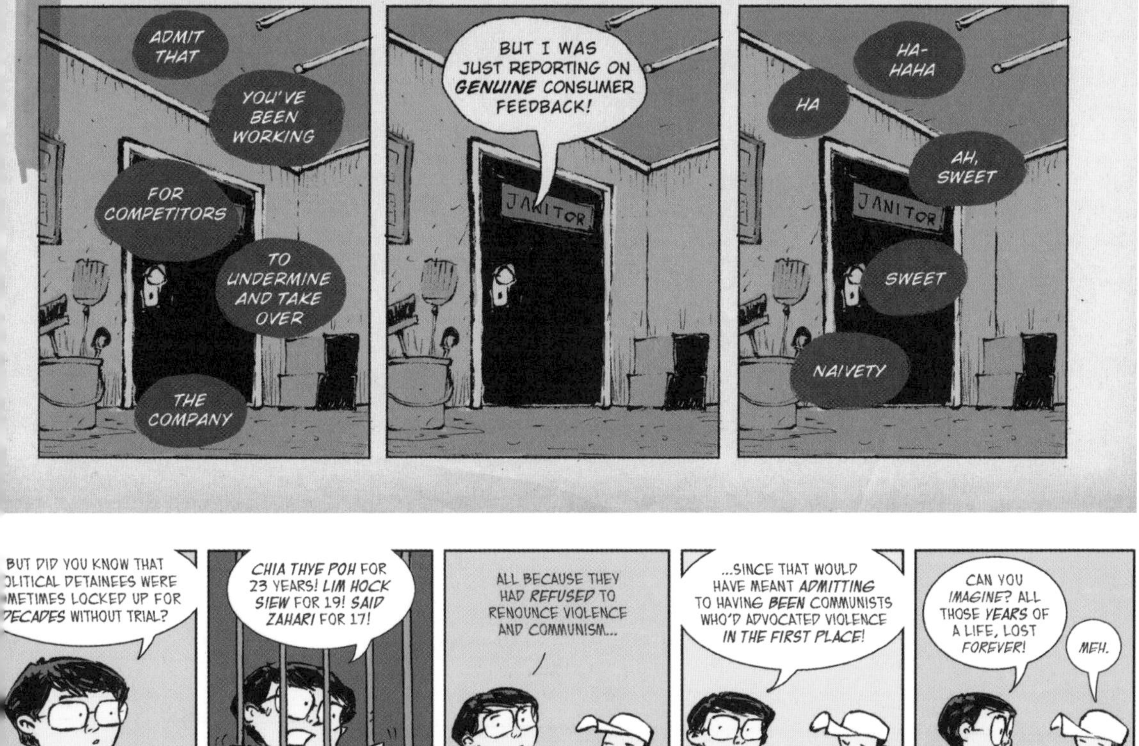
BUT DID YOU KNOW THAT OLITICAL DETAINEES WERE METIMES LOCKED UP FOR ECADES WITHOUT TRIAL?
CHIA THYE POH FOR 23 YEARS! LIM HOCK SIEW FOR 19! SAID ZAHARI FOR 17!
ALL BECAUSE THEY HAD REFUSED TO RENOUNCE VIOLENCE AND COMMUNISM...
...SINCE THAT WOULD HAVE MEANT ADMITTING TO HAVING BEEN COMMUNISTS WHO'D ADVOCATED VIOLENCE IN THE FIRST PLACE!
CAN YOU IMAGINE? ALL THOSE YEARS OF A LIFE, LOST FOREVER!
MEH.

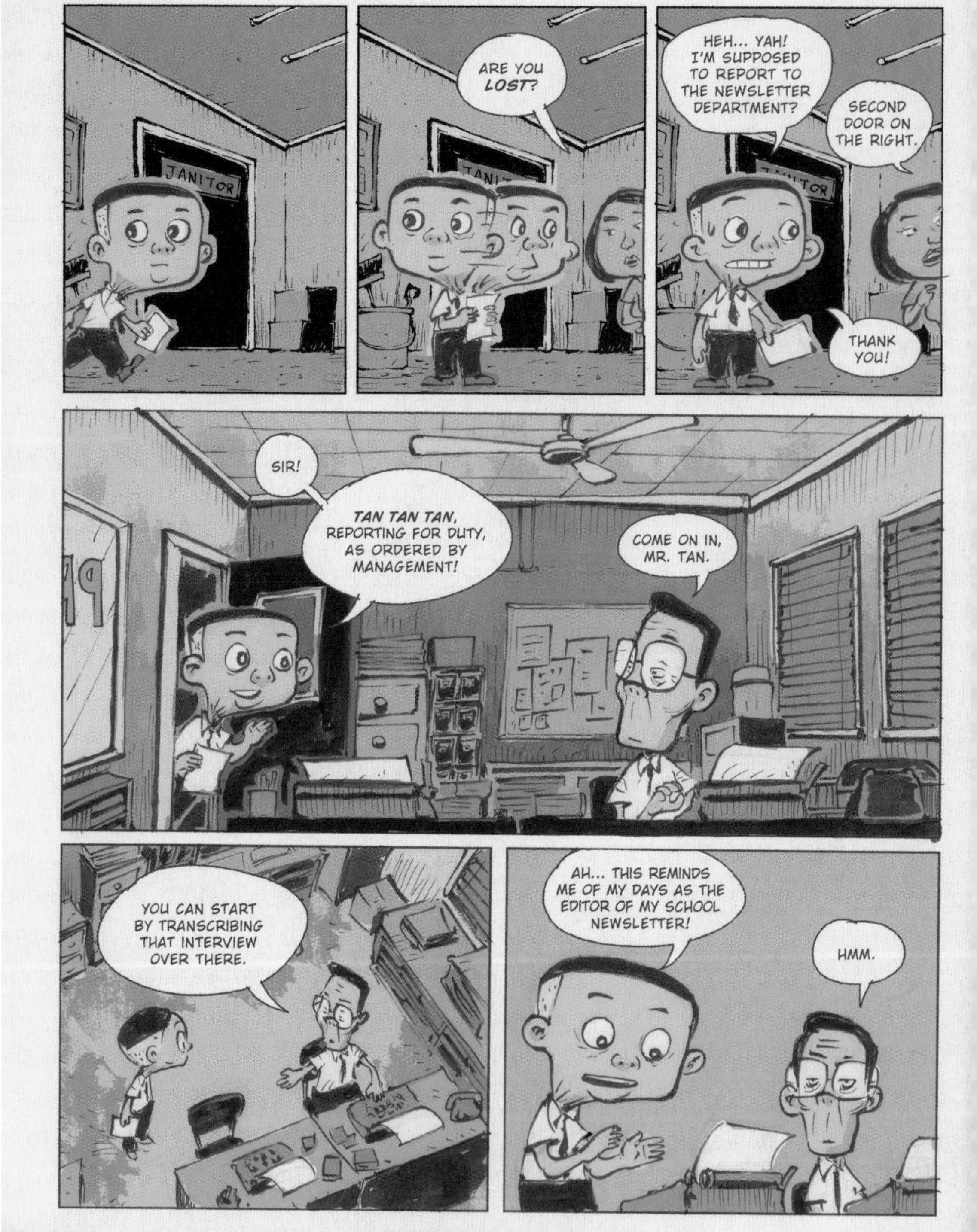
JANITOR
ARE YOU *LOST*?
HEH... YAH! I'M SUPPOSED TO REPORT TO THE NEWSLETTER DEPARTMENT?
SECOND DOOR ON THE RIGHT.
THANK YOU!
SIR!
TAN TAN TAN, REPORTING FOR DUTY, AS ORDERED BY MANAGEMENT!
COME ON IN, MR. TAN.
YOU CAN START BY TRANSCRIBING THAT INTERVIEW OVER THERE.
AH... THIS REMINDS ME OF MY DAYS AS THE EDITOR OF MY SCHOOL NEWSLETTER!
HMM.

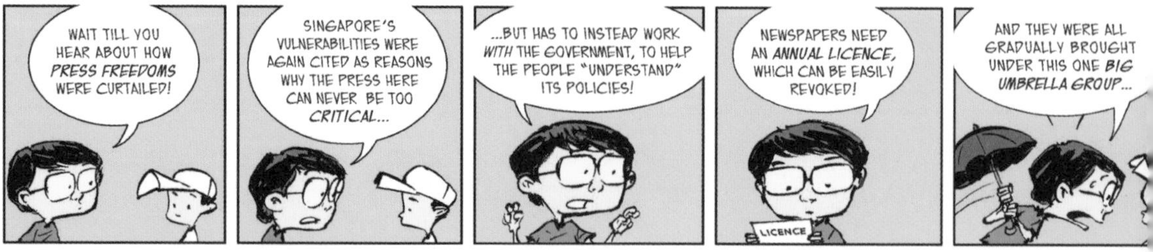
WAIT TILL YOU HEAR ABOUT HOW *PRESS FREEDOMS* WERE CURTAILED!
SINGAPORE'S VULNERABILITIES WERE AGAIN CITED AS REASONS WHY THE PRESS HERE CAN NEVER BE TOO *CRITICAL*...
...BUT HAS TO INSTEAD WORK *WITH* THE GOVERNMENT, TO HELP THE PEOPLE "UNDERSTAND" ITS POLICIES!
NEWSPAPERS NEED AN *ANNUAL LICENCE*, WHICH CAN BE EASILY REVOKED!
LICENCE
AND THEY WERE ALL GRADUALLY BROUGHT UNDER THIS ONE *BIG UMBRELLA GROUP*...

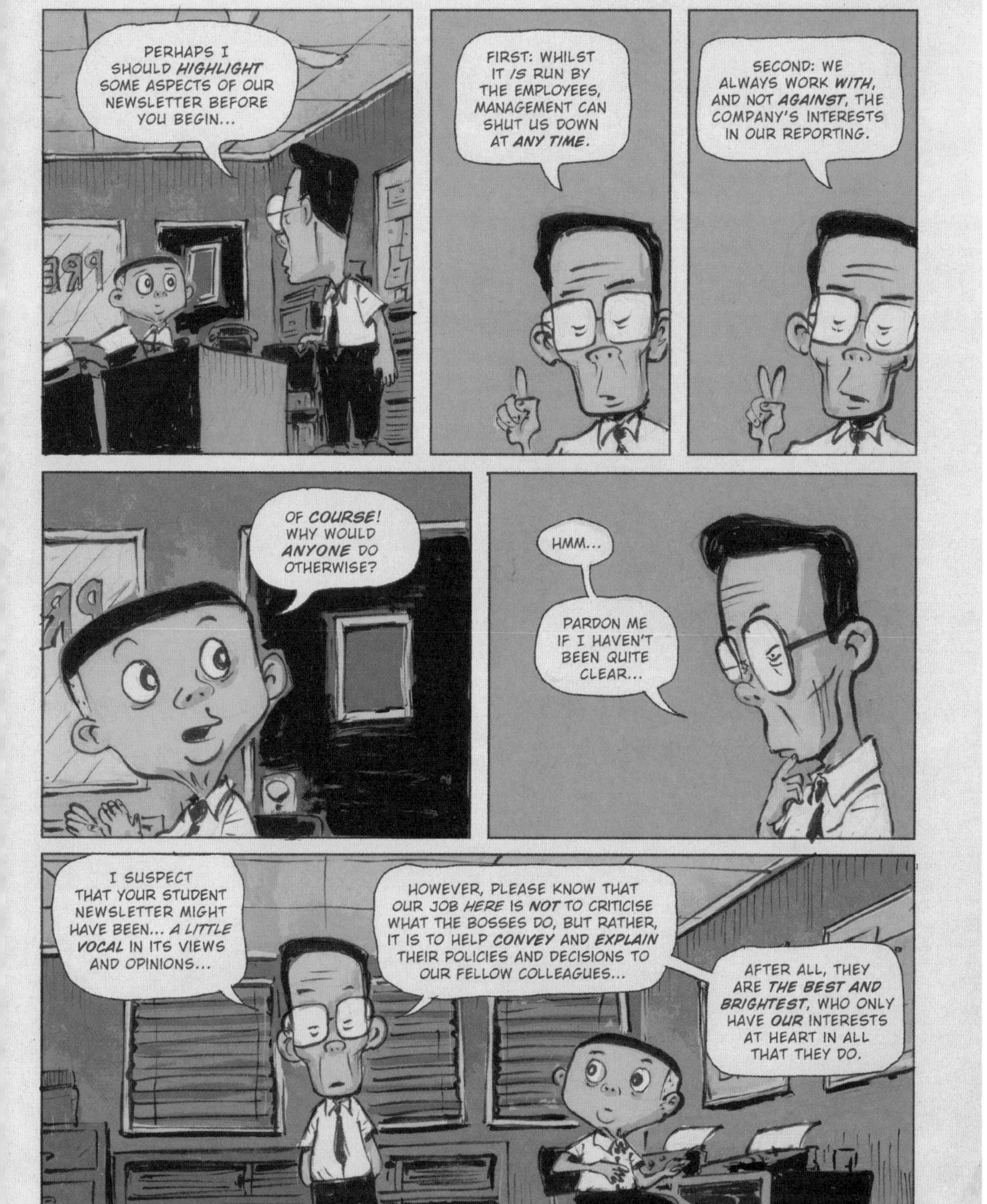
PERHAPS I SHOULD HIGHLIGHT SOME ASPECTS OF OUR NEWSLETTER BEFORE YOU BEGIN...
FIRST: WHILST IT IS RUN BY THE EMPLOYEES, MANAGEMENT CAN SHUT US DOWN AT ANY TIME.
SECOND: WE ALWAYS WORK WITH, AND NOT AGAINST, THE COMPANY'S INTERESTS IN OUR REPORTING.
OF COURSE! WHY WOULD ANYONE DO OTHERWISE?
HMM...
PARDON ME IF I HAVEN'T BEEN QUITE CLEAR...
I SUSPECT THAT YOUR STUDENT NEWSLETTER MIGHT HAVE BEEN... A LITTLE VOCAL IN ITS VIEWS AND OPINIONS...
HOWEVER, PLEASE KNOW THAT OUR JOB HERE IS NOT TO CRITICISE WHAT THE BOSSES DO, BUT RATHER, IT IS TO HELP CONVEY AND EXPLAIN THEIR POLICIES AND DECISIONS TO OUR FELLOW COLLEAGUES...
AFTER ALL, THEY ARE THE BEST AND BRIGHTEST, WHO ONLY HAVE OUR INTERESTS AT HEART IN ALL THAT THEY DO.

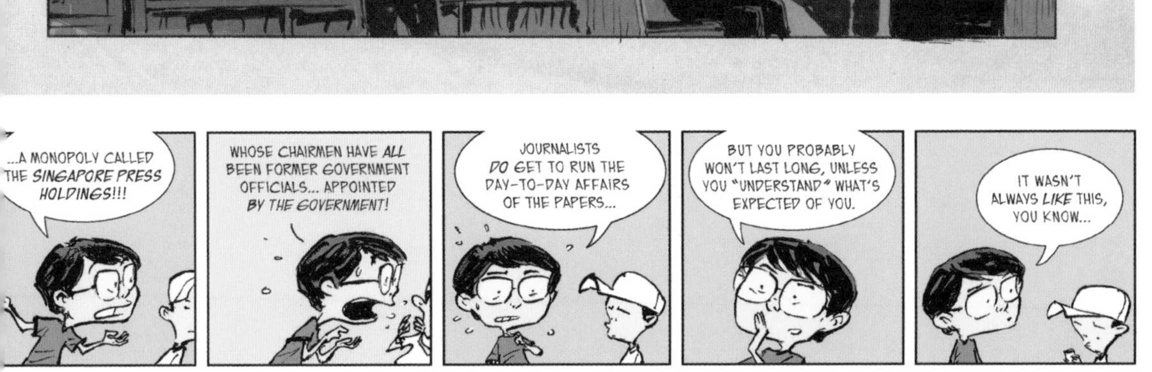
...A MONOPOLY CALLED THE SINGAPORE PRESS HOLDINGS!!!
WHOSE CHAIRMEN HAVE ALL BEEN FORMER GOVERNMENT OFFICIALS... APPOINTED BY THE GOVERNMENT!
JOURNALISTS DO GET TO RUN THE DAY-TO-DAY AFFAIRS OF THE PAPERS...
BUT YOU PROBABLY WON'T LAST LONG, UNLESS YOU "UNDERSTAND" WHAT'S EXPECTED OF YOU.
IT WASN'T ALWAYS LIKE THIS, YOU KNOW...

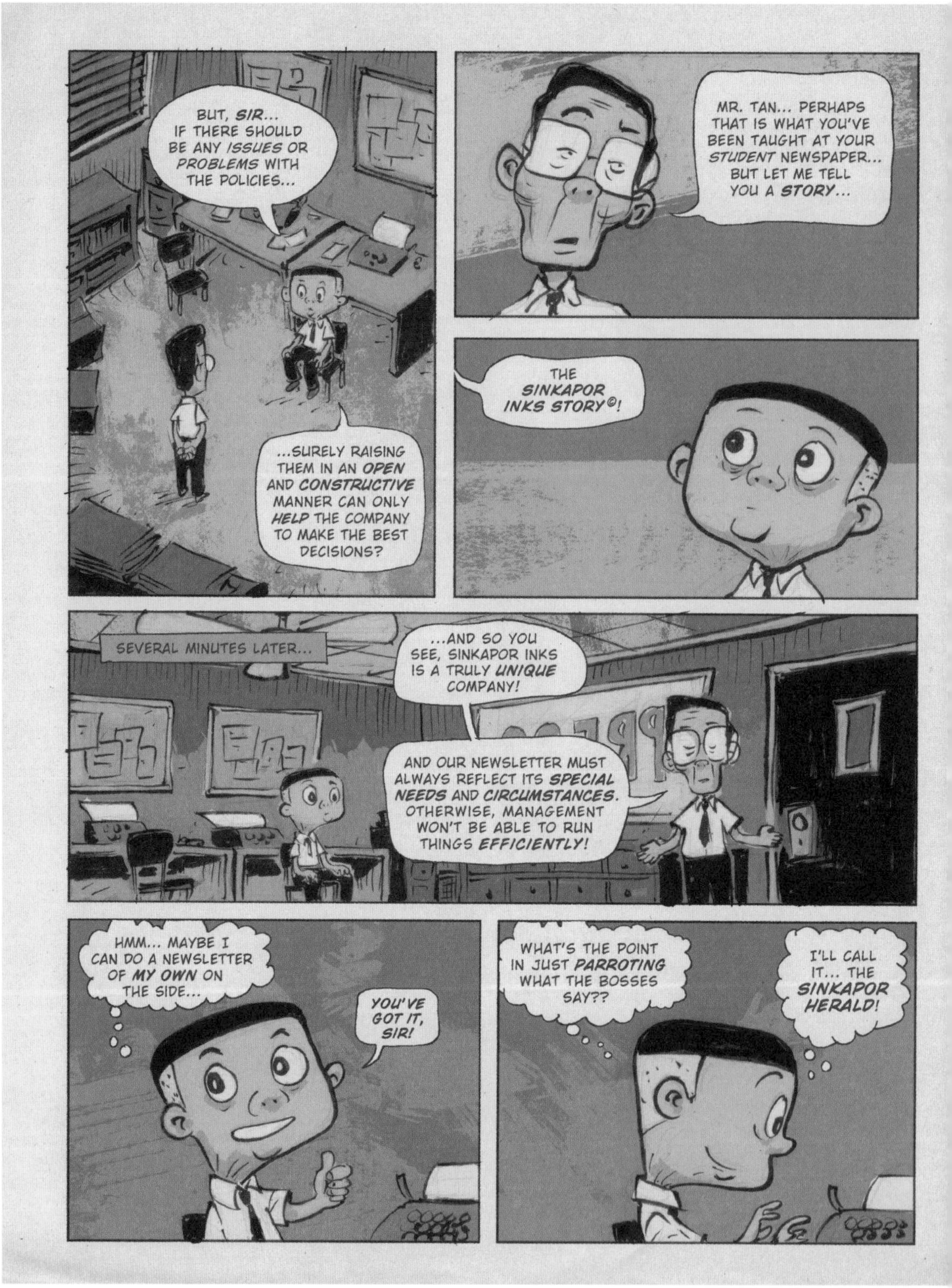
BUT, SIR... IF THERE SHOULD BE ANY ISSUES OR PROBLEMS WITH THE POLICIES...
...SURELY RAISING THEM IN AN OPEN AND CONSTRUCTIVE MANNER CAN ONLY HELP THE COMPANY TO MAKE THE BEST DECISIONS?
MR. TAN... PERHAPS THAT IS WHAT YOU'VE BEEN TAUGHT AT YOUR STUDENT NEWSPAPER... BUT LET ME TELL YOU A STORY...
THE SINKAPOR INKS STORY©!
SEVERAL MINUTES LATER...
...AND SO YOU SEE, SINKAPOR INKS IS A TRULY UNIQUE COMPANY!
AND OUR NEWSLETTER MUST ALWAYS REFLECT ITS SPECIAL NEEDS AND CIRCUMSTANCES. OTHERWISE, MANAGEMENT WON'T BE ABLE TO RUN THINGS EFFICIENTLY!
HMM... MAYBE I CAN DO A NEWSLETTER OF MY OWN ON THE SIDE...
YOU'VE GOT IT, SIR!
WHAT'S THE POINT IN JUST PARROTING WHAT THE BOSSES SAY??
I'LL CALL IT... THE SINKAPOR HERALD!

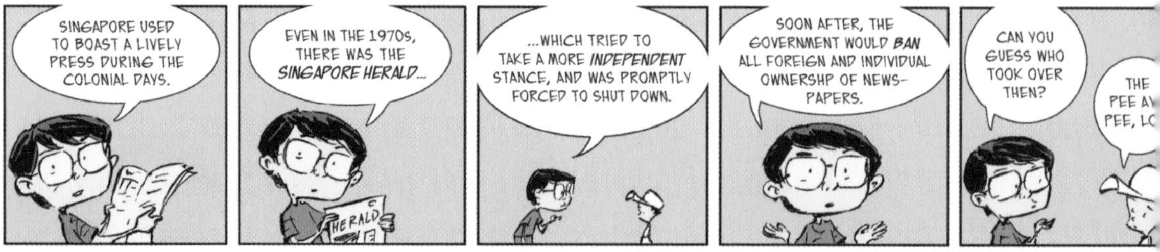
SINGAPORE USED TO BOAST A LIVELY PRESS DURING THE COLONIAL DAYS.
EVEN IN THE 1970s, THERE WAS THE SINGAPORE HERALD...
HERALD
...WHICH TRIED TO TAKE A MORE INDEPENDENT STANCE, AND WAS PROMPTLY FORCED TO SHUT DOWN.
SOON AFTER, THE GOVERNMENT WOULD BAN ALL FOREIGN AND INDIVIDUAL OWNERSHP OF NEWS-PAPERS.
CAN YOU GUESS WHO TOOK OVER THEN?
THE

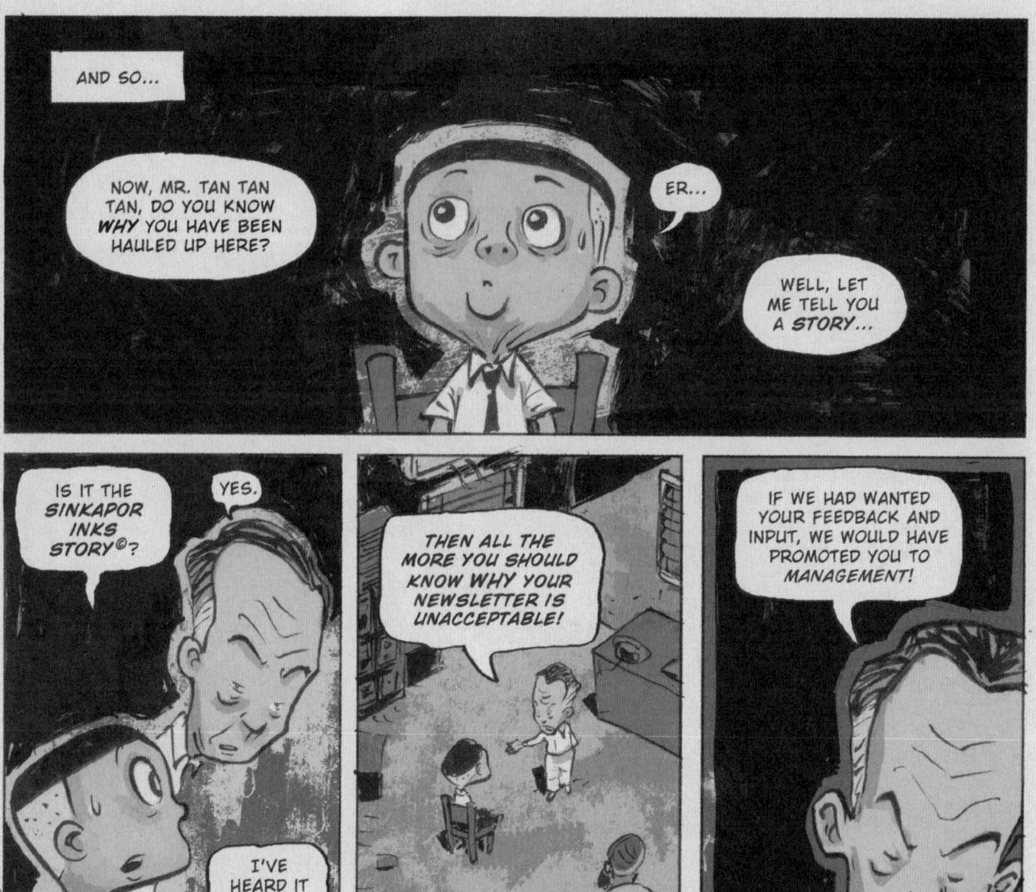
AND SO...
NOW, MR. TAN TAN TAN, DO YOU KNOW *WHY* YOU HAVE BEEN HAULED UP HERE?
ER...
WELL, LET ME TELL YOU A *STORY*...
IS IT THE *SINKAPOR INKS STORY©*?
YES.
I'VE HEARD IT ALREADY.
THEN ALL THE MORE YOU SHOULD KNOW WHY YOUR NEWSLETTER IS UNACCEPTABLE!
IF WE HAD WANTED YOUR FEEDBACK AND INPUT, WE WOULD HAVE PROMOTED YOU TO *MANAGEMENT!*
BUT *THEN AGAIN*, SINCE WE ONLY WANT ***THE BEST AND BRIGHTEST*** TO LEAD THIS COMPANY... WE CAN'T BE PROMOTING THE LIKES OF YOU NOW, ***CAN WE***?
AND SO WE END UP WITH ***DIME-A-DOZEN*** FELLOWS LIKE YOU WORKING IN THE NEWSLETTER DEPARTMENT!

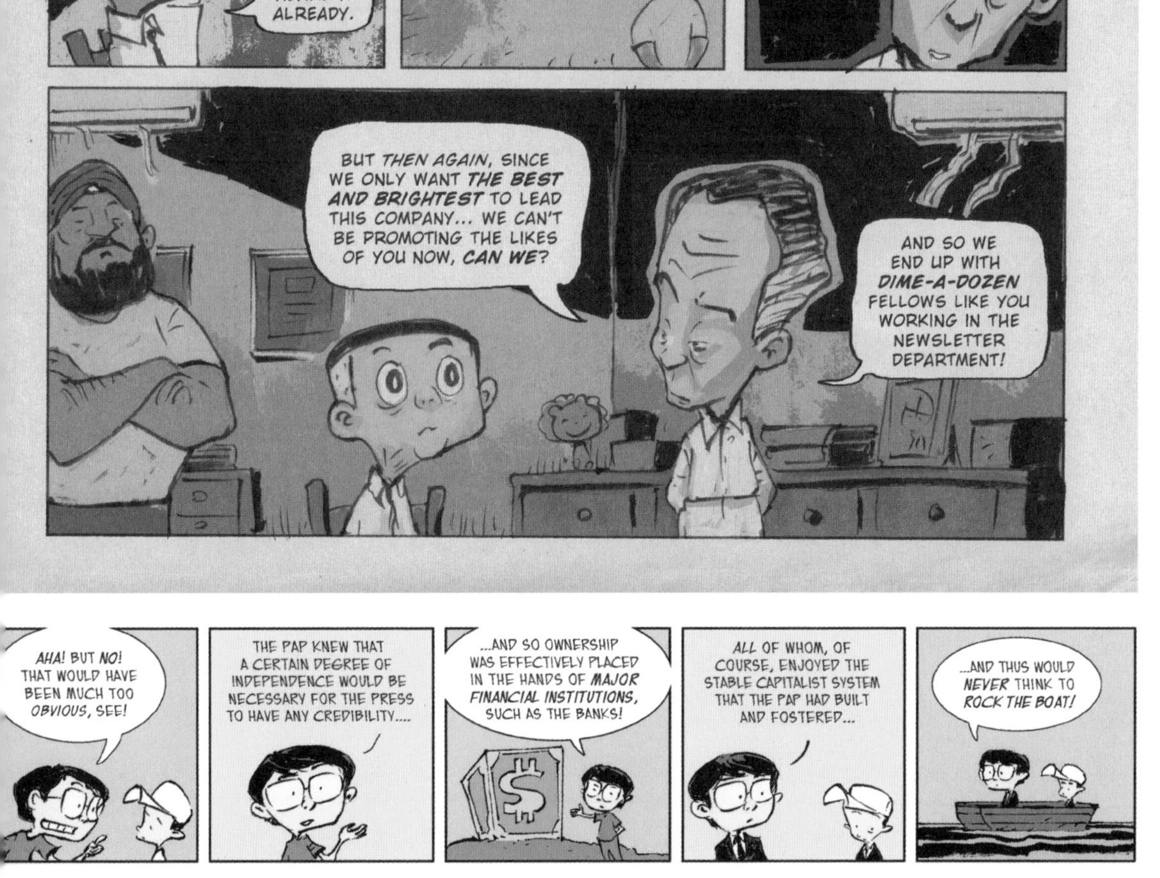
AHA! BUT *NO!* THAT WOULD HAVE BEEN MUCH TOO *OBVIOUS*, SEE!
THE PAP KNEW THAT A CERTAIN DEGREE OF INDEPENDENCE WOULD BE NECESSARY FOR THE PRESS TO HAVE ANY CREDIBILITY....
...AND SO OWNERSHIP WAS EFFECTIVELY PLACED IN THE HANDS OF *MAJOR FINANCIAL INSTITUTIONS*, SUCH AS THE BANKS!
ALL OF WHOM, OF COURSE, ENJOYED THE STABLE CAPITALIST SYSTEM THAT THE PAP HAD BUILT AND FOSTERED...
...AND THUS WOULD *NEVER* THINK TO *ROCK THE BOAT!*

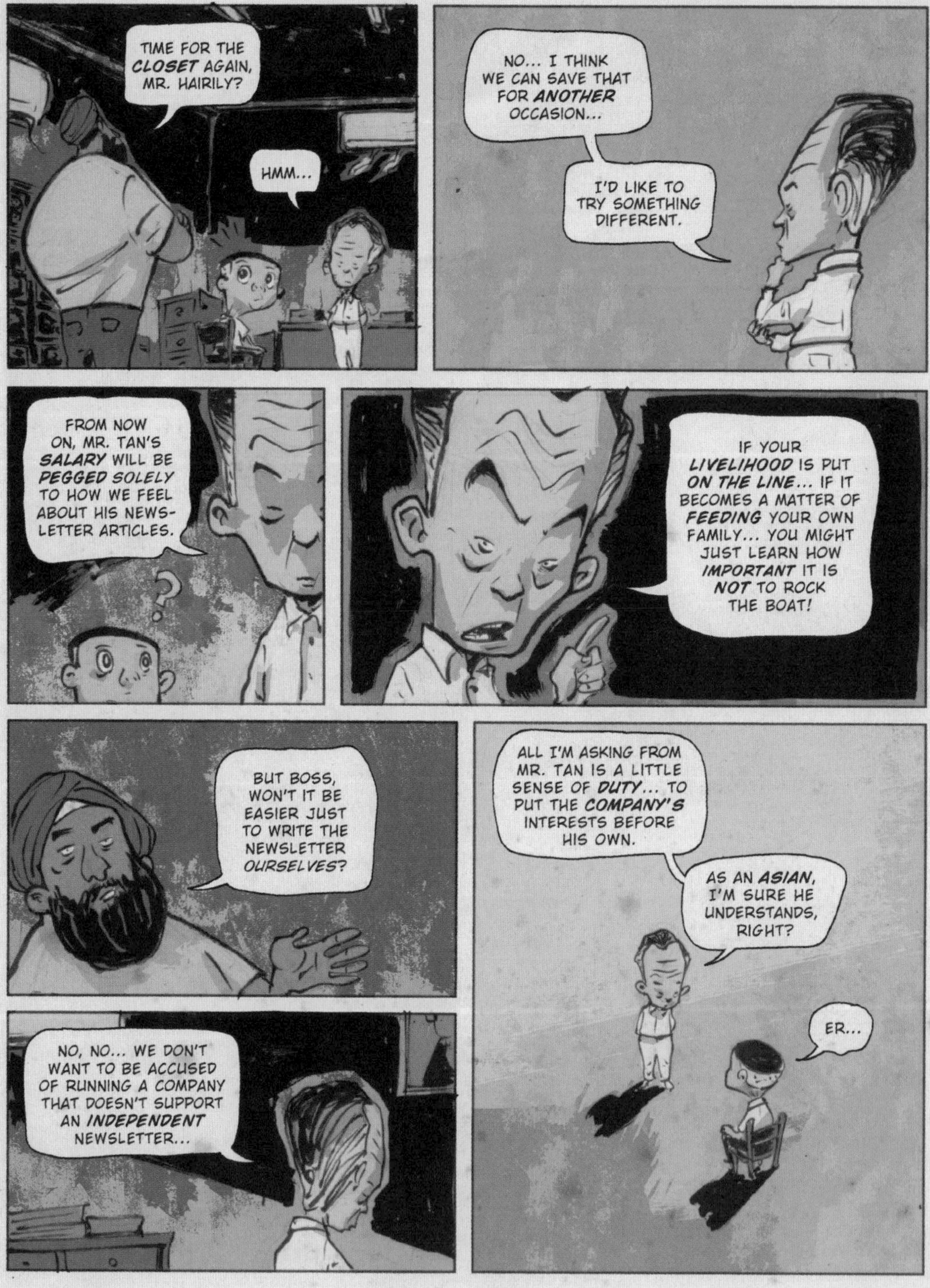
TIME FOR THE CLOSET AGAIN, MR. HAIRILY?
HMM...
NO... I THINK WE CAN SAVE THAT FOR ANOTHER OCCASION...
I'D LIKE TO TRY SOMETHING DIFFERENT.
FROM NOW ON, MR. TAN'S SALARY WILL BE PEGGED SOLELY TO HOW WE FEEL ABOUT HIS NEWS-LETTER ARTICLES.
?
IF YOUR LIVELIHOOD IS PUT ON THE LINE... IF IT BECOMES A MATTER OF FEEDING YOUR OWN FAMILY... YOU MIGHT JUST LEARN HOW IMPORTANT IT IS NOT TO ROCK THE BOAT!
BUT BOSS, WON'T IT BE EASIER JUST TO WRITE THE NEWSLETTER OURSELVES?
NO, NO... WE DON'T WANT TO BE ACCUSED OF RUNNING A COMPANY THAT DOESN'T SUPPORT AN INDEPENDENT NEWSLETTER...
ALL I'M ASKING FROM MR. TAN IS A LITTLE SENSE OF DUTY... TO PUT THE COMPANY'S INTERESTS BEFORE HIS OWN.
AS AN ASIAN, I'M SURE HE UNDERSTANDS, RIGHT?
ER...

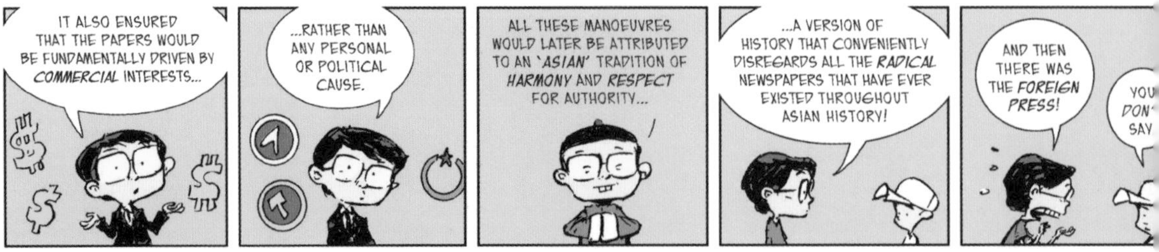
IT ALSO ENSURED THAT THE PAPERS WOULD BE FUNDAMENTALLY DRIVEN BY COMMERCIAL INTERESTS...
...RATHER THAN ANY PERSONAL OR POLITICAL CAUSE.
ALL THESE MANOEUVRES WOULD LATER BE ATTRIBUTED TO AN 'ASIAN' TRADITION OF HARMONY AND RESPECT FOR AUTHORITY...
...A VERSION OF HISTORY THAT CONVENIENTLY DISREGARDS ALL THE RADICAL NEWSPAPERS THAT HAVE EVER EXISTED THROUGHOUT ASIAN HISTORY!
AND THEN THERE WAS THE FOREIGN PRESS!

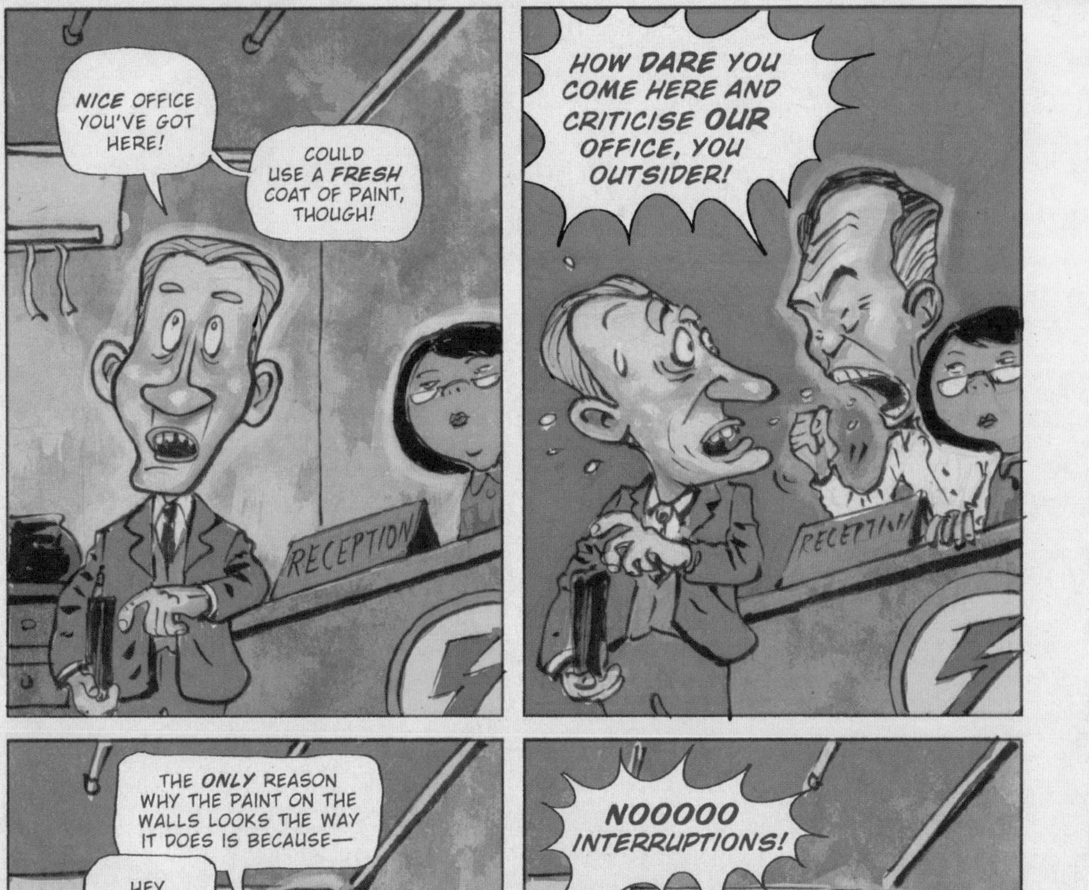

NICE OFFICE YOU'VE GOT HERE!
COULD USE A FRESH COAT OF PAINT, THOUGH!
RECEPTION
HOW DARE YOU COME HERE AND CRITICISE OUR OFFICE, YOU OUTSIDER!
THE ONLY REASON WHY THE PAINT ON THE WALLS LOOKS THE WAY IT DOES IS BECAUSE—
HEY, I JUST MEANT—
NOOOOO INTERRUPTIONS!
YOU'D BETTER LET ME RESPOND TO YOUR ACCUSATIONS IN FULL, SO THAT EVERYONE CAN SEE FOR THEMSELVES WHO'S RIGHT!

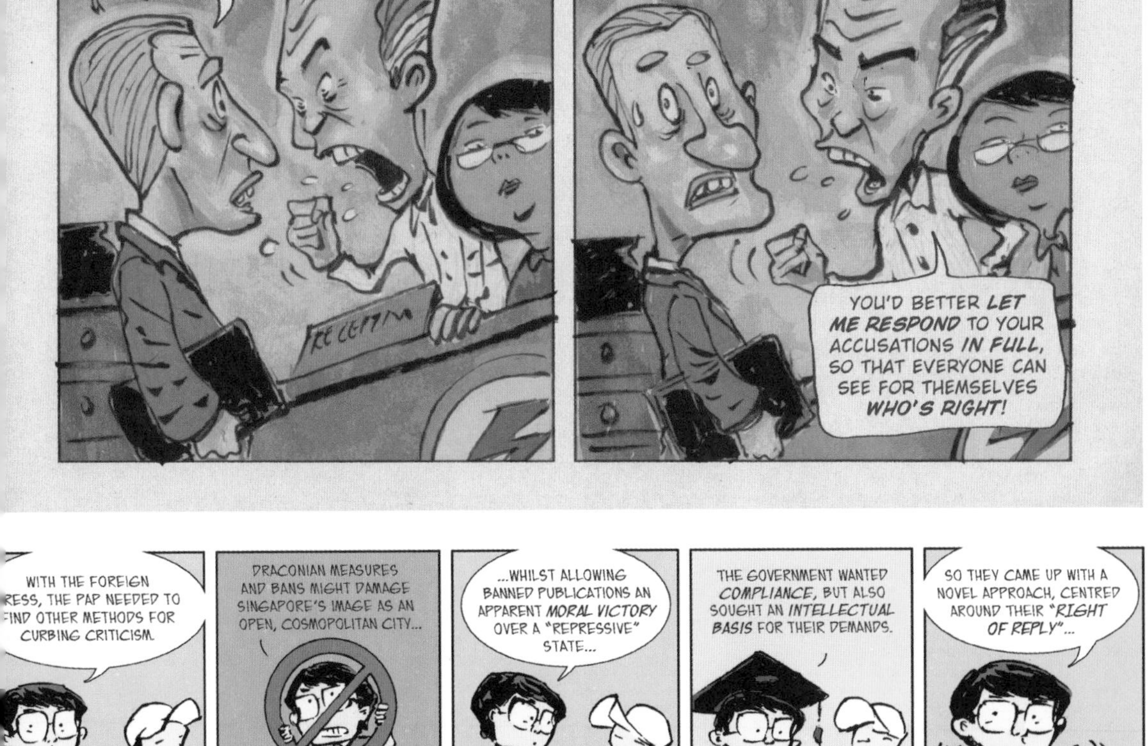

WITH THE FOREIGN RESS, THE PAP NEEDED TO FIND OTHER METHODS FOR CURBING CRITICISM.
DRACONIAN MEASURES AND BANS MIGHT DAMAGE SINGAPORE'S IMAGE AS AN OPEN, COSMOPOLITAN CITY...
...WHILST ALLOWING BANNED PUBLICATIONS AN APPARENT MORAL VICTORY OVER A "REPRESSIVE" STATE...
THE GOVERNMENT WANTED COMPLIANCE, BUT ALSO SOUGHT AN INTELLECTUAL BASIS FOR THEIR DEMANDS.
SO THEY CAME UP WITH A NOVEL APPROACH, CENTRED AROUND THEIR "RIGHT OF REPLY"...

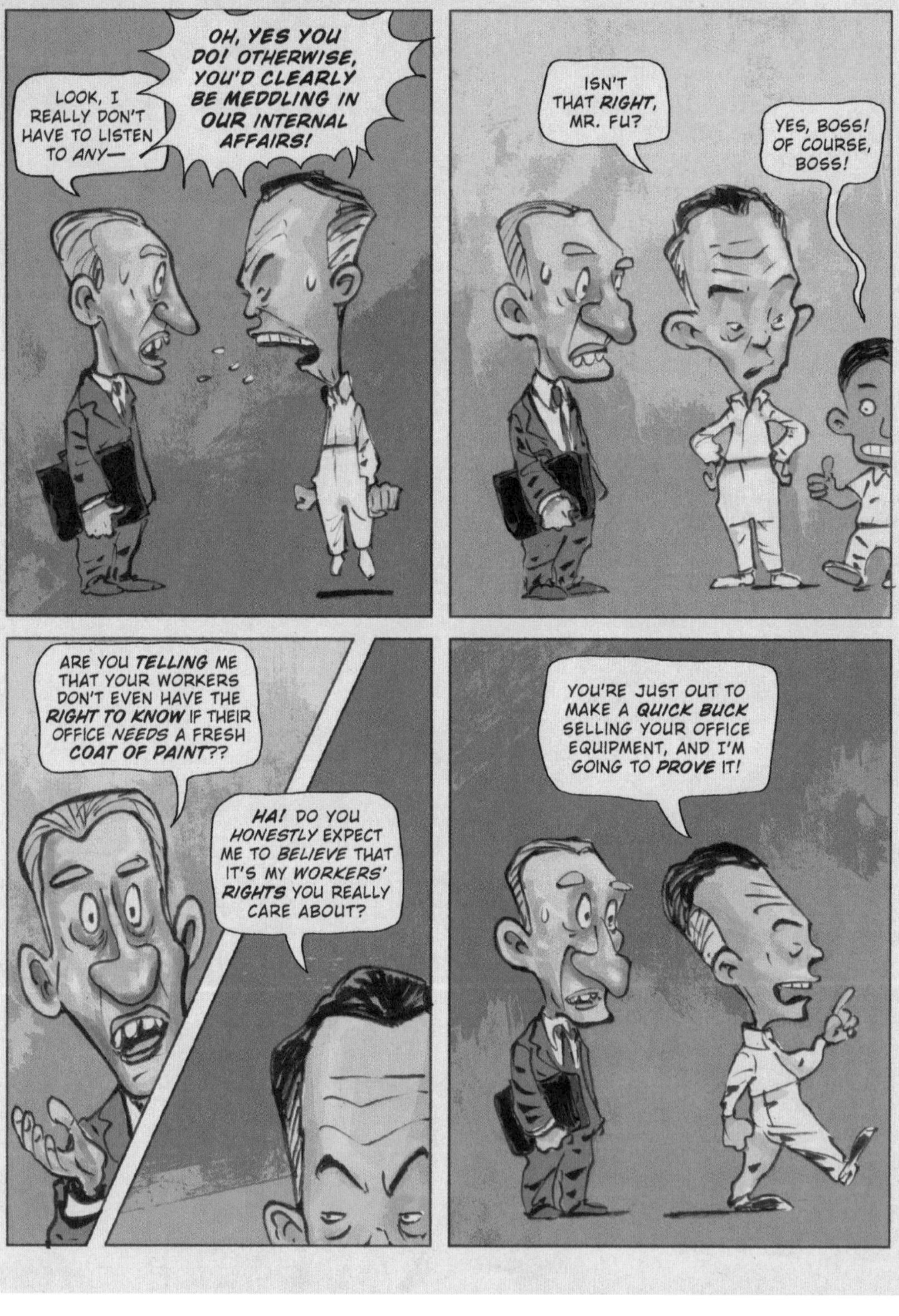
LOOK, I REALLY DON'T HAVE TO LISTEN TO ANY—
OH, YES YOU DO! OTHERWISE, YOU'D CLEARLY BE MEDDLING IN OUR INTERNAL AFFAIRS!
ISN'T THAT RIGHT, MR. FU?
YES, BOSS! OF COURSE, BOSS!
ARE YOU TELLING ME THAT YOUR WORKERS DON'T EVEN HAVE THE RIGHT TO KNOW IF THEIR OFFICE NEEDS A FRESH COAT OF PAINT??
HA! DO YOU HONESTLY EXPECT ME TO BELIEVE THAT IT'S MY WORKERS' RIGHTS YOU REALLY CARE ABOUT?
YOU'RE JUST OUT TO MAKE A QUICK BUCK SELLING YOUR OFFICE EQUIPMENT, AND I'M GOING TO PROVE IT!

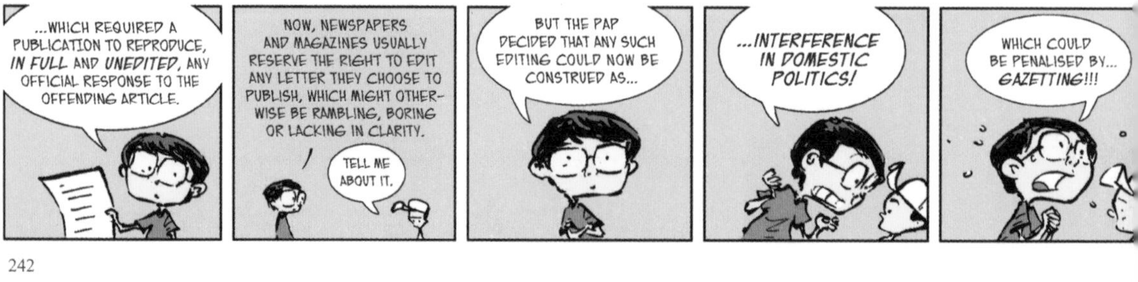
...WHICH REQUIRED A PUBLICATION TO REPRODUCE, IN FULL AND UNEDITED, ANY OFFICIAL RESPONSE TO THE OFFENDING ARTICLE.
NOW, NEWSPAPERS AND MAGAZINES USUALLY RESERVE THE RIGHT TO EDIT ANY LETTER THEY CHOOSE TO PUBLISH, WHICH MIGHT OTHERWISE BE RAMBLING, BORING OR LACKING IN CLARITY.
TELL ME ABOUT IT.
BUT THE PAP DECIDED THAT ANY SUCH EDITING COULD NOW BE CONSTRUED AS...
...INTERFERENCE IN DOMESTIC POLITICS!
WHICH COULD BE PENALISED BY... GAZETTING!!!

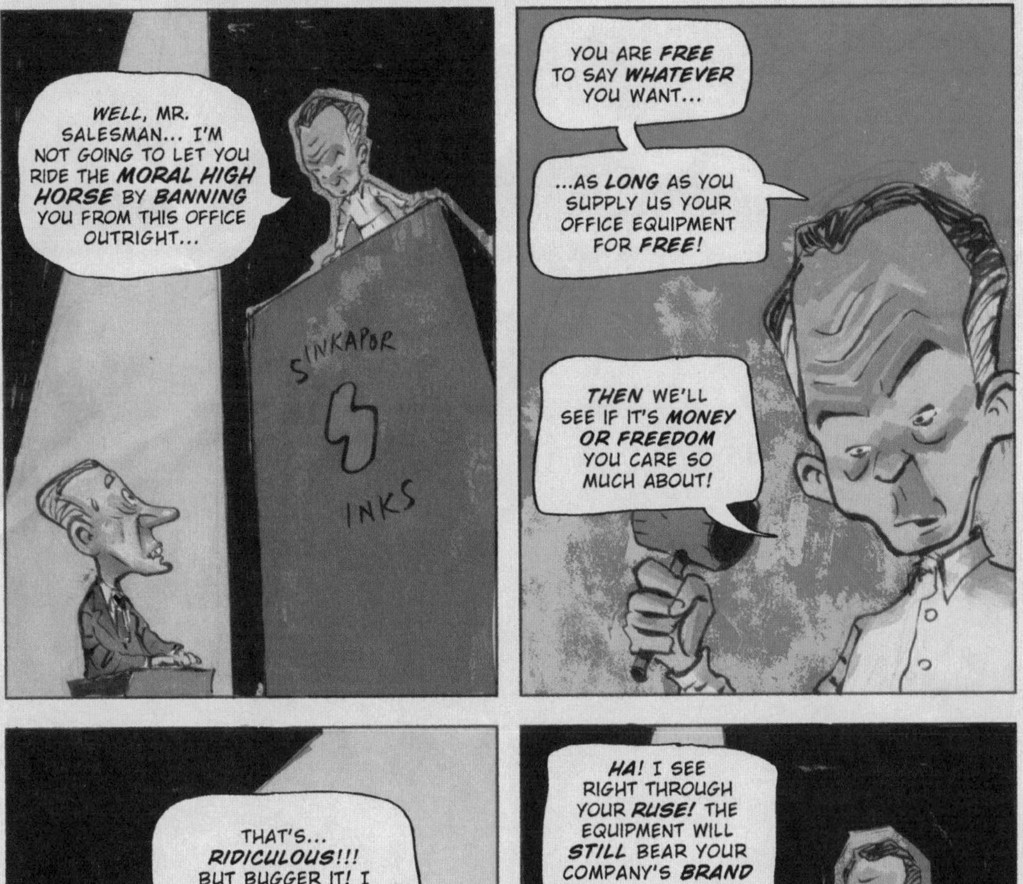
WELL, MR. SALESMAN... I'M NOT GOING TO LET YOU RIDE THE MORAL HIGH HORSE BY BANNING YOU FROM THIS OFFICE OUTRIGHT...
SINKAPOR
INKS
YOU ARE FREE TO SAY WHATEVER YOU WANT...
...AS LONG AS YOU SUPPLY US YOUR OFFICE EQUIPMENT FOR FREE!
THEN WE'LL SEE IF IT'S MONEY OR FREEDOM YOU CARE SO MUCH ABOUT!
THAT'S... RIDICULOUS!!! BUT BUGGER IT! I CAN ALWAYS MAKE MY MONEY ELSEWHERE...
...SO, FINE! YOUR COMPANY CAN HAVE ALL THE EQUIPMENT FOR FREE, IF THAT'S WHAT IT'S GONNA TAKE!
HA! I SEE RIGHT THROUGH YOUR RUSE! THE EQUIPMENT WILL STILL BEAR YOUR COMPANY'S BRAND NAME. WHICH MEANS THAT YOU'LL STILL BE ENJOYING FREE ADVERTISING!
REMOVE THOSE, THEN WE'LL TALK!
INKS

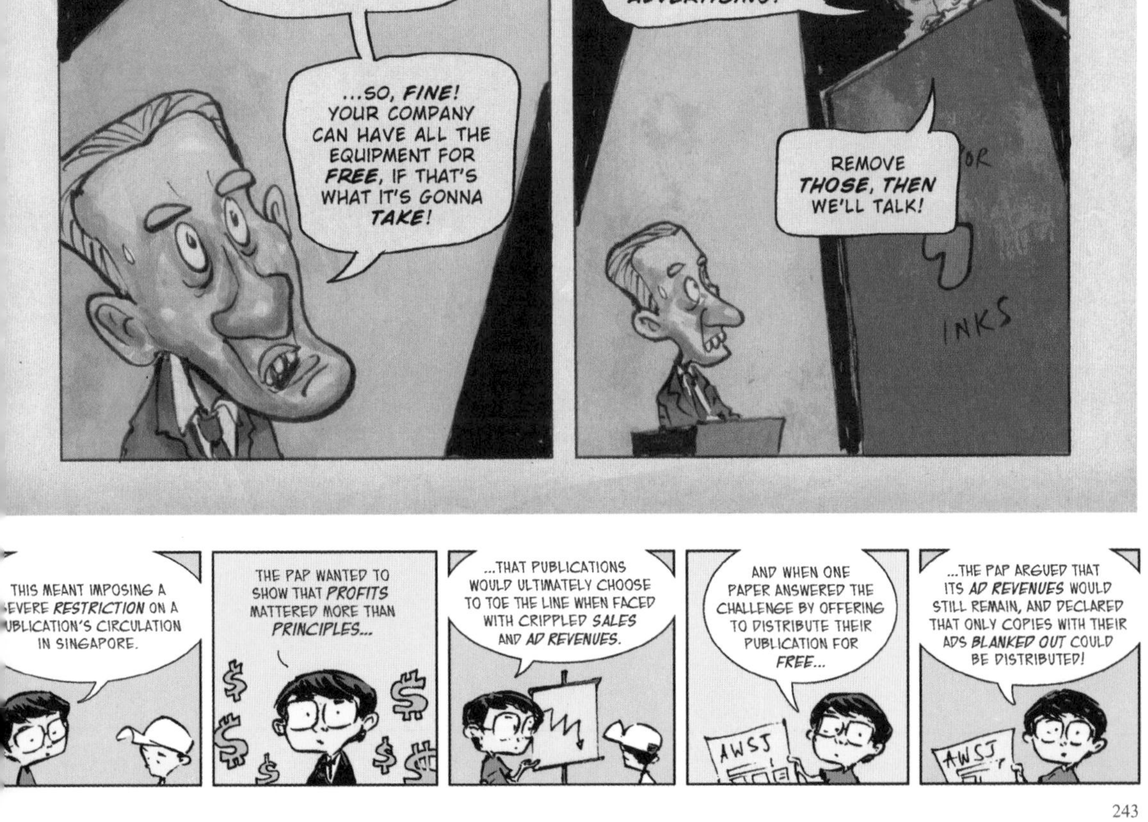
THIS MEANT IMPOSING A EVERE RESTRICTION ON A UBLICATION'S CIRCULATION IN SINGAPORE.
THE PAP WANTED TO SHOW THAT PROFITS MATTERED MORE THAN PRINCIPLES...
...THAT PUBLICATIONS WOULD ULTIMATELY CHOOSE TO TOE THE LINE WHEN FACED WITH CRIPPLED SALES AND AD REVENUES.
AND WHEN ONE PAPER ANSWERED THE CHALLENGE BY OFFERING TO DISTRIBUTE THEIR PUBLICATION FOR FREE...
AWSJ
...THE PAP ARGUED THAT ITS AD REVENUES WOULD STILL REMAIN, AND DECLARED THAT ONLY COPIES WITH THEIR ADS BLANKED OUT COULD BE DISTRIBUTED!
AWSJ

I AM **NOT** PLAYING THIS **SILLY** GAME WITH YOU ANYMORE! GOODBYE!
WAIT!
I WOULDN'T WANT ANYONE TO THINK THAT WE'RE **DEPRIVING** OUR STAFF OF THE **USE** OF YOUR EQUIPMENT...
MR. FU! A **MEMO**!
FROM NOW ON, IT SHALL BE **PERFECTLY LEGAL** TO **REPRODUCE** ANY EQUIPMENT FROM THIS FELLOW'S COMPANY, FOR USE HERE, IN **THIS** OFFICE, FOR **FREE**!
MAY I REMIND YOU THAT ALL OF OUR EQUIPMENT IS **PATENT-**PROTECTED??
THAT'S *OKAY*... WE WON'T BE VIOLATING THE **SPIRIT** OF THE PATENT LAWS, SINCE **NO ONE** WILL BE MAKING ANY PROFIT OUT OF IT! **HA HA**!

WHEN ANOTHER PUBLICATION DECIDED ON PRINCIPLE TO *STOP SELLING* IN SINGAPORE ALTOGETHER...
FEER
THE GOVERNMENT CONTENDED THAT THIS WOULD RESTRICT THE *FREE FLOW OF INFORMATION* INTO THE COUNTRY...
...AND PROMPTLY MADE AMENDMENTS TO THE LAW...
...THAT ACTUALLY ALLOWED FOR THE *REPRODUCTION* OF THE PUBLICATION, *WITHOUT* THE PUBLISHER'S PERMISSION!
OH, THE *MADNESS!*
UH-HU

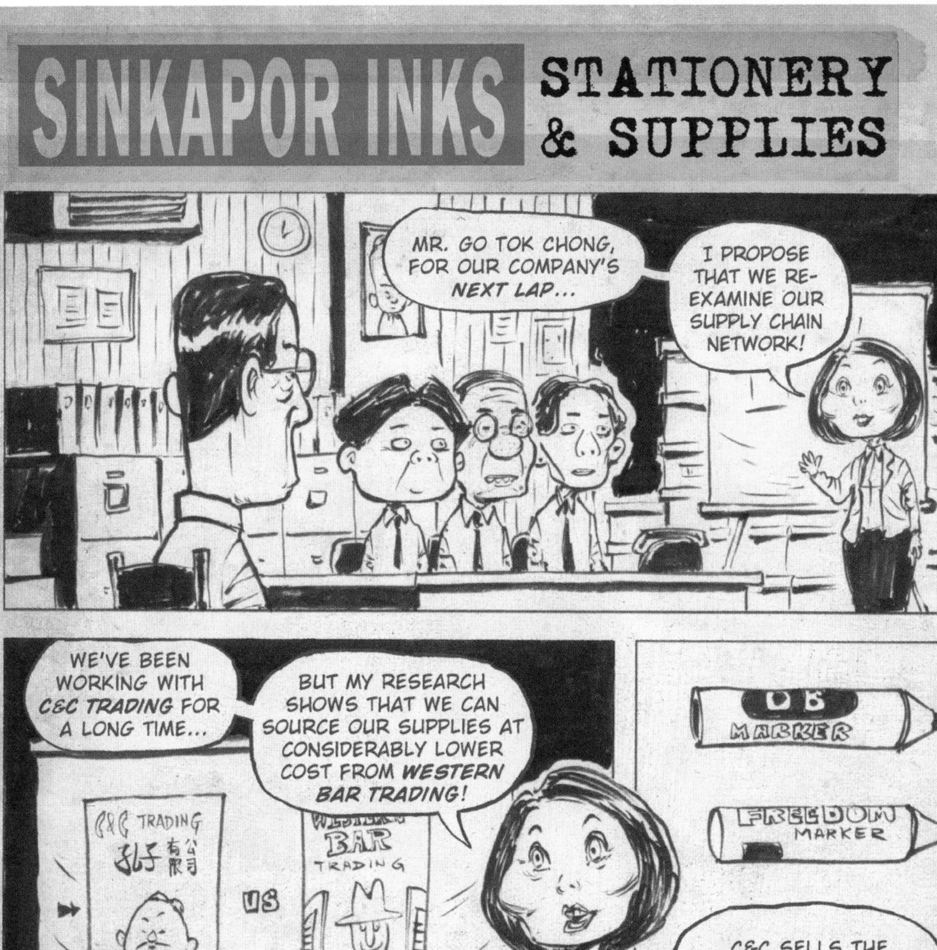
SINKAPOR INKS
STATIONERY & SUPPLIES
MR. GO TOK CHONG, FOR OUR COMPANY'S NEXT LAP...
I PROPOSE THAT WE RE-EXAMINE OUR SUPPLY CHAIN NETWORK!
WE'VE BEEN WORKING WITH C&C TRADING FOR A LONG TIME...
BUT MY RESEARCH SHOWS THAT WE CAN SOURCE OUR SUPPLIES AT CONSIDERABLY LOWER COST FROM WESTERN BAR TRADING!
C&C TRADING
孔子有限公司
VS
BAR TRADING
OB MARKER
FREEDOM MARKER
C&C SELLS THE ONG BENG MARKER FOR 50 CENTS EACH, BUT WESTERN BAR HAS A SIMILAR ONE—
STOP

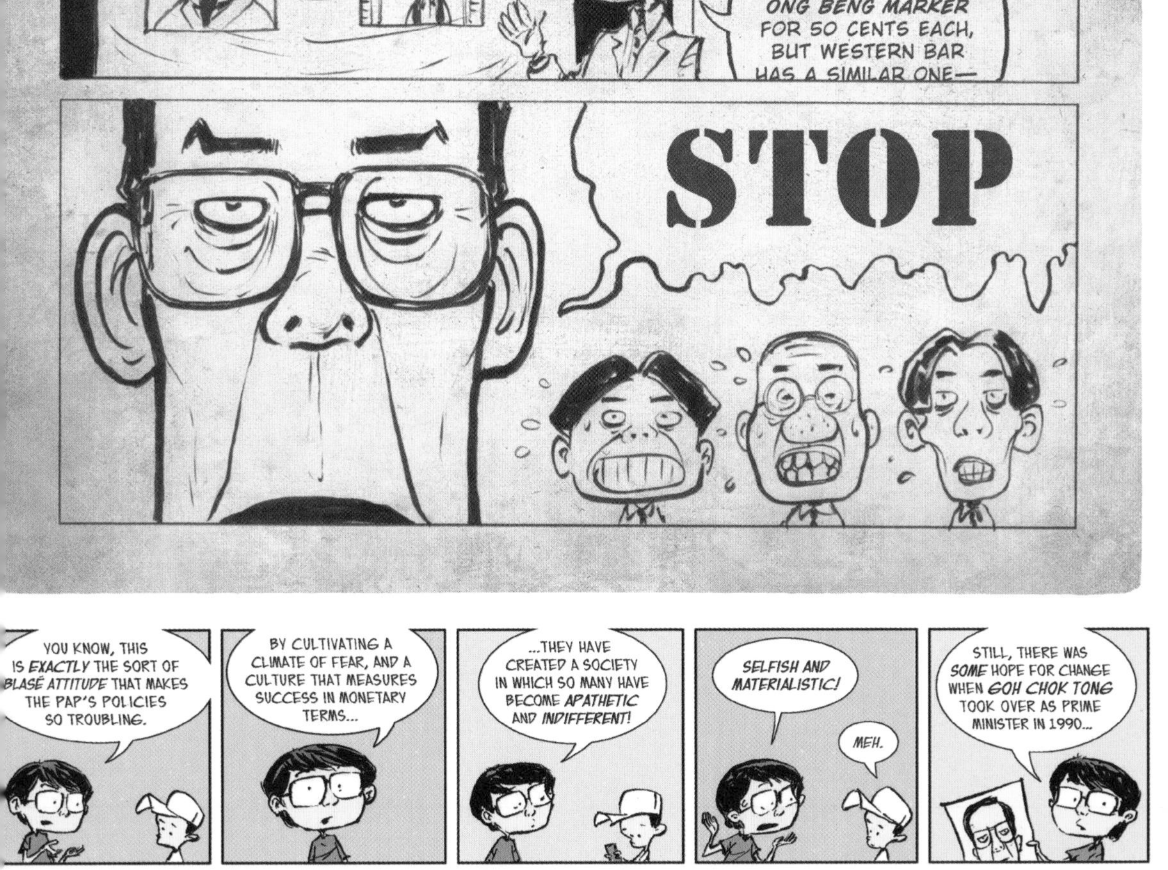
YOU KNOW, THIS IS EXACTLY THE SORT OF BLASÉ ATTITUDE THAT MAKES THE PAP'S POLICIES SO TROUBLING.
BY CULTIVATING A CLIMATE OF FEAR, AND A CULTURE THAT MEASURES SUCCESS IN MONETARY TERMS...
...THEY HAVE CREATED A SOCIETY IN WHICH SO MANY HAVE BECOME APATHETIC AND INDIFFERENT!
SELFISH AND MATERIALISTIC!
MEH.
STILL, THERE WAS SOME HOPE FOR CHANGE WHEN GOH CHOK TONG TOOK OVER AS PRIME MINISTER IN 1990...

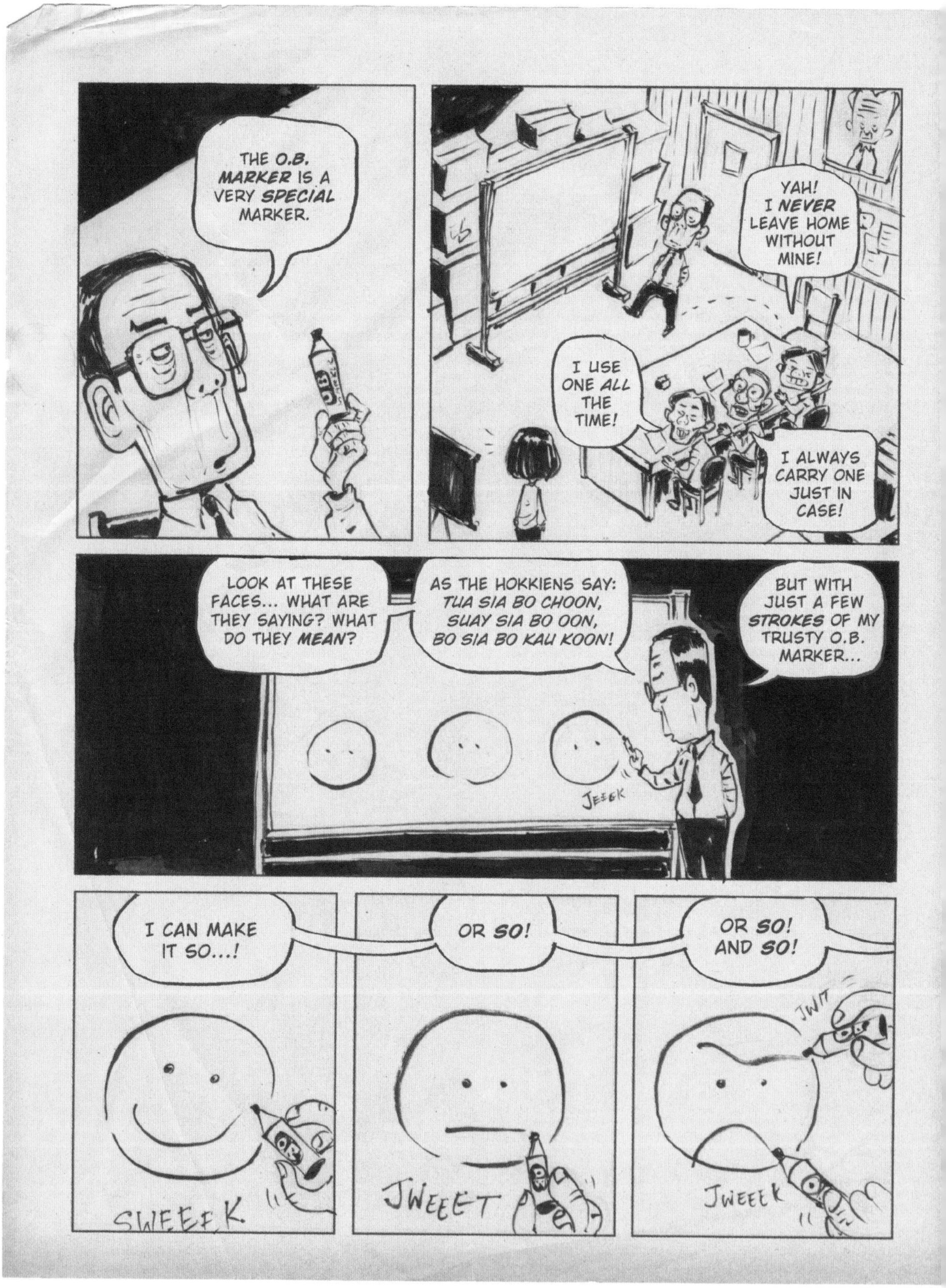
THE O.B. MARKER IS A VERY SPECIAL MARKER.
YAH! I NEVER LEAVE HOME WITHOUT MINE!
I USE ONE ALL THE TIME!
I ALWAYS CARRY ONE JUST IN CASE!
LOOK AT THESE FACES... WHAT ARE THEY SAYING? WHAT DO THEY MEAN?
AS THE HOKKIENS SAY: TUA SIA BO CHOON, SUAY SIA BO OON, BO SIA BO KAU KOON!
BUT WITH JUST A FEW STROKES OF MY TRUSTY O.B. MARKER...
JEEEK
I CAN MAKE IT SO...!
SWEEEK
OR SO!
JWEEET
OR SO! AND SO!
JWIT
JWEEEK

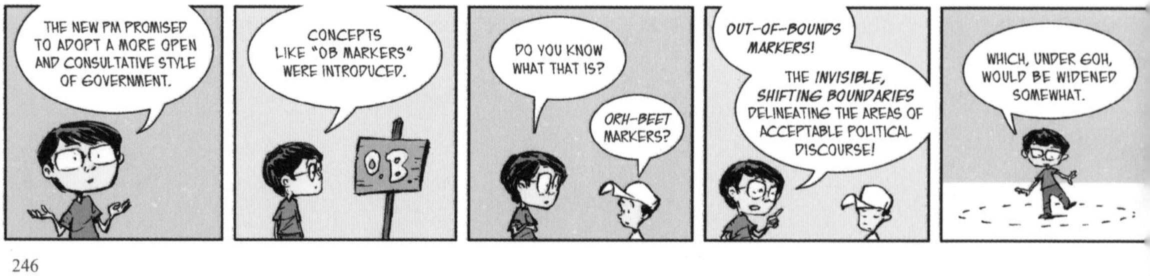
THE NEW PM PROMISED TO ADOPT A MORE OPEN AND CONSULTATIVE STYLE OF GOVERNMENT.
CONCEPTS LIKE "OB MARKERS" WERE INTRODUCED.
O.B.
DO YOU KNOW WHAT THAT IS?
ORH-BEET MARKERS?
OUT-OF-BOUNDS MARKERS!
THE INVISIBLE, SHIFTING BOUNDARIES DELINEATING THE AREAS OF ACCEPTABLE POLITICAL DISCOURSE!
WHICH, UNDER GOH, WOULD BE WIDENED SOMEWHAT.

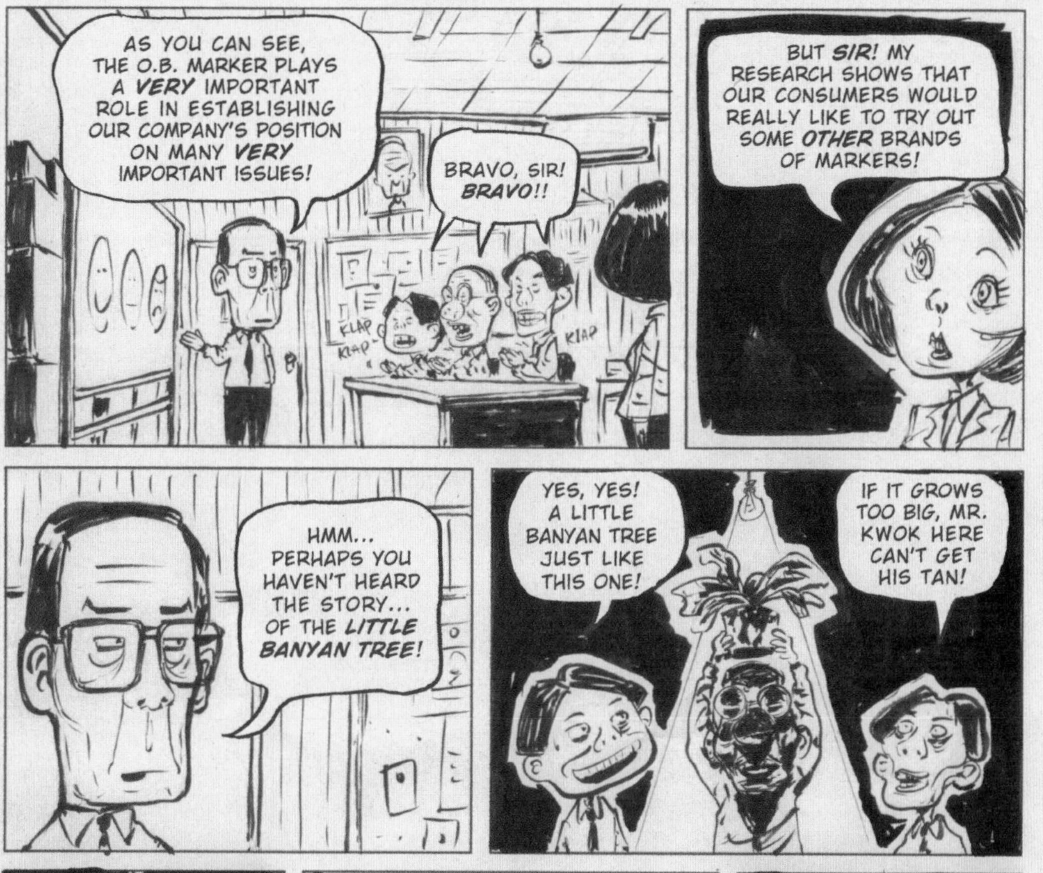
AS YOU CAN SEE, THE O.B. MARKER PLAYS A *VERY* IMPORTANT ROLE IN ESTABLISHING OUR COMPANY'S POSITION ON MANY *VERY* IMPORTANT ISSUES!
BRAVO, SIR! *BRAVO!!*
KLAP
KLAP
KLAP
BUT *SIR!* MY RESEARCH SHOWS THAT OUR CONSUMERS WOULD REALLY LIKE TO TRY OUT SOME *OTHER* BRANDS OF MARKERS!
HMM... PERHAPS YOU HAVEN'T HEARD THE STORY... OF THE *LITTLE BANYAN TREE!*
YES, YES! A LITTLE BANYAN TREE JUST LIKE THIS ONE!
IF IT GROWS TOO BIG, MR. KWOK HERE CAN'T GET HIS TAN!
BUT REMOVE IT *ENTIRELY,* AND I'D BE *TOO* HOT!!
SO, WE HAVE TO *PRUNE* IT JUDICIOUSLY!
SNIP
SNIP
WOW! *VERY* JUDICIOUS!
WELL-PRUNED, SIR!
NOW, IT'S IN *PERFECT HARMONIOUS BALANCE!*

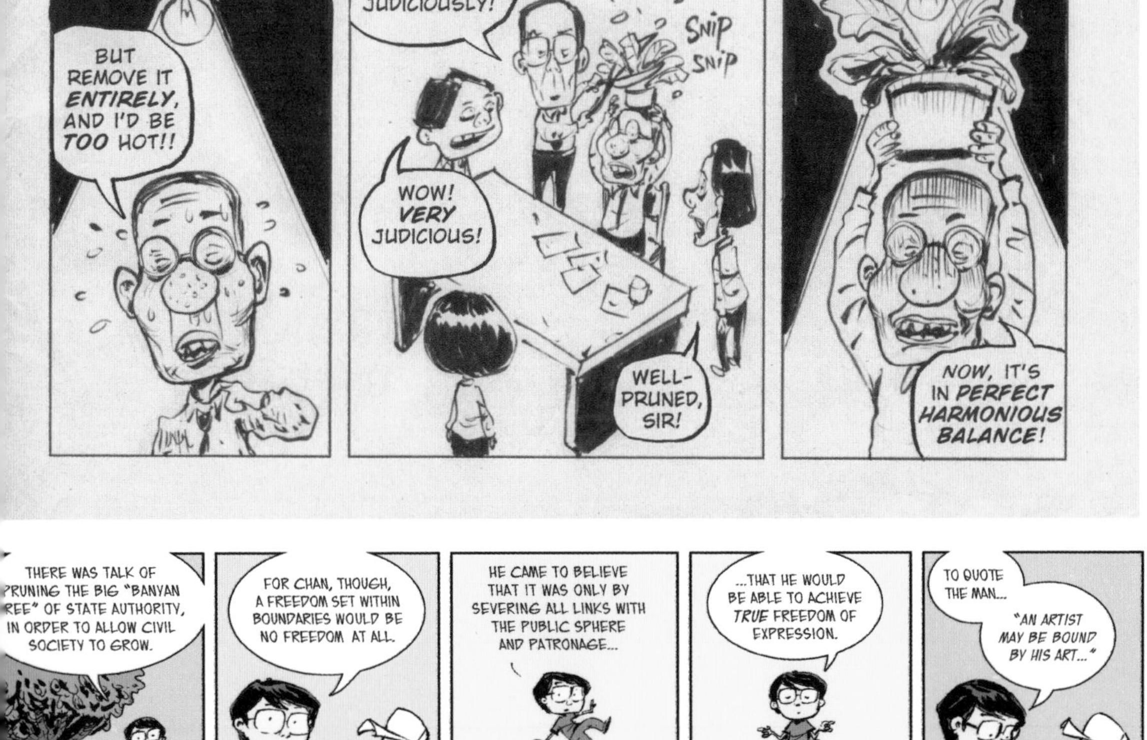
THERE WAS TALK OF PRUNING THE BIG "BANYAN REE" OF STATE AUTHORITY, IN ORDER TO ALLOW CIVIL SOCIETY TO GROW.
FOR CHAN, THOUGH, A FREEDOM SET WITHIN BOUNDARIES WOULD BE NO FREEDOM AT ALL.
HE CAME TO BELIEVE THAT IT WAS ONLY BY SEVERING ALL LINKS WITH THE PUBLIC SPHERE AND PATRONAGE...
...THAT HE WOULD BE ABLE TO ACHIEVE *TRUE* FREEDOM OF EXPRESSION.
TO QUOTE THE MAN...
"AN ARTIST MAY BE BOUND BY HIS ART..."

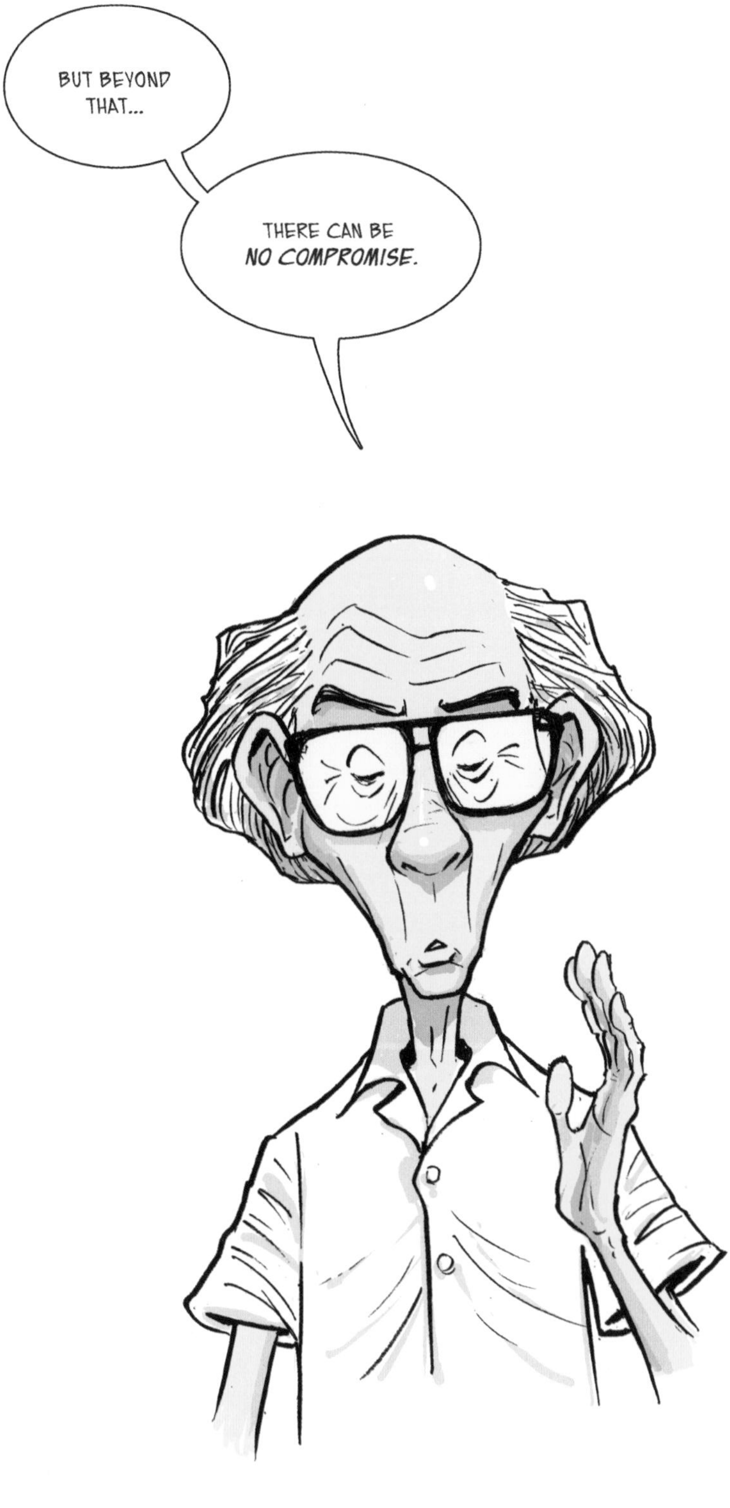
BUT BEYOND THAT...
THERE CAN BE NO COMPROMISE.

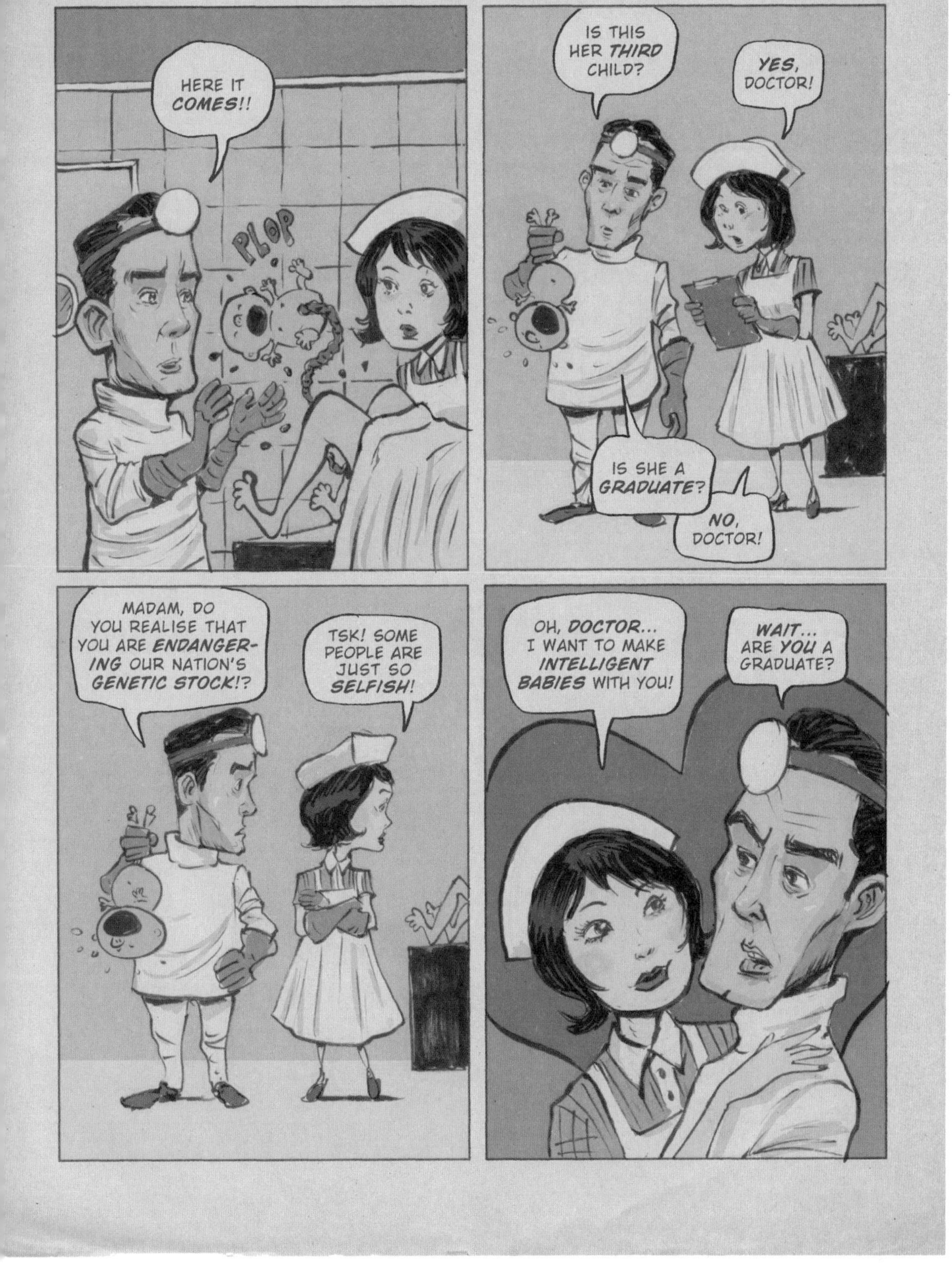
HERE IT COMES!!
PLOP
IS THIS HER THIRD CHILD?
YES, DOCTOR!
IS SHE A GRADUATE?
NO, DOCTOR!
MADAM, DO YOU REALISE THAT YOU ARE ENDANGER-ING OUR NATION'S GENETIC STOCK!?
TSK! SOME PEOPLE ARE JUST SO SELFISH!
OH, DOCTOR... I WANT TO MAKE INTELLIGENT BABIES WITH YOU!
WAIT... ARE YOU A GRADUATE?

Above **STOP AT TWO** (1984) | Chan Hock Chye | Unpublished

The 1980s provided fertile ground for Chan's critiques of government policies. Population control policies such as the **Graduate Mothers Scheme** (1984) and the "**Have Three Or More, If You Can Afford It**" (1986) campaign were, in his eyes, symptomatic of a state bent on shaping its citizenry according to the particular intellectual convictions and idiosyncrasies of then Prime Minister Lee Kuan Yew.

Right
TRASH CAN BABY
1984
Chan Hock Chye
Unpublished

In 1984, the government introduced a slew of social and financial incentives that were designed to entice better-educated women to bear more children, while less-educated mothers were encouraged to undergo voluntary sterilisation.

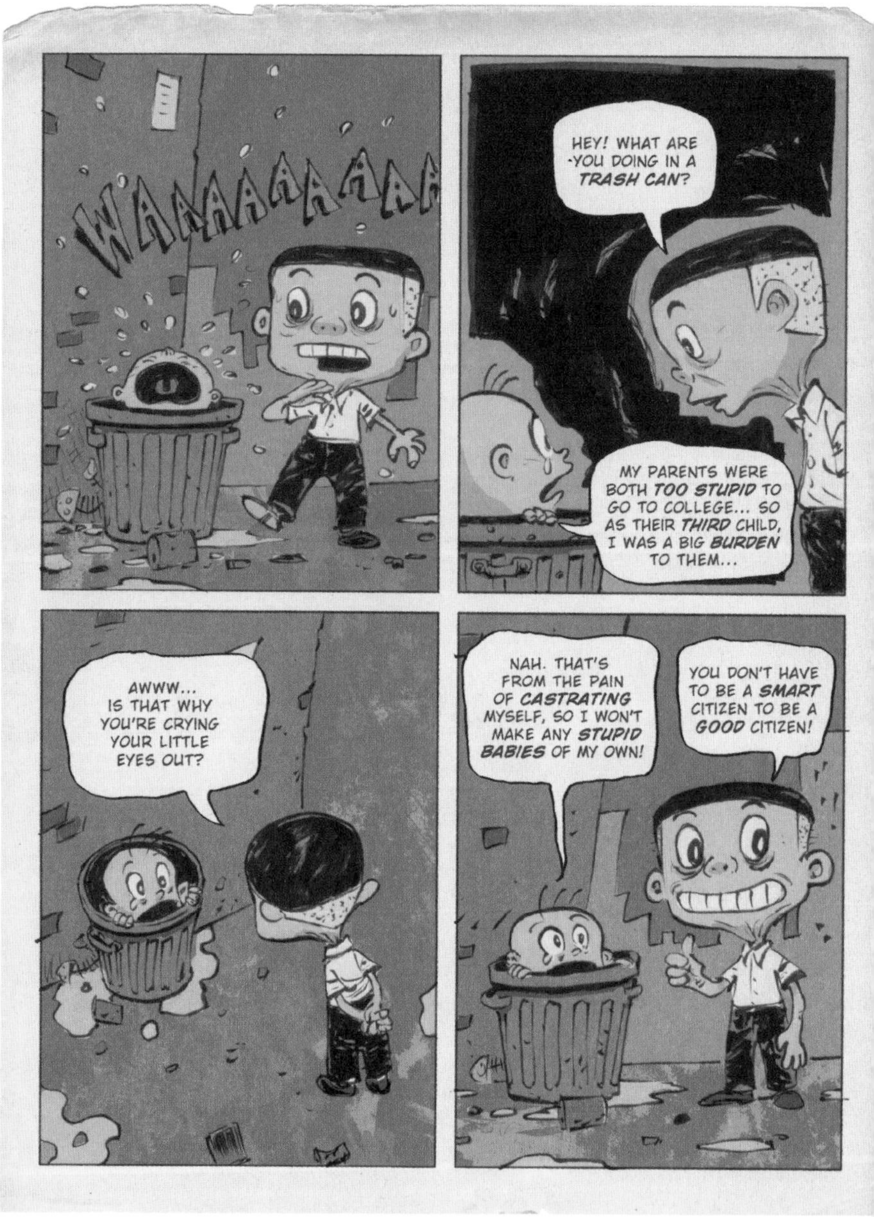

WAAAAAAAAAH
HEY! WHAT ARE YOU DOING IN A TRASH CAN?
MY PARENTS WERE BOTH TOO STUPID TO GO TO COLLEGE... SO AS THEIR THIRD CHILD, I WAS A BIG BURDEN TO THEM...
AWWW... IS THAT WHY YOU'RE CRYING YOUR LITTLE EYES OUT?
NAH. THAT'S FROM THE PAIN OF CASTRATING MYSELF, SO I WON'T MAKE ANY STUPID BABIES OF MY OWN!
YOU DON'T HAVE TO BE A SMART CITIZEN TO BE A GOOD CITIZEN!

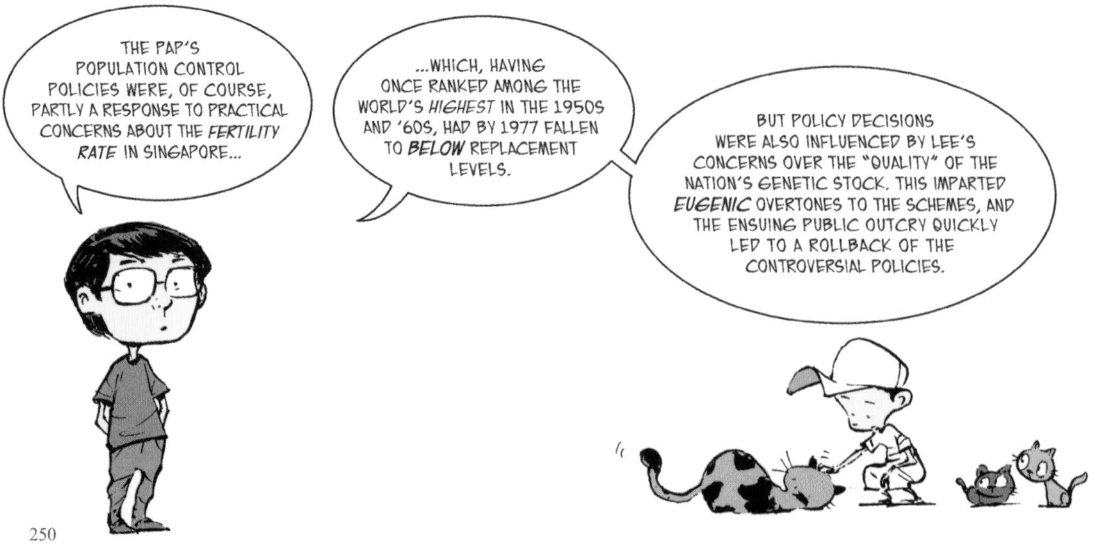

THE PAP'S POPULATION CONTROL POLICIES WERE, OF COURSE, PARTLY A RESPONSE TO PRACTICAL CONCERNS ABOUT THE FERTILITY RATE IN SINGAPORE...
...WHICH, HAVING ONCE RANKED AMONG THE WORLD'S HIGHEST IN THE 1950S AND '60S, HAD BY 1977 FALLEN TO BELOW REPLACEMENT LEVELS.
BUT POLICY DECISIONS WERE ALSO INFLUENCED BY LEE'S CONCERNS OVER THE "QUALITY" OF THE NATION'S GENETIC STOCK. THIS IMPARTED EUGENIC OVERTONES TO THE SCHEMES, AND THE ENSUING PUBLIC OUTCRY QUICKLY LED TO A ROLLBACK OF THE CONTROVERSIAL POLICIES.

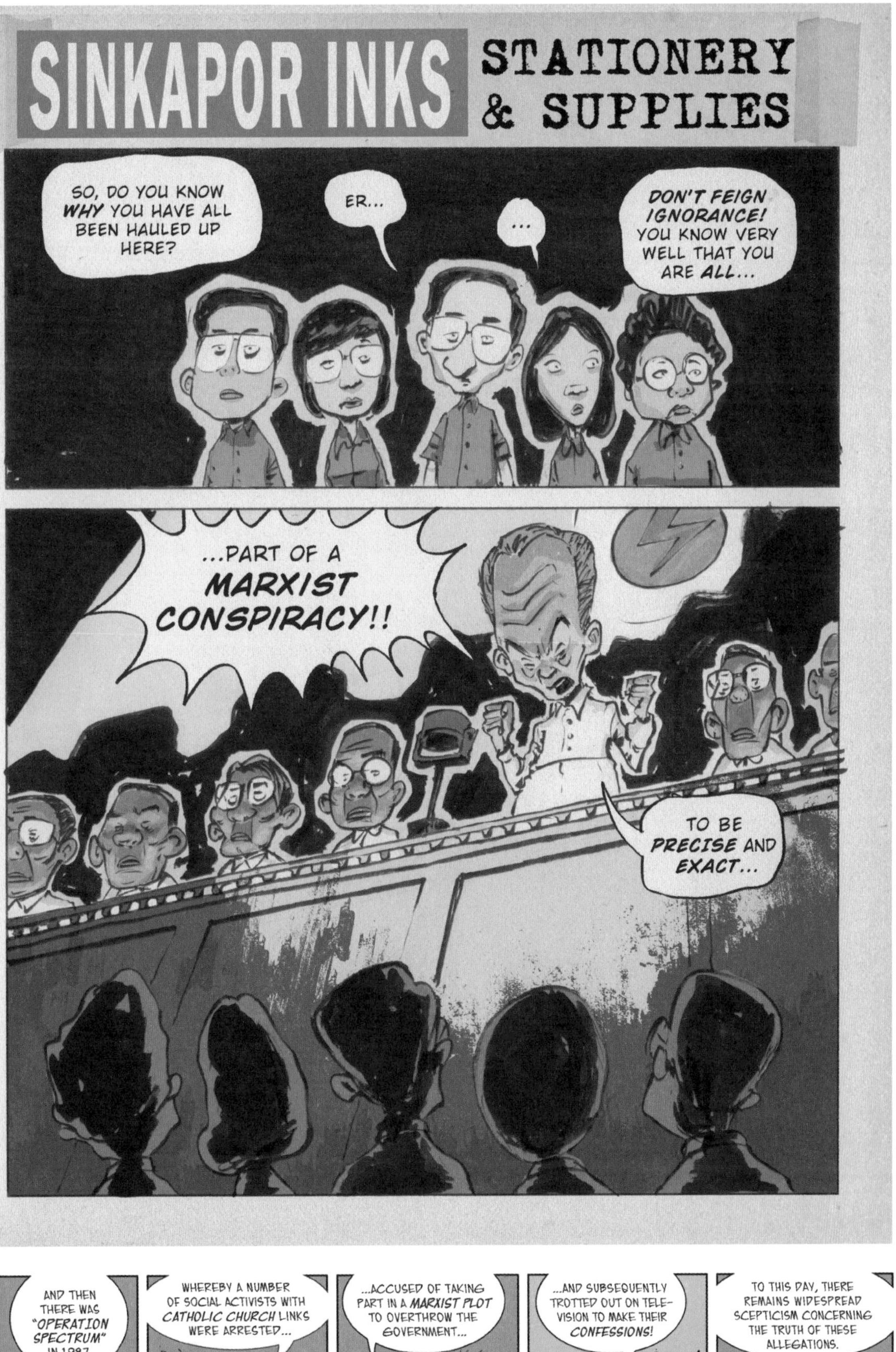
SINKAPOR INKS
STATIONERY & SUPPLIES
SO, DO YOU KNOW WHY YOU HAVE ALL BEEN HAULED UP HERE?
ER...
...
DON'T FEIGN IGNORANCE! YOU KNOW VERY WELL THAT YOU ARE ALL...
...PART OF A MARXIST CONSPIRACY!!
TO BE PRECISE AND EXACT...

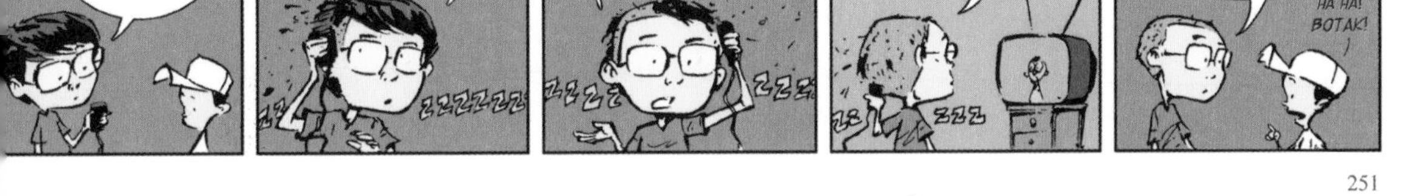
AND THEN THERE WAS "OPERATION SPECTRUM" IN 1987.
WHEREBY A NUMBER OF SOCIAL ACTIVISTS WITH CATHOLIC CHURCH LINKS WERE ARRESTED...
ZZZZZZ
...ACCUSED OF TAKING PART IN A MARXIST PLOT TO OVERTHROW THE GOVERNMENT...
...AND SUBSEQUENTLY TROTTED OUT ON TELE-VISION TO MAKE THEIR CONFESSIONS!
TO THIS DAY, THERE REMAINS WIDESPREAD SCEPTICISM CONCERNING THE TRUTH OF THESE ALLEGATIONS.
HA HA! BOTAK!

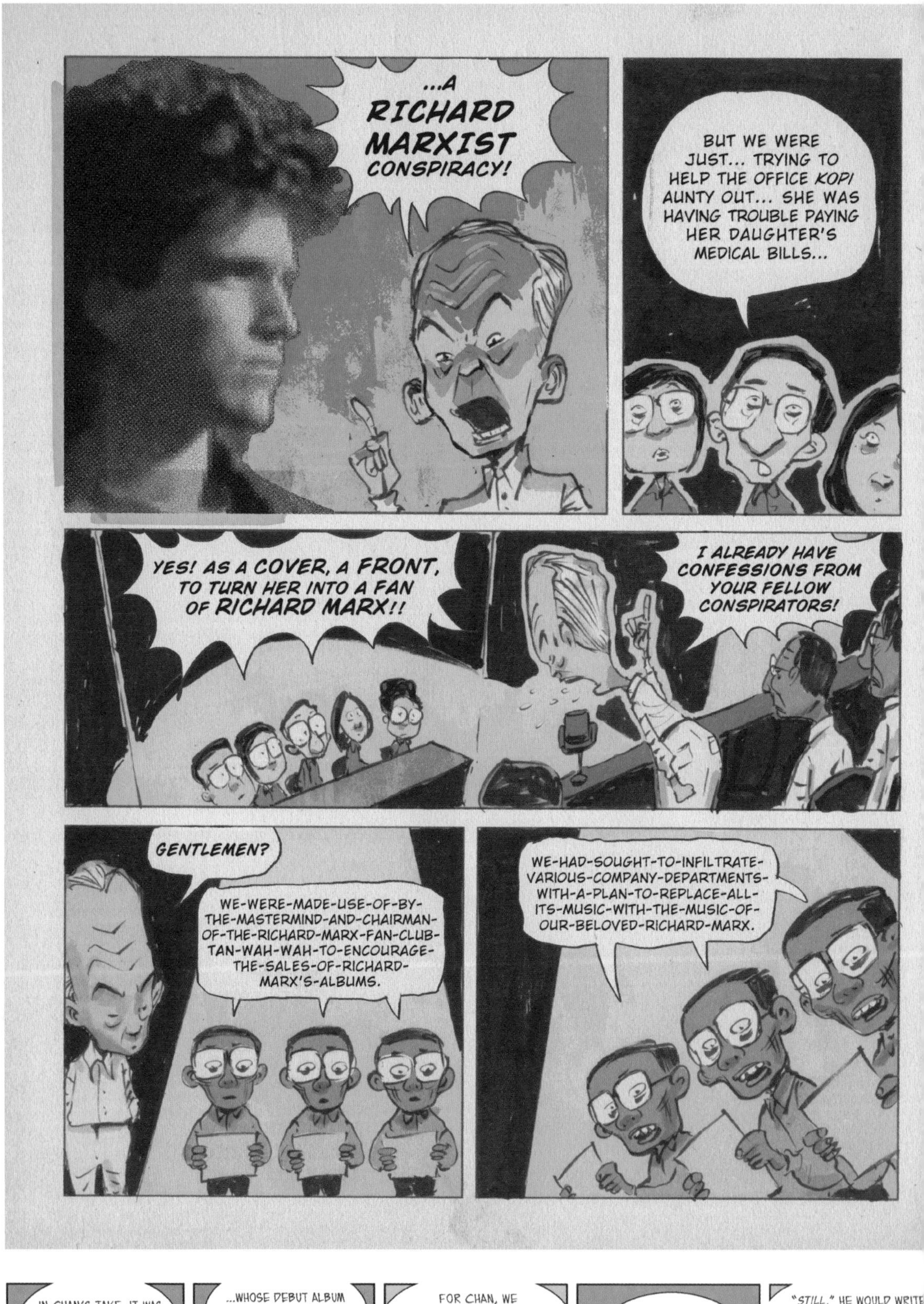
...A RICHARD MARXIST CONSPIRACY!
BUT WE WERE JUST... TRYING TO HELP THE OFFICE *KOPI* AUNTY OUT... SHE WAS HAVING TROUBLE PAYING HER DAUGHTER'S MEDICAL BILLS...
YES! AS A COVER, A FRONT, TO TURN HER INTO A FAN OF RICHARD MARX!!
I ALREADY HAVE CONFESSIONS FROM YOUR FELLOW CONSPIRATORS!
GENTLEMEN?
WE-WERE-MADE-USE-OF-BY-THE-MASTERMIND-AND-CHAIRMAN-OF-THE-RICHARD-MARX-FAN-CLUB-TAN-WAH-WAH-TO-ENCOURAGE-THE-SALES-OF-RICHARD-MARX'S-ALBUMS.
WE-HAD-SOUGHT-TO-INFILTRATE-VARIOUS-COMPANY-DEPARTMENTS-WITH-A-PLAN-TO-REPLACE-ALL-ITS-MUSIC-WITH-THE-MUSIC-OF-OUR-BELOVED-RICHARD-MARX.

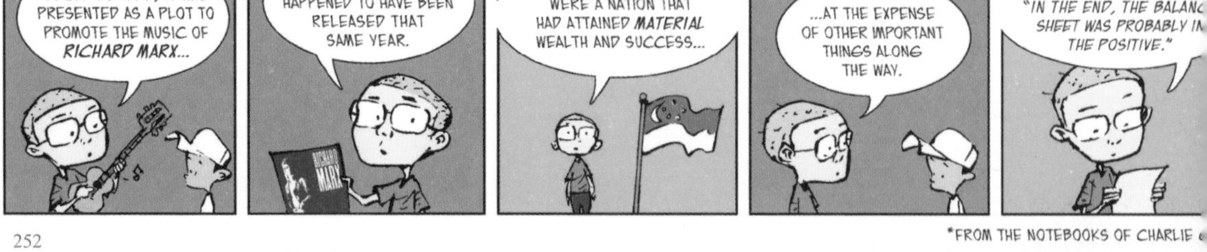
IN CHAN'S TAKE, IT WAS PRESENTED AS A PLOT TO PROMOTE THE MUSIC OF *RICHARD MARX*...
...WHOSE DEBUT ALBUM HAPPENED TO HAVE BEEN RELEASED THAT SAME YEAR.
FOR CHAN, WE WERE A NATION THAT HAD ATTAINED *MATERIAL* WEALTH AND SUCCESS...
...AT THE EXPENSE OF OTHER IMPORTANT THINGS ALONG THE WAY.
"STILL," HE WOULD WRITE "*IN THE END, THE BALANC SHEET WAS PROBABLY IN THE POSITIVE.*"

*FROM THE NOTEBOOKS OF CHARLIE C

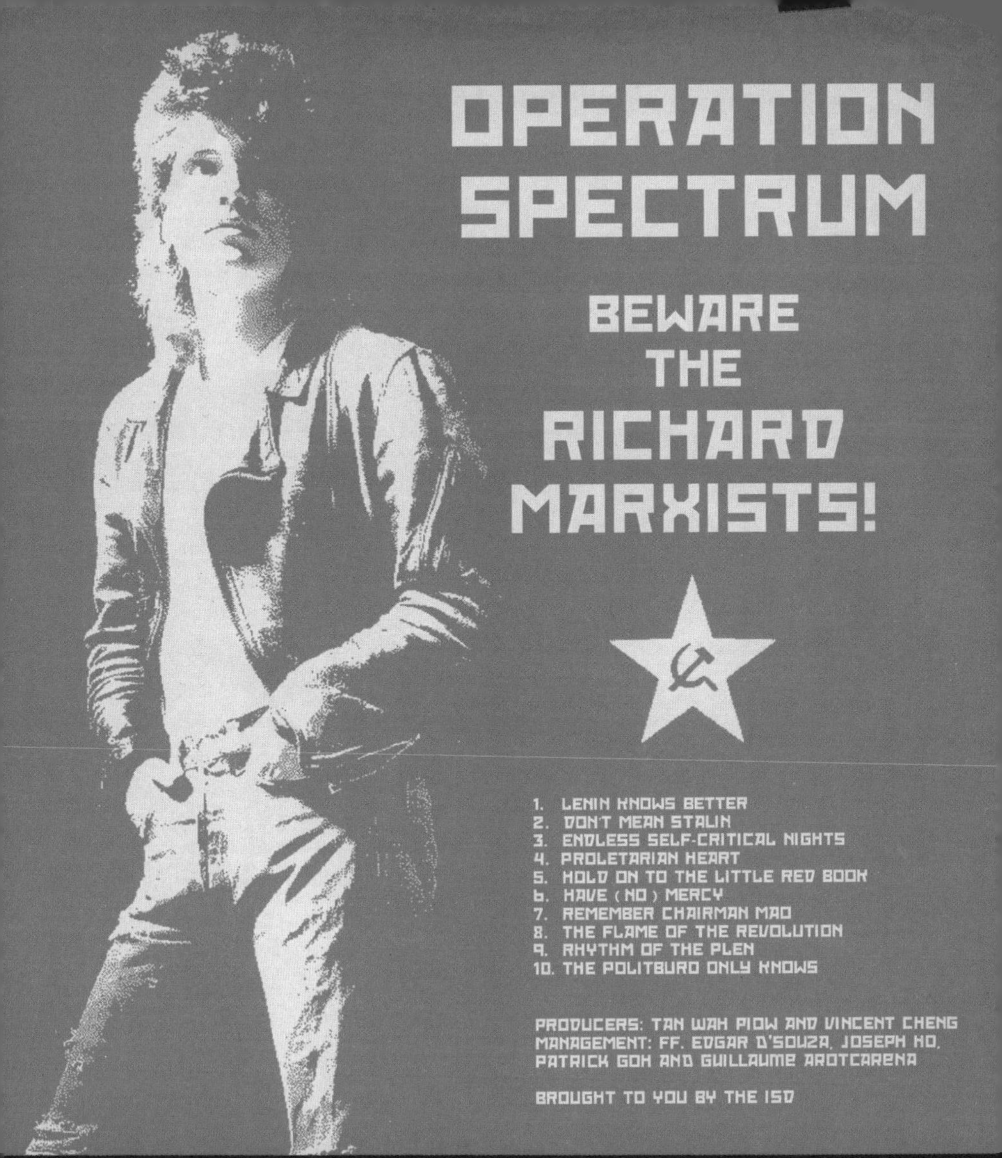
OPERATION SPECTRUM
BEWARE THE RICHARD MARXISTS!
1. LENIN KNOWS BETTER
2. DON'T MEAN STALIN
3. ENDLESS SELF-CRITICAL NIGHTS
4. PROLETARIAN HEART
5. HOLD ON TO THE LITTLE RED BOOK
6. HAVE (NO) MERCY
7. REMEMBER CHAIRMAN MAO
8. THE FLAME OF THE REVOLUTION
9. RHYTHM OF THE PLEN
10. THE POLITBURO ONLY KNOWS
PRODUCERS: TAN WAH PIOW AND VINCENT CHENG
MANAGEMENT: FF. EDGAR D'SOUZA, JOSEPH HO, PATRICK GOH AND GUILLAUME AROTCARENA
BROUGHT TO YOU BY THE ISD

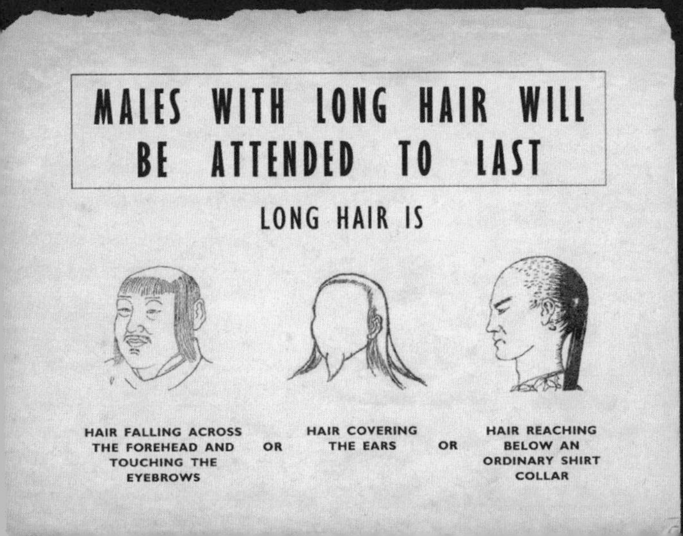
MALES WITH LONG HAIR WILL BE ATTENDED TO LAST
LONG HAIR IS
HAIR FALLING ACROSS THE FOREHEAD AND TOUCHING THE EYEBROWS
OR
HAIR COVERING THE EARS
OR
HAIR REACHING BELOW AN ORDINARY SHIRT COLLAR

Above
OPERATION SPECTRUM
1988
Concept by Chan Hock Chye
Layout by James De Souza
Self-published

Chan often sought out his former publisher's son, James De Souza, who had taken up graphic design, to help him realise his ideas for mock poster designs.

Left
LONG HAIR IS...
1982
Chan Hock Chye
Self-published

A spoof of official flyers discourag long hair for men, which had come under attack by the government a symbol of decadent Western cultu and mores.

Bring on a smile.
Say 'Please'.

A little thought means so much

Make
urtesy
r way
f life

人讲求礼貌

**TAKE YOUR TIME
TO SAY "YES"**

TO MARRIAGE
HAVING YOUR FIRST CHILD
AND YOUR SECOND

学华语
讲华语

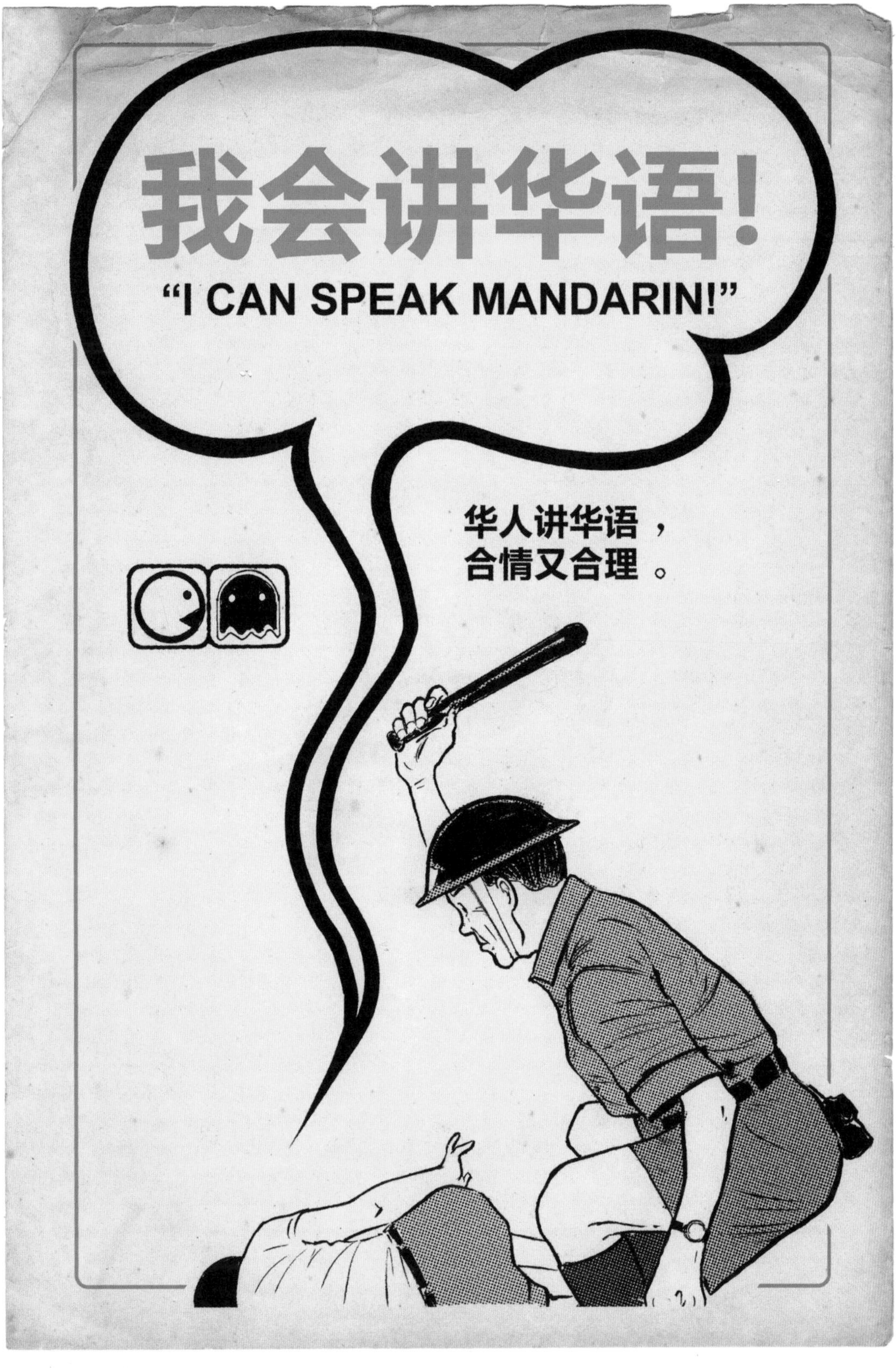

我会讲华语!
"I CAN SPEAK MANDARIN!"
华人讲华语，
合情又合理。

Above **I CAN SPEAK MANDARIN!** (1985) | Art and Concept by Chan Hock Chye, Layout by James De Souza

Drawing on the '**Speak Mandarin**' campaign posters and images of the 1956 Chinese Middle School riots, Chan's mock poster was a commentary on the shifting fates of Chinese education in Singapore. Marginalised from the 1950s to the 1970s over its perceived links with communism and Chinese chauvinism, it would later be rehabilitated as a means of helping Singaporean Chinese maintain their values, culture and identity.

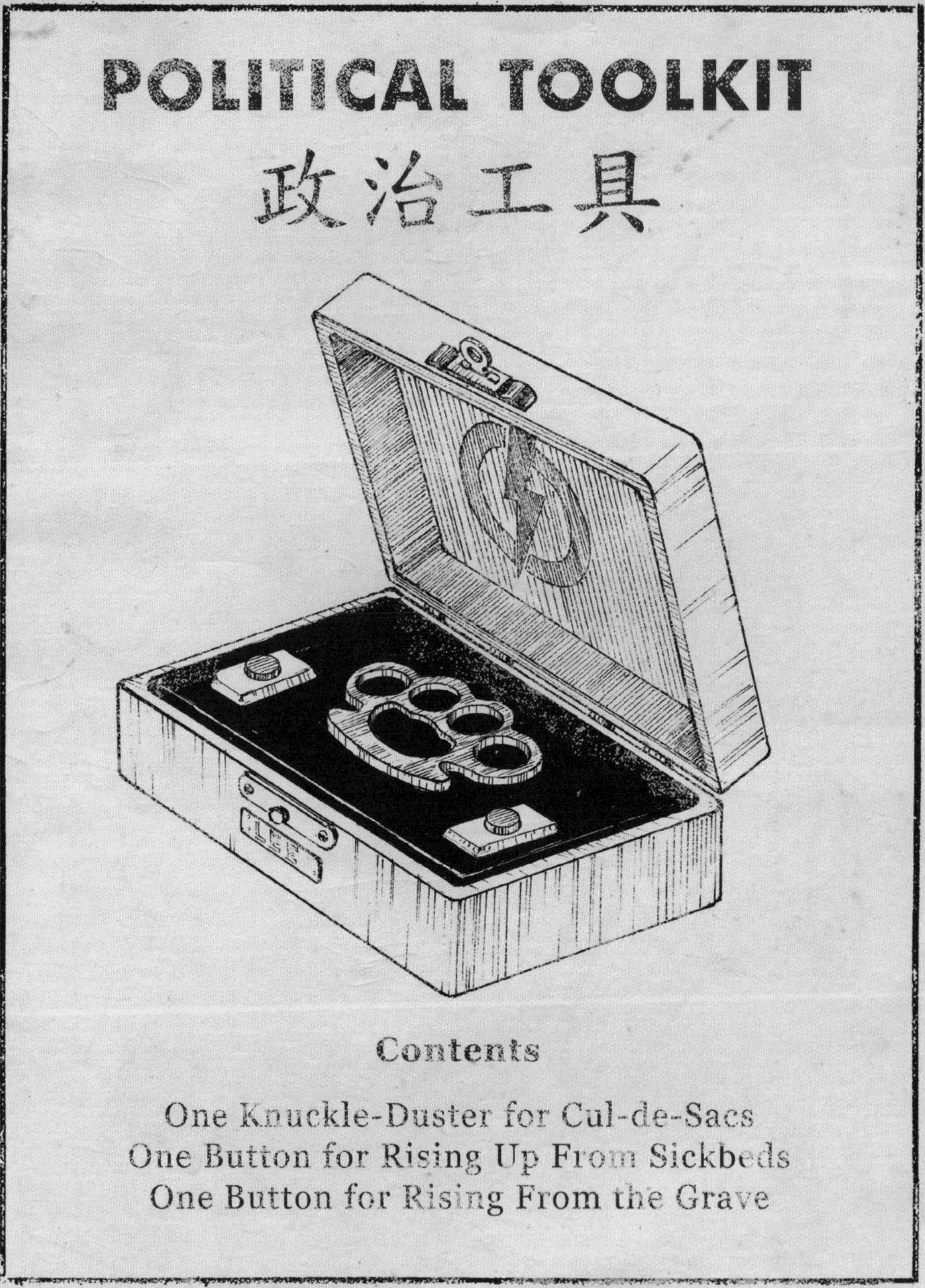

POLITICAL TOOLKIT
政治工具

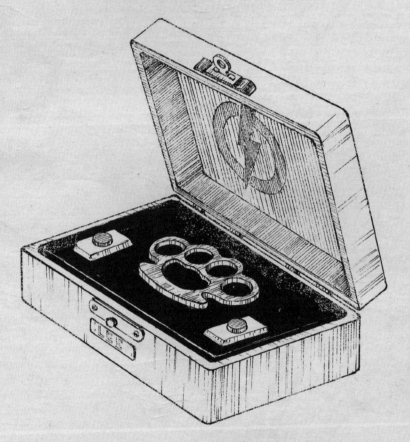

Contents

One Knuckle-Duster for Cul-de-Sacs
One Button for Rising Up From Sickbeds
One Button for Rising From the Grave

Above **POLITICAL TOOLKIT** (1997) | Chan Hock Chye | Unpublished

One of the few personal illustrations done by Chan in the style he had used for advertising illustrations in the 1950s and '60s. The idea was based on the speeches and writings of Lee Kuan Yew. At the National Day Rally in 1988, Lee had assured Singaporeans that *"Even from my sickbed, even if you are going to lower me into the grave and I feel something is going wrong, I will get up."*

He would claim on another occasion that *"[M]y posture, my response has been such that nobody doubts that if you take me on, I will put on knuckle-dusters and catch you in a cul-de-sac... Anybody who decides to take me on needs to put on knuckle-dusters. If you think you can hurt me more than I can hurt you, try. There is no other way you can govern a Chinese society."* (from *Lee Kuan Yew: The Man and His Ideas*, 1998).

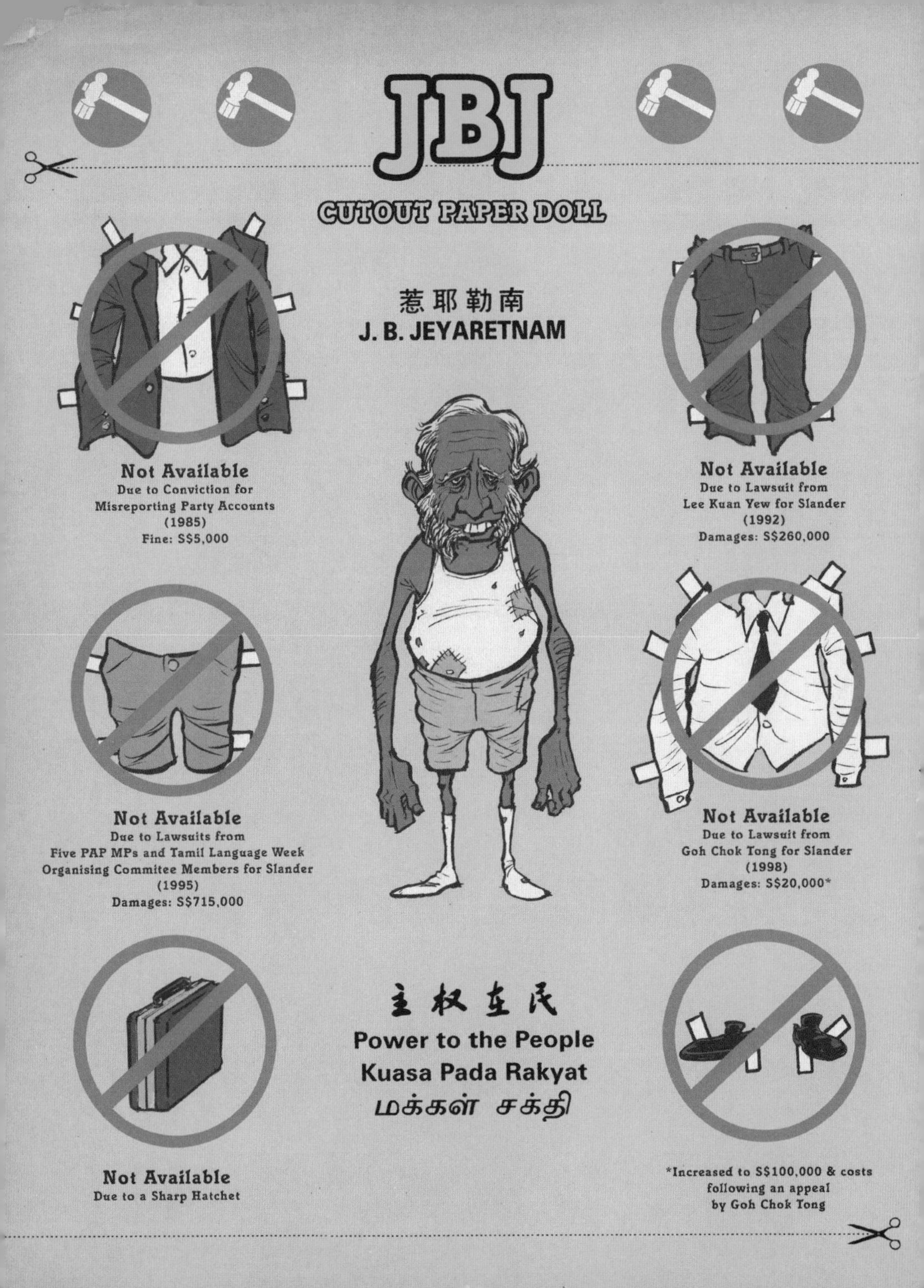
JBJ
CUTOUT PAPER DOLL
惹耶勒南
J. B. JEYARETNAM
Not Available
Due to Conviction for
Misreporting Party Accounts
(1985)
Fine: S$5,000
Not Available
Due to Lawsuit from
Lee Kuan Yew for Slander
(1992)
Damages: S$260,000
Not Available
Due to Lawsuits from
Five PAP MPs and Tamil Language Week
Organising Commitee Members for Slander
(1995)
Damages: S$715,000
Not Available
Due to Lawsuit from
Goh Chok Tong for Slander
(1998)
Damages: S$20,000*
主权在民
Power to the People
Kuasa Pada Rakyat
மக்கள் சக்தி
Not Available
Due to a Sharp Hatchet
*Increased to S$100,000 & costs
following an appeal
by Goh Chok Tong

Above **JBJ CUTOUT PAPER DOLL** (1998) | Chan Hock Chye | Self-published

Joshua Benjamin Jeyaretnam (JBJ) won the 1981 Anson by-election and became the first opposition politician to capture a seat in Parliament since Singapore's independence in 1965. He was twice disqualified as a Member of Parliament and further declared a bankrupt as a result of a series of high-profile lawsuits. Chan says that he created the paper pattern mock-up as "My impression was that he was getting sued in court all the time, sued until *terng kor*, as they say."

Terng kor Hokkien, literally to lose one's pants; describes a person who has lost all of his possessions, often as a result of some ill-calculated gamble

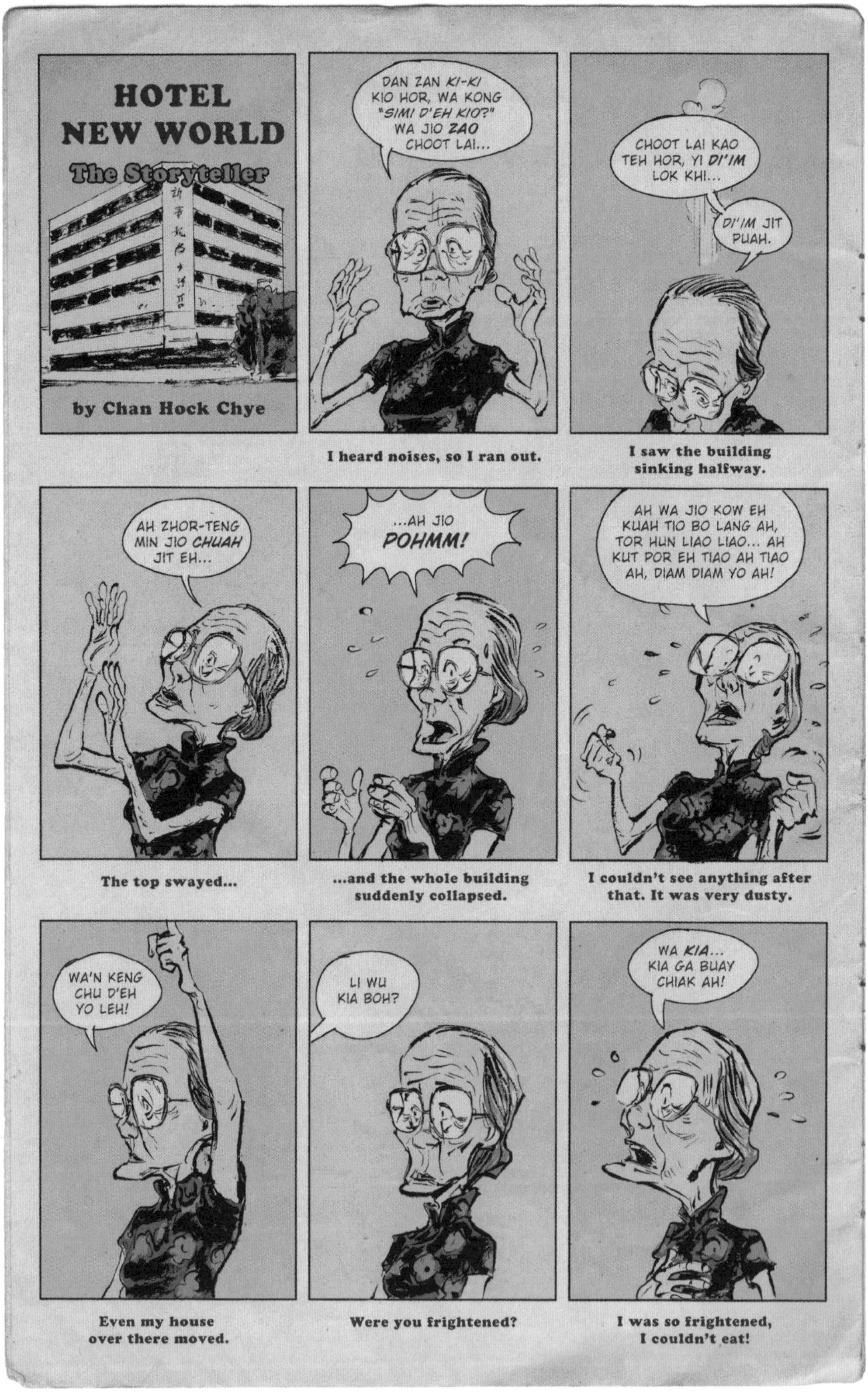
HOTEL NEW WORLD
The Storyteller
by Chan Hock Chye
DAN ZAN KI-KI KIO HOR, WA KONG "SIMI D'EH KIO?" WA JIO ZAO CHOOT LAI...
I heard noises, so I ran out.
CHOOT LAI KAO TEH HOR, YI DI'IM LOK KHI...
DI'IM JIT PUAH.
I saw the building sinking halfway.
AH ZHOR-TENG MIN JIO CHUAH JIT EH...
The top swayed...
...AH JIO POHMM!
...and the whole building suddenly collapsed.
AH WA JIO KOW EH KUAH TIO BO LANG AH, TOR HUN LIAO LIAO... AH KUT POR EH TIAO AH TIAO AH, DIAM DIAM YO AH!
I couldn't see anything after that. It was very dusty.
WA'N KENG CHU D'EH YO LEH!
Even my house over there moved.
LI WU KIA BOH?
Were you frightened?
WA KIA... KIA GA BUAY CHIAK AH!
I was so frightened, I couldn't eat!

Above **HOTEL NEW WORLD: THE STORYTELLER** (1988) | Chan Hock Chye | Self-published

The collapse of Hotel New World in 1986 left 33 dead, and would go down as one of Singapore's deadliest civil disasters. Based on a television interview with a witness to the incident, Chan's comic sought to illustrate the gap between the interviewee's rich and expressive dialect and the colourless English translated captions provided by the televison programme. He had conceived of the comic after watching a staging of Kuo Pao Kun's *Mama Looking for Her Cat*, a play that explored the breakdown in communication between different generations in Singapore as dialect knowledge and usage plummeted among the younger generation.

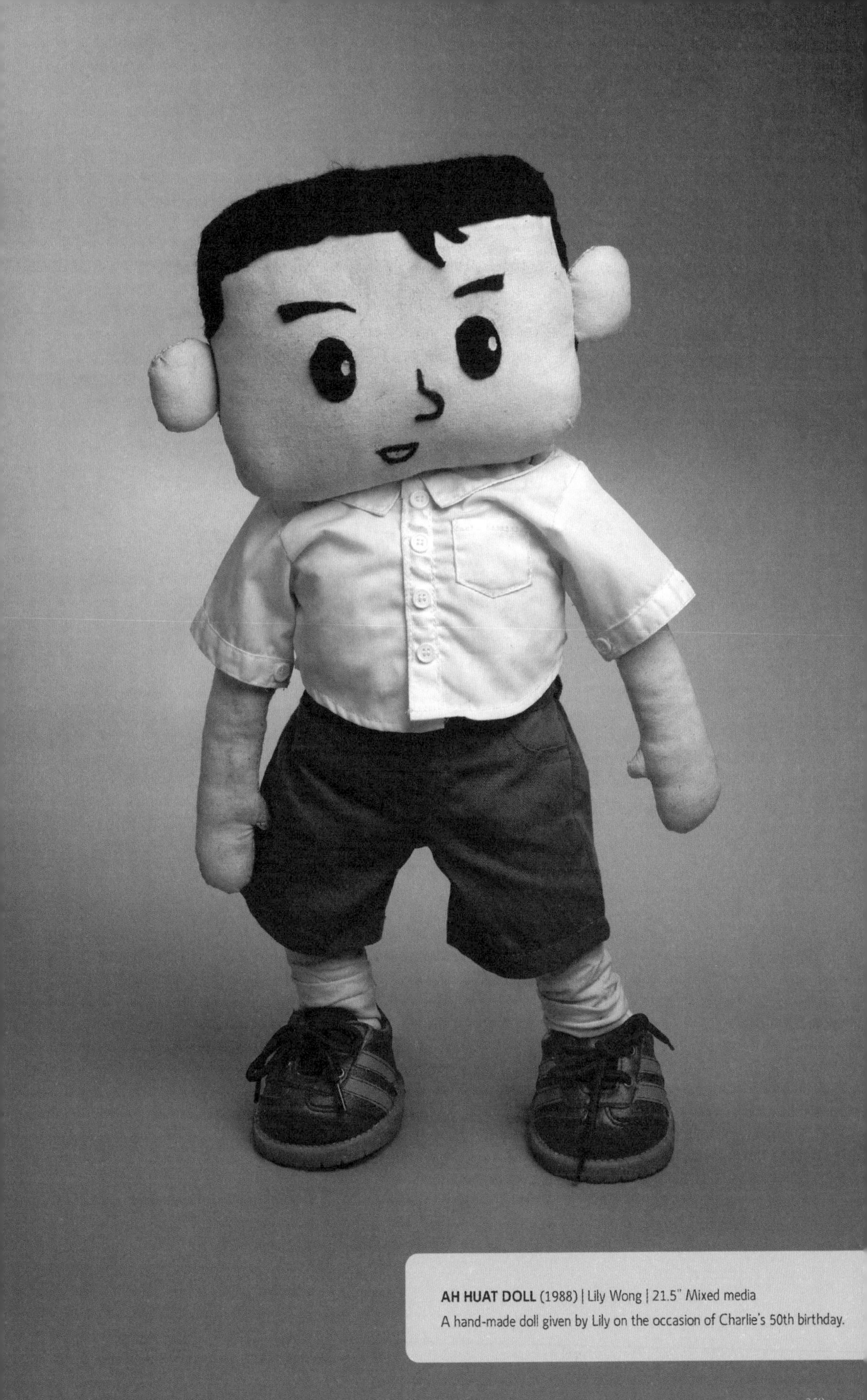

AH HUAT DOLL (1988) | Lily Wong | 21.5" Mixed media
A hand-made doll given by Lily on the occasion of Charlie's 50th birthday.

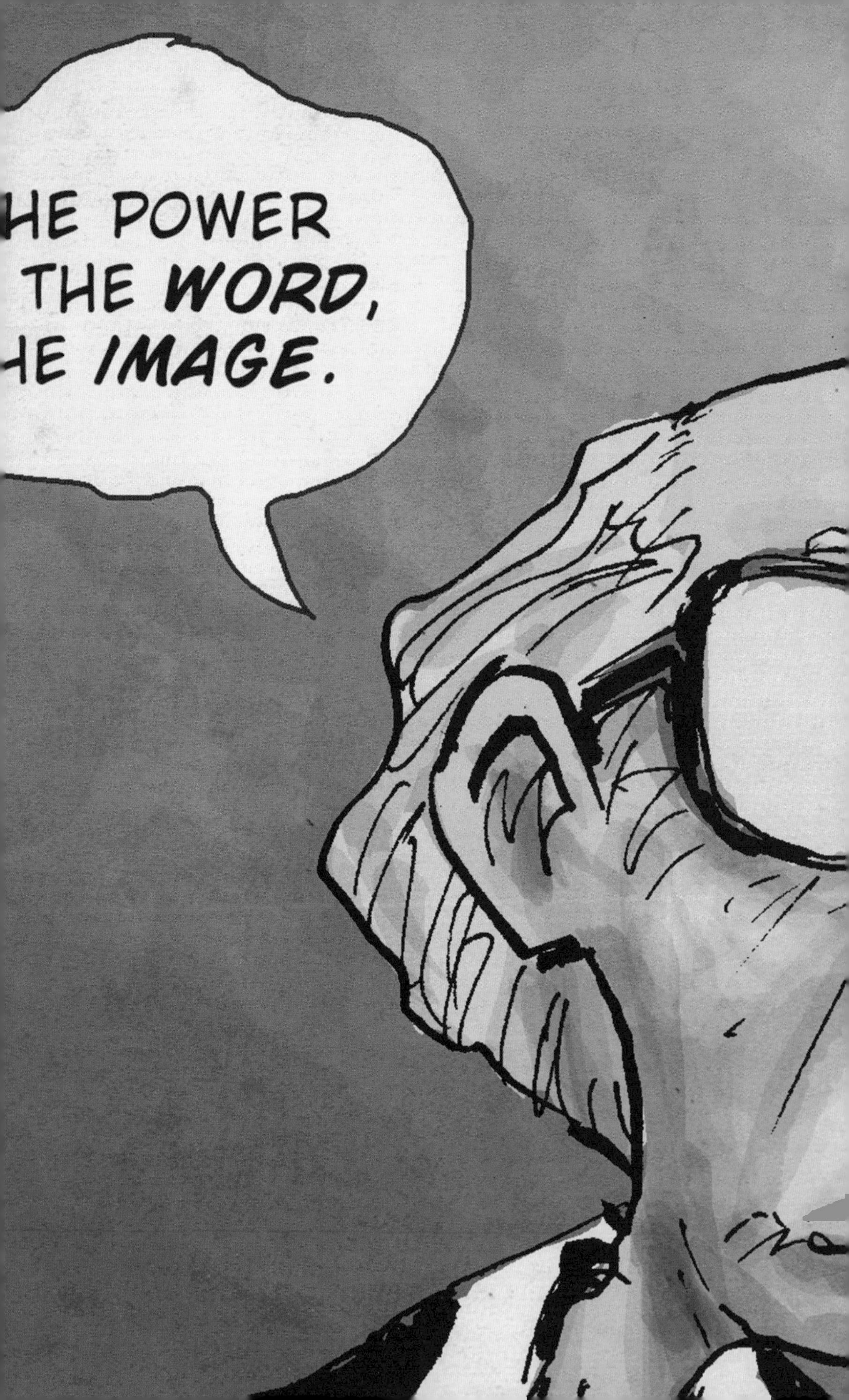
HE POWER
THE WORD,
HE IMAGE.

Chapter Eight

THE KING OF COMICS

漫画之王

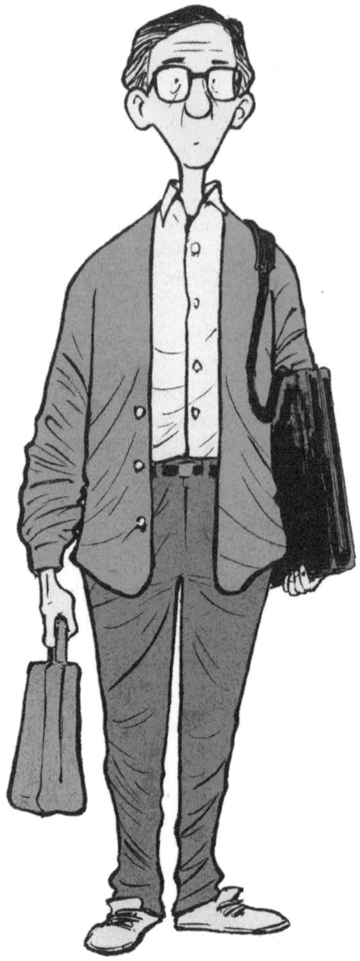

Charlie Chan Hock Chye, aged 50, 1988

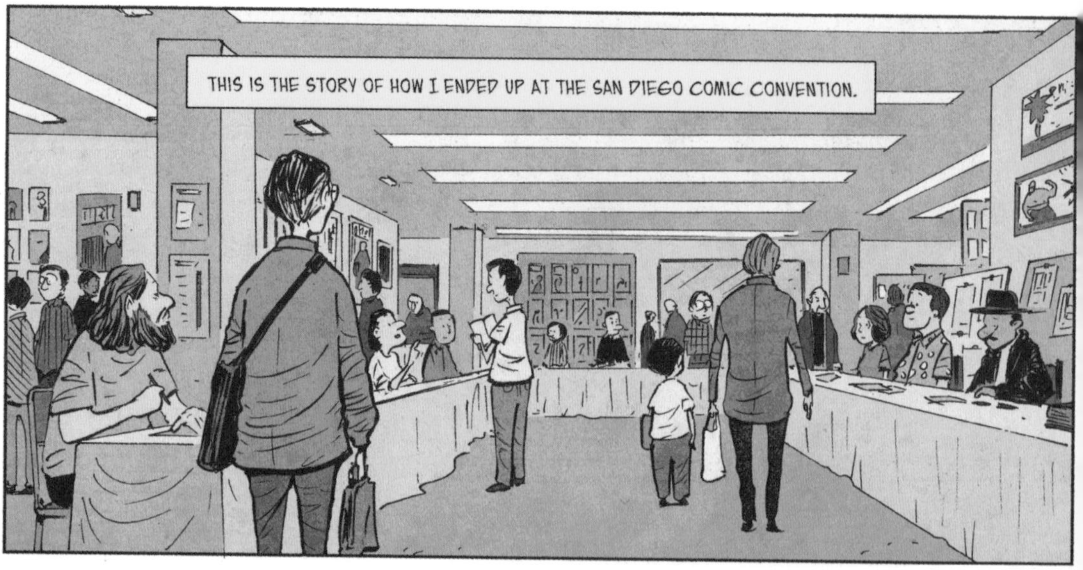
THIS IS THE STORY OF HOW I ENDED UP AT THE SAN DIEGO COMIC CONVENTION.

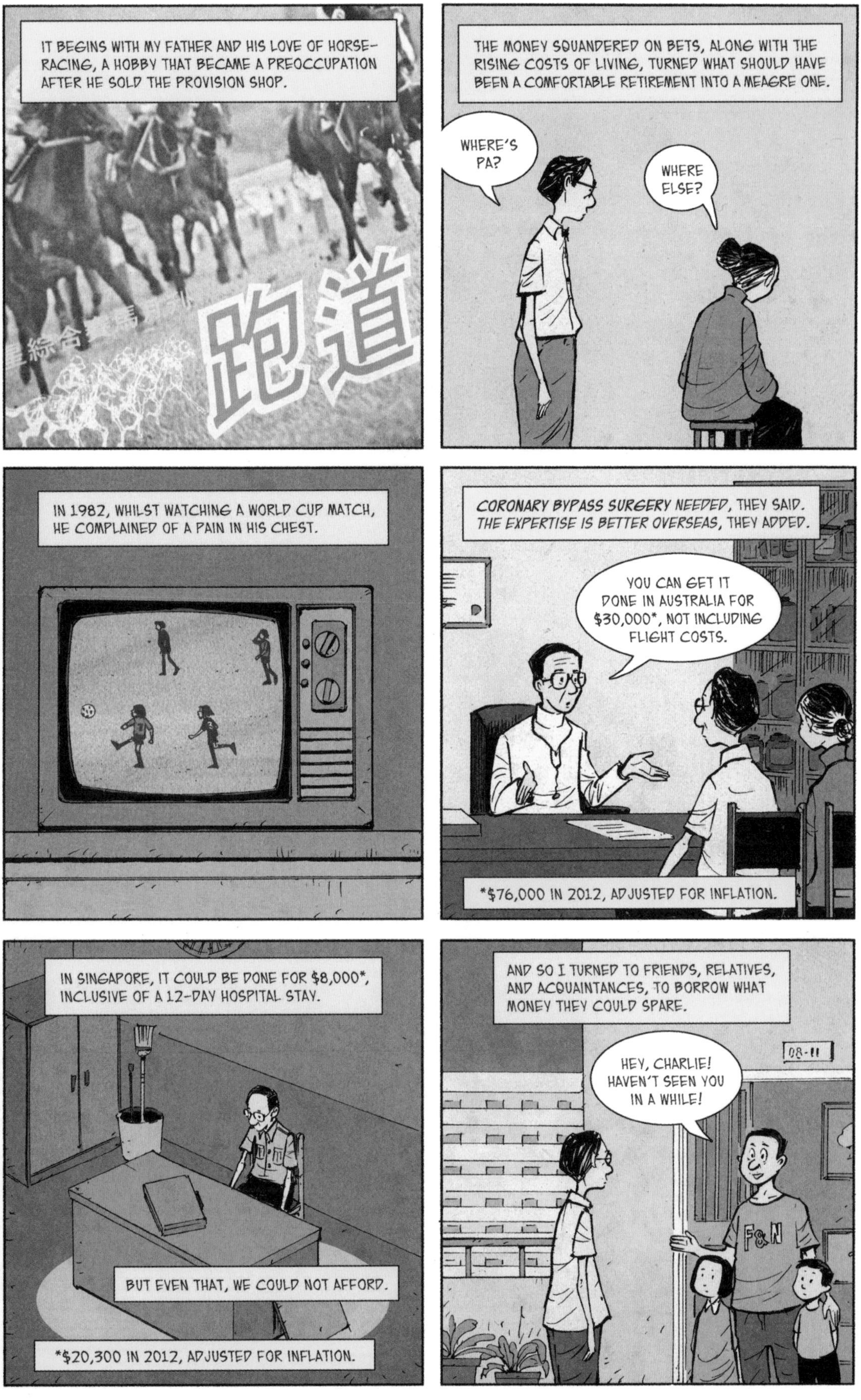
IT BEGINS WITH MY FATHER AND HIS LOVE OF HORSE-RACING, A HOBBY THAT BECAME A PREOCCUPATION AFTER HE SOLD THE PROVISION SHOP.
跑道
THE MONEY SQUANDERED ON BETS, ALONG WITH THE RISING COSTS OF LIVING, TURNED WHAT SHOULD HAVE BEEN A COMFORTABLE RETIREMENT INTO A MEAGRE ONE.
WHERE'S PA?
WHERE ELSE?
IN 1982, WHILST WATCHING A WORLD CUP MATCH, HE COMPLAINED OF A PAIN IN HIS CHEST.
CORONARY BYPASS SURGERY NEEDED, THEY SAID. *THE EXPERTISE IS BETTER OVERSEAS*, THEY ADDED.
YOU CAN GET IT DONE IN AUSTRALIA FOR $30,000*, NOT INCLUDING FLIGHT COSTS.
*$76,000 IN 2012, ADJUSTED FOR INFLATION.
IN SINGAPORE, IT COULD BE DONE FOR $8,000*, INCLUSIVE OF A 12-DAY HOSPITAL STAY.
BUT EVEN THAT, WE COULD NOT AFFORD.
*$20,300 IN 2012, ADJUSTED FOR INFLATION.
AND SO I TURNED TO FRIENDS, RELATIVES, AND ACQUAINTANCES, TO BORROW WHAT MONEY THEY COULD SPARE.
08-11
HEY, CHARLIE! HAVEN'T SEEN YOU IN A WHILE!
F&N

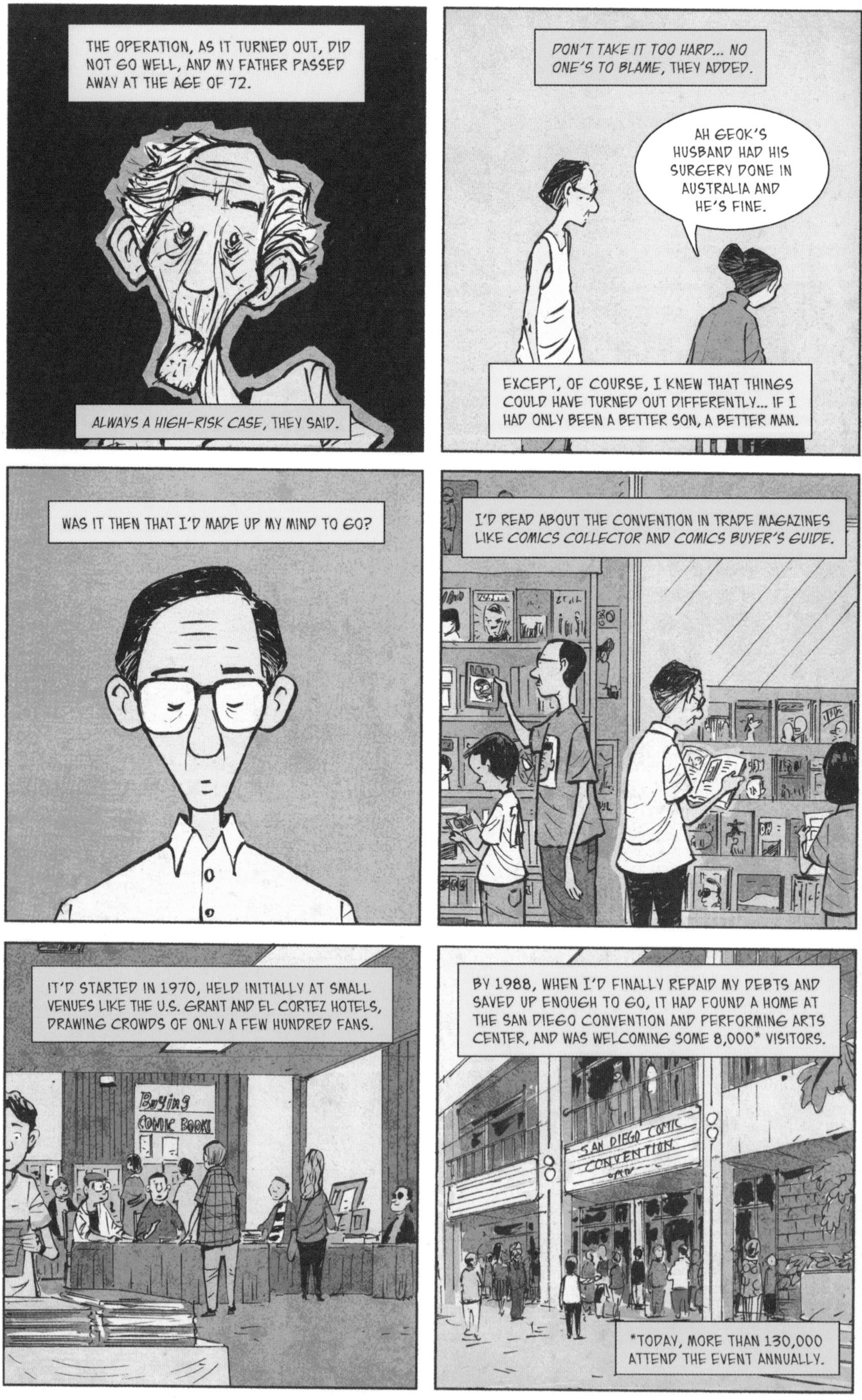
THE OPERATION, AS IT TURNED OUT, DID NOT GO WELL, AND MY FATHER PASSED AWAY AT THE AGE OF 72.
ALWAYS A HIGH-RISK CASE, THEY SAID.
DON'T TAKE IT TOO HARD... NO ONE'S TO BLAME, THEY ADDED.
AH GEOK'S HUSBAND HAD HIS SURGERY DONE IN AUSTRALIA AND HE'S FINE.
EXCEPT, OF COURSE, I KNEW THAT THINGS COULD HAVE TURNED OUT DIFFERENTLY... IF I HAD ONLY BEEN A BETTER SON, A BETTER MAN.
WAS IT THEN THAT I'D MADE UP MY MIND TO GO?
I'D READ ABOUT THE CONVENTION IN TRADE MAGAZINES LIKE COMICS COLLECTOR AND COMICS BUYER'S GUIDE.
IT'D STARTED IN 1970, HELD INITIALLY AT SMALL VENUES LIKE THE U.S. GRANT AND EL CORTEZ HOTELS, DRAWING CROWDS OF ONLY A FEW HUNDRED FANS.
Buying COMIC BOOKS
BY 1988, WHEN I'D FINALLY REPAID MY DEBTS AND SAVED UP ENOUGH TO GO, IT HAD FOUND A HOME AT THE SAN DIEGO CONVENTION AND PERFORMING ARTS CENTER, AND WAS WELCOMING SOME 8,000* VISITORS.
SAN DIEGO COMIC CONVENTION
*TODAY, MORE THAN 130,000 ATTEND THE EVENT ANNUALLY.

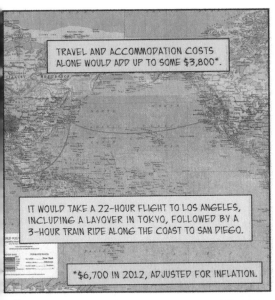

TRAVEL AND ACCOMMODATION COSTS ALONE WOULD ADD UP TO SOME $3,800*.

IT WOULD TAKE A 22-HOUR FLIGHT TO LOS ANGELES, INCLUDING A LAYOVER IN TOKYO, FOLLOWED BY A 3-HOUR TRAIN RIDE ALONG THE COAST TO SAN DIEGO.

*$6,700 IN 2012, ADJUSTED FOR INFLATION.

IT WAS A LOT OF MONEY FOR SOMEONE IN MY CIRCUMSTANCES, BUT I KNEW THAT IT WAS SOMETHING I *HAD* TO DO.

SO I STARTED TO PUT TOGETHER A PORTFOLIO OF MY BEST WORK.

BECAUSE AMERICA WAS THE PROMISED LAND.

SINGAPORE WAS TOO SMALL, OUR POPULATION OF 3 MILLION LACKING THE *CRITICAL MASS* TO SUPPORT A REAL COMICS INDUSTRY.

THE FEDERATION IS IMPORTANT. WITHOUT THIS ECONOMIC BASE, SINGAPORE WOULD *NOT* SURVIVE.

READERS HERE WOULD NEVER APPRECIATE LOCAL COMICS. THEY WOULD ALWAYS SEE US AS POOR IMITATORS OF THOSE FROM THE U.S., JAPAN, HONG KONG AND TAIWAN.

WOULD YOU LIKE TO CARRY MY COMIC IN YOUR SHOP?

NAH, IT'S OK.

AND MOST OF ALL... I KNEW THAT, AWAY FROM THIS STERILE COUNTRY AND CULTURAL BACKWATER WITH ITS CLOSED AND SHALLOW MINDS, I WOULD AT LAST BE ABLE TO FIND OTHER MEMBERS OF MY OWN TRIBE.

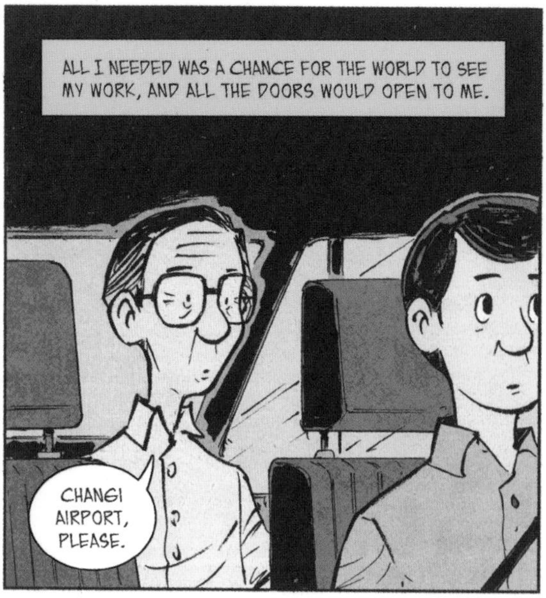
ALL I NEEDED WAS A CHANCE FOR THE WORLD TO SEE MY WORK, AND ALL THE DOORS WOULD OPEN TO ME.
CHANGI AIRPORT, PLEASE.

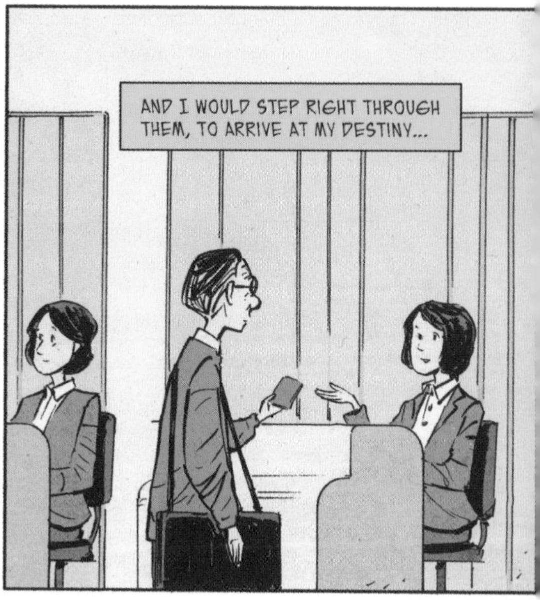
AND I WOULD STEP RIGHT THROUGH THEM, TO ARRIVE AT MY DESTINY...

CALLING OUT TO ME FROM FAR ACROSS THE PACIFIC, LIKE A SIREN SONG.

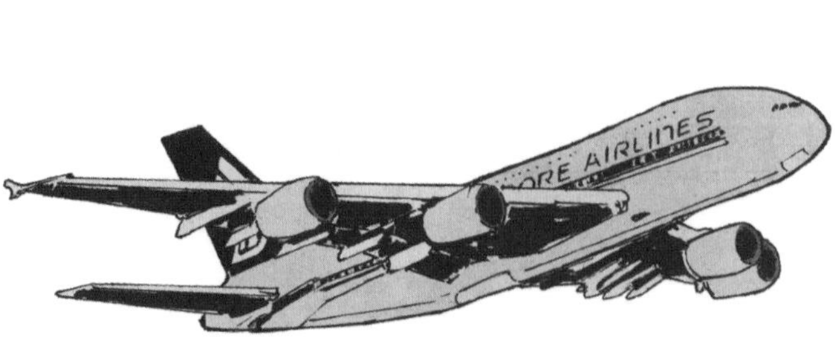
ORE AIRLINES

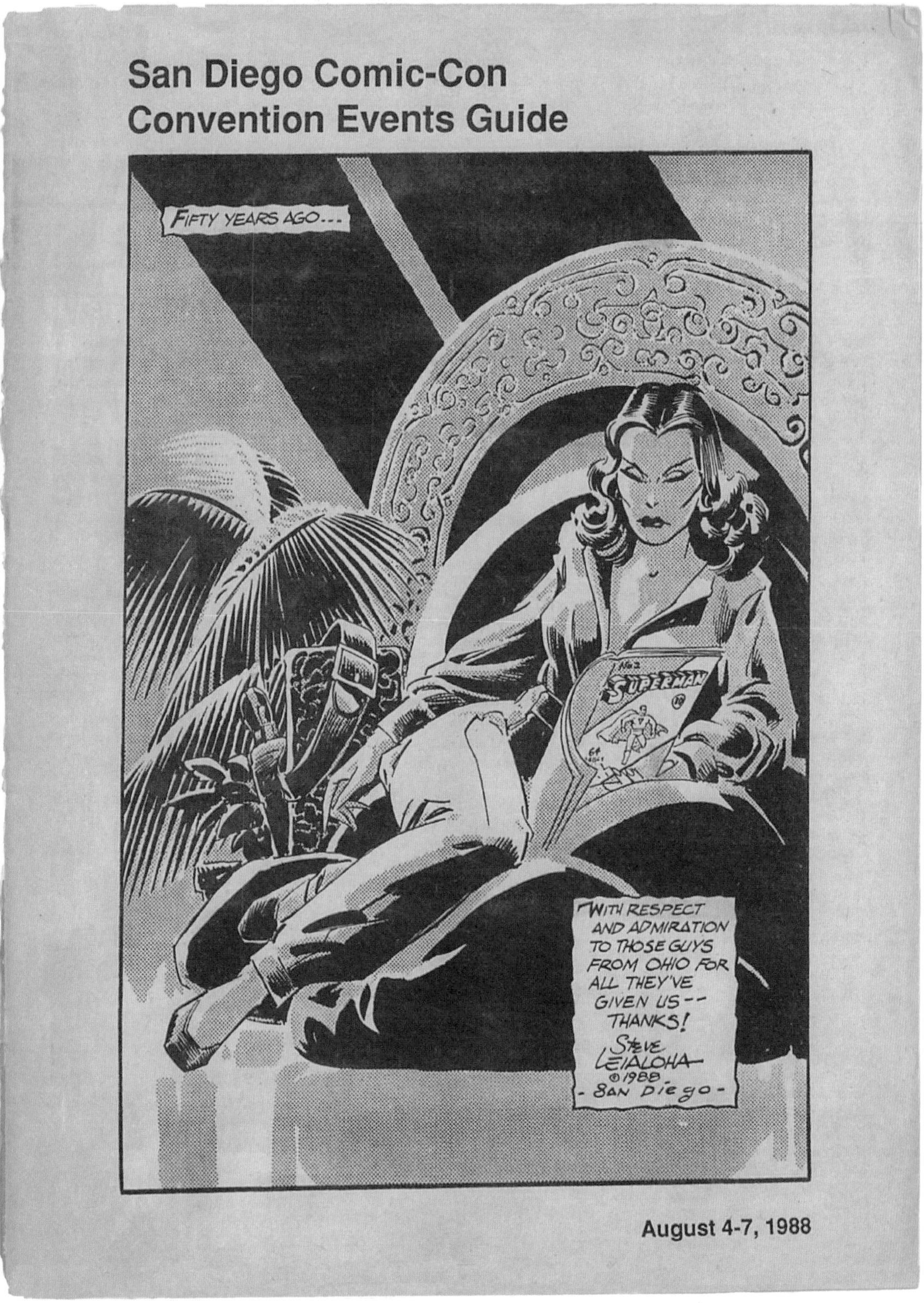
San Diego Comic-Con
Convention Events Guide
FIFTY YEARS AGO...
No. 2
SUPERMAN
WITH RESPECT AND ADMIRATION TO THOSE GUYS FROM OHIO FOR ALL THEY'VE GIVEN US -- THANKS!
STEVE LEIALOHA ©1988 - SAN DIEGO -
August 4-7, 1988

Above
SAN DIEGO COMIC-CON
Events Guide
1988
Art by Steve Leialoha
Collection of Chan Hock Chye

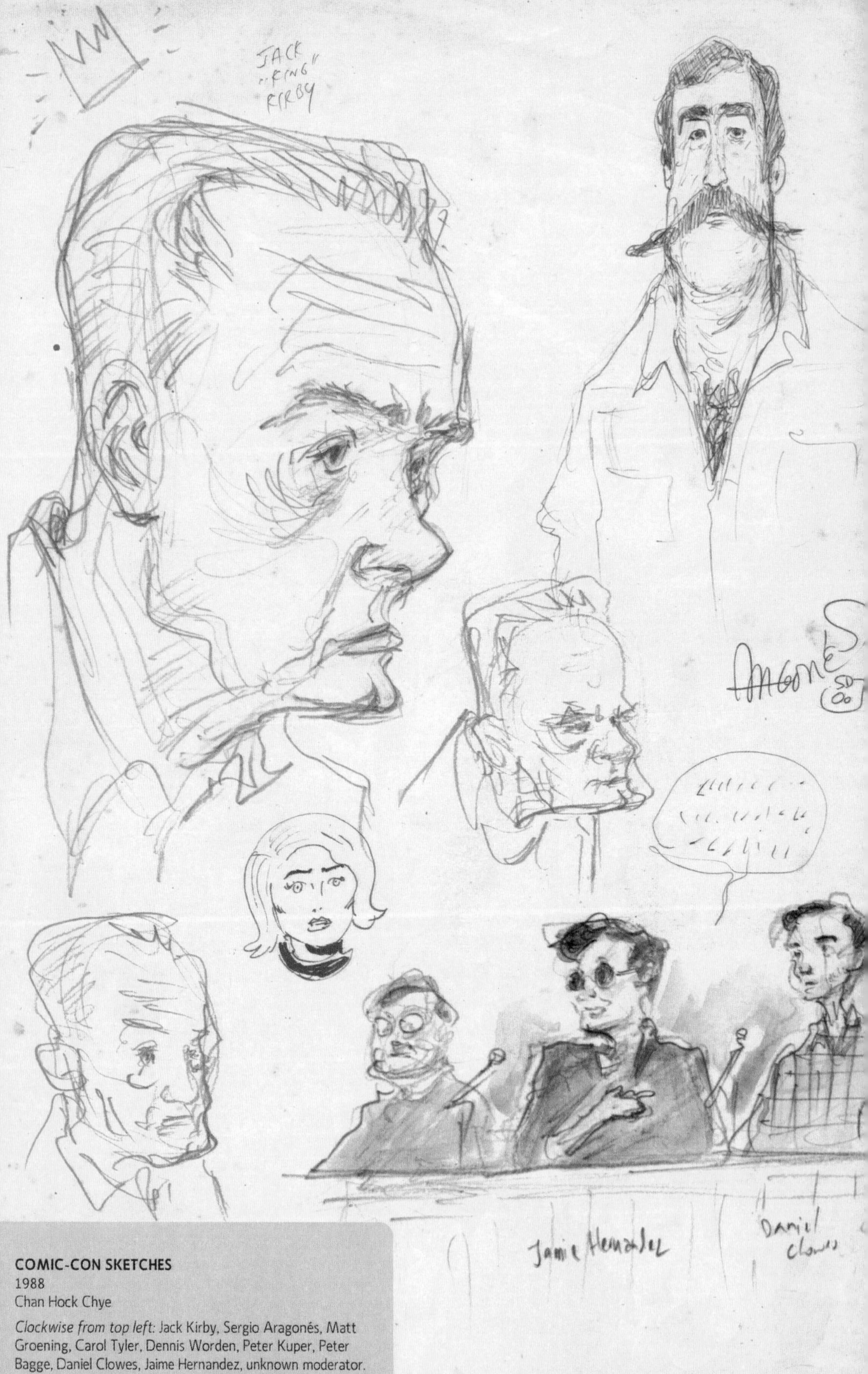
JACK "KING" KIRBY
Jamie Hernandez
Daniel Clowes

COMIC-CON SKETCHES
1988
Chan Hock Chye

Clockwise from top left: Jack Kirby, Sergio Aragonés, Matt Groening, Carol Tyler, Dennis Worden, Peter Kuper, Peter Bagge, Daniel Clowes, Jaime Hernandez, unknown moderator.

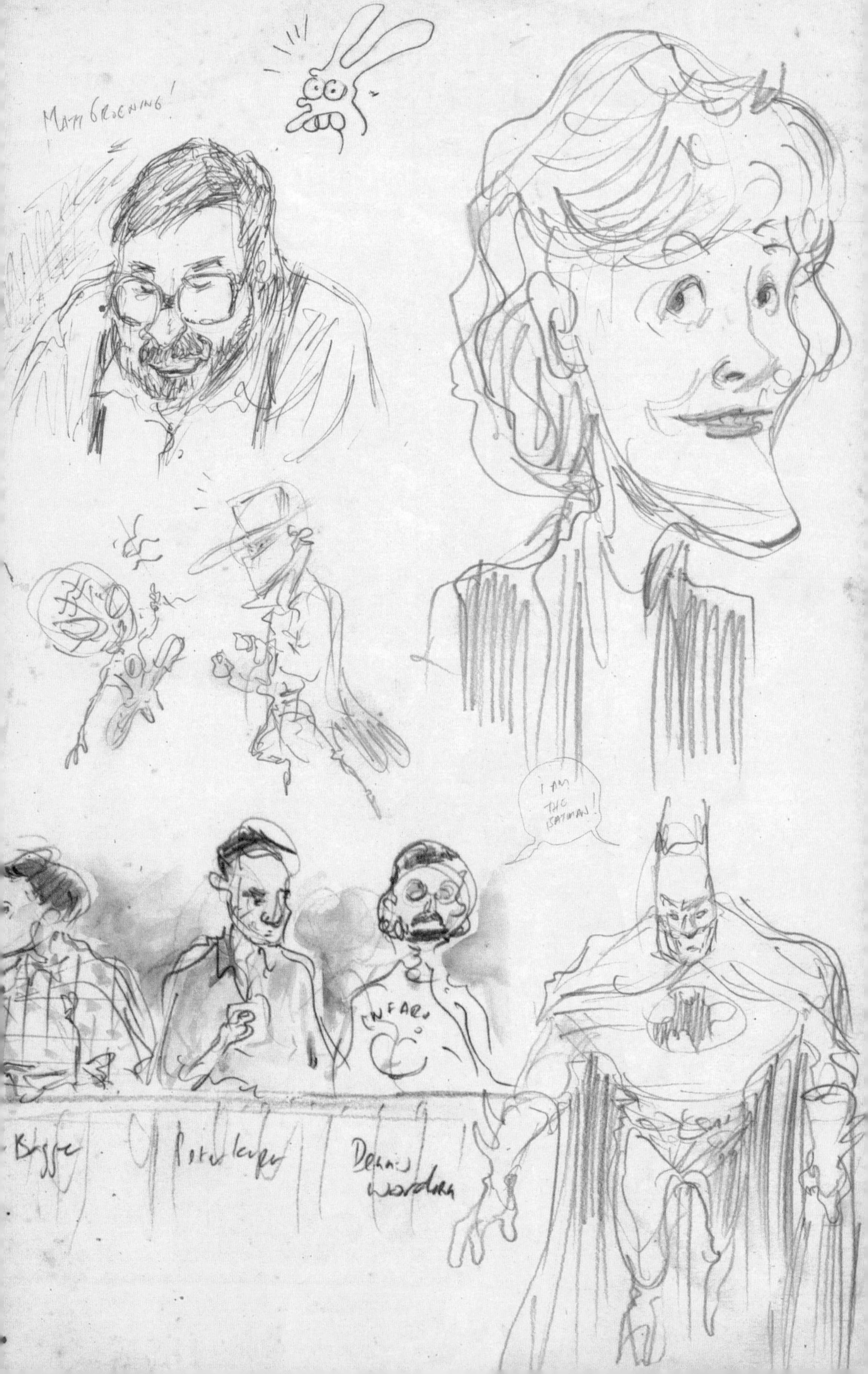
MATT GROENING!
I AM THE BATMAN!
Peter Kuper
Dennis Worden

THE KING OF COMICS

PART ONE

by Charlie Chan

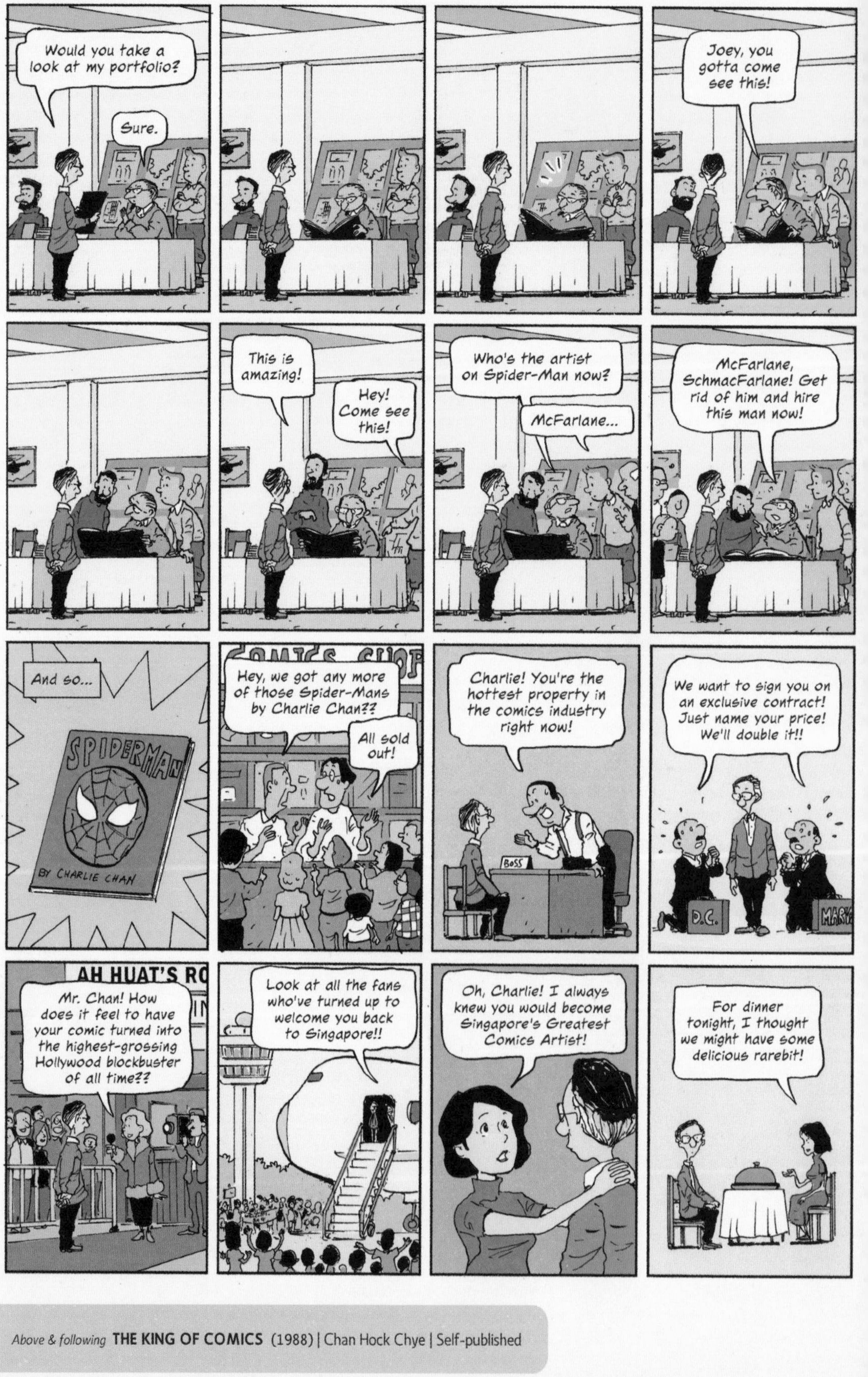

Would you take a look at my portfolio?
Sure.
Joey, you gotta come see this!
This is amazing!
Hey! Come see this!
Who's the artist on Spider-Man now?
McFarlane...
McFarlane, SchmacFarlane! Get rid of him and hire this man now!
And so...
SPIDERMAN
BY CHARLIE CHAN
Hey, we got any more of those Spider-Mans by Charlie Chan??
All sold out!
Charlie! You're the hottest property in the comics industry right now!
BOSS
We want to sign you on an exclusive contract! Just name your price! We'll double it!!
D.C.
AH HUAT'S RO
Mr. Chan! How does it feel to have your comic turned into the highest-grossing Hollywood blockbuster of all time??
Look at all the fans who've turned up to welcome you back to Singapore!!
Oh, Charlie! I always knew you would become Singapore's Greatest Comics Artist!
For dinner tonight, I thought we might have some delicious rarebit!

Above & following **THE KING OF COMICS** (1988) | Chan Hock Chye | Self-published

THE KING OF COMICS

PART TWO
by Charlie Chan

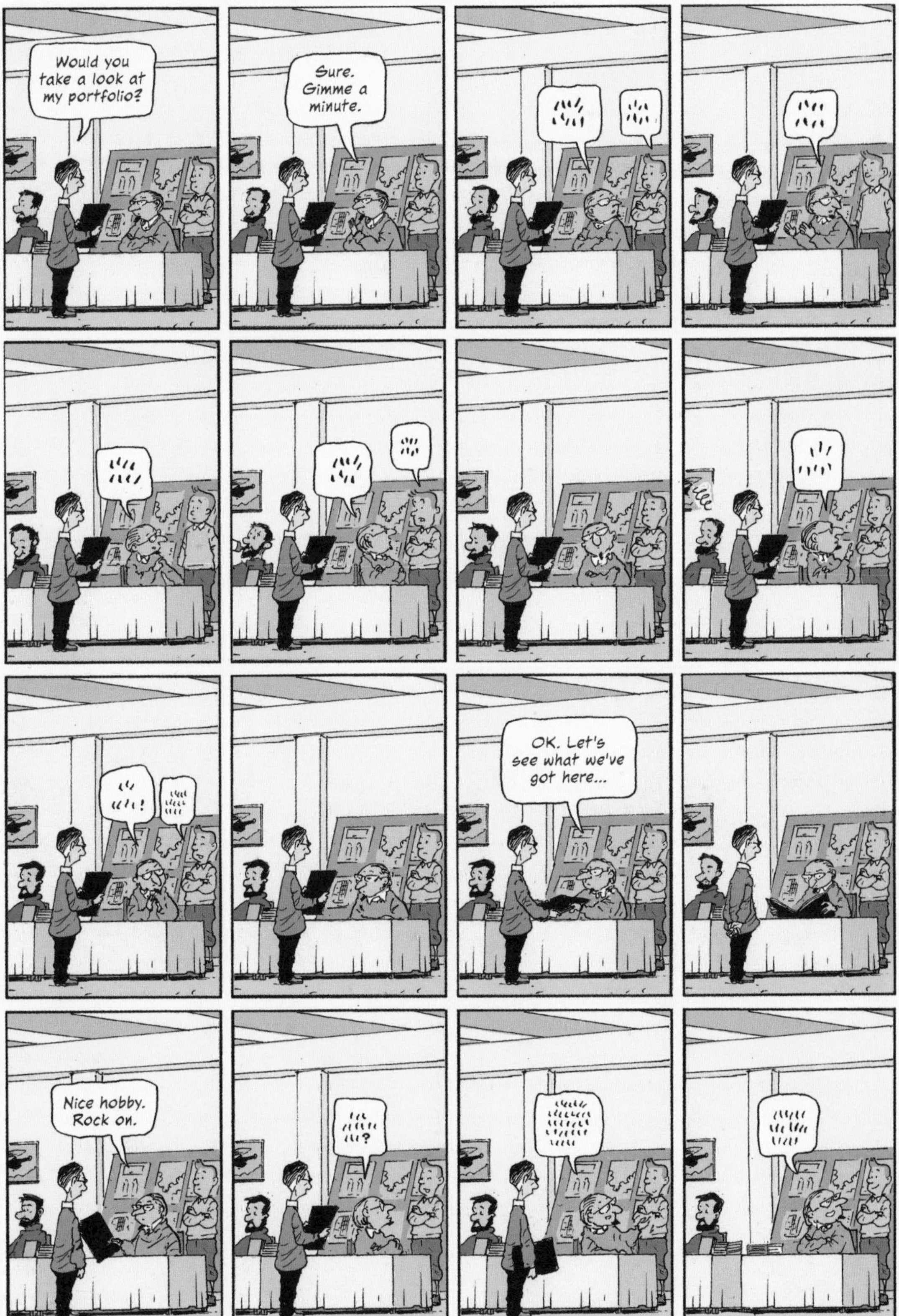

Would you take a look at my portfolio?
Sure. Gimme a minute.
OK. Let's see what we've got here...
Nice hobby. Rock on.

THE KING OF COMICS

PART THREE
by Charlie Chan

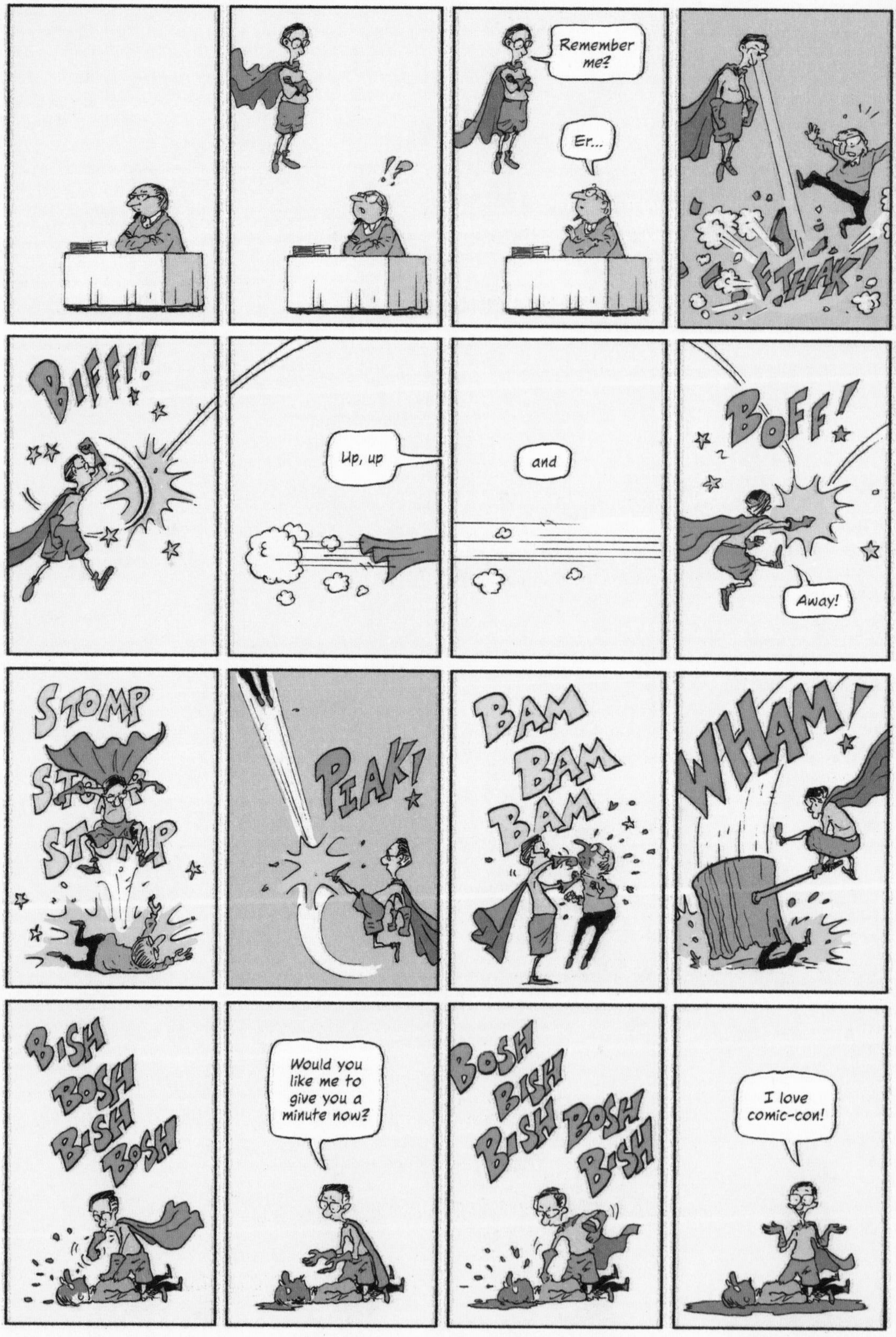

Remember me?
Er...
FTHAK!
BIFF!
Up, up
and
BOFF!
Away!
STOMP
PIAK!
BAM
BAM
BAM
WHAM!
BISH
BOSH
BISH
BOSH
Would you like me to give you a minute now?
BOSH
BISH
BISH
BOSH
BISH
I love comic-con!

Chan's San Diego Comic-Con experience turned out to be a mixture of excitement and disappointments. He would write that "*It had given me a glimpse of what comics and a comics community could aspire to be. But I remained an outsider looking in, unable to become a member of the club, however much I longed to do so.*"

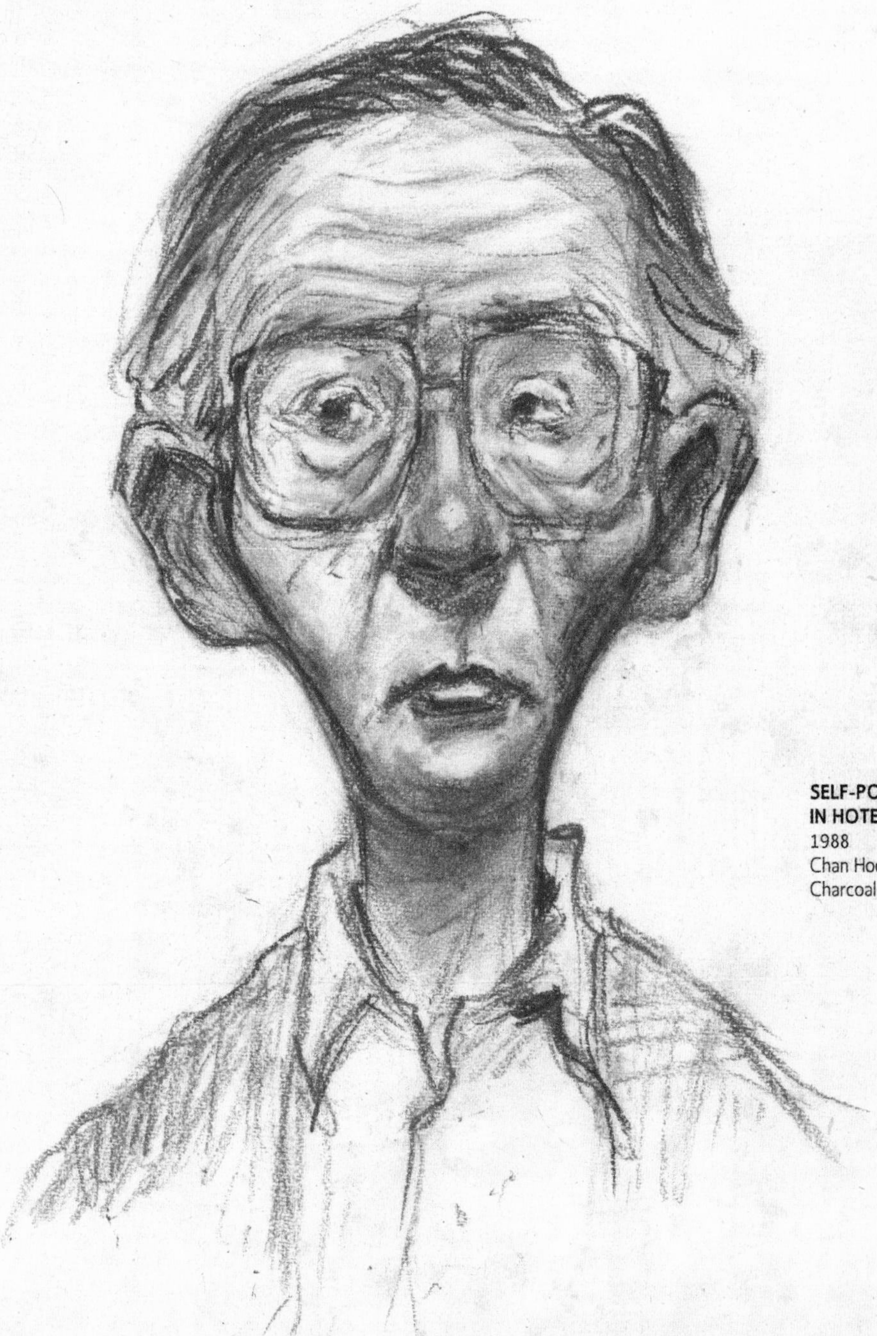

SELF-PORTRAIT IN HOTEL ROOM
1988
Chan Hock Chye
Charcoal on paper

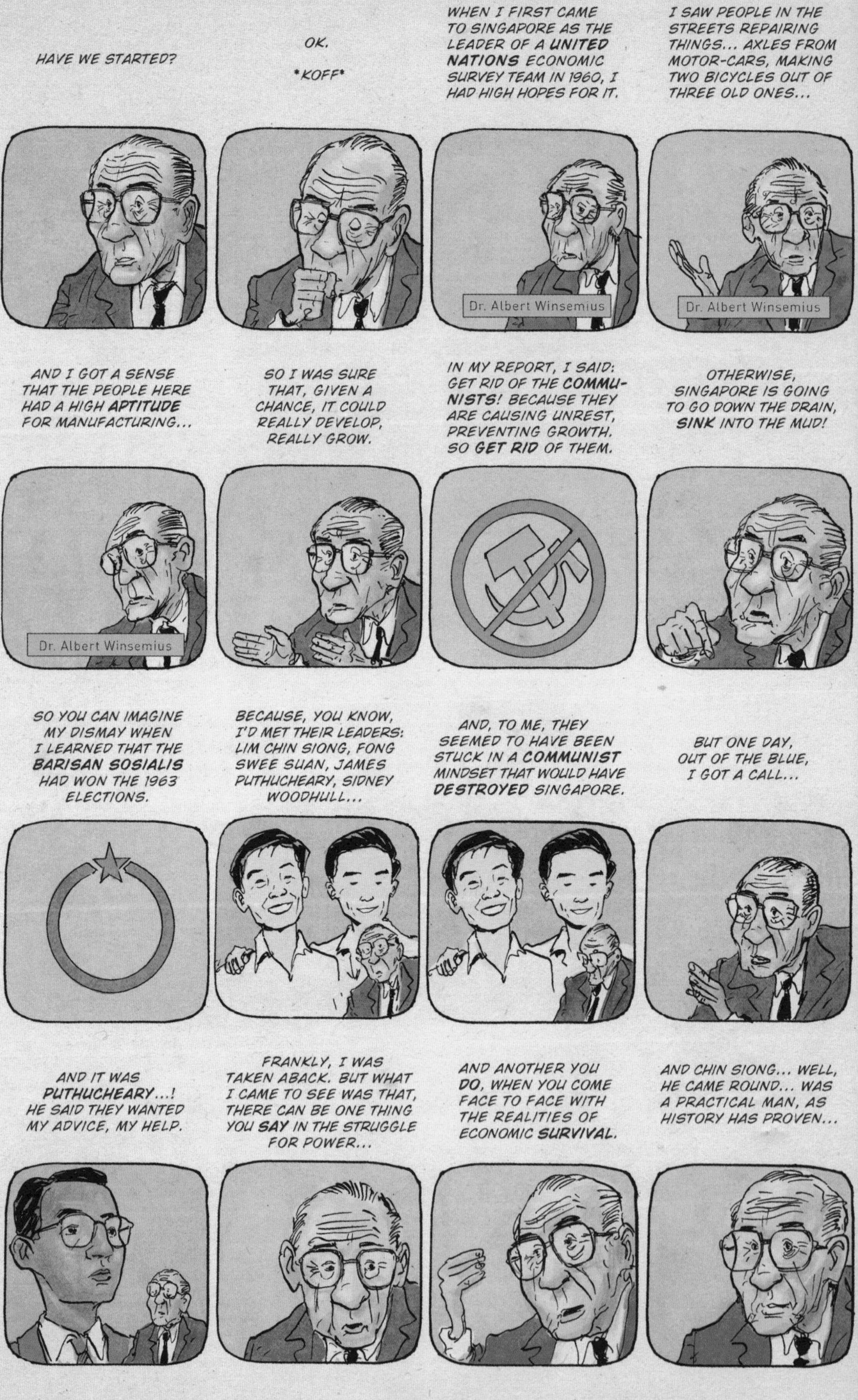
HAVE WE STARTED?
OK.
KOFF
WHEN I FIRST CAME TO SINGAPORE AS THE LEADER OF A UNITED NATIONS ECONOMIC SURVEY TEAM IN 1960, I HAD HIGH HOPES FOR IT.
Dr. Albert Winsemius
I SAW PEOPLE IN THE STREETS REPAIRING THINGS... AXLES FROM MOTOR-CARS, MAKING TWO BICYCLES OUT OF THREE OLD ONES...
Dr. Albert Winsemius
AND I GOT A SENSE THAT THE PEOPLE HERE HAD A HIGH APTITUDE FOR MANUFACTURING...
Dr. Albert Winsemius
SO I WAS SURE THAT, GIVEN A CHANCE, IT COULD REALLY DEVELOP, REALLY GROW.
IN MY REPORT, I SAID: GET RID OF THE COMMUNISTS! BECAUSE THEY ARE CAUSING UNREST, PREVENTING GROWTH. SO GET RID OF THEM.
OTHERWISE, SINGAPORE IS GOING TO GO DOWN THE DRAIN, SINK INTO THE MUD!
SO YOU CAN IMAGINE MY DISMAY WHEN I LEARNED THAT THE BARISAN SOSIALIS HAD WON THE 1963 ELECTIONS.
BECAUSE, YOU KNOW, I'D MET THEIR LEADERS: LIM CHIN SIONG, FONG SWEE SUAN, JAMES PUTHUCHEARY, SIDNEY WOODHULL...
AND, TO ME, THEY SEEMED TO HAVE BEEN STUCK IN A COMMUNIST MINDSET THAT WOULD HAVE DESTROYED SINGAPORE.
BUT ONE DAY, OUT OF THE BLUE, I GOT A CALL...
AND IT WAS PUTHUCHEARY...! HE SAID THEY WANTED MY ADVICE, MY HELP.
FRANKLY, I WAS TAKEN ABACK. BUT WHAT I CAME TO SEE WAS THAT, THERE CAN BE ONE THING YOU SAY IN THE STRUGGLE FOR POWER...
AND ANOTHER YOU DO, WHEN YOU COME FACE TO FACE WITH THE REALITIES OF ECONOMIC SURVIVAL.
AND CHIN SIONG... WELL, HE CAME ROUND... WAS A PRACTICAL MAN, AS HISTORY HAS PROVEN...

AND THAT WAS JUST A **SNIPPET** OF OUR INTERVIEW WITH DR. WINSEMIUS...

MUCH MORE COMING UP LATER TONIGHT, FROM THE MAN THEY CALL THE **FOUNDING FATHER** OF SINGAPORE'S ECONOMY...

...AS PART OF OUR CELEBRATION OF OUR GREAT LEADER LIM CHIN SIONG'S **63**RD BIRTHDAY!

WHO'S STILL LOOKING AS **SUAVE** AS EVER! DON'T YOU THINK, SIMON?

DAYS OF AUGUST

BY
CHAN HOCK CHYE

HA HA HA, YOU KNOW IT, LISA! MEANWHILE, ALONG ORCHARD ROAD, BIT OF A TRAFFIC SNARL BUILDING UP WITH THE EVENING RUSH HOUR...

OTHERWISE, IT'S BEEN YET ANOTHER **BEAUTIFUL DAY** HERE ON OUR LITTLE ISLAND PARADISE!

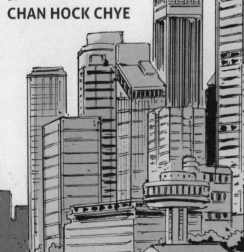

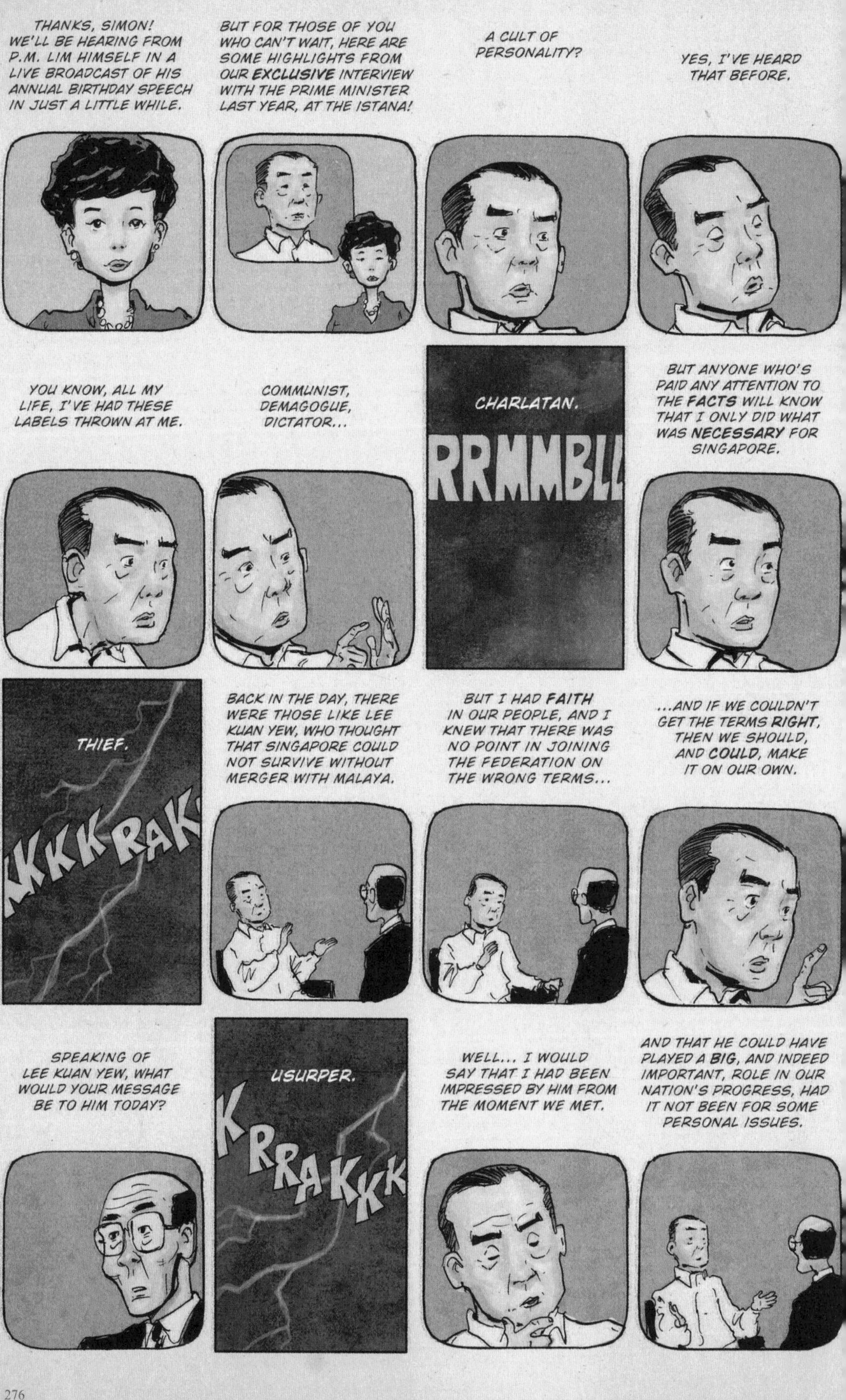
THANKS, SIMON! WE'LL BE HEARING FROM P.M. LIM HIMSELF IN A LIVE BROADCAST OF HIS ANNUAL BIRTHDAY SPEECH IN JUST A LITTLE WHILE.
BUT FOR THOSE OF YOU WHO CAN'T WAIT, HERE ARE SOME HIGHLIGHTS FROM OUR **EXCLUSIVE** INTERVIEW WITH THE PRIME MINISTER LAST YEAR, AT THE ISTANA!
A CULT OF PERSONALITY?
YES, I'VE HEARD THAT BEFORE.
YOU KNOW, ALL MY LIFE, I'VE HAD THESE LABELS THROWN AT ME.
COMMUNIST, DEMAGOGUE, DICTATOR...
CHARLATAN.
RRMMBLL
BUT ANYONE WHO'S PAID ANY ATTENTION TO THE **FACTS** WILL KNOW THAT I ONLY DID WHAT WAS **NECESSARY** FOR SINGAPORE.
THIEF.
KKKKRAK
BACK IN THE DAY, THERE WERE THOSE LIKE LEE KUAN YEW, WHO THOUGHT THAT SINGAPORE COULD NOT SURVIVE WITHOUT MERGER WITH MALAYA.
BUT I HAD **FAITH** IN OUR PEOPLE, AND I KNEW THAT THERE WAS NO POINT IN JOINING THE FEDERATION ON THE WRONG TERMS...
...AND IF WE COULDN'T GET THE TERMS **RIGHT**, THEN WE SHOULD, AND **COULD**, MAKE IT ON OUR OWN.
SPEAKING OF LEE KUAN YEW, WHAT WOULD YOUR MESSAGE BE TO HIM TODAY?
USURPER.
KRRAKKK
WELL... I WOULD SAY THAT I HAD BEEN IMPRESSED BY HIM FROM THE MOMENT WE MET.
AND THAT HE COULD HAVE PLAYED A **BIG**, AND INDEED IMPORTANT, ROLE IN OUR NATION'S PROGRESS, HAD IT NOT BEEN FOR SOME PERSONAL ISSUES.

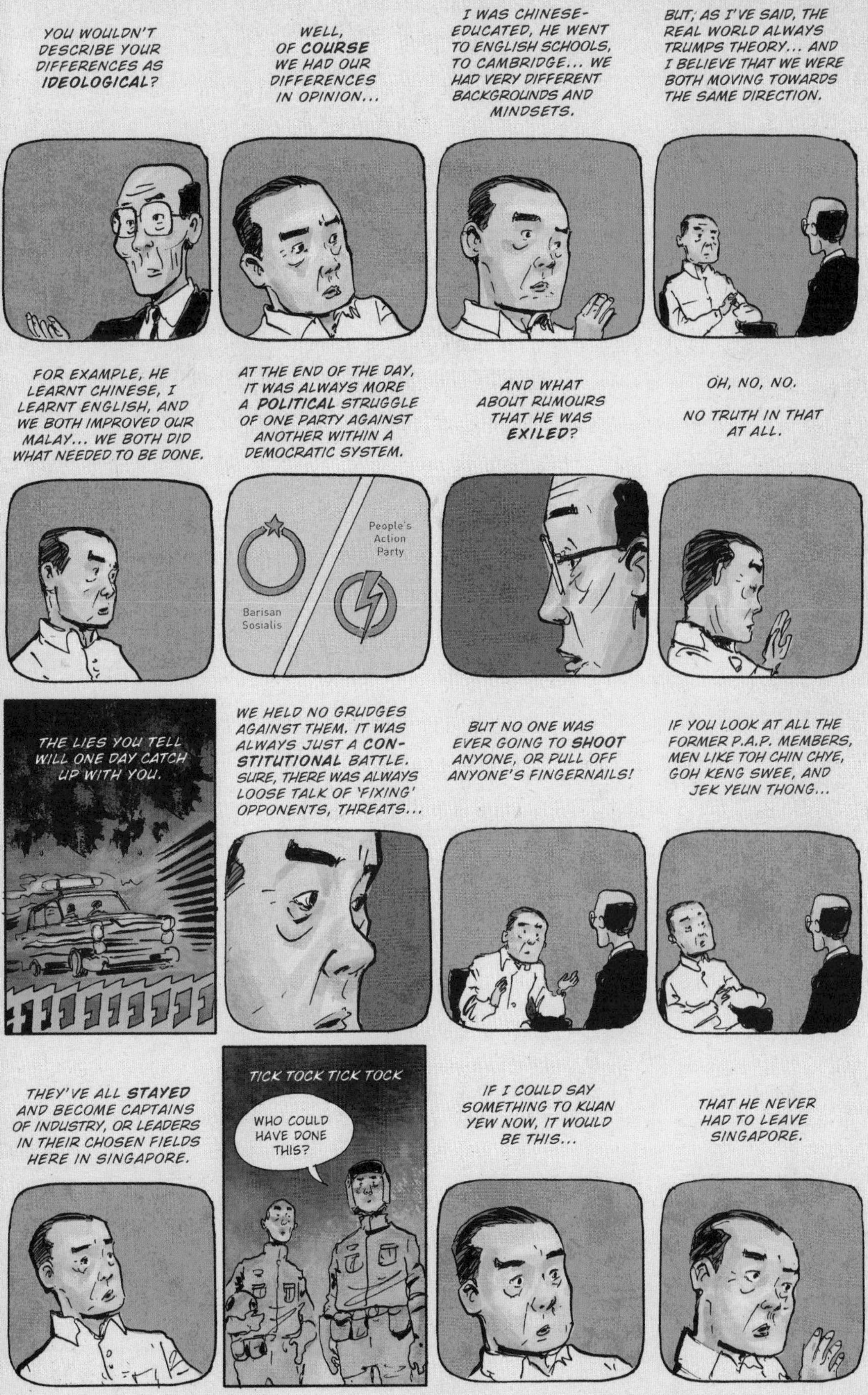
YOU WOULDN'T DESCRIBE YOUR DIFFERENCES AS IDEOLOGICAL?
WELL, OF COURSE WE HAD OUR DIFFERENCES IN OPINION...
I WAS CHINESE-EDUCATED, HE WENT TO ENGLISH SCHOOLS, TO CAMBRIDGE... WE HAD VERY DIFFERENT BACKGROUNDS AND MINDSETS.
BUT, AS I'VE SAID, THE REAL WORLD ALWAYS TRUMPS THEORY... AND I BELIEVE THAT WE WERE BOTH MOVING TOWARDS THE SAME DIRECTION.
FOR EXAMPLE, HE LEARNT CHINESE, I LEARNT ENGLISH, AND WE BOTH IMPROVED OUR MALAY... WE BOTH DID WHAT NEEDED TO BE DONE.
AT THE END OF THE DAY, IT WAS ALWAYS MORE A POLITICAL STRUGGLE OF ONE PARTY AGAINST ANOTHER WITHIN A DEMOCRATIC SYSTEM.
Barisan Sosialis
People's Action Party
AND WHAT ABOUT RUMOURS THAT HE WAS EXILED?
OH, NO, NO.
NO TRUTH IN THAT AT ALL.
THE LIES YOU TELL WILL ONE DAY CATCH UP WITH YOU.
WE HELD NO GRUDGES AGAINST THEM. IT WAS ALWAYS JUST A CONSTITUTIONAL BATTLE. SURE, THERE WAS ALWAYS LOOSE TALK OF 'FIXING' OPPONENTS, THREATS...
BUT NO ONE WAS EVER GOING TO SHOOT ANYONE, OR PULL OFF ANYONE'S FINGERNAILS!
IF YOU LOOK AT ALL THE FORMER P.A.P. MEMBERS, MEN LIKE TOH CHIN CHYE, GOH KENG SWEE, AND JEK YEUN THONG...
THEY'VE ALL STAYED AND BECOME CAPTAINS OF INDUSTRY, OR LEADERS IN THEIR CHOSEN FIELDS HERE IN SINGAPORE.
TICK TOCK TICK TOCK
WHO COULD HAVE DONE THIS?
IF I COULD SAY SOMETHING TO KUAN YEW NOW, IT WOULD BE THIS...
THAT HE NEVER HAD TO LEAVE SINGAPORE.

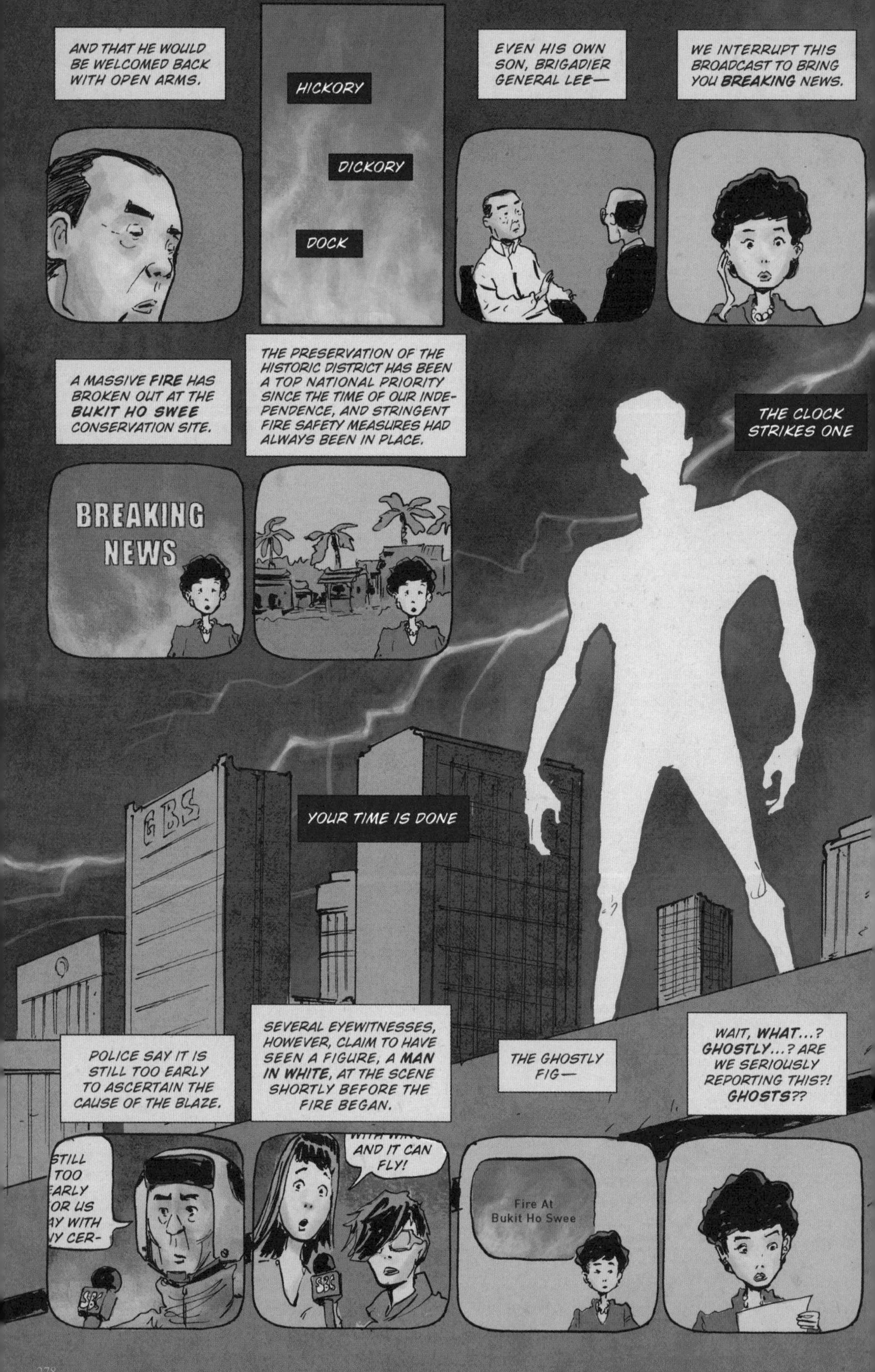

AND THAT HE WOULD BE WELCOMED BACK WITH OPEN ARMS.

HICKORY

DICKORY

DOCK

EVEN HIS OWN SON, BRIGADIER GENERAL LEE—

WE INTERRUPT THIS BROADCAST TO BRING YOU **BREAKING NEWS**.

A MASSIVE **FIRE** HAS BROKEN OUT AT THE **BUKIT HO SWEE** CONSERVATION SITE.

THE PRESERVATION OF THE HISTORIC DISTRICT HAS BEEN A TOP NATIONAL PRIORITY SINCE THE TIME OF OUR INDEPENDENCE, AND STRINGENT FIRE SAFETY MEASURES HAD ALWAYS BEEN IN PLACE.

THE CLOCK STRIKES ONE

YOUR TIME IS DONE

POLICE SAY IT IS STILL TOO EARLY TO ASCERTAIN THE CAUSE OF THE BLAZE.

SEVERAL EYEWITNESSES, HOWEVER, CLAIM TO HAVE SEEN A FIGURE, A **MAN IN WHITE**, AT THE SCENE SHORTLY BEFORE THE FIRE BEGAN.

THE GHOSTLY FIG—

WAIT, **WHAT**...? GHOSTLY...? ARE WE SERIOUSLY REPORTING THIS?! GHOSTS??

STILL TOO EARLY FOR US AY WITH NY CER-

AND IT CAN FLY!

Fire At Bukit Ho Swee

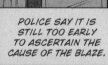

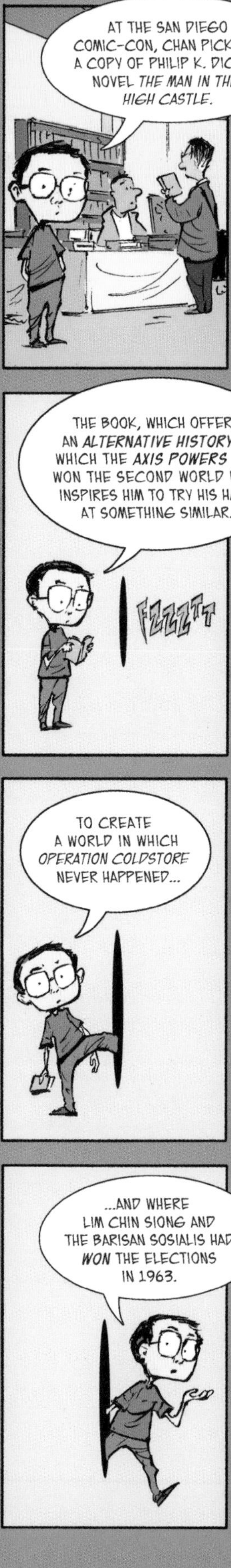
AT THE SAN DIEGO COMIC-CON, CHAN PICKS UP A COPY OF PHILIP K. DICK'S NOVEL *THE MAN IN THE HIGH CASTLE*.
THE BOOK, WHICH OFFERS AN *ALTERNATIVE HISTORY* IN WHICH THE *AXIS POWERS* HAD WON THE SECOND WORLD WAR, INSPIRES HIM TO TRY HIS HAND AT SOMETHING SIMILAR.
FZZZTT
TO CREATE A WORLD IN WHICH *OPERATION COLDSTORE* NEVER HAPPENED...
...AND WHERE LIM CHIN SIONG AND THE BARISAN SOSIALIS HAD *WON* THE ELECTIONS IN 1963.

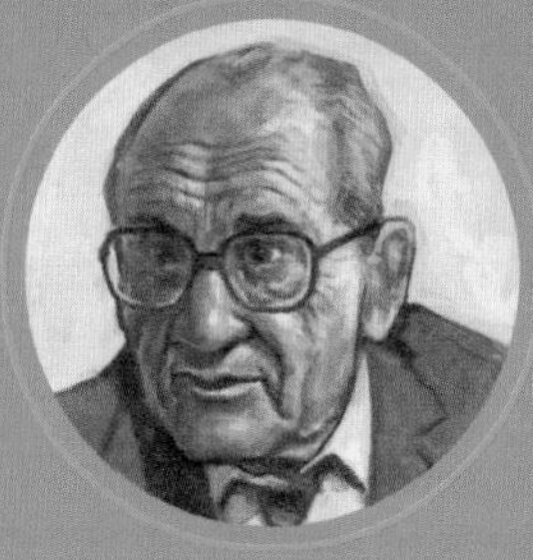

ALBERT WINSEMIUS
Dutch Economist

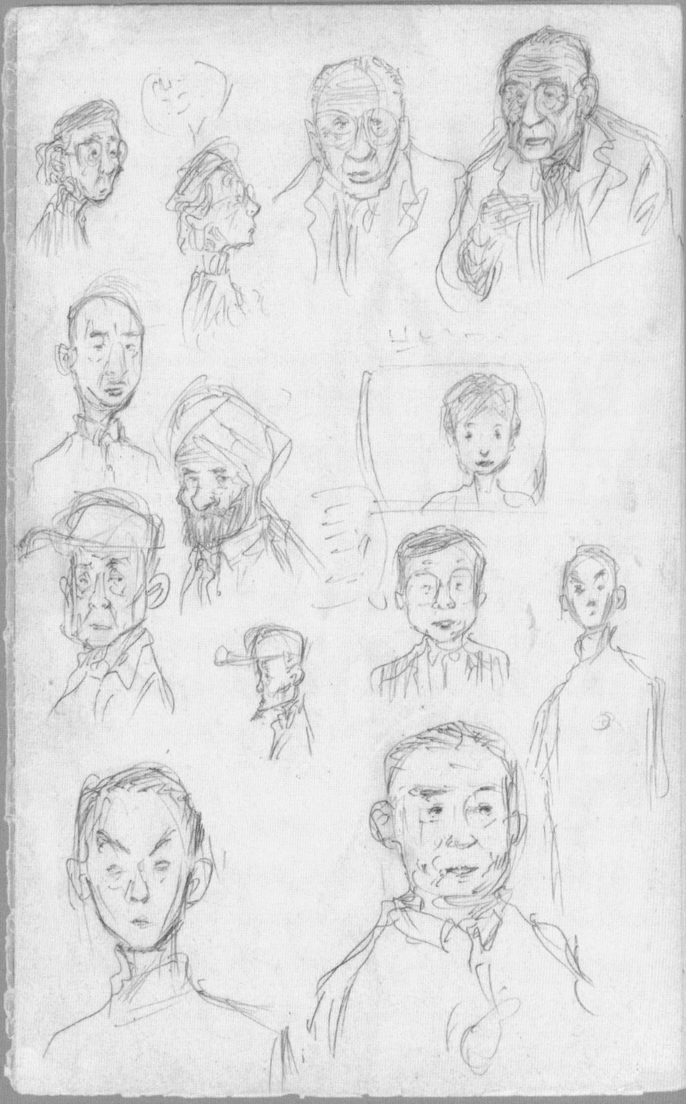

LIM CHIN SIONG

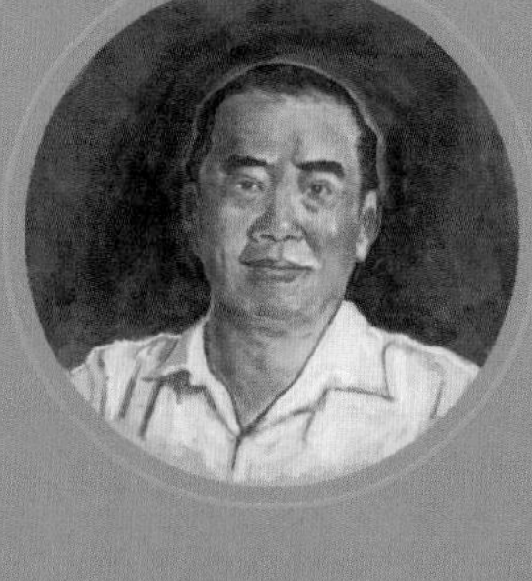

Above
DAYS OF AUGUST
Character Sketches
1988
Chan Hock Chye

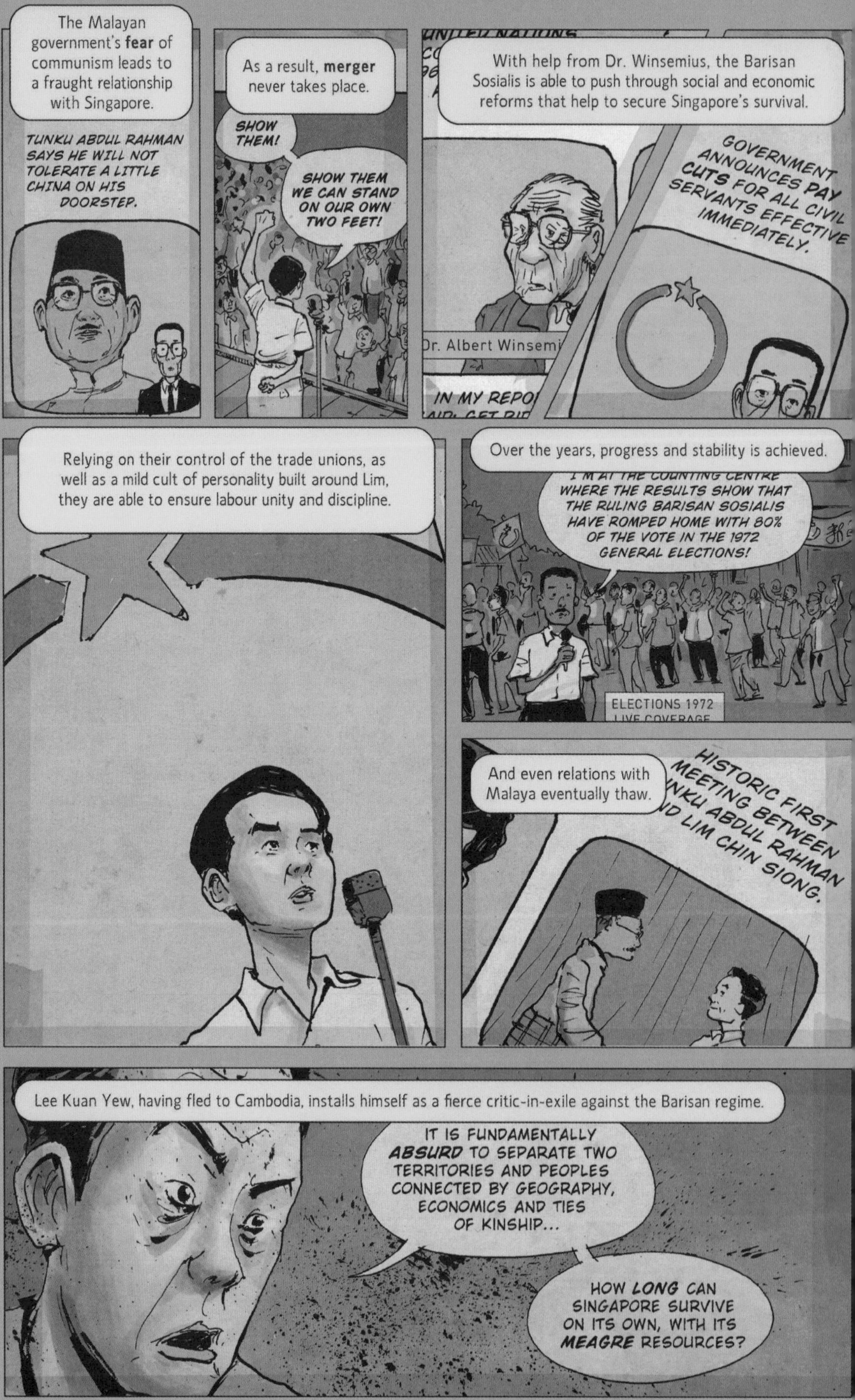
The Malayan government's **fear** of communism leads to a fraught relationship with Singapore.
TUNKU ABDUL RAHMAN SAYS HE WILL NOT TOLERATE A LITTLE CHINA ON HIS DOORSTEP.
As a result, **merger** never takes place.
SHOW THEM!
SHOW THEM WE CAN STAND ON OUR OWN TWO FEET!
With help from Dr. Winsemius, the Barisan Sosialis is able to push through social and economic reforms that help to secure Singapore's survival.
GOVERNMENT ANNOUNCES PAY CUTS FOR ALL CIVIL SERVANTS EFFECTIVE IMMEDIATELY.
Relying on their control of the trade unions, as well as a mild cult of personality built around Lim, they are able to ensure labour unity and discipline.
Over the years, progress and stability is achieved.
I'M AT THE COUNTING CENTRE WHERE THE RESULTS SHOW THAT THE RULING BARISAN SOSIALIS HAVE ROMPED HOME WITH 80% OF THE VOTE IN THE 1972 GENERAL ELECTIONS!
ELECTIONS 1972
And even relations with Malaya eventually thaw.
HISTORIC FIRST MEETING BETWEEN
Lee Kuan Yew, having fled to Cambodia, installs himself as a fierce critic-in-exile against the Barisan regime.
IT IS FUNDAMENTALLY ABSURD TO SEPARATE TWO TERRITORIES AND PEOPLES CONNECTED BY GEOGRAPHY, ECONOMICS AND TIES OF KINSHIP...
HOW LONG CAN SINGAPORE SURVIVE ON ITS OWN, WITH ITS MEAGRE RESOURCES?

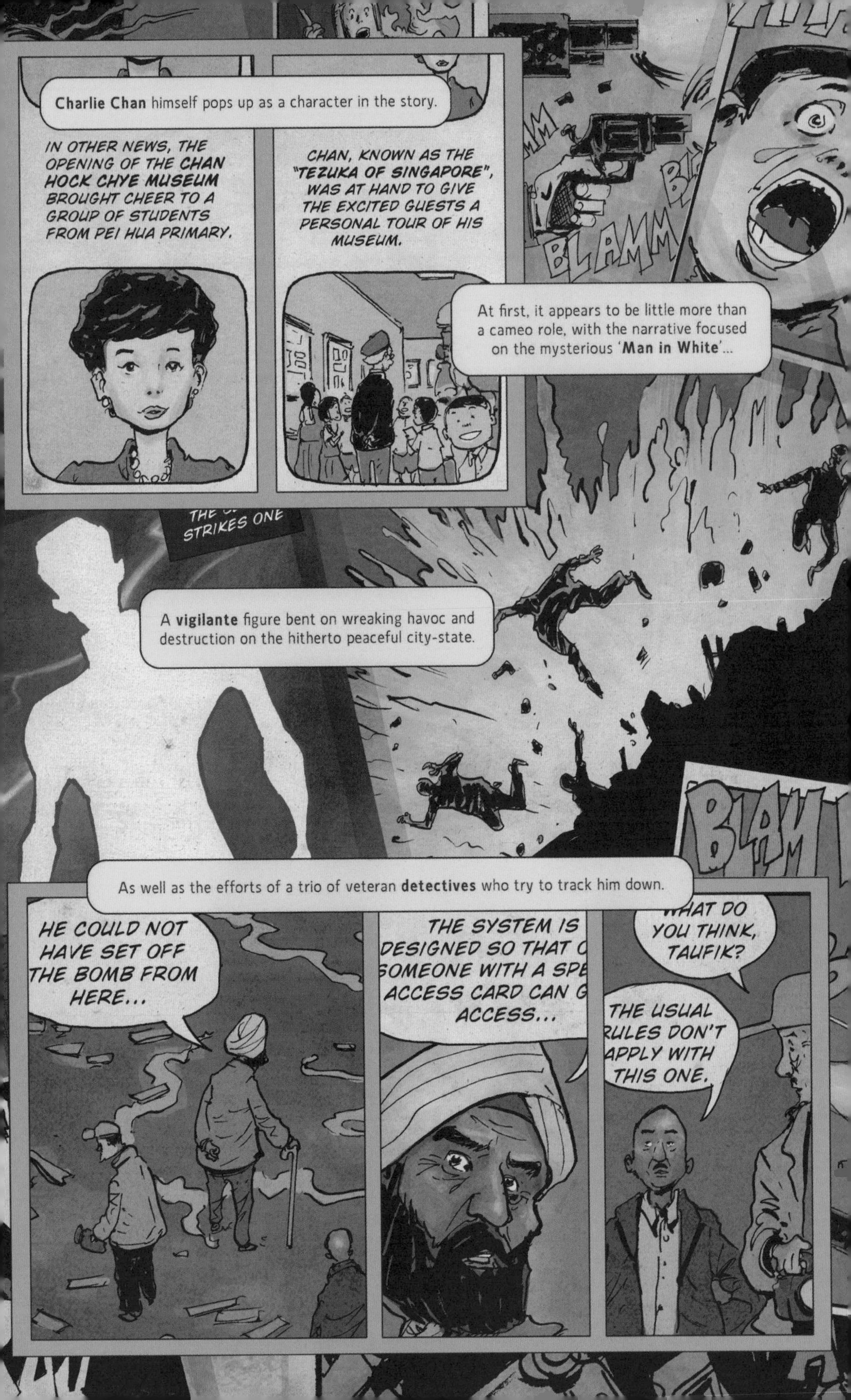
Charlie Chan himself pops up as a character in the story.
IN OTHER NEWS, THE OPENING OF THE CHAN HOCK CHYE MUSEUM BROUGHT CHEER TO A GROUP OF STUDENTS FROM PEI HUA PRIMARY.
CHAN, KNOWN AS THE "TEZUKA OF SINGAPORE", WAS AT HAND TO GIVE THE EXCITED GUESTS A PERSONAL TOUR OF HIS MUSEUM.
BLAMM
At first, it appears to be little more than a cameo role, with the narrative focused on the mysterious 'Man in White'...
STRIKES ONE
A vigilante figure bent on wreaking havoc and destruction on the hitherto peaceful city-state.
BLAM
As well as the efforts of a trio of veteran detectives who try to track him down.
HE COULD NOT HAVE SET OFF THE BOMB FROM HERE...
THE SYSTEM IS DESIGNED SO THAT O SOMEONE WITH A SPE ACCESS CARD CAN G ACCESS...
WHAT DO YOU THINK, TAUFIK?
THE USUAL RULES DON'T APPLY WITH THIS ONE.

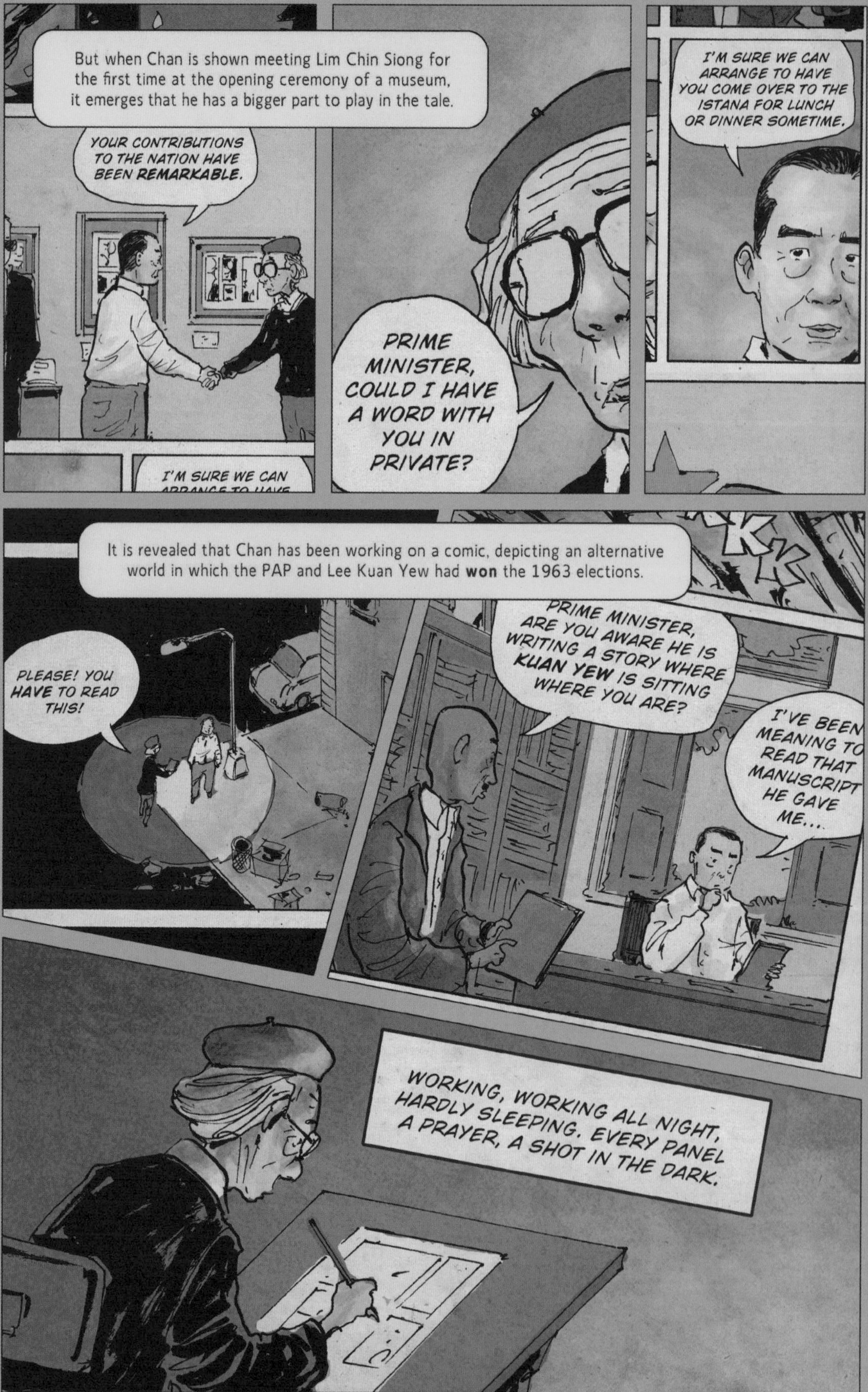

But when Chan is shown meeting Lim Chin Siong for the first time at the opening ceremony of a museum, it emerges that he has a bigger part to play in the tale.
YOUR CONTRIBUTIONS TO THE NATION HAVE BEEN **REMARKABLE**.
I'M SURE WE CAN
PRIME MINISTER, COULD I HAVE A WORD WITH YOU IN PRIVATE?
I'M SURE WE CAN ARRANGE TO HAVE YOU COME OVER TO THE ISTANA FOR LUNCH OR DINNER SOMETIME.
It is revealed that Chan has been working on a comic, depicting an alternative world in which the PAP and Lee Kuan Yew had **won** the 1963 elections.
PLEASE! YOU **HAVE** TO READ THIS!
PRIME MINISTER, ARE YOU AWARE HE IS WRITING A STORY WHERE **KUAN YEW** IS SITTING WHERE YOU ARE?
I'VE BEEN MEANING TO READ THAT MANUSCRIPT HE GAVE ME...
WORKING, WORKING ALL NIGHT, HARDLY SLEEPING. EVERY PANEL A PRAYER, A SHOT IN THE DARK.

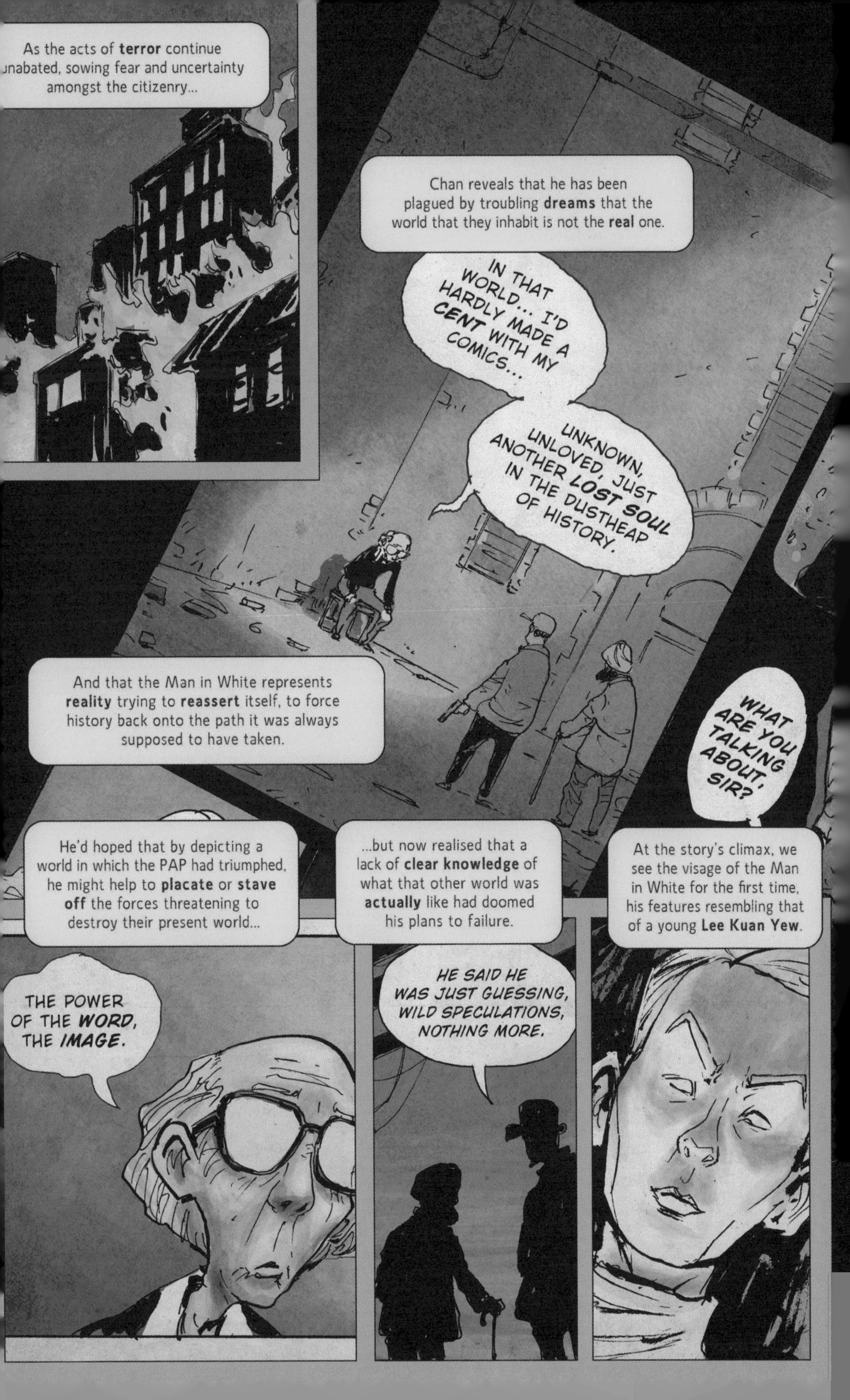

As the acts of **terror** continue unabated, sowing fear and uncertainty amongst the citizenry...
Chan reveals that he has been plagued by troubling **dreams** that the world that they inhabit is not the **real** one.
IN THAT WORLD... I'D HARDLY MADE A ***CENT*** WITH MY COMICS...
UNKNOWN, UNLOVED, JUST ANOTHER ***LOST SOUL*** IN THE DUSTHEAP OF HISTORY.
And that the Man in White represents **reality** trying to **reassert** itself, to force history back onto the path it was always supposed to have taken.
WHAT ARE YOU TALKING ABOUT, SIR?
He'd hoped that by depicting a world in which the PAP had triumphed, he might help to **placate** or **stave off** the forces threatening to destroy their present world...
THE POWER OF THE ***WORD***, THE ***IMAGE***.
...but now realised that a lack of **clear knowledge** of what that other world was **actually** like had doomed his plans to failure.
HE SAID HE WAS JUST GUESSING, WILD SPECULATIONS, NOTHING MORE.
At the story's climax, we see the visage of the Man in White for the first time, his features resembling that of a young **Lee Kuan Yew**.

The inhabitants of this world make their final stand...

THIS IS MY WORLD, AND I'M NOT GIVING IT UP WITHOUT A FIGHT!

WE BUILT
STRONG, PROS
SINGAPORE...
DOES IT MATT
DID IT AND H

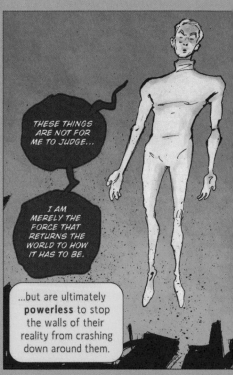

THESE THINGS ARE NOT FOR ME TO JUDGE...

I AM MERELY THE FORCE THAT RETURNS THE WORLD TO HOW IT HAS TO BE.

...but are ultimately **powerless** to stop the walls of their reality from crashing down around them.

Chan and Lim Chin Siong now find themselves thrown back in time to pre-independence Singapore.

Restored to their youth, and having seemingly been given a chance to reconsider all their choices, knowing now, to some degree, what the future has in store...

Lim Chin Siong

Chan Hock Chye

(This is accompanied by a stylistic shift, with the 4x4 panel grid previously used in the book abandoned in favour of looser configurations.)

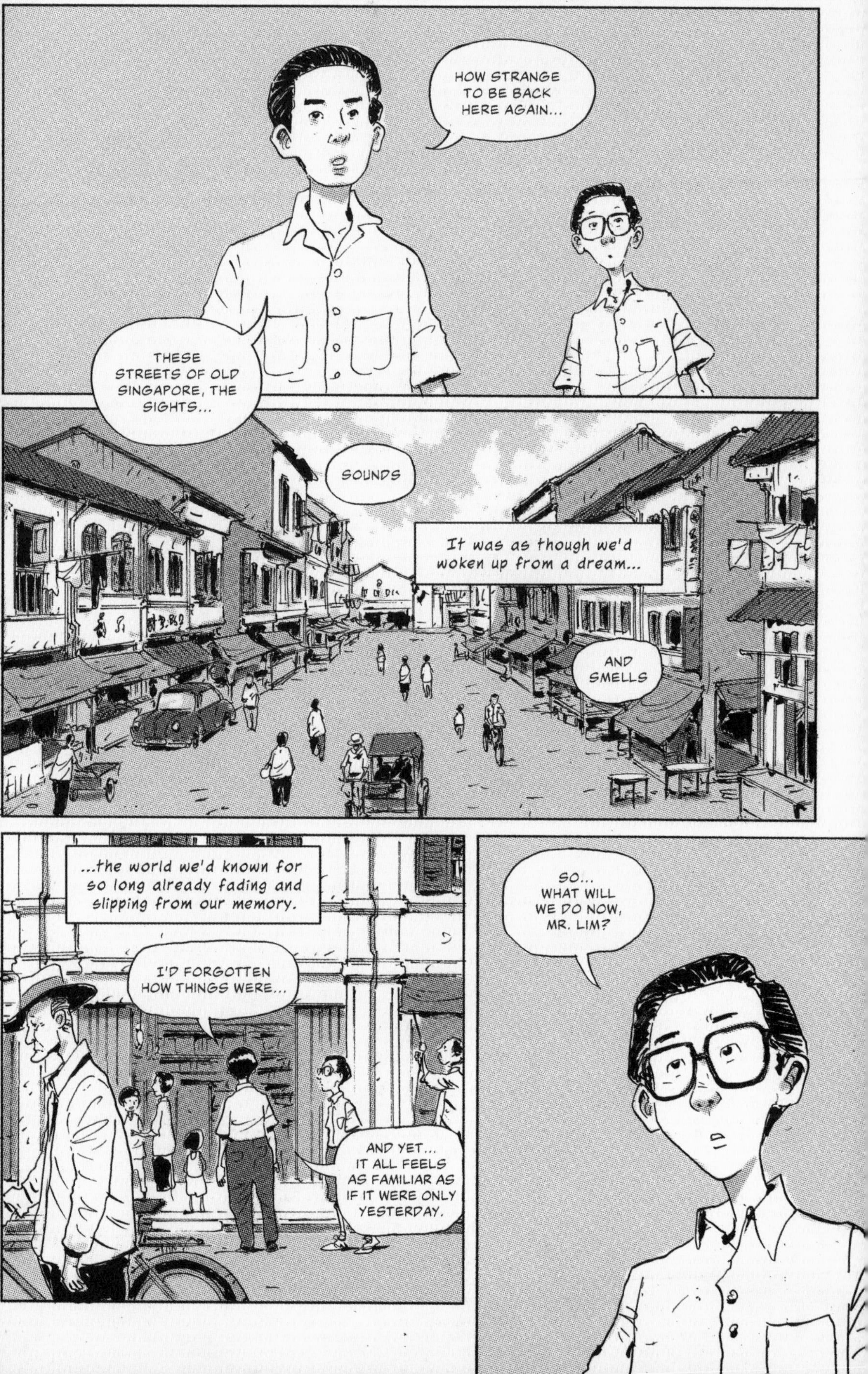
HOW STRANGE TO BE BACK HERE AGAIN...
THESE STREETS OF OLD SINGAPORE, THE SIGHTS...
SOUNDS
It was as though we'd woken up from a dream...
AND SMELLS
...the world we'd known for so long already fading and slipping from our memory.
I'D FORGOTTEN HOW THINGS WERE...
AND YET... IT ALL FEELS AS FAMILIAR AS IF IT WERE ONLY YESTERDAY.
SO... WHAT WILL WE DO NOW, MR. LIM?

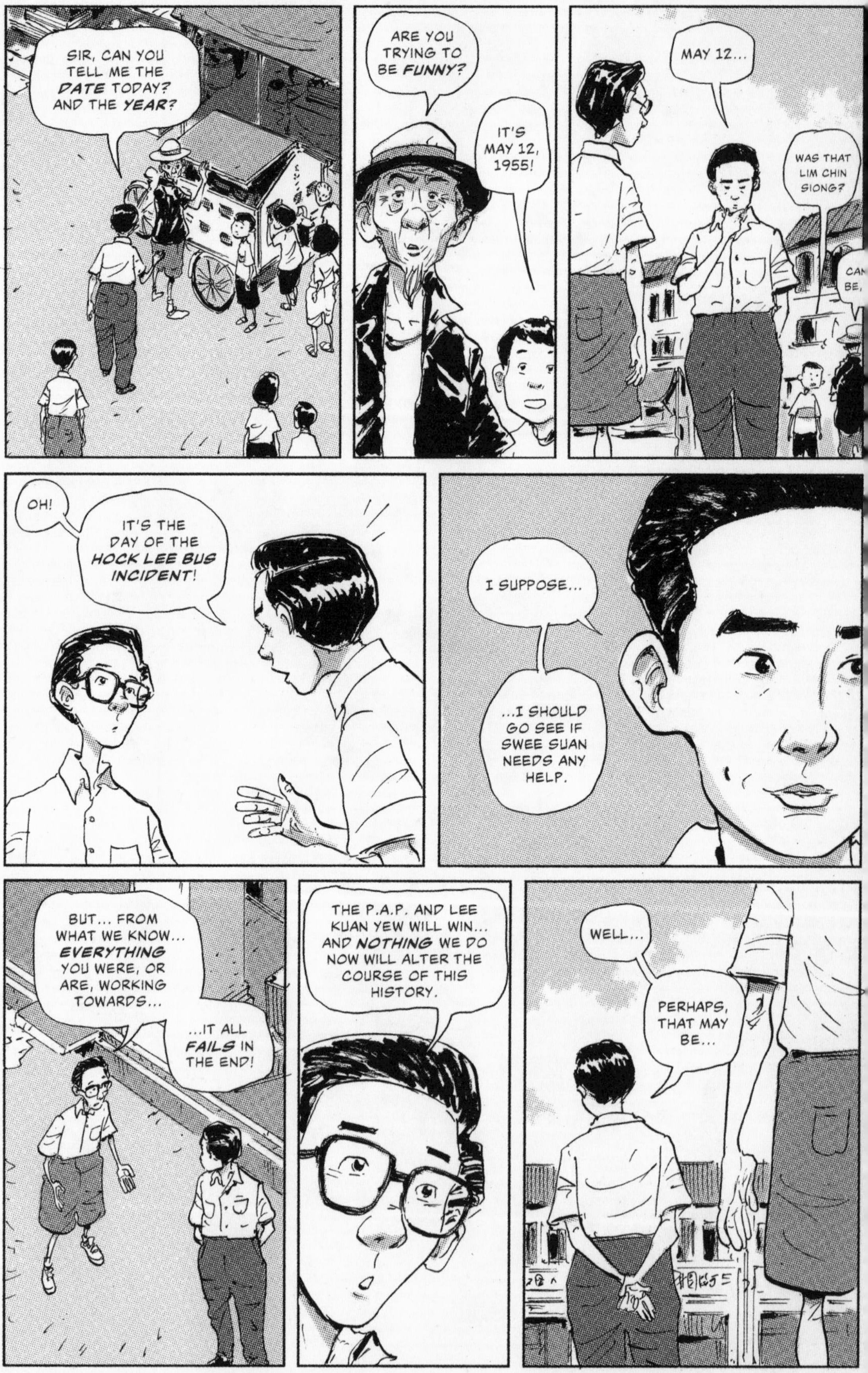
SIR, CAN YOU TELL ME THE DATE TODAY? AND THE YEAR?
ARE YOU TRYING TO BE FUNNY?
IT'S MAY 12, 1955!
MAY 12...
WAS THAT LIM CHIN SIONG?
OH!
IT'S THE DAY OF THE HOCK LEE BUS INCIDENT!
I SUPPOSE...
...I SHOULD GO SEE IF SWEE SUAN NEEDS ANY HELP.
BUT... FROM WHAT WE KNOW... EVERYTHING YOU WERE, OR ARE, WORKING TOWARDS...
...IT ALL FAILS IN THE END!
THE P.A.P. AND LEE KUAN YEW WILL WIN... AND NOTHING WE DO NOW WILL ALTER THE COURSE OF THIS HISTORY.
WELL...
PERHAPS, THAT MAY BE...

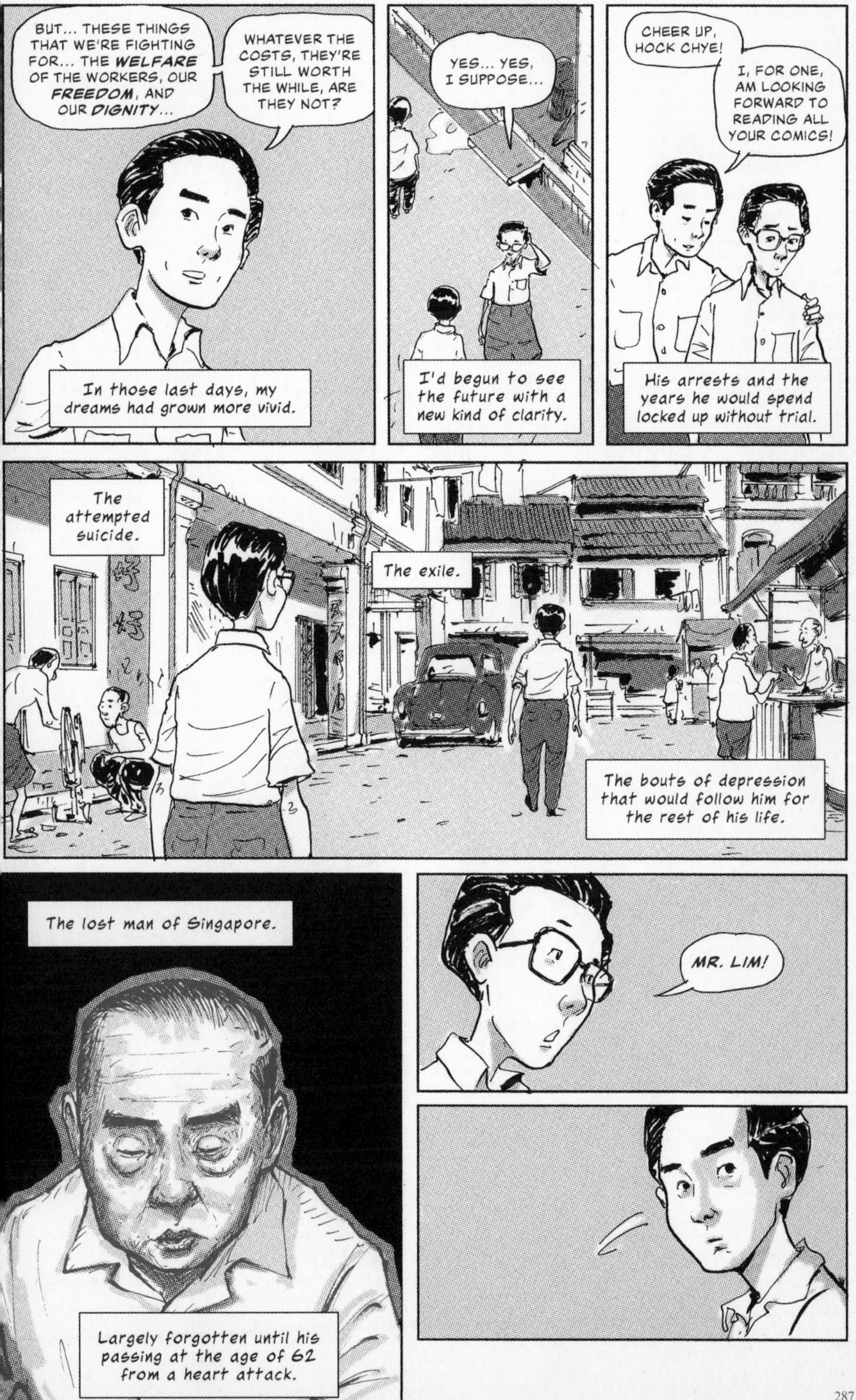

BUT... THESE THINGS THAT WE'RE FIGHTING FOR... THE **WELFARE** OF THE WORKERS, OUR **FREEDOM**, AND OUR **DIGNITY**...
WHATEVER THE COSTS, THEY'RE STILL WORTH THE WHILE, ARE THEY NOT?
In those last days, my dreams had grown more vivid.
YES... YES, I SUPPOSE...
I'd begun to see the future with a new kind of clarity.
CHEER UP, HOCK CHYE!
I, FOR ONE, AM LOOKING FORWARD TO READING ALL YOUR COMICS!
His arrests and the years he would spend locked up without trial.
The attempted suicide.
The exile.
The bouts of depression that would follow him for the rest of his life.
The lost man of Singapore.
Largely forgotten until his passing at the age of 62 from a heart attack.
MR. LIM!

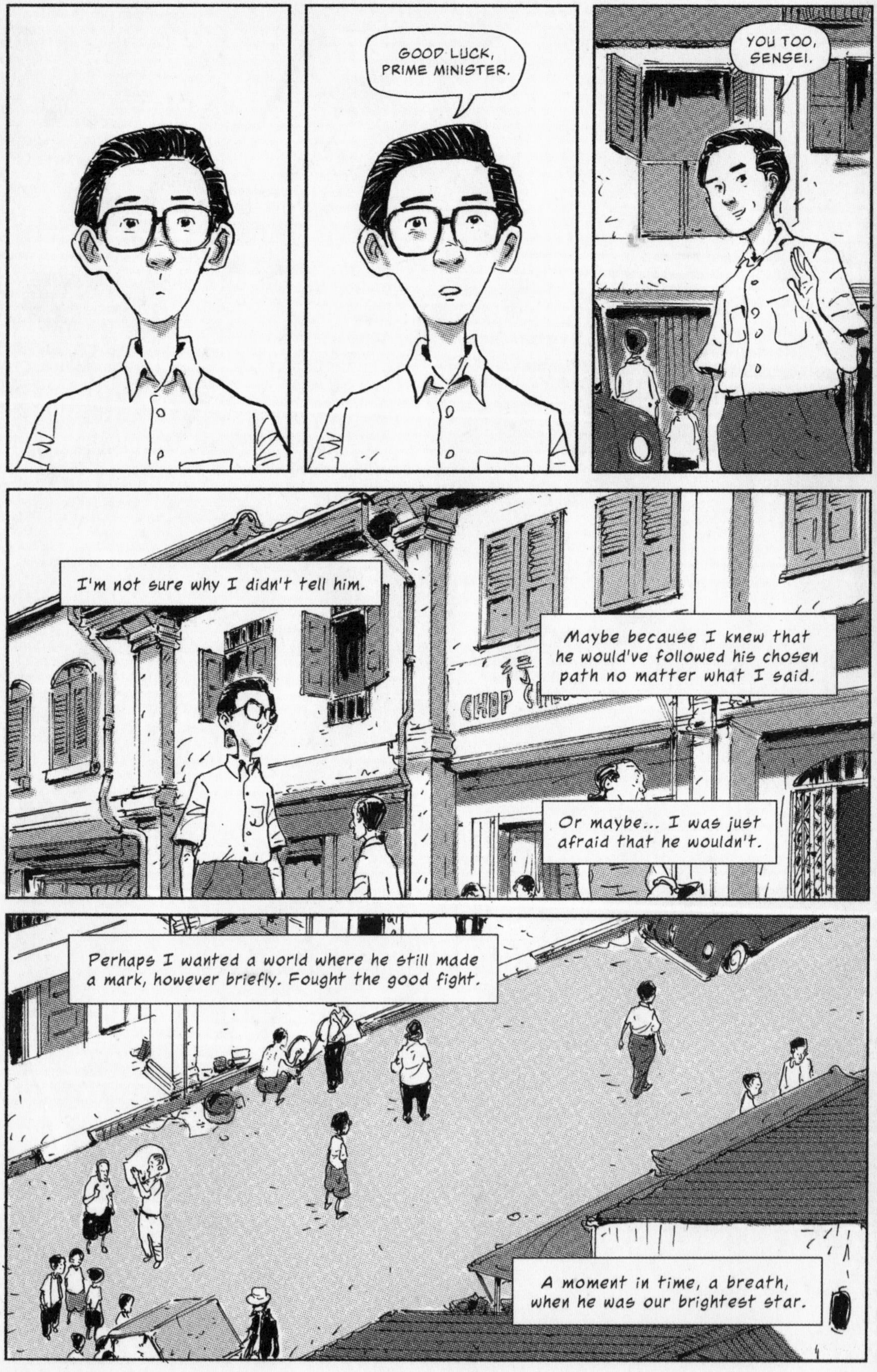
GOOD LUCK, PRIME MINISTER.
YOU TOO, SENSEI.
I'm not sure why I didn't tell him.
Maybe because I knew that he would've followed his chosen path no matter what I said.
Or maybe... I was just afraid that he wouldn't.
Perhaps I wanted a world where he still made a mark, however briefly. Fought the good fight.
A moment in time, a breath, when he was our brightest star.

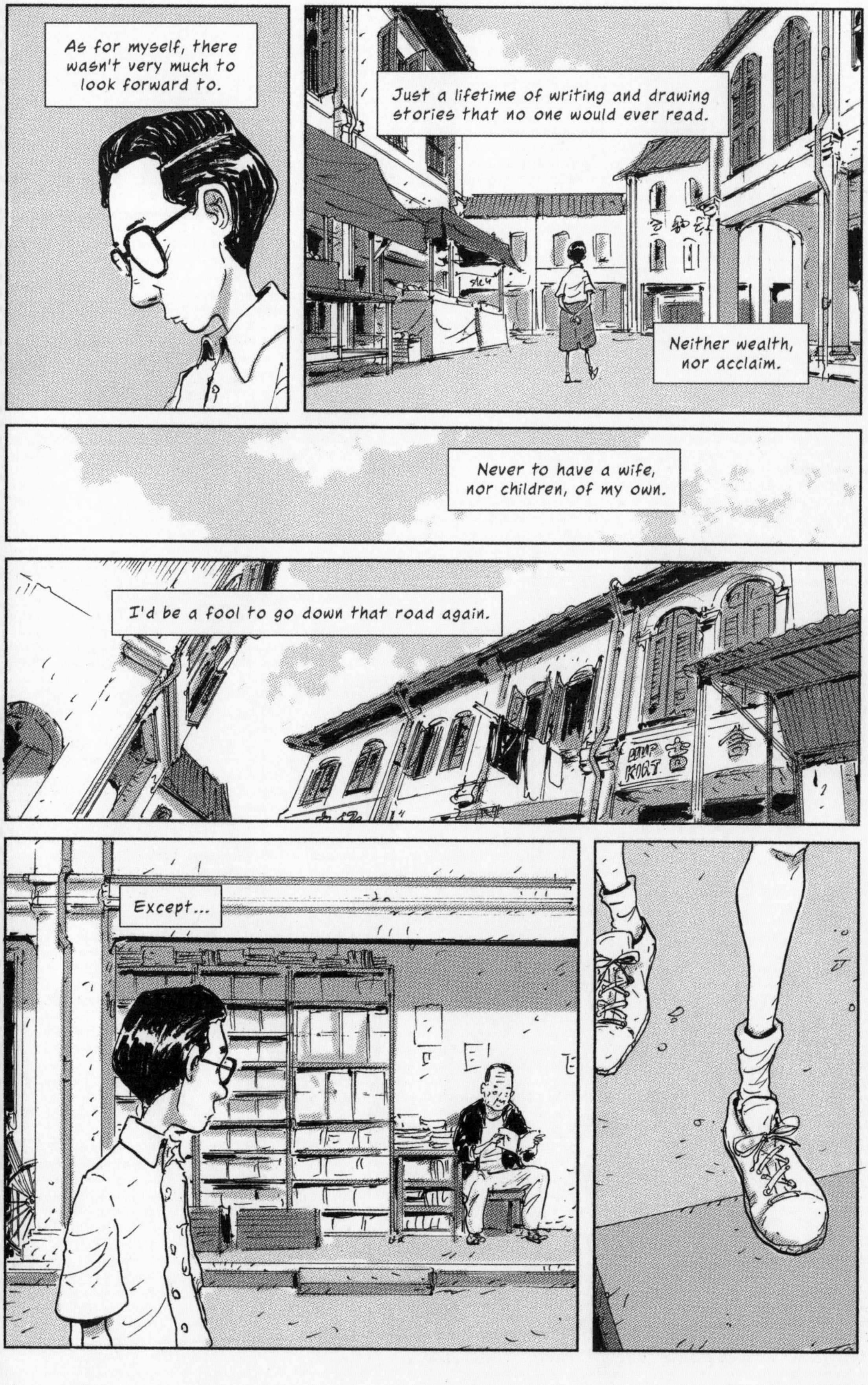
As for myself, there wasn't very much to look forward to.
Just a lifetime of writing and drawing stories that no one would ever read.
Neither wealth, nor acclaim.
Never to have a wife, nor children, of my own.
I'd be a fool to go down that road again.
Except...

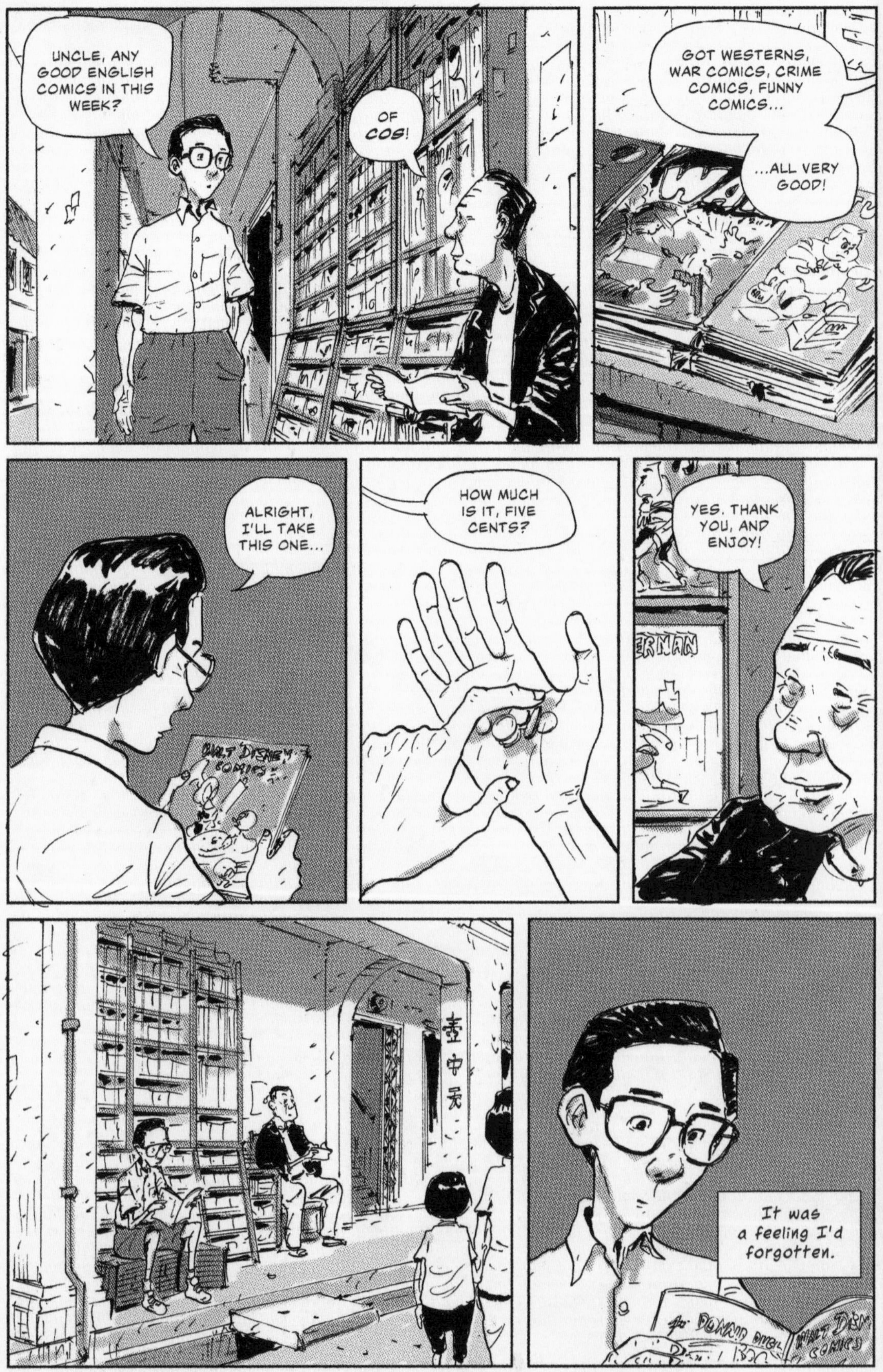
UNCLE, ANY GOOD ENGLISH COMICS IN THIS WEEK?
OF COS!
GOT WESTERNS, WAR COMICS, CRIME COMICS, FUNNY COMICS...
...ALL VERY GOOD!
ALRIGHT, I'LL TAKE THIS ONE...
WALT DISNEY'S COMICS
HOW MUCH IS IT, FIVE CENTS?
YES. THANK YOU, AND ENJOY!
It was a feeling I'd forgotten.
DONALD DUCK
WALT DISNEY'S COMICS

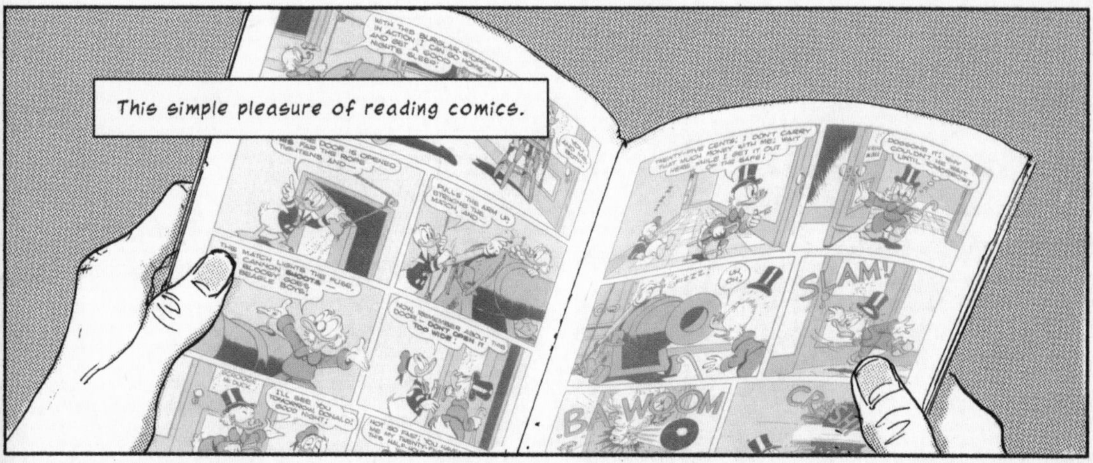
This simple pleasure of reading comics.
SLAM!
BAWOOM

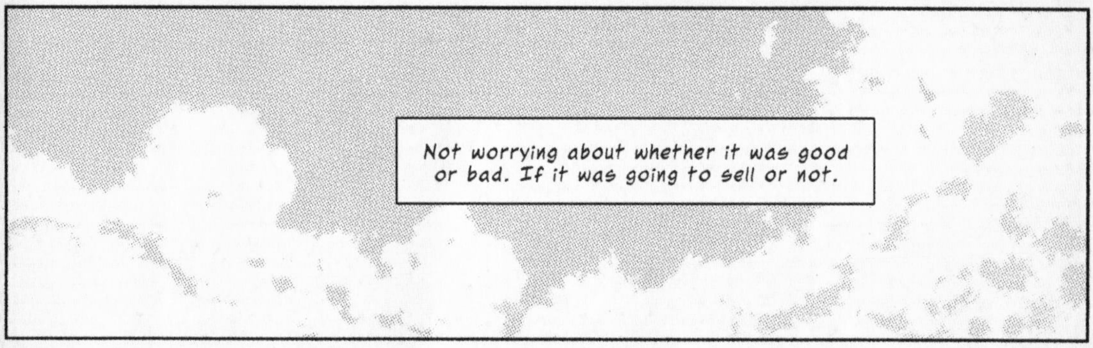
Not worrying about whether it was good or bad. If it was going to sell or not.

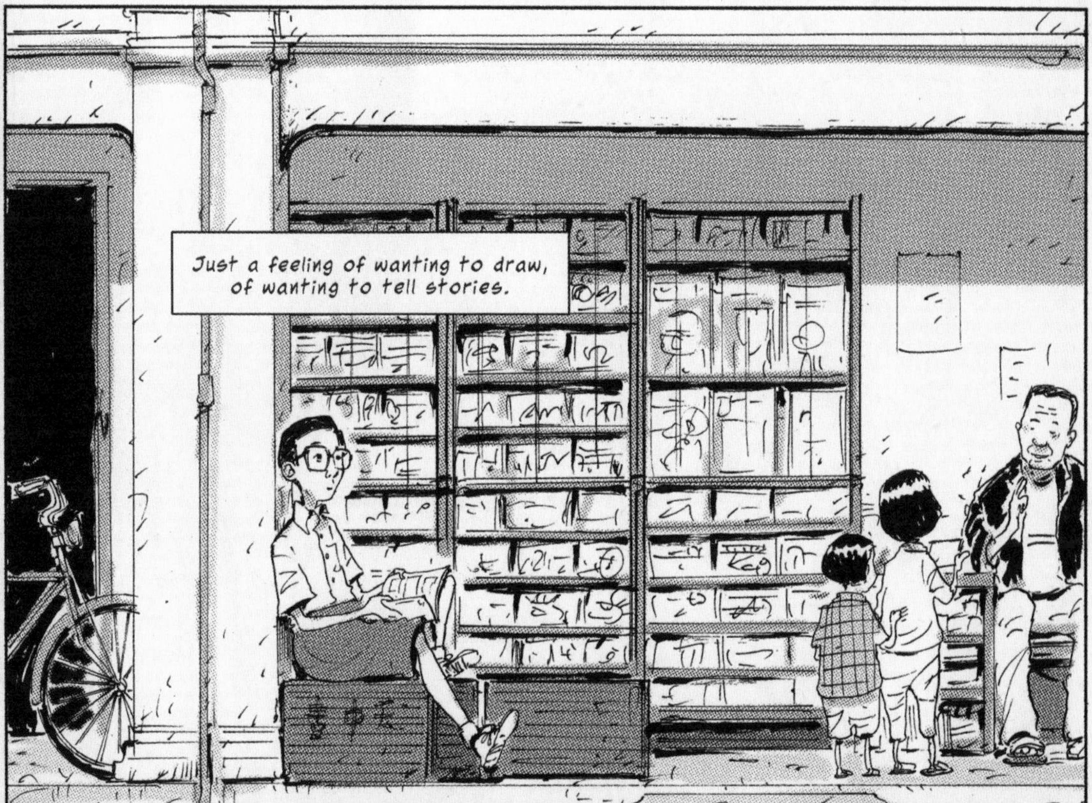
Just a feeling of wanting to draw, of wanting to tell stories.

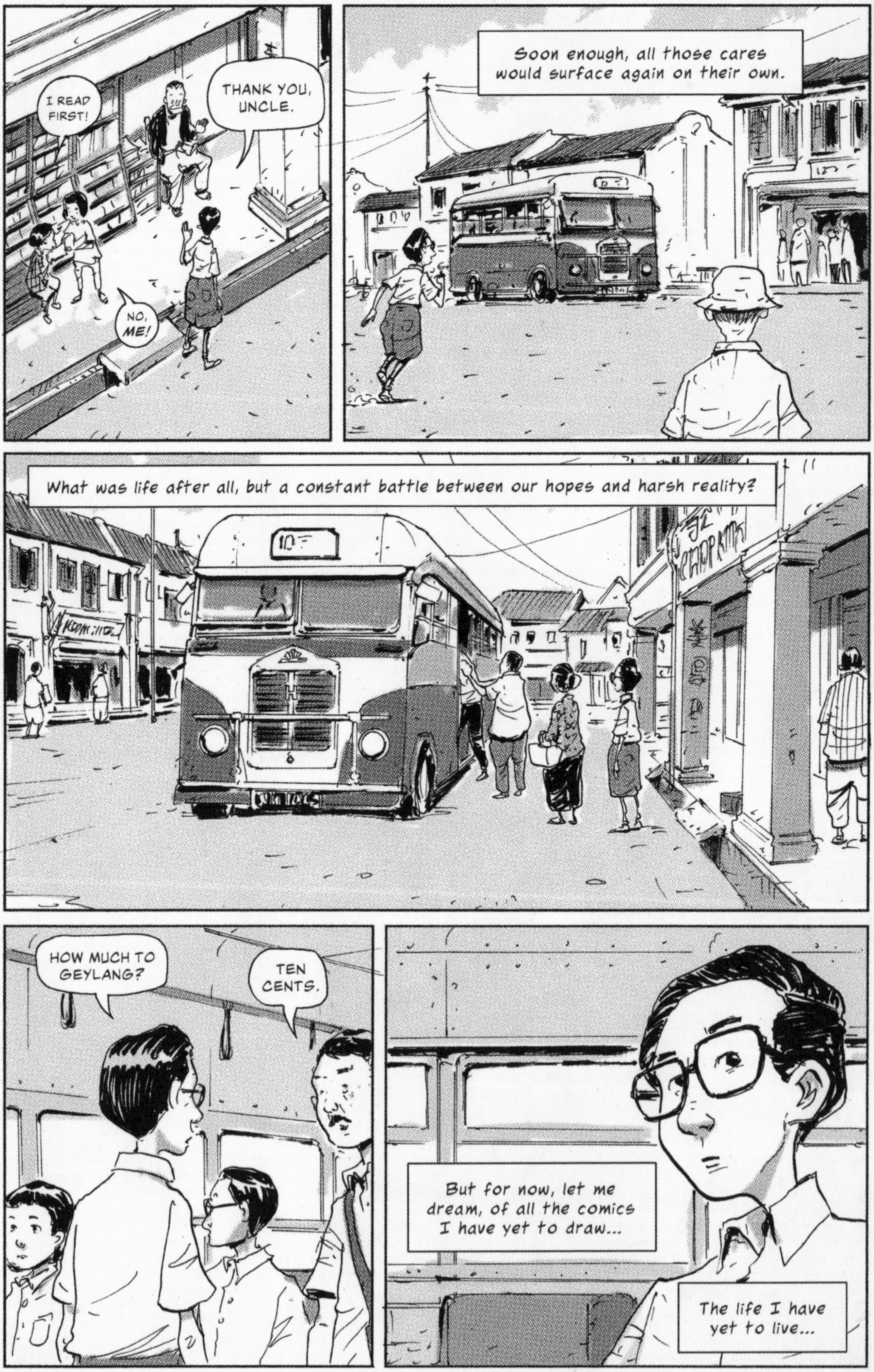
I READ FIRST!
THANK YOU, UNCLE.
NO, ME!
Soon enough, all those cares would surface again on their own.
What was life after all, but a constant battle between our hopes and harsh reality?
HOW MUCH TO GEYLANG?
TEN CENTS.
But for now, let me dream, of all the comics I have yet to draw...
The life I have yet to live...

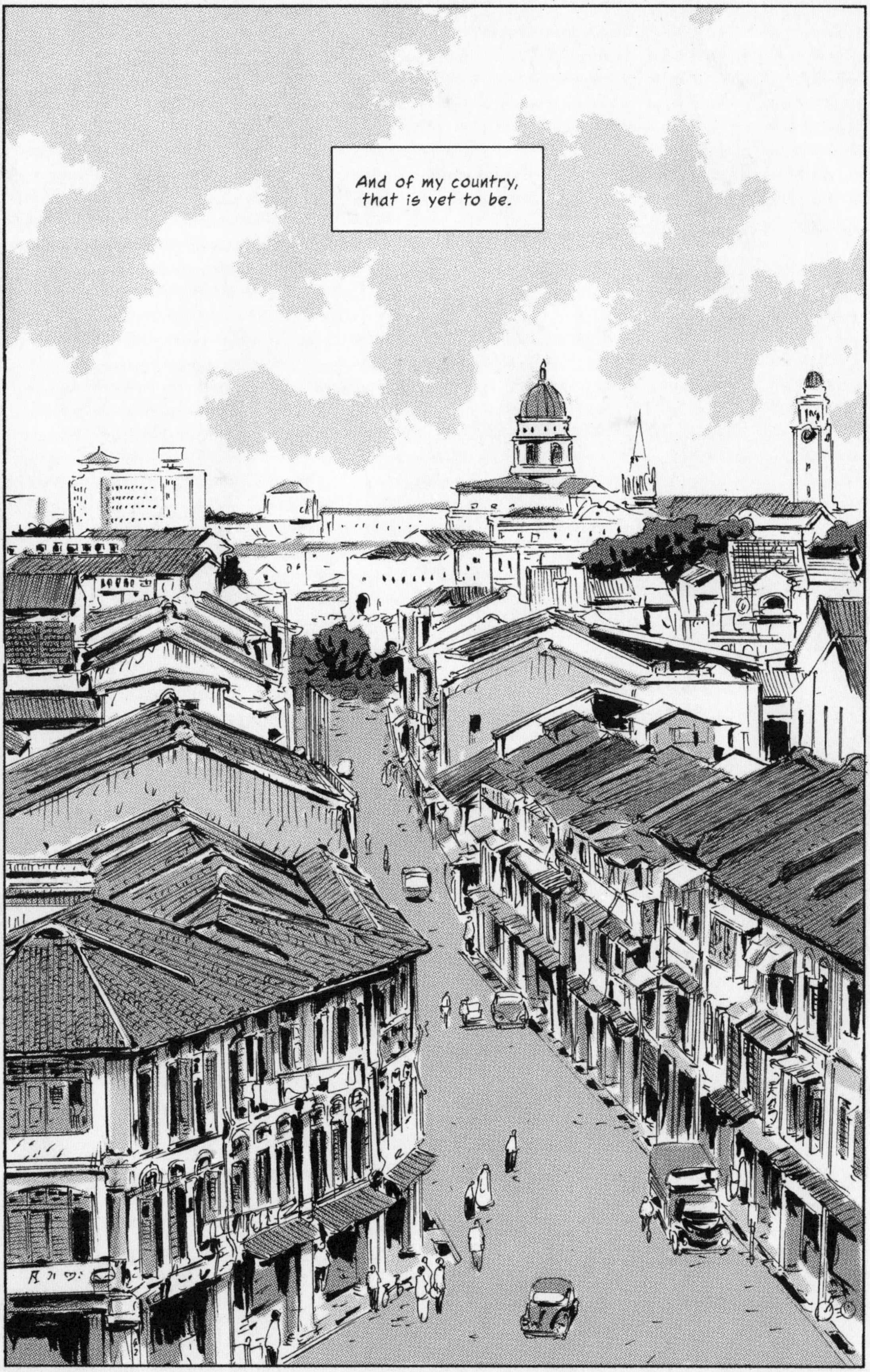
And of my country, that is yet to be.

First embarked on in 1988, "*Days of August*" remained unfinished for many years. Chan says, "*I never quite knew how to finish the story... until I heard about Lim Chin Siong's passing. Although historical closure may be ever elusive, for the story at least, it marked an ending of sorts.*"

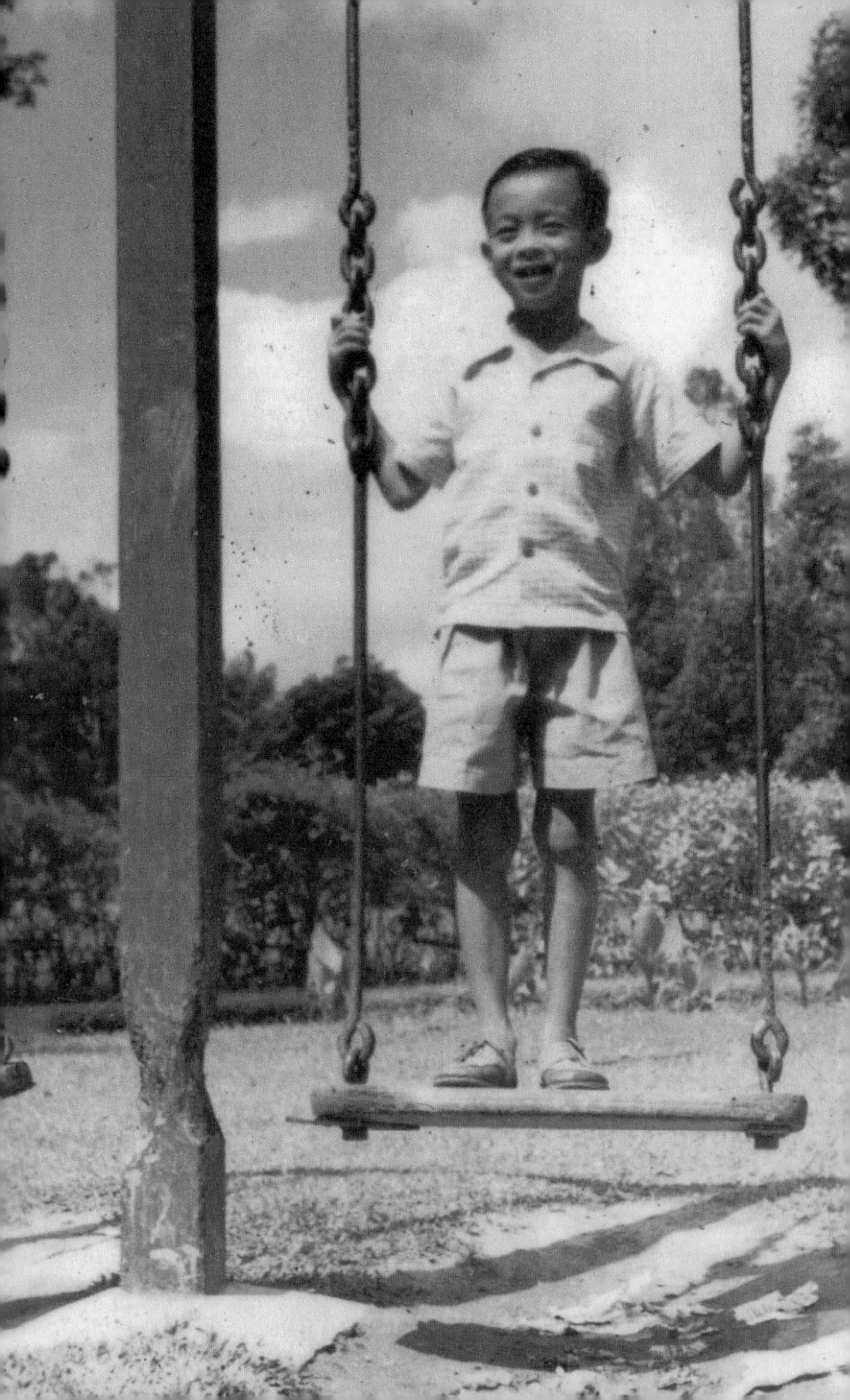

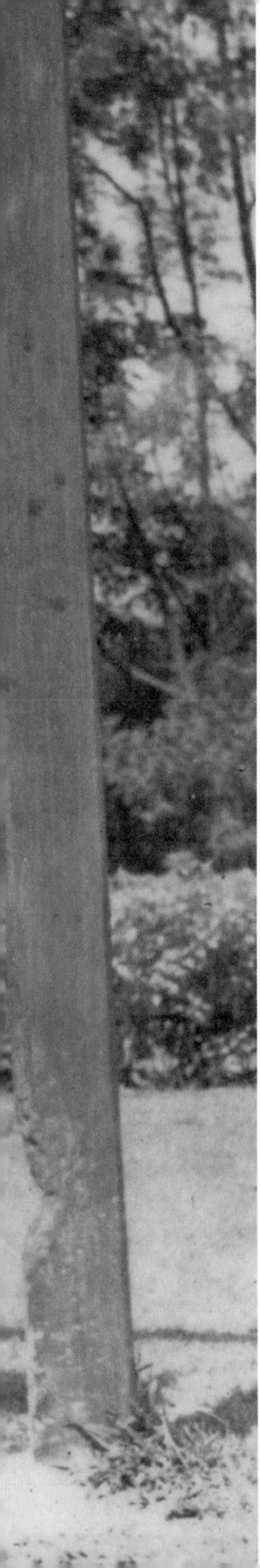

Epilogue

AN OLD MAN NOW, AFTER ALL

野草苺

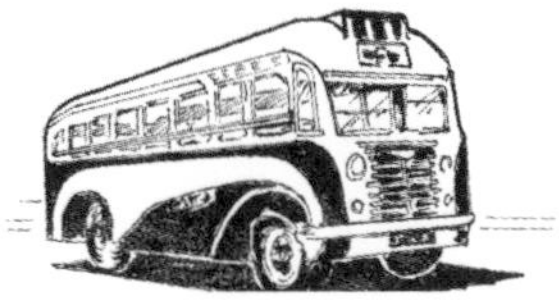

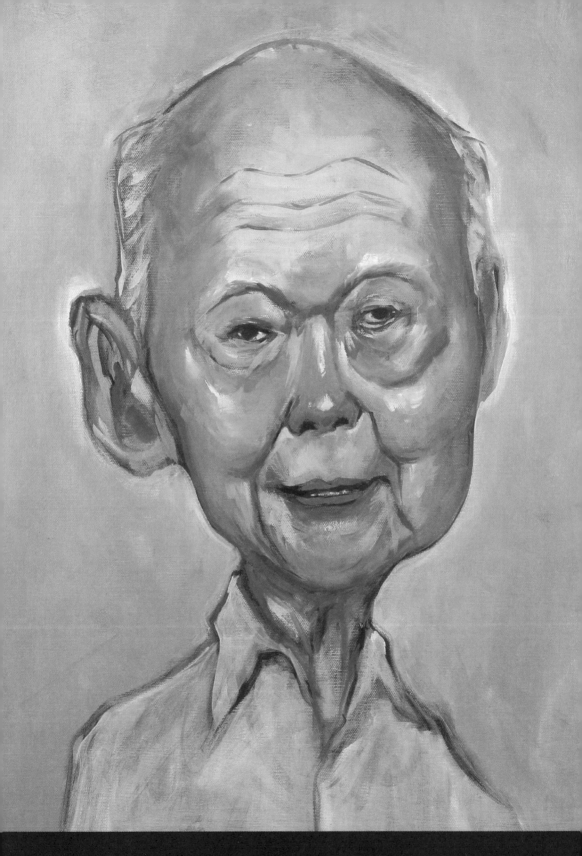

TIME AND TIDE (2012) | Chan Hock Chye | Oil on canvas

Portrait of Lee Kuan Yew at the age of 88. By the time he retired from office in 1990, Lee had served as the Prime Minister of Singapore for 31 years. He would continue to play an active and vocal role in the nation's politics until declining health led to a gradual withdrawal from public life in his final years. Lee's passing in 2015 prompted an unprecedented outpouring of public tributes and appraisals of his legacy, a testament to the profound impact he'd had on the development of the nation and its people.

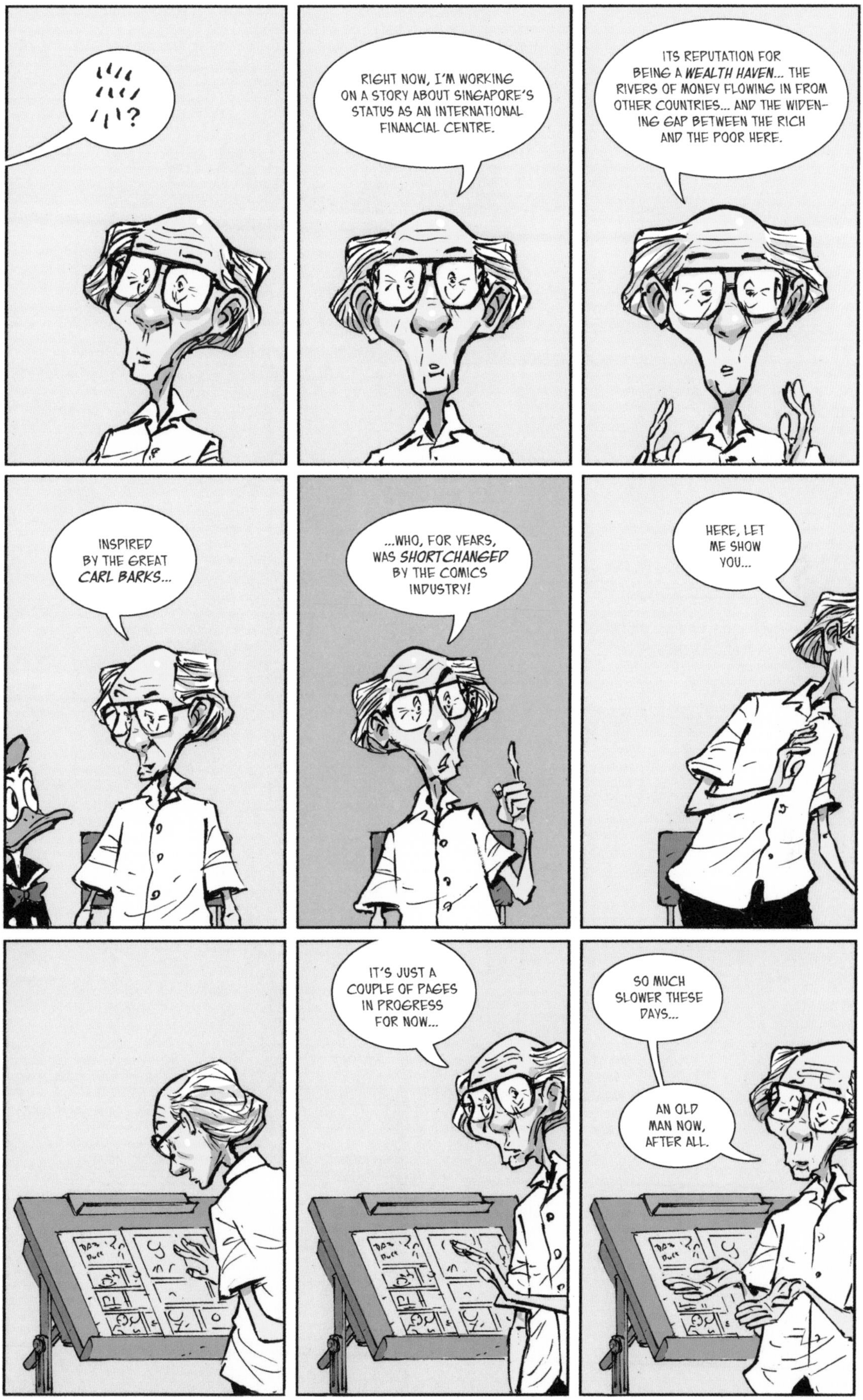
???
RIGHT NOW, I'M WORKING ON A STORY ABOUT SINGAPORE'S STATUS AS AN INTERNATIONAL FINANCIAL CENTRE.
ITS REPUTATION FOR BEING A *WEALTH HAVEN*... THE RIVERS OF MONEY FLOWING IN FROM OTHER COUNTRIES... AND THE WIDENING GAP BETWEEN THE RICH AND THE POOR HERE.
INSPIRED BY THE GREAT *CARL BARKS*...
...WHO, FOR YEARS, WAS *SHORTCHANGED* BY THE COMICS INDUSTRY!
HERE, LET ME SHOW YOU...
IT'S JUST A COUPLE OF PAGES IN PROGRESS FOR NOW...
SO MUCH SLOWER THESE DAYS...
AN OLD MAN NOW, AFTER ALL.

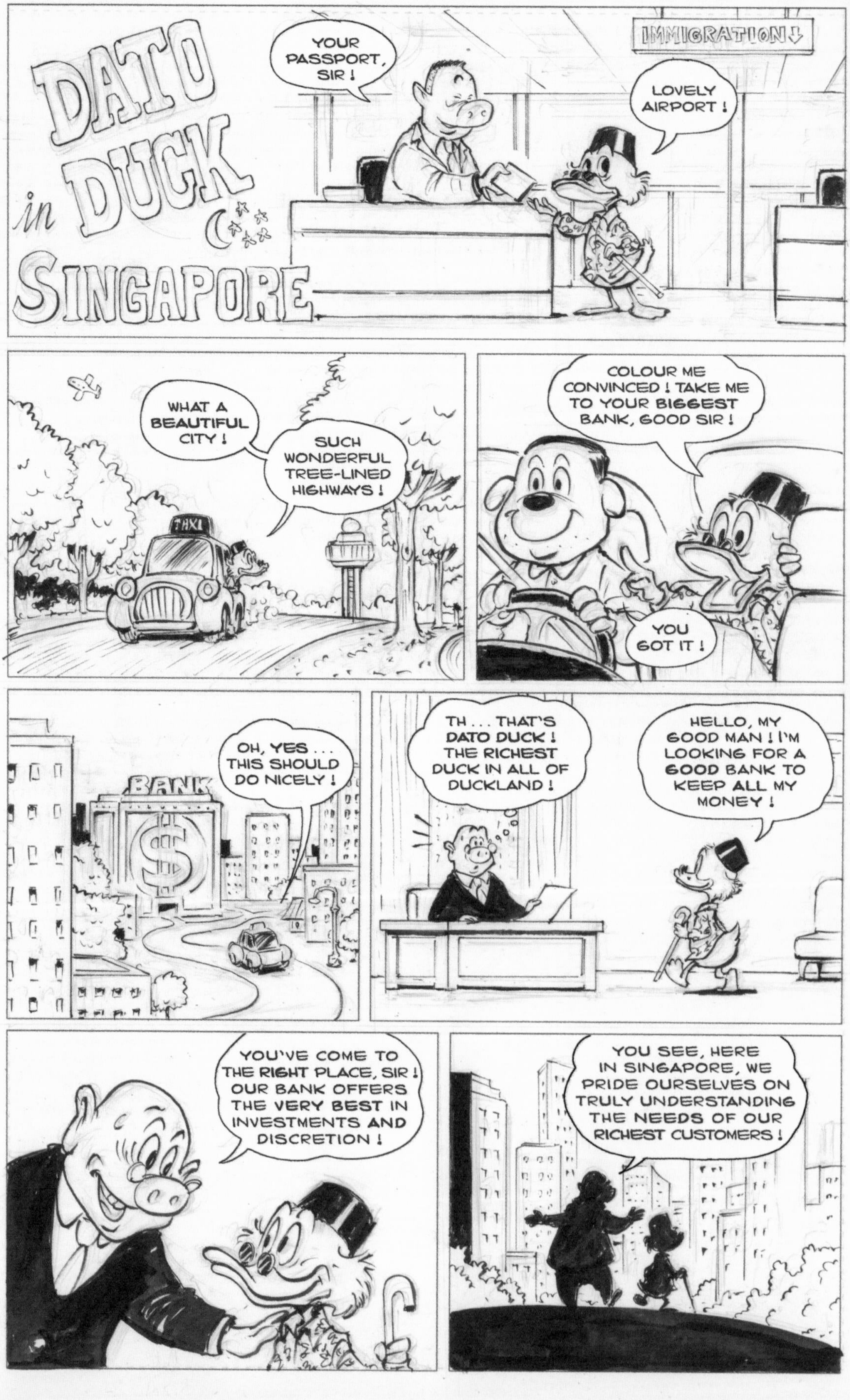
DATO DUCK in SINGAPORE
YOUR PASSPORT, SIR !
IMMIGRATION
LOVELY AIRPORT !
WHAT A BEAUTIFUL CITY !
SUCH WONDERFUL TREE-LINED HIGHWAYS !
TAXI
COLOUR ME CONVINCED ! TAKE ME TO YOUR BIGGEST BANK, GOOD SIR !
YOU GOT IT !
BANK
OH, YES . . . THIS SHOULD DO NICELY !
TH . . . THAT'S DATO DUCK ! THE RICHEST DUCK IN ALL OF DUCKLAND !
HELLO, MY GOOD MAN ! I'M LOOKING FOR A GOOD BANK TO KEEP ALL MY MONEY !
YOU'VE COME TO THE RIGHT PLACE, SIR ! OUR BANK OFFERS THE VERY BEST IN INVESTMENTS AND DISCRETION !
YOU SEE, HERE IN SINGAPORE, WE PRIDE OURSELVES ON TRULY UNDERSTANDING THE NEEDS OF OUR RICHEST CUSTOMERS !

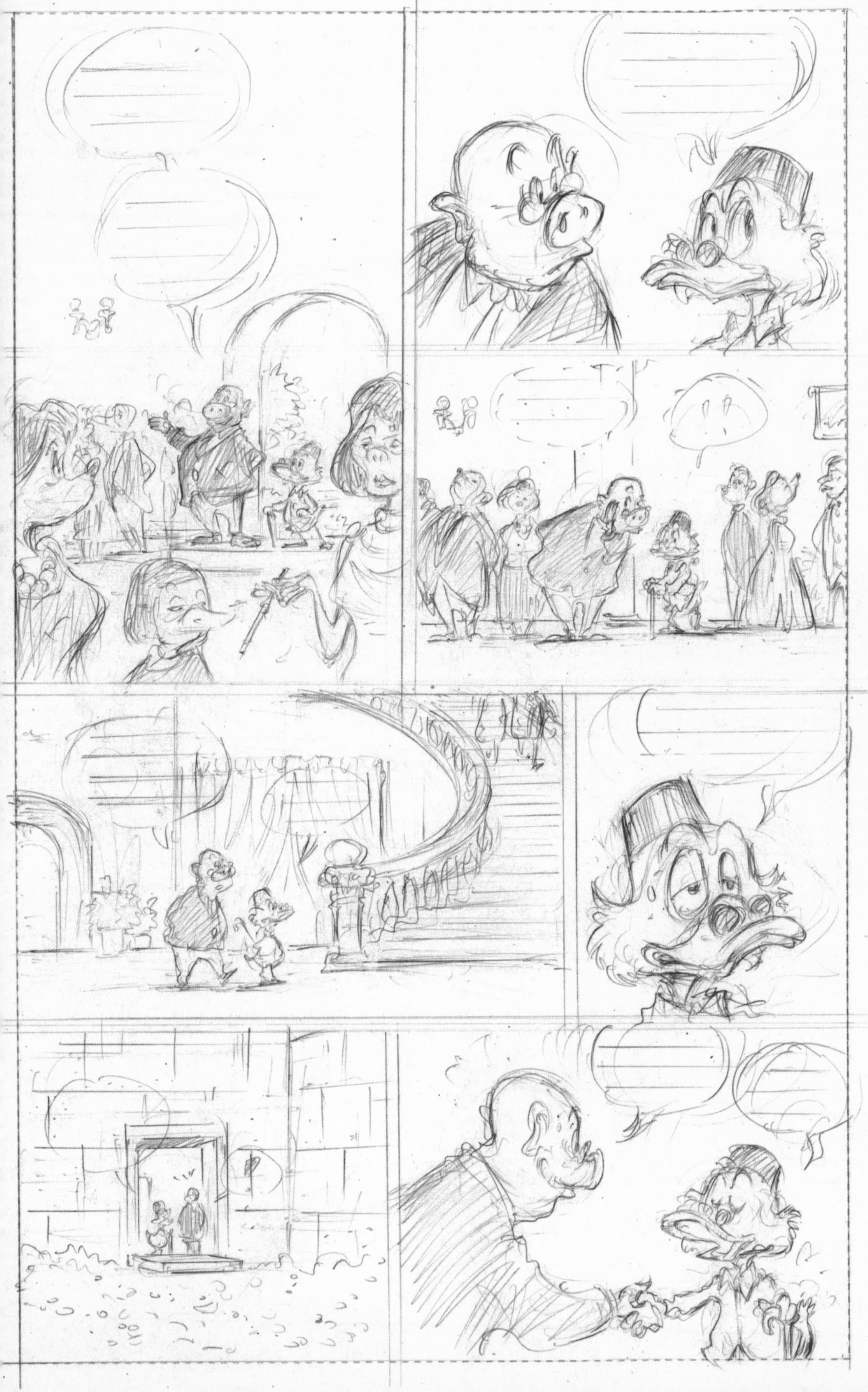

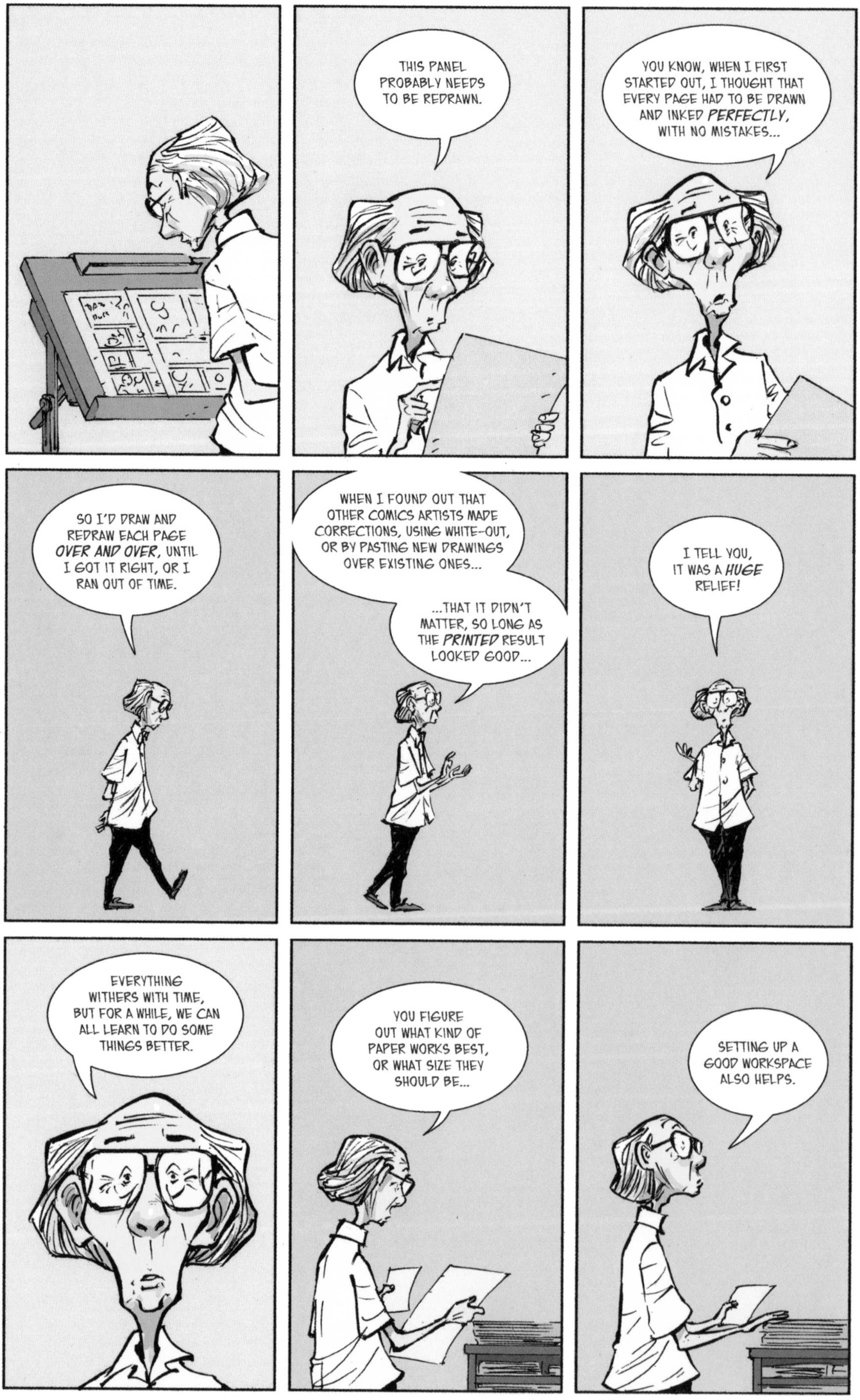
THIS PANEL PROBABLY NEEDS TO BE REDRAWN.
YOU KNOW, WHEN I FIRST STARTED OUT, I THOUGHT THAT EVERY PAGE HAD TO BE DRAWN AND INKED *PERFECTLY,* WITH NO MISTAKES...
SO I'D DRAW AND REDRAW EACH PAGE *OVER AND OVER,* UNTIL I GOT IT RIGHT, OR I RAN OUT OF TIME.
WHEN I FOUND OUT THAT OTHER COMICS ARTISTS MADE CORRECTIONS, USING WHITE-OUT, OR BY PASTING NEW DRAWINGS OVER EXISTING ONES...
...THAT IT DIDN'T MATTER, SO LONG AS THE *PRINTED* RESULT LOOKED GOOD...
I TELL YOU, IT WAS A *HUGE* RELIEF!
EVERYTHING WITHERS WITH TIME, BUT FOR A WHILE, WE CAN ALL LEARN TO DO SOME THINGS BETTER.
YOU FIGURE OUT WHAT KIND OF PAPER WORKS BEST, OR WHAT SIZE THEY SHOULD BE...
SETTING UP A GOOD WORKSPACE ALSO HELPS.

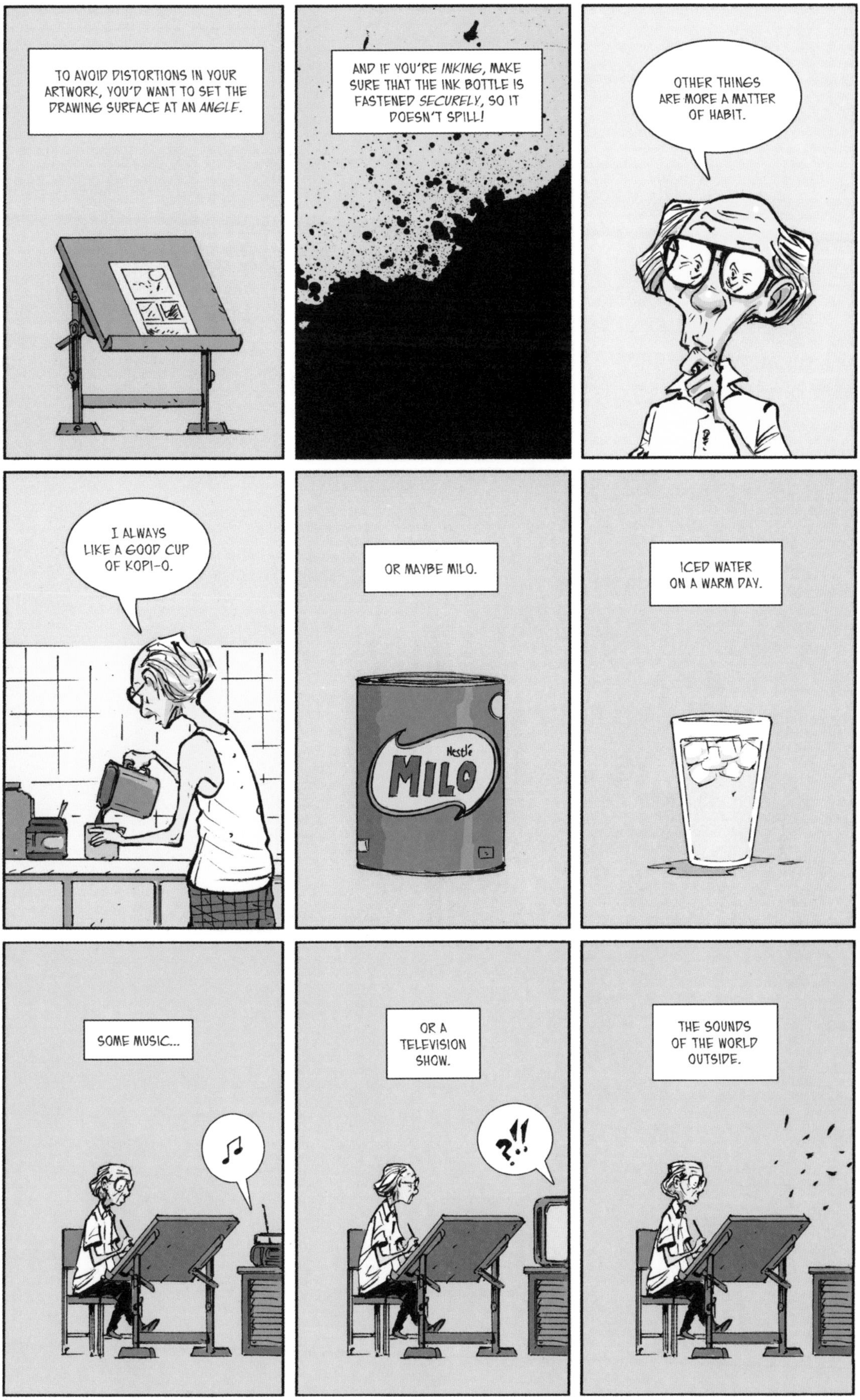
TO AVOID DISTORTIONS IN YOUR ARTWORK, YOU'D WANT TO SET THE DRAWING SURFACE AT AN *ANGLE*.
AND IF YOU'RE *INKING*, MAKE SURE THAT THE INK BOTTLE IS FASTENED *SECURELY*, SO IT DOESN'T SPILL!
OTHER THINGS ARE MORE A MATTER OF HABIT.
I ALWAYS LIKE A GOOD CUP OF KOPI-O.
OR MAYBE MILO.
Nestlé
MILO
ICED WATER ON A WARM DAY.
SOME MUSIC...
OR A TELEVISION SHOW.
?!!
THE SOUNDS OF THE WORLD OUTSIDE.

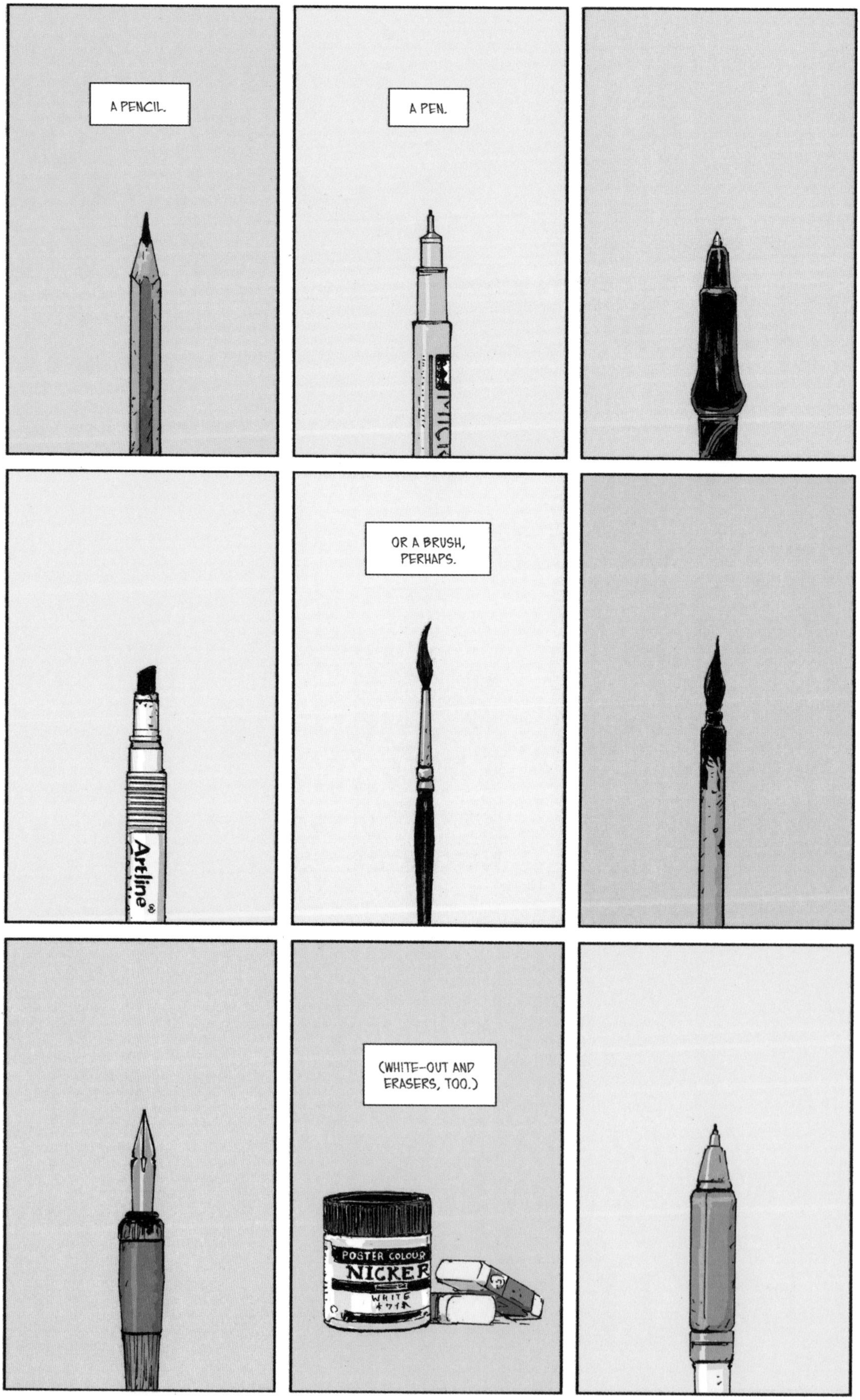
A PENCIL.
A PEN.
Artline
OR A BRUSH, PERHAPS.
(WHITE-OUT AND ERASERS, TOO.)
POSTER COLOUR
NICKER
WHITE

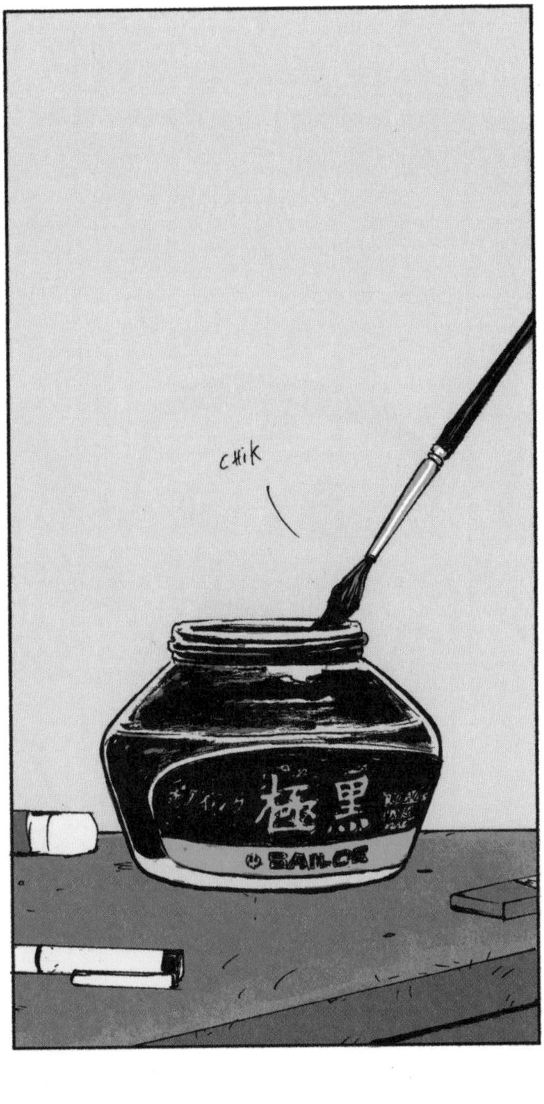
CHIK
極黒

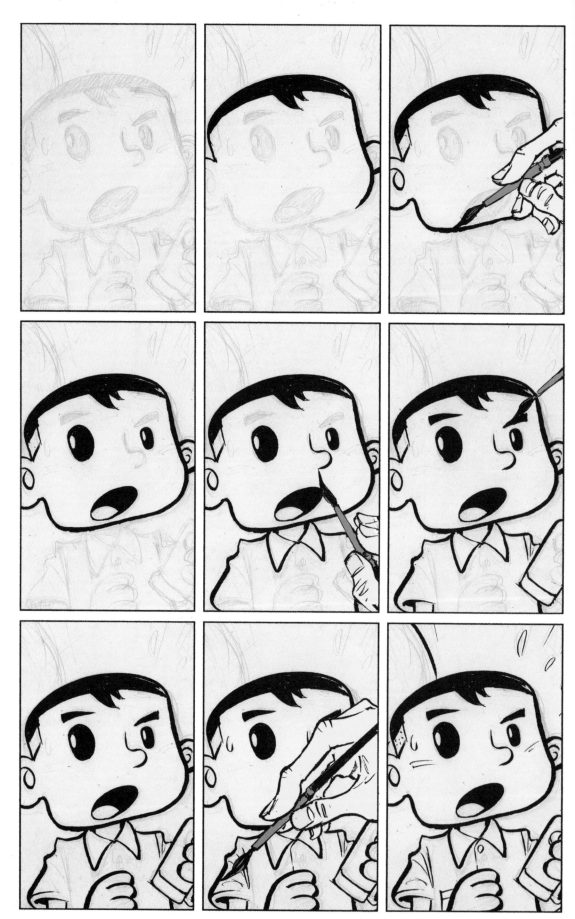

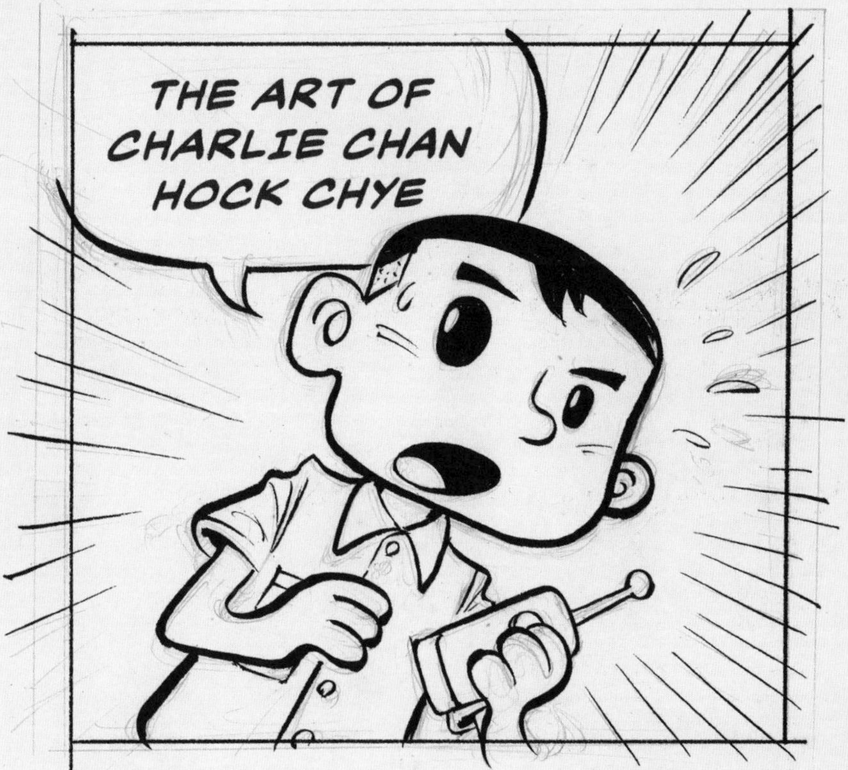
THE ART OF CHARLIE CHAN HOCK CHYE

Charlie Chan Hock Chye, aged 76, 2014

Notes

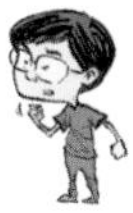

Listed by page number

1 This theory of the origins of the "si" in "Malaysia" is, by most accounts, anecdotal.

7 It is difficult to overstate Japanese comics artist Osamu Tezuka's (1928–1989) prodigious output and profound influence on the development of manga and anime. Over the years, his debut work *Shin Takarajima* (1947) has acquired an almost mythical, cult-like status. For a more nuanced and revisionist account that challenges mainstream notions of the book's impact and Tezuka's role in its creation, see Ryan Holmberg, "Tezuka Outwits the Phantom Blot: The Case of New Treasure Island cont'd," *The Comics Journal,* February 22, 2013 *<www.tcj.com/tezuka-osamu-outwits-the-phantom-blot-the-case-of-new-treasure-island-contd>*.

18 English-medium schools had become increasingly attractive in post-war Singapore, owing to the better educational and employment opportunities they afforded students. Thanks to generous funding by the British, these boasted superior facilities and standards of teaching. 1954 marked the first year that the new intake in English-medium schools outstripped that of the Chinese schools. See Jim Baker, *Crossroads: A Popular History of Malaysia and Singapore* (Singapore: Marshall Cavendish Editions, 2006), p. 263–65; and C. M. Turnbull, *A History of Modern Singapore, 1819–2005* (Singapore: NUS Press, 2009), pp. 247–50.

31 The May 13 incident, which saw a clash between Chinese Middle School students and the police, helped kick-start a period of increased political activism in Singapore. Although its significance tends to be downplayed in official histories, those involved often recall the events with some degree of pride and fondness. For a more detailed account by May 13 participants, see Tan Jing Quee, Tan Kok Chiang and Hong Lysa (eds.), *The May 13 Generation: The Chinese Middle Schools Student Movement and Singapore Politics in the 1950s* (Petaling Jaya, Malaysia: Strategic Information and Research Development Centre, 2011).

37 D. N. Pritt, a renowned Queen's Counsel and left-wing champion, was brought in to defend members of the University of Malaya Socialist Club (USC) against the British colonial government during the *Fajar* sedition trial of 1954. Lee Kuan Yew, who was legal adviser to the club, served as Pritt's legal assistant in defending the USC's eight-member editorial committee against charges that they had published seditious articles in the May 10 issue of the club journal, *Fajar.* The students' strongly negative response to the military initiative to establish the Southeast Asia Treaty Organisation (perceiving it as continued Anglo-American aggression in the region) in the journal belied the usual framing of English-educated intellectuals as mostly politically apathetic, and stoked the British government's fears that they had managed to bridge the divide between English-educated and Chinese-educated anti-colonial activists. The case was quickly dismissed, with the trial boosting Lee's reputation in left-wing circles, thereby helping to pave the way for his becoming the leader of the progressive People's Action Party formed later that year. For more, see Kah Seng Loh, Edgar Liao, Cheng Tju Lim and Guo-Quan Seng (eds.), *The University Socialist Club and the Contest for Malaya: Tangled Strands of Modernity* (Amsterdam: Amsterdam University Press, 2012).

50 Lim Chin Siong and Fong Swee Suan were leading trade unionists in the 1950s. Coming from Chinese-educated backgrounds, a combination of ability, commitment and charisma brought them to the forefront of the trade union and anti-colonial movements. Fong was one of the founding members of the People's Action Party (PAP), and Lim, one of the party's first assemblymen in the groundbreaking 1955 Legislative Assembly, alongside Lee Kuan Yew and Goh Chew Chua.

Representing the radical left-wing of the party, Lim and Fong would later be accused of being communists. Dominant historical narratives in Singapore tend towards this interpretation, but recent divergent accounts have questioned the unequivocal vilification of the radical left. See Tan Jing Quee and Jomo K. S. (eds.), *Comet in Our Sky: Lim Chin Siong in History* (Kuala Lumpur: Insan, 2001); and Mark R. Frost and Yu-Mei Balasingamchow, *Singapore: A Biography* (Singapore: Editions Didier Millet / National Museum of Singapore, 2011), pp. 409–10.

52 For a largely mainstream interpretation of the Hock Lee Bus Riots, see Channel NewsAsia's TV documentary "Days of Rage: Hock Lee Bus Riots" *<www.channelnewsasia.com/tv/tvshows/daysofrage/hock-lee-bus-riots/968850.html>*. For an alternative approach, see "Politics of the Chinese-speaking Communities in Singapore in the 1950s: The Shaping of Mass Politics" by Hong Lysa in *May 13 Generation*, pp. 80–84.

54 Article on Chong Lon Chong taken from *The Straits Times*, July 2, 1955, p. 8.

63 Wally Wood (1927–1981) is widely recognised as one of the greatest comics artists to emerge in the 1950s, working on various titles for EC Comics, DC Comics and Marvel Comics, including *Weird Science*, *Mad* magazine and *Daredevil.* By 1980, however, problems with alcoholism as well as declining health and career prospects would lead him to take on work drawing pornographic comics. Wood took his own life with a gun in 1981.

67 *Children's Paradise* <<儿童乐园>> magazine, founded by editor-artist Lo Koon-Chiu (1918–2012) in 1953, was the first full-coloured children's comic in Hong Kong. With its well-crafted and beautifully drawn stories, it proved to be immensely popular and influential, with 1,006 issues published by the end of its run in 1994.

80 *"Kia kee lai!"* ("Stand up!" or "On your feet!") was a phrase used by Lim Chin Siong. " 'Look friends, only dogs have licences and numbers…The British say you cannot stand on your own two feet. Show them that you can stand!' – at which point, according to one eye witness, 40,000 people 'leapt up – shining with sweat, fists in the air – shouting '*Merdeka*' " (Frost and Balasingamchow, *Singapore: A Biography*, pp. 355–56).

81 "I Love My Malaya" was a nationalistic song adapted from the popular Taiwanese folk song "Taiwan Is My Home" <<我爱我的台湾岛>>.

82 Force 136 was a special operations task force set up in 1940 by the British to gather intelligence, as well as to incite, organise and support indigenous resistance groups in enemy-occupied territory in Southeast Asia. In Malaya, its recruits consisted mainly of Kuomintang Chinese, as well as some Malay and Indian agents. After the Japanese conquest of Malaya and Singapore, Force 136 fighters worked with the Malayan People's Anti-Japanese Army (MPAJA) in fighting the Japanese. The MPAJA, formed by the Malayan Communist Party (MCP) after the fall of Singapore, had built up to a force of some six to ten thousand guerrilla recruits by 1945, but the war would be won before any large-scale joint operation with Force 136 was launched. Made up of predominantly Chinese working class youths, these MPAJA guerrillas would later form the core of the MCP's anti-British armed insurgency. For more on Force 136, see Tan Chong Tee, *Force 136: Story of a WWII Resistance Fighter* (Singapore: Asiapac Books, 3rd ed., 2007).

86 American comics publisher EC Comics started out as Educational Comics before becoming known as Entertaining Comics. Under William Gaines, it enjoyed popular success from 1949, publishing horror, crime, science fiction and war titles. The war comics line (*Two-Fisted Tales* and *Frontline Combat*), edited, written and sometimes drawn by Harvey Kurtzman (1924–1993), stood out for their meticulously researched stories and anti-war stance. The horror comics titles (*Tales From the Crypt*, *The Vault of Horror* and *The Haunt of Fear*), however, were notorious for their gleeful depiction of gruesome acts, and helped spur the mounting public criticism of the comics industry. Psychologist Fredric Wertham led the way in linking comics reading with juvenile delinquency. The publication of his book *Seduction of the Innocent* in 1954 helped pressure a move towards self-regulation within the comics industry, and culminated in the introduction of the Comics Code that same year. Wertham's influence arguably stunted the growth and development of American comics for decades, although more recent studies have found multiple flaws in his methodology and approach. See Dave Itzkoff, "Scholar Finds Flaws in Work by Archenemy of Comics," *New York Times*, February 19, 2013 <www.nytimes.com/2013/02/20/books/flaws-found-in-fredric-werthams-comic-book-studies.html>.

91 After their conquest of Singapore, the Japanese tapped into nationalist passions amongst Indian prisoners of war and set up the Indian National Army (INA) as part of its "Asia for Asiatics" propaganda campaign. The ostensible goal was to fight for India's independence from the British. The INA would gain real traction with the arrival in Singapore of Subhas Chandra Bose, the charismatic leader of the Indian Independence League, in July 1943. By the time it set out to join the Indian front in 1944, however, the tide of war had already turned, and the army was pushed back to Burma along with the Japanese army without making any significant advances. See Turnbull, *A History of Modern Singapore,* pp. 216–50, and Lee Geok Boi, *The Syonan Years: Singapore Under Japanese Rule 1942–1945* (Singapore: National Archives of Singapore and Epigram, 2005), pp. 231–40.

92 The Malayan Communist Party under Chin Peng had been treated as anti-Japanese heroes after WWII, but when it became clear that British and communist aims could not find common ground, the MCP sought an armed struggle instead. Known as the Malayan Emergency, the insurgency war lasted from 1948 to 1960. So-called New Villages were set up as part of the Briggs Plan, a British strategy to eliminate communist influence in Malaya by relocating some half a million predominantly Chinese squatters into highly policed gated compounds, in a bid to cut off supplies and other support to the communist guerrillas. Faced with the vast counter-insurgency resources of the British army, the MCP's effectiveness as a fighting force was largely curtailed by the mid-1950s.

108 First published in 1990, *Mr Kiasu* became one of the most commercially successful and iconic comics series from Singapore. The *kiasu* (Hokkien for "being afraid to lose") mentality, defined by the Oxford English Dictionary as a "grasping, selfish attitude," was thought to be a peculiarly Singaporean trait. With its recognisable home-grown character, the comic so resonated with local readers that it even established a tie-up with fast food behemoth McDonald's for a "Kiasu Burger" in Singapore at one point.

109 A pioneer in animation and comics, Winsor McCay (1867–1934) is best remembered for his innovations in the 1914 vaudeville animation feature *Gertie the Dinosaur*, as well as his comic strips *Little Nemo in Slumberland* (1905–1911, 1924–1926), and *Dream of the Rarebit Fiend* (1904–1913, 1923–1925). Both comics featured their characters having fantastical dreams. *Little Nemo* was a full-coloured, lushly illustrated strip aimed at younger readers, while *Rarebit Fiend* dealt with more adult anxieties, often revealing certain unflattering or terrifying aspects of the dreamer's psyche.

110 *Eagle* was a British children's comics weekly founded by an Anglican vicar, Marcus Morris (1915–1989), and the artist Frank Hampson (1918–1985). Morris sought to produce a comic that could provide an edifying alternative to the popular horror and crime comics from the United States. In 1949, Morris and Hampson put together a dummy issue of the comic, sparing no expense

in building models and costumes in order to provide their artists with proper references for their drawings. The idea was seen as a risky venture, and they were turned down by several publishers in London until Hulton Press finally decided to take a gamble on it. *Eagle* turned out to be a resounding success, with the first issue released in April 1950 alone selling 900,000 copies.

113 The British colonisation of Singapore began in 1819 with the arrival of Sir Stamford Raffles, who would ink a formal agreement with the Johore prince Tengku Hussein, granting the British the right to establish a trading post in Singapore. The portrayal of the British as "invaders" as such is not strictly accurate, although British colonial rule was arguably predicated on the belief in the superiority of Western culture and technology. It would continue until the Japanese conquest of Malaya in 1942.

114 The court hearing shown on these pages is based on an actual postal workers' strike in 1952. Lee Kuan Yew, a recent graduate from Cambridge University and newly employed at the law offices of Laycock & Ong, became the legal adviser to the postal workers union, which was in the middle of a wage dispute with the British government. The successful resolution of the dispute, with plenty of glowing press centered on Lee's skill and effectiveness in handling negotiations, further burnished the young lawyer's growing reputation as a left-wing champion of the underdog.

116 The British Empire was no longer financially sustainable after WWII, and the British recognised the need to withdraw from the colonies stretching from India to Malaya. They had hoped, however, to maintain their economic and strategic interests in the regions by handing power over to "acceptable" members of the local elite: conservative, right-wing leaders who would be sympathetic to British interests. In Singapore, the conservative Progressive Party (SPP), made up of English-educated, Western-oriented upper-class commercial and professional men advocating for a gradual approach towards constitutional reform and self-government, was initially earmarked for the role. Despite the self-interested nature of many of their actions, the British commitment to an orderly decolonisation in Malaya and Singapore, manifested through socioeconomic programmes designed to reshape education, housing and labour, can scarcely be disregarded. These would go on to play an important role in Singapore's eventual viability as a city-state. For more, see Turnbull, *A History of Modern Singapore*, pp. 238–43.

117 The Rendel Constitution led to the 1955 elections, which would provide Singapore with limited self-government (defence, internal security and foreign affairs would remain under British control). The electoral roll was expanded, with the aim of engaging more Singaporeans in the political process. The results took both the British and the contesting parties by surprise, with the SPP's conservative approach soundly rejected at the polls (ibid., pp. 244–60).

The Labour Front under David Marshall, championing a much faster route to independence, emerged victorious, garnering 10 of the 25 seats. It was invited to form a coalition government with the Singapore Alliance, and Marshall became the first Chief Minister in Singapore's first elected government in 1955. The People's Action Party (PAP) won 3 seats to become part of the opposition. It was a calculated decision by the party leadership to contest only a handful of seats. They saw the 1955 election as a transitional one, since the government would only have restricted powers under the Rendel Constitution. By positioning itself as a strong and vocal left-wing opposition in the Legislative Assembly, the new party sought instead to win over the Chinese-educated masses, with the intent to bolster their electoral base until full self-government could be realised.

118 Singapore would not be fully independent, since the British retained control over defence and non-commercial foreign affairs, while a council was set up to handle internal security. For more on the issue of internal security, see notes to pp. 130–31.

119 The postal workers' negotiations helped bridge Lee Kuan Yew with the trade unions and the student movements, who in turn promised the support base that would be necessary for his aspirations to set up a viable anti-colonial political party. The young lawyer was at the forefront of a group of English-educated moderates seeking to lead Singapore to independence on a Fabian socialist model. Joining forces with Lim Chin Siong and the other trade unionists provided them with the mass support of the Chinese-speaking majority, whilst the Chinese-educated leaders saw Lee's considerable legal and political acumen and knowledge of constitutional practice as an advantage in their struggles against British colonialism. For more, see Frost and Balasingamchow, *Singapore: A Biography*, pp. 350–55.

123 The Lim Chin Siong anecdote referred to here was recounted by David Marshall in an interview in Melanie Chew, *Leaders of Singapore* (Singapore: Resource Press, 1996), p. 79.

128 The incident depicted here refers to Marshall's threat to resign as Chief Minister in July 1955, after Governor Sir Robert Black's initial rejection of his request for the appointment of four assistant ministers.

129 *Pogo* was a comic strip created by Walt Kelly (1913–1973) that featured anthropomorphic funny animal characters, including the titular Pogo, a possum, and his alligator friend Albert. It ran from 1948 to 1975, and at its peak was syndicated in nearly 500 newspapers in 14 countries.

130 Despite facing numerous obstacles, ranging from British scepticism to political opposition from both the right and radical left, David Marshall succeeded in introducing reforms and ideas that addressed the fundamental grievances of Singaporeans during his tenure as Chief Minister. His genuine and principled sympathy for student and worker causes, however, made him unwilling to crack down on

their actions, and made the British wary of handing over full powers of internal self-government to Singapore. Whilst amenable to making many concessions, the colonial government was adamant about retaining powers over internal security. Marshall's flamboyant and uncompromising style of politics arguably doomed negotiations during constitutional talks in London, and led to his resignation as Chief Minister in June 1956 (see Turnbull, *A History of Modern Singapore*, pp. 262–65).

131   The new Chief Minister, Lim Yew Hock, was much more willing to act against the students and workers. There is some evidence to suggest that he might even have sought to provoke confrontations in order to justify the arrests of left-wing leaders such as Lim Chin Siong (see "Lim Chin Siong in Britain's Southeast Asian De-colonisation" by Greg Poulgrain, from Tan and Jomo [eds.], *Comet in Our Sky*, p. 117). The arrest of Lim and 18 Middle Road union leaders during the student riots in October 1956 gave the British enough assurance to grant Singapore greater powers of self-government. The deal offered to the new Chief Minister was, in fact, very similar to the one rejected by David Marshall in 1956. The British were now willing to cede nominal control of internal security, however, by transferring power to an Internal Security Council comprising three representatives from Singapore, three from Britain and one from the Federation of Malaya. Given that the tussle over internal security was largely centred around the detention of leftist elements, this change could be seen as essentially cosmetic in nature, with the British confident that the deciding Federation vote would always favour any moves against the radical left.

The new constitution was to come in place after the 1959 elections. Having taken the necessary actions to win favour as well as concessions from the British, Lim Yew Hock's government was unable to reap any electoral benefits. The PAP's decision to consolidate mass support by playing the role of the anti-colonial opposition during the transitional period proved to be prescient, however. It swept to power in 1959, capturing 43 of the 51 seats contested. See Baker, *Crossroads*, pp. 271–76.

144   The post-war period in Japan saw a boom in manga publishing. *Akabon* or "red books" (赤本, so-named for their prominent use of red ink to add tone to black-and-white line art) were a low-cost alternative to expensive pre-war hardback manga collections. This cheaper new format, primarily distributed via rental libraries, gave many struggling manga artists their first big break, among them Osamu Tezuka.

The late 1950s saw the emergence of a grittier, more realistic breed of manga aimed at older readers, known as *gekiga* (劇画, meaning "dramatic pictures"), a genre distinct from the traditional *manga* (漫画, meaning "whimsical pictures") produced for children. The term was coined by Yoshihiro Tatsumi (1935–2015), although the form's leading light was arguably Yoshiharu Tsuge (b. 1937). The movement had a profound effect on Tezuka as

well, leading him to create multi-volume works such as *Phoenix* and *Message to Adolf*, which featured more mature content focused in part on the turbulent sociopolitical changes wrought on Japan after the war.

146   After the PAP's election victory in 1959, eight of the detained Middle Road union leaders including Lim Chin Siong, Fong Swee Suan, James Puthucheary, Devan Nair and Sidney Woodhull were released. Lee Kuan Yew's insistence on their release was, as he had anticipated, a popular move, although there are suggestions that he had in effect manoeuvred both the left-wing elements of his party as well as the British over the issue of their detention (see "Lim Chin Siong and the 'Singapore Story'" by T. N. Harper, in Tan and Jomo, *Comet in Our Sky*, pp. 18–48). Many others arrested in 1956 remained in detention, including Lim's brother, Lim Chin Joo.

164   The Bukit Ho Swee Fire, the biggest ever recorded in Singapore, broke out at 3:20 p.m. on May 25, 1961. The cause of the fire has never been firmly established, although official accounts place the onus on the inherent flammability of the squatter settlement, which could have easily been set ablaze in the event of a household accident. Unsubstantiated rumours of arson have always persisted, however, with some placing the blame on the government, which had been seeking to redevelop the land for some time. Among these were claims that the fire could have served as convenient grounds to force the eviction of recalcitrant kampong residents. In the larger scheme of things, the Bukit Ho Swee Fire marked the beginning of the end of large-scale squatter dwellings, and helped push Singapore towards its modern incarnation as an urban city-state, where the majority of the population live in public housing. For a nuanced account of the fire and its impact, see Loh Kah Seng, *Squatters into Citizens: The 1961 Bukit Ho Swee Fire and the Making of Modern Singapore* (Singapore: NUS Press, 2013).

167   *Catch-22* is a novel by Joseph Heller published in 1961. Set during WWII, the book satirised the murderous insanity of war and captured the anti-military zeitgeist of the Vietnam War (1954–1975) era. The title, which refers to a fictional bureaucratic military stipulation, became a byword for unsolvable logic puzzles, the only solution for which is made impossible by a circumstance or rule inherent in the puzzle.

168   Superhero comics arguably became the mainstream comics genre in the United States from the mid-1950s onward, thanks to the Comics Code, which frowned upon the excesses of war, crime and horror comics, but was open to the bloodless punch-ups depicted in superhero comics. Marvel Comics in particular helped reignite the genre through the talents of artist Jack Kirby (1917–1994) and editor-writer Stan Lee (b. 1922). Kirby's explosive, kinetic style made his characters' superhuman feats seem believable, and the Lee-Kirby team was able to create "humanized, troubled characters ambivalent about their powers" (Roger Sabin, *Comics, Comix & Graphic Novels*, London: Phaidon, 1996). Their successes included

The Fantastic Four (1961), *The Incredible Hulk* (1962), and, most of all, *The Amazing Spider-Man* (1963).

174 The alliance between moderate and left-wing elements in the PAP finally fell apart in July 1961. Events were kicked off when the vulnerability of the PAP's moderate wing was exposed by its losses in two by-elections in Anson and Hong Lim earlier that year. The Malayan Prime Minister, Tunku Abdul Rahman, was alarmed by the prospect of a more radical – and in his mind, communist – government taking over in Singapore. Having previously balked at the difficulties involved in a merger between the two territories, he now came to the conclusion that merger with Singapore and the Borneo territories would be necessary to prevent the possible emergence of a "second Cuba," which could be dangerous to Malaya's security.

The Tunku's change of heart alarmed Lim Chin Siong and his supporters, as they recognised that the move was directed at suppressing leftist influence. Lim subsequently sought and received assurances from Lord Selkirk, British High Commissioner for Singapore and Commissioner-General for Southeast Asia, that the British would not intervene if the leftists were able to unseat then Prime Minister Lee Kuan Yew through constitutional means. This meeting, which came to be known as the "Eden Hall Tea Party," angered Lee, who called for a vote of confidence in his leadership in an emergency meeting of the Legislative Assembly. The vote was won by a narrow margin, and 13 left-wing PAP members who had abstained from voting, including Lim, Sidney Woodhull and Fong Swee Suan, were expelled from the Party.

This splinter faction went on to form a new party, the Barisan Sosialis, with Lim Chin Siong as its Secretary-General, on July 29, 1961. Large-scale defections to the new party followed, leaving the PAP in a critically weakened and precarious position. See Turnbull, *A History of Modern Singapore*, pp. 277–80; and Frost and Balasingamchow, *Singapore: A Biography*, pp. 396–99.

186 Apart from its role in curtailing the perceived communist threat, a merger between Singapore and Malaya was also seen as inevitable and a historical necessity by many. Along with the strong historical, cultural and geographical ties connecting the two territories, merger presented the allure of a common market, whilst providing a roadmap to independence that was acceptable to the British. See John Drysdale, *Singapore: Struggle for Success* (Australia: George Allen and Unwin, 1984), pp. 258–60, 294–95.

There was, however, some opposition to the merger. Indonesian leader Sukarno saw the formation of the Federation of Malaysia as an attempt by the British to maintain colonial rule and influence in the region, and launched the *Konfrontasi* (Confrontation) campaign in response. The military operation was aimed at destabilising the new federation, with numerous armed infiltrations launched in the Borneo territories and the Malaysian Peninsula, as well as

indiscriminate bombings in Singapore, including the MacDonald House bombing on March 10, 1965. *Konfrontasi* formally ended with the signing of a peace treaty in 1966, soon after Suharto replaced Sukarno as president. See Marsita Omar, "The Indonesian-Malaysian Confrontation," <*eresources.nlb. gov.sg/infopedia/articles/SIP_1072_2010-03-25.html*>.

187 Within Singapore, the Barisan Sosialis opposed merger on various grounds, some of which were self-serving, and others perhaps more forward-looking. They were outmanoeuvred by the PAP in any case. For a closer look at the events leading up to the National Referendum on Merger in September 1962, see Drysdale, *Singapore: Struggle for Success*, pp. 283–312; and Albert Lau, *A Moment of Anguish: Singapore in Malaysia and the Politics of Disengagement* (Singapore: Times Academic Press, 1998).

189 Toh Chin Chye on the formulation of the ballot papers for the referendum on merger, in Chew, *Leaders of Singapore*, p. 92. For more on the PAP's strategy leading up to the referendum, see Willard A. Hanna, *The Formation of Malaysia: New Factor in World Politics* (New York: American Universities Field Staff, 1964), p. 116ff.

191 Between 1960 and 1963, the PAP demonstrated tremendous zeal and pragmatism in introducing social and economic reforms to improve standards of living in Singapore. They built more than 24,000 public housing units under the Housing Development Board scheme, and significantly increased expenditure on education and healthcare. The newly established Public Utilities Board introduced basic amenities ranging from running water to electricity and improved sanitation, whilst 4,000 acres of swamp and wasteland in Jurong were turned into an industrial estate that would eventually lay the foundations for Singapore's economic growth. Measures were also taken to combat crime and improve women's rights.

Having successfully won independence from British rule and accomplished merger with Malaysia, the PAP had sufficient grounds for optimism in the 1963 elections, even if its grassroots base had been decimated by the split with the Barisan Sosialis just two years earlier. Aside from their tangible achievements, they had consolidated ground support via community centres and the effective control of public broadcast channels such as television. As the incumbent party, the PAP was certainly in a position to make electoral and constitutional laws work in its favour.

In February 1963, the launch of Operation Coldstore saw the detention of Lim Chin Siong and other leading members of the Barisan Sosialis, thus greatly weakening the opposition. For all that, the decisiveness of the PAP's electoral victory in September that year, in which they won 37 of 51 seats, still came as a surprise. In retrospect, this was partly due to the first-past-the-post electoral system, which allowed the party to win three-quarters of the seats contested, despite receiving only 46.5% of the popular vote. The split in the opposition vote in many constituencies is also estimated to have cost the Barisan as many as 17 seats. For more, see Turnbull, *A History of Modern Singapore*, pp. 282–86; and Lau, *A Moment of Anguish*, pp. 48–53.

193   The question of Lim Chin Siong's association with the Malayan Communist Party has occupied a central place in the narrative of Singapore's modern history. On the one hand, the "us vs. them" Cold War mentality of the era promoted the identification and vilification of any person or group with leftist leanings with the Communist United Front. This was certainly how Lim and the Barisan Sosialis have been portrayed in official histories. However, while the radical left did not shy away from using more militant action in the form of strikes and protests, the actual degree of direct communist influence remains debatable. Declassified documents of British colonial government records in recent years have provided additional fuel to revisionist accounts. For more, see "Lim Chin Siong and the 'Singapore Story'" by T. N. Harper and "Lim Chin Siong in Britain's Southeast Asian De-colonisation" by Greg Poulgrain, both in Tan and Jomo, *Comet in Our Sky;* and Frost and Balasingamchow, *Singapore: A Biography*, pp. 374–78 and 409–10.

Lim's image as a rabble-rouser has often been bolstered by popular accounts of his speech at a PAP rally on October 25, 1956, which claim that he had instigated the crowd to "*pah matah*" (Hokkien for "beat the police"), which led to widespread rioting. Historian Thum Ping Tjin's recent research, however, points to evidence in the British Archives that suggests that Lim had in fact entreated the crowd *not* to vent their discontent on the police. See <*www. theonlinecitizen.com/2014/05/lim-chin-siong-was-wrongfully-detained*> and another historian's refutation of Thum's claims: <*www.ipscommons.sg/lim-chin-siong-and-that-beauty-world-speech-a-closer-look*>.

194   The PAP's victory in the 1963 elections included wins in the predominantly Malay constituencies of Geylang Serai, Kampong Kembangan and the Southern Islands, this despite opposition from the Singapore Alliance, which had received the backing of Federal leaders, including Tunku Abdul Rahman himself. Their proven ability to appeal across racial lines emboldened the PAP to take part in the Malaysian federal elections in 1964, a premature and ultimately disastrous move that ended up raising the ire of federal political leaders and eventually contributed to Singapore's ouster from Malaysia in 1965. For more, see Lau, *A Moment of Anguish*.

Lee Kuan Yew had made an initial commitment to the Tunku that the PAP would not take part in the first Malaysian federal elections, but the exact nature of this agreement remains disputed (see Sonny Yap, Richard Lim and Leong Weng Kam, *Men in White: The Untold Story of Singapore's Ruling Political Party* [Singapore: Singapore Press Holdings, 2009], pp. 264–65). In any case, Lee had stated in a speech that "We will not take part in the 1964 elections in the Federation" (*Sunday Times*, September 29, 1963).

195   The movement towards merger as a means of containing the influence of the radical left in Singapore had arguably led to hurried negotiations where certain issues had been glossed over, amongst which was the role Singapore would play in federal politics. The United Malays National Organisation (UMNO) leaders appeared to envision, at best, a slow integration of the PAP into their conservative and communalist style of governance, while the PAP leaders sought a much quicker timetable in which they could take an active role in Malaysian politics. The latter's consequent push towards a greater voice and influence would lead to conflicts with threatened pro-Malay elements within the Federation, as well as the conservative Malaysian Chinese Association (MCA). See Turnbull, *A History of Modern Singapore*, pp. 287–90.

196   Although the PAP performed poorly in the 1964 federal elections, they had effectively presented themselves as a potential threat to UMNO's approach to politics. The latter now sought to attack the PAP within Singapore, with its secretary-general Dato Syed Ja'afar Albar spearheading attempts to exploit and stir up discontent amongst Singapore Malays. See Turnbull, *A History of Modern Singapore*, pp. 290–92; and "The Alliance Strikes Back" in Lau, *A Moment of Anguish*, pp. 131–60.

197   MCA president Tan Siew Sin was able to use his position as Federal Finance Minister to curtail Singapore's economy when he felt that the MCA's position as UMNO's main ally was being threatened. His proposals, such as a punishing tax plan raised during budgetary parliamentary debates in November 1964, would badly hamper Singapore's own Finance Minister Goh Keng Swee's plans for the industrialisation of the island state. Goh eventually became a prime mover behind Singapore's split from Malaysia, convinced as he was that, for all the intimidating challenges it would face, Singapore would stand a better chance of achieving economic growth as well as swifter development as an independent nation free of Federal interference (see Turnbull, *A History of Modern Singapore*, pp. 287–300; and Lau, *A Moment of Anguish*, pp. 214–17).

Once the PAP's hopes of supplanting the MCA as the ruling Malaysian Alliance Party's second partner had been quashed, its decision to step into the role of an active opposition party within the Federation arguably set it on a collision course with UMNO, in which neither side was willing to give way. By espousing a non-communal policy of "a democratic Malaysian Malaysia" that repudiated the provision of special rights and privileges for Malays, and in further attempting to form a non-communal opposition bloc under the banner of the Malaysian Solidarity Convention (MSC), the PAP had upset the Malaysian politico-communal status quo by presenting a challenge to what UMNO saw as an inviolable component of the Malaysian social and political contract. For more, see "'We Are on Collision Course'" in Lau, *A Moment of Anguish*, pp. 211–52.

198   Rising rhetoric on both sides led to communal riots in Singapore in July 1964 during a Muslim procession to celebrate the Prophet Muhammad's birthday. Conflicting explanations of what had sparked the riots remain unresolved (see Baker, *Crossroads*, pp. 314–15). Further outbreaks of violence occurred in August and September, resulting in 36 deaths, with more than 550 injured over the three months of rioting. Even though the riots came as a shock to the leaders on both sides of the straits, it failed to generate anything more than a brief truce. By July 1965, a select group of senior leaders on both sides had embarked on secret negotiations that would lead to the official separation of Singapore from Malaysia on August 9, 1965. For more, see "The Singapore Riots" in Lau, ibid., pp. 161–210.

210   The "Singapore Story" depicted here represents the official narrative of Singapore's history. The satirical take anticipates the launch of the National Education programme in 1997. This was a major push by the PAP government to "engender a shared sense of nationhood" in youths and students, by instilling core values and beliefs in newer generations that had not experienced the nation's early struggles, with the expressed aim to "ensure [Singapore's] continued success and well-being."

231–47   The PAP's attempts to control the media, alongside its claims of requiring a new media model to suit Singapore's unique circumstances, have been the subject of much analysis. Sources include Cheong Yip Seng, *OB Markers* (Singapore: Straits Times Press, 2013); Cherian George, *Freedom from the Press: Journalism and State Power in Singapore* (Singapore: NUS Press, 2012); and Francis Seow, *The Media Enthralled: Singapore Revisited* (USA: Lynne Rienner Publishers, 1998).

251   Operation Spectrum was a security operation in which the Internal Security Act (ISA) was invoked for the arrest and detention of 22 activists with suspected Marxist links, including many church social workers, in May and June 1987. It continues to be an uncertain and somewhat chequered part of Singapore's history. With the absence of any official re-examination or analysis, an abundance of rumour, speculation and educated guesses at best instead surrounds the actual events. Historian C. M. Turnbull concluded that "[t]he alleged Marxist Conspiracy and the Liberation Theology menace turned out to be myths" (Turnbull, *A History of Modern Singapore*, p. 339). The exact reasons for developing and perpetuating such "myths" remain murky, however, with theories ranging from a genuine fear of a communist threat to attempts to prevent the Catholic Church from possibly becoming a legitimate political force in post-independence Singapore.

255   The Chinese Communist Party's successes in the post-WWII era were a source of pride for many overseas Chinese, and moderate leaders of the PAP came to see the Chinese-educated as being particularly susceptible to communist influence. Nanyang University, largely funded by businessman Tan Lark Sye, was thought to have been a hotbed of communist and communalist activity. Consequently, it was merged with the University of Singapore in 1980 to form the National University of Singapore. Often portrayed as chauvinists, Chinese activists championing Chinese education from the 1950s to the '70s have argued that their fears that the PAP's policies would lead to the eventual decline and erosion of the Chinese language and culture in Singapore have turned out to be well-founded.

256   Lee Kuan Yew's claim about putting on knuckle-dusters to tackle his critics (see Han Fook Kwang, Warren Fernandez and Sumiko Tan, *Lee Kuan Yew: The Man and His Ideas* [Singapore: Times Editions, 1998], p. 126) was made in response to writer Catherine Lim's criticism of Prime Minister Goh Chok Tong in 1994. The *Straits Times* had published several pieces of her political commentary, for which she had received a stern slap on the wrist. The authors and Lee himself contended that such political commentary would never have been risked when Lee was still Prime Minister, given his reputation for taking on his critics with an iron fist.

This no-nonsense brand of state authoritarianism was often justified by the argument that respect for leaders and hierarchy constituted a cardinal principle of Asian Confucian societies. When speaking about China's Tiananmen Incident of 1989 at the Institute of International Relations in Paris, May 23, 1990, Lee said: "You cannot mock a great leader in an Asian Confucian society. If he allows himself to be mocked, he is finished" (Lianhe Zaobao [ed.], *Lee Kuan Yew on China and Hongkong after Tiananmen* [Singapore: Shing Lee Publishers, 1990], p. 136). Even amongst leaders within Asia, however, there has been a distinct lack of agreement concerning this concept of an all-encompassing umbrella of "Asian core values," which include a deference to societal interests over the individual, respect for authority and prizing consensus over confrontation. For example, see "What Would Confucius Say Now?," *The Economist*, July 23, 1998 <www.economist.com/node/169045>.

During his 1988 National Day Rally speech, while discussing the transition of leadership to his successor Goh Chok Tong in 1990, Lee Kuan Yew vowed to "get up" from his grave if he sensed that Singapore was in trouble. It appeared to convey his intention to continue playing a role in Singapore's politics even after stepping down as Prime Minister.

257   Joshua Benjamin Jeyaretnam (commonly known as J. B. Jeyaretnam or JBJ) was Secretary-General of the Workers' Party for 30 years (1971–2001). He stood for Parliament five times from 1972 onwards before making a breakthrough in the 1981 Anson by-elections, when he defeated PAP candidate Pang Kim Hin. The last opposition candidates to successfully contest in general elections had been members of the Barisan Sosialis in 1963, but their decision to walk out of Parliament and boycott it in protest kicked off an unbroken run of 18 years of uncontested governance for the PAP, which enjoyed a single-

party domination of the legislature without any opposition. Jeyaretnam retained his Anson seat in 1984, and was joined then by the Singapore Democratic Party's Chiam See Tong, who became the second opposition MP. Jeyaretnam passed away in 2008 at the age of 82. See Geoffrey Robertson, "Joshua Jeyaretnam," *The Guardian*, October 7, 2008 <*www.theguardian.com/world/2008/oct/07/2*>.

258   Kuo Pao Kun (1939–2002) was a pioneer in Singapore theatre, writing plays in both Chinese and English, including *The Coffin Is Too Big for the Hole*, *No Parking on Odd Days*, *Mama Looking for Her Cat* and *Lao Jiu*. His work combined traditional and experimental elements, and often incorporated acute social commentary and critique. The agitprop elements in his early plays led to his detention under the Internal Security Act from March 1976 to October 1980, and the revocation of his citizenship from 1977 to 1992. Following his release, Kuo continued with his theatre work and went on to become one of the most influential forces in the local arts scene, founding both the Practice Theatre Ensemble, a bilingual theatre group that was later renamed the Theatre Practice (1986), and the independent arts centre the Substation (1990). For his lifework, Kuo was awarded the Cultural Medallion in 1990, the highest honour for a Singapore artist.

262   The San Diego Comic Convention (SDCC) or Comic-Con was founded by comics artist and letterer Shel Dorf, comics bookstore owner Richard Alf and publisher Ken Krueger in 1970. Early incarnations of the event were held at various venues such as the U. S. Grant and El Cortez Hotels, and attended by just a few hundred fans. The numbers grew steadily, however, and by 2010, thanks to increased Hollywood interest and participation, media attention and a widened fan base, Comic-Con had become a major pop cultural event attracting more than 130,000 attendees annually. SDCC moved to the relatively small San Diego Convention and Performing Arts Center (CPAC) in 1979, and relocated to its present home at the newly built San Diego Convention Center in 1991.

274   Famed Dutch developmental economist Albert Winsemius came to Singapore as part of a United Nations industrial survey mission in 1960, and served as the nation's long-time chief economic adviser from 1961 to 1984. Working closely with Lee Kuan Yew and successive Finance Ministers Lim Kim San, Goh Keng Swee and Hon Sui Sen, Winsemius is credited with providing the PAP with a blueprint for Singapore's "economic miracle." In particular, the Dutch economist emphasised the importance of making the country attractive to foreign investors and industry through infrastructural development, political stability, labour discipline and education. See Turnbull, *A History of Modern Singapore*, pp. 281, 302, 358; and Kees Tamboer, "Albert Winsemius, 'Founding Father' of Singapore," *IIAS Newsletter #9*, Summer 1996 (Leiden, Netherlands: International Institute for Asian Studies, 1996) <*www.iias.nl/iiasn/iiasn9/soueasia/winsemiu.html*>.

279   *The Man in the High Castle* is a 1962 science fiction alternative history novel by Philip K. Dick, which imagines a world where the Axis Powers of Japan and Nazi Germany had emerged as the victors of WWII. The book features a story within the story, in the form of a novel titled *The Grasshopper Lies Heavy* read by several characters, which in turn offers an alternate history where the Allied Powers had won the war, the details of which differ from our real world history.

280   During the height of tensions between Singapore and Malaysia, there were calls from some UMNO quarters for Lee Kuan Yew and other PAP leaders to be arrested. Plans were made for a Singapore government-in-exile to be set up under Minister for Culture S. Rajaratnam in Cambodia, owing to Lee's personal friendship with head of state Prince Norodom Sihanouk. For more, see Drysdale, *Singapore: Struggle for Success*, p. 380; Alex Josey, *Lee Kuan Yew: The Crucial Years* (Singapore: Marshall Cavendish Editions, 2012), pp. 282–87; and Michael Leifer, *Singapore's Foreign Policy: Coping with Vulnerability* (London: Routledge, 2000), p. 52.

281   The phrase "men in white" refers to the PAP's practice of appearing at public events all decked out in white, as a symbol of the party's purity and incorruptibility. Since the party's inception in 1954, white has been the adopted colour of choice for all formal party occasions. All symbolism aside, the PAP's commitment to a stable and clean government has been, by most conventional measures and accounts, recognised as one of its key defining traits and enduring achievements. See Drysdale, *Singapore: Struggle for Success*, p. 226; and Frost and Balasingamchow, *Singapore: A Biography*, pp. 383–86.

297   After leaving his job as an animator at Disney in 1942, Carl Barks (1901–2000) ended up working on Donald Duck stories for comics publisher Western Publishing. He created many memorable characters from Scrooge McDuck to the Beagle Boys, but remained largely anonymous, as Disney animations and comic book licences carried only Walt Disney's name. Barks's recognisable style, however, led him to be dubbed "The Good Duck Artist." It was not until 1960 that two of his fans were able to track down the identity of the man behind the comics. Gifted with the ability to imbue comics characters with unforgettable personalities, Barks has been hailed as one of the most important comics artists of the 20th century, and was famously referred to as "the Hans Christian Andersen of comic books" by fellow cartoonist Will Eisner (1917–2005).

302   The writing tools shown here, from top left to right, are: Faber-Castell HB Pencil, Sakura Pigma Micron 03, Ballpoint Pen (brand unknown), Artline Calligraphy Pen 2.0, Winsor & Newton Series 7 Size 1 Sable Brush, Chinese calligraphic brush (brand unknown), Nikko Comic Pen Nib G-model with nib holder, Nicker Poster Colour (White, No. 51) and Pentel Hi-Polymer Erasers, and Pentel Selfit 0.5 mm Mechanical Pencil.

ACKNOWLEDGEMENTS

Special thanks to:

Bernadette Baker-Baughman, Charlie Beckerman, Mike Carey, Chan Shiuan, Janice Chiang, Choo Zheng Xi, Fong Hoe Fang, Cherian George, Goh Eck Kheng, Goh Soon Chye, Paul Gravett, Vera Greentea, Sam Holmes, Iskander, Nicholas Jainschigg, jooja!, Ambrose Khaw, Chip Kidd, Koh Boon Long, Dan Koh, Koeh Sia Yong, Lee Han Shih, Lee Tse Ling, Paul Levitz, Alwyn Liang, Cheryl Liew, Lim Cheng Tju, Lim Li Kok, Bob Mecoy, Kiruthiga Mahendran, David Mazzucchelli, Aaron McConnell, Mom & Dad, Jean-Paul Moulin, Akshita Vijay Nanda, Zaleha Othman, Pang Xueling, Derek Royal, Siew Kum Hong, Sara Siew, Joyce Sim, Harminder Singh, Rizal Solomon, Gary Tan, Tan Hwee Ann, Kevin YL Tan, Sarah Tan, Tan Shufern, David J. Sung, Tan Thiam Chye, Aaron Thng, Sudhir T Vadaketh, Edmund Wee, Drew Williams, Gene Yang, Danny Yee, Sue Yee, Yeo Oi Sang, Yeo Hak Sim, Robert Yeo, and Yong Wen Yeu.

ABOUT THE AUTHOR

Sonny Liew is an award-winning comics artist, painter and illustrator whose work includes the *New York Times* bestseller *The Shadow Hero* with Gene Luen Yang (First Second Books), *My Faith in Frankie* with Mike Carey (DC Vertigo), *Sense & Sensibility* with Nancy Butler (Marvel Comics) and *Doctor Fate* with Paul Levitz (DC Comics).

He has received Eisner nominations for *The Shadow Hero* and *Wonderland* (Disney Press), as well as for spearheading *Liquid City* (Image Comics), a multi-volume comics anthology featuring creators from Southeast Asia. His *Malinky Robot* series is a 2004 Xeric grant recipient and winner of the Best Science Fiction Comic Album Award at the 2009 Utopiales SF Festival in Nantes. He received the Singapore National Arts Council's Young Artist Award in 2010.

Born in Malaysia, he lives in Singapore, where he sleeps with the fishes.

ALSO BY SONNY LIEW

THE SHADOW HERO with Gene Luen Yang
MALINKY ROBOT
GEORGETTE CHEN: WARM NIGHTS, DEATHLESS DAYS
MY FAITH IN FRANKIE with Mike Carey
SENSE & SENSIBILITY with Nancy Butler
WONDERLAND with Tommy Kovac
DOCTOR FATE with Paul Levitz

All rights reserved. Published in the United States by Pantheon Books, a division of Penguin Random House LLC, New York, and distributed in Canada by Random House of Canada, a division of Penguin Random House Canada Ltd., Toronto. Originally published in paperback in Singapore by Epigram Books in 2015.

Pantheon Books and colophon are registered trademarks of Penguin Random House LLC.

Grateful acknowledgment is made to the following for permission to reprint previously published material: **DC Comics**: p. 2 (9th panel), p. 265 (3rd panel); **Ministry of Culture, Singapore**: p. 254 (leftmost and 2nd from right); **Ministry of the Environment, Singapore**: p. 254 (bottom, 2nd from left); **Ministry of Information and the Arts, Singapore, courtesy of the National Archives of Singapore**: p. 110 (photos), p. 134 (2nd panel); **Mr. Kiasu character image, used with permission of Johnny Lau**: p. 108 (3rd panel); **National Productivity Board, Singapore**: p. 254 (rightmost); **Photograph from *Comet in Our Sky: Lim Chin Siong in History*, used with permission of GB Gerakbudaya Enterprise Sdn Bhd**: p. 179; **Singapore Family Planning and Population Board**: p. 254 (middle, 2nd from left).

Library of Congress Cataloging-in-Publication Data
Liew, Sonny.
The art of Charlie Chan Hock Chye / Sonny Liew.
pages ; cm.
ISBN 978-1-101-87069-3 (hardcover : alk. paper). ISBN 978-1-101-87070-9 (eBook).
1. Singapore—Politics and government—Comic books, strips, etc. 2. Singapore—Economic conditions—Comic books, strips, etc. I. Title.
PN6790.S553L54 2016   741.5'95979—dc23   2015023576

Editor: Joyce Sim
Managing Editor: Altie Karper
Production Manager: Andy Hughes
Production Editor: Kathleen Fridella
Design Director: Chip Kidd
Editorial Director: Dan Frank
Layout and cover design by Sonny Liew
Author portrait © Sonny Liew

www.pantheonbooks.com

Printed in China
First American Edition
9 8 7 6 5 4 3 2 1

一山不容二虎

ONE MOUNTAIN CANNOT ABIDE TWO TIGERS

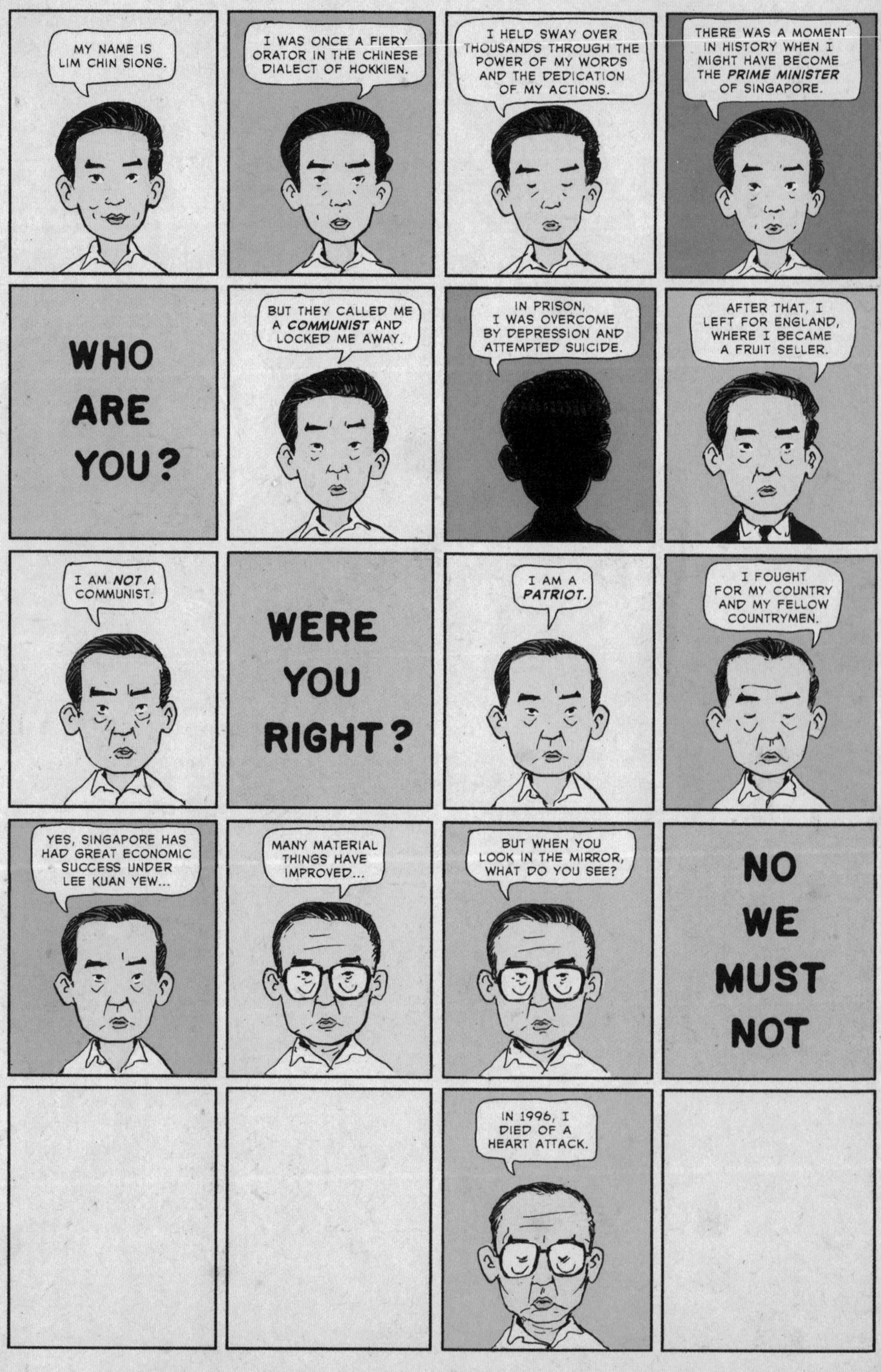
MY NAME IS LIM CHIN SIONG.
I WAS ONCE A FIERY ORATOR IN THE CHINESE DIALECT OF HOKKIEN.
I HELD SWAY OVER THOUSANDS THROUGH THE POWER OF MY WORDS AND THE DEDICATION OF MY ACTIONS.
THERE WAS A MOMENT IN HISTORY WHEN I MIGHT HAVE BECOME THE *PRIME MINISTER* OF SINGAPORE.
WHO ARE YOU?
BUT THEY CALLED ME A *COMMUNIST* AND LOCKED ME AWAY.
IN PRISON, I WAS OVERCOME BY DEPRESSION AND ATTEMPTED SUICIDE.
AFTER THAT, I LEFT FOR ENGLAND, WHERE I BECAME A FRUIT SELLER.
I AM *NOT* A COMMUNIST.
WERE YOU RIGHT?
I AM A *PATRIOT*.
I FOUGHT FOR MY COUNTRY AND MY FELLOW COUNTRYMEN.
YES, SINGAPORE HAS HAD GREAT ECONOMIC SUCCESS UNDER LEE KUAN YEW...
MANY MATERIAL THINGS HAVE IMPROVED...
BUT WHEN YOU LOOK IN THE MIRROR, WHAT DO YOU SEE?
NO WE MUST NOT
IN 1996, I DIED OF A HEART ATTACK.